THE LAST GASP

Trevor Hoyle

Jo Fletcher
BOOKS

First published in Great Britain in 1983 by Random House
This edition published in Great Britain in 2016 by

Jo Fletcher Books
an imprint of
Quercus Editions Ltd
Carmelite House
50 Victoria Embankment
London EC4Y 0DZ

An Hachette UK company

A CIP catalogue record for this book is available
from the British Library

PB ISBN 978 1 84866 455 5
EBOOK ISBN 978 1 84866 456 2

10 9 8 7 6 5 4 3 2 1

Typeset by CC Book Production
Printed and bound in Great Britain by Clays Ltd, St Ives plc

In memory of my beautiful sister Julie.

May she at last have found the peace she sought,
on her final journey.

'. . . Let us strike the keynote, Coketown, before pursuing our tune.

It was a town of red brick, or of brick that would have been red if the smoke and ashes had allowed it; but as matters stood it was a town of unnatural red and black like the painted face of a savage. It was a town of machinery and tall chimneys, out of which interminable serpents of smoke trailed themselves for ever and ever, and never got uncoiled. It had a black canal in it, and a river that ran purple with ill-smelling dye, and vast piles of buildings full of windows where there was a rattling and a trembling all day long, and where the pistons of the steam engine worked monotonously up and down like the head of an elephant in a state of melancholy madness. It contained several large streets all very like one another, and many small streets still more like one another, inhabited by people equally like one another, who all went in and out at the same hours, with the same sound upon the same pavements, to do the same work, and to whom every day was the same as yesterday and tomorrow, and every year the counterpart of the last and the next'

HARD TIMES by Charles Dickens

'Half of all the energy consumed by man in the past two thousand years has been consumed in the last one hundred'

FUTURE SHOCK by Alvin Toffler

'If the present growth trends in world population, industrial pollution, food production and resources depletion continue unchanged, the limits to growth on this planet will be reached sometime within the next one hundred years'

THE LIMITS TO GROWTH by Donella H. Meadows

'All progress is based upon a universal innate desire on the part of every organism to live beyond its income'

Edmund Burke

2016

2016

I

I

The mystery man arrived just before the five-month Antarctic night set in. Two days later and he would never have been found.

Like a mole from its burrow, Gavin Chase emerged that morning from the prefabricated bunker eight feet below ground. Ten years ago the bunker had been on the surface. Now, shored up with buckled iron ribs and creaking timbers, it was gradually sinking deeper and deeper into the ice with the warming summer temperatures. Soon it would be necessary to abandon and build anew.

It was still dark. The spread of stars was etched into the firmament with hard, diamond-like precision. Above the icebound continent of five million square miles – nearly twice the area of Australia – the insulating troposphere was so shallow, half that of the equator, that the marine biologist felt as if he were directly exposed to the vacuous cold of outer space. Welcome to the Antarctic winter: cold enough to turn gasoline into jelly and make steel as brittle as porcelain.

Chase stepped carefully from the slatted wooden ramp that led below. He was a bulky, shuffling figure in outsize red rubber boots, swaddled in waffle-weave thermal underwear and navy-issue fatigues, all zipped up inside an orange parka. Protecting his vulnerable hands, felt gloves inside thick mittens were thrust into gauntlets that extended to his elbows. A thin strip from eyebrows to the bridge of his nose was the only part of him open to the elements. He moved across the wind-scoured surface of packed snow to the weather-instrument tower, eyes probing the darkness.

Yesterday the temperature had fallen to -46.8°C. Once it dropped past -51°C there would be no more scuba diving till next summer. But he hoped there was time for at least one more dive. There were specimens of planktonic algae he wanted to collect, in particular a subspecies known as *silicoflagellates*, which abounded beneath the pack ice of the Weddell Sea, here on the western rim of the Antarctic Plateau. Amazing really – that there should be such an abundance of microscopic life teeming below when up above it was as bleak and sterile as the moon.

It was an odd phenomenon. While surface temperatures stayed very low, sea temperatures underneath the ice were rising. One of the positive results for him was that the diving window had been extended: even this late in the season there were patches of open water in the pack ice, whereas a few years ago it would have been a solid mass. Impenetrable.

With slow, calculated movements he gripped the metal ladder and hauled his six-foot frame twenty feet up to the first platform. Young and fit as he was, honed to a lean 160 pounds after nearly six months at Halley Bay Station, Chase knew that every calorie of energy had to be budgeted for with a miser's caution. Inactive, the body used up about one hundred watts of power, which went up tenfold with physical activity. The trick was to keep on the go without overtaxing yourself. That way you kept warm, generating your own heat – but there was another trap if you weren't careful. At these extreme latitudes the oxygen was low, the equivalent of living at ten thousand feet on the side of a mountain. With less oxygenated blood reaching the body's tissues any exertion required double the effort and energy expenditure. Too much exertion and you could black out – as quickly as a light snapping off – and that would be that.

Chase knelt down and brushed away the thick coating of frost from the gauges.

Windspeed was up to twenty-two knots, he noted with a frown, then he relaxed slightly and grinned when he saw that the red needle of the temperature gauge was still a few degrees short of sixty. Good. That meant one more day, possibly even two. Nick wouldn't like it, but he'd have to persuade him; he couldn't dive without a backup.

With only two weeks left to serve at the station, Chase was keen to gather as many marine samples as possible before boarding the C-130 for the 1,850-mile flight across the Pole to the American base at McMurdo Sound, then the 2,400-mile haul back to Christchurch, New Zealand.

And a week after that he would be home!

He straightened up and gazed out over the featureless wasteland towards the heart of the polar interior. His breath plumed the air like smoke. On the barely discernible line of the horizon a very faint smudge of crimson indicated the advent of the sun. They would see it for a couple of hours today – a flattened reddish ball resting on the rim of their world – and then it would be dark once more. Soon it would be night until September.

The five-month long night aside, there was another, more urgent reason Chase was glad to be leaving. During the winter months the Antarctic lost nearly half its ozone cover, the earth's protective shield against ultraviolet radiation from the sun. The decline had first been spotted in the early seventies, when atmospheric analysis had revealed the culprit to be CFCs, the chlorofluorocarbons used in aerosol sprays and other products. By the mid-nineties, ozone levels above the South Pole had fallen by forty per cent, and the *Nimbus 7* satellite confirmed it: a gaping hole in the stratosphere of thousands of square miles, as big as the USA.

Twenty years on, the hole was not just still there; it was growing. Come September, anyone at Halley Bay foolish enough to spend a few hours exposed to direct sunlight ran the risk of developing melanoma. And Chase was quite certain he could do without a dose of skin cancer, thanks very much.

Directly below him elongated slivers of deep purple shadow edged out from the weather gantry and radio mast – the 'bird's nest' as it was called by everyone on the station. The shadows crept slowly across the smooth humps that were the only visible sign of the warren of living quarters and labs and the thirty-six men beneath.

The arc of red tipped the rim of the world.

Chase held his breath. An Antarctic sunrise was awesome, no matter how many times you witnessed the miracle.

From dingy grey to misty pearl and then to blinding white: the landscape was illuminated like a film set. Chase shielded his eyes against the reflected glare. Even though the horizontal rays were weak, the albedo effect of the white blanket of snow and ice threw back every photon of light in a fierce hazy dazzle that seared the eyeballs. Under certain conditions this caused a whiteout, land and sky melting together with no horizon to align the senses, all contours and topographical features lost in a blank white dream.

Chase watched and marvelled, and then he focused . . .

Something was moving out there on the ice. *Hell, no, must be mistaken.* He was gazing towards the Pole. Nothing could be coming from that direction, from the barren heart of all that emptiness.

In the next instant he was scrambling down the ladder, rubber boots slithering on the ice-coated rungs. In his haste he forgot about the thinness of the atmosphere, about energy budgets. He hadn't gone more than a dozen yards before his chest was heaving. Sweat ran from his armpits: always a danger signal, because damp clothing quickly lost its insulation properties and you could end up freezing in your own perspiration.

Steady now, idiot, take it easy. Whatever was out there – *if* anything was out there – it had survived until now. Steadying himself, he sucked in long deep gulps of air. He'd look bloody foolish if he were found dead within fifty feet of the entry ramp.

A little over ten minutes later, pacing himself, he came in sight of the object he'd seen. It was a sled. The team of eight dogs was, quite literally, on its last legs, too exhausted to do anything except sag in their harness straps and pant weakly.

Chase leaned over the sled and pulled back the stiffened canvas sheet. It cracked like breaking timber. A shapeless mound of ice-encrusted furs concealed the body of a man. His head was sunk deep in a cavity of fur. He was heavily bearded and blackened by the sun. Dark goggles, the old-fashioned type, with tiny circular lenses, covered the eye-sockets.

Dead – must be, Chase reckoned and then saw the blistered lips move. Bloody impossible. The man had come out of nowhere, appeared from a thousand miles of icy wilderness and – incredibly – he was alive.

2

The wedge of light sliced through the darkness as if the blackness itself were a tangible substance. Wielding the heavy battery of arc lamps, Chase swam deeper. He was the searcher, Nick the collector. Above them the lid of ice, forty feet thick, sealed them in a freezing watery tomb, save for a single tiny aperture that was their entry and exit point. It was very easy to feel trapped and claustrophobic.

No wonder Nick had grumbled and cursed. 'For Christ's sake, are you a masochist or what, Gav? No, I get it, a bloody sadist, that's what you are. Nick Power thinks the tour's over, no more work to be done, so I'll show the bastard. Make him suffer.'

Except that Chase didn't think of it as suffering. He rather enjoyed it, as a matter of fact. When diving like this he felt suspended, a tiny fragment of warm life, on top of the world (top, bottom – in an astronomical context they were interchangeable), with everyone and everything else beneath him.

All the continents, oceans, cities and the whole of mankind were way down *there*.

At a hundred and thirty feet he swung the battery of lamps around. Nick hadn't a clue what to look for; he merely followed the wedge of light and swooped when Chase gave the signal. It could look a bit ridiculous, grabbing at nothing, and Chase grinned behind the full-facemask at Nick's apparently pointless pantomime. They were after microscopic plants, the *silicoflagellates*, and it was more good luck than fine judgement if they happened to snare the ones Chase wanted.

He chose what looked a likely spot, just above the ocean floor and hoped for the best.

Nick turned towards him, his faceplate flashing like a silver coin in the milky light. The net trailed after him, a long swirling cocoon. He'd closed the neck, Chase saw, and was gesturing upwards. He'd obviously had enough. Probably the cold was starting to seep through his insulated suit – he could feel a creeping numbness in his own feet. If you ignored it – and you could, it wasn't painful – you felt fine, at least until you got back to the surface and began to thaw out. Then you were wracked with the most excruciating agony and, eventually, if not treated promptly, you'd find all your toes had dropped off.

Chase gave a thumbs-up in the cone of light, indicating they were done, but Nick continued gesturing, his movements sluggish, dreamlike. What was the daft clown playing at?

Chase kicked with his flippered feet and swam nearer to see Nick's panicked eyes bulging at him through the faceplate. He gestured frantically over his shoulder towards his double cylinders . . . something was the matter with his air supply.

It was difficult, trying to manoeuvre the awkward battery of lights with one hand while he spun Nick around with the other. The blackness surrounding them was total, just a speck of light in countless cubic miles of inky black water.

The first cylinder was empty; its gauge registered zero. The second cylinder should have kicked in automatically, but it hadn't, and Chase saw why at once: the exposed brass feed-pipe was flecked with ice and the valve had frozen. Nick was eking out his existence on what little oxygen remained in the first tank.

They were below 130 feet, and if they were to avoid the bends, that meant an ascent lasting several minutes – much too long for Nick to survive. And Chase couldn't feed him from his own mouthpiece: air supply and mask were an integral unit, and if you removed your mask in these waters, the cold would strike needles into your skull and kill you with the shock.

For several seconds Chase's mind was locked in paralysis. Nick had only a few gasps of air left; even if he managed to get him to the surface alive, the lack of oxygen would cause irreparable brain damage. It was an unwelcome reminder that the Antarctic was an implacable enemy: relax your guard for even one instant and it would exact the full penalty. Negligence was death.

Heat.

You fought cold with heat. The only source available was the battery of lamps. Chase grasped Nick by the shoulder, using the leverage to force the cowled arc light against the brass feed-pipe. If he didn't get direct contact, the water would dissipate what little heat there was.

Together they floated in darkness, the muted thump-and-gurgle of Chase's air supply the only sound. Everything became topsy-turvy; they were no longer at the top of the world but the bottom, the immense weight of the planet pressing down on them. So that must mean the thick slab of ice was *beneath* them, and beyond that the tenuous troposphere, and then nothing but bottomless space . . .

Wake up, wake up! he told himself savagely. He was starting to hallucinate, lose orientation. The cold was getting to him. If he didn't concentrate he might start swimming towards the seabed, thinking it was the surface.

Nick had ceased to move and Chase found himself praying to God, in whom he didn't believe – then Nick's arm twitched under his gloved hand. His head turned, the faceplate misty with expired water vapour. For the second time in as many days Chase thought he had a dead man on his hands – and both times, thank God, he had been wrong.

The valve, at last, was free; the ice on the feed-pipe had melted. With huge relief Chase saw that the gauge was registering again. A wavering chain of silver bubbles rose from Nick's exhaust release and surged upwards.

Nick still held the net in an instinctive grip. Guided by the weighted guide-line, Chase rose slowly, his other hand grasping Nick's shoulder-harness firmly. He had to pause three times on the ascent and count out the minutes for decompression, until eventually the two scientists were in sight of the circle of green lights that marked their entry point through the ice, then gratefully hauling themselves on to the diving platform. Wooden steps led to a plywood-lined corridor that ran from the edge of the Weddell Sea on to the Filchner Ice Shelf – the actual Antarctic Plateau. There the corridor led directly into the basement of the station. It took them fifteen minutes to reach it. Chase had wanted to leave their scuba sets on the platform to be collected later, but Nick insisted he could manage.

'Are you dead sure we didn't come up with an empty net?' he remarked, not altogether jokingly.

Chase dumped his tanks on the rack and lifted the stainless-steel lid of the collecting vessel, in which the net sloshed in six inches of seawater.

Nick's face was circled with a fine red mark where the lip of the rubber hood had clung. It looked even more incongruous because surrounding it was a frizzy mop of reddish hair and a straggly reddish beard. For reasons Chase could never understand, the beard was neatly razor-trimmed in a crescent below the mouth while left to flourish unchecked elsewhere: an art student's beard; odd, since Nick was a glaciologist.

Chase filled the galvanised tub with steaming hot water while Nick stripped off his rubber suit down to a pair of boxers with a saucy motto on the crotch. His pale skin was tattooed with blue patches from the cold. Chase helped him into the tub. 'I just hope those two pints of seawater are worth it,' Nick mumbled, teeth chattering. 'Allow me the privilege of accompanying you on your next suicide mission.'

'Shut up and sit down,' Chase said. He filled another tub, stripped off his own suit and sank into the warm water with a blissful sigh. At first he felt nothing, then, slowly, came the luxurious tingle of returning life through his frozen limbs. They'd been under the ice for nearly an hour, at these temperatures the absolute limit before serious damage was done to the body's tissues.

It would be his last dive, no question about that. It had very nearly been Nick's last dive, period. He felt a pang of guilt, mingled with heartfelt relief. Down there it was ball-freezing, black and dangerous and they were both well out of it, thank Christ: alive, and with all extremities intact. He cradled his privates in the hot soapy water and thought of Angie.

The warmth began to seep through him, making him pleasantly drowsy.

Only a few days more and then homeward bound, he dreamed, slipping into his favourite reverie. Angie's blonde hair, like pale seaweed. Angie's smooth skin, firm buttocks, and long legs. He'd always had a fatal weakness for leggy blondes with cut-glass accents. Coming from Bolton in Lancashire, he wondered whether it wasn't some murky atavistic impulse: the caveman desire to possess and dominate, a bit like the childhood thrill of planting his feet in a field of virgin snow, despoiling the serene white canopy.

Perhaps for Angie it was the reverse, that she fancied a bit of rough: the kid from the back streets who'd elevated himself to the status of professional research scientist. A BA in oceanography and marine sciences at Churchill College, Cambridge, a Master's in advanced complex ecology at Durham University and a Ph.D. on the feeding ecology and energetics of intertidal invertebrates at the Stazione Zoologica, Naples.

If he hadn't known the *curriculum vitae* was his own, it would have impressed him.

Thinking about Angie wasn't such a good idea. It inevitably started him off on a fantasy seduction that tantalised his libido without satisfying it; better to postpone that line of thought until reality was made flesh.

'How's the Creature from the Black Lagoon?' he called out.

Nick wafted his hand through the steam. 'After a great deal of thought I've come to the conclusion that you're a northern nutcase, Chase.' He sniffed. 'Or should that be Nut-Chase? Heh-heh. Anyway, the original mad scientist.'

'How's that?' Chase enquired, leaning back, eyes closed.

'Why make it hard on yourself and difficult for the rest of us? If Banting doesn't give a flying fuck – and he doesn't, we know that – why should you?'

'What do you mean, difficult?'

'By setting a bad example,' Nick clarified in a pained voice. 'The tour's nearly over. You're off home soon and I've only got a month to do. Haven't you done enough work?'

'There were some specimens I needed and it was my last opportunity. All right for you popsicle boys – you can get samples any time you want.'

Nick Power's work as a glaciologist involved extracting ice cores from a mile-and-a-third beneath the polar cap to research their 100,000-year-old history. Nick and Gavin were the same age, twenty-seven. The two had met for the first time at the station and become friends. In their off-duty hours they alleviated the boredom by listening to Chase's collection of Muddy Waters and John Lee Hooker and smoking Nick's prime Lebanese Red, which a friendly American pilot brought in on the monthly supply run. This was Nick's number-one priority; on the same scale glaciology came a poor seventh.

'I've got a year to eighteen months' lab work when I get back to Newcastle. I'll need all the specimens I can get hold of.'

He towelled himself briskly, body tingling and aglow. While they were getting dressed, standing on the slatted wooden boards, Nick asked him if he'd heard anything more about the mysterious Russian.

Chase glanced up, frowning. 'How do you know he's Russian?'

'Well, whatever he's babbling it sure ain't English, according to Grigson. Could be Serbo-Croatian for all the sense it makes.'

'Have you looked in on him yourself?'

Nick buttoned up his plaid shirt and pulled on a navy sweater. 'I called in the sickbay after breakfast. Grigson was feeding him soup and the guy was staring into tomorrow-land with peas and carrots lodged in his beard. What I can't understand is where he came from. How the hell did he get here?'

'It's a mystery all right.'

'I mean, Bloody Norah – how far is the Russian base?'

'Five, maybe six hundred miles. But it hasn't been used in over two years. Their main research facility is Mirnyy Station, and that's two thousand miles away on the edge of the Amery Ice Shelf.'

The Mirnyy Station had a dubious claim to fame: the lowest-ever recorded temperature on the planet, -89.2C, had been charted near there some time in the early eighties.

Nick combed his fingers through his tangle of a beard. 'One man and an eight-dog team never made it *that* far,' he asserted positively. 'No-fuckin'-way, Jose.'

'Did Grigson say anything about his condition?'

'The medic put his neck in a brace, which could mean he's injured his spine.'

Chase finished lacing his boots and stood up straight, a good three inches taller than Nick. 'Anybody here speak Russian?'

Nick thought for a moment. 'Nope. Perhaps the mad raving Russkie speaks English.'

Chase raised his eyebrows. 'Shall we investigate?'

'By all means.'

Chase extended an arm. 'After you, Carruthers.'

'No, after you, Fortescue, old bean.'

3

Dim green globes burned in the tiny sickbay, one above each of the four beds. The other three beds were empty, sheets and blankets folded in neat piles. The man in the bed nearest the door appeared to be sound asleep. He had a broad Slavic face and a flattened nose, the skin above the full black beard dark and crazed like old parchment. It was impossible to tell his age, though Chase guessed he was in his late forties, early fifties.

He was lying half-raised on a bank of pillows, the plastic surgical collar holding his head at a stiff, unnatural angle like that of a mummy in a sarcophagus. The green wash of light added to the eerie impression of a body recently excavated from the grave.

Grigson, the medical orderly, was absent.

It didn't seem right to disturb the man, who might have been in a coma. But when Nick, in his usual direct fashion, went straight up to the bed and stared down inquisitively, the man opened cloudy eyes and mumbled in a hoarse broken voice. The words were unintelligible.

From the foot of the bed Chase asked softly, 'Is he sedated?'

Nick gave a slight shrug. He peered down and pressed the backs of his fingers to the man's forehead, on which there was a faint sheen of perspiration. 'You know something, I think he is mad. Look at his eyes.'

'Could be fever.'

'Mmm.' Nick shot a swift glance at Chase. 'Maybe being out on the ice for so long snapped his mind. I think it would have snapped mine.'

'Possible,' Chase conceded. 'But how could we tell?' He leaned forward, seeing the cracked lips moving, straining to hear what he said. It was a word, all right. Sounded like *Stan-or-Nick*.

'So,' Nick pondered, 'it's either Stan or me, is it?' He enunciated very slowly and carefully. 'We do not understand. Do you speak English? English – yes?'

'English,' the man said distinctly. Nick brightened. The man said, 'Nyet,' and Nick's face fell.

'Try him with French,' Chase suggested.

'I don't speak French, what about you?'

'Enough to ask the way to the Eiffel Tower and not understand a word of the reply.' Chase became thoughtful, his dark eyes narrowing in his tanned face. 'If he is Russian, which he sounds to be, he's either a scientist or with the military.'

'Or he might have been prospecting for gold,' said Nick glibly.

'You don't have much sympathy for a sick man.'

'Sorry. Next time I'll bring him some grapes and a Danielle Steele novel.'

Chase came forward and gently took hold of the man's weathered right hand. 'Remind me to send for you when I'm on my deathbed,' he said, examining the small callous on the side of the middle finger, the kind caused by holding a pen. Which might mean he was a scientist with a lot of desk work, writing up copious research notes.

He was about to lay the hand down when it tightened on his in a surprisingly strong grip and the cracked lips blurted out a torrent of words. The incomprehensible babble went on and on, leaving the man choking for breath. Again Chase caught the word or phrase sounding like *Stan-or-Nick*. The Russian was obviously desperate to communicate something; his eyes were glazed, staring blankly upwards at the plywood ceiling, yet he spoke with force and conviction, desperation even: a man with an urgent message to convey.

'Let's try him with a pad and pencil.'

'So you can't speak Russian but you can read it. Clever.'

'We'll find a way to get it translated,' Chase said. He found a pen on the orderly's night table and pressed it into the man's fingers. 'At least it'll give us the gist of what he's trying to say.'

Nick tore a leaf out of a small black notebook. He affixed it to the clipboard holding the temperature chart, then supported the clipboard at a convenient angle. Chase guided the Russian's hand. The man held the pen as though it were an alien artefact; then he realised what was required of him. His eyes unfocused, head held stiffly, but he did manage to scrawl something down, though for all his babbling it was only a single line before his hand shook and the pen slipped from his fingers.

Chase held up the clipboard for them to read what the man had written.

$$CO_2 + CO_3 = +H_2O \rightleftharpoons 2HCO_3$$

Nick tugged at his beard. 'What's that?' he frowned. 'Something to do with the carbon cycle?'

'It's the chemical interaction that takes place when carbon dioxide is dissolved in seawater.'

'So what?'

Chase studied the equation. 'Search me.'

At the sound of voices in the corridor he thought it prudent to slip the piece of paper into his pocket, without quite knowing why. Quickly he replaced the clipboard on its hook at the foot of the bed. He straightened up as the project leader entered the sickbay followed by Grigson.

Professor Banting's head shone like a polished green egg in the dim light, close-set eyes in a narrow skull. He glared suspiciously at Nick and Chase. 'Don't you know this man is very ill and shouldn't be disturbed?'

'What's wrong with him?' asked Nick, unintimidated.

'His back is broken,' Grigson stated without emotion: a medical fact. He went over and checked the Russian's pulse.

Banting pointedly stood aside, waving a hand. 'Please leave at once. You shouldn't be here at all. It's totally irregular.'

'What's going to happen to him?' Chase wanted to know.

Banting breathed out slowly, controlling his annoyance. 'They're sending a C-130 from McMurdo. So now you know. All right?'

'What's this got to do with the Americans? Why inform them?'

'Because, Dr Chase, they have the facilities and we haven't.'

As well as project leader, Professor Ivor Banting was head of the British Section Antarctic Research Programme. More administrator than serious scientist, he commanded little respect from the team under him. He was more preoccupied with keeping an eye on the stores' inventory than in conducting research experiments and actually collecting scientific data. Chase thought him a petty-minded bureaucrat and had little time for him.

Banting cleared his throat. 'There's also the matter of security, which I doubt would have occurred to you. The Americans want to know what he was doing here.'

'Don't tell me they think he's a spy,' Chase said, not sure whether he ought to laugh or not. 'We find a man with a broken back out on the ice, two thousand miles from nowhere, and the Americans regard him as a security risk?'

But Professor Banting was not in the mood to debate the point. He said curtly, 'As head of station, Dr Chase, this is my responsibility. And my decision. The Americans are the right people to deal with it.' He stuck both hands into the pockets of his shapeless tweed jacket in the pose of someone whose patience was rapidly evaporating. 'Now, if you and Dr Power would be so good . . .'

At the door Chase paused and glanced back at the figure on the bed, the black beard enclosing the soundlessly miming lips. Even now a reflex part of the Russian's brain was striving to communicate . . . what exactly? What could be so important? A simple chemical equation known to every first-year chemistry student? Chase curled his hand around the piece of paper in his pocket.

'I just hope you know what you're doing, Professor.' He controlled his irritation. 'This man is gravely ill. Moving him could be a fatal mistake.' Why hadn't Grigson objected? Too intimidated, maybe.

'Well, if so' – Banting deliberately turned his back – 'it is mine to make and not yours, Dr Chase.'

In the corridor Chase said, 'Heartless bastard.'

Nick said, 'I hope he dies of worms.'

4

Wearing only ragged shorts and a pair of canvas shoes with holes in them, Theo Detrick sat in the stern of a small wooden rowboat in the middle of a placid lagoon, surrounded by a bracelet of dazzling pink coral. He was a short, robust man with a boxer's torso and shoulders burned a deep mahogany. Whereas many men his age had thickened and grown slothful, Theo kept to a strict regimen: the discipline of his scientific calling extended into every area of his hermetic life. Each morning without fail he swam two laps around the lagoon. He had the strength, muscle tone and stamina of a man half his age. Beneath a spiky crew cut of snow-white hair his face was grizzled and etched with lines, his eyes of transparent blue screwed up against the sunlight reflected on the water.

Canton Island is the tiniest of a loosely scattered group, the Phoenix Islands, fractionally below the equator; no more than flyblown specks in the vast blue expanse of the tropical Pacific. For Theo Detrick, Canton Island was important precisely because of its location. Nearly twenty years before, at the age of forty, he had come to the island and stayed here, its sole inhabitant. What had begun as a routine research project in marine biology, sponsored by a two-year Scripps Fellowship, had turned into his life's work.

Behind the boat trailed a surface-skimming net. Its fine silk mesh had captured a kind of greenish goo, which he was careful not to disturb as he hauled the net over the stern. Later, in his laboratory in the clapboard house with the sagging porch, Theo would cut the silk into three-inch squares and examine each one patiently and painstakingly under the microscope. But even with the naked eye the evidence was plain enough, to his practised eye at any rate. The phytoplankton index was in decline. It was a trend that had been noted in all the oceans of the world, but never plotted so carefully, so thoroughly, over such a long period of time.

The scientist shielded his eyes and looked beyond the coral reef to the open sea, a thousand glittering facets in the unbroken arc of blue.

It was out there, in the narrow belt along the equator, that the upwelling of colder water brought with it a rich soup of microorganisms from the ocean depths. These were the countless billions of minute unicellular planktonic algae that formed the staple diet of most fish. And a significant proportion of the world's constantly replenished oxygen supply came from these tiny free-floating plants. Like all green plants they absorbed the energy of the sun and by means of photosynthesis converted water into its constituent parts of hydrogen and oxygen. The hydrogen they used to produce carbohydrates for their own needs, dumping the oxygen as a waste product into the atmosphere.

This 'waste' was vital to all animal life on the planet.

There wasn't any man living who knew as much about this microscopic form of marine life as Theo Detrick did. His book on the subject, nine years in the writing and published a decade ago, was now regarded as the standard text. From the royalties on the book and the grant he still received from Scripps, he was able to continue his research, although he had a hunch that at the institute he existed merely as an entry on the departmental balance sheet. (*'Old Theo? Thought he was dead.'*) He visited the mainland at the most twice a year, so he couldn't really blame them. His wife had died fourteen years ago. His daughter, Cheryl, herself a postgraduate at Scripps, must feel she was corresponding with a distant relative – a stranger even – when they exchanged their infrequent texts and emails.

He rowed back to the jetty, the oars smooth in his leathery palms. The years of isolation had engendered a fear and distrust of the outside world. By choice he would have preferred to be left alone on his island. He wanted nothing more than to work at what he knew best, at the subject to which he had devoted the greater part of his working life.

But for *the* question: what good was that work, that research, all that dedication, if not used for the benefit of mankind? He had a duty not only to himself. He was a forgotten man and wouldn't have had it any other way, but the time had come to consider other things. For the past two years, he had tried to deny the truth, yet daily he saw the evidence, and it was inescapable. It was building up, sheet after written sheet, graph after graph, in the mass of notes lying between mildewed green covers on his workbench. Detrick could afford to ignore it no longer.

Who would pay heed to a forgotten man? Theo wondered, holding the skimming net in one hand while he pulled himself up with the other. Especially the apocalyptic warning of a lone scientist long vanished from civilisation? A crank, deranged, even.

He went up the beaten path to the house, knowing what had to be done. Like a fire-and-brimstone prophet of ancient times, he was about to preach death and destruction. His sermon concerned nothing less than the end of the world.

5

Nick Power lounged back in the canvas chair, his calf-length combat boots with the thick-ridged soles propped on the corner of the trestle table. 'The guy's off his rocker, Gav, we both know that.'

Chase disagreed. 'Feverish, yes, and in pain – probably drugged to the eyeballs – but he was definitely trying to tell us something.'

'Like what, for instance?'

'Dunno,' Chase said with a shrug.

'Because it doesn't mean anything! You said it yourself: an elementary equation that can be found in any standard chemistry textbook. The guy was deluded, just babbling nonsense. Something he'd learned as a peasant back in Vladivostok.'

Chase gazed thoughtfully across the small cluttered mess-room with its half-dozen late diners idling over coffee. It was the comfortable hour of the evening at Halley Bay, the station battened down against the searing wind and cold and dark. Primaeval man seeking the shelter of the cave, the warmth of companionship in a hostile environment.

The others had retired to the rec room along the corridor to play cards or chess, or have a game of table tennis on the battered table supported by packing crates. Some would be hoping to call home on their mobiles or tablets, if the ionospheric storms didn't play havoc with the signal. There were any number of satellites passing over the South Pole – the European Space Agency's Cryo-Sat for one, designed for mapping of ice sheets and ocean levels – but such was the turbulent nature of the earth's magnetic field that getting a decent reception was a risky business. On the odd occasion there had been total tele-communications blackout.

Following two winters of severe flooding, Nick was always anxious to have news of his parents in the West Country. Their farm near the village of Muchelney Ham had twice been under five feet of water.

The Somerset Levels were prone to flooding, but the torrential rains of recent years had been the worst in living memory. This year – so far, at least, touch wood – the farmhouse had remained dry and secure.

'When are they transferring the Russkie to McMurdo?' asked Nick, hands behind his head.

'Tomorrow. The transport is due in at fourteen hundred hours.'

Nick perked up. 'Wow-weee, brother! If Jim Carlson is in the crew we could have a fresh supply of Red.' He puffed out his chest happily. 'That's made my day, Tonto.'

'You'll have to smoke it all yourself,' Chase reminded him. 'Blast off into outer space all on your own, Sonny Boy. Very soon I shall be gaaaaawn . . .' His hand took off like a plane.

'Lucky bastard.'

'You've not got too long. A few more core samples and you're done.' Chase sipped the last of his lukewarm coffee. 'What's the dating you're working on?'

'Oh, pretty recent . . . about fifteen hundred BC.'

'It actually is amazing,' Chase marvelled, 'how in hell you can date it so accurately.'

'Well, between you and me and Sophia Loren, it's more an educated guess – give or take two or three hundred years. But in the total span of fifty thousand years, what's a couple of centuries between friends? Interesting result the other day. A dark band which is probably the residue of volcanic ash. We dated it by carbon-14 at about two and a half thousand years, so there must have been a huge eruption about that time.'

'And the ash got this far?'

'Sure. Most airborne pollution does.'

'That's right – the Industrial Revolution,' Chase remembered. He had been intrigued when Nick told him one band of darkening in the ice core was caused by smoke and soot from the cotton mills in his home town and the surrounding area, starting about two hundred and fifty years ago. It was generally accepted that Bolton in Lancashire was the model for Coketown in Charles Dickens's novel *Hard Times*, set in the industrial north of England; it was certainly true that Dickens had visited the town when researching the book.

Nick had explained that every year ten to twenty inches of snow fell on Antarctica, which, with the accumulated pressure, gets squeezed down into four to eight inches of pure ice, which trapped a permanent record of the climate at any given moment. They had even detected traces of leaded petroleum. As Nick had observed, 'Here I am, shut up in this bloody ice-hole at the arse-end of the globe, studying the effects of the Los Angeles freeway system.'

Now Chase said, 'Pollution down here – and it's supposed to be the cleanest, purest air anywhere in the world.'

In the dim light his hair had a blue-black sheen and the whites of his eyes stood out beneath the dark bar of his eyebrows. Someone had once described his looks as 'satyric'. He'd felt flattered until he looked up the definition and found that it meant a Greek wood-demon with a tail and long pointed ears.

'If the mad Russkie *is* a scientist,' Chase said, 'what's his field?'

'That's easy.'

'Yeah?'

'Professor Boris reading Pornography.'

'Highly amusing.'

'Well, here's an idea. Why not contact Mirnyy Station and ask if they've lost anyone.'

'Are you serious?'

'It's one way to find out.'

Chase was doubtful. 'That might not help the guy – supposing he doesn't want them to know where he is for some reason.'

'What the hell, Gav, does it really matter? He'll be in the tender loving care of the Yanks soon. Let them worry about his pedigree.' Nick swung his boots down. He stood up and flexed his shoulders. 'Let's go to the rec room. With any luck there's a poker game tonight.'

They went in single file along the narrow wooden corridor, which was lined with silver-clad pipes and lit by caged bulbs. Faintly above their heads they could hear the wind howling; on the surface it was 57°C below, with a wind-speed of forty-two knots. Chase smiled as he recalled an expression of his mother's: *Not fit to turn a dog out,* she'd say when the wind and rain swirled around their little terraced house. He missed her, found himself recalling more silly inconsequential things – mannerisms, sayings – with each passing year, like sediment building up. His dad, Owen, still lived in the same house. He had acquired a lady friend, though Chase had yet to meet her.

Nick fetched two cans of Old Speckled Hen from the communal fridge. Payment was on the honour system; you were supposed to write down whatever you consumed. Settled in a sagging armchair, Chase peeled back the tab and took a mouthful. A group in the corner was clustered round a small screen, watching *Inglourious Basterds* for the umpteenth time. They never got tired of that movie. Poker was not on the menu tonight.

Chase fished out the crumpled piece of paper and continued to sip his beer while he studied it. This simple equation must mean something. The fact that it *was* so simple was what agitated him the most.

The absorption of carbon dioxide in seawater, after all, was a commonplace chemical interaction. Readings using an infrared analyser were taken over huge tracts of ocean every day of the week. What they invariably showed were different rates in equatorial regions than nearer the poles. The reason was well understood: gases were less soluble in warm water than in cold. This produced the cycle of an outgassing of carbon dioxide into the atmosphere near the equator – because the warmer water couldn't hold it – and a corresponding sink for carbon dioxide at higher latitudes. So everything was evenly balanced. The ocean was an extremely efficient exchange mechanism, maintaining a constant level of atmospheric CO_2 of about 0.03 per cent. It had been stable for millions of years.

The increase in carbon dioxide, leading to the greenhouse effect, had been known and documented since the 1930s. In the fifty years leading up to 1936, humanity's industrial activities added an extra 150 billion tons of carbon dioxide to the atmosphere. The actual amount was very small compared to the huge flux of gases in the forests and the oceans. That was of little concern. What *was* problematic was how would a carefully balanced ecosystem cope with all this extra CO_2 floating around?

To that nobody had an answer. Since about 1850 – when the Industrial

Revolution really got cooking – there had been a ten to fifteen per cent increase in carbon dioxide (which was where the greenhouse effect came from). Most people didn't realise that the atmosphere was heated not from above, but from below – radiated heat from the earth's surface. The sun's rays passed through the atmosphere, heated up the planet and then, because of the added carbon dioxide and water vapour, were trapped and couldn't escape.

The big question still begged an answer. If twenty-five to thirty billion tons of CO_2 were being produced every year, and yet less than fifty per cent of the increase had been detected in the atmosphere, where had all the extra carbon dioxide gone? Anyone who could supply an answer was on the way to winning the Nobel Prize.

Chase himself was a marine biologist, not an atmospheric physicist, so he was out of the running. He swigged his beer and frowned at the piece of creased paper on his knee; wouldn't that be something, if the Russian had found an answer to the puzzle. Or even a few clues. Some new evidence that the extra CO_2 was being absorbed into the polar oceans. They were the usual CO_2 sinks—

Then something struck him with a chilling shock, something he'd only this moment realised. Of course the absolutely crucial question was how long could the oceans *keep on absorbing* the extra carbon dioxide that was building up year on year due to man's industrial activities? Surely there must come a time when they reached saturation point – so what then? How would that affect the complex interweaving of atmosphere, oceans, land-mass – the entire biosphere – and the life-forms that depended on its viability?

Nick said, 'You look like somebody who's lost a quid and found a rusty nail, Gav. Stop fretting over it; the Russkie isn't your problem.'

Chase finished his beer and felt like throwing the can at the wall. It wasn't the Russian he was thinking about but that damned chemical equation scrawled on a piece of paper. He gazed round at the cramped, muggy room with its tired sagging furniture and the motley collection of scientists, most of them bearded and unkempt.

'Can't wait to get out of this damn rat-hole,' he said with genuine feeling. 'Back to sanity and civilisation.'

'And sex,' said Nick with such lugubrious envy that Chase couldn't help burst out laughing.

6

The four-engined ski-shod C-130 landed the next afternoon right on schedule, taking advantage of the paltry rays cast by an inch of sun peeping reluctantly over the horizon. It was a clear day, the sky a magnificent deep magenta, with the wind down to fifteen knots, and everyone not engaged with some pressing duty was above-ground to greet the aircraft. Any diversion was a welcome break in routine.

With typical thoroughness the Americans had sent a three-man medical team equipped with a special stretcher on which the injured man was carefully placed, made comfortable, and strapped down. Chase had to admit that he was receiving the best possible care and attention.

He stood with Nick Power and several others watching the stretcher being taken on board through the rear bay, wide enough for a tank. Professor Banting was stood a little way off with a young executive officer named Lloyd Malden. The American in charge of the operation wore a red parka that looked smartly pressed, and knee-high boots lined with fox fur. He had the alert, gimlet-eyed look of a military automaton. Probably brushed his teeth the regulation number of strokes, Chase reckoned.

When the stretcher had disappeared into the hold of the Hercules, Chase went over to join them. Banting paused in mid-sentence and gave him a hostile stare, which Chase ignored. He came straight to the point.

'I'm very concerned about this man. Do you think he's in any condition to be moved?'

The young lieutenant narrowed his eyes, making his hatchet face inside the red parka hood sharper still. He said bluntly, 'Excuse me – are you offering a medical opinion?'

'Yes.'

'Then I take it you're a doctor?'

'Yes I am.'

Malden was taken aback. 'Very sorry, I didn't realise. Pardon my rudeness—'

'Chase is a doctor – of marine biology,' Banting cut in, his voice thick with anger. 'He has no medical expertise whatsoever. And this has *nothing* to do with him. Ignore this intrusion, Lieutenant. My apologies on his behalf.'

'Don't apologise for me, Professor. As I'm the person who found this man out on the ice, I believe I have a legitimate interest in how he's looked after.'

Banting reached out a mittened hand as if to physically push Chase away, but Malden said, 'One moment, Dr Chase. Was he conscious when you found him? Did he say anything?'

'No. I thought he'd pissed on his chips.'

'You thought he—?'

'Was dead. Zilch. Kaput,' Chase said. 'Nearly but not quite.'

Lieutenant Malden raised his smooth chin and brought it down in a swift, decisive nod. Chase smelled rosewater on the wind. 'Right, I understand what you mean,' the lieutenant said, as if having deciphered a garbled message over a faulty landline.

'Have you any idea who he is?'

'Not yet. We're hoping to find out.'

Chase wasn't good at placing American accents but this one sounded to him to be cultured New England: precise, polite, with no strong American inflection. The studied politeness, he suspected, was an exceedingly thin veneer.

'He's Russian, wouldn't you say?'

Lieutenant Malden's pale blue eyes shifted in Banting's general direction, then snapped back. 'Yes. That is, we think he might be.'

It was going to take a stick of dynamite in every orifice to make the American offer a candid opinion. Chase said, 'You're pretty keen to get hold of him, considering you've no idea who he is.'

'I don't follow. In what way?'

Chase gestured. 'You've sent an aircraft nearly two thousand miles on a special flight. Here you are in person to oversee the operation.

And you're moving somebody in a serious condition who ought not to be moved at all.'

'I'm led to understand you're a marine biologist, Dr Chase, not a medical practitioner.'

The same gentle voice and polite tone. But the demarcation between Chase's personal concern and professional standing had been clearly drawn. In other words, butt out and shut the fuck up.

Professor Banting closed ranks. 'We've had this discussion already, Dr Chase. You're beginning to try my patience. The fact is that Lieutenant Malden and I are acting on instructions from a higher authority. We are simply doing our best to carry them out.'

Chase said stubbornly, 'Even if it kills the patient.'

Banting was close to apoplectic. 'You are being offensive to a decorated officer of the United States army, Dr Chase! Lieutenant Malden served in Iraq. He was in the vanguard of the offensive in Fallujah. Show some respect, man!'

'Dr Chase, please . . . don't be unreasonable.' Malden raised his hands in appeal. 'At McMurdo we have a complete range of medical facilities. The patient will receive the very best attention, you have my word.' The lieutenant's eyes thawed a little. 'Look here – I'll even have the senior medic send you a progress report, how's that?'

Did that corny approach really work with some dimwit? Malden must think him stupid, and Chase didn't like being taken for a mug.

'You can't seriously believe he's a security risk. Not with a broken back.'

'This has nothing to do with security. Leastwise, not military security.' Malden lowered his voice, as if taking Chase into his confidence. 'I can tell you this, Dr Chase. Between us, we think he's possibly a member of a Russian oil-prospecting team. We suspect that the big Russian corporations have been secretly exploring the continent for oil deposits. Which, I expect you know, is in contravention of the Antarctic Treaty, ratified by twenty-four nations. If we can come up with actual dates and locations from an eyewitness, then it might persuade them to pull out before the whole thing blows up into a major international incident. Of course we don't want the Russians looking for oil behind our backs. But neither are we seeking a confrontation over what, until now, has been neutral ground.'

Chase breathed twin plumes of steam into the blisteringly cold air. He remained silent. Banting stamped his feet, looking almost relieved.

Lieutenant Malden leaned forward. 'I'd appreciate it, Dr Chase, if this didn't go any further.' One intelligent man appealing to the integrity and good sense of another. 'You understand?'

'Oh, absolutely.'

The American's thin lips twitched into something resembling a smile. He shook hands with them both, gave a courtesy salute, and walked briskly across the packed snow to the waiting gunship, whose engines had been kept idling all the time it was on the ground to avoid the fuel freezing.

The Hercules taxied into the wind and after a long run-up finally took off, snow spurting from its skis in a billowing cloud; in seconds the wing and fuselage lights were bright winking stars against a sky already darkening into the twenty-two-hour night.

Chase strolled back with Nick to the entrance ramp, ignoring his friend's complaints that Jim Carlson, the lousy bastard, hadn't material-ised with the expected little plastic bag. Instead he was thinking of the perfectly sincere expression on the sharp young features of Lieutenant Lloyd Malden, and of his equally sincere explanation, so confidential, so plausible, so well-rehearsed.

That Gavin Chase hadn't believed a word of.

Three days later, during the changeover at McMurdo Station, Chase learned from a US Army doctor that the Russian had died of a brain haemorrhage on the operating table. He was shocked, but not surprised. The poor sod hadn't stood a chance. From a hard plastic bucket seat forward of the cargo compartment in the smooth silver belly of a C-121 Lockheed Super Constellation, Chase gazed down on the swathes of blue and green that marked the varying depths and different currents of the ocean. They were six hours out from Antarctica, with another four to go before landing at Christchurch.

As the C-121 droned on he thought about the dead man, about the piece of paper carefully folded in his diary, about the absorption of carbon dioxide in seawater. But none of it got him anywhere at all.

2

I

The research vessel *Melville*, two days out from San Diego, steamed at quarter-speed through the gently rolling Pacific swell. On a towline one hundred yards astern, the RMT (Rectangular Mid-Water Trawl) scooped surface water to a precisely calibrated depth of two metres, capturing the tiny mesopelagic creatures on their upwards migration from the middle depths.

Part of the fleet belonging to the Scripps Institution of Oceanography, the *Melville* was on a shakedown cruise for the Marine Biology Research Division, testing a new type of opening-closing release gear. It was operated from the afterdeck on instructions from the monitoring room amidships, and it was the task of Cheryl Detrick and Gordon Mudie to watch and report on the trawl's performance. After nearly two hours Cheryl was bored to tears, not so much with deck duty as with Gordon and the fact that despite nil encouragement, he kept coming on strong. He was tall and skinny, with lank mousy hair that straggled in the breeze, and a gaping loose-lipped grin that reminded her of the Disney dog Pluto. She thought him unattractive and charmless, while he clearly thought he was making a first-rate impression.

Gordon stood by the winch, happy in his ignorance, while Cheryl kept lookout through Zeiss binoculars. Both were graduate students working on a research project for Dr Margaret Delors, who for ten years or more had been gathering data on the eastern subequatorial Pacific.

'Jeez, it's hot,' Gordon complained, fanning himself and stating the obvious. 'Don't you think so, Sherry?'

Cheryl continued watching the RMT. Another thing that irritated her about him, she hated being called Sherry. 'Release gear open,' she reported into the button mike and received the monitoring room's acknowledgement over the headset. Now another fifteen minutes of Gordon's witty repartee and inane grin. *Lord deliver us . . .*

Moving to the rail she did a slow sweep of the placid ocean. After a moment she removed the headset and dangled it on a metal stanchion. The breeze ruffled her cropped sun-bleached hair. All through university she'd never cut it, until it reached her waist, and then a friend had advised her that she really ought to style it to suit her height and figure, which Cheryl interpreted as meaning that girls of medium stature with a voluptuous figure looked dumpy with waist-length hair.

Gordon leaned his bony forearms on the rail and beamed at her, full of bright, sincere lecherous interest. She might have liked him if he hadn't been so damned obvious. He was probably too honest, she reflected. The guys she fancied were devious bastards, some of them real chauvinist pigs at that, which was a trait she didn't admire in herself. But there had to be a physical turn-on, no matter who it was, and Gordon just didn't qualify.

'It was your dad, wasn't it, who wrote the book? You're the same Detrick, aren't you?' He was trying manfully to keep the conversation rolling and Cheryl felt a slight twinge of compassion.

'That's me.' Cheryl smiled. 'The nutty professor's daughter.'

'Somebody told me he could have been really big at Scripps – even the director if he'd wanted – but he just went off into the blue.' Gordon waved his hand. 'An island a zillion miles from nowhere. What made him do it?'

'He hates people,' Cheryl said flippantly. She was tempted to add, 'It runs in the family,' but didn't. Gordon was a pain in the ass, but she didn't want to make a cheap remark for the sake of it.

'Is that right? Does he really hate people?' Gordon was giving her his intense moony stare, perhaps hoping he'd discovered a topic of mutual interest.

Cheryl shrugged, scanning the ocean through the binoculars. 'I don't know. To be honest, I don't know him all that well. I get a Christmas card every February and there isn't much room for a life story between the holly and the snow-covered turtles.'

'Jeez, Sherry, you're his *daughter*.'

'So you keep reminding me, *Gordy*.'

Gordon mused on this and then came up unaided with the thought for the day. 'They do say that geniuses are very weird people. Not like the rest of us. You know – kinda inhuman, cold, no emotions.'

'I'm sure he'd be thrilled to hear that.'

Gordon was immune to irony. 'Jeez, I'd love to meet somebody like that, Sherry. I bet he's a fascinating guy. I mean to say, the *dedication* it takes to go off like that, leaving civilisation and all that stuff behind, living purely and simply for your work. That's terrific.'

'Is it?' Cheryl lowered the binoculars and stared at him, her tone sharper than she intended. 'It's terrific to live with relatives for most of your life, being shipped around like a package? To be an orphan when one of your parents is still alive? That really is terrific, Gordy.'

The resentment, the hurt, so long buried, still had a raw edge to it. Especially when dredged up by a casual or thoughtless remark, and Gordon Mudie was turning out to be an expert in that department.

The bass throb of the engines faltered, missed a beat and then resumed its pounding rhythm. Cheryl felt the vibrations through her rope-soled sandals. The ship was labouring. She leaned right over, holding the binoculars aside on their leather strap and peered down into the churning water.

Normally it was a cream froth but now it was red, the colour of blood.

'Gordon, look at that!'

'Jeez-uz!'

'What have we hit?'

'Must be a seal – or a shark, maybe.'

But it was neither. Cheryl looked around and discovered that the *Melville* was suddenly afloat on a red ocean. She'd been so distracted by Gordon that she'd failed to notice that the vessel was struggling to make headway through a thick spongy mass of minute planktonic organisms. It was this which was giving the sea its reddish hue.

She knew there'd been several outbreaks in recent years: vast blooms of the microcellular organism *Gymodinium breve* had appeared without warning off the coasts of America, India and Africa. Nobody knew what caused the growth, nor why it suddenly came and went. But the 'red tide' was deadly, to both sea life and man.

She clamped the headset back on and spoke into the mike. 'Monitoring room? We'd better wind in the RMT. We're in the middle of an algae bloom. I think it's the poisonous variety.'

The headset squawked a reply and Cheryl said, 'We're to close the release gear and bring the trawl in.' When Gordon didn't immediately respond, she snapped, 'What are you waiting for? If we pick up any of this crap it'll take days to clean out.'

Gordon backed away from the rail, his high forehead creased in a perplexed frown. 'Where's it come from? There must be a squillion tons of the stuff.' Still frowning, he went over to the winch and began winding.

Cheryl gazed down at the water. Her nose wrinkled as she caught a whiff of something rotten . . . and in the churning red wake she saw the white upturned bellies of hundreds of fish: a shoal of poisoned sea bass.

In spite of the warmth of the sun a shiver rippled down her spine. What had caused it? A natural ecological foul-up, or man-made thermal pollution?

And just imagine, she thought, if the bloom kept right on multiplying and spreading and poisoning all the fish. It would eventually take over, filling all the oceans of the world with a stinking red poisonous mess. Every sea creature would die, and the bloom might not stop there – when it had conquered the oceans it could infiltrate the river systems and lakes and streams. It might even gain a root-hold on the land . . .

Cheryl shook herself out of the nightmare. Thank God it was only imagination.

2

Bill Inchcape – or Binch, as everyone called him – was seated at the keyboard of the computer terminal in the cavernous air-conditioned basement where DELFI was housed behind hermetically sealed three-inch steel doors. This precaution was less for security reasons than to protect the germanium circuitry and memory disks against changes in temperature and humidity.

Data from all parts of the world were received at the National Climate Prediction Foundation, Boulder, Colorado, and fed into the computer. It was the physicist's job to extract the climatic anomalies and prepare a summary, which was circulated to various government agencies. What these agencies did with this information nobody knew; it was Binch's hunch, as he confided to Brad Zittel, that it served merely to justify Washington's funding of the centre, made them feel they were getting sufficient 'drudge for their dollar'.

At the moment he was trying to monitor five screens simultaneously. Down here it was quite cool, though Binch still sweated, the garish strip-lighting reflecting on his damp scalp through rapidly thinning baby-fine hair.

'You wouldn't think it could get any worse, but it always seems to,' Binch complained in his reedy voice. 'Just look at all this stuff!'

Brad Zittel slumped down in the next chair. He wasn't at his best this morning. Dark circles ringed his eyes. For two months or more he'd been waking at 4 a.m. and making a pot of Darjeeling, then watching the sky slowly brighten from his study window.

'Worse in what sense?' he asked dully. 'The anomalies are getting worse or there are more of them?'

'Quality and quantity both up. This is supposed to be a two-day job and it's going to take a week.' Binch pointed to the screens. 'Sweden: Rainfall increased by ninety per cent with some areas recording average monthly amounts in one day. Finland: Warmest December on record in Helsinki since measurements began in 1829.'

He touched the master screen and scrolled through the latest input.

Brad took a breath, trying to quell the too-familiar panic rising in his chest, trying to tell himself not to be such a prick.

| Libya: | Highest maximum December temperature since 1924. Precipitation during December and January exceptionally low. |
| Belgium: | Coldest winter since 1962-1963. Fifth coldest this century. |

Brazil:	Northeast state of Caera experienced worst drought in living memory. Frost reported on 6–7 days in the south and snow fell in Rio Grande do Sul (extremely rare event).
Czechoslovakia:	Severe cold temperatures during early January accompanied by heavy snowfall.
Australia:	Record maximum temperatures in Western Australia. Town of Cocklebiddy reported a new max of 55.7°C.
Antarctica:	McMurdo and South Pole stations measured record max temperatures during late December.
Arctic Ocean:	Both Canadian and Russian sources report temperatures 14°C below normal, making it the coldest February on record.

Brad discovered that his hands were shaking. He couldn't read any more. He pushed himself away from the desk on the swivel chair.

'What's the matter?' asked Binch alertly. 'You okay?'

Brad Zittel smiled diffidently and scratched at his grey stubble. He suddenly realised he'd forgotten to shave this morning. A NASA pin flared in the lapel of his cotton jacket. 'I haven't been sleeping too well, I guess. Joyce keeps telling me I need a vacation. Could be she's right.'

'You do look kinda beat.' Binch eyed him shrewdly. 'Still got that pollution bee in your bonnet? Come on, Brad, buddy, you're taking it far too seriously. This old ball of mud ain't gonna peg out just yet.'

Brad gestured. 'These anomalies . . . every month more of them . . .'

'We've always had them, ever since records were kept. In fact we're probably finding *more* freak conditions today precisely because every Tom, Dick, and Harry is monitoring the climate more closely. Ever think of that?'

'I've thought about it.'

'But you're not convinced.'

Brad kneaded his palms, his eyes downcast. 'Do you remember the preface you wrote to the last summary?' he said quietly. 'I can't get one line out of my head: "Reports of long-standing records being broken were received almost daily from all seven continents." Those are your words, Binch, not mine.'

The physicist squirmed a little in his chair. 'Yeah, all right,' he conceded, 'so the weather isn't behaving normally just now. But what in hell *is* normal? You've got to see it over the long term, Brad. What we consider "average weather" for the first half of this century needn't necessarily be "average" for the latter half. Most of the records we use for comparison stretch from 1900 to 1970 – but maybe *that* period was abnormal and the climatic pattern today is the normal one.' He shrugged elaborately. 'Plain fact is, we don't know.'

'And what about DELFI? What does it have to say?'

'DELFI can only come up with a prediction based on existing data; it's merely an extrapolation of present trends.' Even in Binch's ears, this sounded like an evasive reply, which it was. If the computer's forecasts weren't worth a row of beans, why pay any heed to them at all? The truth was that Binch couldn't explain the system's predictions, and yet he relied on those Washington dollars to keep the show on the road.

In the manner of such beasts it was named after the rather forced acronym for Determining Environmental Logistics for Future Interpretation. In plain English its function was to analyse and correlate changes in global weather and to predict climatic patterns in the future. To this end it was directly linked with NORPAX (North Pacific Experiment) and CLIMAP (Climate Long-Range Investigation Mapping and Prediction). Taken together, these three should have provided the most accurate forecasts of what would happen to the global climate over the next fifty years. So far, however, the conclusions had been contradictory, which was what upset Binch. The system was his brainchild, but it was showing itself a somewhat recalcitrant offspring.

Against his will, Brad felt his attention wrenched to what DELFI was spewing out. He began to hum a tune, repeating the same fragment of melody over and over again. A Joni Mitchell track from way back, something about 'a marbled bowling ball'.

Binch glanced up uneasily. Brad was staring into space, oblivious, humming his tune.'

3

One of Major Bradley E. Zittel's keenest pleasures was to stand at the wide window of his third-floor office and lose himself in contemplation of the picture-postcard scenery. The view warmed his soul and calmed his mind: the icy backbone of the Rockies thrusting sharply against the translucent blue of a cloudless sky; sunlight, so pure and clean, reflecting from the snowy peaks with an intensity that hurt the eyes.

For millions of years the mountains had stood thus, aloof and daunting, indifferent to what went on around them. They didn't seek to be admired. Their grandeur and awesome beauty were sufficient unto themselves. His eye beheld them and they didn't give a damn whether he looked or not, but remained uncompromising, a savage act of nature arrested in time and space.

His first sight of the earth from the region of the moon had evoked the same response in him.

It had also changed his life.

Born in San Antonio, Texas, a graduate of the Carnegie Institute of Technology, he had enlisted in the navy and continued his studies at MIT, emerging with a master's in aeronautics and astronautics. Then came four years with NASA, during which he took part in three missions, the longest being an eighty-one day stint in Skylab, which had a profound effect on his whole philosophy.

Up to that point, aged twenty-nine, he had thought no more or less about the environment and matters of ecology than it was fashionable to do. In fact he was rather weary of hearing people refer to the earth as 'a spaceship with finite resources'.

Then he went into space. As he looked down upon the earth, he thought it was so damned beautiful. He'd been expecting it, of course, having seen with every other person living the colour shots of the swirling blue-white planet set against the velvety blackness of space. But by God, it *was* beautiful, no denying it – and vulnerable. That's what threw him. This incredibly beautiful, peaceful-looking planet floating all alone in the infinite reaches of the cosmos. And although he'd always known this to be true intellectually, now he actually felt the truth of it. He remembered thinking: This is our home – and it's all we've got!

In that moment, 130 miles in space, he ceased to be an American citizen and became a citizen of the planet. Every astronaut he knew felt the same. From out there it was all so painfully obvious that mankind, squabbling and falling out like a pack of ignorant loutish children, was in danger of fouling its own nest. Humanity was mindlessly overpopulating the planet, squandering its resources, filling it with deadly pollution. And all the while demanding more, grabbing more, pushing one another out of the way in a selfish, greedy scramble.

That experience, that revelation, five years ago, still had the power to make him tremble. It had fuelled his determination to do something about it. But what? Wage a one-man crusade against the despoilment of the planet? That was naïve, worse, futile.

A solution of sorts presented itself when, on leaving NASA for the big cruel world outside, he'd been invited by Bill Inchcape, a former MIT alumni, to join him at the National Climate Prediction Foundation. Bill said they needed somebody with his kind of experience to take charge of satellite photography and evaluation, so for the past three years Brad had been head of the department, working in collaboration with the centre's meteorologists and atmospheric physicists: people, he felt, with their hearts in the right place. Yet still it wasn't enough. In a way he couldn't explain – even to Binch, who possessed far more technical knowledge and expertise than he did – Brad was gripped by a mounting sense of panic. What really scared him – what *haunted* him – was that the world might be sliding headlong towards an inescapable ecological doomsday, with nothing for mankind to do but slide helplessly with it.

Brad turned away from the window with its magnificent mountain panorama and sat down at his desk, a tall, slightly stooping man with a gentle, worried face. He was in his early fifties now, though he looked older, and certainly felt it. He wasn't eating or sleeping properly. It also upset his wife that he never had much time for the boys any more. Their two teenage sons, Gary and Pete, couldn't understand why Dad showed little interest in them and their joyful enthusiasms.

Joyce blamed it on Brad being forever and totally preoccupied with his work – but it wasn't that.

How could he explain that he was thinking about them, his own flesh and blood, and deeply concerned in the most drastically real way possible? That in his mind's eye there was an image that revolved endlessly like a closed spool of film: the bleak future his generation was bequeathing theirs.

A dead, polluted, uninhabitable planet.

Brad Zittel looked at his taut, outstretched hands and pressed them to his face. He had to find the answer, for the sake of his children and all the future generations. What terrified him was that, as far as he could see, there wasn't an answer to be found.

4

Bo Anyango knelt in the baked red earth and fingered the mottled leaves of a coffee bush. The rising sun had just cleared the peaks of a distant mountain range so the air was still pleasantly cool; yet it was tainted with the sour odour of decaying vegetable matter.

Bo was mystified. Every single bush on his four-acre plot had been ruined. Shrivelled discoloured leaves were scattered all around, several inches deep in the furrows he had hoed with his own hands, using implements supplied by the Bakura Institute of Agriculture. Like his African neighbours, he had followed the instructions and tended his crops just as the *mzungu* – the European agricultural officer – had shown him. And just like the crops of his neighbours, the coffee bushes had wilted and died. The only means of livelihood for himself, his wife and five children was now so much rotten, stinking vegetation.

What had gone wrong?

Squatting on his skinny haunches, Bo looked disconsolately around him. Three years' work to prepare the land for the coffee crop he had been assured would fetch a good price, totally wasted. He had been told of the miracles the Europeans could bring about with their powders and sprays, and he had been eager to try. JEG was the magic word on the side of the canisters. It was an English word, he supposed, though no one had told him its meaning. He had believed in JEG because he had seen the results with his own eyes. Crops that normally would have been stripped bare by hordes of voracious insects, commonplace in this remote region of western Kenya, had flourished and grown to maturity. The valley, once a barren waste, had blossomed. The insects had been defeated – for a while.

Recently, however, some of the pests had reappeared, and in far greater numbers than before. The spider-mite – not an insect but a member of the scorpion family – had returned in the millions. Its razor-sharp mouth was specially adapted for piercing and sucking chlorophyll from leaves, and it had a prodigious appetite. In the past the spider-mite population had been kept in check by predatory insects and birds, most of which had disappeared since JEG had been used so widely. Some animals too, he observed, had also gone, too many of them found floating belly-up in the streams. Soon the valley would be denuded of vegetation, silent of birdsong, devoid of animal life. Only the vultures and the spider-mites would be left.

Bo knew one thing for sure. Without the coffee crop he would be unable to barter for goods, unable to feed himself and his family. He knew also that he was worse off now than he had been before the *mzungu* came to the valley bringing the miracle of modern science.

3

I

Squeezing the rubber bulb between thumb and forefinger, Chase gingerly deposited a globule of fluid on the glass slide and positioned it under the microscope. He adjusted the magnification to a scan of 0.3 mm and the bead of water became a subminiature menagerie of marine life. Sharpening the focus, he concentrated on a particular group and after a few moments identified two subclasses of diatoms called *Centricae* and *Pennatae*.

Why such diversity in such tiny organisms less than one millimetre in length? Obviously each was suited to a specific purpose and mode of life, fitted perfectly into its niche, yet he couldn't help but marvel at the seemingly endless proliferation of design and the incredibly minute adaptations to environment.

By his right elbow lay his notebook and several sheets of graph paper, and next to those on the bench his heavily annotated copy of the standard work, Detrick's *Diatom Growth and Development*. Taking up the book and opening it at one of the sections marked with slips of paper, he refreshed his memory. Most species of diatoms were widely distributed throughout the world and were probably, Detrick had said, the most abundant and adaptable creatures in the oceans, if not on earth.

Chase wrote up his notes, frequently going back to the eyepiece to check a detail, and made rough sketches of the various subclasses to complement his descriptions. He found the ordered routine of lab work deeply satisfying. The slow, painstaking accumulation of observed data, the classifying and cross-referencing, the fragmentary picture slowly emerging – though after four months of steady work he was still a long way away from reaching any kind of conclusion. He shook his head in mute wonder at the amount of work Detrick must have put in to write his monumental study, surely a lifetime's dedication. Did he have that kind of perseverance? He doubted it; for instance, that specimen of brine he'd examined yesterday. He'd spent damn near three hours distilling it and setting up the test, and he might as well have been looking at tap water. The sample had obviously been spoiled, contaminated somewhere between collection and the lab. It had come from his last dive, he recalled, when Nick was handling the net. Maybe that explained why it had been so low on what one would have normally expected to find in the ocean under the Antarctic Ice Shelf – low on phytoplankton, diatoms and *Ceratium*.

Anyway, he'd written off the sample as a botched job and thrown the whole bloody lot down the sink. So much for the objective, dispassionate scientist. No, he thought wryly, a 378-page treatise on marine biology wouldn't be appearing under the name of Dr Gavin Chase any time soon.

He stretched and yawned and glanced at his watch: twenty past four. This being Friday he didn't have any qualms of conscience about packing up early. It took him only a few minutes to clear away and return the specimen jars to the freezer.

As he hung up his white coat and reached for his jacket, his mobile trilled.

'Carruthers! How are you, old bean?'

'What ho, Fortescue! And how's the Lebanese Red?'

Nick chuckled. 'The good stuff? Too bloody expensive. I'm thinking of cultivating my own crop. What are you up to?'

'The same,' Chase replied, leaning against a bench. 'Developing a squint from staring down a microscope all day. What's happening with you?'

'Well now, matey, that's just it. How does a long weekend away, *sur Le Continent*, all expenses paid, grab you?'

'Go on.'

'Conference in Geneva in two weeks' time, the ninth onwards for four days. The EU is sponsoring delegates from British universities. I've put my name down, but there are still a few places open. How about it? You could take time off, couldn't you?'

'What's the gig?'

'The International Conference on the Environmental Future. All the usual stuff, plus rich food, plenty to drink. And the rest.'

'The rest?'

'Sex and rock'n'roll. Like the sound of it?'

'I'm a happily kept man.'

Nick made a gurgling noise. 'What you hear is the sound of hollow laughter. Of course we might have to put in a couple of appearances, just to show willing. But nobody keeps a check on who does what.'

'Or with whom.' Chase drummed his fingers on the work bench and looked at the sealed specimen jars inside the hermetic cabinets. 'I don't think so, Nick, thanks all the same. I've got a full schedule of lab work planned. Anyway, what do I know about the environmental future?'

'What does anybody?' Nick Power responded.

Much as he'd have liked to see Nick again, Chase didn't see how he could justify a long weekend in Geneva at the EU's expense. Better that someone who was genuinely interested should make the trip. Besides, what would Angie have to say? He'd only been back a few months and they were just getting used to each other again; she might dream up the notion that he was grabbing at any opportunity to flee the nest.

He repeated his excuse about the pressure of work.

Nick sounded disappointed. 'Your trouble is you're too damn serious for your own good, Gav. How's it going with you and Angie?'

'Never better.' He said it automatically, and then wondered if it was true. They were talking of getting married, so it must be, he supposed. 'Sorry Nick – what was that?' He'd missed what Nick was saying.

'. . . the Russian who kept going on about Stan-or-Nick and we couldn't figure out what he meant? The conference brochure lists all the delegates and one is a Professor Stanovnik. Get it? *Stan-ov-nik.*'

'Is he Russian?'

'Yeah, think so.' There was a riffling of paper and a tuneless whistle and then Nick said, 'Professor B. V. Stanovnik of the Hydro-Meteorological Service, Academy of Sciences, Moscow. Perhaps Stanovnik and the guy we found were colleagues.'

It was a possibility, Chase thought. By the sound of it the

Hydro-Meteorological Service was certainly in the right area. Oceans. Climate. So who was Stanovnik? Climatologist? Oceanographer?

'Is Stanovnik giving a paper at the conference?'

'He's on the list of speakers, but doesn't give the title of his paper. If you like – and assuming he speaks English – I could ask him what he knows about the absorption of carbon dioxide in seawater.' Nick's gruff chuckle came over the phone. 'That was it, wasn't it?'

'It was,' Chase agreed, 'but you'd be better off asking him what he *doesn't* know about it. If the Hydro-Meteorological Service is carrying out research, presumably it's to fill a gap in their knowledge. Something they're keen to find out.'

Nick said he'd keep it in mind, that he was sorry Chase couldn't drag himself away, and they said their goodbyes.

2

The conversation ran around his head as he walked up the three flights of stairs to the flat and let himself in. Normally Angie didn't finish at the studio till six-thirty, and then went for a drink or two – usually three or four – with her colleagues from the newsroom. But today she was sitting in an armchair with her feet propped up, clasping a large gin and tonic.

'Like to go to a party, darling?'

'When?' Chase said as if enquiring about the date of his execution.

'Tonight.'

'Where?'

'Archie's. Somebody's leaving bash and Archie kindly offered to do the honours. I said yes for both of us.'

Chase draped his jacket over a chair, taking his time and doing it carefully to show he wasn't annoyed, which he was. He didn't like Archie Grieve, Angie's boss. Archie was one of the breed of brash young Scottish journalists who had infiltrated the media south of the border. They all had trendy credentials as the grandsons of spot-welders in the Clydeside shipyards or as grassroots activists for New Labour. Gavin Chase wasn't convinced by Archie, not in the slightest. They had met only once and had nothing in common; Chase genuinely came from working-class stock and he could sniff out a bogus flat-cap revolutionary before they even shook hands.

For the sake of peace and harmony, he nodded and even managed a smile.

In the first hour Chase had three stiff whisky-and-sodas to get him through the rest of the evening. After that he lost sight of Angie, nodded vaguely at three or four people and wandered in a mellow haze from room to room of the large old house. Everything was stripped down to the bare wood. Their host had greeted them at the door attired in a plum-coloured shirt, faded denims and fashionably scuffed trainers. He obviously watched endless re-runs of *Top Gear*, Chase thought uncharitably. And the little squirt – he was under five feet six – had kissed Angie not on the cheek but on the lips. Chase detected a warmth that didn't befit an employer–employee relationship, which led to speculation about whether she'd been unfaithful while he was away. He himself had had no opportunity to stray, but had temptation come his way, would he have fallen? He didn't honestly know.

Chase stood in the lee of a monstrous growth of dark green shrubbery that sprouted from a Victorian urn. He was content with the whisky for company. What was it about media folk he didn't like? They inhabited a world he didn't understand, glossy and slick – 'trendy' in the worst possible meaning of the word. As if they were centre-stage, while everyone else faded off into shadow and was thus relegated to trivial anonymity.

Steady, he told himself. *Your paranoia is showing.* He took a measured sip of his drink, hoping to eke it out, and tried to remain inconspicuous.

'You're Angie's fella.' A small dark-haired girl had appeared at his elbow. Obviously not inconspicuous enough.

Chase looked down into large brown eyes ringed with spiky black lashes. She wore an embroidered sleeveless jacket over a loose linen dress with a generous neckline. He could see where her tan ended. Thin gold bracelets clinked on her arms.

'I guessed you must be. We know all about the intrepid Arctic explorer.'

'Right bloke, wrong continent,' Chase replied.

The girl bit her lip in mock horror. 'Ooops! Geography was never my best subject. That's at the bottom, isn't it?'

Chase nodded. 'Or the arse-end of Mother Earth is the technical term we intrepid *Antarctic* explorers prefer to use.'

The girl tilted her head to the side as she laughed. 'Great! I've found a scientist with a sense of humour! Gavin, isn't it? I'm Jill. I work with Angie in the newsroom. PA.' She clinked his glass with hers and they both drank.

'What does that entail?'

'Oh, mostly running around getting everything organised. Production assistants get shunted about a lot: news, current affairs, documentaries. Without us the television industry would collapse.'

Chase had never thought of television as an industry. Its product seemed so ephemeral: in one eye and out the other. But he was starting to relax and as the whisky warmed his gut he felt a benign sense of letting it all go hang. For three months he'd been completely absorbed in his work and it was high time he got smashed. The mood beckoned to him like a seductive lover.

'What are you grinning at?'

'Plenty of excellent single malt and attractive company.'

'And what do you do when you're not exploring?' she asked him.

'I'm in the marine biology department at the university. Right now I'm classifying specimens I brought back with me. Microscopic plant life from the oceans.' Chase waved his hand dismissively. 'Not very interesting to the layman, I'm afraid. Or the laywoman.'

'That's plankton, isn't it?' Jill said.

'Yes it is.'

She gave him a shrewd look. 'I may get my continents mixed up, but I'm not completely stupid.'

'Yes, well . . . the name "plankton" is a general term for all floating plant and animal life in the seas and rivers. My speciality is *Halosphaera, Phaeocystis, silicoflagellates* and *Bacillariophyceae.*'

That'd teach her not to be such a smart arse.

Jill laughed again. 'That's easy for you to say.'

'More like a bloody miracle after three whiskies. It's the stuff most fish feed off – phytoplankton, that is, the plant form. They're a very primitive organism, one of the oldest on the planet. Been around for at least two thousand million years.' Through the crush of people in the next room Chase glimpsed Angie standing next to Archie Grieve. Angie and Archie. How cosy that sounded. They looked to be at the centre of a laughing group of chums, all very easy in each other's company. As Chase watched, Archie's hand slid around Angie's waist in what might have been an innocent friendly gesture. Or not so innocent.

'So without it there'd be no fish suppers,' Jill said.

'Sorry? What?'

'The fish feed off the plankton you said. No plankton, no fish . . .'

'Yes. Right. That's true.' Archie's hand was moving imperceptibly lower, resting just above Angie's right buttock. 'And they allow us to breathe too.'

Jill looked puzzled. 'Do they?'

'If you look at a pond you'll see the bottom carpeted with millions of tiny silver bubbles. That's oxygen. The phytoplankton releases oxygen after splitting water into hydrogen and oxygen.'

'Isn't that photosynthesis?'

Chase nodded. 'Most of the oxygen we breathe comes from the oceans.' He was tall enough to look over Jill's curly dark head, but there were other bodies in the way now, so he couldn't see how far the errant hand had strayed.

Jill said, 'I always thought trees did that – the rain forests in South America and Asia. That's really frightening. Destroying millions of acres and burning them down.'

'All green plants take in carbon dioxide and give off oxygen; forests give us about thirty per cent, but the phytoplankton in the oceans provides most of the oxygen we need, roughly seventy per cent. And without phytoplankton there wouldn't be any trees in the first place.'

'It isn't dull at all, is it, microbiology?' Jill said. 'It's fascinating really.'

'I like to think so,' Chase said. 'It's what I spend my life doing.'

A space cleared between the crush of bodies. Archie's hand was on the demarcation line between friendly and indecent. Or maybe Angie didn't consider it so. Chase swirled his whisky, making the ice cubes clink.

'The whole bag of tricks depends on microscopic plant life. Most people don't realise that the early atmosphere was highly poisonous – to us, that is. Mainly hydrogen, ammonia, methane. It was only when the first primitive forms of algae came along and started releasing oxygen into the atmosphere . . .'

What to do? Go for a refill or barge into their cosy group and ask Archie Grieve what the fuck he was trying on? Ask Angie too, for that matter. She didn't appear to mind her boss fondling her bum in public.

'I can understand it, even though I'm slightly pissed,' Jill said, 'so you must have explained it okay.'

Chase grinned and finished off his drink. 'Thanks. I appreciate the compliment. People live their lives and never give a second thought to the way the biosphere works. They just take it for granted. If you're enthusiastic and start talking about it they go glassy-eyed and fall into a doze. You really have to be a genius like David Attenborough to make them see the big picture.'

'Or Sir Frederick Cole. He's got the knack as well. You've heard of him, I take it?'

There was a gleam in her brown eyes and a hint of mockery in her tone. Was it his turn to be patronised?

'We had a nickname for him: "Firebrand Fred".'

'You know him then?'

'He was one of my lecturers at Cambridge.'

'He's coming into the studio next week to do an interview. We're recording it on Wednesday afternoon and I'm the gofer.'

'I think he'd be rather good on the telly,' Chase said. 'Blunt Yorkshire humour, straight from the shoulder. A natural TV pundit, or whatever they call them.'

The laughing group of cronies was still there but Archie and Angie had moved off. Chase did a slow survey of the room but couldn't spot them.

Jill was shaking her head and grinning. 'We had to ask him to wear a new suit for the interview filming. You won't believe it – well you would, perhaps, having known him – Sir Fred turned up at the office wearing a pullover with holes in it and the crotch of his trousers somewhere down near his kneecaps. "Firebrand Fred",' she said, collapsing into giggles. 'I'll call him that next time I see him.'

'Be my guest – but don't mention my name.'

It occurred to Chase that if he wanted to pick someone's brains, he couldn't do better than Sir Fred. He'd earned his knighthood for an impressive body of research in the eighties and early nineties and was still regarded as one of the most eminent people in the field, even though he'd given up the lab bench for the lecture platform.

'What time is he there?'

'He'll be arriving about one and will probably have lunch in the canteen. We're in the studio at two-thirty and it'll take forty minutes to an hour. Do you want to come along?'

'I wouldn't mind,' Chase said.

'What is it, a reunion with an old prof? Or work-related?'

'Something or nothing. A small matter of marine chemistry.'

Jill pointed at his empty glass. 'That looks like a small matter of alcohol deficiency. Another malt whisky?'

Chase was about to thank her when who should stroll up but his old mate Archie Grieve, the famous Clydeside spot-welder, with Angie in tow.

'Enjoying yersel, Gav?' Archie enquired in an overly familiar way, given that this was only their second meeting. 'The gorgeous Jill looking after you, is she?'

Chase grinned. 'And listening to my boring lecture on microscopic plant life into the bargain.'

'Ah, Gav,' Archie said with a crooked grin. 'Tales of the wild frontier with daredevil scientists and all that guff. The old charisma never fails, eh?' He combed his long floppy hair back with both hands and gave Angie a sly wink. Her long hollow cheeks, usually pale, were rather flushed, Chase noticed. Was this the effects of alcohol or Archie's roving hands?

'Jill tells me you've got Sir Fred Cole in the studio next week,' Chase said.

Archie pulled a face. 'We have, but it's none of my doing,' he said disparagingly. 'I get sick and bleddy tired of these so-called experts – ha! – bleating on about global warming. Clever scheme to rake in taxpayers' dosh from the government, that's my view. Big fat juicy grants for telling us we're all gonna fry. Nice work if you can get it.'

'You honestly think Fred Cole is a charlatan?' Chase asked.

Archie shrugged. 'Got himself a handy little earner on the lecture circuit, hasn't he? In his best interest to constantly spread panic stories, keep us all shit-scared.'

'I thought the War on Terror was supposed to do that,' Chase said glibly. 'And I don't think Sir Fred is deliberately spreading panic. Global warming is a scientific fact, not a scare story.' He wondered whether Archie Grieve was drunk or was he always this offensive?

'Angie didn't mention you were another of the climate change brigade. D'you go around preaching this stuff for fun or do you get paid?'

Jill must have been watching Chase and saw his expression alter, for she touched his arm and said, 'I promised to refresh your drink, Gavin. Another Scotch?'

'I'm fine, Jill. Thanks. Perhaps it's time we were going.'

'I should've warned you,' Angie said, 'that Archie doesn't have much time for academics. He was educated in the school of hard knocks . . .'

'I was so – too bleddy right! None of that academic bullshit, ta very much. University of Life for Mrs Grieve's wee lad.'

'Did you get a pass grade?' Chase enquired.

Archie Grieve's eyes narrowed. He stared up at Chase. 'What d'you bleddy mean by that? Ye taking the piss, matey?'

'No. I'm trying not to be rude either. As if you'd notice.'

'Then what are ye tryin to say?' His belligerence brought out Archie's Glaswegian accent.

'That if you don't know anything about a subject, it's better to keep quiet and let people guess at your ignorance rather open your mouth and confirm it. Otherwise you end up looking like a prize tit. *Matey.*'

Jill squeezed her eyes shut and bit her lip, as if she might explode with mirth. Archie Grieve just stood breathing hard and glowering. Angie was livid, shooting dagger-glances at Chase, who politely took Jill's hand and thanked her for the pleasant chat.

On the way home in the cab Angie was still seething. She sat with her arms tightly folded and snapped at him from the corner of her mouth, 'He's my boss, for heaven's sake. He could decide to fire me first thing Monday morning. Did you have to insult him like that? In front of his work colleagues? It was unforgivable – Archie's sensitive about his educational qualifications.'

'Or lack of them.'

'Was it worth the effort, riling him like that?'

'It wasn't any effort,' Chase assured her. 'And I doubt you'll lose your job.'

'How do you come to that conclusion?'

'Obviously, he fancies you. Maybe the reverse applies. You spent more time with him this evening than you did with me.'

Angie said in a small/ sullen voice, 'You looked well enough entertained.'

In the light of a streetlamp he saw that her cheeks were shiny. Chase sighed and said, 'I'm sorry, Angie. I didn't mean those stupid remarks to harm your career in any way.'

'Forget my career. It doesn't matter.'

'Of course it matters.' He put his arm round her shoulders.

'In the future maybe. Not for a while anyway. I'm planning on taking a break from it.'

'Just because I upset your boss?' Chase said, mystified. 'But why?'

'That little prick's not the reason,' Angie said, and snuggled her head against him. 'Can't you think of any other?'

Chase looked ahead through the windscreen at the rows of street lamps. It took him only a moment, and then he could. He nodded slowly. 'Ah . . .'

3

The blonde secretary with the silver claws reacted perceptibly when he appeared in front of her desk. Most of the men who passed through her office on their way to see the deputy director of the World Oceanographic Data Center were conservatively dressed in dark business suits, crisp shirts and polished shoes. A few of the younger ones, it was true, wore open-necked shirts, casual jackets, jeans. But here was somebody in late middle age who looked for all the world like a beachcomber down on his luck.

She half-rose in alarm, appraising with distaste the dingy crumpled T-shirt under the cord jacket with torn pockets; the jacket was a peculiar shade of green that might almost be mildew (the secretary looked closely and saw that it *was* mildew). Completing the ensemble, dirty white twill trousers with ragged bottoms and sneakers, minus laces, which might have been – many, *many* moons ago – white.

And no socks . . .

Quite stunned by this apparition in the sanctity of her Washington office on an otherwise unremarkable Tuesday morning, Ms Weston could only stare speechlessly, and it was left to Theo Detrick to introduce himself. In his soft guttural accent, a remnant of his German ancestry, he reminded her of his appointment with Dr Parris Winthrop, the deputy director.

'You – you are Dr Detrick?'

'That is correct,' he said patiently.

Parris Winthrop was less taken aback than amused. 'Theo, marvellous to see you!' he said in greeting, striding around his huge walnut desk. He towered over Theo, clad in a bespoke dark grey suit with a matching tie flecked with pale yellow. 'Say, you look wonderful! But Theo, good grief, what the hell are you wearing?'

'What I always wear.' Theo swapped his bulging briefcase with the broken clasp from right to left in order to shake hands. 'Macy's haven't got around to opening a store on Canton Island as yet.'

Winthrop patted his shoulder, genuine pleasure on his ruddy, well-fed face, and indicated a leather armchair. 'Like something to drink?'

'Coffee, black, will be fine.'

'I was thinking of something with a bit more bite. Don't tell me you've become Spartan in everything,' Winthrop said jovially.

'I like to keep a clear head during the day.' Theo sat back holding the briefcase flat on his knees with both hands. It was worn and scratched and some of the stitching had come adrift.

'Coffee it is then.' Winthrop smiled and leaned across the desk to press the intercom tab. A gold signet ring flashed on his little finger.

The white-haired scientist let his eyes roam around the spacious office. Slats of sunlight from the Venetian blinds imprinted gold bars on the thick carpet. Parris had every reason to be expansive and highly pleased, both with the world and with himself. He had climbed impressively high on the ladder since their student days at McGill. Both had come from poor homes and non-intellectual backgrounds; both had finished top in their respective subjects. Then Parris had had the good fortune to receive a Travelling Fellowship, which he chose to spend at the Kaiser Wilhelm Institut in Dresden. While Theo had doggedly embarked on the long hard slog of underpaid research in small laboratories up and down the country, Parris had been given the luxury of several prestigious options, including the post of director of the Pacific Fisheries Experimental Station, then based in Hawaii.

After that it was plain sailing. Or maybe it wasn't, Theo considered, knowing how the outward show of a person's life could often be misleading.

Perhaps Parris had struggled and fought as much as the next man, the difference being that he had taken his chances – and had the good sense to stay near the centre of influence.

From Theo Detrick's point of view, the prestige was of less importance than the fact that Parris was on PSAC: the President's Scientific Advisory Committee.

'When was it, three, four years ago?' Winthrop said. He snapped his lean fingers. 'Dedication ceremony at Scripps for the physical oceanography annexe, right?'

Theo nodded. 'You'd just been appointed deputy director here.'

'And I met your daughter there. She was at Scripps, taking her Ph.D. Where is she now?'

'Still there, doing postgraduate work. According to her last email.'

'Haven't you seen her recently?'

'Not for more than a year.' Theo examined his brown grizzled hands. 'I don't get to the States very often. On this trip I shipped into San Francisco and flew directly here.'

Winthrop waited a moment. Whatever had brought his old friend seven thousand miles, it wasn't merely to pay a social call. 'I guess it must be pretty important then.'

'I think so.' Theo cleared his throat and opened the one remaining clasp on his briefcase. He carefully extracted a thick stack of papers loosely contained between stiff covers and tied together with black tape. It was bulky enough to require both hands as he placed it on the gleaming expanse of desk. 'My research,' he said quietly.

Winthrop looked at it and then at Theo. 'Over how long?'

Theo stared beyond him to the Venetian blinds, lost in speculation. He blinked slowly and said, 'Altogether, twenty-eight years. Most of it is over the last ten years, as regards actual conclusions. But the records are complete from 1988.' There was no smugness or boasting; it was a statement of fact. 'I'd like you to study it, if you would, and then we can see the President together.'

A corrugation of V-shaped lines appeared below the deputy director's silvery widow's peak. He looked at the heap of soiled documentation in its dog-eared covers despoiling his beautiful desk and then regarded Theo blankly.

'I don't understand. The *President*?'

'You're still a member of the advisory committee?'

Winthrop nodded, a little more warily now.

Ms Weston tapped and entered discreetly, leaving a tray with coffee. Theo waited until she had gone.

'That's the reason I came to see *you*. I don't know of any other way, except through you, Parris, old friend.'

'No, you don't understand me. What I meant was, *why* do you have to see him? About what?'

Theo's expression was calm, stoical. His clear blue eyes, the colour of a washed sky, showed no emotion as he said, 'We are in danger of running out of oxygen. The amount in the atmosphere will decline quite sharply over the next quarter-century – I'm not certain when exactly – but it will fall below the level capable of supporting life on this planet. All animal life, that is, including mankind.' His square brown hand made a gesture towards the heap of paper. 'The evidence is all there. Records from over nearly thirty years of the decline in the phytoplankton index, which is continuing to decrease at a steadily increasing rate.'

'Theo, old man,' Winthrop said faintly, 'do you seriously expect me to tell the President that the world is about to perish through asphyxiation?'

'No,' Theo corrected him at once, 'I want you to arrange a meeting so that I can tell him. That is why I'm here, why I came in person. This is my task, my responsibility, Parris, not yours.'

Winthrop's healthy, urbane face had frozen into a mask of pained unease. He'd read what isolation could do the mind. Was he seeing it at first hand in the ragged figure sitting before him? He pushed such thoughts away for a moment and tried to concentrate on what Theo was saying.

'I'm not asking you to take my word alone. If I were, I'd be as mad as you're beginning to think I am. What I ask is that you consider this information objectively, as a scientist, and draw your own conclusions.'

'Which you believe will be the same as yours.'

'If you're honest and consider the data without prejudice, yes,' Theo told him frankly. 'It's all there in the records. I don't have to convince you; study them and you'll see.'

'The evidence is completely incontrovertible?'

'Yes.'

'Then why not publish it?'

Theo smiled, his head craggy and solid as a carving in the filtered light. 'I intend to, but I know it will be seen by many people as yet another doomsday prophecy: another fanciful way for the world to end.' He clenched his fist and leaned forward. 'What I need – must have – is the support of an organisation such as yours and ultimately, the support of the President. Only then will people begin to listen and take the threat seriously.'

'But is it as serious as you make out, Theo?' Winthrop asked. 'You've taken readings from a specific fixed location, remember. I've seen a number of recent reports on phytoplankton growth in the Atlantic and yes, while it's true that there *has* been a decline north of fifty-nine degrees north, there's actually been in *increase* in southern latitudes.

As you know better than anyone, Theo, the phytoplankton population is subject to cyclical change and seasonal variation. How do you know that what you've been observing isn't simply a local phenomenon, confined to the equatorial Pacific?'

'Fair point,' Theo said, helping himself to coffee. He stirred in a spoonful of sugar, sipped, and nodded appreciatively. 'I've been used to instant.' He took another sip and said, 'I chose Canton Island as my base because it lies in the ten-degree belt where cold-water upwelling takes place for most of the year. This provides the ideal conditions for abundant growth of micro-organisms – in the first place because the water rising from two- to three-hundred-metre depths is rich in nutrients; and, second, because phytoplankton thrives in cooler water. Also, phytoplankton cannot grow at extreme depths because of insufficient light, which blocks photosynthesis. But given all these conditions – ample sunlight, cooler water, plenty of nutrients – it should bloom copiously. And that's precisely what isn't happening.'

Winthrop twisted the signet ring, working it around and around, his face sombre. 'What you're saying is that if the phytoplankton is declining in the ocean around Canton Island, where conditions are the most favourable, then the situation must be the same if not worse elsewhere in the world.'

'A logical conclusion, I'd say. Wouldn't you?' Theo met the deputy director's eye squarely. 'Unfortunately that isn't all.'

'What else?' Winthrop said stonily. He wasn't sure that he wanted to hear any more.

'Well . . .' Theo placed his cup and saucer on the tray. '. . . this part, I admit, is hypothesis. But it follows on directly from my research findings. We know that the tropical oceans accumulate a net surplus of solar energy over the year, while the subArctic and Arctic oceans show a net loss. Through the various poleward currents, such as the Gulf Stream, this excess heat is transferred from the tropics to the higher latitudes. At the same time there's a deep return flow of cooler water towards the equator, resulting in upwelling. This is the mechanism that keeps the planet in thermal equilibrium.' Theo tapped the bulky folder. 'But if the phytoplankton is declining, as my records show, one possible cause is a temperature increase in the deep return flow to the tropics. It could be gradually getting warmer.'

It took Winthrop several moments to see what the scientist was driving at. Warmer currents from the polar oceans could mean only one thing: that the polar oceans themselves were getting warmer. Which in turn meant that something was warming them. He grimaced as if in pain and shut his eyes. 'We're back to the CO_2 problem.'

Theo nodded and poured himself more coffee.

Winthrop said hopefully, 'This is all supposition, though, isn't it? You've no concrete proof.'

'About the warming of the polar oceans caused indirectly by a build-up of carbon dioxide in the atmosphere, yes. About the decline in the phytoplankton index leading to oxygen depletion, no.'

'Theo, come on now – you can't be that certain!' Winthrop objected, nervously smoothing his tie with a manicured hand. 'We're not even sure how much oxygen the phytoplankton contributes to the atmosphere. Nobody agrees on a precise figure—'

'But everybody agrees it's well over sixty per cent,' Theo reminded him. 'Possibly as high as seventy per cent. How long could we survive if *more than half* our oxygen supply was cut off?'

Winthrop didn't know how to answer, or how to refute Theo's reasoning. There was something wrong with it, there had to be. But he couldn't spot the flaw. Like every other ecological process, the manufacture of oxygen by photosynthesis was inextricably bound up with a host of other atmospheric and oceanic factors. Nothing operated independently as of itself. So therefore, if the oxygen level was being disturbed or disrupted in some way, in *any* way, it should be apparent elsewhere in the system. Other indices – biological processes – would be affected. But what processes? Where to look? Where to *begin*?

He breathed a long sigh. 'This is a helluva lot to ask, Theo.'

'I'm asking only one thing,' Theo maintained stolidly, his rugged face grim. 'Evaluate the data. Is that asking too much?'

'And if I think you're wrong?'

Theo sat in silence. Finally he said, 'Then I'll go somewhere else. The World Meteorological Organisation or the National Climate Prediction

Foundation in Colorado – somebody somewhere will listen eventually. They'll have to.'

'Maybe so, but do you honestly believe the President will pay heed to a warning like this?' There was a thin note of asperity in his voice. Theo was an old friend, a scientist whose selfless dedication he had always admired, even envied. But by God, how naïve! A romantic idealist in the murky world of government, with its half-truths and compromises and machinations. Whereas he was well-practised in such expediency, as of course he had to be, for the sake of his own survival.

He gestured angrily at the heap of paper. Angry because this ragged-trousered innocent out to save the world had walked into his office on a perfectly ordinary morning and threatened to upset the apple cart. Winthrop wouldn't have minded so much if it hadn't been his damn apple cart!

'Supposing the President took you seriously. Just what do you think he could do? Have you thought of that? The CO_2 problem, if it exists, is global. Every developed nation is pouring billions of tons of the stuff into the atmosphere every year from power plants and furnaces and factories. What in hell is he supposed to do, Theo? Stop the fucking world?'

Theo gazed unwaveringly at the immaculately groomed man behind the desk. 'I'm a marine biologist,' he said, 'not a politician. I'll do everything I can. But then it's up to others, to people like you, Parris. I don't know what more I can do.'

Winthrop rose wearily and came around the desk. He didn't feel like smiling, though he managed to find the ghost of one. 'All right, Theo, I'll have my staff look it over and come up with an evaluation. That's all I can promise.'

'That's all I ask,' Theo said, standing up. He looked down at his feet. 'Perhaps I should have worn socks.'

Winthrop patted him on the shoulder as they walked to the door. 'Are you staying in Washington?'

'For a few days, that's all. I was thinking of flying out to the West Coast to see my daughter.'

'Okay, call me before you leave. Just one thing . . .' Winthrop said, pausing with his hand on the knob. 'Is there any way we can verify this? If your hypothesis is right about warmer currents from the poles, there must be other signs, other factors we can look for.'

'There ought to be several,' Theo said, staring hard at the swirling walnut veneer on the door. 'Unfortunately the ecological changes will be so gradual – almost imperceptible – that it might take years for them to become apparent. But one of the first signs will be the absorption level of carbon dioxide in polar seawater. If the CO_2 has reached saturation point, then we'll know for sure.'

When the scientist had gone, the deputy director of the World Oceanographic Data Center sat at his desk and stared broodingly at twenty-eight years of work between bent and discoloured covers, twisting the gold signet ring around and around.

4

Kenichi Hanamura fought his way to street level, feeling like a minnow among a pack of barracuda. His spectacles were fogged and he experienced blind helplessness as he was carried bodily along, jammed shoulder to shoulder, in the crush of morning commuters.

How many more people were they going to cram into Tokyo before the city collapsed under the strain? Even the subway system, supposedly the most advanced and sophisticated in the world, was barely able to cope. So what about next year when it was estimated that the city's population would exceed thirty-three million?

On the street it was less congested, but now Hanamura had the fumes to contend with. He debated whether or not to wear his mask. He ought to, of course, because the doctor had advised it after he'd complained of chest pains six months ago. But he hated the damn thing.

Stupid, really, because as an insurance claims investigator he was well aware of the risks. He'd seen the statistics for himself, the endless grey columns of figures which to the trained eye made horrifying reading. People suffering from bronchitis and emphysema up one third in the past five years. Death toll increased by nine per cent in the last year alone, directly attributed to toxic pollution in Japan's major cities and industrial areas. Premiums would have to go up again to cover the escalating risk.

The thought of those figures nagged him as he passed the sheer glass-and-aluminium façade of the Mitsukoshi department store. Numbers, graphs, charts always seemed more real to him, made a sharper impact somehow, than the evidence of his own eyes. Especially because at forty-four years old, a city dweller with a sedentary occupation, he was right there in the danger zone. It was small comfort to know that his American wife, Lilian, and Frank, their thirteen-year-old son, were adequately covered in the event of his death by the company's Blue Star plan, one of the perks of the job.

From habit Hanamura glanced across the busy street at the huge illuminated sign on the corner of the Kyoto Banking Corporation building. The sign looked anaemic in the bright sunlight, but even so he could clearly read the daily pollution index spelled out in electronic digits in parts per million.

carbon monoxide	310 PPM
sulphur dioxide	0.46 PPM

The warning was stark enough even for Kenichi Hanamura.

Moving out of the throng of hurrying people he fumbled in his briefcase for his mask. The straps were entangled with something and he tugged impatiently, losing his temper. And now his glasses were misting over again and he couldn't see!

It wasn't his glasses, he suddenly realised with panic; it was his vision. Whenever he tried to focus on a particular object there was a round white blob in the way. His heart jumped. He swayed and thrust out his hand to steady himself against the polished granite base of the building. Even though he knew what was happening to him he couldn't understand why there wasn't any pain. He tried to draw breath and couldn't. His chest was locked tight.

Where was the nearest oxygen-dispenser point? Somewhere nearby there would be a row of plastic cowls with masks attached to oxygen lines. For a few yen you could suck in several pure lungfuls, enough to brace yourself against the city-centre smog.

But where? How near? Could he get there?

A pounding steam engine started up inside his head and whined to a shrill crescendo, blocking out the sound of traffic and scurrying feet. The shimmering white blob swelled like a monstrous balloon, cutting off his vision completely.

In the instant that he slithered down the granite wall to the pavement, Hanamura's last conscious thought was tinged with regret that he would never have the opportunity to tell the doctor he was wrong.

For there was no pain. None at all. It was just like going to sleep in a blizzard next to a steam engine.

4

I

The banks of lights dimmed one by one until the studio became a shadowy twilit cavern. Chase looked down from the angled window of the control gallery, fascinated.

'That's a wrap,' said the director at the console behind him. She spoke into the microphone. 'Thank you, studio.'

Through the glass walls either side Chase could see people stirring and stretching. Jill beckoned to him and he followed her into the corridor. She was wearing a loose pink T-shirt imprinted with UCLA and green cord trousers that showed off her backside.

'Does Sir Fred know I'm here?'

Jill nodded as they went down the stairs. 'He remembered you straight off.' She gave him a sneaky sideways grin. 'Told me you once tried to hoax him with a fake specimen and he nearly fell for it.'

Chase stopped on the bottom step and cringed. He'd completely forgotten about the spoof. Three of them had soaked some blue-green algae in a beaker of Guinness and taken it along to Sir Fred with carefully rehearsed expressions of bafflement. Could he identify this mutant bloom? How come it had such a peculiar smell? The professor had carried out a series of tests with his usual thoroughness before issuing a formal lab report with 'Brown Ale Algae (North Sea)' under the species classification.

The professor had had the last laugh too. He'd taken his revenge on the three culprits by setting them the long and laborious task of identifying the percentage carbon yields of the marine food chain all the way from phytoplankton to third-stage carnivores. They didn't pull any more tricks.

After bringing coffee, Jill left the professor and his former student to chat in one of the small reception rooms. Chase had been wondering how to broach the subject (what the hell *was* the subject?), but his trepidation melted away in the warmth of Sir Frederick Cole's welcome.

Chase remembered him as a sloppy dresser, though today, wearing the suit Jill had mentioned, he was positively smart – even though the material was stiff, enclosing his chest in a kind of blue shell, and there was an excess of it in the sleeves and trouser legs. He still had an untidy thatch of mousey-coloured hair, greying at the temples, and lively brown eyes peering out from beneath bushy grey eyebrows.

'Enjoy yourself in the Antarctic?' he asked when they'd shaken hands, his flat Yorkshire voice unchanged.

'You know about that?'

'Oh, aye, I keep in touch. I saw your name in *Geographical* magazine, in a list of personnel at Halley Bay.' Sir Fred's eyes twinkled. 'And I could hardly forget one of the perpetrators of the Brown Ale incident. Ruined my reputation and chance of a Nobel.'

Chase grinned weakly. 'Actually, sir, it was Guinness.'

'Was it? Never knew that. Thought it was Newcastle Brown. So there you are, lad, none of us can be right all the time.' He took out a meerschaum pipe, gazed at it with regret and cradled it in his palm. 'What is it, Gavin, career problem? Advice you want?'

Chase went over the problem quickly and briefly, mentioning the Russian found on the ice, the scrawled chemical equation, his death at McMurdo Station, all the while acutely aware that he was wasting Sir Fred's time. Here, in this comfortable lounge with its easy chairs and potted shrubbery, the whole thing seemed preposterous and he cursed himself for being such a fool. Then he remembered to add the bit that Nick had told him about, the scientist who was to be one of the speakers at the conference in Geneva.

Sir Fred didn't immediately see the connection, and Chase explained, 'The Russian – the man we found on the ice – kept repeating something over and over that sounded like Stan-ov-nik. We thought it was a word, or a phrase, but it could have been a name – maybe this scientist called Stanovnik who's going to be in Geneva. Have you heard of him?'

'Aye. I've also met him, two or three times. Boris Stanovnik. He's a microbiologist with the Hydro-Meteorological Service in Moscow, or whatever it's called these days, after the privateers took it over and made a killing. Good chap, Boris. Old school.' Sir Fred sucked on his empty pipe and observed Chase keenly. 'Got the equation with you?'

Chase took the slip of paper from his diary and handed it over. After a minute's scrutiny Sir Fred raised his eyes and gave Chase a sceptical glare.

'Is this another leg-pull?'

'No – no, sir, really. It's perfectly genuine.'

'What we have here is the basic dissolution of CO_2 in seawater.'

Chase nodded. 'That's what I don't understand – why go to the trouble of writing it down? A perfectly ordinary chemical interaction. Another thing. He couldn't speak a word of English, and yet he was able to use our chemical symbols.'

Sir Fred waved that away. 'Normal practice. Many foreign scientists use them as an international code. But it is odd, must admit. As you say, Gavin, why bother in the first place? He must have been trying to communicate something he felt was important.' Sir Fred folded the paper and gave it back. 'You didn't find out his name then?'

'No. Perhaps the Americans did.'

'Didn't you ask them?'

'It didn't occur to me,' Chase confessed. 'We should have flown in our own medical team – or even waited till he was stronger. I got the impression that Professor Banting was afraid of offending the Americans by refusing.'

'Professor Banting is afraid of offending his own shadow,' Sir Fred commented drily. He rubbed the side of his nose with a stubby forefinger. 'I'm trying to remember. Last time I met Boris Stanovnik – about two years ago, must be – he was working on a climatic project.'

'Really?' Chase was puzzled. 'I thought you said he was a microbiologist?'

'He was investigating the effects of pollutants and chemical runoff on micro-organisms in coastal seawater. You're familiar with eutrophication, I take it?'

Chase nodded. When a river or lake received an overabundance of nutrients (usually caused by the spill-over of farm fertilisers with a high nitrogen content) this encouraged the growth of dense algae blooms. As these decayed and died, they consumed all the oxygen in the water. Deprived of oxygen, other plants and animals also perished, with the result that the water became biologically dead. This was the process of eutrophication; it had the effect of speeding up the natural evolutionary cycle. Lake Erie in the United States and the land-locked Mediterranean were often-cited examples where the natural organic processes had been accelerated by some two hundred years, leading to extinction.

'We had a long chat about it,' Sir Fred recalled. 'His main interest was how eutrophication on a large scale might affect the climate. When a lake dies and becomes stagnant and turns into swampland, it alters the local weather patterns in the same way that clearing a forest can either increase or decrease rainfall. The Russians are keen to find out what affect that has on the climate.'

'I don't see the direct connection between climate and carbon dioxide absorption in seawater.'

'Now you come to mention it, neither do I,' Sir Fred conceded. 'Though it could have something to do with the greenhouse effect. Indirectly.'

Chase said, 'I've thought about that myself, but I don't see how.'

'If you like I'll mention this particular topic to Banting next time I see him,' said Sir Fred, getting up. He seemed to inhabit the blue suit rather than wear it. 'The Americans could have confided in him.'

'Are you likely to see Professor Banting?'

'We serve on half a dozen committees together.' Sir Fred gave Chase a long-suffering look and rolled his eyes. 'Professor Banting and the committee might have been made for each other.'

Chase went ahead and held the door open.

'You know, Gavin, if you're all that curious you could find out yourself,' Sir Fred told him. 'Go and see Boris Stanovnik in Geneva. He speaks excellent English.' He chuckled gruffly, apparently finding that highly amusing. 'Better than mine, in fact.'

'Thank you again for taking the time to see me, sir. I appreciate it. I'll watch out for your interview.'

They shook hands and Sir Fred wandered off down the maze of corridors, obviously knowing where he was bound. The thought in Chase's mind was not Boris Stanovnik or the conference in Geneva, but Angie. Following her news, he might have reason to feel guilty about taking off abroad for a few days. But after all, he reasoned, the trip *was* connected with his work. In a kind of sort of roundabout way. And it would only be for a few days. And he hadn't seen Nick Power in months . . .

<h2 style="text-align:center">2</h2>

Brad Zittel had the car radio on, though he wasn't really listening. It was a meaningless babble. Fragments of insanity caught and snagged at his private inner sanctum of peace:

. . . no sireee! you won't find a better deal this side of the Rockies . . . buy three and get the fourth free! . . . we're offering discounts on the discounts at J. C. Broughton's . . . looking for the little gift to please the special lady in your life? . . . ten ninety-five and you get a chrome set for the low low price of . . .

The world was manifestly mad; to Brad Zittel it was perfectly clear. In fact it was screaming for attention, for action. The planet was drowning in its own excrement and nobody gave a damn . . .

Take that car in front. He'd been unseeingly watching it pumping out poisonous fumes for the last ten minutes. What the hell did the driver care? The air was still clear and breathable, wasn't it? Nobody had actually dropped dead on the highway. Not yet.

Without a moment's further consideration Brad pulled over and ran the small red Honda on to the sloping grass shoulder. The traffic behind honked and swerved. Somebody shook a fist. Brad switched off the engine and slumped back in the seat, all the strength leaking from his fingertips. His head felt curiously tight and his temples throbbed.

. . . at the Temple of Divine Worship this coming Sunday . . .

It was too big a mess for one man to sort out – and why should he bother? Let them sink in their own sewage. His stomach tightened in a spasm of virulent rage that swelled inside him like a growth until he felt that he must burst.

Still the endless stream of cars and trucks blurred past, filling the air with a soft blue haze.

Brad got out and faced the oncoming surge of oxygen-breathing monsters spewing out poison. Movable instruments of death, like the Nazi gas ovens on wheels. He stumbled on to the concrete lip of the highway and began to walk towards them. This, it seemed to him, was the only logical thing to do.

He felt very calm.

Traffic streamed past on either side, incredulous faces and gaping mouths. He walked diagonally across the five-lane freeway, angry and yet calm, impotent and yet defiant.

A huge truck bore down, silver exhaust pipe burnished by the sun, the driver wrenching at the wheel and cutting across the path of a car, which braked sharply, setting up a cacophony of horns.

Miraculously the traffic continued to flow all around him, a river of hurtling murderous metal, the warm breeze and pungent fumes wafting against his face and filling his nostrils. A long-haired motorcyclist went by, shouting something that was snatched away, and then a car with a trailer rocking crazily as the driver tried to avoid him.

Brad walked on.

The cars and trucks had malevolent eyes and snarling mouths. He could smell their stinking breath. Another sound insinuated itself above the steady roar, a thin, high-pitched braying. He didn't see the patrol car, lights flashing, slew to a stop on swaying springs. But he did feel the force as something with a powerful grip yanked him from behind, and moments later he was being lifted bodily and carried, then thrust face-down on to dimpled plastic that smelled strongly of stale sweat.

A hand held the back of his neck in a choking grip and a long-suffering voice said, 'Why the fuck can't you take an overdose like the rest of them and get it over with quietly?'

3

Winthrop had expected scepticism from the other members of the subcommittee whose brief was to vet the agenda for the next monthly session of PSAC, when the President himself would be in attendance. He had expected incredulity from some of them, even scornful laughter – but not the open hostility he now faced.

The attack had been led by General George N. Wolfe of the Department of Defense, who wasted no time and little breath in calling the proposal alarmist and unscientific. Winthrop had actually flushed and only just stopped himself blurting out that the general should stick to military matters and leave others better qualified to decide what was 'unscientific' and what wasn't. But this would have opened an old wound (the presence of a Defense Department spokesman on the President's Scientific Advisory Committee) and have served no useful purpose. It wouldn't help his career any either. If word got back to the Pentagon that the deputy director of the World Oceanographic Data Center was an awkward son of a bitch . . . well, anyway, better to ease down a little and not get excited.

Parris Winthrop wanted to see his name on the director's door, not on a list of has-beens circulating Washington for the post of washroom attendant.

'It amazes me, Winthrop, that you even considered putting this crackpot notion forward in the first place.' Wolfe hunched forward over the polished circular table, his tanned face a maze of cracks and lines that was a legacy of Southeast Asia. His eyes were like fissures in sandstone. 'Jesus Christ, man, this is a government-appointed body, not a goddamn college debating society. We're supposed to deal in hard scientific fact. Instead you come up with some ludicrous concoction dreamed up by a lunatic living on—' He turned his craggy head abruptly to his aide for clarification. Lieutenant Malden murmured in his ear. General Wolfe swivelled back to bark at Winthrop, 'Canton Island, wherever the hell that is.'

Winthrop smoothed his silvery hair with long slender fingers.

'General, I feel I ought to point out that Dr Detrick is an eminently respected scientist with an international reputation. His book *Diatom Growth and Development* is the standard work on the subject. Anyone acquainted with marine biology knows of his contribution to—'

General Wolfe snorted rudely. 'Just because the guy's written a book doesn't make him a divine oracle.'

Esther Steinbekker, the chairwoman, an emeritus professor at Johns Hopkins, said crisply, 'Many of us are familiar with Dr Detrick's work, Parris. We know of his important contributions to the field. But really, on the basis of unsupported and unverified data you can't seriously expect us to include this item on the PSAC agenda.'

Everyone looked at Winthrop, who was at pains to define his position. The last thing he wanted was to be lumped with Theo in the cranks and screwballs category.

'Of course I agree that the research is unsupported by others in the field. And no, I don't for one second accept all the conclusions that Detrick draws. But I do think we should at least consider what is, after all, the fruit of thirty years' effort. If Detrick is conceivably right—'

'Then I'm a Dutchman,' General Wolfe grated, getting a few chuckles and covert smiles.

Winthrop eyed him stonily. This bastard was out to make him a laughing-stock. He could feel perspiration prickling the back of his neck.

Two seats along to his left, Professor Gene Lucas spoke up in his mild southern voice. Lucas was with the Geophysical Dynamics Laboratory at Princeton: a small, slim man with a clipped grey moustache, one of the country's leading experts in the study of the biosphere.

'You say in your summary, Dr Winthrop' – peering through bifocals at the briefing paper before him – 'that Detrick expects the decline in phytoplankton production to have an effect, quote "appreciable effect" unquote, on the oxygen level within twenty years.' He looked up. 'Surely, if that were the case, shouldn't we see the start of such a trend right now? Those things don't happen overnight.'

Before Winthrop could respond, one of the other scientists, a particle physicist, directed a question at Lucas. 'As we're not as well-acquainted with atmospheric dynamics as yourself, professor, perhaps you could tell us how such a change would be detected? And if in fact there has been any change?'

'No change at all,' Lucas stated emphatically. 'The most recent measurements indicate that the percentage of oxygen in the atmosphere has remained stable at 20.94 for the past one hundred and fifty years; that's to say, since continuous reliable records were kept. There is absolutely no evidence to suggest either a rise or fall in oxygen content.' He turned to regard Winthrop over his spectacles. 'Furthermore, it has been calculated that if the entire fossil fuel reserves of this planet were to be burned, the combustion would reduce the oxygen to only 20.80 per cent. An insignificant change, which would have nil effect on lifeforms, including man.'

Winthrop was beginning to regret that he'd raised the subject. Two of his senior staff had studied Theo's massive dossier of research and both agreed that its implications were serious enough to warrant a hearing before PSAC. As for Winthrop himself, he felt that this was the least he could do in the light of his friendship and Theo's personal entreaty.

Yet this vehement reaction from the military had taken him aback. It was almost as if they had an ulterior motive. But then why should this be a concern of national security when it was plainly not a national but a *global* threat? Because, of course, any depletion in oxygen would threaten every nation in the world – every single person, every living creature on the planet, in fact.

'To put this in perspective,' Professor Lucas went on in his gentle drawl, 'we have to remember that the atmosphere weighs fifty-seven thousand trillion tons. Any anthropogenic effect would be negligible in comparison with the natural flux of gases on such a vast scale.'

'What's that in plain English?' demanded General Wolfe, fixing Lucas with his steely gaze.

'I'm referring to any man-made interference in the ecological balance. The effect of mankind's activities would be hardly noticed.'

'Uh-huh,' the general said dubiously, casting a sideways glance at his aide.

'While this is true about there being no apparent signs of oxygen deficiency at the present time,' Winthrop said, addressing everyone around the table, 'it's worth pointing out that changes in the atmosphere can and do happen, and over a short time period at that. There's been a significant increase in carbon dioxide over the past hundred years, for example—'

'Which has been noted and measured,' Lucas stated quietly.

'Well, yes, it has, of course.' Winthrop moistened his lips and plunged on, conscious that all eyes were upon him. 'But what ought to concern us is the speed . . . the – erm – the suddenness of that increase. If it can happen with carbon dioxide, why not with oxygen? Couldn't Dr Detrick's work be the first sign, the first hint, so to speak, of a possible decline in the oxygen level?'

'Well, for one, I don't accept Detrick's hypothesis,' said an elderly white-haired man opposite. 'He might know all there is to know about marine biology, but his grasp of atmospheric physics is highly suspect, it seems to me.'

There were nods and grunts of assent on all sides.

Winthrop saw that the general's aide, the lieutenant with the sharp features and pale blue eyes, was watching him with hawk-like intensity. He had the ghost of a smile pasted on his thin lips. What the hell was going on here? Some kind of subversive political ploy, a conspiracy to have him removed from PSAC? If that happened, his chances of making director were zilch.

'We seem to have arrived at a consensus,' said Esther Steinbekker, with what sounded in Winthrop's ears to have a ring of finality about it. 'As chairwoman I can't recommend that this committee include the item on the agenda for the next presidential meeting. Need we take a vote?'

She looked from face to face, her scrutiny finally coming to rest on Winthrop.

The room went quiet. Any committee member had the right to insist on a vote. Winthrop stared down at his manicured hands and laundered cuffs resting on either side of the neatly stacked files on the leather-bound blotter. He swallowed carefully, making sure that the movement in his throat went unnoticed. A vote would be recorded in the minutes, become part of the official archives of PSAC. It would be there in perpetuity, referred to and quoted forever into the future. However, no vote, no record.

Winthrop took care not to move a muscle.

4

When the meeting was over, Lieutenant Lloyd Malden gathered the documentation together, locked it inside his briefcase and stood by the door while the general made his farewells. A few minutes later the two of them were striding along the corridor. They crossed the marble-floored reception hall, passed through the glass doors and down the broad shallow steps onto Virginia Avenue.

A warm breeze stirred the branches of the maple trees along the wide thoroughfare as General Wolfe and his aide ducked inside the black limousine with the triangular Defense Department pennant on its nearside wing. It was now 11:28 a.m. and they were only three minutes adrift, Malden was pleased to note; considering the useful morning's work it was a trifling discrepancy, even given the general's fetish for living his life to a gridiron timetable.

As they passed the State Department and headed for Constitution Avenue, General Wolfe clasped his hands together and stared out through the tinted windows while he puffed away at a fat Amorvana Regios. Malden didn't break the silence, knowing how the general liked to savour his personal triumphs.

'Fucking children,' remarked the general eventually through the swirling cigar smoke.

'Beg your pardon, sir?'

'Just fucking kids, the lot of them. And some even say we should leave the decisions to the scientists. Jesus Christ, where would we be, Lloyd?'

'I thought you handled the situation with consummate skill, sir.'

Was that too fulsome? No, not with Blindeye, Malden decided. General George Nelson Wolfe hadn't acquired the nickname only because of his middle name. His ego was armour-plated. You could pour on the crap until he was up to his knees in diarrhoea and he'd breathe it in like Chanel No. 5.

'What you might call a preemptive strike,' Wolfe chuckled. 'Want to know something, Lloyd? Let me tell you. If there's one thing I detest more than a scientist, it's a fucking deskbound scientist. Just sits there passing paper back and forth. Neither fish nor fowl.' He savoured his cigar. 'Watching them try to play at politics is like watching kids in a sandpit.'

'Incidentally, General, have you seen the latest budget estimates from JEG Chemicals? They're now talking of 1.4 billion dollars to develop new strains in the symmetrical triazines group. That's on top of the eight hundred and ten million for chloraphenoxy acid compounds. I think we ought to give that some prime time.'

The general was dismissive. 'Money is the least of our worries. If that's what it takes, that's what we pay.' He frowned across at Malden, the cigar jutting out of his face like a post sticking out of parched red earth. 'Help me here, Lloyd. I still get confused with those two. With Operation Download, which is Laptop and which is Tablet?'

'Symmetrical triazines is Laptop, chloraphenoxy acid is Tablet. I didn't actually mean that, sir. My concern is focused primarily on the fact that the combined amount for the WCD programme is large enough to start attracting attention from the State Department. Till now we've managed to marginalise these sums under contingency funding, supplementary budgets and the like – kept them off the books in effect. But together they're now exceeding two billion. Sooner or later someone is going to want a breakdown.' Malden smiled his mirthless smile. 'Rather a piece of change to allocate to keeping the Pentagon lawns and flowerbeds free from weeds.'

'You're right, Lloyd,' General Wolfe brooded. 'As usual, you're right. We'll have to do something about it.'

Not that Blindeye had the faintest notion what to do about it. The general didn't have a clue and never bothered to grasp even the most basic elements of the plans to develop Weapons of Climate Degradation. He might have a vague notion that it involved interfering with the biosphere, messing around with the climate, but beyond that his mind wouldn't travel. So the general's next move would be to wait for Malden to come up with a strategy. Then he would mull it over for a couple of days and issue the instruction to proceed – verbally, of course. Blindeye wouldn't commit himself to anything, least of all an incriminating chain of decision-making and command responsibility.

The reasons Lieutenant Malden had zero respect for his superior were many. It was true that the general had served in Southeast Asia, but never in a combat role. Throughout his career he'd been an administrative officer, up to his hairy nostrils in paperwork and computer files, whiling away the hours with endless meetings and pointless briefings. Not that he'd bothered to read any of the documents that passed before his dull-eyed gaze or immersed himself in the minutiae of policy planning. He had junior officers like Malden to do the donkey-work. The officer-lackeys digested the mountains of stuff and passed on the gist of it for the general to pretend he had a grasp of the subject.

So Blindeye had ascended through the ranks with barely any effort, whereas Malden had grafted every inch of the way. And of course he'd seen action from his early days after leaving boot camp and ten-week basic training. Aged eighteen, Malden had been with the Third Battalion, Eighth Marine Regiment at the battle of Fallujah in Iraq.

It was the military who termed it a 'battle'; in reality, it was a bloodbath.

The initial assault on Iraq's third-largest densely populated city of three hundred thousand people had begun when four US private security contractors were ambushed in the city centre. Their armoured four-wheel drive received a direct hit from a rocket-propelled grenade, flipped over and burst into flames. The four men were killed instantly, but just to make sure, a chain of small boys passed along jugs of petrol to pour on the bodies. The charred remains were then hung from a bridge over the Euphrates.

President Bush vowed to teach the people of Fallujah a lesson. He also wanted revenge. The Eighth Marine Corps launched its first attack in April 2004. Malden hadn't been involved in this action, which had killed more than eight hundred people, nearly half of them women and children, in the first week of fighting.

After that, the city was supposed to be evacuated of its civilian population. Not all of them were able to flee. Between 50,000 and

60,000 non-combatant civilians remained behind when Malden and his platoon took up positions in the abandoned housing blocks on the edge of the city. There was a fever infecting his comrades, one he had never experienced before. It seeped through the ranks. Preparing for the first assault, their commanding officer addressed his men. 'The enemy has got a face,' he told them. 'He is called Satan. He is here in Fallujah. And we're going to destroy him.'

The unit's pastor rallied them to battle: 'The wrath of God will be called down upon the terrorists and evil-doers in Fallujah. And you, the US Marine Corps, are the instrument of that wrath.'

From the third-floor balcony of the apartment block, Malden had a grandstand view. It was risky up there, with sniper-fire a constant threat. But the odds were pretty well stacked in favour of the good guys. To soften them up, the 3rd Marine Aircraft Wing dropped more than 700 bombs on Fallujah and strafed it with 93,000 machine-gun and cannon rounds. Over several days the US 1st Marine Division fired 5,685 high-explosive 155mm shells and deployed white phosphorus and depleted uranium munitions.

Later estimates by the UN said about sixty per cent of all houses in the city were totally destroyed or seriously damaged; in addition, 9,000 shops, sixty-five mosques, sixty schools and a heritage library had been demolished. Hundreds of thousands of people were displaced.

By the end of the victorious battle, in January 2005, the director of the main hospital reported that 700 bodies (including 550 women and children) had been recovered from just a third of the city's neighbourhoods.

The US military deemed the operation a resounding success and rubber-stamped it *Mission Accomplished*.

Malden had been thrilled and in awe of the immense destructive power unleashed during the campaign. To witness the buildings endlessly pounded in that way, with no quarter asked and none given, was a sight to see. He reckoned the news would spread far and wide that the US Marine Corps was one tough mean hombre you wouldn't want to mess with, no sir, if you had any sense. He'd heard a Red Cross worker describe what was left of Fallujah as a 'City of Ghosts'.

Dammit, that was the truth – and serve 'em right. Maybe in future the locals wouldn't go around murdering innocent private contractors who were just doing their jobs and setting their bodies on fire in the streets.

'Know what still bugs me?' the general said, scattering flaky ash over the cushioned armrest that separated them. 'Astakhov. If only that bastard had talked we'd have a pretty good idea what the Russians are up to in Antarctica.'

'We did our best, sir, but he was in bad shape. Interrogating somebody with a broken spine isn't easy.' Malden shrugged his narrow shoulders in the tailored tan uniform. 'What do you threaten him with?'

'I'm not blaming you, Lloyd.'

And you'd better not, you tub of useless lard, Malden thought viciously. The meaty hand holding the cigar patted his arm and Malden almost flinched with revulsion; he held himself tense.

'I'm confident you did all you could to extract the information,' General Wolfe assured him, scattering more ash. 'You win some, you lose some.'

Malden surreptitiously brushed ash from his sleeve while pretending to examine his thin hands with the polished square-cut nails. 'I wish we could lose Detrick the same way,' he said softly.

'Detrick?' The general turned to gaze at him, his eyes screwed up tight. 'Why? Who's gonna listen to him now? That crackpot!'

'I don't know, General. Maybe no one. But it's an added risk, and one we don't have to take. Winthrop was right about one thing: Detrick still has an international reputation. All right, so we've choked off Winthrop – you made certain of that, sir – but there might be others who are prepared to listen.' Malden looked into the general's eyes. 'And he's close to the mark. Very close.'

General Wolfe nodded slowly.

'Very well, Lloyd. In that case we'd better do something about it.'

5

I

'Will you need both suitcases?' Nina Stanovnik called to her husband. 'Or just the large one?'

She stood in front of the open doors of the massive mahogany wardrobe, hands on hips, head cocked for his reply. She knew he didn't like to be encumbered with too much luggage, but left to his own devices her shambling bear of a husband would have gone off without even a change of underwear, never mind fresh socks.

'The small one. Just the small one,' he said, appearing in the doorway. Despite his greying hair, cropped close to the scalp, Boris Vladimir Stanovnik might reasonably have passed for someone in his late forties if it hadn't been for the purple pouches underneath his eyes. His voice was deep and resonant, his manner gentle and withdrawn.

He inclined his head and smiled, seeking her assent.

'I'll do the packing,' Nina announced firmly, tapping her shapeless bosom beneath the floral print dress. She manhandled the larger of the two suitcases on to the bed, lid yawning wide. 'You can't possibly wear the same suit and shirt all week, for goodness' sake.'

The chiding in a long-suffering voice was part of the game. Thirty years of marriage had hardened habit into familiar, comfortable ritual.

'Socks,' she muttered to herself, going to the chest of drawers near the window. Boris watched her fondly for a moment and then returned to the living room, his face creased in a smile.

His laptop lay on the inlaid leather surface of the open bureau. Next to it was a disordered heap of papers, files, newspaper clippings, books and magazines. The smile faded. How much ought he to take with him to Geneva? None of it was sensitive material; the hard-core classified data were locked away in the Hydro-Meteorological Service archives or encrypted behind a series of firewalls. Boris shook his head as he recalled the days before the demise of the Soviet Union. Back then, in the eighties, any trip abroad entailed interrogations by anonymous officials – every detail of the itinerary was scrutinised, every minute of time had to be accounted for. Unless Soviet scientific research had already been published in official journals (and was thus available to the West) there was an absolute embargo on working notes and calculations leaving the country. This sometimes led to the ludicrous situation of not being allowed to take out commonplace material that could be found in the pages of American and European science journals sold on thousands of newsstands.

Boris opened his laptop and then had to hunt for his glasses, feeling a twinge of arthritic pain in his right shoulder as he did so. Moscow was cold and damp and dismal at this time of year and he cursed the apartment's feeble heating system, which even at full blast was unable to take the chill from his bones.

'Sweaters,' floated his wife's voice from the bedroom. 'You'll need sweaters in Switzerland, I should think. They have snow there all the year round.'

'Leave out the English woollen one. I'll wear it on the journey.'

There were a dozen emails awaiting his attention, but just the one from his office on Dzerzhinsky Square. It was somewhat an irony that the seven-storey building had once been the headquarters of the KGB. Now it housed dozens of quasi-official government departments that had been taken over (*handed over to*, more accurately) by private companies and were being run as profit-making enterprises. Which was precisely what had happened to the Hydro-Meteorological Service. Yes, Boris was still nominally in charge, though the man at the top (and reaping the rewards) was a weasel called Yuri Malankovitch, who fifteen or so years ago had been just one of a dozen lowly lab assistants. And a damn useless one at that. Boris could and should have fired him for his incompetence and slovenly personal habits. But he'd been too soft-hearted, and was now paying the price.

The email was an internal memorandum, addressed to 'HEAD

OF SECTION', an update on the disappearance of Peter Astakhov. It was still a mystery, several months later, what had happened while Peter was on a scientific assignment. Based at Mirnyy Station on the East Antarctic Plateau, he had been engaged on climatic field research of a fairly routine nature. Boris missed him terribly, and not only on a personal level; Peter was a first-rate scientist, a good man to have around. Yet he had vanished without trace somewhere out there in the frozen wastes.

'Slippers,' said his wife from the doorway, making him blink. 'Shall I pack your slippers?'

Boris shook his head. 'No!' He gave her a pained look. 'Nina, dear, I can't wear slippers to the conference. It isn't a rest home for retired scientists.'

She gestured to heaven and went back into the bedroom.

When his wife had finished packing she prepared a meal, which they ate in the living room, the television news turned low.

'Will Theo Detrick be there?' she asked as they were finishing off their meal with *syrniki* – little fried cheesecakes – and drinking their tea.

'I've no idea,' Boris replied. 'It must be three or even four years since I heard from him. He was in the Pacific at the time, still working on his precious diatoms.'

'Such a pity you lost touch,' Nina said sadly. 'We could have visited him again; those six months in America were wonderful.'

'Things have changed,' Boris said grimly.

'Well, of course they have, dear . . .'

'I meant here.'

'Oh,' Nina said quietly. 'Yes.'

Glasnost now had a hollow, mocking ring to it. There had been such high hopes during the Gorbachev era that things were going to get better. In many ways they had, with a surge in prosperity and plentiful consumer goods in the stores. What no one had quite realised, or been prepared for with the rise of unfettered capitalism, was that the grey men of the former Soviet bureaucracy – the *apparatchiks* – would come out of the woodwork and take over the economy. Party officials were transformed in a matter of months into rouble millionaires. People with no professional qualifications or appreciable talents of any kind – such as Malankovitch – went from menial clerical and low-skilled jobs to running companies and being chauffeured around in half-million-dollar Bentley Continentals.

For the criminal element, it was a perfect storm. They had been there all along, of course, keeping their heads below the parapet while the old order was banished and society went through its upheavals, biding their time. Their time had come – with a vengeance.

Even during the Gorbachov era, the dying gasp of the Soviet empire, Boris reflected, he had been permitted to take his wife with him; that's how they had come to spend the summer in the States, while he was the visiting professor at Scripps Institution of Oceanography, and had become close friends with Theo Detrick. Now the rampant paranoia of the Cold War period had come full circle. The corporations and companies run by oligarchs – Malankovitch being a prime example – were loath to allow their brightest brains and senior academics to go unchaperoned on overseas trips in case they gave away valuable commercial secrets. Or not so much 'gave away' as 'sold to the highest bidder'.

The oligarchs trusted no one, Boris suspected, because they themselves were so untrustworthy.

For this particular trip, Yuri Malankovitch had done something totally unprecedented: he had personally invited Boris to his gated mansion north of Moscow. Boris had been there once, at a reception for foreign investors, but never before had he been summoned for drinks and a private chat. The mansion was one of half a dozen properties Malankovitch owned in New York, Paris, and the latest, a forty-five-million-pound London town house in Belgravia, which had nine bedrooms, an underground pool and a thirty-seat cinema.

From the moment he sat down opposite his 'boss', Boris was transported back to the days when the pale, pockmarked Yuri had rinsed out test tubes and mopped the floor of the lab. What did it were two striking physical traits. The first was his odd-coloured eyes, one brown, the other a misted-over blue. The second was that this disconcerting gaze was fixed coldly and unmoveably on the dead centre of Boris

Stanovnik's forehead. He remembered it so well: Yuri's inability – or refusal – to look anyone directly in the eye.

'You're to make a speech at the conference in Geneva,' Malankovitch began without any preamble.

'Not so much a speech as delivering a treatise,' Boris said, wondering if Malankovitch would know the difference.

'I asked my people to give it the once-over, but they tell me it's not available on the internal company website. They searched the database and it's not there. Which I find very strange and perplexing, Stanovnik. Wouldn't you say?'

Boris was so distracted by the odd-coloured eyes boring into his forehead that it took him a moment or two to gather his thoughts.

'Strange and perplexing? No, not really. I don't prepare a set text. I have notes in front of me on my laptop and I extemporise from those. I prefer to speak spontaneously.'

'But to the point, I trust,' came the response, accompanied by a faint, cold smile. 'I assume you have a title, Professor? You don't make that up on the spot . . . ?'

'Oh, yes. I had to submit it to the vetting committee for approval. "Micro-Organisms and Climate Change". The theme of the conference is the environment,' Boris said.

'Does your "speech" – or your whatever-you-call-it – make any reference to the information compiled by our research bases in the Antarctic?'

'Can you be more specific? That's a huge area – both scientifically and geographically.'

Malankovitch frowned and his gaze drifted off somewhere. 'Err, well, I mean generally, Professor . . . in relation to . . . um, you know . . .'

Boris let the imbecile dangle. Obviously he had no idea what he was talking about. The ex-lab orderly was asking questions he didn't understand, clearly fed to him by his technical advisors. *Dangle on*, he thought, *little odd-eyed toad*.

'. . . well, err, the latest findings from our team at Mirnyy Station . . .'

'All depends what you mean by "latest findings", Yuri. As of three months ago? One of our principal staff there, Peter Astakhov, has been reported missing, and this has disrupted the research programme. Our people there are naturally distraught.'

'I have been informed of that,' Malankovitch said. He cleared his throat. 'Most upsetting.' He reached out to a side table and picked up a sheet of paper. Boris could see that it had the Hydro-Meteorological Service logo at the top, but nothing more.

'You've been in touch, I understand, with someone at the Scripps Institution of Oceanography in California. A person called Theo Detrick.'

'Not correct,' Boris said.

'No?' Malankovitch kept his eyes lowered, his sallow face expressionless.

'No. I did try to contact him by email but got no reply.'

'For what purpose?'

'I was hoping he'd be attending the conference in Geneva so we could meet up.'

'And will you be meeting him there?'

'I have just explained,' Boris said patiently, 'that I haven't had a reply, so I don't know if Dr Detrick will be there or not.'

'The email contains personal news and friendly salutations.'

'So it does.' That Malankovitch and his henchmen read his emails and other communications came as no surprise to Boris, but nonetheless it infuriated him. This gang was nothing more than a pack of arrogant mafia goons lining their own pockets, and doing it by using the talents of those like him and other dedicated scientists seeking to pursue knowledge and enlightenment.

'I've visited and worked with Dr Detrick in the past. I consider him a friend as well as a colleague. He would think it "strange and perplexing" if my message wasn't couched in personal terms; in fact he'd find it rather insulting.'

Malankovitch blinked a number of times, frowning into the middle distance. He slowly nodded. 'I see. Yes, ah, well, that would explain it. I understand.'

'Good. Glad you do. Now you know. Anything else?'

Boris loaded the terse phrases with several shades of meaning: condescending, impatient, intimidating, challenging, even a hint of bullying. As if to say *I am Professor Boris Vladimir Stanovnik, one of this*

country's leading experts in marine microbiology, and you, Yuri Malankovitch,
whatever status you might have attained, and however much loot you might
have plundered, and whoever you think you are, will always remain the
incompetent, shifty, snivelling lab orderly with poor complexion and bad breath.

The glow of vengeful satisfaction Boris felt didn't last long. This
evening, having supper with Nina as they watched the news together,
the bitter taste left by Malankovitch's final words as he was leaving the
gated compound to the north of Moscow hadn't faded.

Fixing his odd-coloured eyes on Boris for the first time, Malankovitch
had said, in a voice empty of expression, 'Have a pleasant stay in Geneva,
Professor. Don't forget to bring back a present for your wife.'

His meaning had been all too clear. While Boris was free to leave
the country to attend the conference, he should never forget for one
moment that Nina remained behind in Mother Russia. Shades of the
old Soviet regime. What was the time-honoured phrase? The more
things change, the more they stay the same?

2

From his seat one over from the window, Theo Detrick looked out at the
huge circular cowling of the GE90, bathed in diamond-bright sunlight.
As part of his research, Theo had made a special study of commercial
aero engines. The GE90 on this Delta Boeing 772 long-haul was the
largest and most powerful engine so far in aviation history, producing
130,000 pounds-force thrust. The engine was slightly ahead of him,
so he couldn't see the gaping turbofan mouth gulping in rarefied air
35,000 feet above Greenland. But he knew that every minute of the
flight this one engine consumed more than one hundred pounds of
oxygen, which, times two, meant the aircraft burned up eighty-six tons
of oxygen every time it crossed the Atlantic.

He couldn't begin to guess at the number of flights on the transatlantic route. And God knew how many other private, commercial
and military aircraft were flying every hour of the day and night. Add
them all together and it amounted to a global oxygen loss of millions
of tons every twenty-four hours.

And that in itself was only a tiny proportion. Man was greedily consuming more and more oxygen in his industrial plants, his power stations, his home furnaces, his automobiles – every form of combustion was destroying oxygen in quantities that the natural cycle of the biosphere wasn't designed to cope with, nor able to replenish.

There was also – and this was a thought never far away from Theo's mind these days – the world population of 7.2 billion human beings, each one needing seven pounds of oxygen every day to stay alive. By the year 2030, at the current rate of growth, there would be an estimated eleven billion people inhabiting the planet; the question was, would there be any air left for them to breathe?

And those cretins in Washington couldn't see – refused to admit – there was a problem. Were they mad, or was he?

In the window seat next to his, Cheryl leaned forward, blocking his view. Resisting the impulse to touch her hand, Theo asked instead, 'You're not regretting this, are you?'

'Not so far,' Cheryl answered briefly. She spared him a cool glance and turned away, a shaft of pure sunlight gilding her razored cap of hair and snub-nosed profile.

He had no right to expect anything more. All those years of absence and neglect couldn't be simply wiped away by the promise of a week in Geneva. He remembered his resolve not to rush her into a kind of false father/daughter intimacy that would embarrass them both. No, if any real affection was still there it would have to evolve naturally, unforced, at its own pace. It came as a shock that for years he had experienced not a twinge of guilt, only now to discover that it was his strongest emotion.

He said diffidently, 'This trip will be useful to you. You'll meet other marine biologists and people with different views, be able to get involved in seminars and debates—' Then he hastily reconsidered and thought it wise to add, 'Of course, for you, I want it mainly to be a vacation.'

Still not looking at him, Cheryl said, 'I thought maybe you'd invited me along to take notes. Work comes first, doesn't it? And second. And third.'

'Yes, my work is important to me,' Theo acknowledged soberly.

'But it is also important to me that you are involved – that you believe in what I am doing – I hope—' He was fumbling for the words and making a mess of it. He looked down at his hands, gnarled mahogany. 'I wanted you to be with me because . . .'

The truth was he didn't know himself what the reason was. He suspected it had something to do with a need to find understanding. Sympathy. Affection? One person in all the world who might believe in him.

Cheryl shook her head, looking out of the window. 'You don't have to explain. If I wanted reasons I'd have asked for them. I'm here. Let's leave it at that.'

Theo found a smile. 'If nothing else, you're an independent young woman.' He meant it as a compliment, but it was a day when he could say nothing right.

'Yes,' Cheryl said. 'I've had plenty of practise.'

Theo shifted uncomfortably, his broad torso hampered by the narrow seat, and wisely decided to abandon this pretence at conversation.

In the battered briefcase between his legs rested the paper he was to read at the conference. It was a summation of all his years of research and thought, worked on and sweated over during the past three weeks until he had pared it down to eleven double-spaced typed pages. More a predictive document than a list of facts and figures, he had given it the title 'Back to the Precambrian': a reference to the period more than 2.5 billion years ago, when the atmosphere was composed of hydrogen, methane and ammonia and no free oxygen; a time to which he believed the earth was returning.

Theo dozed while Cheryl stayed awake and watched a movie.

She felt confused and vulnerable. It was a massive understatement to say it had been a shock when her father turned up unannounced at Scripps less than a week ago. That shock turned into bewilderment when he produced two airline tickets and hotel reservations. She couldn't actually remember accepting his invitation, or even having time to regret it. As fate would have it, she had ten days before the *Melville* sailed on its next research voyage, this time to Guadalupe Island off Mexico. There had been no obstacle, no real reason why she shouldn't go. And, she argued to herself, it would be valuable and stimulating to attend a convention with such high-profile delegates, most of them leaders in their field. So here she was.

Travelling with the spin of the earth, they saw dusk come upon them with the dramatic abruptness of a thundercloud. After passing over the northernmost tip of Scotland, the aircraft began to lose altitude in preparation for the long descent into European airspace. To one fitfully dozing passenger the muffled shriek of engines sounded like the howl of a greedy machine sucking the breath from his lungs.

3

It was Chase's first visit to Geneva and his preconceptions that it would be clean, somewhat austere, and filled with the all-purpose breed of European technocrat seemed depressingly close to the mark.

He and Nick were booked into the Inter-Continental, a fifteen-minute drive from Cointrin Airport, which conveniently enough was also the conference centre. In the wide carpeted lobby a laser display board gave the conference itinerary, with details and locations of the various speakers and their subjects.

Chase paused to scan the board. His spirits sank. This was heavy stuff.

GLOBAL ENVIRONMENTAL MONITORING:
    Dr J. N. Ryman
HAZARDS OF TOXIC WASTE:
    Professor I. V. Okita
DEMOGRAPHIC PATTERNS IN THE 21ST CENTURY:
    Professor D. S. Smith
THE CARBON DIOXIDE CONUNDRUM:
    Dr P. Straube
GLOBAL WARMING – FACT OR FICTION?:
    Lord Derker of Hollingworth

Nick said, 'Who in hell is Lord Derker? Is he one of ours?'

'I guess he must be a Member of the House of Lords.' Chase

shook his head. 'Though what he knows about global warming, real or otherwise, is double bollocks wrapped in tissue paper.'

OZONE – A VANISHING PROBLEM?:
Professor C. Hewlett
WHERE IS SCIENCE TAKING US?:
Dr E. B. Salem

Where indeed? The list was long and Chase didn't come to the name he was looking for until near the end.

MICRO-ORGANISMS AND CLIMATE:
Professor B. V. Stanovnik

Suitably noncommittal, Chase reckoned, for a paper from a Russian scientist. He saw that Stanovnik was down to speak on the Tuesday morning, three days from now. Perhaps he'd get the opportunity to have a word with him before then. Sir Fred had mentioned that he spoke good English, which was fortunate. Chase didn't relish the idea of conversing via an interpreter. It might easily lead to *mis*interpretation.

The hotel – 'Holiday Inn with Hiltonian pretensions', according to Nick – was bustling and frenetic. After unpacking and cleaning up they kept to Nick's plan and headed for the main bar. Chase felt ill at ease alongside the conservatively suited conference crowd sporting plastic name tags on their lapels. The atmosphere was one of forced conviviality, with everyone busily consuming pre-dinner drinks.

'Oh, Christ, no . . .' Nick sucked in a breath and lowered his head.

'What's up?'

Nick swivelled his head as a signal and stared hard. Through the bar-dwellers Chase glimpsed a narrow bald head and close-set eyes like raisins in dough. In his usual tweed jacket and grey cords Professor Ivor Banting was talking to a large bull-necked man with shorn greying hair.

'Has he spotted us?' Nick asked tremulously. 'I had to put up with the bastard at Halley Bay and I'll be damned if I'm going to here.'

'Last person I expected to see,' Chase said, turning to face the other way. 'Would you have said Banting the Terrible was all that interested in the future of the environment?'

Nick was scathing. 'He bloody well isn't. A week in Geneva at somebody else's expense, though? A fucking freeloader . . .'

Chase looked down on him with a flinty grin. 'Unlike present company, you mean?'

'He's an arse-licker,' Nick insisted. 'Why do you suppose he was so accommodating to the Yanks in taking the Russkie?'

'You tell me.'

'Because they've got the funds to underwrite big research projects, dummy. Banting keeps in with the guys with the bucks. He couldn't give a damn who they are and what the project is providing they're willing to cough up—' He glanced furtively over his shoulder. 'He hasn't seen us, has he?'

'What makes you think he's all that keen to meet us anyway?' Chase said. 'Could be he's as anxious to avoid—'

Unfortunately he wasn't; the next moment Professor Banting had excused himself and was beginning to push his way towards them through the crowd.

Nick swore under his breath and threw back his drink in one quick gulp.

After they'd shaken hands – Nick with barely concealed bad grace – Banting gestured around, saying with a knowledgeable air, 'Some excellent people here. I'm looking forward to it, aren't you? Have you seen the agenda?'

Chase said he had. 'Anyone you'd recommend?'

'Straube and Ryman, and Colin Hewlett's paper should be worth hearing – I was his tutor at Loughborough, you know. And Stanovnik and Professor Okita; all first-rate chaps. I've been to the last two conferences, in Iceland and Miami, and this looks like the best so far.'

'What's that?' Nick said, peering intently at Banting's lapel badge. Unlike all the others, his ID was mounted in a thin silver frame, in the bottom corner of which was the tiny embossed emblem of a silver conch shell.

'I'm a sponsored delegate,' Banting explained. 'The JEG Corporation. They're very much concerned with environmental matters.'

'American?'

'International,' Banting said. 'Their interests are worldwide – electronics, chemicals, lumber, transportation, aerospace. A very large organisation with dozens of subsidiaries.'

Nick's expression remained deadpan, which was eloquent enough in itself.

Chase said, 'So you reckon Stanovnik will be worth listening to?'

'It's always useful to find out what the Russians are up to,' Banting said. He gestured towards the bar. 'That's the chap I was with a moment ago. Decent type, quite friendly, not a grump like most of his colleagues.'

'That was Stanovnik?' Chase said, craning to see, but the big Russian had gone. Apparently random events and disconnected factors, somehow drawn together. He had the feeling that he was on the edge of something. He was intrigued, and also strangely excited. Half-listening to Banting, he nodded abstractedly, and heard Nick utter a low groan of deep anguish.

Chase had just accepted Banting's invitation for the three of them to dine together, a sort of British Antarctic Expedition reunion. Shit and Corruption.

4

In common with the seventeen hundred other people in the hall, Chase hadn't a clue what the rumpus was about.

Scheduled to start at 3 p.m. – it was now ten past – on the Sunday afternoon, this first session was billed in the programme as 'Welcome to the Sixth International Conference', followed by a 'Symposium of Views': a cosy get-together, he had imagined, to ease everyone as painlessly as possible into the rigours of the week ahead. Like everyone else he hadn't been prepared for the commotion by the steps leading up to the platform.

What the hell was going on? A protest?

If so then the protestors were an unlikely pair – a stocky, tanned, white-haired man and a girl who might have been a student in a grey parka with faded denims tucked into knee-high boots. It was the girl who was doing all the talking while the man was standing there holding a dilapidated briefcase under his arm, his expression calm, resigned, a little weary.

Several officials had closed ranks while others were scurrying around gesticulating to one another. The girl, attractive and obviously incensed, was by turns raging at and then pleading with a harassed-looking official. Above them the conference chairman, a Norwegian, waited unhappily at the microphone, uncertain whether to ignore the commotion and carry on regardless, or hang on in the hope that it might, like a summer thunderstorm, quickly blow over.

'And I thought this was going to be dull,' Nick said, enjoying the spectacle, straining his curly head to get a better view. 'Who *are* they?'

Chase shook his head. 'No idea. But the girl sounds American.'

They watched as the officials escorted the man and the girl along the aisle and through a side door, the girl arguing as fiercely as ever. The auditorium, silent and rapt till now, droned with speculation like a beehive disturbed by an intruder.

Nick grinned delightedly. 'I hope the next act is as good,' he said, but his face fell when the Norwegian began to speak in that unrhythmic swaying singsong that either grated or sent people to sleep.

It sent Nick to sleep.

5

The official held up his hands, palms outwards, and said, 'The governing committee is not required to give a reason, mademoiselle. It is their decision alone. You understand?' He gave a weak smile.

Cheryl, now icily calm, said, 'I see. The fact that my father has flown halfway round the world to be here doesn't matter a damn to your committee. They can decide, just like that, and we don't have the right to ask why or to receive an apology or even a reply? That's how you run things here, is it?'

'I am sorry, Mademoiselle. The decision is not mine.'

'You won't even give us a *reason*.' She looked towards her father, who so far had shown neither anger nor disappointment – no emotion at all, in fact.

'As I have said, it is not required. The rules of the conference state that all papers must receive prior approval—'

'But the paper was accepted!'

'No, not so in this instance, mademoiselle. It was provisionally agreed that Dr Detrick would be allowed to address the conference, subject to his paper being cleared by the committee. The committee has now seen the paper and made its decision.' Again the half-shrug, the tepid smile.

Cheryl ground her teeth. It was her father's passive attitude, his air of resignation that angered her almost as much as this bland, round-shouldered bureaucrat in the dark suit with shiny elbows. Didn't he *care*? To be treated in such a despicable fashion and told that not only was his paper disbarred but he would not be permitted to take part in any discussion from the platform? Christ, it was galling!

'By all means Dr Detrick and you are free to attend the conference as delegates.' The official spoke directly to Cheryl, having decided that she was the one to appease. 'The conference is, after all, international, and we are pleased that you have decided to attend.'

The young woman swallowed her anger. 'That's most kind of you, Monsieur—'

'Carpentier.' He made a little bow.

'Monsieur Carpentier.' She breathed and said in a low voice, 'But if you think that's the end of the matter, you're very sadly mistaken.'

His smile faded around the edges.

'My father didn't come all this way to sit around exchanging small talk. He came to deliver a paper, and you haven't given us one reason why you won't let him. You say the decision isn't yours; okay, I accept that. You also tell us that we can't talk to the people whose decision it is. Right. But you can't stop us talking to the press. Maybe what this shambles of a so-called conference needs is a rocket up its ass.'

'Monsieur, please . . .' The official looked pained and appealed to Theo. 'I can do no more. I am the spokesman, that is all. I have much to do. You will excuse me, please.' His shoulder twitched and he walked away.

Theo turned to leave, his face impassive.

'Aren't you going to say anything?' Cheryl cried, enraged by his docility. 'Just let these people walk right over you? My God, I thought your work *meant* something to you. I got the impression that nothing else did for the past thirty years,' she added bitterly.

There and then she could have cut her tongue out, but it was too late. It had been said.

'It's all right. I do understand,' Theo said to her later, at dinner, when she had fumbled her way towards an apology. He brought his hand across the white tablecloth and covered hers. 'You have every right to feel I have neglected you. But I would like to say thank you.'

Cheryl gazed at him with a slight frown. 'For what?'

'Speaking up for your shit of an old man.'

She felt herself colouring. Dammit, why wouldn't her emotions stay still? One minute she hated him, the next she felt compassion – affection – even genuine love. One thing she did know, and this had never wavered: her respect for him as a scientist. And maybe, she thought, that was the way of it: he couldn't have been both devoted father and dedicated scientist.

She tossed her sun-streaked head in mocking self-disdain. 'Oh sure, I always insist on my rights. I'm good at that.'

The waiter placed an avocado salad in front of Cheryl. Another waiter poured lentil soup into Theo's bowl.

'I must be dumb or something,' Cheryl said, 'but I still don't understand. I mean, why come all this way and then give in without a fight? Without even a protest?'

Theo picked up his spoon and paused, staring down at the steaming soup. He said, 'When you've worked on something for years, and invested your will and purpose and strength in it, you suddenly find that you've no energy left. It's been used up. My work is important to me, of course it is, but after so long I find that I'm—' He broke off, searching for the word.

'Tired?'

Theo said slowly, 'Disillusioned. People don't want to listen. I tried in Washington, but it was no good, so I came here, thinking that these people would be different, more open, receptive. It appears I was wrong.' He dipped into his soup. 'People don't wish to face the truth.' He drank, and dabbed his lips. 'It's much easier that way.'

'But the least they could do is *listen*. And come to a judgement. What have they to lose?' It was the question of a naïve schoolgirl and Cheryl winced at the tone of righteous indignation in her voice.

'It's a matter of interpretation,' Theo explained. 'It's quite feasible to accept the data as genuine and yet to disagree with the predicted outcome. The worldwide decline in phytoplankton is not in dispute – but what that might mean in terms of oxygen depletion is open to debate.'

'Then you could be wrong?'

'It is always possible to be wrong,' Theo answered gravely. 'Scientists by nature are conservative creatures. They don't like change, especially of this magnitude. My predictions will hardly be popular with the scientific community.' He looked down at his powerful hands, the palms ridged with calluses; not the hands of a scientist. 'I was stupid to expect otherwise. I've been away too long.'

Cheryl had been distracted by someone across the restaurant. She touched Theo's arm, who leaned back in his chair, a slow smile lighting up his face. The man came over to their table and as she watched the reunion a childhood memory stirred within her.

'You will not remember me,' Boris Stanovnik said in his deep Russian voice, taking her hand. 'You were a little child, with golden hair and . . . I forget the word – what are they called?' He tapped his cheeks and nose.

Cheryl laughed, delighted. 'Freckles. I still have them in summer, but not the golden hair unfortunately. Yes, I do remember you. I was tiny and you were a giant,' she said.

Boris chuckled. 'And children never forget giants, eh?'

Cheryl shook her head, smiling. It pleased her immensely that her father had found a friendly soul in a desert of indifference.

It was still quite early, a few minutes after nine-thirty, and she could see that Theo was in the mood to chat for hours yet. Feeling tired, she rose and excused herself. As she passed the display board in the lobby the words seemed to leap out at her:

Global . . . Climate . . . Toxic . . . Ozone . . . Hazards . . . Carbon Dioxide . . . Problem . . . Waste . . .

It was all there, screaming to be heard. So why had that damned committee turned him down? Were they frightened that what her father had to say was too controversial? Too alarmist? Maybe the committee's attitude was typified by the official with his round shoulders and meek eyes and closed mind.

As the elevator doors slid open and she stepped inside, Cheryl had a remembered glimpse of the red algae bloom churning up from under the stern of the *Melville*. Surely to God it was proof that what Theo foretold was fact and not fantasy: he had seen a prophetic vision that she had witnessed for herself in the broad light of day.

The doors were halfway closed when a man slipped through. He was tall, broad-shouldered, burned dark by tropical sun, and wearing a white suit. Preoccupied, Cheryl didn't think it odd when he didn't enquire which floor she wanted, but pressed the button that happened to be her floor, too.

6

'I don't fancy yours,' Nick said.

'I don't fancy either one.'

'Come on, Gav, don't be like that. The one with the big bumpers hasn't taken her eyes off you all night. The little redhead will suit me fine. How about it?'

Chase drained the last few drops of pilsner beer and set the glass down. He wiped his mouth and said, 'Not tonight, chum. But you go right ahead. Only please don't come crashing in at two in the morning, will you?'

'Great!' Nick said without enthusiasm. 'Thanks a bunch.' He scratched his beard morosely.

'See you at breakfast,' Chase said, sliding down from the barstool.

'You're not really going?'

'Looks like it.' At the foliage-shrouded entrance to the bar he turned and saw Nick semaphoring with his eyebrows to the two young women, one of whom, he had to admit, was rather attractive. As Chase went out he saw her gazing after him, and for just a moment regretted his decision. Truth be told, he was still struggling with the hot-off-the-press news of Angie's pregnancy; the revelation hadn't sunk in yet. He couldn't stop himself juggling with dates – it was ungallant, if not downright nasty, to think such thoughts, but the worm of suspicion had burrowed deep inside him and he couldn't kill the little bastard. The worm looked a lot like Archie Grieve.

Chase walked across the lobby, and made it to the elevator just as the doors were closing. The woman inside, wearing a ridiculous feathery hat above a face like a weathered prune, glared at him as he tried to contain a rippling belch of warm beer fumes.

Much to his relief the feathery prune got out at the second floor. Chase carried on to the third and walked along the carpeted corridor, trying to remember if his room was on the right or the left when a sharp cry – female – stopped him in his tracks.

'You heard me – get out, you bastard!'

An angry voice, frayed at the edges with fear.

The corridor swallowed up the sound. There was silence.

'Get out now! I mean it, you bastard – *get out!*'

It was coming from the room two doors down from his. Chase's first instinct was not to interfere – it was probably a domestic quarrel. He moved softly onwards until he was level with the door, where he paused and stood listening. There was a mumbled sound, almost a growl, and then a kind of strangled shout.

Chase rapped on the door. 'Are you all right in there?' It sounded fatuous, but he didn't know what else to say. 'Hello?'

'Get in here. Don't go away. Come in, please – *right now!*'

He pressed the handle down but the door was locked. Something hit the door, hard, and disintegrated with a tinkle of glass and metal. Again he heard the low mumbling growl. He banged on the door with his fist. The woman started yelling and almost at once there was a click as the lock was released and the door opened a couple of inches.

Chase put his shoulder to the door and pushed. Something blocked it.

'If you're coming in, for Christ's sake get in here!'

Chase used his full weight and the impediment shifted. Across the room, on the far side of the bed, a young woman with short sun-streaked hair was holding aloft a hairbrush. As an object of aggression it was pretty underwhelming. As Chase stepped inside, his shoe crunched on something: the broken remnants of a travel alarm clock, the missile she must have hurled at the door.

Then Chase saw a row of broad brown fingers, thickly matted with hair, gripping the edge of the door. As the door opened further he saw the other participant in the drama. He was blond, tanned, wearing a white linen suit, and while Chase was six feet tall, this fellow topped him by a good three inches.

Still holding the door, not looking at Chase but facing the girl, the man said in a low American growl, 'Give the message to your father. I think we understand one another, you and me. Stay calm and keep your mouth shut.'

The girl swung the hairbrush behind her head. 'Take a running jump, you dickless creep.'

That seemed to have the right effect. The man in the white suit elbowed the door open and barged past Chase without bothering to look at him. As he disappeared into the corridor the girl said in a quivering rush of breath, 'Shut the door, quick. Make sure it's locked. I don't want that bastard coming back.'

'Is he likely to?' Chase said. It was then that he recognised her – the girl from the conference hall who had been arguing with the officials. 'You seem to cause trouble wherever you go,' he said conversationally.

She breathed in deeply and closed her eyes. 'Can't tell you how grateful I am for stepping in. Thanks.'

'In that case would you mind putting the brush down?' Chase tested the handle to make sure the door was locked; he wasn't keen on any more surprises. 'Who the hell was that? Do you know him?'

Cheryl shook her head. She was massaging her left wrist, which he now saw was inflamed, with fingermarks. 'That bastard was in the elevator. He followed me to the room and when I tried to shut the door in his face he grabbed me and threw me inside.'

'It sounded like he was threatening you.'

'I should have gone for his privates. That's if he's got any.'

'Hadn't you better call the management and report it? The guy's too dangerous to just let wander around.'

Cheryl was rummaging through a leather valise. 'I should, you're right. But first I want to see my father. He's in the hotel restaurant.'

'Why don't you call him?'

'He doesn't carry a phone. I know I'm imposing.' She came round the bed. 'Will you do me a great favour and come downstairs with me? If you don't mind, Mr—'

'No, that's fine,' Chase said. Then it would be her father's problem and not his. 'Gavin Chase,' he told her.

On the way to the elevator she said, 'I'm grateful to you, Mr Chase. Thank God you were in the hallway and heard me. I'm Cheryl Detrick, by the way.'

'Glad to be of help, Ms . . .' There was a moment's delayed reaction before he said, 'Detrick? Is your father Theo Detrick? The marine biologist?'

'Yes. You know of him?' It appeared to please her.

'He wrote the bible,' Chase said sincerely.

'Are you a delegate?'

'Yes, sort of. That's my field too.'

'And mine. Postgraduate at Scripps.'

'We marine biologists should stick together,' Chase said, smiling down at her.

'My sentiments precisely,' Cheryl said, thumbing the elevator button.

6

Perhaps coincidence ran deeper than anyone suspected. Conceivably there was an ordered pattern, some kind of system, to which everyone was blind, perceiving it only as a series of random events. And when these events came together at a particular point in time and space, people called it 'coincidence'. How else to explain it?

'Can I get you a drink?'

Chase started, broke from his contemplation.

'The mini-bar is well stocked, and my father doesn't drink. What'll you have?' Cheryl asked.

'Um, yes. Whisky with ice. Thank you.'

Coincidence upon coincidence, Chase was thinking: that after encountering Cheryl Detrick in such bizarre circumstances, he should now find himself sitting in her hotel room having drinks with Boris Stanovnik – the very man he had come all this way to meet.

The big Russian was leaning forward, elbows on knees, a glass of beer looking tiny in his clasped hands. 'You think what happened is to do with what we were discussing?' he asked Theo.

'Of course it is.' Sitting in the bright halo of light from the corner lamp Theo Detrick's face seemed darker and craggier than ever. 'They warned me officially, through the proper channels, and then obviously thought it necessary to make the warning more direct. More personal.'

'They?' Boris said in amazement. 'The conference committee?'

'No, the people acting through the committee.'

'But who *are* "they"?'

'Some political lobby or other, with corporate connections. Big pharma maybe. Chemical companies with agricultural interests. I don't know the specifics, Boris, but somebody with something to lose.' Theo smiled thinly. 'I wouldn't put it past our State Department or the CIA.'

Boris was still frowning. 'Is it possible – the man who attacked Cheryl was with your State Department?'

'Maybe.'

'He would make the threat so openly?'

'Oh sure,' Cheryl said, making herself comfortable at the foot of the bed. 'Threats, coercion, blackmail, frame-ups . . .' She gave a sardonic smile. 'America is a democracy, don't forget. You're free to threaten anybody you want.'

Chase was bewildered. 'The paper you were supposed to deliver must be pure dynamite, Dr Detrick. What were you intending to speak about?'

'Its title is "Back to the Precambrian",' and when he saw Chase's blank expression, went on, 'Precambrian is the term I have given to describe the reversion of the earth's atmosphere to what it was 2.7 billion years ago. In that epoch the constituents were principally a highly corrosive mixture of hydrogen, ammonia and methane. But no oxygen,' Theo added significantly.

'You believe the earth is reverting to that state?'

'Unfortunately, I do,' he said gravely. 'I wish I could draw other conclusions from the work I've done, but . . .' He shook his head.

'Your work on diatoms, you mean?'

'Yes, the phytoplankton species at large. In the equatorial Pacific, which is normally one of the most productive regions of the ocean, all classes of this organism are in drastic decline. As the oceans provide most of the oxygen requirement there must inevitably come a time when the amount is reduced. Worst case, I'd say within the next twenty to fifty years. Within a hundred years all the free oxygen at present circulating in the atmosphere will either have been consumed or will be locked up in various oxidation compounds such as rocks, decaying matter and so on. When that happens we shall be left with an atmosphere similar in composition to what it was in the Precambrian period.'

Theo gazed across the room, his smile weary and resigned. 'Man is a most arrogant species, Dr Chase. He forgets that for billions of years this was a sterile planet with a poisonous atmosphere. It was only with the liberation of oxygen into the air that our form of organic life was able to evolve – but the biosphere doesn't owe us a living. We take it as a God-given right that oxygen is there for us to breathe, when in fact it is an accident, a biological quirk, so to speak, of nature.'

Chase said diffidently, 'I don't question the validity of your research, Dr Detrick, not at all. But frankly I find your prognosis hard to accept. I don't know the actual figure, but the amount of oxygen in the atmosphere is immense—'

'One thousand, one hundred and forty trillion tons,' Theo said.

'Surely that's more than enough to meet our needs for the foreseeable – indeed, the *unforeseeable* – future? I assume that phytoplankton growth won't cease altogether, so presumably the oxygen level will continue to be topped up. And there are the green plants on land that supply a sizeable proportion of oxygen, at least thirty per cent.'

Theo sipped his iced tea, lost for a moment in thought. 'I take your point, Dr Chase,' he said finally. 'And it's a fair one. But in considering the oxygen yield of the biosphere and whether it is sufficient for our long-term needs, there are two sides to the equation. Let us call them "profit and loss" and draw up a global balance sheet.

'On the profit side we have an abundance of green plants, in the oceans and on land, which daily perform the miracle of photosynthesis. These absorb the rays of the sun and produce energy that is used to break down water molecules into their component parts. The hydrogen thus released is combined with carbon to supply sugar for the plant's own needs, while the oxygen is given off as a waste product.' Theo held up his fist, which shook slightly. 'This process, far more complex than that taking place in a petrochemical plant – and, what's more, happening inside a group of cells less than one billionth of an inch in diameter – is the unique factor that allows animal life to exist on this planet. Without it' – the fist sprang open to become a knife blade that sliced the air – 'nothing!'

'I think it's safe to assume that Dr Chase is familiar with the miracle of photosynthesis,' Cheryl said in mild rebuke.

'Yes, of course. Please forgive me.' Theo spread his hands in apology. 'You must understand that little else has occupied my thoughts for a long time.' He eased back in the chair, his profile etched against the lamplight. 'That, as I say, is the profit side of the equation. On the loss side we have the consumption of oxygen: every form of life that respires, including man, and every kind of combustion process – power plants, factory furnaces, automobiles, aircraft, domestic boilers – everything in fact that burns fossil fuels.

'Now, it has been estimated, based on the most reliable sources available, that every year we consume between ten and fifteen per cent of the free oxygen in the atmosphere. Until today that annual deficit has, as you point out, been topped up by the photosynthetic activity of green plants.

'However, we must now take into account several new factors. First, the increase in world population, which by 2030 will be over eleven billion, possibly nearer twelve. If we progress as we have been doing, this will mean more of everything – power plants, factories, cars, aircraft – all of which will demand more and more oxygen. Each year that ten to fifteen per cent deficit will grow larger. Maybe that wouldn't matter too much if the production of oxygen continued at its present rate, but when we look closely at the balance sheet we find that the profit side is getting more and more into the red.

'As well as the declining phytoplankton we're also losing the world's major forests. Deciduous forests have an oxygen-producing capacity one thousand times greater than the average land surface; in the United States alone we cover an area the size of Rhode Island – five thousand square miles – with new roads and buildings *every year*.

'We all know about the great forests in South America, Southeast Asia, Borneo, New Zealand. They're being destroyed at an alarming rate. But even more disastrously they're being *burned* – which at a stroke turns that item on our balance sheet from profit to loss. Instead of being net *producers* of oxygen, the forests have become net *consumers*.' Theo looked at Chase, a tired smile plucking at the corner of his mouth. 'I could go on, but I think you see my point.'

'Which is,' Boris put in sombrely, 'less profit, more loss. The equation does not balance. We consume more of what isn't there no longer.'

The Russian, with his quaint English, had come up with a clumsy yet telling description, thought Chase. *We consume more of what isn't there no longer.*

He said, 'Isn't there another possibility? Another direction it might take? The earth reverting to its primordial atmosphere can't be the only option.'

Theo was prepared to admit he might be wrong, but added a killing rider: 'I've tried to make the equation balance and found it impossible; believe me, Dr Chase, I have tried.'

For all that man had done to the environment, the planet's complex web of self-regulating mechanisms had always, in the past, managed to compensate for his use and abuse of natural resources. But that, as Chase now realised, was not the question. Theo Detrick wasn't talking about what had happened *in the past*. It was the earth's ability to cope *in the future* – with all the additional burdens man was imposing on it year by year – which concerned him.

Boris drank some beer and said, 'You were perfectly correct, Dr Chase, to speak of the hugeness of our planet.' He smothered a belch and went on, 'In a single year the volume of water recycled by evaporation is three hundred and eighty thousand cubic kilometres. In one year more than one hundred thousand million tons of carbon dioxide are absorbed in the oceans and nearly two hundred thousand million tons are converted into plant material by photosynthesis. To recycle a single molecule of water from the ocean, via the atmosphere, through photosynthesis, and return it to water by animal respiration, takes two million years. The resources are enormous, true, the processes incredibly complex, yes. But I am forever mindful of something Buckminster Fuller once said. You remember, Theo?'

After a moment Theo said, 'The steel ball.'

The Russian smiled. 'Fuller said that to get a true picture of the depth of the atmosphere, from the earth's surface to the edge of space, imagine a steel ball the height of a man. Breathe on the steel ball and your condensed breath represents the depth of the atmosphere. You see what this means? While it is true that man lives on a planet that is vast in comparison with himself, he actually *survives* thanks to a thin layer of biosphere no more than twelve miles deep.'

Cheryl took Chase's empty glass and went to make him a fresh drink. He watched her clunk the ice in and pour the whisky while questions skittered through his mind. As she brought the drink to him, he asked, 'This is happening because of the decline in phytoplankton. So what's causing that?'

Theo Detrick roused himself. 'Not one specific thing. More likely a combination of factors, some operating independently of the others. In my opinion – and it's no more than that – the cause is linked to the build-up of atmospheric carbon dioxide. This is leading, as we know, to a global increase in temperature, bringing warmer oceans. And the warmer the ocean means phytoplankton is less able to thrive. Another factor might be that photosynthetic activity is inhibited by higher temperatures.' He shrugged. 'In short, Dr Chase, I don't really know.'

Seawater and carbon dioxide: the reason he was here in the first place. Chase could hardly bring himself to ask the question. 'If this is the cause, Dr Detrick, how would we know? What are the signs to look for?'

Theo looked at Boris. 'Let's ask the expert,' he proposed. 'Professor Stanovnik has spent many years studying such causes and their effects at the microbiological level.'

Chase felt a tightening in his chest, as if he were slightly out of breath.

Boris smoothed his knees, rocking slowly back and forth. 'It so happens that a colleague of mine, Dr Astakhov, was interested in this very problem and conducted many field experiments all over the world to discover where the excess carbon dioxide was going. We've known for more than a hundred years that the amount of CO_2 is increasing but have been unable to account for more than half of it. Dr Astakhov's theory was that the excess production was being absorbed into the oceans. Possibly he was near to reaching a definite conclusion, but . . .' He raised and let fall his shoulders in a ponderous shrug, then concluded, 'Dr Astakhov disappeared before his research was completed. We do not yet have the answer to the mystery of the missing carbon dioxide.'

Chase thought for a moment before he spoke, phrasing his question with care. 'Is it correct to assume, Professor, that *if* the oceans had absorbed this extra carbon dioxide – reached saturation point, in fact – that this would confirm Dr Detrick's theory?'

'Yes,' Boris answered without hesitation, 'almost certainly. It would be a strong indication that the increase in carbon dioxide and the rising temperature of seawater have a causal link. But as yet we do not have the research data to make such a claim. Had Dr Astakhov returned—'

'From the Antarctic?' Chase said feeling the last piece of the jigsaw slide into place.

'Yes, he was based at Mirnyy Station, and the last report we have . . .' The Russian's dark pouched eyes narrowed and remained fixed on Chase. 'How do you know this?' His curiosity bordered on distrust. 'Do you know Dr Astakhov?'

'No. But I talked with him. After a fashion.'

'Where?'

'At Halley Bay.'

'The British base in the Antarctic?'

'Yes.'

'You speak Russian?'

'No.'

'Then that is most strange, Dr Chase,' Boris said bluntly. 'Peter hardly knew one word of English.'

'No,' Chase corrected him, 'your colleague didn't know *any* English. But under the circumstances I don't think his lack of English mattered. I imagine even you would have had some difficulty in understanding him. He was half out of his head, on the verge of coma. He had a broken back. In fact it's a bloody miracle we managed any kind of communication at all. But we did.'

Boris was watching him with the intensity of a hawk. 'He told you of his research – what he had found?'

Chase shook his head. 'He wrote down a chemical equation.'

'What equation?'

Everyone was watching Chase intently as if he were about to produce a rabbit out of a hat.

'Okay, you got it,' Cheryl said, with a faint touch of exasperation. 'Our undivided attention. Put us out of suspense. What the hell was it?'

Chase told them.

2

Afterwards it was his turn to listen while Theo Detrick narrated a horror story. He had been living with the knowledge of what a return to the Precambrian era would mean to the human race, had spent years brooding over it in his tiny island retreat, and now, without emotion, he gave them his scenario for the future.

The first victims would be the very young, the very old, and those already suffering from cardiac and respiratory conditions. Anoxia – the medical term for a deficiency of oxygen to the tissues – would initially affect these three groups. Mortality statistics would show a gradually steepening rise as they succumbed to the impoverished atmosphere.

This Theo classified as Stage One.

Stage Two would begin when the oxygen level had fallen by several per cent. Conditions then would be similar to those on a fifteen-thousand-foot-high mountain. Dizziness, nausea and blackouts would become commonplace. There would be a sharply increased incidence of infertility. By this time the decrease in oxygen would start to have serious and widespread effects on all animal life.

Stage Three. By now the composition of the atmosphere would be radically altered as the planet reverted to its primordial state. The ozone layer – or what was left of it after the attack by CFCs and pollution of the atmosphere – would thin out and disappear completely, allowing cosmic rays and solar radiation to penetrate to the earth's surface. This would cause severe burns, skin cancers and leukaemia.

Then would come the mutants: weird forms of life whose genetic structure had been warped in the womb. Whether such forms of life could continue to thrive and prosper on a planet going backwards to its own past was doubtful, but for a time at least the earth would be inhabited by monsters. These, Theo believed, like the dinosaurs, would eventually die out.

Then what?

'And then,' Theo said, 'we come to Stage Four. The final act. The earth will have returned to the Precambrian: defunct of all animal life and denuded of all vegetation. What's left will be the most primitive form of bacteria, the rest biologically dead.'

'But it isn't,' Chase protested, '*inevitable*. Surely the process can be halted or reversed? It *must* be possible.'

'Must it?' Theo said gently. 'As I've made clear, Dr Chase, we have no God-given right to survive. The biosphere doesn't owe us a living.' He gazed around vaguely, not seeing them. 'One thing is absolutely certain. It cannot be stopped and it won't be stopped if the world refuses to listen and take heed.'

3

The second whisky was a mistake. The first had been a treble; the next one Cheryl poured him was if anything even larger. Nursing the glass, Chase leaned on the balcony rail, the lights of Geneva's riverfront panorama spread somewhat blearily before him. In the near distance he could see headlights moving along the Rue du Rhône, and a little further off the sparkling necklace of diamonds marking the Pont du Mont-Blanc spanning the river itself.

He half-turned as Cheryl came out onto the balcony and joined him at the rail.

'Does your father usually take a dip at' – Chase checked the time – 'coming up to midnight?'

Theo Detrick had wished them goodnight and returned to his own suite, wondering aloud if the hotel pool was open at this hour. Boris Stanovnik had left earlier, saying he had notes to prepare for his lecture.

'On that subject,' Cheryl said, 'I wouldn't really know. He's been out of the country most of the time, living on Canton Island in the Pacific. But he did tell me he swam twice round the lagoon every morning before breakfast. So I guess staying in a five-star hotel in the middle of a city feels like being in captivity. And he misses the exercise, maybe . . .'

She took a sip of her drink, then noticed the nearly empty glass in his hand. 'Can I freshen that for you?'

Chase shook his head, smiling. 'I'd love to, but better not. There's a

pretty heavy schedule tomorrow. But you know, it's a funny thing . . .
it'll feel weird.'

'What will?'

'Listening to the papers and discussion on climate change in light
of what your father's been telling us tonight. It'll be like . . . well, as
if we're only being given half the story. Or even just a fraction of the
real picture, of what's actually happening.'

'I think most people already know we're on a *catastrophic* course.'

She slurred the words slightly, making Chase realise he wasn't alone
in feeling the alcoholic effects of strong liquor. Or in Cheryl's case it
might also have to do with the nervous aftershock of her encounters with
the American thug. The incident in Cheryl's room had been reported
to the hotel management, who said they would inform the police.

Chase looked down at Cheryl; she seemed steady on her feet right
enough, though her eyes were heavy-lidded.

'It's been a tough day for you. You need your rest. I'll let you turn
in.' He finished the few drops of whisky left in his glass.

'I really shouldn't ask this after all you've done. You've been terrific,
Gavin.' Cheryl gave a small tired smile. 'I nearly said "a real life-saver".
Which actually is what you were.' She hesitated. 'Can I beg a favour
of you?'

'Yes of course. What is it?'

'Would it be okay,' Cheryl said, 'you not leaving right this minute?'

'Why, sure. I'll stay as long as you wish. I just thought – after all
that's happened – you could do with a good night's sleep.' He touched
her shoulder reassuringly and was startled to feel her trembling. The
night air was cool but not cold, so it couldn't be that. 'Are you all right?'

At his tone, gentle and concerned, she moved closer. Her head of
sun-streaked hair came no higher than his shoulder. Chase felt the
girl's arms slide around his waist and the full softness of her as Cheryl
snuggled herself into his embrace. It was the delayed reaction of fear,
and the need for comfort, that drove her, he knew, rather than passion;
but this genuinely innocent desire for closeness lasted not much longer
than ten seconds before his natural impulse took over and stirred into
life, and Cheryl responded to him. She lifted her mouth to his.

For several moments they were both lost in the kiss. Chase didn't know how long the phone inside the room had been ringing. Cheryl also became aware of its persistent tone and she broke away and went to answer it. Chase paused outside the sliding door, waiting for his ardor to subside.

'Yes, yes, this is she . . . What?' Cheryl was running her hand through her short tousled hair, the phone pressed to her ear. As Chase stepped inside the room she turned slowly to face him, still listening. 'Yes. I understand.' And then: '*Where?*'

Her face was a mask as she slammed the phone back in its cradle before grabbing Chase's arm. Her fingers dug into his forearm. 'Come with me. *Please.*'

'What is it? What's wrong?'

The fitness suite and health spa were in an annexe at the rear of the hotel. Two white-coated male attendants were waiting for them at the entrance. They tried to bar their way. 'Ms Detrick? No, I'm sorry, no further! I'm afraid you're not allowed to—'

Cheryl pushed them aside and with Chase close behind, she barged through a pair of swing doors into a tiled enclosure which led to the poolside. The atmosphere was humid and stifling, with a tang of chlorine. The surface of the water was a shimmering green, disturbed by spreading ripples. On the opposite side of the pool were two more attendants, kneeling over a prostrate figure with arms spread wide. The figure had a broad, tanned back and cropped white hair.

'Ms Detrick! Excuse me, please . . .' It was the business-suited under-manager who scurried up to them. 'But on behalf of the hotel, I am sorry to enquire – if your father, Herr Detrick – was he a poor swimmer? Or did he suffer from a bad heart, perhaps? It is important we know . . .'

Cheryl was standing quite still: nothing showed on her face, no expression at all.

Chase turned on the man and caught hold of both neat lapels of his business suit. He shook him once, hard. 'If I were you, I wouldn't say one more word. You get it? Not one.' Chase pushed him away. The under-manager said nothing.

4

The moon floated serenely in a magenta sky, lighting the peaks of the Rockies with a soft ambience like ethereal snow.

Major Bradley E. Zittel had hardly moved in the past hour, gazing out of his study window, unconscious of time, of it passing or standing still; aware only of the moon's decaying arc across the night sky, looking down with a blandly smiling face on a dying planet.

A young planet, only 4.5 billion years old.

He remembered once trying to explain to seven-year-old Gary the age of the earth, but it was a difficult concept for the youngster to grasp – simply too vast a number. So Brad had asked his son to imagine the earth as a human being of forty-six years of age.

Not much was known about the first ten years of this person's – Planet Earth's – life, and it wasn't until it reached the age of forty-two that plants and primitive life-forms started to appear. Dinosaurs didn't arrive on the scene until one year ago, when Planet Earth was forty-five. Mammals appeared eight months ago, and it was only in the middle of last week that apes evolved into men.

The last Ice Age happened at the weekend.

Modern man had walked the planet for four hours. In the last hour he had developed agriculture. The Industrial Revolution began one minute ago. In these final sixty seconds, out of forty-six years of life, Brad explained, mankind had done to Planet Earth everything we saw around us. He didn't know if any of this had sunk in, but he had tried his best. Maybe Gary would retain some of it as he grew older.

The tea had gone cold in the pot, but that was to be expected, Brad thought. The ineluctable law of the universe. Entropy. Everything was creeping towards slow death: himself, earth, moon, sun, stars. The dying fall. Fall from grace.

As it was in the Beginning, so it shall be in the End . . .

He didn't hear the door open and close, nor detect the presence in the darkened room until it laid warm fingers against his cheek. 'Come to bed, darling. Please. You can't go on like this.'

Why not? 'Entropy,' Brad said. 'Falling. Dying. End.'

His wife's nightgown rustled as she settled herself on the arm of the chair. She cradled his head, holding him close, as one might comfort an ailing child.

'I want to understand you, Brad. Let me help you.'

'They don't know. How can they, when they've never seen the earth? They don't *know*.'

'Who? Know what?' She was scared. Her fingers moved tentatively over his forehead, feeling the lines that lately had become deeper, permanently engraved. What was it, this obsession that had taken over his waking hours? And even while he slept – his nightmares told her that.

She was losing the gentle man she had married, whose children she had borne, whom she loved dearly. She couldn't reach him any longer, and now it had become much worse – that incident on the highway, the police bringing him home, the fuss to keep it quiet, out of the papers, the doctor putting it down to overwork, because medically, he was lost.

Brad hardly slept but spent hour after hour of the night, every night, sitting by the study window and staring, literally, into space.

'Brad, honey, please tell me what it is so I can help you.' There was a plaintive note of fear in her voice. She felt sick. 'Can't you say it, for me?'

She enfolded him in her arms, but he made no effort to respond to her embrace. He sat indolently and she was reminded of pictures she had seen of mental patients, vacant-eyed, slack-jawed, trapped in mad dreams . . . dear God, no, not him.

'Brad. Darling,' she murmured, holding him, near to tears. 'You've got to talk about this. You've got to tell someone. How can you go on carrying this burden all the time? You need help, Brad.'

'Not me. The world needs help,' he contradicted her. He began to tremble, his hands shaking in spasm. 'I have seen the earth in all its glory, one of the chosen few. There was a purpose in that, don't you see?' His hand fastened on hers, crushing, hurting. 'My purpose is clear,' Brad said through clenched teeth. 'I must do what I can. Let me go, Joyce. *Let me go!*'

'Go where?' she asked in terror. 'Wait, I'll call Dr Hill,' she said quickly. She prised her hand free. 'I'll call him now – this minute.'

In a moment of lucidity, as if his thoughts had suddenly pierced a bank of fog, he said matter-of-factly, 'Doctors can only be of help to the sick or the mentally ill, Joyce. I'm neither. I'm the healthiest, sanest person on this planet. There *has* to be an answer. I know it. I'll find it.'

He rose and strode from the darkened study. Joyce heard him climbing the stairs. She went after him. In the bedroom he was throwing things into a suitcase.

Joyce watched him from the doorway, her knees weak, trembling. 'Brad, what are you doing? What's happening? Where are you going?'

He was totally absorbed in packing. 'If there's an answer I'll find it.'

Fear. Grief. Panic. Incomprehension: Joyce experienced them all over the next few minutes as he packed, kissed her almost absently and walked out the door.

She knew somehow he had gone for ever and she would never see him again.

2021

2021

I

Cheryl Detrick emerged wearily from the long grey tunnel into the arrivals hall of Los Angeles Airport. The metal attaché case containing her laptop and documents file dragged at her arm and she had a dull ache in the small of her back. Airline seats were fine for ergonomic dolls, rotten for human beings.

She skirted a group of youths wearing red bandannas who were playing craps on the worn green carpet, walked determinedly past an old man offering his hat for change and tried to make it to the door without being accosted. The trip to Chicago had been paid for by Scripps, so legitimately she could charge the cab fare into the city, though she objected to the expense – they'd take it out of her lab allocation and she needed every cent.

Cheryl was almost at the exit and steeling herself at the prospect of stepping from the air-conditioned arrivals hall into the LA steambath.

'Hi, Sherry, it's me!'

She was too preoccupied to notice him, so the tall, gangling man with thinning hair plucked at her sleeve. 'I checked your return flight and decided to meet you.' Gordon Mudie beamed down at her. Though married with a couple of kids, he never missed even a half-chance to hang around, ever hopeful, especially now that she was unattached again.

Cheryl groaned inside, but on the outside she was all smiles. No way she was going to turn down a ride home, even if it meant putting up with Gordy. Once they were cruising at fifty-five on the interstate with the radio turned low she kicked off her shoes and stretched out in the seat; it would have been bliss to stay quiet and relax, but he was keen to learn about her trip.

Eyes half-closed, Cheryl said, 'It was the usual rigmarole. They sat and heard me out – politely, as usual – and then made the usual remarks. Then we did some chitchat and shook hands. Same old, same old, as ever.'

'You make it sound as if you don't care.'

Cheryl sighed and said, 'Of course I care. Why do you suppose I keeping knocking myself out? Whether the trip was worth it and whether it'll do any good, I honestly don't know . . . Gordon, would you mind stepping on it? I'd really like to get home before midnight.'

The car speeded up at once. Gordon was apologetic. 'I was just taking it easy till we cleared the basin. Visibility's down to two hundred yards today. They've had to ground the police helicopters.'

Cheryl looked out and noticed for the first time how bad it was: headlights on the other side of the freeway appeared like dim glowworms in the thick sulphurous gloom. At one time it had taken less than thirty minutes to get clear of the city; now it took the best part of an hour. There was a reason for it: the Los Angeles Basin was the most notorious thermal inversion trap in the world. Contrary to normal, the warmer air was on top, at about two thousand feet, and the cooler air underneath, so there was no natural upwards flow. Sunlight acted on the lethal outpourings of seven million car exhausts, which combined with industrial pollution to produce dense photochemical smog. This was the 'air' that Basin residents had to breathe, containing carbon monoxide, aldehydes, ketones, alcohols, acids, ethers, benzpyrene, sulphur oxides, peroxacetyl nitrates and alkyl nitrates.

No wonder a hundred thousand people every year were advised by their doctors to move out in order to avoid – or at any rate, to relieve – lung diseases like bronchitis and emphysema.

The irony wasn't lost on Cheryl that while this earthbound problem got steadily and inexorably more critical, the government was spending thirty million dollars *a day* on military space systems – the manufacture of which, at NASA's Space Division in nearby El Segundo, just added to the miasma they were ploughing through.

It was a relief at last to see the pale golden light of the evening sky. The Carlsbad sign went by. On their right the Pacific was a flat dark mass in the deepening twilight. Gordon switched off the filtration unit and Cheryl wound the window down to breathe in relatively fresh cool air.

'I really admire you, Sherry,' Gordon said, playing the same old tune. 'Your father's work is vitally important. I truly believe that.'

'If only the people in Washington, New York and Chicago felt the same there'd be no problem. Well, there *would* be a problem,' she qualified, 'but at least we'd be pulling together and finding ways to overcome it.' Why hadn't she said 'solve it'? Because she didn't believe there was a solution?

Gordon frowned through the windshield. 'But action by just one country alone, one government, isn't enough, is it? Gotta be a concerted effort.'

'That's what I keep on telling 'em,' Cheryl said dismissively, as if losing patience with a stubborn child. 'But with a really staggering lack of success. To them I'm just one more eco-nut.'

'Stop running yourself down. You're an intelligent woman, Sherry. I've always had the greatest respect for you . . . ' He glanced across at her. 'Women with both looks and brains are pretty rare.'

Cheryl was too weary to be annoyed or even amused. Over the years Gordon Mudie hadn't altered by a decimal point.

'You say the nicest things to a girl.'

But even such blatant mockery sailed past his head and vanished in the slipstream, as she was quick to realise when he reached for her hand and said soulfully, 'You know damn well how I feel about you, Sherry. Always have; ever since we were on the *Melville* together.'

Cheryl extricated her hand from his heated grasp. 'Yes, Gordon – but in those days we were both single, with no kids.'

'*You're* single,' he said, as if pointing out a salient fact that had somehow escaped her.

'I am. *You're* not.'

'Would it make a difference if I weren't married?'

'Gordon, I really appreciate your driving all the way to the airport. Thank you. But let's leave it like that, if you don't mind. As friends.'

He stopped outside the single-storey wooden house on Borrego Avenue where Cheryl lived alone since Jeff had gone off to Colorado –

possibly the reason why Gordon was being so attentive, the departure of her live-in lover. But that particular episode had played itself to a standstill months before he got the job in Boulder with the National Climate Prediction Foundation.

Cheryl scooped up the mail from the mat and left it on the hall table without looking at it, and went straight into the kitchen, switching on the radio to drown the silence of the empty house. She made lemon tea, trying to decide whether or not she was hungry, and carried the glass into the living room, flicking on the TV for company. Clint Eastwood was killing somebody with a Magnum .45. In the next scene there was a uniformed police officer filling out a report. It triggered in her the same reaction it always did, and had for the past five years: the recollection of the 'investigation' carried out by the Swiss police and coroner, and the conclusion that Theo's death had been 'misadventure'. Cheryl had thought it ludicrous then and her opinion hadn't changed. Her father had had a powerful body and strong constitution; he lived on a small island and was an *excellent* swimmer. To have drowned in the safe environment of a hotel pool without external circumstances was simply not credible.

Despite her testimony, corroborated by Gavin Chase, that there had been a man in the hotel that very same evening, threatening her verbally and with physical violence, the authorities dismissed his possible involvement through lack of evidence. The man in the white suit was never identified, and no other witnesses came forward. How could they start a murder investigation, the authorities wondered, on such a paucity of corroborative facts?

Theo's death might have been an accident – *might* have been, but *wasn't*. The reason was simple: because her father had been a pain in the ass to the powers in the shadows. Because he'd badgered the folk in Washington and got the alarm bells ringing. Because he knew what was coming, and it was a dangerous message from a prominent scientist that threatened too many important interests – military and industrial. And while Cheryl didn't know which agencies were responsible, she knew damn well that political chicanery was at the bottom of the turgid, dirty brew.

Her mind was a muddle. It had been a long trip and she was tired. Cheryl had taken on her father's crusade, and as with him, it had become an obsession.

She finished the tea and went through the hall to the bedroom, collecting her attaché case on the way; the mail she left untouched, and therefore didn't see the envelope with the Russian postmark, which was third in the pile.

The mail would still be there in the morning, and tomorrow, thank God, was another day.

2

'Everyone needs a label,' Marcus Barrett said. 'That's why I'd like you to do this series for us. You've established a reputation and the public trusts you.'

Chase was ill at ease, not just with the compliments, but with the surroundings. He wasn't used to lunching at such high-class places as the Colony Bar & Grill in the Beaumont Hotel, Mayfair; already he'd spotted at least three TV celebrities and a couple of high-profile journalists.

He was a little in awe of Marcus Barrett too. The editor was a very distinct and unusual combination: his parents had arrived in the UK as penniless immigrants from Guyana in South America. By the time Marcus came along, the company his father had founded – a mail-order business selling perfume and cosmetics – was worth more than thirty million sterling, and eventually Barrett senior sold it to an international consortium for more than three times that sum. So the first-generation son of a lowly immigrant family received a private education at Marlborough and then went on to Cambridge, where he acquired a first-class degree in history and philosophy. Even at university, Marcus had been something of a maverick. He wasn't interested in a high-flying career in the city or in academe, but he was passionate about world affairs in general and alternative political structures in particular. As a wealthy man with a rebellious streak, he had the means and the ambition to indulge his passion. *Sentinel* was a print and online journal that was influential and well-respected, though it hadn't been out of the red since it was founded nine years earlier.

Not that Marcus gave a damn; making money held zero interest for him. Instead, he was committed to radical new ideas and spreading them as widely as possible through social media and grassroots campaigning.

'The programme you did for the BBC was pitched at just the right level. Intelligent and informed, without being too academic or stuck up its own arse. I spoke to several people and they were most impressed.'

'I'm glad several people watched it,' Chase said wryly.

Marcus laughed. The contrast of smiling brown eyes and straight white teeth against glowing dark skin brought glances from every woman in the room. The other unusual – and somewhat intimidating – aspect about Marcus Barrett was his appearance. The Savile Row-tailored suit and hand-stitched Italian shoes marked him out as a City stockbroker, as did his cultured, expensively educated accent – so the shiny jet-black hair worn in long dreadlocks draping his shoulders was a startling contradiction.

This meeting, and the offer of work, had come about through a chance encounter in the BBC bar at Broadcasting House. Marcus had liked *Personal Crusade*, the programme Chase had written and presented. The two had been introduced by a producer and from this had sprung the idea for Chase to research and write a series for the magazine on how the environmental debate was viewed from an international perspective.

'What I'm after is hard-hitting factual stuff,' Marcus went on, fingertips tapping the table-top for emphasis. 'And it must be attributed – accountable. None of that "a spokesman said" or "a highly placed source divulged" crap. Opinions from faceless bureaucrats and PR lobbyists aren't worth a damn. You get the idea?'

Chase did get the idea, and he liked it. Most of the work he had done previously was to a tight brief and an even tighter budget. As a freelance contributor he wasn't used to a generous travel and living allowance.

'How soon can you leave for the States?'

'Early next month,' Chase said, having already thought about it. He'd need that length of time to make family arrangements and finalise travel plans.

'What about your journalism and spots on TV? No contractual obligations?'

'I'm not under contract. They call me in on an *ad-hoc* basis whenever they need an *expert's* viewpoint.' Chase spoke casually, with a gentle hint of irony. 'As you say, Marcus, everyone has to have a label.'

'I have a good feeling about this, Gavin. It's a project I've had in mind for years but the right person wasn't available, or the timing was off. Now it's all come together – and you are definitely the right man at the right time.' Marcus raised his brandy glass. 'Here's to a successful research trip and a terrific series. You never know, we might even have a bestseller on our hands.'

3

Chase took a chance that the tube was running and walked from the Beaumont up to Bond Street station: you could never be sure since London had gone bankrupt which services were operating and how frequently. He was in luck and rode all the way to Chigwell, practically at the utmost end of the Central line. Living anywhere near the centre of town was impossible these days, unless you'd inherited a family home or were nudging the millionaire bracket. People were being forced further and further out; with his precarious freelancer's income Chase was just about clinging on in one of the less salubrious outskirts.

He walked through the drizzle to his flat in Lambourne Road. How bloody typical of the British climate to remain damp and miserable, even though average temperatures worldwide were the highest ever recorded. And each year's record high topped the last one. Over in the American Midwest, Chase knew from his close study and constant tracking, it was back to the dustbowls of the thirties. Droughts had devastated vast areas of Asia and Africa, with millions of refugees aimlessly on the move. Even the Antarctic permafrost was heating up. These crazy extremes of global climatic change meant that while some places were being burned off the map, others lay sodden under a perpetual downpour.

At Belgrave Court (fancy name for a bog-standard mansion block) he went up to the second floor and let himself into the three-room flat. Fortunately he had a standing arrangement with a neighbour whose little girl Sarah went to the same school as Dan: whenever Chase had a business meeting she'd collect his son and look after him till he got back. Sarah fussed around Dan like a mother hen, but Chase was content that the boy was safe and well looked after.

The plain wooden table that served as his desk in the book-lined living room was inches deep in copies of *Science, Nature, New Scientist* and *Science Review*. A dozen or so heavyweight academic tomes were scattered about. All this was the mother lode of background research on a two-thousand-word piece on predictive climate modelling, as yet only half-written, for the *London Review of Books*.

Meeting Theo Detrick in Geneva five years ago had changed his life; the marriage to Angie, which hadn't lasted two years, had had an even greater effect. In fact he owed his ex-wife for his new career. She *had* been seeing someone else – not her former boss Archie Grieve, as it turned out, but a tall, balding scriptwriter called Terry Steel who wrote soaps. Angie moved in with him – they were welcome to one another. The question of a custody battle had never arisen because Angie had never contested it. Chase couldn't bring himself, even now, to think of Angie abandoning her son, although it was the brutal truth.

While still married he'd been contributing fillers and short summaries to the scientific press so it wasn't a completely new departure when he terminated his ICI Research Fellowship at Durham and came to London to try his hand at freelance journalism, though it was one hell of a gamble. The first year had been tough, especially with a young child to bring up. For a while he was reduced to graveyard-shift lab work, but then the journalism started to pay and he got a lucky break as resident 'science expert' on a television news programme. The pay was nominal, but the profile-raising was brilliant and suddenly he was on the inside track, meeting producers and commissioning editors, which led to more TV projects as contributor or presenter. At last he was able to provide a reasonable standard of living for Dan and himself. At thirty-two he was beginning to feel just a tad more secure, though the career of a freelance was always on a knife-edge, and he never forgot that.

At lunch, Marcus Barrett had made something of the fact that he was becoming well known and respected as a science populariser; very true, but Chase wasn't daft, he knew his 'success' could vanish just as swiftly in a puff of smoke.

The sight of the piles of books and periodicals and scientific papers signalling *work to be done!* made him restless, though it was probably pointless until two cups of strong black coffee had cleared away the brandy fumes. Besides, there was the welcome ritual of bathtime and some quality father-son time to come first.

The end of the world would have to wait until after Dan's bedtime story.

The kettle was on the boil when his phone went: could he sit in on a discussion on fourth-generation nuclear energy for a phone-in on BBC Radio 5 this coming Thursday? Chase automatically said yes, he could. After he put the phone down it occurred to him that soon – by the end of *this* week – he'd have to turn down future offers: three weeks from now he'd be on his way to America. There was a heap of stuff to sort out, not least Dan and his care. Marcus Barrett had been especially generous in offering to provide and pay for a full-time nanny. He had a son of his own, Titus, who was just three months older than Dan, and he had mooted the possibility that Dan might do an extended sleep-over with Titus and his carer while Dad was away. Chase needed to think some more about that.

Already he had outlined to Marcus Barrett what the five-week trip would entail. The itinerary would cover an eastern swathe of New York, New Jersey, Boston, Washington, DC, MIT . . . then it would be over to the West Coast, Scripps, the National Climate Prediction Foundation in Colorado . . . and several stops in between that hadn't been set in stone; Chase wanted the flexibility to respond to new leads and pursue intriguing possibilities as they sprang up.

Shortly after five o'clock Dan appeared. He was escorted to the door by the conscientious eight-year old Sarah, taking her role as surrogate mother *very* seriously.

'Daniel has been a *very* naughty boy,' she informed Chase primly, standing there in pinafore and pigtails, arms folded. 'He won't do as he's told!'

'I'm sorry to hear that. What's the matter?'

'He would *not* go to the toilet,' Sarah said, frowning through her dimples.

Father and son silently regarded each other with identical blue-grey eyes. Like Chase's, the boy's hair was dead straight and hung over his eyes in a sweeping curve, though it was fair and fine, not thick and black.

'Oh. I see.' Chase appeared to give the matter some thought. 'Well, never mind, Sarah. Perhaps he didn't want to go. And thank you so much for looking after him.'

Duty discharged, Sarah gave a firm nod and trotted off along the corridor.

'I did want to go,' Dan confided as his father closed the door. 'To the toilet.' And then in a burst of scandalised five-year-old indignation, 'But her, Bossy Boots, wanted to come with me and pull my pants down!'

'Pity,' Chase told his son. 'That's probably the best offer you'll get for at least ten years.'

4

Secretary of Defense Thomas J. Lebasse was dying of cancer of the bowel, and he knew it. At best the doctors had given him two years, which was a year longer than he had given himself. His body disgusted him; it stank of putrefaction, the sweetish sickly odour of death.

He was sixty-one years old, a small, round-shouldered man with a bald dome of a head that seemed too big for his body. Superficially he looked healthy, having just returned from ten days in Florida, but his tan had a grey pallor and the skin of his face sagged in flaccid folds underneath his dull eyes.

Right now his body wasn't the only thing that disgusted him; he found this meeting, and in particular these people, utterly distasteful.

'You keep insisting we have no choice but to implement this plan, Major Malden. As I see it, that's precisely what we do have: *a choice*. We still have our nuclear capability, which is superior to anything the Russians or the Chinese can muster.'

From his position at the head of the table Lebasse looked along the two rows of faces, all turned attentively towards him. Three members of the Joint Chiefs of Staff. An admiral who had made a special study of deep-draught cargo vessels. Two high-ranking air force officers, experts in missile deployment. A civilian scientist named Farrer whose function here today Lebasse wasn't entirely clear about.

Plus the two prime movers of Operation Download: General George N. ('Blindeye') Wolfe and his henchman, Major Lloyd Malden.

'Mr Secretary, with respect,' Major Malden was saying in his cultured New England voice, 'we are faced with a radical new situation.'

Appearance matched voice perfectly: neat dark hair, carefully parted, smooth sharp-featured face, tailored uniform with lapel badges burnished to winking brightness. His was the kind of face that became more youthful with the passing years, in contrast to General Wolfe, who at sixty-two could have passed for a man of seventy.

'The use of nuclear weapons is becoming an outdated concept in terms of global strategy.' Malden spoke with the smug self-confidence of a schoolboy who thinks himself brighter than his teacher but isn't smart enough not to show it. 'The MX missile system will be obsolete even before it's deployed. Already the budget is way off the graph and it's nowhere near fully operational. With respect, Mr Secretary—'

'Forget the respect,' Lebasse snapped. 'Say what you have to say.'

'We must adopt a strategy of domination by the use of Weapons of Climate Degradation. If we don't – and don't do it urgently – others will succeed where we have failed. We have to be ready to meet this new threat, sir. The balance of power must be in our favour if we're to safeguard the nation. After all, that is our prime responsibility.'

'Thank you, Major Malden,' said Lebasse icily. 'I don't need *you* to remind me of my – our – responsibility to the nation. According to you, nuclear weapons are becoming obsolete as a means of defending ourselves. Instead, your proposal is to adopt a completely new strategy of what might be described as environmental warfare. Have I got it right?'

'Yes, Mr Secretary. Correct.' Malden hesitated. 'Though that isn't the phrase we like to use. Our preferred terminology is WCD.'

'And your contention is that we must develop WCD before the Russians have the same idea and develop their own?'

'We know they already are, sir. They've been working on such a plan for at least six years.'

Lebasse said slowly, 'I think if they had, Major, I'd be the first to know about it.' He added dryly, 'I'm usually kept in the loop on such matters.'

'If I may say so, sir, not necessarily. You see, this wouldn't be reported as falling within the remit of defense intelligence. It wouldn't be perceived as a threat to national security at all, in fact.'

Lebasse leaned back in his chair and folded his arms. 'Go on, Major.'

'Some years ago we interrogated a Russian scientist at one of our bases in the Antarctic. His name was Astakhov. He divulged that his government was experimenting with a process to alter the chemical balance of seawater—'

'You say he was interrogated,' Lebasse interrupted.

'Yes, sir. Under EPT.'

Lebasse sighed. 'Speak English, Major.'

'Sorry, sir. Enhanced Persuasion Technique.'

'Was he kept in permanent detention afterwards?'

'No, sir.'

'So when he returned to Russia, he'd report this "enhanced persuasion" interrogation, wouldn't he? And they'd know what our interest was and draw their own conclusions.'

'He never returned to Russia.' Malden's thin lips curved in a faint smile. 'He died. His masters in Moscow learned nothing. Our involvement was known to only a small number of military and scientific personnel.'

'I see. And from this flimsy evidence – one man's testimony obtained under duress – you conclude that the Russians have an active and ongoing programme to develop WCD.'

'Not that alone, sir. We have other verifiable—'

'Much of this is supposition and guesswork, major, isn't it? You don't have any hard facts to support your theory. You might just as easily say the Russians have colonised the far side of the Moon on the basis that some crank is selling bottles of moondust in Red Square.' Thomas Lebasse looked up and down both sides of the table, spreading his hands as if to say *Am I right or am I right, goddamnit?*

Nobody took the bait. It would be a fatal error, Lloyd Malden knew, to engage the Secretary of Defence in a stand-up argument. He gripped a pencil and started cross-hatching on the blank pad on the desk blotter, holding himself tight inside. Better not to further arouse this sick old man who should have stayed in Florida with the rest of the gibbering senile geriatrics. So he would bide his time; there were allies in the room. Let somebody else take the lead, Malden decided, doodling an erect cock and huge pair of balls.

That somebody else couldn't have been any better than a four-star general: US Air Force General Walter Stafford of the Joint Chiefs of Staff. He was known to be a moderating influence, so not unduly hawkish. More important, he'd known Lebasse since they were students together at Columbia in the early eighties.

'Frankly, Tom, I share some of your doubts and uncertainties. But the major has spoken of a specific threat and I'd like him to share it with us. What have the Russians got that we haven't, Major Malden?'

'The Methane Gun.'

Every head turned towards him, followed by ten seconds of total silence.

The army's representative on the Joint Chiefs, General Smith said, 'And what the fuck of a fart in a wind-tunnel is the "methane gun"?'

'Potentially it's a very real and dangerous weapon, General,' Malden said. 'We've been monitoring it for some time.'

'And yeah! – so what the tarnation is it? An actual *gun*?'

Malden looked up from the pad with its doodles and gave an almost imperceptible nod to Farrer. The scientist had been exhaustively briefed and rigorously rehearsed; he launched in confidently, 'The Russians have developed a method of thawing the permafrost beneath the sea in Eastern Siberia. Under controlled conditions this fires fifty-gigaton cannon shells of methane gas into the atmosphere – hence the term Methane Gun. A single shell of methane is equivalent to one thousand gigatons of carbon dioxide. There's enough methane trapped beneath the Siberian permafrost to push global warming up by a factor of ten to a hundred. Eventually this would bring the planet close to an atmosphere very like that of Venus.'

'But how does that impact our security concerns?' Smith wanted to know. 'What does it mean to the US?'.

'The first effects on the mainland will bring a rise in sea levels of between seventy and one hundred and fifty feet. This is sufficient to cause flooding of many of our coastal cities and towns, including New York, Los Angeles, San Francisco, Miami, New Orleans and many others.

'Second, it will almost certainly affect the circumpolar wind pattern in the Northern Hemisphere. This disruption will alter the climate of the United States by increasing the average temperature of the Midwestern states by something like four to seven degrees, which will effectively wipe out all grain production in that region.'

'That's happening already,' Lebasse interrupted. 'The Midwest has suffered near-drought conditions for the last three years out of five. Grain yields are down twenty per cent or more.'

'This time it won't be a blip on the graph, Mr Secretary,' Farrer said. 'It'll be permanent and total. We'll lose the lot.'

'I see.' Lebasse nodded, tight-lipped. 'Go on.'

'Third – and while this is impossible to predict accurately – the shift in climate patterns over the entire United States will become much more erratic: torrential rainfall on the scale of monsoons in the southeast and prolonged droughts in the western desert regions.'

'Floods. Starvation. Drought,' barked Blindeye Wolfe, spelling it out in headlines. He looked grimly along the table towards the Secretary of Defense, his eyes like slits so that they almost disappeared in the creases of his face. 'Jesus, the Russkies have the perfect weapon – the Methane Gun! No call to use their nuclear capability. They'll just drown, starve, and fry us into submission!'

'Tell me, Mr Farrer,' Lebasse said very quietly, 'how much of this dramatic scenario is scientific fact? And how much is hot air?'

Farrer's fair complexion coloured a little. 'Well, sir, it's difficult to prove, I admit. But even a minor change in global climate can have disastrous long-term effects.' He cleared his throat. 'An increase of only 4°C would melt the entire polar ice cap. The Russians won't achieve that, but even a fraction of the increase would be enough to bring about the effects I've outlined.'

General Stafford raised his head slowly to look at Lebasse.

'I'd like it placed on record, Tom, that I gotta go with Major Malden on this one. He and General Wolfe have put a tremendous amount of effort into Operation Download. It isn't something they've just dreamed up. In my book we have to give them the green light. If we don't, the Russians and maybe the Chinese too will steal a march on us. Let's give this our blessing and proceed to full operational status as quickly as possible. Nothing else will deter the Russians, that's a dead certainty.'

'"Dead" being the operative word,' Lebasse remarked stonily. He was thinking of his four grandchildren, ranging in age from seventeen to five. Global environmental death was a fine legacy to bequeath them. He ruminated with bleak despair whether it had been any different since the moment – 5:30 a.m. 16 July 1945 – when the atomic bomb stopped being a row of symbols in a physicist's notebook and was transformed into a five-thousand-degree fireball above the Trinity site in Arizona . . .

Was what he was being asked to sanction any more monstrous than that? No, except that he would not live to see the consequences. The seeds of death were already within him, his escape route to eternity. History would judge him on this one decision – always supposing there was any history worth writing about. Or anyone left to write it.

5

Lebasse was being forced to go somewhere he didn't wish to go. A plan to degrade the environment made no kind of sense at all to him. Countries weren't sealed off from one another. Disrupt the climate in one country and its effects would be felt in every other region as well. The nations of the world shared the same eco-system, the same biosphere. It wasn't as if each one inhabited a separate planet.

A thought occurred to the Secretary of Defence: a glimmer of hope. It might even be a lifeline. He glanced towards Malden, who was intent on whatever he was doodling on his pad.

'Central to this proposal is consideration and evaluation of a subject requiring specialist knowledge. I would have thought the President's senior scientific advisor should be present at this meeting today. Why isn't he?'

Malden stirred himself and looked up from his drawing of a penis, which now had a dagger through it, dripping blood. 'Operation Download retains a high-security status, Mr Secretary. Access is denied to all but designated military personnel.'

'Are you seriously telling me that that excludes Professor Lucas?'

'Yes, sir.'

Lebasse said irritably, 'How am I supposed to reach a decision on the scientific validity of this scheme of yours without recourse to expert advice?'

'That's the purpose of Farrer being here,' Malden said, indicating the civilian scientist.

'But he's not independent, is he?' Lebasse pointed out. 'He's one of your people. From your outfit, Advanced . . . whatever it's called . . .'

'ASP, sir. Advanced Strategic Projects.'

'Before I make my recommendations to the President I want to be absolutely sure I understand the ecological implications of what you're proposing. Your data and statistical analysis, for example.'

At a nod from Major Malden, Farrer spoke up. 'The vast bulk of the information we based our study on came from the DELFI computer modelling facility at the National Climate Prediction Foundation. Which is located at Boulder, Colorado,' he supplied helpfully. 'It's acknowledged to be the most sophisticated capability anywhere in the world.'

'I know all about computer predictions,' Lebasse muttered darkly. 'They can be made to prove just about anything you care to name. Or disprove it. Otherwise known as GIGO. Garbage In, Garbage Out. And I'll be damned if a decision of this magnitude is going to be based on the whim of a box of microchips and gee-jaw processors. No matter how "sophisticated" it happens to be.'

Lebasse addressed General Wolfe and Major Malden directly. 'I don't see any logical reason why Professor Lucas can't be given clearance for Download, do you? And by that I mean all matters pertaining to it. Lucas is the President's senior advisor, for God's sake.'

Malden straightened up. 'If I may speak frankly, sir, I'm not completely happy and at ease about that—'

'What? Dammit all, man, why not? Do you seriously believe Gene Lucas is a security risk?'

If the Secretary of Defence decreed it, Malden knew, then of course it would have to be, but this was dangerous. Professor Lucas wasn't in anyone's pocket. He would give an unbiased appraisal based on the facts as he saw them. Which might be in their favour, or might not. Which was a gamble Malden wasn't prepared to take. They'd have to head this off somehow.

Correction. *He* would have to head it off.

'Yes, Mr Secretary, I'll look into it right away.' Malden gave his thin, joyless smile. 'I'm pretty sure something can be arranged.'

'Not can – *will* be arranged,' Lebasse said, his icy tone returning.

Malden shrugged, to show he wasn't intimidated. 'It will have to go through ASP, of course, under whose auspices Download has been developed.'

'How long?'

'Sir?'

'Before Professor Lucas is granted security clearance?' asked Lebasse impatiently.

'Forty-eight hours, depending.'

'Depending? On *what* exactly?'

'No historical impediment or conflict of interest.'

'What on earth are you talking about, man?' Lebasse rested his fists on the table. 'Conflict of interest? Such as?' He was watching Major Malden suspiciously and making no attempt to conceal it.

Without a moment's hesitation Malden replied smoothly, 'When ASP was set up, six years ago, one of the directives was to the effect that no military or scientific personnel who had spoken out against Agent Orange were to be permitted access to, or knowledge of, Operation Download. Hence, sir, the special security classification.'

Malden's face didn't betray for an instant how close to the wind he was sailing.

Agent Orange was the chemical defoliant widely used in Vietnam. Years after the war ended, its indiscriminate use across the countryside was found to have maimed and killed thousands of Vietnamese peasants as well as American combat troops and aircrew. The virulent chemical caused cancer, skin diseases, ugly growths on various parts of the body and all manner of severe genetic damage. Many of the native children – and some American kids too – had been born with malformed limbs, blindness, heart defects, duplicate reproductive organs and internal organs growing outside their body.

Anyone who had voiced strong opinions of moral outrage over Agent Orange certainly would never countenance Operation Download and the deployment of WCD. Lebasse thought about it, and he had to admit the logic made sense. So what stance had Gene Lucas taken on the issue? Pro or anti? Outspoken or in agreement? He didn't know.

Neither did he know that Lloyd Malden two minutes previously had invented the ASP directive about barring those critical of Agent Orange. None such existed. In any case, Malden was confident he could dig up some dirt on Lucas, if not about Agent Orange, then something else. And if he couldn't find any he'd invent that too – just as Farrer, who wrote science fiction in his spare time, had invented the Methane Gun scare story and written it up in a 'Technical Briefing Paper', based on one of his own imagined weapons. The science behind it was true: huge belches of methane were indeed being released into the atmosphere from deep within Arctic permafrost deposits. But this had nothing to do with the Russians and was quite beyond their control. It was in fact the result of global warming, caused mainly by burning fossil fuels in the USA, China and Europe.

Malden didn't like Farrer – couldn't stand the fellow – but had to admit the Methane Gun black propaganda ploy was a stroke of genius.

Lebasse said, 'I'll leave it to you, Major. Run a check on Professor Lucas and inform my office the minute you receive clearance.'

Malden nodded and as if making a note, drew a bold thick arrow from the bleeding penis to the name of the Secretary of Defence heavily ringed in black.

General Stafford raised his hand. 'One question I'd like to ask Major Malden, Tom, before we wind up.'

'Of course, Walt. Go ahead.'

'If we get Presidential approval – assuming we do – how soon before Operation Download comes into operational mode? By that I mean deployment-ready?'

'Fourteen months.'

'You sound pretty sure of that, Major.'

'That's because I'm *very* sure, General. We already have the component parts of the plan: chemical compounds code-named "Laptop" and "Tablet". Also the self-destruct supertankers which can be modified from existing mothballed stock and standby missiles for targeting remote or inaccessible waters. What remains is a matter of command control, deployment and implementation. Simple logistics.'

Lebasse rubbed a whitish substance from the corner of his mouth and looked at his fingertips. 'Assuming you get Presidential approval for your WCD,' he said quietly.

6

Whenever he was at the Pentagon, General Wolfe loved to ride the electrified light-rail transit system that ferried the thousands of military and intelligence personnel across the vast complex. It would have taken a fit individual more than two hours at a brisk jog to do a lap of the outer ring.

As they left the meeting, Lloyd Malden was feeling buoyant and in good spirits and thus prepared to indulge his chief in this childish diversion. Malden was confident he had the measure of that sick old husk Lebasse; even better, he had him at his mercy.

No question, Operation Download was going ahead, with or without Lebasse's blessing.

They boarded the light transit and rode side by side through the brightly illuminated tunnels to the open-air viewing platform which overlooked the Potomac River. Blindeye Wolfe asked for his cigar case and led the way to the smoking area. It had been raining earlier but now it was fine and the humidity was rising. While the general enjoyed his cigar Malden checked his pad for messages. There were at least a dozen, but nothing requiring immediate attention. He turned at the sound of some commotion or other: a boisterous group of senior army officers and civilians were gathered at the balustrade, guffawing and pummelling each others' backs, some engaging in bear-hugs. A young officer was relaying information from a hand-held curved news-screen, each fresh item bringing more whoops and clenched-fist salutes.

About to make some joking reference to the celebration, Malden was stalled when his upper arm was seized in a painful grip. General Wolfe's face had undergone a striking transformation – screwed up, red verging on purple, brows drawn together. The general snatched the cigar from his mouth, leaving a string of spittle trailing from its chewed end.

Malden was genuinely alarmed. 'What's the matter, General?'

'Let's get the fuck outta here.'

'Very well – but what is it?'

'The bunch making all the racket – you don't know who the guy is with the ridiculous pompadour of dyed straw on his bonce? Don't you recognise him?'

Major Malden took a moment to scrutinise the individual, who stood out from the others with his big, broad-shouldered bluster: florid complexion, thick chestnut-brown moustache trimmed by a laser. And as the general said, a spectacular sculpted crown of hair the same vibrant shade as the 'tache. Malden had seen him before, but couldn't recall where.

'Who is he?'

'Chesney Poulton.' Blindeye Wolfe uttered the name as if it tasting cyanide. 'Runs a lobby group here in DC: the American Advanced Alliance or some such. Reckons he calls the shots big-time and knows everybody worth knowing.'

'Maybe he does,' Malden said, remembering now. 'Wasn't Poulton an advisor to Rumsfeld and Wolfowitz when they were running State and Defense? I didn't realise you two had some history, General.'

'If we have,' Wolfe said, glaring at Malden, 'it's between him and me and nobody else.'

'Yes, sir. I understand.' The major's expression was deadpan; this was just the kind of mystery he thrived on. Any juicy little tidbit from the general's murky past was meat and drink to Lloyd Malden. 'I wonder what the jubilation is all about?'

'Knowing Poulton, somebody just died of cancer.'

The rancour went deep, no doubt about it. More intrigued now he knew who the man was, Malden turned towards Chesney Poulton, watching him covertly, and was startled to find Poulton staring straight at him. It was unnerving. Their two gazes locked. Malden felt the colour rise in his cheeks. Even worse, the man with the ludicrous hairstyle excused himself from the group and strode towards them. He towered over Wolfe and was at least three inches taller than the major. Looking down on Malden, he said to General Wolfe, 'And who do we have here, George? Another of your protégés?'

'Happens to be none of your business, but Major Malden is my senior executive officer. If I had my way, Poulton, they'd bar lobbyist time-wasters like you from setting foot inside the Pentagon. This is a top-level intelligence facility for planning military operations, not a cocktail lounge for peddling propaganda and salacious gossip.'

'Nice speech, George. Did your pretty boy write it for you?'

Malden flinched as if he'd been struck. The riposte that came instantly to mind was a mocking remark on Poulton's elaborate hair-do. But making an enemy of such a powerful Washington player maybe wasn't such a clever idea. He bit his tongue and straightened up defiantly, his gaze sullen.

Poulton appraised the major in his smartly tailored tan uniform. He looked puzzled. With a frown he inclined his head to inspect the triangular shoulder-flash, which depicted an adder. The coiled-up snake was a visual representation of Advanced Strategic Projects, or ASP. Malden was proud of both the title and the symbol, having dreamed them up himself.

'What kinda dumb name is that for a military outfit?' Poulton enquired blandly, raising his bushy eyebrows. 'And what's ASP stand for anyway? As Soon As Possible? No, I have it – Ass-Wipe.'

'Your status doesn't grant you the privilege to know the projects we're involved in,' General Wolfe said, twisting his lips in a superior smile. 'This is real man's work, Poulton, not frivolous PR dabbling on the fringes.'

'Is that so?'

Wolfe dismissed him with a waft of the hand. 'Go back to your partying with the rest of the zombie goons. You've evidently found something silly enough to keep your little brains amused.'

'Tell me, George, you know what today's date is?'

Wolfe regarded him suspiciously. 'Of course. April 21. So what?'

'In future you'll remember it as a "Big Day" – maybe not up there with 9/11, but it's a date you won't forget. Remember the name Santa Clara too. For your information, it's a small town in the middle of Cuba. What happened in Santa Clara today is gonna have a major impact: the first stage in a project your status doesn't grant you the privilege of knowing *anything* about.'

Malden's curiosity was fired up. He couldn't stop himself from asking, 'What is it that's so momentous? A coup of some kind?'

'You're a bright boy, Major,' Poulton said with grudging respect. 'Not too far wide of the mark for a blind guess. A perfect shitstorm is about to descend on that prime piece of real-estate.' He smiled at Malden. 'I'll be keeping an eye on you.'

'Stay off my turf,' Wolfe barked at him, jabbing his finger in Poulton's broad chest. 'You know what? Fixing stuff in a two-bit banana shit-hole like Cuba is a good fit, I'd say. You've found your own level at last. Congratulations. Well done.'

Chesney Poulton looked untroubled. He gazed down on Wolfe, then leaned over and put his mouth close to the general's fleshy ear. Even though the big man kept his voice low, Malden heard every word.

'My advice to you, George, is simple. Don't meddle in politics. I've heard about you and Operation *Dumpload* or whatever it's called. This is my game. You and your fancy boy are out of your depth. Listen to me, and pay close attention: keep outta my way, or I'll have you and Ass-Wipe fucked over. Comprehensively and permanently.'

Poulton's tone was reasonable and unthreatening; he might have been offering a friendly word, except for the message. Major Malden wasn't to forget it.

2

I

Chase stood before the tinted, angled window looking out at the serrated mountain peaks etched against the bright blue Colorado sky: so incredibly sharp and clear you felt you could touch them, even though they were twenty miles away.

'Don't you find the view distracting, Bill?'

'Binch,' said Bill Inchcape with a smile. 'Everybody calls me Binch.' He heaved his bulk out of the chair and wandered over to the window. 'It is pretty spectacular, I guess, but after eighteen years it's just part of the scenery.' He caught Chase's eye and chuckled. 'What am I saying? It isn't part of the scenery, it *is* the scenery.'

'It certainly beats the view from my London flat,' Chase remarked enviously. 'If I had this to look at I'd never get a thing done.'

After three weeks and two days of being continually on the move he was starting to feel jaded and travel-weary. The National Climate Prediction Foundation at Boulder, Colorado, was near the end of his itinerary. These magnificent mountains and wide-open spaces were a tonic: just what he needed to buck up his spirits and restore his mental edge.

'What do you think, Gavin, is the information of any use?' Binch wanted to know, tucking his pudgy hands into the pockets of his voluminous trousers.

Chase nodded. 'I'll have to work the technical stuff into the text somehow, soften it up. The pieces are aimed at the layman, not scientists, so it'll have to be pitched at that level.'

'Let me tell you something,' Binch said frankly. 'A few years ago I'd have kicked you out the door as one more environmental crank. I used to think it was a load of hogwash; you know, reporters, TV pundits trying to jump on the scare bandwagon.'

'But not anymore?'

Binch shook his head so that his jowls quivered. 'There's too much going on up there we don't know about.' He gestured towards the empty blue sky. 'And what we do know isn't exactly reassuring. Living with DELFI has taught me that much.'

'You use DELFI for climatic prediction modelling,' Chase said.

'Right. Stands for Determining Environmental Logistics for Future Interpretation.' Binch made a face. 'Damn-fool name, I know, but I guess we're stuck with it.'

Chase's research for his piece on computer weather modelling had come in useful here. He'd already learned that as far back as the 1980s the major nations had cooperated in mounting a climate-monitoring survey, known as the Global Weather Experiment. It was an ambitious multi-million-dollar programme involving the simultaneous launching of five geostationary satellites and two polar-orbiting stations. Aircraft from a score of nations fitted with sensitive measuring equipment carried out a systematic probing of the atmosphere and the oceans. More than forty surface vessels were used to make oceanic and atmospheric observations in the Southern Hemisphere. A network of automatic data buoys supplied a constant update on currents, wind strength, and rainfall.

The purpose of the Global Weather Experiment had been to collect data as a basis for computer modelling studies; it was then realised that the existing computer power was hopelessly inadequate – swamped by such a cornucopia of information. What was needed was a new, state-of-the-art computer facility, one that could handle the fiendishly complex global climate system. In addition, it would require the capacity to simulate natural and man-made changes in the atmosphere and oceans, and from this data come up with accurate long-term predictions.

Thus, in 2002, DELFI came into being. Acknowledged from the start as the most powerful and sophisticated facility of its kind, DELFI had been upgraded to process microwave signals direct from ATOP 7 (Astronomical and Terrestrial Observation Platform), the latest US orbiting station, completed only two years before.

'How far ahead are you forecasting?' Chase asked.

'Currently we're running three predictive programmes – ten, fifteen, and twenty years.' Binch was about to say something else, and hesitated.

'Restricted?' Chase said astutely.

Binch nodded, meeting Chase's eye with a sour smile. 'As you might know, the military have a hand in this, as in everything else. I guess they think the Russians should have to sweat for their own climatic predictions instead of getting ours for peanuts.'

'I can see that. But I don't see the military application.'

'Me neither. If CO_2 is going to be a problem twenty years from now, it'll be the same for everybody. There's no military value in that so far as I can figure out.'

'Unless you happen to be the first country to know about it and plan accordingly,' Chase said, testing a speculation. Yet even supposing DELFI predicted a sharp rise in carbon dioxide over the next twenty years, so what? Such an increase had been recognised and plotted for decades. Did Bill Inchcape know something else that he couldn't reveal?

Binch returned to the desk and eased himself down. 'Can't say more, Gavin. Sorry. If ASP got to hear I'd even been talking to you they'd ball me out and cancel my pension.'

'ASP?'

'Advanced Strategic Projects. They're a scientific offshoot of the army based at the Pentagon. I don't know a lot about them except they rank pretty high in the Defense Department.'

'How often do you submit reports to them?'

'Hey now,' Binch protested mildly. 'Don't dig too deep. Off the record, we give them an update when there's been any significant change. There's no set schedule. Maybe every three months or so.'

Chase stared at him. 'Every *three* months? You mean things change that rapidly?'

'Let's just say that as we feed in additional data our predictions become more accurate,' Binch amended. 'Right now, in fact, we're working on new software that will sharpen up our accuracy by at least fifty per cent. We've got a new computer specialist, an ex-Scripps guy, who's absolutely brilliant.'

'What does ASP do with the information?'

'I don't know,' Binch replied, giving him a level stare. 'And if I did I wouldn't tell you.' His expression softened. 'Hey, how'd you like to come to dinner this evening . . . if you've no other plans? My wife Stella, she's a terrific cook – as you can see.' He patted his lavish paunch.

2

Chase had met with this kind of hospitality throughout his trip, and he was delighted to accept. Americans on their home ground, he had found, were the warmest and most generous of people.

To his relief the occasion was quite informal. As Binch had promised the food was delicious, and Bill and Stella Inchcape the perfect hosts. Nothing was too much trouble, yet they didn't fuss over him, treating him rather as an old friend of the family. There were two other guests, Jeff Henshaw – the 'ex-Scripps guy who's absolutely brilliant' – and his companion for the evening, Ruth Brosnan, a doctor specialising in diagnostic research at a hospital in Denver.

After the meal they went out on to the deck and sprawled in comfortable loungers, drinking coffee and brandy under the stars. The night was warm and the air fragrant with the scent of pines. There was a sharper, almost bitter smell too that Chase couldn't identify.

'Cactus flower,' Stella Inchcape informed him. 'They don't usually grow so far north, but this is the third or fourth year we've had them. They're all over the place. I've asked Binch to cut them back but he's too lazy to get off his derrière.'

'What I hate about gardening is that it's a waste of time,' Binch said. 'Once it's been cut, why can't grass stay cut!'

'We'd be in trouble if it did,' Chase said.

Ruth Brosnan asked him about his assignment and he explained about the series of articles he'd been commissioned to write for *Sentinel*.

'You don't somehow sound like a journalist to me,' she said, appraising him with dark eyes. She was a slender, rather elegant woman with dark curly hair that framed a sensitive, intelligent face.

He gave her a lazy smile. 'That's probably because I'm a marine biologist by training and inclination. I've been writing science articles for round about four years.'

'What made you switch?' asked Jeff Henshaw.

Chase had been asked this before and it was tempting to evangelise. As an individual, a lone scientist, he had felt his influence was limited, whereas as a science writer (he didn't use the word journalist) he might conceivably make a real difference. It was his way of focusing attention on the environment debate.

'You don't actually believe we're heading for the final showdown,' said Jeff Henshaw, his face creasing in a pained smile. He wore heavy horn-rimmed glasses which were somehow out of keeping with his compact, powerful build; his air of mocking cynicism was rather patronising.

Chase wouldn't be lured. 'I'd have thought that you, Jeff – along with Binch and DELFI – could answer that better than I could,' he said easily.

'No, you've got it wrong, my friend.' Henshaw was almost scoffing. 'What you gotta understand is that DELFI predicts how conditions *might* change and the probable extent of those changes; it cannot and *does not*, believe you me, foretell the end of the world.'

'Well,' Chase said, 'let's hope I am wrong and you're right. I'd hate to say goodbye to all this.' With his glass he indicated the five of them, the lawn and flowering bushes fading away into darkness. Above them the sky was an ocean of stars.

'We had this guy who used to work here,' Binch spoke up, 'had the same feeling as you, Gavin. An ex-astronaut called Brad Zittel. That was indeed a very strange thing: he just took off – disappeared – leaving his wife, family, home, everything.' He shook his head reflectively. 'Never heard a word to this day. Weird.'

'His kind usually are,' Henshaw said, not looking at Chase, though the faint smile of condescension was back.

Stella Inchcape frowned, remembering. 'Joyce – Brad's wife – did everything she could to locate him. She called in the police, the FBI, the State Department . . . but they never found him, not a trace.'

'Perhaps he had some kind of nervous breakdown,' Ruth said.

Binch agreed. 'I guess could be. What happened – he'd get all wrought up over the weather anomalies, sat there slumped in his chair looking at the screens, staring at the print-out like it was the Doomsday Book, grey in the face. Couldn't shake him out of it; he just kept insisting we had to do something before it was too late.'

'Isn't it just possible that he was right?' Chase mused. From the corner of his eye he noticed that Binch was staring moodily into his glass, his lower lip jutting out. It was bloody infuriating not to know what DELFI was predicting. If a hardened sceptic like Bill Inchcape was starting to have doubts, then the data must be pretty hair-raising.

'Who else are you seeing?' Ruth asked him, as if trying to steer the conversation into less choppy waters.

'Some people on the West Coast at UCLA and Scripps. And if there's time I'd like to go up to Oregon. They have an enlightened attitude towards environment issues up there, I believe.'

'Do you have a contact at Scripps?' Binch asked.

'Dr Cheryl Detrick. She's the daughter of Theo Detrick.'

Binch nodded. 'Right, yes, heard of her. Read some of her stuff in fact. *Science Review*, I think. Very contentious, pretty outspoken.' He craned his head around. 'Did you know her when you were at Scripps, Jeff?'

Jeff Henshaw nursed his drink, shoulders hunched forward. He laughed suddenly, for no apparent reason. 'Yeah, knew her pretty well, as a matter of fact. We did some work together . . . amongst other things.' He cocked an eyebrow in Chase's direction. 'Cheryl's another environmental nut-job.'

Ruth glanced at him disapprovingly. As if in apology, she said to Chase, 'Jeff thinks all environmentalists are anti-science, that their mission is to turn the clock back and return civilisation to the Stone Age. He doesn't believe that's possible or practicable.'

'Jeff is right,' Chase said. 'On the contrary I want to use science to *solve* our problems. The way I see it, science is ethically neutral; it's scientists who have ethics – or lack them. Science should be used for the benefit of mankind, not its detriment.'

'I bet you were an Eagle Scout too,' Henshaw said, grinning.

Chase didn't bother responding. He'd debated the subject with better opponents than Jeff Henshaw; no way he was going to be a decoy duck for cheap entertainment value.

'For my ten cents' worth,' Binch said, 'I don't think we scientists should get involved. I do my job and let somebody else worry about the ethical rights and wrongs.'

'Maybe you *should* worry about it,' his wife put in quietly.

'And wind up like Brad Zittel? No thanks.' Binch waved the suggestion away and helped himself to more cognac.

Ruth Brosnan said, 'We've got a patient at the hospital with a condition that's possibly environmentally related. Very disturbing from a clinical point of view: a case of chloracne.'

Chase stared at her. He couldn't believe he'd heard correctly. 'You mean dioxin poisoning?'

Ruth nodded. The light from the patio lanterns cast spiky shadows from her eyelashes across her cheekbones. 'In actual fact,' she went on reluctantly, 'more than one. Three cases, as of yesterday. Nobody suspected dioxin poisoning at first – why would we? It wasn't until we'd eliminated everything else . . . but the tests confirm it.'

Chase was sitting up in the lounger. 'To the best of my knowledge there hasn't been a case of dioxin poisoning for the last ten years. Have you been able to trace the source?'

'Not definitely, but it's most likely agricultural. All three cases come from southeast of here, beyond Denver, which is mainly – in fact, exclusively – farmland.'

Binch asked, 'How serious is this, Ruth? I mean, is it likely to spread, become an epidemic?'

'All depends how many other cases turn up over the next two to three weeks.'

Chase begged to differ. 'Forgive me, that's one hell of an understatement. This isn't chicken pox or measles.'

'What is the lake?' Stella asked. 'Is it dangerous?'

'Dioxin is a lethal compound – highly toxic. Even a minute leakage is a serious risk for everybody within a forty–fifty-mile radius.'

Stella was aghast. 'Why produce something so highly dangerous? What on earth is it used for?'

'It isn't used for anything,' Chase said. 'Dioxin is a by-product in the manufacture of the herbicide 2,4,5-T, which is more commonly known by the acronym TCDD. One of the first symptoms of dioxin poisoning is chloracne, a very nasty skin complaint. I'll spare you the details.' He looked at Ruth, his eyes clouding. 'How is it possible to have three cases of chloracne when there's been a worldwide ban on the manufacture of 2,4,5-T for at least thirty years? They can't still be using it on farmland around here.'

'No, they're not,' Ruth confirmed. 'At least, the big combines aren't, because we've checked up on them. But there are hundreds of smaller farms and thousands of smallholdings with just a few acres of land.' She sighed. 'We just don't have the resources. It'll take months for a complete investigation to try and pinpoint the source.'

There was something that didn't quite fit, that Chase couldn't put his finger on. Chloracne was caused by dioxin poisoning, which implicated herbicides. So what didn't?

'Could it be a leak from a chemical plant?' Jeff Henshaw suggested.

'The nearest chemical plant is two hundred and fifty miles away,' Ruth said. 'We checked it, but it processes oil-based products, not herbicides.'

'Isn't that the stuff they used in Vietnam to defoliate the jungle?' Binch asked Chase. 'A lot of the military personnel who served out there developed symptoms of dioxin poisoning.'

'That's what led to the ban. There was a whole range of genetic disorders caused by—'

Chase stopped, realising what Binch had just said. *Of course!* 2,4,5-T was used in Vietnam because it checked the growth of broad-leaved plants in jungles and forests; it had little effect on the narrow-leaved grasses of the sort found in croplands. So farmers in this part of the US wouldn't use 2,4,5-T anyway; it would be ineffective.

'Are there any military bases in the area?'

Binch had to think for a moment, scratching his chin. 'I guess the nearest is NORAD.'

'What's that?'

'The North American Air Defense Command. It's based at Colorado Springs, inside Cheyenne Mountain. But it's a command and control centre, deep underground; it's non-operational in terms of aircraft and missiles.'

'Don't forget the space centre near Cheyenne,' Ruth put in. 'That controls all the spy satellites and military shuttles launched from the Vandenberg Spaceport in California.'

Chase recalled that for thirty years the United States had been spending billions of dollars developing space platforms for beam weapons and killer-satellite launch pads. The Vandenberg Spaceport on the Californian coast was a miniature city, with its own schools, shopping malls, housing projects, hospitals. But Vandenberg was nearly half a continent away. He said, 'Do they launch anything in this vicinity – say within fifty or sixty miles?'

Ruth glanced uncertainly at Binch. 'Don't they carry out test-firings of experimental prototypes from the Martin Marietta Space Center?'

'Where's that?' Chase asked.

'Near Denver. Sorry, Gavin, I don't follow your drift,' Ruth said perplexedly. 'What's any of this got to do with TCDD and dioxin poisoning?'

'You know what?' Chase said. 'Nothing that I know of. I'm just praying that it's so.' Which he hoped was the truth and nothing but the truth.

3

Even though Boris lay quite still, from the sound of his breathing, shallow and irregular, Nina knew her husband was awake. She moved her hand beneath the covers, found and gripped his.

'There's nothing else you can do,' she murmured in the darkness. 'You tried your best, my love. Stop blaming yourself. It isn't up to you any more.'

'Then who?'

'Somebody else. Somebody younger.'

Boris laughed, a rumble deep in his chest. 'The younger people are committed to greed and the pursuit of pleasure just as we were to the party and socialist progress. Most of them live for today, and let the future go hang. Let it take care of itself, the fools!'

'They're not all like that,' Nina said. 'There are some who still care.'

'Perhaps so. But they're powerless or afraid.'

'Aren't you afraid?'

His hand returned the pressure. 'Nina, dearest, I've worked as a scientist in this country for getting on forty years. I have always tried to do my best, to work with integrity, for the benefit of mankind. If I'm unable to publish my research any longer, what has been the point of it all? Being afraid to speak the truth defeats the object of my calling . . .'

Boris had to break off because there was a husky tremor in his voice. He felt his wife's grip tighten.

'There are scientists in the West engaged in the same work,' Nina pointed out. 'Your old friend Theo Detrick, until he passed away—'

'"Passed away" is the kind of deceitful phrase our leaders use,' Boris said. 'An evasion of the truth. Theo was murdered. Let's speak of things as they are, not use weasel words.'

He was angry, his voice harsh, and he was immediately contrite. 'I'm sorry, dearest, that was uncalled for. It's wrong to take my frustration out on you. Forgive me.' He turned his head towards her on the pillow. 'I should have spoken out when I discovered what happened to Peter Astakhov in the Antarctic. The signs were there for us all to see – the oceans reaching saturation point, unable to absorb another cubic centimetre of carbon dioxide. The level of oxygen production was bound to be affected. It was inevitable.'

'You did what you did in good faith.'

'No,' Boris said bitterly, 'in blind ignorance.'

'It isn't your fault!' Nina insisted. 'You've written articles and done all you possibly can to have them accepted by the science journals. What more can you do?'

'Publish them abroad. Malankovitch has the clout to block them here, to stall me, but not in the West.'

'But why should it matter to him, to that bonehead, if your research is published here in Russia or anywhere else?' Nina asked. She was bewildered.

'I have two thoughts on that,' Boris said. 'The first is we mustn't share our findings about oxygen depletion – and our fears – with other countries because we can use that knowledge to our advantage. Don't you see, Nina? It could be used as a potential weapon.'

'No, I don't see. How is it—?'

'A weapon of global environmental warfare,' Boris said patiently.

'But that's crazy! Whoever thought that up must be off their heads. If you're threatening somebody with oxygen depletion, you're threatening yourself as well. My God, Boris, it's like aiming the gun at your own head . . .'

'So tell me, wise one, how is that any different from when the Soviet Union and the West squared up to one another with nuclear weapons and threatened mutual destruction? It makes just as much sense, doesn't it? And as little.'

Nina was silent.

Boris said, 'My second thought is that multi-billionaire Malankovitch and his mafia pals are dead against me leaving the homeland ever again. There's a lot of classified research material he doesn't want leaking to the West – well, not before he's made his millions out of it.'

'You've been to America,' Nina pointed out, 'more than once. He didn't stop you going.'

'I was free to go,' Boris agreed, 'so long as you stayed here, remember. That was the deal.'

'Did Malankovitch actually say that to you?'

'Of course not.'

'Then how can you be sure the threat was real?'

'Nina, dearest, he didn't have to spell it out in ten-metre block capitals for me to know what he meant. Anna Politkovskaya – remember her?'

'The journalist who died?'

'She was murdered. It was a contract killing. In the lift of her block of flats. And then there was Gadzhimurat Kamalov, a reporter investigating the mafia. He was shot six times in a drive-by shooting outside the newspaper office. Alexander Khodzinsky, another journalist. Stabbed to death. Kazbek Gekkiev, a TV reporter. Shot dead in the street. Akhmednabi Akhmednabiev, deputy editor of a current affairs magazine. He was shot a dozen times in his car when he was fifty metres from his house. More than two hundred journalists and media workers assassinated by the mafia or unknown forces.'

'What about these people? What are you saying?'

'You asked me if the threat was real. It was real enough for them.'

'Do you seriously believe Malankovitch was behind those murders?'

'My guess is they were ordered by the FSB, or the Moscow Mafia – which amounts to much the same thing. The message couldn't be clearer: step out of line, do something we don't approve of, and this is what'll happen to you.' Boris turned his head restlessly on the pillow. 'It's because I know how their minds work that I'm certain what he meant. He didn't need to draw me a diagram!'

Nina was silent for a while, thinking, yet hardly daring to think. Then she said, 'It would be highly dangerous sending this information to the West. Even if the articles were published under another name. With Malankovitch watching you . . .'

'Very dangerous,' Boris agreed. 'For both of us.'

She was relieved, thinking he'd changed his mind, and an instant later knew she was a fool. There was something in his voice that made her body tense itself. Her hand gripped his tightly.

'What are you going to do?' Heart in her mouth.

'I have no choice. Get out.'

'You mean leave Russia?'

'Yes.'

'For ever?' The words were like the taste of iron on her tongue.

'Yes.'

'It can't be done,' she whispered.

'Yes, it can,' Boris said very calmly. 'I've already begun to make the arrangements. All my internet communication is heavily monitored, so I've written to Theo's daughter by airmail. I'm just hoping they won't think to intercept such an old-fashioned method. And even if they do, it's just a friendly letter with greetings and gossip. Cheryl will read between the lines, I hope, and see what I'm getting at.'

'What are these "arrangements" you speak of?'

'I'll know within a few days. I'll be given a date, and details of what I have to do . . .'

Fear crept in, shrinking her mind to nothing. She became numb. Tears leaked out of her eyes and ran down the sides of her head on to the pillow.

'Boris, I don't want to lose you,' she sobbed. 'Oh, please, God, no. No—!'

He gathered her body in his arms and held her close, feeling her heart shuddering in her chest. 'Woman. *Woman!* You're not losing me. Did you think after all these years I'd leave you behind? We stay together, whatever happens. I'd rather lose my life than lose you.'

4

The silver helicopter clattered in low over the trees and shimmied down on to the yellow crisscrossed landing pad. Sunlight flared off the clear thermoplastic canopy and glinted on the conch-shell motif aft of the starboard door. The door swung open, and even before the helicopter had properly settled the man in the white linen suit was striding across the pad. He went down the steps to where the lawns swept in their rolling green perfection up to the house, passing through the ring of plainclothes guards standing idly with curled hands and hard, immobile faces.

Two more guards stood aside as he entered the glass-walled elevator, which took him smoothly to the rooftop. A covered area extended to a sundeck overlooking the orderly ranks of firs descending to the blue haze of the Pacific. To the south, just visible beyond the ridge, the white ramparts and Gothic follies of San Simeon gleamed like bleached bone. Cars hummed distantly on US 1 below, and a light aircraft droned somewhere over the placid ocean.

A pink-coated Javanese manservant stood near the mirror-tiled bar, his sallow face expressionless. The man in white passed quickly through and out into the sunlight. He came to a halt and looked down, wraparound sunglasses masking his eyes, arms hanging by his sides, hands loosely flexed. 'The Lebasse situation checks out, Mr Gelstrom. It's as we thought. The condition is terminal.'

'How soon?'

'One year. Maybe longer.'

'You've seen the medical records?'

The man in white nodded.

Joseph Earl Gelstrom opened his vivid blue eyes for the first time and squinted up. The man in white watched him. The same thought hovered in the hot motionless air between them; they understood each other so well that words were superfluous.

Gelstrom looked along the length of his lean, bronzed body and suddenly tautened his abdominal muscles into a set of symmetrical hard brown pebbles. With the effort, his head was thrust forward, long sun-streaked hair smoothly gathered at the nape of his neck. He was forty-nine years old and possessed the looks and physique a man twenty years younger would have envied. He didn't drink or smoke and exercised obsessively. Nothing could touch him.

Just as suddenly Gelstrom relaxed, lay back, and breathed out slowly through flared nostrils. The man in white waited, casually appraising the topless sun-basking girl, apparently asleep. The other person, the man with the narrow bald head in a loose robe he ignored completely.

Gelstrom rose lithely and went to the white wooden rail. He was barefoot, even though the tiles were scorching. Though exactly six feet tall, he seemed smaller and slighter when the man in white moved to stand alongside him. The two of them stood looking out into the distance, not speaking.

It had never been calculated, but Joseph Earl Gelstrom was possibly one of the top half-dozen most wealthy citizens in the United States.

His empire had been founded at the age of nineteen, started on the building blocks of his father's New Jersey interior-decorating business, which at the time employed nine people. Few people knew about his beginnings. Nothing was known about him publicly prior to his takeover, at the age of twenty-three, of a small run-down chemical company that had a contract for the supply of detergents to the US Army. The contract amounted to a paltry ninety thousand dollars a year – until Gelstrom came up with a proposition to rationalise the army's vehicle-cleaning programme, thereby saving them several million dollars annually. What he omitted to mention was that he had costed the new contract on the number of vehicles to be cleaned rather than the quantity of detergent to be supplied. In fact he had achieved the promised saving simply by halving the recommended amount of detergent per vehicle. His only expense was in re-labelling the drums to that effect.

From there he went into chemicals for industrial and agricultural use, which led to timber and ranching. Like the old Soviet Union, he had a series of five-year plans. In each of these periods he concentrated all his attention and efforts on a particular group of industries. Thus timber and ranching occupied him from the ages of twenty-four to twenty-nine. From twenty-nine to thirty-four it was electronics, computers and plastics. From thirty-four to thirty-nine it was aerospace research and armaments, and in later years he had extended the JEG Corporation's interests into road and rail transport, TV and movie production and the electronic home leisure and information market. Along the way he had acquired holdings in publishing, car rentals, sports equipment, motels, fast food franchises and multiple spin-offs.

Over the years the media had repeatedly tried to expose the man to the public gaze. On three occasions the press had come close enough to cause him serious concern. On two of these occasions he had arranged through his grapevine of highly placed and influential contacts to have the story blocked and the reporters warned off. The third attempt, by a young and eager female TV reporter, had unfortunately succeeded – unfortunate, that's to say, for the reporter. She was hit by a truck while out jogging near her apartment in the Twin Peaks district of San Francisco. At about the same time her car had been stolen, which was later recovered minus a briefcase, laptop, mobile phone, digital camera and two memory sticks.

Two attempts had been made on Gelstrom's life. Both sources had been identified, although only one had been satisfactorily resolved. This was the disgruntled ex-owner of a vending-machine company the JEG Corporation had taken over, leaving him with little more than the shirt on his back. A Vietnam veteran, he shot Gelstrom at point-blank range with a sawn-off shotgun and blew his head clean off. His aim was excellent; his identification of the target less so. He happened to have killed an Italian arms dealer with whom Gelstrom was negotiating a deal.

The other source (the one not resolved) was the Mafia. It was the first and only time Gelstrom had heeded a warning and backed off. The deal involved a casino in Las Vegas and Gelstrom had unwisely employed his usual strategy to gain a controlling interest. It wasn't appreciated, and he should have known better – and soon did when the car he was supposed to be travelling in erupted in a fireball on Interstate 15 en route to Los Angeles. Two of his best people died while he was nine thousand feet above Death Valley on his way to San Francisco. Gelstrom immediately pulled out of the deal, wrote it off as a failure and counted himself lucky. Gambling, he decided, was Mafia business and they were welcome to it.

Unlike *this* business, which he was going to do something about, though he hadn't as yet decided what. He gripped the rail. 'Having a sick man in the administration doesn't say a lot for the President's judgement.'

'That's if he knows.'

'He must know. Lebasse would have had to tell him.'

'The media would tear Hernandez apart,' said the man in white, who was called Sturges. His face beneath the blond crew-cut was hard and brutal, the curved strip of smoked plastic making him seem blind and menacing. Gold glinted at his throat and on both hairy wrists.

'It's Lebasse we have to work on, not the President,' Gelstrom said. 'If the Secretary of Defense approves Download, President Hernandez will go along. But should Lebasse recommend the opposite and reject the proposal, *then* we have a problem. It puts the President on the spot. He can't go against the guy he himself appointed.'

'We can break Lebasse easily enough – leak it to the media . . . but Hernandez will get as much flak.'

'He's only just into his second year,' Gelstrom said speculatively. 'Barely out of the honeymoon period. I think his stock of goodwill is still pretty high.'

The first President of the United States with a Hispanic background had been elected to office in 2020. It had been a risky strategy – Gelstrom had taken some convincing. But what had finally swung his support behind that option was the powerful lobbying carried out by AAAV, a Washington-based pressure group. The Alliance for the Advancement of American Values was headed by Chesney Poulton. Gelstrom had been highly sceptical until he saw the demographic stats provided by the AAAV: a steep rise in the proportion of Hispanics eligible to vote, which outnumbered the black electorate by three to one. After that, it was a done deal, the only remaining question of choosing the right candidate with the necessary attributes: tall, slim, photogenic, nice smile, good English (no accent) and not too dark-skinned.

Chesney Poulton had had a hand in that too, seeking out a law professor of Costa Rican descent: Oscar Hernandez, a third-generation American. Poulton and the AAAV had personally selected, groomed, promoted him: he was 'their man', as Poulton assured Gelstrom and the group of business leaders and heads of corporations who'd backed the candidate – each of whom had divvied up tens of millions of dollars of campaign funding, with some hefty behind-the-scenes arm-twisting for good measure.

Gelstrom was more than happy with the choice of Oscar Hernandez, who reminded him physically of the 1950s Hollywood star Fernando Lamas. Married to an attractive wife, with two lovely daughters, Hernandez was also bisexual, with an active and promiscuous past involving both sexes, which meant he was tightly and securely under their control.

'We can't take a risk on that sick fuck.' Gelstrom's tone was flat, without emotion. 'If he's gonna die anyway, what has he to lose? Lebasse has to be neutralised and somebody we can trust put in his place. Who do we have?'

Sturges gazed blindly over the ocean. 'What about Zadikov? We've supplied him with enough girls.'

'Good old Ralf.' Gelstrom smiled without humour. His dark eyebrows came together above the broad ridge of his nose. 'What's Lloyd Malden's pitch on this?'

'He says it's our move.'

'Has he found some way to block the other guy – what's he called – the science advisor?' He snapped his fingers. 'Lucas.'

Sturges nodded. 'He made up something Lucas is supposed to have said about Agent Orange years ago. It should be enough because it bars Lucas from having access to ASP material. So basically he's in the dark.'

'Which just leaves Lebasse,' said Gelstrom thoughtfully. He swung around to face the man under the sunshade whose bald head was pink and glowing. 'We need an opinion, Ivor, old chap, old man.'

'What? I'm sorry?' Ivor Banting jumped, craning forward with a tentative smile. He was pretending not to have heard what they were discussing. Gelstrom spelled it out. 'We can't wait a year for Lebasse to die. We need approval of Operation Download as of now. As of right this minute, old chap. How do we dispose of him?'

5

At that same moment, though due to the different time zone three hours later by the clock – 7:25 p.m. Eastern Standard Time – Thomas J. Lebasse and Gene Lucas were attending a garden party at the lake-side home of Senator Crawford P. Bright and his wife, Sonia, on the outskirts of Belvedere, a fashionable residential area fifteen minutes' drive from Capitol Hill.

Circulating among the 150 or so guests it was easy and natural for the two men to meet without causing comment or arousing suspicion. At this time of year this was only one of countless social events, which was why Lebasse had accepted the invitation and arranged through an intermediary to have the names of Professor Gene Lucas and his wife, Elizabeth, included on the guest list.

As for Lucas, he regarded the invitation, even though he didn't know Senator Bright personally, as perfectly normal and above-board; after all, he was the President's senior scientific advisor, and he went along with no other intention but to relax and enjoy himself and breathe in the rarefied atmosphere of the Washington socialites, an opportunity that didn't come his way all that often.

His benign and relaxed disposition lasted up until the moment he found himself strolling with the Secretary of Defense down by the lake – which at that relatively early hour was molten with the light of the setting sun.

Wildfowl made desultory muted sounds in the reeds as they settled down for the night and behind the two men a garland of fairy lamps marked the perimeter of the festivities – voices, laughter, the clink of glasses, a Chopin 'Nocturne' – twenty yards away on the darkening velvety lawn.

'Oh, yes, a number of times,' Lucas said in answer to a question. 'We've served on various presidential committees together since 2016. In those days General Wolfe was, as I recall, a colonel and Malden a lieutenant.'

'Do you know anything about the work they're engaged upon?'

Lucas exhaled pipe smoke, his mouth small and prim beneath a neatly clipped moustache. He was only an inch or two shorter than Lebasse, which made a change from having to crane his neck in order to converse. 'On the military side, you mean? I know they're both with Advanced Strategic Projects at the Pentagon. But no, not specifically.'

They walked on, Lucas puffing his pipe and watching Lebasse covertly. The man was ill, shrunken, his eyes dull, his movements lethargic. Ulcer? Liver trouble? Something pretty serious, Lucas guessed. The germ of suspicion entered his mind that this meeting wasn't as incidental as it appeared.

'Then I take it you know nothing about a project code-named Operation Download?'

Lucas shook his head. 'Never heard of it.'

'You sure?' Lebasse persisted in a low voice.

'No. Never.' Lucas stood aside to allow the other man to ascend the four concrete steps leading up to the short wooden jetty. It was just wide enough for them to walk side-by-side. They came to the end without speaking, Lebasse's breath whistling in his chest. Lucas stood and waited, curiously ill at ease. His party mood was fading with the sun's last rays behind the Blue Ridge of Shenandoah National Park.

'I'm breaking my oath of office by what I'm about to tell you,' said Lebasse, his face ruddily imbued with a fake glow of health by the sunset. 'This is for your ears only. "Download" has special category classification and isn't to be divulged to anyone without ASP clearance. Now, Gene – okay if I call you that?' and at Lucas' brief nod, went on, 'Two reasons I'm telling you this, Gene. One, I need advice. You're qualified to give it and I trust you. Two, I *don't* trust General Wolfe, and Malden even less. They both have a vested interest in seeking approval for this project and will go to any lengths to get it. Are you with me?'

Lucas nodded slowly, pipe clamped between his teeth. This reeked to high heaven of political and military intrigue, which he abhorred.

'Operation Download is part of a long-term strategy to threaten Russia and China with total environmental war,' Lebasse went on. 'According to ASP intelligence the Russians have a plan of their own to tamper with the ecological balance of the Arctic Circle, which will lead to a widespread disruption of our climate here in the United States. They – Wolfe and Malden, that is – take the position that nuclear and bacteriological modes of warfare are outdated. In their place they propose we up the ante with WCD. We have to be ready with a war-plan that will stalemate the Russian threat and maintain the balance of power.'

'I'm not familiar with the acronym WCD,' Lucas said.

'Weapons of Climate Degradation.'

'God in heaven! So they've decided the current methods of wiping ourselves out aren't sufficient? We need new and better methods, do we?'

'I'm relating what Wolfe and Malden expressed to me, Gene. I'm not advancing my own opinion. It's their contention—' Lebasse broke off, choking on something. He fumbled for a tissue and wiped spittle from the corner of his mouth.

Lucas waited. In the dwindling light of dusk the face before him assumed a sickly grey pallor, the eyes sunken in their sockets. Was this the reason for the secrecy, the urgency? The Secretary of Defense had to make one last vital decision before time ran out?

'But I'm not a scientist, Gene,' Lebasse went on, recovering. 'I have to know whether sanctioning Download as a viable plan of defence is a greater risk than having no deterrent at all. It could pose a bigger threat to our security here at home than anything the Russians or the

Chinese might throw at us. That's why I need your honest, considered opinion. The final decision is mine and I have to be right.'

'I'll need a complete dossier on the operation, of course,' Lucas said. 'Projections. Stats. All the analysis you have relating to both the scientific and military logistics.'

'It's on a memory stick,' Lebasse said, 'in the glove compartment of your car. I realise I'm putting you on the spot, but I need an answer within two weeks.' Lebasse was speaking more quickly now, as if time was indeed running out. 'Report to me and only to me. Not through my office. Here's an unlisted number you can call.'

'Do you want a verdict over the phone?'

'No, face to face. We'll arrange to meet. In the meantime if you need more information, call that number.'

'Very well. I'll do whatever I can . . .' Lucas was about to add something, but there didn't seem much else to say.

Lebasse turned. 'Let's get back before we're missed.' He took two paces and halted. There was a figure on the jetty. In the deepening twilight it was possible to make out only a white dinner jacket and the glowing tip of a cigar.

'He said it was teeming with trout, but I don't believe it,' Lebasse chortled jovially, moving on. 'Crawford spinning a line again! That sneaky old bastard, eh?'

'Yeah, what a joker. Ha-ha,' said Gene Lucas, in what sounded in his own ears to be an incredibly bad piece of ham acting.

3

'You say he's worried about something. Or that he's asking for help.' Chase scooped up a forkful of mashed potatoes and peas. 'The letter doesn't say that. In fact it says nothing at all, really.'

'My, how quick you are, Gav. That is exactly my point!'

'Okay, smarty-pants. Cut the sarcasm.'

Cheryl swallowed the morsel of steak she was chewing. 'Think about it for a second. Boris sends a letter – a *letter* by airmail – for chrissakes. Could have sent it by Morse code and the intent wouldn't have been plainer. He was trying to evade any form of interception, and playing safe by making it bland and chatty.'

'So how are you supposed to know there's anything wrong?'

'Because I've just proved to you I *did* know, dummy. By what *wasn't* in the letter. It was far too dangerous.' Cheryl took a sip of water, ice cubes clinking in the tall glass. 'I think I know Boris. He was trying to tell me something.'

'It was weeks ago, almost a month, you said, and you haven't heard anything since.'

They were in the Scripps refectory eating a late lunch among tables that bore the debris of several hundred people, now departed, with staff moving along the aisles.

'That's what worries me. I wrote back at once – just a few lines, to say I'd received it – and haven't heard another word.' She dug into another piece of steak.

The scrape and clatter of the clean-up operation made it difficult to concentrate. Wiping his mouth with a paper napkin, Chase said, 'You have to admit, Cheryl, this is pure speculation until you hear something more. You're whistling in the dark.'

It was four years since their last meeting. At that time Cheryl had been in shock still, the grief of her father's death churned up with anger and frustration at the intransigence of the Swiss authorities. They had marked the case 'Closed' and that was it – *finito*.

Cheryl pushed her plate away. 'It really gets to me. The world is full of closed doors. You bust through one and, boy, sure enough, there's another – locked and barred and plastered with NO ENTRY signs.'

'I just had one slammed in my face,' said Chase with some feeling. He told her about his meeting with Bill Inchcape, of the predictions that the DELFI climate-modelling programme was supplying to ASP in Washington – Highly Confidential.

'I know about DELFI. What's the other?'

'Advanced Strategic Projects. One of these cloak-and-dagger organisations that breed like flies at the Pentagon. It isn't even supposed to exist. I could tell Bill Inchcape regretted mentioning it the minute he had.'

They left the refectory and strolled in the sunshine to Cheryl's office in the glass-walled annexe of the marine biology division, set among lawns and shrubs and gravel paths. Much of her work these days concerned the distribution of marine life in the Pacific Basin. 'I do the stuff I'm required to do for Scripps,' Cheryl explained. 'The rest of the time I spend trying to raise public awareness about oxygen deficit, and that it's an urgent problem— '

As they settled in armchairs, she pointed to a graph on the wall.

'Good luck with that,' Chase said sardonically. 'You know as well as I do it's going to take something cataclysmic – like the Tokyo Alert, say, but on a global scale – to shake people up. On the human time-scale the process is barely discernible, just creeping up on us until we reach the point of no return.'

'Creeping could turn into a gallop,' Cheryl said. 'As our friend over there discovered.'

On the window ledge stood a two-foot-high model of Tyrannosaurus rex, its terrible plastic jaws agape, rows of pointed teeth gleaming in the sunshine through the blinds.

She was referring to the theory that the dinosaurs were wiped out in just a few short years, possibly less than twenty. An asteroid several kilometres in diameter had hit the Earth and shrouded the planet in a mantle of dust. Lack of sunlight killed off the animals and most of the plant life and very soon 80 per cent of the entire species were extinct.

'The dinosaurs died of starvation,' Chase pointed out, 'not oxygen deficiency.'

'It isn't important what they died of, Gav, but how quickly it happened. One minute they were there, the next . . .' She snapped her fingers. 'It could happen just as fast to us, in less than twenty years, ten, even five.'

'That's human beings for you. We go merrily on our way, ignoring everything around us, then one morning we wake up gasping for air.'

'That could be literally true,' Cheryl said. 'We're burning up millions of tons of oxygen every year. The balance between profit and loss is one part in ten thousand; precious little to be putting in the bank when we're already deep in the red.'

'It wouldn't take much to push us over the edge, would it? Say by accident or by design.'

Cheryl gave him a quizzical look. 'Don't follow you, Gav. By design?'

'What do you know about dioxin?'

'Connected with the manufacture of fertiliser, isn't it? I'm pretty sure the Environmental Protection Agency banned it years ago.'

'It seems not everyone's obeying the ban. When I was in Colorado I met this physician, Dr Ruth Brosnan, who's got several cases of chloracne in the local hospital. Only one thing causes chloracne as far as I know . . .'

'Dioxin poisoning. Has she found the source?'

'Dr Brosnan thinks some of the small share-croppers are using up old stocks of 2,4,5-T, but that can't be right. It's the wrong type of herbicide for the grasslands in that area.'

Cheryl was leaning forward, elbows propped on her knees. 'Maybe I'm dumb, but I'm not following this. What has dioxin poisoning got to do with somebody deliberately tampering – you said *by design* – with the biosphere?'

'There might be a connection.'

'If there is, I don't see it.'

'Well, consider.' Chase ticked off the points on his fingertips. 'Let's assume Dr Brosnan's diagnosis is correct. That means someone is either manufacturing 2,4,5-T or using it in the area. Not farmers, as I've said. What other applications are there? Suppose it's the military? There's an experimental missile base near Denver, so that's a feasible assumption—'

'If somewhat unlikely.'

'Why? The military have used it before to defoliate jungles; why shouldn't they be using it now for some other purpose?'

Cheryl went over to the window. She stared at the shrubbery outside, wondering aloud, 'What other purpose is there apart from killing off green stuff?'

'You put it in a nutshell yourself, Cheryl. Tampering with the biosphere. Using the environment as a strategic weapon.'

'That's the craziest conspiracy theory I've ever heard,' Cheryl scoffed, turning to face him. 'Why would they do it?'

'Why wouldn't they?'

That stopped her. Both of them knew that if something was technically feasible and could be made to work, then somebody would want to try it.

'For God's sake, Gavin, how long have you been thinking this?'

'Since I talked to Ruth Brosnan a few days ago.'

Cheryl went to her desk and sat down at the console. She tapped a few keys and waited.

'What are you up to?'

Cheryl was about to answer, and then raised her hand for silence when the voice recog came over the speaker.

'*Please identify yourself,*' it said.

'Dr Detrick, Marine Life Research Group.'

'*Audio ID validated,*' it responded at once. '*Please continue.*'

Cheryl thought for a few moments while she formulated the question.

'Give me a list of companies that fit the following indices. One: Suppliers of herbicides to US armed forces within the last ten' – she looked a query at Chase, who nodded – 'years. Two: Companies with current contracts with the US Defense Department. Three: Chemical companies with the capability of manufacturing 2,4,5-T—'

Chase leaned across and scribbled on a pad.

'—also known as chloraphenoxy acid herbicides,' Cheryl added. 'How long to evaluate?'

'*One moment, Dr Detrick.*'

'Process of elimination?' Chase asked.

'No more than four, maybe five companies fit those criteria.'

'If the data's not classified,' Chase said dubiously, 'and are in your Big Brain to begin with. That's a bloody big "if".'

'Take the bet?' Cheryl taunted him. Her grin was mischievous.

'You sound pretty sure of yourself.'

'I am. Any industrial yearbook off the shelf will tell you which companies have Department of Defense contracts.'

She had her father's confidence and sense of purpose, he saw; the traits had been handed down. Chase said, 'All right, Sherlock, let's say you come up with the names of the companies. What then?'

'We find out which of them is breaking the EPA regulations by continuing the manufacture of 2,4,5-T. Simple enough.'

'This is anything but simple,' Chase said, torn between being annoyed by her cockiness and yet admiring her positive directness: the brash American can-do attitude all over.

The voice recog said, '*We have one result, Dr Detrick. The following matches all criteria: JEG Chemical Corporation, Bakersfield, California, USA.*'

'That is all. Goodbye.'

'*Thank you, Dr Detrick. Enjoy the rest of your day.*'

Cheryl sat back, folding her arms. 'There we go,' she said, smiling sweetly, with a suspicious lack of guile. 'You just lost your bet, buddy-boy.'

2

About midmorning the heat had started to settle over Washington and by midday the air was dense and sultry, threatening a thunderstorm. In his fourth-storey office in the southwest wing of the Pentagon,

Thomas Lebasse had the distinct impression that the weather bore him a personal grudge. Even with the air conditioning and sustained by iced lemon tea, Lebasse was dogged by a dull nagging headache that made every thought a wearisome effort.

His doctor had warned him what to expect, so he was hardly surprised. Fatigue. Nausea. Lack of concentration. Deteriorating motor function. It was all happening just as predicted: the long slow slide into death, with the world growing dimmer as the cancer devoured him alive.

Resolutely he pushed the nightmare away. *Move on, you old bastard*, he ordered himself. *Don't dwell on it. Just keep going.*

Answering a buzz on the intercom, Lebasse listened to his senior aide, David Peralta, who told him he'd had a call on his unlisted private line while he'd been in conference with the budget steering committee. Lebasse sat forward in his red leather wing chair, the pain and fear momentarily forgotten. 'Did the caller leave a name, Dave?'

'No, sir. Said he'd call back later.'

'The caller was male?'

'Yes, sir. But the line was bad. Must have been in a grey spot.'

He'd been expecting Gene Lucas to call any day now. If Operation Download really was as monstrously unthinkable as he suspected, Lucas was the man to confirm it.

If he achieved nothing else in the short time left to him, the Secretary of Defense had pledged to stop that evil scheme before it got started. By comparison, chemical warfare was positively humane.

He buzzed his secretary and told her he was going to lunch at his desk and asked her to bring him a sandwich – corned beef and pickle on rye – a glass of milk and a cream doughnut. He'd given up counting calories; not much point now. And anyway, over recent months he'd noticed that no matter what he ate, or whatever quantity, he continued to lose weight. Only this morning he'd pulled his belt in another notch.

His head still throbbed. He couldn't shake it.

Giving in, he took a plastic vial from a side drawer, shook a red-and-white capsule into his hand and washed it down with water. Phenoperidine, a narcotic analgesic, had side-effects similar to those of morphine, and the doctor had warned him not to take more than three in any twelve-hour period. It was an effective painkiller, although it tended to make him light-headed and euphoric. Hardly the right frame of mind for dealing with sober matters of state, he thought sombrely.

He ate his lunch seated on the couch, and then rested for a while. The sultry throbbing had eased, but when he tried to get up – too quickly, it seemed, because all of a sudden he felt giddy – Lebasse had to steady himself against the corner of the desk. The light from the window was burning his eyes. With careful small steps he moved to close the Venetian blind. The slender cord in his hand had the feel and texture of thick rope. He tugged at it and the large office was plunged into restful twilight.

Turning away, Lebasse was mesmerised by the pattern the filtered sunlight made on the pastel green carpet . . . thin gold rods arranged in perfect symmetry.

Hell, that was so pretty!

A lump of emotion rose up in his throat. That's what he'd miss the most: vibrant golden light. It was light from heaven – God's light. He'd never been a religious man, but he supposed that the prospect of death heightened one's awareness of the Infinite. He'd soon know. Nothing surer.

It was restful in this aquarium. Everything was cool limpid green, peaceful and calm and for the first time in his life he had absolutely no fear of death. 'Death, where is thy sting?' he mocked; death was pure golden light all the way to infinity, beckoning him. He welcomed it, in fact. To be at one with the Infinite, shimmering in green and gold light . . .

What more could any man want?

Woman.

And miracle of miracles, there she was, golden-haired, arms outstretched, drifting towards him. She was holding something, an offering, and he, in turn, opened his arms to her. But now she was turning away. Oh, no! He needed this woman to share eternity with him; sure he did. Nothing surer.

At once, as if in answer to his plea, something beautiful took place. The woman began to sing. Her mouth opened and a high note pierced his brain with such exquisite intensity that he wanted to weep. He was uplifted, his spirits soaring, floating, flying towards the Infinite.

Why had he never flown before?

Everyone ought to try this, he told himself, flying towards the bars of light, which parted before him in glittering splendour as he crashed through the window headfirst, taking the tangled Venetian blind with him.

When his secretary entered with his senior aide they found an empty office filled with a humid breeze. One complete window had disappeared from its aluminium frame and sunlight streamed like a golden searchlight on to the pastel-green carpet.

Ex-Secretary of Defense Thomas J. Lebasse lay mangled on the concrete paving four floors below: the images invoked by having chosen the one capsule containing a large dose of LSD-25 wiped clean from his brain.

3

Cheryl was lying full-length on the couch wearing a loose halter-neck dress, her brown arms and shoulders bare. They had eaten a pleasant dinner together and Chase felt warm and relaxed, but now she had to spoil it by badgering him.

'It was you, remember, who told me about the dioxin poisoning,' Cheryl said, waving her wine glass at him. 'You set the hare running and now you don't want to do anything about it . . .' The wine spilled and she tossed back what was left in one gulp.

Chase picked up his brandy glass. 'What am I supposed to do about it? I agree that we know – or suspect – that JEG Chemicals is up to something. And you're right, a story like that is just what I'm looking for. After nearly four weeks all I've got is a hard-drive of background stuff – worthy but dull. You don't have to convince me.' He swirled the brandy and drank.

'So let's do it,' Cheryl said.

Chase laughed without humour. 'You think a chemical company producing 2,4,5-T is going to welcome a journalist poking his nose in?

"Oh, I just happened to be in the vicinity and I heard you're supplying a highly dangerous banned chemical to the US Army. Mind if I look around?" Yes, that'll work.'

'You're a science writer, not a journalist,' Cheryl said, pointing at him. 'Right?'

'Which still won't get me into the JEG plant.'

'You keep bragging you've made programmes for the BBC.'

'I don't *keep on* bragging . . . I've mentioned it once.'

Cheryl lay back, a small smile on her lips. She was enjoying herself. 'Is your BBC accreditation still valid?'

'I hadn't given it a thought.'

'Well, *think* about it.'

'Yes, probably. So? I can't see it getting past their security.'

'There might be another way.' Cheryl was studying her empty wine glass. 'What if you were an accredited faculty member of the Scripps Marine Life Research Group?'

'Go on,' said Chase warily.

'We could invent a story that Scripps is interested in purchasing supplies. You show up with valid ID and have a nosy around the plant.'

Chase took a few moments to think about the idea. It might be risky, but what the hell, this was the purpose of his trip, wasn't it? And the story had landed in his lap – he'd be a fool to dismiss it. He said, 'If we go ahead I'll need a few more days. I'll call Marcus Barrett in the morning. How long will it take to set up?'

'Are you sure you want to do it?'

Chase was exasperated. 'It was you who thought it up!'

'I realise that,' Cheryl said, 'but I might have had too much wine. I don't want you to be . . .' she fumbled her words, 'to be put in any . . .'

She did sound woozy. 'Any what?'

'Danger.'

'The plant is in Bakersfield. How far away is that?'

'About a six-hour drive.'

'Contact JEG and fix up an appointment, soon as possible. Try for the day after tomorrow.' The more Chase thought about it, the keener he was to try. 'I can spare an extra couple of days.'

Lying back on the cushions, Cheryl was watching him through half-closed eyes. 'You can stay here. If you'd like to.'

'Is that what's called making me an offer I can't refuse?' Chase said.

'That's for you to decide, Gav.' Cheryl held up her glass. 'Why don't you get me another drink while you think about it?'

Chase picked up the wine bottle on his way over to the couch.

'Didn't take you very long . . .'

'I'm a quick thinker,' Chase said.

4

On his way to the gloomy back of the bar on G Street, Gene Lucas asked for a light beer.

He couldn't think what else to order; bars like this weren't exactly his natural environment. He'd come in off the street for the air-conditioning above all else, and to sit in a quiet booth to make his call to the Secretary of Defense. It was supposed to be urgent, and yet he couldn't get through. He'd tried already five times . . .

The booth stank of alcohol, and faintly of vomit. He watched the barman set up some beers and turn back to the TV screen above the array of bottles. Four customers, all male, slouched at the bar over their drinks. The lead story all week had been the Tourist Bus Massacre in Cuba: thirty-three American tourists slaughtered in a machine-gun and grenade attack as their bus drove through a small town called Santa Clara. Rebels from the mountains had been blamed. Already there were outraged demands from US media pundits and blowhards for economic reprisals against Cuba, some demanding military intervention.

Before reading the Download document, Lucas had thought all this cloak-and-dagger stuff stupid and pretty infantile. But his mind had been changed quickly enough – or as long as it took him to read the file.

It was the most horrifyingly scary future scenario he'd ever read. No wonder Lebasse had gone about it in such a furtive, undercover manner. That there were agents of the state who could contemplate putting the world in peril for some spurious 'strategic advantage' by building Weapons of Climate Degradation . . . it chilled his blood. Lucas saw immediately, as would any sane person, that such a plan would affect East and West in exactly the same way. These madmen thought that oxygen depletion could somehow be confined or contained: as if certain areas of the globe would be immune from its effects, when in reality every living, breathing thing on the planet was at risk.

Gene Lucas was just humbly thankful that Lebasse had had the sense to seek a scientific opinion. It was a small mercy that Operation Download existed only in the warped brains of a bunch of military psychopaths. That it would take many years of research and billions of dollars, which the Secretary of Defense, ailing man as he was, would never sanction.

Come on, come on, Lucas fretted, listening to the dialling tone. *For God's sake, somebody answer* . . . from the dark booth at the rear of the long room his attention was drawn to the four barflies blearily watching the TV. They'd suddenly sat up and were craning their necks. From this angle Lucas' view of the screen was acutely slanted and he could just make out a distorted news presenter. Then he was back concentrating on the phone as the burring tone ceased and someone finally answered – praise the Lord!

'Hello? Hello! I've been calling for ages. Can I speak to—'

The name he was about to utter stuck in his throat like a peach stone. Lucas found himself staring goggle-eyed at the image on the screen: a face he recognised, even at this sharp angle. He strained to listen, the phone in his hand forgotten.

'. . . *having suffered a heart attack at his office in the Pentagon. In a brief statement released a few minutes ago, Senior Aide David Peralta is quoted as saying, "Defense Secretary Thomas J. Lebasse appeared to be in full health this morning, having participated in a full schedule of meetings. There was no reason to suppose . . ."'*

Lucas stumbled from the booth. There was a roaring vacuum in his brain.

He walked along G Street in the direction of the White House, massing purple clouds rolling in from the west, oblivious to the large warm spots hitting his face. The threatened thunderstorm was nearly upon them.

His mind kept repeating numbly over and over, *Lebasse is dead. I have the Download file. Lebasse is dead. I have the Download file and Lebasse is dead . . .*

4

I

The research laboratories of Advanced Strategic Projects were situated some thirty miles southeast of Washington, DC, along Highway 301, down an unmarked road leading nowhere.

A few fishermen did use the road to get to Patuxent Creek, which meandered northwards until it lost itself in young plantations of spruce and firs, though none were aware of the square grey single-storey building with smoke-blue windows that blended in with the picturesque Maryland landscape.

Unobtrusive as it was to the casual eye, the installation kept its real secret even more closely guarded. Below ground it extended to five sub-levels containing offices, recreation and living quarters, laboratories and test chambers.

The 230 acres of woodland were monitored by guards dressed as hunters in checked shirts and windbreakers and hiking boots. They patrolled with Alsatian dogs, double-barrelled shotguns and shortwave transceivers attached to throat mikes. Infrared scanners planted in the trunks of trees detected every form of life down to the size of a dormouse. A web of lasers crisscrossed the approach to the building, trapping the unwary in a deadly electronic maze.

Inside the building security was equally as tight. Two elevators, monitored by closed-circuit TV, were the only means of access below. Every visitor had to present an electro-sensitised identification disc whose microchip circuitry held a record of the holder's unique physiological profile: fingerprints, voiceprint, biorhythms and ECG trace. Should anyone attempt the subterfuge of presenting another's disc, the system would automatically seal the elevator doors, locking the intruder inside a vault of titanium and steel.

The deepest and most extensive vault housed the laboratories and test chambers. In the largest room, row upon row of rubber-lined stainless-steel tanks contained a profusion of marine animal and plant life. Temperature and salinity ranged from sub-zero to equatorial, with all the graduations in between. Ultraviolet panels mimicked the action of sunlight and sprinklers supplied calibrated amounts of rainfall.

From the observation booth behind the yellow gantry rail, Dr Jeremiah Rolsom, scientific director of ASP, watched three masked and rubber-suited operatives manhandling a drum along the gantry to the feeder-chute of tank nine. The drum was painted bright pink with a large black N on its side.

'Is this the last of the batch?' Rolsom asked a technician seated at the instrument console.

'Yes, sir.'

'What concentration?'

'Thirty-four per cent.'

Rolsom nodded and nibbled his lower lip, his round black face shining under the reflection of the arc lights high up in the vaulted ceiling.

'We're testing inorganic nitrogen in varying concentrations. It's pretty much the same as the fertiliser used by farmers, except the proportion is boosted to what a lake might receive in runoff over five years.' He turned to face Major Malden, who was standing with his arms behind his back, pointed chin slightly raised. 'Essentially it's the same process, only speeded up by a factor of fifteen.'

'How soon before you get results?'

'Three to four weeks. We're trying to duplicate the Lake Erie experience.' Rolsom was referring to how rainwater draining from the farmlands of the Midwest leeched the nitrogen from the soil equivalent to the sewage of about twenty million people, double the population of the Lake Erie hinterland at that time. With the nitrogen balance of the lake disturbed, huge algae blooms grew unchecked, and as the blooms decayed, the bacterial action consumed most of the lake's free oxygen, killing off fish and plants. The result was one dead lake.

Malden looked past him into the chamber. 'It might work with a lake, but will it work with an ocean?'

'Sure, given time, plus vast amounts of nitrogen-rich fertiliser.' Rolsom indicated the rows of tanks through the window. 'That's only one of several options open to us. Out there you've got just about every conceivable combination of herbicidal overkill. It all depends what you want to happen and how quickly.'

The sharp angles of Malden's face were softened by the booth's dim lighting. He looked like a boy, except for his eyes, which were black and hard. 'Are we talking about months or years?' he asked.

'Everything depends on deployment, and whether you're going for land or sea targets. Now take Tablet – the chloraphenoxy acid group – which acts as a plant hormone, causing metabolic changes so that the plant grows at a phenomenal and uncontrolled rate. In effect it grows itself to death.'

'So more suited to land vegetation.'

'That's right,' Rolsom said. 'Our other main group, symmetrical triazines – Laptop – interferes with photosynthesis. The plant's biochemical processes are halted and eventually it dies of starvation. Laptop would be more effective in the oceans, killing off the phytoplankton. But speed of deployment is the key.'

'Well, we've got missiles and supertankers,' Malden said. 'We've tested Tablet at the range in Colorado and it's looking good. A single payload targeted on South America could wipe out fifty square miles of rain forest. As for the oceans, supertankers at strategic locations could dump Laptop within hours. As far as anyone knew they'd be commercial vessels on regular trade routes. Not a nuke to be seen.'

Rolsom led the way into the corridor.

'You'll want to see the bacteriological section while you're here.'

'How's it coming along?'

'We're experimenting with a number of mutant strains of bacteria that consume oxygen at a far greater rate than normal.' Rolsom was using his hands for more graphic displays. 'The bacteria don't actually interfere with photosynthesis, rather, they eat up the oxygen as fast as the phytoplankton can produce it. With that rate of growth you could turn the whole of the Pacific into bacterial soup in two, maybe three months.'.

The image was arresting and Lloyd Malden felt a pleasurable shudder down the length of his spine. As a kid he'd gone around with an imaginary machine-gun wiping out everything that moved, *rat-ta-ta-ta-ta-ta-ta-ta-tat!* It had been a harmless pastime for a lonely boy. He still vividly remembered seeing archive news footage of a Vietnamese peasant being shot in the head at point-blank range, an experience that gave him his first proper erection. Emaciated yellow corpses strewn about a paddyfield excited the same reaction. And best of the lot, the thick of a live-action massacre in Fallujah . . .

They took the elevator up to sub-level D and entered the laboratory, lit by glareless ceiling panels. He felt an almost sensual pleasure. This was his achievement, all these people working away to realise his ambition! While it was true that General Wolfe was ostensibly head of ASP (and it had been his rank that had persuaded the Pentagon to fund this pilot scheme), the real driving force and inspiration had come from him . . . from the kid with the imaginary machine-gun.

Now, looking around at what he had created, Lloyd Malden felt an ecstatic thrill and the most profound satisfaction.

There was a tiny blot, a mere irritating speck, to spoil this oasis of perfection. Malden had been proud of the name ASP until the confrontation at the Pentagon with that oaf Chesney Poulton – the way he had mocked Malden's creation, calling it Ass-Wipe, for chrissakes! – ate at him like acid indigestion. It reminded him of being bullied, and the agony of impotence.

Banishing the thought, Malden strolled with the director past rows of white-coated researchers crouching over lab benches. At the far end of the long room an illuminated red sign warned STERILE AREA. Beyond, through a double pane of glass, masked and rubber-suited figures moved like priests among massive transparent tanks mounted on metal racks. Everywhere there was a cathedral calm and quiet.

Beneath the red sign Rolsom stopped and pointed through the panel into the sterile inner chamber. The tanks were half-filled with seawater in which a greenish-brown scum floated.

'You can see how the bacteria progressively affect the phytoplankton. Each tank represents a time lapse of one week, and by the sixth or seventh week the bacteria outnumber the marine organisms, which then start to decay. The phytoplankton is being choked to death.'

'The change in colour is an indication of how the bacteria are consuming the oxygen?' Malden said, wanting to be quite sure he understood.

'The green is the healthy phytoplankton and the colour darkens and turns brown as the bacteria multiply.' Rolsom tapped the glass with his fingernails. 'The real beauty of this method is that we need only a small amount of chemical bacteria to start the process rolling – after that it's self-generating. Not only is it highly effective, but it's also very economical.'

'And very fast,' Malden mused. 'In three months we could virtually eliminate all phytoplankton growth.'

'Don't be too optimistic,' Rolsom said, sounding a note of warning. 'It's at least a year before we're ready for field trials. And we still don't know what happens over the long term, after the bacteria have taken over. It could be that it will continue multiplying—'

But Malden didn't want to hear. He said brusquely, 'That's irrelevant as far as we're concerned. Have you tested it at Starbuck yet?' He was gazing fixedly through the glass panel at the rows of tanks.

Starbuck was an island on the equator, in the dead centre of the Pacific Ocean. Once used for naval weapons testing, it had been taken over by ASP for marine trials on herbicides. Its location tickled Malden, being near Canton Island where Theo Detrick had spent nearly thirty years researching his precious diatoms.

'No, no, it's too soon,' Rolsom said a shade uneasily. He glanced around at the researchers nearby and dropped his voice to a murmur. 'What about the other problem?'

'What other problem?'

'The political one.'

'I thought you knew better than to ask.'

'It does concern me, Major.'

'What concerns you, Rolsom, is right here—' He gestured towards the tanks containing their swill of greenish-brown scum.

'But if the Secretary of Defense is going to veto the project I think I have a right to—'

'That won't happen,' Malden said, turning away. 'Didn't you catch the news this morning? The problem you refer to has been taken care of.'

'We still need presidential approval,' Rolsom persisted, following him to the door.

Malden's nostrils were pinched and white. His face had the consistency of wax under the bland lighting. 'Do you suppose I am not fully aware of that fact?'

There was a finality to his tone that debarred further discussion.

They took the elevator up to the director's office on sub-level B, not exchanging another word.

Malden collected his cap and gloves. 'I'm going out to the West Coast to look over the Bakersfield plant. Any problems with supplies?'

Rolsom stood stiffly. He shook his head. 'No, sir. We get excellent service from JEG. Tell them we have no complaints.'

'Glad to hear it.' About to go, Malden paused. He said, 'From midnight of the 22nd, this research department will no longer be known as ASP. Its new designation is Future Crisis Operations Executive, with the Pentagon acronym Fut/COE. You will be officially notified in a day or so of the name change.'

With that, Major Malden departed, without bothering to shake hands.

2

The train left Moscow at four o'clock on a rainy afternoon and arrived in Riga at eleven-fifteen the following morning, having been delayed at Ludza on the Latvian border for almost three hours. No one had bothered to explain why, and for Boris and Nina it was the one worrying moment of the journey. Boris had carefully rehearsed the reason why they were travelling to the Baltic port and had made sure their papers were in order, though the explanation lacked plausibility even to his own ears. The Gulf of Riga was not noted as a vacation spot – certainly not a *kurort*, or a health spa, so popular with Russian vacationers. And the capital itself was hardly a tourist attraction, filled as it was with shipping and textiles and telecommunications industries.

Thankfully the stop at the border hadn't been to check papers. At least they'd assumed that, because they hadn't seen any police, and the guards on the train didn't interrupt their naps, as if the delay were a routine occurrence.

Boris sat gripping his wife's hand and staring out at the ethereal dawn landscape, which consisted of trees in endlessly regimented rows marching down the hillside. At long last the train moved on; they breathed easily again, and had a nip of brandy from Boris' flask to celebrate and take the chill from their bones.

In Riga they took a taxi to a small spartan hotel overlooking the river Dvina frequented by travelling salesmen, where a room had been booked for them; they were to remain here until contacted. Boris had no idea whether they would have to wait hours or days, no clue as to what was to happen next or where they would be sent. The extent of his knowledge was confined to this shabby, cheerless house in a city he had never visited before and where he didn't know a solitary soul.

He had taken everything on trust, as he had to, praying that these people knew what they were doing and wouldn't let them down. It was only now he realised what a blind, foolhardy gamble it all was: entrusting their lives to an organisation he knew nothing about – and actually, not even an organisation, but just one person. Andrei Dunayev was a student of his from the old university days. Boris had lost touch, and then, quite by chance had run across Dunayev in, of all places, the furnishing department of GUM, Moscow's mammoth department store. They chatted for a while and Boris learned that his ex-student was working as a cleaner on the railways.

Boris was shocked. 'With your qualifications?' How could this be? Dunayev had been one of his best students, and had graduated with honours.

'I ran afoul of the *nachalstvo*,' the young man confessed, referring to the new regime of privileged ruling class who wielded all the power; displease them and you found yourself blacklisted from any well-paid occupation.

After that they kept in touch, meeting occasionally for a drink in the evenings. It soon struck Boris that for someone in a badly paid job, Dunayev always had plenty of money to spend – he once showed up wearing a pair of expensive English tan brogues. And the reason then became clear. He was *na levo*, he explained – literally, 'on the left' – which meant he dealt in the black market. The cleaning job was merely a cover.

When Boris made the decision to skip the country, naturally, it was to Andrei Dunayev he turned for help. The young man could fix just about anything, from under-the-counter Swiss watches at half the imported price to the best seats at the Bolshoi. First a brief phone call, a meeting in the park and everything, according to Dunayev, would be arranged. For this service, of course, there was a price. Boris was to get his hands on as much money as he could, in cash; he and Nina should pack two suitcases (as if they were going on a weekend trip) and be ready at twenty-four hours' notice to leave.

The word came. They were to take the overnight train to Riga where accommodation had been booked for them. They were to travel under their own name until out of the country – as if this were indeed a short vacation. False papers would be supplied. He trusted Dunayev implicitly, Boris kept telling himself, and yet now that they were on their way – they had taken that crucial and dangerous first step – he was beginning to have qualms.

After a light lunch of chicken and salad he and Nina walked arm in arm along the embankment that bordered the river. The port itself was some three miles away. They could see the tangle of cranes and the funnels of ships to the west. Hereabouts the river traffic was mainly strings of coal barges, tugs and other small craft. Boris carried his phone, but he didn't want to be away too long from the hotel in case someone tried to make contact there; after ten minutes they turned and strolled back. He couldn't help glancing nervously at every car that passed, wondering if they were being followed: he wouldn't put it past Malankovitch to have him under constant surveillance. Even the middle-aged female receptionist behind the desk made him nervous. Her eyes bored right through him as she handed him the old-fashioned room key.

'Where will it be?' Nina asked, holding tightly on to his arm. 'Sweden? Finland?'

Towering beside her, hunched inside his overcoat, Boris shook his head morosely. 'I wish I knew. Wherever they send us, it won't be easy.'

His wife was silent for a while. 'Are we doing the right thing, Boris? There's still time to go back before we're missed.'

'We can't go back. I must get to America.'

'But why – why *you*?' she cried suddenly, clutching his arm, and Boris looked around fearfully. Nina bent her head and lowered her voice, even though there was no one else on the wide paved embankment. 'There must be others who know what's happening – let them do something!'

'Perhaps there are. But somebody has to take the responsibility. How could I just sit back and do nothing?'

'But what can the Americans do?'

Boris stared across the river, sparkling in the weak afternoon sunshine. She had pierced to the heart of his dilemma. He recalled how Theo Detrick had been thwarted in his attempt to change hearts and minds, to convince his own government that something had to be done urgently before the environment took its revenge for the damage inflicted upon it. Theo had been shunned and reviled – even by his scientific colleagues at the Geneva conference. And then he'd been murdered. So what chance had he? All governments, East or West, were tarred with the same brush. Don't upset the economic equilibrium. At all costs maintain the status quo. Climate change mightn't be as bad as we feared. Ignore unpalatable facts and they'll go away.

But these facts wouldn't go away, and still he couldn't answer her.

At breakfast the next morning in the small dining room, Boris heard a car draw up in the forecourt. There was nothing untoward about that, except his nerves were so on edge that he was seeing danger everywhere. For some reason he couldn't get the image of Anna Politkovskaya out of his head. The journalist had been murdered in the lift of her apartment block. Photographs of the bloodstained elevator, with a photo inset of the dead woman, had been on every front page. It was a reminder, if Boris needed one, of the lengths the state and the Moscow mafia would go to when their interests were challenged or compromised.

Nina was looking down at her plate. The sight of her neat grey head, the hair parted in the middle and held in place by two combs, filled him with an ache of tenderness and affection.

A moment later it looked like his worst fears were coming true. The frosty-faced receptionist entered and curtly informed him there was someone to see him. Boris was resigned to it by now; he'd just have to bluff his way through as best he could. Malankovitch might not believe a word, but he had to stick to the prearranged story, that he and his wife had come to Riga for a short break. He just assumed, as he walked into the reception lobby, that Malankovitch and his mafia goons would know where to find him, and they had.

His fatalism was total.

A man of medium height wearing a brown overcoat was standing with his back to Boris, studying a faded sepia photograph of the hotel as it had been in the Soviet era. No change there, Boris thought sourly. Just beyond the main door, on the outside steps, he saw another lurking figure: the man's colleague, no doubt.

The man in the brown overcoat turned casually to reveal a thin young face and deep-set eyes. The deep-set eyes didn't look directly at Boris but past his right shoulder.

'This the one?'

'That's the one.'

The frosty-faced receptionist was standing behind Boris with her arms folded. She gave a jerk of the head. 'Checked in with his wife yesterday about noon. Thought there was something odd about them. Call themselves Stanovnik.'

Boris said, 'What's going on?' and tried a show of bewilderment bordering on righteous indignation: 'My name *is* Stanovnik. Professor Stanovnik, head of the Hydro-Meteorological Service in Moscow.'

The thin-faced young man gave the ghost of a smile. He hadn't shaved, Boris noticed. He looked rather unkempt generally. Malankovitch's Moscow mafia was getting more and more slovenly in appearance these days.

'We already know that, Professor.' He went on in a softer tone, 'We also know why you're here. Cut the bullshit. Did you really think it would be so easy?'

'I have absolutely no idea what you're talking about. What the hell is going on?' Boris let his voice rise. 'What do you want with me?' His bones felt like water. Why had he dragged Nina into this? *In God's name, why?*

'It's pointless, Stanovnik.' The young man shrugged. 'Dunayev told us everything. You should choose your friends more carefully.'

Boris stared at him for a full five seconds. His shoulders sagged. The strain was etched on his face. He shook his head, staring at the floor.

'The wife's in there,' the receptionist said, pointing. 'Shall I get her?'

'You've done great, we're pleased with you,' the young man said. 'You'll be rewarded for the tip-off.'

'How much?'

'Ten thousand roubles.'

'Twenty thousand or nothing!'

'Damn you!' Boris turned on her, his voice hoarse and shaking. 'I hope you rot in hell, you dried-up old hag!' He found himself raising his fist high above his head, and not knowing whether he really intended to strike her.

The young man stepped forward and grabbed his arm. 'You're in seriously deep shit as it is, Professor. Don't make it any worse for yourself and your wife. Are your things packed and ready to go?'

Boris nodded, his head downcast.

'All right. Go and fetch them. Now. *Hurry.*'

When he returned with the two suitcases, breathing heavily, his wife was waiting in the lobby. Nina didn't utter a word as he helped her into her coat. He put his arms around her to give her a comforting hug.

'No time for that,' the thin-faced young man snapped, beckoning his colleague. He tapped one of the suitcases with his shoe. 'Both in the car.' He nodded brusquely to the receptionist as they all went out.

The car pulled away, Boris and Nina in the back, the sharp-featured young man in the passenger seat, his colleague driving. It was a bright sunny day. There was hardly a cloud, though for Boris, the outside world hardly existed. He stared straight ahead, sick and defeated in spirit, sunk fathoms deep in his own thoughts. They hadn't even made it to the border . . .

He came back to the present with a start. The young unshaven man in the brown overcoat was offering him a pack of cigarettes. Boris shook his head, feeling lost and confused. What was going on? The young man lit two and passed one to his colleague. He loosened the collar of his overcoat and Boris glimpsed a grimy shirt collar.

'No introductions,' the young man said, smoke trailing from his nostrils. 'It's safer that way. We're taking you to Pāvilosta, a small town on the coast about a hundred miles west of here. At eight o'clock tonight you'll board a fishing boat. Shortly after midnight you'll be transferred to a motor launch – that's the tricky bit. Then it's a fast run to an island called Bornholm. Ever hear of it?'

Boris shook his head dumbly.

'Sovereign territory of Denmark. We have a contact there. She'll arrange passage to the mainland.' The young man glanced over his shoulder and smiled. 'All being well, you should be in Copenhagen this time tomorrow.'

Boris found his voice. It sounded strange. 'What was all that about? Back there at the hotel? I thought—'

'We had to make absolutely sure. You could be a shill for the mob. Or a decoy, luring us into a trap.'

'I thought *I* was in the trap.'

'Not you. Congratulations, by the way. Your reaction was more than convincing.'

'And the receptionist?'

'Yes, she's good, isn't she?' The young man grinned, shaking his head. *'Twenty thousand or nothing!'* He laughed out loud. 'She almost had me believing it.'

3

Chase drove north along Interstate 5, skirting the fringes of the Los Padres National Forest. The few remaining hectares of trees were being encroached upon by the sprawl of Los Angeles from the south and the ever-greedy Vandenberg Spaceport inland from the coastal strip. He thought of his conversation with Binch and Ruth Brosnan.

The JEG plant was conveniently near Vandenberg – too conveniently for comfort. Was this fanciful paranoia on his part, or was there some actual link between them?

Once past Wheeler Ridge he turned on to Highway 99 and headed for Bakersfield. The ridged folds of ochre-coloured hills shimmered in the heat. The car's thermometer registered an air temperature of 45°C. Chase drove in shirt-sleeves with the windows fully wound up against the searing blast and blessed the marvels of modern technology.

In Bakersfield he looked for the JEG Chemicals sign and was directed by an arrow underneath a huge silver conch shell along a smaller road that followed the meanderings of the Kern River. The plant was eight miles away on the other side of Bakersfield, clearly visible a good three miles away: all gleaming aluminium domes, silver towers and abstract sculptured pipework; it resembled a lunar colony, and in the distorting heat waves it looked surreal.

At the gate he showed his Scripps ID card. It bore the name of Dr David Benson – a person whose identity Cheryl had either borrowed or invented. The guard checked a clipboard and waved him through.

In the large semicircular reception hall he was asked to wait while they contacted Mr Merrick's office. Chase spent the few minutes looking at an illuminated display framed in moulded bronze that took up a complete section of wall. Next to each name was a symbol – oil derrick, space probe, jet fighter, lumber truck, movie camera – meant to represent the particular company's products and services. Chase couldn't help being impressed by the JEG empire in all its splendour.

JEG Electronics Division
JEG Thermoplastics Division
JEG Petroleum Division
JEG Pharmaceuticals Division
JEG Data Systems Division
JEG Aerospace Division
JEG Ranching Division
JEG Lumber Division
JEG Realty Division

JEG Transport Division
JEG Movie & TV Division
JEG Communications Division
JEG Franchising Division

The empire's size and strength was undoubted, Chase reflected, and it would have powerful friends in high places.

Merrick had thinning sandy hair and a wispy ginger moustache, wearing spectacles with green frames that unfortunately clashed with his colouring. Chase got the impression that the moustache and glasses were an attempt to lend authority to a babyish face and timid, retiring manner. They shook hands across Merrick's desk; he was obviously quite willing to accept Chase as an English marine biologist on Scripps' faculty. He listened as Chase explained that the Marine Life Research Group was mounting a deepwater expedition, but when Chase got to the bit about 'investigating the systematics, evolution and spatial distribution of the benthic foraminifera' he raised his hands. 'Sorry, Dr Benson, gotta stop you there. Outside my field.'

Chase affected surprise, as if benthic foraminifera were a regular topic of discussion at every dinner table, though it was the reaction he'd hoped for. He scratched behind his ear. 'How best to explain it? If I say a specialised type of flora-control agent . . .'

'A marine herbicide, you mean?' said a relieved Merrick, at last getting the drift. 'Oh, sure, no problem. We have forty patented compounds, maybe even more.' He touched the keypad on his desk and swivelled it round to show a list on the screen.

Chase tutted apologetically. 'None of which is suitable.'

'How can you be sure?' Merrick was taken aback.

'We've been through all the industrial chemist catalogues. What we're after is a special herbicide that's effective in deepwater conditions at extremely low temperatures.'

'That sounds like something specially formulated for that particular purpose. The cost of producing a completely new herbicide can be substantial, starting at tens of millions—'

'Let's not worry our heads about money,' Chase said. 'Not at this early stage.' He piled it on. 'If it's effective it could become standard procedure for marine biology institutions throughout the world.'

Merrick was leaning forward, hands clasped on the desk, thumbs weaving. His eyes gleamed at the prospect of a contract worth millions. 'You need to talk with our senior research chemist, Dr Hilti. Let me set it up, Dr Benson. Won't take minutes, I assure you.' His eagerness was touching.

'Before we get to that, Mr Merrick—'

'Chuck.'

'Some of our people at Scripps aren't convinced – *Chuck* – that JEG Chemicals has the facilities for a project of this scale. That I should really get in touch with Dow or Monsanto and let them have a shot at it.'

'Dr Benson, have no fears on that score. We've got the R&D facilities, the laboratories, the highest qualified staff. Take my word for it!'

'I wouldn't dream of doubting it,' Chase said, 'but of course I have to satisfy the people at my end that you can handle it.'

'Oh, absolutely.'

'Can I take a tour of your labs?'

Merrick nodded enthusiastically. 'But of course! Let me arrange it now, if you have the time.' He waited anxiously while Chase glanced at his watch and took ages deliberating. His freckled face lit up when Chase said at last, 'Okay, Chuck, I think I can manage that, thanks. I shall tell my people you've been most accommodating.'

Chuck Merrick beamed.

4

In a side ward of the annexe that housed the Diagnostic Research Unit of the Reagan Memorial Hospital, Denver, Dr Ruth Brosnan watched a ten-year-old boy die in agony. His face was a mass of suppurating sores, obscuring his eyes and turning his mouth into a fat raw blister. She felt angry, helpless and near to tears.

The child had been admitted four days ago complaining of chest and abdominal pains, vomiting green bile and with hard, shiny growths on his arms and legs. Unlike the earlier patients, who had had to undergo a long process of clinical investigation before their condition could be identified, the boy had been immediately tested for dioxin poisoning, and the pathology lab had confirmed it within twelve hours.

Not that rapid and accurate diagnosis made a blind bit of difference, Ruth told herself bitterly. Once it had infiltrated the body, dioxin caused irrevocable genetic damage, primarily to the nervous system. Depending on the concentration of the dose and the length of time the patient had been exposed to it, the outcome was slow, agonising death or, at best, permanent crippling of body and brain. There was nothing she, or anyone, could do.

Leaving the ward, she took off her mask and gown and dropped them into the sterilisation chute. Her eyes were dry, her face pale but composed. She smiled briefly at one of the nurses as she went back to her office.

There she wrote up her notes and closed the file.

Case number nine. The third and youngest to die. Two others, a man in his mid-thirties, and an elderly woman, were still on the danger list. The remaining four had been moved to another ward now that their condition had stabilised. Would there be more? An epidemic? She shied away from the dreadful possibility.

Ruth turned her eyes, as she found herself doing countless times a day, to the map of Colorado on the wall. There were nine coloured pins in an arc to the south and west of Colorado Springs, itself a few miles south of the Martin Marietta Space Center. The prevailing wind was from the northeast.

She looked at the map and thought again of what Gavin Chase had said, that evening at the Inchcapes'. Or rather, as she reminded herself, not so much what he had said, as the questions he had asked, the doubts he had raised. Those questions and doubts filled her with a sickly foreboding that grew with each passing day and every new victim.

5

Chase had no need to fake his admiration; the facilities, as promised, were impressive. After being conducted by Merrick and Dr Hilti around the three-storey building, with its large, brightly lit laboratories, and being shown everything he asked to see, Chase expressed himself more than satisfied.

Dr Hilti was a tall, spare man in his early sixties with the austere, scrubbed look of someone who lived his life to a rigid, unswerving discipline. He wore a spotless white coat and had a prominent Adam's apple supported by a blue and white-checked bowtie. Here was a different calibre of intelligence to Chuck Merrick's, and Chase knew he'd have to be extra careful: that piercing stare and tight, prudish mouth advertised to the world that Dr Hilti was nobody's fool.

Chase was less than content, however. He hadn't naïvely expected to come across direct evidence that they were producing a banned chemical at the plant. What he did know was that the manufacture of 2,4,5-T on a commercial scale required continuous laboratory monitoring and ultra-high levels of precaution. Nowhere had he seen anything to set the alarm bells ringing. And Merrick and Dr Hilti were quite willing to take him through the labs, floor by floor, never once hesitant or in the least evasive.

He'd done as much as he could. Cheryl was going to have to dream up some other way of finding out what JEG Chemicals was up to – if indeed the company was up to anything.

He followed Dr Hilti, back ramrod-straight, to his office on the ground floor. With Chuck Merrick chattering in his ear he nearly didn't spot the side corridor leading to a pair of steel doors with portholes in them and a sign above reading – MARINE EXPERIMENTAL CHAMBER.

Chase slowed down while Merrick carried on a few paces, and before Merrick realised what was happening, Chase was heading towards the steel doors.

'This looks interesting, Chuck . . . marine experimentation?'

A smaller red-lettered sign said AUTHORIZED PERSONNEL ONLY. Chase had almost reached the doors when Dr Hilti arrived close behind. 'Not in there, I'm sorry.' His tone was apologetic yet brusque. 'We're conducting a series of tests.'

Chase looked disappointed, while Chuck Merrick in turn scowled at Dr Hilti. 'Come now, we can surely make an exception in this case. Dr Benson represents a very important client.'

Chase had to give him credit for this show of defiance. Dr Hilti blinked several times, his Adam's apple bobbing up and down above the bowtie. 'I don't suppose a few minutes will do any harm,' he muttered, and though still clearly reluctant, he led the way through the steel doors with Chase following and Chuck Merrick bringing up the rear.

It was like entering a shimmering undersea cave.

Enormous translucent tanks were ranged on either side of a central aisle. The only illumination, a gently shifting green light, came from the tanks themselves. A layman might have mistaken it for an aquarium. The bottoms of the tanks were faithful replicas of different seabeds: some with sand and silt, or with small rocks and pebbles, with fantastic coral architecture, and everywhere a profusion of plant life, their fronds rippling rhythmically to an unseen current.

Exactly like an aquarium, Chase thought – except that there were no fish. In fact, no marine creatures of any description.

Down at the far end of the chamber a circular metal staircase led up to a railed gantry. Chase thought he detected movement up there, but in the shifting green patterns it was hard to be sure. Instead he concentrated on his other senses, primarily smell: most herbicides had a distinctive odour that he would have known instantly. He inhaled the humid atmosphere, trying not to sniff audibly.

'Water purification and treatment of effluents,' explained Dr Hilti, close by his side as they moved along the aisle. 'New methods of water pollution control.'

If it was a lie, it was smoothly and plausibly done. So far Chase had no cause to doubt the scientist was telling the truth. But if it was genuinely and entirely innocuous, why forbid entry to rows of tanks containing seawater, sand, rocks and plants?

He couldn't smell herbicides, but something stank.

Chase thought Chuck Merrick deserved a small reward. 'I'm very impressed. Thanks for the tour. I'll be putting in a favourable recommendation to my head of department.'

'And who's that?' Dr Hilti enquired.

'Dr Detrick,' Chase said before he had time to stop himself. He cursed his oversight in not inventing a name – any damn name would have done.

'We haven't had dealings with Scripps before,' Merrick was saying, obviously happy now. 'We very much welcome this opportunity.'

They came to the far end near the metal staircase leading up to the gantry and turned back. A person entered through the double doors, about thirty yards away, and Chase tried not to flinch at the sight of the greenish glow reflecting off a bald head; as if something had caught his interest, he bent close to one of the tanks.

Ivor Banting, large as life and twice as ugly. Even though it had been five years since last they'd met, Banting would recognise him at once.

Bending over, his face close to the glass wall of the tank, Chase listened as Banting's footsteps drew near. He felt an unbearable tenseness in his shoulders as the footsteps approached, and he heard Dr Hilti say, 'Good morning, Professor.' *Oh, by the way, Professor Banting, I'd like you to meet . . .*

But Dr Hilti didn't, and after a grunted reply from Banting, the footsteps carried on. A moment later they were ascending the metal treads of the circular stairway.

Unhurriedly, Chase straightened up and moved towards the double doors, following Merrick into the corridor, where the air felt deliciously cool against his forehead, which he hoped wasn't perspiring too heavily.

Then he had to summon up his concentration and focus because Merrick was speaking to him, saying something about lunch in the cafeteria. Chase thanked him for the offer, but he had to start the drive back to Scripps. With that out of the way, he expressed his gratitude to both Chuck Merrick and Dr Hilti and left.

Behind the double doors, inside the chamber, standing on the high gantry overlooking the rows of tanks, his sharp features bathed in shimmering green light from below, Major Lloyd Malden murmured in a strained, irascible voice, 'Of course I'm sure. I met him at Halley Bay. He was one of your marine biologists. The point, Ivor, is simple: what is he doing here, and what does he *want*? Do you have any answers?'

6

'Isn't that why he gave you the dossier?' Elizabeth Lucas said, bringing the coffeepot to the table. She was wearing a quilted housecoat, her face unmade-up but her highlighted brown hair neatly brushed from its centre parting. She couldn't bear to be seen with untidy hair, even in front of her husband at breakfast.

'Yes, of course it is – but Liz, what am I expected to do now?' Gene Lucas shook pepper over his scrambled eggs and picked up his fork. Grey shadows encircled his eyes. He put the fork down, squinting painfully against the reflecting laminated surfaces and the rack of glinting kitchen utensils. 'If Lebasse couldn't trust his own people in the Defense Department, how can I? Somebody somewhere must have found out what he was doing.'

'How do you know that?' his wife asked sensibly, pouring his coffee. 'Did he tell you that in so many words?'

'Tell me what?' Lucas asked irritably.

'That he didn't trust them?'

Lucas sighed and shut his eyes for a second. Liz didn't understand. She still had a touching faith in authority, still believed that for people to have achieved high office they must, by definition, be steadfast, loyal and true.

He shook more pepper over his eggs and Liz said sharply, 'Gene, you're spoiling it!'

Seeing what he had done he forked the pepper into the eggs. There was no doubt in his mind that Lebasse had been murdered. And if they (whoever 'they' were) could get rid of the Secretary of Defense, they could certainly get rid of him.

He laid his fork down. He had to talk to somebody. 'This is a secret military project called Operation Download, devised by a special Pentagon agency by the name of Advanced Strategic Projects. They want to put this thing into operation – they could even be developing it right this minute, for all I know.'

'Yes, dear,' Liz nodded, buttering a piece of toast. 'You explained it to me before. Eat your eggs before they go cold.'

'Elizabeth, do you understand what I'm talking about?' Lucas tapped the table in time with the words. 'They are deliberately and cold-bloodedly going to alter the ecological balance of this planet. They intend to fill a huge fleet of supertankers with herbicides and wipe out all the phytoplankton in the oceans. They plan to replace missile warheads with payloads of herbicides and drop them into equatorial forests, killing off all the trees and plants. By destroying all the green plants in the oceans and on land they mean to upset the oxygen balance of the atmosphere. It's all part of some insane strategy to protect this country. They're crazy, mad as hatters, the whole bunch of them!'

'Is it possible to do that?' Liz asked, scooping up a forkful of scrambled eggs. 'Could they affect the oxygen in that way?'

Lucas nodded wearily. 'Yes, they can do it. Given sufficient quantities of herbicides over a period of time – months or years; it's hard to know for sure how long it would take.' He leaned over the table, a lock of greying hair falling across his puffy eyelids. 'Liz, we depend on the plants, and once they're gone, our supply of oxygen is gone too – for ever. Without oxygen we're finished, and every other living creature with us.'

The motion of her jaw slowed, became mechanical. 'But that would be committing suicide.'

'That's exactly what it is!' Lucas sipped his coffee and looked at her over the rim of the cup, haunted. 'They can do it – and will – now that Lebasse is out of the way.'

Liz frowned and dabbed her lips. 'What do you mean, out of the way?' she said slowly.

Lucas put his cup down very gently. 'Lebasse was against Operation Download. He wanted it stopped. So they had to find a way of shutting him up. It wasn't an accident, Liz. It wasn't natural causes.'

'But on TV it said he—'

'What did you expect them to say? Everything's been neatly tidied away and no awkward questions asked.'

'Gene, if they know that you have the dossier . . .' His wife's voice trailed away into silence. '*Do* they know? Did Lebasse tell them?'

'*They. Them.* Who are we talking about?' There was a ragged edge to his soft Texan drawl. 'Somebody in the Defense Department? One of the joint Chiefs? Somebody in the White House?' His hands curled into fists on the tabletop. 'I don't know who I can trust because I don't know who "they" are!'

A splash of morning sunlight made a bright rectangle on the wall. In the centre of it a vintage Norman Rockwell calendar showed a small boy sitting alongside a huge policeman at a drugstore counter; at the boy's feet was a red-spotted bundle tied to a stick.

In silence Liz went to the hob for more coffee. When she sat down her face was paler. 'Gene, you must go to the President. He'll listen to you.'

'It's not that easy to arrange. It could take weeks.'

'But if you say it's urgent, a matter of – what do they say—?'

'National security,' said Lucas dully.

'Then that's what you have to do!'

Lucas pushed his untouched breakfast aside. 'If only I could get to him directly, rather than through intermediaries . . . But you're right, I have to try.' He leaned back and rubbed his eyes. 'A few years ago when I was on the Presidential Advisory Committee a marine biologist called Theo Detrick submitted some research he'd spent years working on. According to him the phytoplankton in the oceans was declining. He compiled the evidence, pretty conclusively, that very soon, a few decades at most, the world would be gasping for breath. Well, I can tell you, Liz – I did a terrific demolition job on him and his report. "Ridiculous. Impossible. Science fiction." And you want to know something? Detrick was right all along. I know that now.'

'Would it help if you talked to him?'

'It would, if he was alive. Nobody ever took him seriously, but his daughter is still pushing his work. She's on television now and then, she writes a lot of stuff on the environment.' Lucas was gazing at the Rockwell calendar. 'That's an idea . . . she's in California somewhere, at Scripps, I think. I could send her the file. Sharon Detrick, or something like that. She's well-respected in the environmental lobby.'

He looked up at his wife, who was stacking the dishes and carrying them to the sink. Liz suddenly looked much older, her face cruelly caught in the shaft of sunlight.

'That's what I'll do,' Lucas said, trying to sound cheerful and decisive. 'I'll locate her and—' Liz was hunched over the sink, her shoulders shaking.

Oh Christ, dammit all to hell! Why didn't I keep my damn fool mouth shut?

5

I

Joseph Earl Gelstrom took the call in his office suite in the JEG Tower, which was situated next to the Pacific Coast Stock Exchange on the corner of Pine and Green; like most of downtown San Francisco, the building had miraculously escaped damage in the 2019 earthquake, so nearly all the major corporations had stayed put.

Gelstrom had just finished a workout in the gym on the floor below and his long, sun-streaked hair was damp and straggly from the shower. He had a white towel around his neck, stuffed into his blue silk robe. 'One moment.' He touched a button on the console and told his secretary to find Sturges and then turned back to the screen on which Malden was watching him, waiting.

'All right. Go ahead.'

'Is this channel secure?'

'Yes.'

Malden's lips thinned and he glanced out of shot, a look that could kill. His eyes flicked back. 'I'm at the Bakersfield plant, Mr Gelstrom. We've had a visit from a Dr Gavin Chase, a British marine biologist who tried to pass himself off as someone from the Scripps Institution. Tried – and succeeded. I think we need to do something about it.'

With a lazy gesture Gelstrom combed back his hair. His tanned, handsome face remained composed. 'Is that it, or is there more?'

'Merrick and Dr Hilti showed him around the place, including the marine experimental chamber. He had what appeared to be a bona fide Scripps ID in the name of Dr Benson.'

'So how do you know he's Chase?'

'I recognised him.'

'You know him?'

'I met him once, when he was with Professor Banting at Halley Bay Station.'

'Is Banting there with you now?'

'Yes. Do you want to speak to him?'

'No. What did Chase want?'

Malden's tongue flicked out to moisten his lips. He looked away and back again, fighting to control his anger. 'Professor Banting thinks – that is, he's almost certain – that Chase is a freelance journalist now. He's seen articles by him in the British scientific press—'

'One moment.' Gelstrom held up his finger and in the same movement beckoned to Sturges, who closed the door and came over to the velvet chair, standing with folded arms, gold glinting on his hairy wrists. 'I'm listening,' Gelstrom said.

'Chase has worked for the BBC, so Banting informs me. In view of the fact that he used a false name it's safe to assume he was hoping to dig up something. He also told Merrick that his head of department at Scripps was Dr Detrick.'

'Did he? That was stupid of him,' Gelstrom remarked languidly. 'And what did he say was the purpose of his visit?'

'Some rigmarole about a new kind of marine herbicide for a deep-water expedition. He wanted to satisfy himself about the R&D capability and Merrick believed him without running a check.'

'That was stupid of him, too,' Gelstrom said. There was a silence through which Malden waited, a muscle moving in his cheek. Gelstrom said, 'Could he have seen anything? What was happening in the test chamber at the time? Anything to make him suspicious?'

'Hilti thinks not. The tanks were being prepared for a new series of tests which aren't scheduled to start until tomorrow.'

'But you think he's dangerous. A threat.'

'Let's say a risk. One we don't have to take,' Malden said tersely. 'He's heard a rumour or there's been a breach of security – otherwise why come to the plant in the first place, and why under a false name? Also, Detrick is involved – maybe she put him up to it. That absolutely seals it as far as I'm concerned.'

'What do you want doing?'

'I leave that to you. But something terminal.'

Gelstrom massaged both temples and turned his head fractionally. 'Anything else you need to know?'

'No,' Sturges said, unfolding his arms. 'That should be enough.'

2

The voice of the Scripps central operator said, 'Mr Bryant of the American Press Association is on the line. Will you take it?'

'Yes, all right, put him on.' Standing at the wall phone in the lab, Cheryl wiped her fingers down the side of her white coat, thinking, *Bryant?* She shook her head, puzzled.

There was a click and a hale and hearty voice boomed, 'Hello! Dr Detrick! Pat Bryant, APA. You won't remember me, but I was at the conference in Washington earlier this year. You answered a couple of my questions.'

'The NOAA conference,' Cheryl said. 'I'm sorry, Mr Bryant. I don't recall—'

'That's by the by,' Bryant said breezily, making Cheryl grit her teeth. 'I don't know if you can assist us, Dr Detrick. We've had a request from the New York representative of the British Press Association. They're trying to help in locating a British journalist, Dr Gavin Chase. He's been in the States for several weeks and apparently the BBC want to reach him urgently. You don't happen to know his present whereabouts?'

'Don't they have his cell phone number?'

There was a momentary pause on the line. 'They do, but apparently he can't be reached for some reason. They stressed to me the urgency of the request—'

'So you just said. I'm reluctant to disclose any information regarding Dr Chase's whereabouts without his say-so. Even to the American Press Association.'

'Absolutely, Dr Detrick. Understood completely. You can't be too careful.'

'As it happens, Mr Bryant, the BBC has just missed reaching him here. Dr Chase is on his way back to England as we speak. He left Los Angeles for New York, where he's catching a flight to London.'

There was another pause, a faint crackle on the line. 'Do you happen to know what time his flight to London departs?'

'Not sure I do know,' Cheryl said, trying to recall Gavin's schedule. 'Does it matter?'

'I guess not. Only I could pass that information on to the BBC, if he's due back in the UK in the next twenty-four hours.'

'Dr Chase did complain about the stopover at JFK; I think he said three hours, or maybe more, hanging around the airport.'

Bryant's booming chuckle came over the line. 'I don't envy him!'

'No,' Cheryl said, and winced, moving the phone from her ear.

'You've been most helpful, Dr Detrick. And I do understand your caution about giving out cell phone numbers to strangers. Bad practice.'

'You're welcome, Mr Bryant. Goodbye.'

She was about to hang up when he said, 'Was it the eight o'clock flight out of Los Angeles?'

'The nine-fifteen.'

'Thanks again. I appreciate it. 'Bye.'

Cheryl hung up and walked across the lab and stood unseeingly at the bench, conflicting emotions rising inside her: a quiet, subdued happiness, but tinged with resentment as well. Of course Gavin had to leave, what was she thinking? He had professional commitments and personal ties back home. But acknowledging this didn't make her feel any better.

In the office suite in San Francisco, Sturges terminated the call and brought up airline schedules on the slate resting on his knee. He spent a couple of minutes comparing options, then did some mental arithmetic. Finally he looked across the desk at Gelstrom, leaning back watching him.

'Take one of the fleet,' Gelstrom said, 'if you need to.'

Sturges shook his head. 'I can make it.' He smiled his empty smile. 'Plenty of time.'

3

ATHLETES DIE IN FINALS
Mystery Deaths in 5,000- and 10,000-metre
European Finals in Stockholm
– Officials Blame Heat Stroke

Chase looked for more in-depth coverage of the story on the *Washington Post* 'Hot News' site, then scanned two or three international titles, which added little to the banner headline. Competitors had suffered from dizziness, nausea, and hallucinations for the past ten days. First the food and water had been blamed, then the legal supplements (and illegal drugs) that many athletes took to improve their performance; and now the climate. *The official explanation is ludicrous*, Chase thought. 24°C. was in no way excessive, not for top-class athletes, the fittest people on the planet.

There could be another cause, one that they wouldn't dream of looking for. Cerebral anoxia: an insufficient supply of oxygen to the brain. If the percentage was low enough and the person was exerting himself, he would eventually die.

But who would ever think of testing for altitude sickness in a place such as Stockholm, which was practically at sea level?

He had dozed a little on the flight from LA, then read a little, and now he was reconciled to the bloody stopover at JFK. He had a pass for the VIP lounge, so he decided to wait till then to get some refreshment. First he had to switch from domestic Terminal Five, West Concourse, to international departures, Terminal Four. Or was it Terminal Seven? He could never remember. He hated changing terminals at JFK.

Chase fell in line as the passengers streamed towards the transit area of Terminal Five.

During the past five and a half weeks he had recorded more than forty interviews, audio and video. He'd written up, he estimated, 35,000 words of notes on his e-pad and in three fat notebooks. He'd talked with scientists, state officials, industrial workers, forestry wardens, city engineers, ecologists and environmentalists right across the country, and it was all there, in the tote-bag containing his laptop, e-pad and digital camera slung on his shoulder. He had enough material – more than enough – for the series he had to write, and he knew that Marcus Barrett would be happy with the result. But he didn't have the clincher.

Several times he had come close – he had sensed it was almost within his grasp when Binch had spoken guardedly about DELFI's predictions (and the interest shown by ASP); when Ruth Brosnan had told him about the chloracne victims and that there were military installations in the area; at the Bakersfield plant where he knew damn well that JEG Chemicals were up to something – yet he'd failed to pin down precisely *what*.

All he *really* had was a string of apparently unconnected facts supported by hunch, suspicion and not very satisfactory circumstantial evidence.

The feeling he was left with was one of uneasy calm, as if everyone was holding their breath, waiting for some cataclysmic event to happen, yet at the same time fooling themselves that it never would. Move along there, folks. No cause for alarm. Everything's fine and dandy.

So air pollution is increasing by fifteen per cent a year. So what else is new? Chemical wastes, pesticides and herbicides are being dumped into rivers and lakes at an unprecedented rate. But who says the environment can't cope? Wildlife is being wiped out, entire species decimated. But isn't that the price we have to pay for a modern technological society? World population is up to 8.7 billion and putting a heavy strain on the biosphere, but don't forget that it's levelling off a lot faster than anyone predicted because of the famines in Africa and Asia.

No, Chase decided regretfully, to a sceptic the case was still not proven. Three dead athletes wouldn't prove it either. What was needed was specific, documented, incontrovertible proof, and that he had failed to get.

4

Russ Trambo wiped the folds of his neck with a handkerchief soaked in ice water and gazed wearily up at the young reporter. Outside the newsroom window of WNRB-TV the hotels and casinos of North Las Vegas were baking nicely in a mid-afternoon temperature of 53°C. Across the street a faulty flickering neon sign (WEDD NGS WH LE-U-WA T) was trying wanly to compete with the hard desert sunlight.

'So what are these guys, Jack? Jesus freaks?'

'Couldn't say. They all look alike, dress alike, black suits, neckties, neat haircuts, those who aren't shorn to the scalp. They don't drive in – they arrive by bus, get picked up on Judson Avenue by trucks.'

'They sound like Mormons to me.' Russ Trambo reached behind him to tweak up the air-con but it was already tweaked as high as it would go. 'Or military.'

Jack Chang shook his head. 'I thought Mormons too, so I asked a couple of them. They said not. One of them told me he was a messenger.'

'Who for, Western Union?'

'What's that?' Jack Chang had never heard of it.

'They get picked up in trucks?'

'Yeah. Army surplus, by the look of 'em.'

'And then what?'

'They go east on Highway 604.' Jack Chang rested his knuckles on the desk, his lean sallow face alight. 'There's gotta be a story there, Russ. Let me take a camera and do a couple of interviews. They're weirdos, if nothing else. We can sell it to the networks as a filler.'

'There's nothing up 604 except the Muddy Mountains Wilderness. That's its actual name, Wilderness – and it's not called that for nothing. Except in this case it is: a whole big bunch of nothing. Did you ask any of them where they were heading for?'

'Sure, the pair I talked to. They didn't appear to have any idea.'

'Then where's your story?' Russ Trambo wanted to know.

'What if they're part of a cult?'

'Listen, Jack, here in Nevada, if they *weren't* part of a cult you'd have your story – and I'd say go ahead and cover it.'

'I checked out the map as well.' Jack Chang flipped open his notebook. 'The Atomic Energy Commission's nuke test site is along 604 – and so is the Nellis Air Force Missile Range.'

'What's your brilliant new theory now? These guys in black suits and short haircuts are aliens or clones or zombies?' The news editor propped his chin in the palm of his hand, mechanically wiping the back of his neck with the now-lukewarm handkerchief. 'Wait a second. It might be a protest movement, a demo . . . any of them mention something like that? Were they waving placards around? Posters?'

'Not that I saw, just carrying these little black suitcases. The whole deal was kinda creepy. It reminded me of a pilgrimage, people gathering together from different places, like these religious nuts do.'

'We got our share of End-of-the-World freaks here as well. Nevada is well provided for.' Russ Trambo shook his head. 'Really can't see anything in this, Jack. If they're waiting for Doomsday by global warming, well, we'll cover that story when it happens.' He wadded the handkerchief into a damp ball and tossed it on the desk, grumbling to himself, 'If it is the fucking end of the world, why can't we have a goddamn ice age instead?'

5

From long experience Sturges knew that it wasn't the act itself that presented problems, but what happened afterwards. If the act could be accomplished quickly, quietly, and without fuss, he would simply walk away and vanish into the crowd – although he didn't like working in crowds; too many unpredictable factors. His preferred *modus operandi* was one-to-one, just him and his victim, in a fixed situation that closed the options down to zero. The Detrick case, for example: just him and the target and an empty pool. If any assignment had achieved a perfect ten, that was the one.

Drowning as a murder weapon: a swift silent blow followed by forced submergence and it was all over, with only a small bruise at the back of the head to show for it.

Today Sturges was the Premier Class executive, soberly dressed in a dark grey business suit with a fine pink stripe outlining the lapels and cuffs. Similarly conservative was the soft black vinyl hat, which he wore to hide his spiky blond crew-cut. Nothing he could do to disguise his six feet four or his 210-pound frame or his fifty-four-inch chest; but there were plenty of big men around and he didn't feel conspicuous. Anyway, nobody ever remembered faces at airports, where his would be one among thousands.

He carried two items of hand luggage: a slim, flat black attaché case and a matching camera slung around his neck. The attaché case contained what he termed his 'close' methods: hypodermic, capsules, cigarettes.

If he could get close to his victim, say next to him in a line of people or behind him on an escalator, the hypo shot was easily delivered through the fake index finger of the black glove; his own hand would be clenched inside, working the plunger.

The tiny beadlike capsules would dissolve instantly in hot or cold liquids, so again this depended on whether he could get near enough to slip one into the victim's drink.

The cigarettes, a popular low-tar brand, were a favourite method, because the victim could smoke one all the way down without suspecting a thing – and ten minutes later would be stone-cold dead of an embolism, by which time Sturges would be long clear of the vicinity and going blamelessly about his business.

Concealed in the camera case was a gas-powered ejector dart, effective at up to twenty-five feet, which could penetrate the thickest clothing and kill in less than two minutes. He'd used it twice before and it was absolutely dependable. No need even to pretend to be taking a photograph: There were two viewing and aiming positions, one from above, which meant he could be fiddling with the camera, pretending to adjust it, and line up his victim through the target viewfinder.

Two vital elements remained unresolved: location and recognition. Sturges had not just to find his man, but to be certain it was Chase. Having seen him once before, in Geneva five years ago, was a bonus; most times he had to work from stills. The images of Chase he'd perused on the net weren't all that brilliant. They were mostly taken from television appearances and the quality was crap. But according to Major Malden, Chase had altered very little – a slight thickening around the waist, perhaps, but still the straight black sweep of hair across his forehead, the thick dark eyebrows.

A moving walkway took him around the rim of a large transparent dome and through a maze of plastic tunnels. Below him the main concourse was thronged with people, among them the usual drug cases, mugging trios and beggars. Few carried hand luggage or a shoulder bag that wasn't chained to his person. Sturges didn't bother; his size was an adequate deterrent.

As he stepped off into the transit lounge he checked out the suspended circular display that flashed up the arrivals and departures.

FLIGHT D-049 : LONDON : 21.15 : TERMINAL 7

It was listed as ON SCHEDULE. Sturges allowed himself a fleeting grin, and a glint of gold shone faintly. His preparation and timing were perfect. He had two full hours: as he'd assured Gelstrom, plenty of time.

First he would check out the general in-transit area that linked the various terminals. If Chase was there and hadn't passed through to Terminal Seven, international departures, it would save him the bother of having to buy a ticket for the onward journey. With his Corporate Priority Visa, security clearance was never going to be a problem – he could have strolled through the channel to airside with a couple of handguns tucked in his belt and a jagged-edge sheath-knife strapped to his chest.

6

Lucas had known all along that getting to see the President at such short notice would be a 9+ on a scale of ten.

At first, following protocol, he'd tried the proper channels, and been told it would take up to two weeks, minimum. When he insisted that it was a matter of extreme urgency he was asked to submit the reason for requesting a personal interview, which was of course out of the question.

In the end he had pleaded, cajoled and finally persuaded two senior White House officials and the President's appointments secretary that it was imperative he speak to the President at once, if only for a few minutes – ten, maybe?

'Is that all?' one of the officials remarked drily over the phone. 'Think yourself damn lucky if you get five!'

He was granted an appointment sandwiched between a delegation from the Free Palestinian Trades Council and an awards ceremony in honour of an army ordnance team that had defused a thousand-pound bomb at Grand Central Station. Instead of being shown to the Oval Office, however, as he'd expected, Lucas was stationed between an aide and a Secret Service agent on the steps leading down to the Rose Garden lawn at the rear of the White House.

Then came another surprise – or rather, shock: he was crisply informed that he had however long it would take the President to walk from the steps to the welcoming committee of politicians, dignitaries and military brass in the middle of the lawn to state his case. Dumbfounded, Lucas gazed with sick dismay at the short stretch of trimmed grass. He reckoned he'd have about a minute; perhaps a few seconds more if the President slowed to a dawdle.

So *one minute* in which to explain the technical complexities, the scientific fallacies and the ecological implications of Operation Download.

One minute to warn of global catastrophe.

It was another dismal shock for him to see down there, amongst the mingling crowd, the tall, erect figure of Major Malden; there was no escaping the man. He had, it appeared, an inside track to the President. Lucas couldn't spot General Wolfe anywhere, so perhaps that was a hopeful sign.

There was a flurry of movement as dozens of members of the security corps appeared on the steps leading down to the lawn. They formed a phalanx on either side, facing outwards, stony-featured men wearing shades, ear-pieces in place, smooth bulges under dark jackets where their Glock semi-automatics were holstered.

On the sidelines, Lucas watched and waited as President Hernandez emerged onto the covered walkway. Alongside him strode a tall, bulky figure with a crest of sculpted hair an impossibly vibrant shade of glossy brown as the sun struck it. The two men were laughing together, almost like a couple of frat guys enjoying a private joke, Lucas thought. He recognised the President's companion at once: Chesney Poulton, an influential insider who headed a DC think-tank called the Alliance for the Advancement of American Values.

At the top of the steps the pair shook hands warmly, both wearing broad smiles. Poulton patted the President's shoulder as if wishing him well, then with a brief departing wave he turned aside and moved out of view.

The President was on his way. Lucas swallowed to lubricate his dry throat, trying to get his thoughts in some sort of order. Knowing he had minutes at most to make his case, the scientific advisor was totally unprepared for what happened next. The soft shuffle of rubber-soled shoes on marble. A solid scrum of hulking security guards bearing down on him. Lucas was grasped firmly by the elbows and all five feet four inches of him was lifted off his feet and carried forward. The next thing he knew, he was walking – more like trotting – at the President's side, surrounded and hemmed in by huge hulking men with massive shoulders, their expressions rendered inscrutable by impenetrable shades, blocking out the light. He was in a forest of bodies.

'Gene, good to see you. How's everything?'

Automatically Lucas extended his hand and it was lightly taken by the slender brown one. The President released his hand and said out of the corner of his mouth, 'What is he, Bud, colonel, general, or what?' A low hard voice from the crush answered at once, 'Colonel, sir. Cathermore. Purple Heart in Afghanistan. Prosthetic hip joint, right side.'

'Mr President,' Lucas said breathlessly, running alongside, 'I have to speak with you, sir, on a vitally important subject concerning national security. It's difficult to explain right here and now, sir, but if you can give me a few minutes of your time . . .'

Hernandez smiled down at him, perfect white teeth in a strong, acceptably Hispanic face: virile, sensual, powerful, full of character. 'I appreciate the circumstances aren't ideal, Gene, but that's how it is. Sorry. These people tie me up in so many fucking knots I can't budge an inch. What is it?'

The smile came back, dazzling. No wonder television audiences went wild over him. He was better looking than any movie star.

Lucas gritted his teeth and launched in. 'Shortly before he died, Mr President, Secretary of Defense Lebasse gave me a briefing document about a top-secret project that had been submitted to him for approval. He wanted my opinion – as a scientist – on the advisability of proceeding with this project' – *they had covered half the distance already; this was impossible, ludicrous, crazy –* 'and I know that Lebasse himself had grave doubts. In view of his untimely death, Mr President, I feel that it's my responsibility, as your scientific advisor, to urge you most strongly not to grant approval . . .'

He was babbling. Did any of this make sense? Trying his best to keep his voice under control, Lucas went on, 'This project must *not* be allowed to go ahead, sir. I cannot stress enough my conviction that it must be halted. The consequences are truly horrendous.'

They were only yards away from the flags and the bunting and the groups of waiting politicians and military officers. President Hernandez halted and the phalanx of aides and secret service agents stopped with him, enclosing the two men: one tall, handsome, brown-skinned, the other small, grey-haired, sallow.

President Hernandez was finally paying attention to Lucas, his puzzled expression momentarily spoiling those evenly proportioned features.

'Which project are you speaking of, Gene?'

Gaining confidence, Lucas said rapidly, 'It's code-named Operation Download, sir. Submitted to the Defense Department by Advanced Strategic Projects, under the auspices of the Pentagon.' At last he was being listened to, and by someone who had the power to *do* something.

The President's frown deepened. 'I think you're mistaken, Gene. Download, as far as I am aware, is a project under the auspices of Future Crisis Operations Executive. Am I correct in that assertion?' he asked an aide.

'You are correct, sir. Known by the State Department acronym Fut/COE.'

'But it's the same project,' Lucas said impatiently, 'regardless of any name change. What they choose to call themselves is irrelevant.'

The President was nodding, as if agreeing with him, but what he was agreeing *about*, Lucas wasn't sure. The President produced his famous smile. 'No cause for concern, Gene, all done and dusted. Approval has been granted on the advice of Mr Zadikov.'

'Who?' Lucas mumbled blankly, too dazed to be astounded.

'Ralf Zadikov. Perhaps you didn't hear the announcement? Mr Zadikov is the newly appointed Secretary of Defense.'

And with that, President Hernandez gave Lucas a friendly pat on the shoulder. 'Great to see you, Gene. Drop by again at a future date. Give my warmest regards to your wife' – somebody muttered a name in his ear – 'Elizabeth.'

He flashed his brilliant smile and the entourage went along with him, all except Gene Lucas, who found himself standing alone on a patch of the Rose Garden lawn in the mellow evening sunshine, gazing at nothing.

7

A small smile playing on his lips, Major Malden stood with a group of officers, observing Gene Lucas, now a lone figure once the parade had moved on, looking lost and abandoned. With Lebasse eradicated, Lucas neutralised and Zadikov in place, there were no further impediments to progress; the way was clear.

The major became aware of somebody nearby and turned to find the looming presence of Chesney Poulton at his shoulder. Malden experienced the same sense of unease as he had on the viewing deck at the Pentagon. There was something intimidating about the man, gross and overpowering, almost chilling . . .

'Where's that fat useless turd you call your superior officer this evening, Major? Let you off the leash?'

'I'm not on anyone's leash,' Malden responded coolly.

'No, I think you're doing okay, as a matter of fact. You and Blindeye have swung Operation Dumpload, I hear. So I guess congratulations are in order.'

Even though the sentiment sounded genuine, Malden was suspicious.

'Last time we spoke you were dead against it. You warned the general to keep out of your way.'

'Stick with herbicides and pesticides, Major, and I couldn't give a flying fuck what you and your Ass-Wipe outfit get up to. Just don't get involved in DC power games; you're strictly junior league.' Poulton squared his broad shoulders. 'Besides, sonny, I have other fish to fry.'

'So you said before,' Malden came back, not to be dismissed that easily. 'The "Tourist Bus Massacre" in Cuba, wasn't it? Seems to me you were already celebrating the attack even before it happened. A Big Day event is what you named it, as I recall: April 21, a date we'd always remember, like 9/11, you said. You were right.'

Poulton's generous, ruddy features had the ghost of a smile. 'You figured that out all by yourself, did you, son?'

'It had all the hallmarks of a False Flag operation to me. Rebels down from the mountains with high-calibre machine-guns and grenade launchers. Wipe out thirty-odd US citizens, leaving no survivors and no witnesses; and for what purpose? What's to gain? There's been no rebel insurgence in Cuba for decades.'

Poulton moved in closer, thereby obliging Malden to back away from the group.

'I'd advise you to be careful attributing False Flags without proof,' he said, lowering his voice to almost a growl. 'Rumours like that get folks into trouble. Stick to what you know something about, son—'

Poulton broke off. He poked a finger at Malden's shoulder-flash. It used to be triangular; now it was oval. 'I see you've changed your designation, Major. You're no longer ASP. So what does "Fut/COE" stand for?'

'Future Crisis Operations Executive.'

'Well now,' Poulton ruminated. 'Just so long as we understand one another, you hear? You steer clear of my affairs and I'll let you and "Fuck-Toe" get on with yours unhindered.'

Malden felt the heat rising to his face.

Poulton went on imperturbably, 'Let's have no more dumb speculation about Cuban rebels and False Flags.' He draped a heavy arm across Lloyd Malden's slender shoulders. 'Then you and me will get along just fine, son.'

6

I

Due to the time difference it was late afternoon in California and Cheryl was where he expected her to be, at Scripps.

From her reaction Chase could tell she was both surprised and pleased he had called. Hearing her voice brought back the night before. The memory of their lovemaking swept over him, assailed him so powerfully that he could smell her perfume, relive the curve of her back and thigh.

It was ridiculous, but he felt as tongue-tied as a kid. For something to say he asked Cheryl when she was going to visit him in England.

'Would you like me to? Seriously?'

'I would. I'd like you to meet Dan. And Dan to meet you.'

It was with a great surge of joy to think he'd soon be home with Dan. The ritual of bath time, silly games and bedtime stories – though those childish antics wouldn't last much longer. It felt wonderful, fantastic, to have the kid to go back to; alone he was rootless; together he and Dan made a family. A home.

He tried to picture Cheryl as part of it, making up the triangle. It was difficult to transpose her mentally from friend to lover; trying to visualise a more permanent relationship between them was for the moment beyond him. Had it been just a casual affair, their few days together, headstrong and passionate because it was so short? Or was there a future for the three of them? In all honesty Gavin Chase had to admit he didn't know; he guessed that Cheryl was no wiser.

Chase had found himself a niche in the main concourse. He had a Michelob and a packet of dry-roast peanuts and was seated on a leather-backed stool, facing the crowd. On the far side of the arena a huge curved screen was displaying the evening newscast.

'Maybe next year,' Cheryl said. 'But no promises.'

'I'm not holding you to any.' With some women, he thought, you could talk all night and fail to communicate; with others a world of meaning was compressed into a sentence. Or even a silence. There was a silence now: a hollow echo as the signal crossed three thousand miles coast-to-coast between bouncing into space and back.

'We can't let it finish.'

After another three-thousand mile pause Cheryl said, 'I suppose we can't, Mr Chase.'

'Do you feel that too?'

'Can I have time to think about it?'

'Of course,' Chase said. 'One-two-three, time's up.'

Cheryl laughed, though her heart wasn't in it.

He said, 'I'm going to miss you. I really fucking seriously am, Ms Detrick.'

'I feel the same.'

Silence again, yet a comfortable, intimate one this time. Then Cheryl said, 'Oh, I meant to tell you . . . very strange. This morning, a few minutes after you left, a package arrived in the mail.'

'What's strange about it?'

Chase was watching but barely seeing a procession of buses on the big screen. Young men were stepping down, all dressed identically in black suits, white shirts, black neckties. It was somewhere way out west because the sun was beating down out of a baking, pure blue sky. A Mormon convention?

'At first glance it *looks* like some kind of government report, but there's nothing with it, no sender's address, no covering letter. It's plastered over with classified and restricted circulation notices.'

Now Chase was interested. 'A report about what?'

'Something called Operation Download. It looks genuine to me, Gav. I'll tell you more when I've had chance to read it.'

She broke off and Chase caught a muttered conversation, and then Cheryl came back. 'I have to go, sorry. One of my experiments is leaking all over the lab floor. Please take care. I mean that. I'm seriously going to miss you . . .'

Chase wanted to say more, but there wasn't time. Happiness and regret mingled inside him. He said his goodbyes and in the middle of them Cheryl said, 'Nearly forgot, someone called Bryant, Pat Bryant, from the American Press Association has been trying to reach you.'

'Don't know him.'

'Me neither,' Cheryl said, 'though he insisted we'd met before. Apparently the BBC are trying to get in touch.'

'The BBC have my cell number.'

'I just told him you were on your way home, and the BBC would have to wait till you arrived back in London. To be honest, Gav, there was something about him . . . kinda fishy, I guess. And creepy as well. Like I knew his voice and yet I didn't.' She said to someone, 'Yeah, yeah, right away . . . Gav, gotta go! Goodbye!'

When she'd gone Chase was left wondering how Pat Bryant of the APA knew to call Cheryl at the Scripps Institution in order to find him. No one knew of his movements from day to day, or his exact timetable, not even Marcus Barrett. Should he call the APA? He decided to put the matter aside until he returned to London; he could talk to the BBC then.

Chase had only his dark green tote-bag containing his laptop and audio gear and memory sticks; his main luggage would transfer automatically to the transatlantic flight. He shouldered the bag and headed across the busy concourse to the four escalators which linked domestic flights with international departures. He still had the better part of two hours before the gate opened. He tried to recall where the VIP lounge was situated at Terminal Seven and couldn't – probably because he'd never used it before, he realised. Previous trips to the States had been self-financed, using budget airlines, not underwritten by generous supporters like Marcus Barrett. It made him nervous to think of the amount he had invested, and whether the series would justify his faith.

Gliding upwards on the escalator, Chase glanced across to a heavy, broad-chested man with cropped grey hair travelling towards him on the downwards escalator; he couldn't help staring as they drew level.

Good God! Was that an apparition, or the genuine article?

'Boris!' Chase shouted. 'Is that you? My God, it is you!'

The man visibly flinched, and then lowered his head as if trying to hide. On his face was a look of shock mingled with fright, but a second later the heavy grey eyebrows went up in surprised recognition. His mouth dropped open. Chase gestured downwards to the lower level.

'Wait there, Boris – I'll come back down!'

Chase gave a thumbs-up to make sure Boris Stanovnik understood. It appeared that he did, because he smiled.

2

Sturges had two options; he had yet to decide on the best method. Whichever one he chose depended on proximity to the target: the camera for a range of ten yards (though preferably five) or the glove for person-to-person contact.

But he needed to have sight of his target before he'd be able to decide the method.

And yes, there it was – the target: at a waist-high table drinking beer, speaking on his cell phone. There was no doubt in Sturges' mind that this was Gavin Chase. He'd hardly changed since Geneva. Chase was in conversation, a small, amused, lingering smile on his lips. He was murmuring into the phone rather than speaking curtly or off-handedly, so maybe, more than likely, it was the Detrick woman. Now and then the giant news screen on the far side of the concourse claimed the Englishman's attention, but only for a second or two.

With Chase so intent on the phone, this was the perfect moment to make his approach. Sturges worked his way circuitously, avoiding the target's line of sight. No need to hurry; that was against his instinct anyway. This close, the favoured method had to be bodily contact. He slipped his hand inside the black leather glove; the hypodermic syringe was already primed and set to go. As usual his emotions were frozen: this was simply a job that had to be done, clean and professional.

Ten paces away, his forefinger slid round the curved brace, thumb resting on the plunger. The rest was simple. Walk boldly up to the man, aim for the upper arm between elbow and tricep, press hard and deep, injecting the systolic fluid. Then walk away.

Chase finished the call and drained the bottle of beer and was off, striding across the concourse before Sturges had even a split second to react.

Amazing, how quickly someone could be lost in a crowd. Sturges knew this to be true – he relied on it himself – but now he was cursing it. But Chase was tall and stood out; that was all to the good, for Sturges soon spotted him, heading for the escalator. But there were many people in the way, and the best Sturges could manage was to join the line for the escalator. There were maybe a dozen others between him and the target.

Wait till we reach the top. There is time. He's in no hurry. And when I catch him up . . .

The plan was sensible, but it didn't turn out like that.

Instead, halfway up the escalator, the target called out to somebody going down – a broad, stocky figure with cropped grey hair – and the man's face assumed a haunted, fearful look, as if pursued by demons. The man was of no concern to Sturges; he was a piffling distraction. However, his plan was thwarted when Chase, instead of carrying straight on when he reached the top, immediately joined the downwards escalator, and in moments was sailing past a furious Sturges, who could only stare at the target across the gap.

3

'We had to leave.' Boris reached across the table for his wife's hand. 'It is, I am convinced, for the best.' Chase had to lean closer to hear in the crowded bar, a constant bustle of customers arriving and departing.

Nina smiled timidly and Chase guessed that because her English was poor she understood little of the conversation. But she seemed delighted that Boris had so quickly encountered a friendly face, in the very first few minutes of their arrival in America.

'Have you a place to go to?' Chase asked.

'Yes, I have friends at the Scripps Institution – but of course you know Theo Detrick's daughter. I tried to tell her in a letter, to explain, but I had to be careful. The FSB were most likely intercepting my foreign communications—'

'The FSB?'

'The Security Service of the Russian Federation. Another complicating factor, what you might call "a worm in the ointment".'

Chase suspected Boris was getting his English metaphors mixed up, but let it pass.

'The Hydro-Meteorological Service is in the charge of a man called Yuri Malankovitch. Would you believe, Gavin, he was once my lab assistant; now he's risen to become an oligarch of immense wealth. I've been prevented from publishing my research and it is my guess – no, my *conviction* – that Malankovitch and his advisors are behind this censorship. They have put pressure on academics and science editors to effectively ban my work.'

'Because it's commercially sensitive?' Chase asked, not clear about the motive.

'That might be one reason,' Boris conceded. 'But personally I think it is because my work on micro-biological species continued the research that Peter Astakhov was engaged on. He was the scientist—'

'I remember,' Chase said. 'The man I found nearly frozen to death on the ice. But wasn't Astakhov a marine chemist? He was studying carbon dioxide absorption in the southern ocean.'

'True. But our work overlapped in many respects. Between us, you and me, this is the reason my research is being blocked. The authorities and people like Malankovitch don't want the outside world to obtain such evidence. It might prove very useful in devising a programme of, what would you say . . . tampering . . .' he was fumbling for words '. . . manipulating the biosphere for one country's advantage over another.' Even though he spoke softly, his words lost in the buzz of voices in the bar, Boris couldn't help glancing nervously round.

'Is that what your government is planning to do with your work?' Chase asked. 'Because they're actively pursuing a strategy of climate control?'

'No . . . meaning I do not have personal knowledge of such a project. But what I do know is how the Russian state, and Malankovitch too, how they think. They see themselves as chess-masters. Before them they see the board. It is hateful to them not to know the position of every piece on the board, to know its value and have the power to move every piece at will. That is lifeblood to them – the power!'

Chase was sorely tempted. Should he add another piece to the conspiracy jigsaw by telling Boris what he and Cheryl suspected JEG Chemicals was cooking up? He checked the time. They had only minutes before Boris and Nina had to leave for their flight and he for his. Besides, this wasn't the place.

Boris went on gravely, 'It is difficult, I realise, for any sane person to understand how such minds function. Risking total calamity of the entire world in order to gain superiority, to hold the balance of power? It's futile to expect logic. At my age I thought I'd seen or imagined every kind of wickedness and stupidity. I actually believed that nothing could shock me ever again . . .' He shook his head wearily. 'But this, if it's what they are planning, is beyond reason, beyond humanity, beyond anything.'

Chase sipped his beer. He put the glass down carefully. He said, 'I wish you all the luck in the world, Boris, I really do. But don't expect to be welcomed with open arms here in the US. Cheryl has been fighting the same battle for years. Ever since her father died.'

Murdered would be the more appropriate word.

'I know Theo's warnings went unheeded,' Boris said, 'but I hope at least to be published here. The work will be known to fellow scientists. That is my one goal.'

Chase glanced again at his watch. Time was pressing. As briefly as he could he explained to Boris about his assignment for *Sentinel*. Any information the Russian wished to disclose, which wouldn't jeopardise his position, Chase was prepared to publish in the series of articles. Would Boris consider it carefully and, if he was agreeable, contact him in London? He handed Boris his card.

'Send the material direct if you think it's safe to do so. Of course I'll attribute anything I use to you in the published article, but if you prefer to remain anonymous, I'll respect that also. Your identity will remain secret. Will you think about it, please?' Chase found himself smiling.

'Yes, of course, and thank you so much,' Boris said, reaching across the table and pumping Chase's hand warmly. He had tears in his eyes.

'On the contrary, Boris. You're the one doing *me* the favour.'

He turned and smiled at Nina. 'Please tell your wife, Boris, that my deepest wish is for her to be happy in her new life. You too, of course, my friend.' Still smiling, Chase held out his hand to Nina, but she wasn't paying attention. Instead her eyes were fixed unblinkingly on the entrance to the bar.

In answer to the question her husband asked, she replied in a low, trembling voice that made Boris spin round in his chair. He turned back and grasped her by the wrist, his whisper harsh and urgent. Nina nodded, still not taking her eyes off the entrance.

Chase leaned towards them. 'What is it?'

Boris crouched over the table as if trying to make himself invisible. 'A man near the door has been watching us for several minutes now. Nina is afraid he is someone from the FSB or the Russian embassy. He has a camera, she says.'

When Chase looked cautiously towards the entrance he saw no one lurking there.

'How could state security have found out where you are? Through the group that helped you get away?'

'No, not possible,' Boris said. 'From Copenhagen we flew to London. We told no one we were coming to America. If someone in the group had talked, we would have been detained in London.' He reached for a blue Delta Airlines shoulder bag. 'We're booked on a flight to Los Angeles, leaving in two hours. We must get on board without being observed.'

'They can easily check the passenger lists of all outgoing flights,' Chase said, playing devil's advocate.

'We have false papers.'

'If they traced you to here from London, Boris, they'll already know the name you're travelling under.' No good glossing over reality, no matter how ugly it might be.

Boris slumped in his chair, clutching the shoulder bag. He said something in Russian under his breath, which could have been an oath of anger or an expression of defeat. Nina's face was a ravaged look of despair. It was as if she had just started to believe they were safe, starting life anew – and yet nothing had changed, they were still dodging shadows.

Chase wondered if she might have been mistaken. Understandably she was full of nerves. It was possible that her mind was playing tricks, even though her fear was real enough. Was there anything he could do to help? His mind roamed anxiously, trying to think of something. His own flight left in under an hour – and he had yet to pass through security at Terminal Seven and get to the gate.

'Is your flight nonstop?'

Boris didn't seem to understand.

'Is it direct to Los Angeles or does it put down somewhere en route?'

Boris examined the tickets. 'We fly to Atlanta and change planes,' he said, but still he looked mystified.

Chase leaned in. 'This is what you do. Take the flight as if you didn't suspect anything. When you reach Atlanta, miss your connecting flight. Instead find some alternative transport. Hire a car, or there might even be a train, though I doubt it. Make your own way to Los Angeles. You have some US dollars?'

'Yes, enough, I think. But why do we leave the flight in Atlanta?'

'If someone is following you, there's a chance it'll throw them off your track.' *A chance*, Chase thought, *a bloody slim chance at that*. But it was all he could come up with at short notice. 'It might fool them into believing Atlanta is your real destination and that you booked tickets to Los Angeles in order to confuse them. It's all you can do, Boris. It might work.'

The Russian nodded slowly. 'It's all we can do—' He sounded dazed, as if in a trance.

Chase gathered up his hand luggage. He was deeply upset to leave Boris and Nina in this predicament, but was bereft of any more ideas. Hanging around and missing his own flight would accomplish nothing.

At the entrance to the bar he turned and looked back. Husband and wife looked utterly despondent. Boris was hugging the blue shoulder bag as a lonely person holds on to a familiar object for comfort and protection. Beside him, Nina was small and sad and lost.

4

Flight D-049 to London was boarding at Terminal Seven, gate fourteen. Chase darted and dodged through the crowd on his way to the escalator. He had yet to pass through security and passport control – *fuck shit fuck shit fuck he wasn't going to make it* – into the international departures lounge. On the upwards escalator he was suddenly conscious of the people close to him. What would a Russian secret service agent look like? Or a Moscow mafia hitman? Chase was suddenly and keenly aware of men with cameras slung around their necks – and there were quite a few.

As the escalator carried him over the final curve and levelled out, two things were preying on his mind. First was the anguish at leaving Boris and Nina behind; the second, and even more urgent, was the necessity to take a leak, *now, this minute*. His bladder was about to burst.

Behind and below him, almost halfway up the escalator, Sturges instinctively pulled the soft black hat lower over his eyes, in case the target happened to glance back.

It felt like *déjà vu* to Sturges: following Gavin Chase up and down this fucking escalator was a never-ending repetitive nightmare.

It should have been over and done with by now, and Sturges should have been on his way back to California. The lethal camera dart had been a possibility in the bar while Chase was talking to the elderly couple – he was actually lining up the hit, except the constant stream of customers passing to and fro was too distracting. The precise moment never came; an opportunity lost. But Sturges had long experience and knew better than to let frustration meld into anger. Keep icily calm and emotionally detached. Hasty decisions led to mistakes.

He waited patiently for the escalator to take him over the last curve before levelling off. High above an illuminated sign in blazing red neon proclaimed INTERNATIONAL DEPARTURES – ALL TERMINALS.

He now had a view along the full length of the marble-floored mezzanine level, thronged with people. Given his height, the target should have been easily visible – but wasn't. Moving aside as people spilled off the escalator, Sturges covered all 360 degrees. *How could Chase have disappeared from sight in those few seconds? How was this possible?*

Again, not accepting the evidence of his own eyes, he performed a complete circular sweep, and it was only when his gaze swept past the sign on the wall for the third or fourth time that he registered what he ought to have seen the first time: the sign indicating the men's rest room.

Sturges immediately began his preparation. His left hand was ungloved. He carefully fitted his right hand inside the soft black leather, his forefinger snug in the curved brace, his thumb lightly on the plunger. It was important to shield the loaded glove from accidental contact, so he kept the glove close to his side, fingers pointing downwards.

With everything ready, Sturges crossed the floor and entered the rest room.

Chase shook the drops of water off his hands. He'd chosen the washbasin nearest the hot-air dryer so he could shuffle his tote-bag along between his feet. None of the other half-dozen men using the facilities looked like a thief, but you could never be too careful at airports.

Drying his hands, Chase looked himself over in the mirror, thinking those tired eyes were in need of eight hours' solid sleep. The men's room with its several mirrors afforded him a kaleidoscope of views and in one reflected image he glimpsed a young man with an Asiatic cast to his features and lank black hair to his shoulders. It was not so much his appearance that aroused Chase's suspicion as the furtive manner in which he was sidling up behind somebody drying their hands. Fascinated, Chase watched this performance in the mirror. The young man reached down, momentarily out of sight, and when he straightened up he was holding a dark green tote-bag in his fist, very similar, Chase thought, to his own dark green tote-bag – no, it wasn't very similar at all; it was the same. And glancing down, Chase saw that his tote-bag had gone.

The Asian kid was fast – so fast that he was nearly at the exit before Chase could even turn round.

'Somebody stop him, that kid, he's got my bag!' he yelled, but everyone just stood in frozen attitudes; no one was quick enough to hamper the Asian kid's flight as he reached the exit, free and unimpeded, when a big man in a grey suit wearing a black vinyl hat appeared, and going full pelt, the kid, despite his razor-sharp reflexes, had no chance to avoid him. With an instinctive gesture, the big man raised a gloved hand to take the brunt of the collision. Both of them staggered back at the impact, the kid falling against the tiled wall. He was young and fit and lithe and he recovered in a trice. Still clutching the tote-bag, he barged his way out and was gone.

Sturges was stunned for a second or two. He recovered instantly when he saw Chase moving towards him. There was panic and desperation in his expression as he tried to get past Sturges, heading for the exit. So the bag the kid was holding must have been the Englishman's, Sturges figured. He knew also that this was his one chance, and he took it.

His right arm came up and he aimed the black leather glove with its stiffened fingers at the target's shoulder, which might have appeared to an onlooker as nothing more than a defensive reaction. But something was amiss. With his thumb hard down, Sturges couldn't understand why the hypodermic wasn't responding. It was stuck. Had it jammed? *Why wasn't the fucking thing sliding home?*

Suddenly Sturges realised why: because the syringe had been discharged already. The vial was empty. The evidence was the tiny hole at the tip of the index finger of the glove, where the hollow needle had pierced the leather. The needle itself was gone.

Pushing frantically past the big oaf blocking the exit, Chase emerged from the rest room and saw the Asian kid straight off – he was on the escalator, already halfway down. The little bastard was employing the tote-bag as a weapon, swinging it back and forth to clear a path. Chase felt sick, in a nightmare of despair, because he knew that once the young Asian kid hit the main concourse, there wouldn't be a cat in hell's chance of catching him.

Nearly at the bottom of the escalator – a few more strides with the swinging tote-bag – and the Asian kid was certain of escape. Soon he'd vanish and be lost in the hurrying throng of people.

But in those last few strides something happened. The Asian kid made it onto the concourse all right, but he'd managed only three or four paces when his legs went rubbery, as if he were drunk. He stumbled over his own feet, his scuffed Nikes getting caught up, before his legs gave way altogether.

With a hollow clunk his head hit the marble floor and he slid forward on his face.

Chase's first priority when he got to him was not the Asian kid; it was the tote-bag, with its store of five weeks of interviews and background notes contained on his laptop and video devices. Chase tucked the tote-bag securely under one arm while he knelt over the motionless kid, who appeared to be out for the count. A small crowd had gathered. There was a flurry of activity among the bystanders and an airport security guard pushed through them. He wore a blue forage cap and his upper body was encased in a bullet-proof vest. Going down on one knee, he held a Glock semi-automatic, both arms fully extended.

'Don't move! Keep both your hands away from your body. Raise your hands!'

Chase was still panting from the headlong pursuit down the escalator. 'This guy's a thief, he stole my bag,' he started to say, his breathing ragged.

'Do what I tell ya! Now! Raise both hands!'

Two other guards, dressed the same, similarly equipped, arrived. They took up crouching positions alongside the first guard. There was something in the demeanour of all three that made Chase feel as if he were the guilty party.

'Move away from the guy on the ground. Leave the bag where it is.'

When Chase had obeyed, stepping back with his hands raised, the first security guard approached and knelt over the prone figure. From where Chase stood, he could see a smear of blood on the marble floor, most likely from the kid's nose when he cracked his skull and slid forward. The guard turned the body over, and Chase saw something else: the jagged stump of a hypodermic needle sticking out of the kid's left collarbone, right through his T-shirt. It was seeping pinkish fluid, spreading a stain.

The guard saw it too and turned round to look at Chase.

'Well, man, you made damn sure he wasn't going anywhere. You a dealer or what?' He pressed two fingers to the side of the Asian kid's neck, feeling for the carotid artery.

One of the other guards pointed his weapon at Chase's head from only a yard away.

'Down on your knees. I said *down.*'

'Wait one second. That wasn't me. I didn't do that.' The Asian's sallow complexion had turned grey, his lips tinged with blue. 'Is he—?'

'As a doornail,' the kneeling guard said. 'You did for him good.' He started speaking into the transceiver clipped to his bullet-proof vest. 'We have a Code Red. Suspected homicide in main transit concourse, Alpha-Zeta, foot of escalators.' He raised his eyes. 'Perpetrator apprehended—'

'You've got this all wrong. Listen, please – it wasn't me who did that.'

The other guard moved closer and put the barrel of the Glock to within an inch of Chase's right ear. 'Don't get your funny accent, bub. Makes me uncomfy. So shut-the-fuck-up.'

Chase did as he was told. He always did when someone was pointing a loaded gun at his head, which had never happened before.

This farcical situation had come about out of the blue, because he was bursting for a piss. It was going to take hours now to explain what was a very simple occurrence. Simple, that is, except for the remnant of a hypodermic needle protruding from the Asian kid's upper chest. Was the kid an addict? Had he impaled himself as he fell on his own hypodermic? But that didn't fit what Chase had witnessed. In fact the kid had staggered forward and collapsed *before* he hit the ground, and presumably before the needle penetrated his chest.

Chase said urgently, but in a low voice, 'There are several people up there who can vouch for what happened.' He pointed to the top of the escalator. 'My bag was stolen by this kid in the men's room. Everyone saw him run out, and saw me go after him—'

Chase looked upwards in the direction he was pointing and the words died on his lips. For a brief couple of seconds he glimpsed a big man in a black vinyl hat at the top of the escalator before the man stepped back smartly out of sight. It was the man at the door to the rest room, Chase was certain, who had collided with the Asian kid. A series of random and yet connected impressions frittered through his mind . . .

The Asian kid had encountered no one except the big man in the black vinyl hat. The big man had a camera slung around his neck. He was wearing a black leather glove which had been thrust, forcibly, Chase recalled, straight at him as Chase tried to exit the rest room.

A memory stirred – a memory from years ago he couldn't place – of chunky gold jewellery on a hairy wrist. The big man was wearing a heavy gold bracelet on his hairy wrist.

Chase stood mutely trying to make sense of all this while the curious crowd jostled forward and gawped at the little drama. He was still trying and failing to make the connections fit when a squad of security guards arrived and led him away at gunpoint.

7

I

It was a chamber of death's heads. Beamed straight down from recessed spotlights in the ceiling, the light bounced off the papers spread across the horseshoe-shaped table, with President Hernandez at its apex, and lit everyone from above and below.

Directly in front of the President, through a floor-to-ceiling glass wall, holographic displays hovered ghostlike in the middle of the darkened chamber. Beneath them sat controllers and military personnel at hooded consoles, while officers stood in the shadowy background in small groups.

Along the table to the President's left, General Deaver, one of the three Joint Chiefs present, said, 'Satellite photo reconnaissance confirms the intelligence picture, sir. Taken together, I should say we have a good probability rating, in the high seventies.'

'That still leaves a better than twenty per cent shortfall, General.'

'With all respect, sir, it can only be conclusive when the Russians actually implement the scheme,' General Stafford pointed out.

The President's famous vote-winning smile was absent today at this meeting ninety feet underground in the concrete, steel and lead-lined installation known as the Prime Situation Center. Connected to the White House by a two-mile tunnel that ran under the Potomac River, the PSC was located directly beneath Arlington National Cemetery. Another tunnel, also with an electric rail shuttle, linked it to the Pentagon, a mile to the east.

General Smith, the army chief, voiced the opinion that they were in danger of losing credibility. 'If somebody's going to act, it ought to be us,' he argued. 'Our countermeasures are more than adequate and at operational status. Isn't that so, Colonel Malden?'

Malden added, 'That's correct, General.'

'Christ, George, this isn't the old nuclear scenario of a preemptive strike,' said General Stafford. 'Nobody comes out of this one looking good and smelling sweet. We all go down the goddamn drain together!'

'Not necessarily all,' said Ralf Zadikov, seated on the President's left. The Secretary of Defense was a gaunt figure, pointed chin resting on clasped scarecrow hands.

General Stafford's lips tightened. Along the table several people shuffled papers and avoided one another's eyes. It was bad form to admit, or even mention, the existence of the sealed oxygen-enriched enclosures reserved for high-ranking politicians and military personnel. This was another key element in the Fut/COE master plan, thoughtfully provided by Malden and designed and built by JEG Construction.

To cover this lapse General Deaver said hurriedly, 'Can we see our deployment pattern on display, Colonel?'

As soon as Malden gave the order a brightly coloured azimuthal projection of the globe shimmered in the black air behind the glass. Missile sites were red; tankers in black against the blue ocean. Nine of the missiles and four of the tankers had the Greek letter β, beta, in silver in the centre of each symbol.

There was silence while everyone contemplated the pleasing design. Then General Smith said, 'What's our present state of readiness, Colonel?'

'Three hundred and ninety-five missiles payloaded with Tablet are targeted on key areas of jungle and rain forest on all continents outside North America. We have thirty-eight tankers of two hundred thousand to two hundred and fifty thousand tons capacity cargoed with Laptop constantly on the move in all major oceans. By the end of this year we will have fifty-two tankers. The missiles and tankers designated beta contain a new bacteriological herbicide that is much more powerful and effective than conventional chemical compounds. We're proceeding as fast as possible to make the conversion to all our missiles and tanker fleet.'

'Will this be enough to give us herbicidal overkill?' General Smith asked.

'Yes, sir.' Malden used the electronic indicator, a glowing white dot. 'As you'll have noted, the tankers are grouped in convoys and not scattered at random. These areas' – the white dot danced about – 'the equatorial Pacific, the North Atlantic, the Southern Ocean around Antarctica, and parts of the Indian Ocean near the Madagascar Basin are richest in phytoplankton and therefore contribute most of the global oxygen yield. We estimate that with our present fleet we can eliminate up to eighty-five per cent of marine plant life.'

'Then why upgrade the fleet at all if we already have that capability?' General Stafford wanted to know. As Air Force chief of staff he could see the need to deploy more missiles, but who the hell wanted more tankers? The defense budget was tight enough without wasteful and unnecessary expenditure.

Malden read the general's mind and had his answer ready. 'The time factor, sir. With more tankers we can speed up the process.'

'Why not more missiles and speed it up even more?'

'Because the forest and jungle targets are less important, General. They contribute only about thirty per cent of the oxygen in the atmosphere; the oceans are the major supplier.'

General Smith seemed mesmerised by the display floating in the darkened chamber. 'How long will it take?' he asked in a faraway voice.

'For elimination of marine plants we estimate six to nine months – with the existing fleet. When our tanker programme is complete we can reduce that to between three and six months. Also our new bacteriological herbicide will be far more efficient. These organisms are biologically alive as distinct from chemically dead, so they reproduce themselves and actually increase their effectiveness from the moment of dispersal. The longer they're in the water the more abundant they become.'

An army colonel down the wing of the table said, 'How soon before there's an appreciable drop in oxygen content?'

'We have no idea,' Malden said evenly.

'No idea?' General Deaver said. 'None at all?'

Malden shook his head, unperturbed by this admission. 'Scientific opinion is at variance. At one extreme it's thought that a reduction in atmospheric oxygen will be apparent within five years. At the other, twelve thousand. We simply don't know.'

'Can I amplify that?' Farrer put in, raising his hand like a schoolboy asking to leave the room. A civilian member of the scientific liaison team, he was here in the Prime Situation Center for precisely this purpose.

'I wish someone damn well would,' General Deaver said icily.

Farrer smiled diffidently. 'There are two factors that make an accurate forecast extremely difficult, if not impossible. The first is the sheer volume of the earth's atmosphere: fifty-seven hundred million million tons. The second factor is the complexity of the biosphere and the interaction of its various components: oceans, atmospheres, landmass, living organisms and so on. Interpretation of the figures, as Colonel Malden has explained, varies a great deal. Some forecasts have it that oxygen depletion will become noticeable in just a few years – maybe five, ten, twenty. Others say that were photosynthesis to cease altogether, less than one per cent of our present oxygen stock would be used up, in which case it would take many thousands of years.'

'It was my impression, Colonel,' said General Deaver, fixing Malden with a stony eye, 'that DELFI had provided us with an accurate prediction – isn't that so?'

'Correct, General, up to a point.'

'What . . . point?' General Deaver said ominously.

'DELFI extrapolates from data we already possess, not from hypothetical factors such as the implementation of Operation Download. Computer weather modelling is still an inexact science and is subject to the same constraints I mentioned a moment ago; that's to say, a lot depends on individual interpretation.'

'So where does this leave us in relation to the Russian threat?' General Smith demanded. 'Can anyone answer me that?'

'Where we've always been,' Malden said promptly. 'Holding the balance of power.'

'Explain that to me, Colonel.'

'Well, sir, the Russians have their Methane Gun Project, exploiting the release of gas plumes in the Arctic Circle, we have Download. Neither of us knows what the effects might be should these schemes be implemented; it's precisely this uncertainty that each side is seeking to exploit.'

'Dammit, Colonel Malden!' General Smith exploded. 'More than a year ago, you and – and—' He jabbed his finger.

'Farrer,' Malden supplied.

'You and Farrer stated with absolute certainty what the effects would be on the United States if Russia went ahead with their Methane Gun programme. Your report, as I distinctly recall, stated these specifics' – he ticked them off on his fingers – 'droughts, flooding of our major coastal cities and towns, widespread crop failures throughout the Midwest. Are you now saying that this isn't likely to happen?'

'Not at all, sir. Those effects were predicted as accurately as we know how. But as Farrer has made clear, the biosphere is an extremely complex mechanism. Neither we nor the Russians know precisely what might happen.' Malden smiled blandly. 'Just as no one could say with total certainty how nuclear warfare would affect the planet, General. The same applies to environmental war. It's a gamble.'

'Come on, George, we knew that all along,' General Stafford admonished his fellow chief of staff. 'Hell, if we dealt in copper-bottomed certainties we could hook up a computer and let it make all the decisions. As far as I'm concerned Colonel Malden has laid it on the line.'

'So we're back to stalemate,' said General Deaver with a heavy sigh. He looked directly at the President. 'Until the Russians decide to go ahead while we're still dithering.'

It seemed that the President hadn't heard – or chose to ignore – the criticism. He was watching the display, eyes half-closed. But then he said, 'When they make their move we'll be ready. Mr Zadikov assures me that Download is superior to the Russian threat. They know we can wipe out the biosphere any time we feel like it.'

2

Of late, Binch had begun to channel-surf the global news feeds on the fourteen screens in the Foundation's communications hub. Whenever a disturbing report came along he flagged it up and made a hard copy.

Overnight bulletins containing key words were automatically segregated and copied for his attention; this morning, as usual, there was a pile on his desk which he skimmed through before he did anything else. It had become a kind of ritual.

His secretary, Janis Swan, poured a cup of coffee, added the three regulation heaped spoonfuls of sugar, and placed it by his elbow. 'Is the world still in one piece?' she enquired laconically.

'Just about,' Binch muttered, distracted, intent on the reports.

BRAZIL, JULY 14, REUTERS — LONGEST DROUGHT IN LIVING MEMORY CONTINUES IN EXTREME SOUTH, WITH EXTENSIVE LOSSES TO SOYBEAN, CORN AND RICE PRODUCTION.

SEVERE FLOODING IN MINAS GERAIS AND RIO DE JANEIRO STATES IN SOUTHEAST, WITH ESTIMATED 6,000 HOMELESS AND MANY CROPS LOST. FLOODING IS REPORTED ALONG THE SÃO FRANCISCO VALLEY WHERE SEVERAL DAMS BURST, CONTRIBUTING TO HEIGHT OF FLOOD.

Drought in one part of the country, floods in another. Not unheard of, Binch thought, sipping his coffee, but happening on too regular a scale – which *was* unheard of. He picked up the next off the pile.

CHINA, JULY 13, REUTERS — DROUGHT FROM PREVIOUS SEASON CONTINUES TO AFFECT CROPS IN HEILONGJIANG, ANHWEI, ZHEUANG AND HUBEI PROVINCES.

WUHAN (CENTRAL CHINA) HAS RECEIVED ONLY 426 MM OF RAIN BETWEEN MARCH AND JUNE, THIS BEING THE LOWEST LEVELS SINCE RECORDS BEGAN IN 1880.

TORNADOES HIT PARTS OF ZHEUANG PROVINCE IN LATE JUNE DEPOSITING HAILSTONES ONE METRE DEEP IN PLACES.

'These really set you up for the day,' Janis said, leaning over his shoulder. 'Couldn't you just read the obituaries instead?'

'Haven't you got anything to do?' Binch grumbled at her.

'What exactly are you looking for?'

Binch slid another report in front of him, sighing. 'Wish I knew.'

13 JULY 71256 AP

BULLETIN: MOSCOW, RUSSIAN FEDERATION

FLOODS CAUSED BY HEAVY RAIN HAVE AFFECTED THE DON, SIM
AND OKA BASINS. WATER LEVELS HAVE RISEN 7–11 METRES AND
INUNDATED 270,000 HECTARES OF FARMLAND, THE REGION'S
WORST FLOODS IN 80 YEARS. DURING MID-JUNE 750 SQ KM
OF FOREST AND AGRICULTURAL LAND WERE UNDER WATER IN
THE KIEV OBLAST REGION.

THE PRIPET RIVER NEAR CHERNOBYL RAYON HAS NEVER
BEEN SO HIGH DURING 96 YEARS OF OBSERVATION.

FLOODING HAS ALSO BEEN REPORTED ALONG THE VOLGA AND
YENISEI RIVERS DUE TO THE MELTING OF THE SNOWPACK. THIS
IS THOUGHT TO BE RELATED TO AN EARLY START TO NAVIGATION
ON THE OB AND YENISEI RIVERS FOLLOWING LAST WINTER.

'Looks like the floods have it today,' Janis observed. 'Do you want
some more coffee?'

'No,' Binch said. 'Thanks.' He riffled through the rest of the pile,
his round face set in a pugnacious expression, as if the man in the
moon were scowling.

Poland . . . serious flooding . . . river Warta 1.5 metres above danger
level.

France . . . wettest spring and summer on record.

India . . . snow and hailstorms . . . 1500 people and 4000 cattle dead.

Indonesia . . . torrential rain brings floods . . . seventy people reported
killed by landslides.

Egypt . . . 500,000 people threatened . . . flooding of Upper Nile
Delta . . . potentially worst disaster ever.

It suddenly occurred to Binch that he was acting just as Brad Zittel
had: looking for signs of catastrophe and finding them – as of course
you would if you surveyed the world at large.

And it wasn't as if any of this hadn't been predicted. The gradual warming of the atmosphere had been known for a couple of centuries or more. Over the past hundred years it had been measured at around half a degree centigrade. All those billions of tons of carbon dioxide pouring into the atmosphere, plus the widespread use of CFCs – one molecule of which trapped 10,000 times more heat inside the 'greenhouse' than a molecule of CO_2. If the heating went on unchecked and global temperatures rose by a further two to three degrees, as was likely, conditions would revert to what they had been millions of years ago, long before the appearance of mankind.

And this, Binch thought, looking at the reports spread before him, was just what you'd expect to find: widespread flooding. Water expanded as it heated up. With the steady reduction of the polar icecaps releasing even more water, sea-levels would rise between eight inches and four-and-a-half feet, depending on melt-rate. An average increase of eight inches didn't sound much – until you realised that a rise of only one foot would erode the Gulf and Atlantic coastal areas, wiping out New Orleans, Atlantic City, New York and Boston. He'd seen one gloomy forecast that predicted a rise by the end of the twenty-first century of twenty-six feet . . .

If he was starting to think and act like Brad, he had good cause. It wasn't only these reports. A month ago Jeff Henshaw's updated climatic modelling programme for DELFI had revealed a new and disturbing trend. Based on data supplied by WIMP – the World Integrated Monitoring Programme – there was a small yet significant decrease in atmospheric oxygen, possibly within the next ten years.

At first Binch had been sceptical. After all, the predicted deficiency was only a couple of percentage points, 2.19 to be exact, well within the permitted margins of error. He'd noted the decline without becoming too alarmed by it. Computer weather modelling couldn't handle such minor fluctuations over short time periods. He couldn't take it seriously, and dismissed it.

Two weeks later, Jeff Henshaw was back with another set of figures. These took the projection beyond 2025. And what he'd found was nothing less than a nightmare.

Beyond 2025 the upwards curve went off the graph. In just over ten years further on – by 2036 – the oxygen content was in rapid decline, four per cent down. If that trend continued the decrease would plummet unchecked, dropping from today's level of around twenty per cent of breathable oxygen to just over ten per cent. Which meant that in twenty years from now, or less, the oxygen content of the atmosphere would be only about half of what it was today. Clearly, as Binch now realised, this couldn't be shrugged off as statistical error or a freak climatic anomaly. This was the best, most accurate data available; based on these reports, DELFI was predicting a significant alteration in the composition of the earth's atmosphere.

They weren't going to fry or drown after all; they were going to suffocate.

Binch pushed the stack of flood reports to one side. Did any of it support the prediction that the world was running out of oxygen? No; not directly at any rate. What would confirm it? That was the nub of the problem. He'd looked closely at the most recent figures on oxygen sampling, all of which had shown the oxygen content of the atmosphere to be perfectly stable. If the effect wasn't apparent now, was it really conceivable that within ten years there would be an actual, measurable decline?

Maybe DELFI had turned into GIGO after being fed spurious information. *Garbage In, Garbage Out*, as the computer jocks called it. But in his heart, Binch didn't really believe that to be the case, and for one very good reason: the change in Jeff Henshaw, from hardened cynic to a guy who walked around with a haunted look in his eye.

'Shall I file these?' Janis asked, gathering the press reports together. When Binch hardly glanced at her, she said, 'Why do you keep reading this stuff, Binch? No wonder you're so moody these days. It's enough to depress anybody.'

'If I didn't bother, who would?' Binch replied. 'Because somebody has to, for chrissakes!' He checked himself. Jesus, he was even starting to sound like Brad Zittel. Whatever had happened to poor Brad? Was he dead? A down-and-out bum somewhere? Drugged to the gills in a psycho ward? *Well now, old chum*, he cautioned himself, *take damn good care you don't go the same way. Snap out of it, man. Think positive!*

Binch chuckled gruffly at this hoary piece of shopworn advice, and Janis said, 'That's better. Just as long as you don't start talking to yourself.' She gave him a stern, meaningful look over her shoulder as she went out.

3

Later in the morning Ty Nolan from the satellite photo reconnaissance section came up to see him with a stash of twenty-by-fifteen-inch glossy prints taken by the geostationary Comsat above the Pacific, then transmitted to the receiving station at Temecula near the Mount Palomar Observatory in California. After being computer-enhanced the images had been sent on here by fibre-optic transfer. The service was as regular as a milk run and Binch didn't see every batch that came through; only now and then, when the photo recce section had a problem, which was the case today.

'It shows up here,' Ty Nolan said, pointing to an area south of the New Hebrides, 'and here, southwest of the Solomon Islands.' Ty was old-school and preferred the tactile nature of glossy prints to images on a screen. He pulled another image from the sheaf and placed his finger on the spot. 'Also here, see, near the Ellice Islands, longitude one hundred eighty degrees. It isn't cloud shadow or lens distortion. At least we're pretty sure it isn't.'

Binch held a print in either hand, peering at each in turn. 'What am I supposed to be looking at? I don't get it.'

Ty Nolan handed him a magnifying lens. Binch leaned closer.

'Fuzzy dark patches. Do you see them now?'

'Yes,' Binch said slowly. He reached for another print and examined it through the magnifier. 'What do you estimate their size to be?'

'The one near the Solomon Islands is roughly twenty miles by nine. The other two are slightly smaller. Though it's hard to be exact because the edges are blurred.'

'They're too big for fish shoals.'

'Plus the fact they don't move,' Ty Nolan said, delving into the file and laying three more prints on the desk. 'These were taken twenty-four hours earlier and the positions are identical.' He pushed his hand through straggly blond hair. 'We've all had a crack at it but nobody can figure out what it is. Or what they are, I should say. Then somebody suggested you.' He grinned.

'I'm flattered,' Binch said drily. *And none the wiser*, he thought. 'What about an infrared scan?'

'This Comsat doesn't have it.'

'What's the depth of the ocean hereabouts?'

'Pretty shallow, less than 3000 feet. It's the Melanesian area, bordered by the Coral Sea and the South Fiji Basin. Hell of a size, more than 4000 square miles.'

'Any eye-sightings to confirm these?'

'No reports so far, but then all three are some distance from land. And whatever they are, they could be below the surface and therefore not visible at sea level.' The young research analyst perched himself on the corner of the desk, his boyish face set in a perplexed frown. 'Any ideas, Binch?'

Binch stared at the prints scattered across the desk. Droughts. Floods. Fuzzy dark patches in the western Pacific. Were these the signs he was looking for? He was reluctant to think they might be – and almost as reluctant to believe that DELFI was wrong.

What if the human race had sown the wind and was about to reap the whirlwind? A whirlwind devoid of oxygen?

Dear God, what if DELFI was right?

4

Elaine Krantz came drowsily awake in the hot pressing darkness. For one horrific moment she thought she was suffocating.

By her side in the double bunk her husband, Jay, slept soundly, his faint snoring oddly muffled in the small airless cabin of the thirty-eight-foot fibreglass sloop *Seabird II*. After several weeks at sea she was accustomed to the sound and found it comforting.

Boy, it was stifling! The wind must have dropped altogether, she decided, moving her tanned legs from beneath the single sheet. There were times, even now, when she reckoned she must have been crazy to agree to the trip. Jay had called it their 'honeymoon adventure' – and adventure it was, all right. Tossed about in a plastic eggcup, drenched with spray, stung by wind, and baked crisp under a pitiless Pacific sun. Now that she'd endured her baptism at sea, though, she felt rather proud, and just that bit superior. Starting out by detesting the little craft, she'd come to love every inch of it, and endeavoured to keep the cabin and tiny galley as neat and shiny as if it were her first home.

From Fanning Island, almost on the equator, they had sailed to Pago Pago in the Samoan group, then Neiafu, Suva and Vila, island-hopping through the Fijis and New Hebrides. They were now on the last lap, having left Honiara three days before, with Malaita less than twenty-four hours away, given a good breeze.

Though there wasn't a whisper of air tonight, much less a decent breeze. And that was strange, Elaine thought, cocking her head – she couldn't even hear the familiar swish and gurgle of water against the hull.

Careful not to disturb her husband, she slipped down from the bunk and padded naked to the companionway, so sure of her bearings that she put her hand unerringly on the rope handrail in the pitch-blackness and hauled herself on deck.

The stench hit her in the stomach.

She caught her breath, gagged and screwed up her face as she fought back the nausea in her chest. In the next instant even this discomfort was forgotten as she looked around at what should have been a boundless expanse of ocean glittering in the moonlight. There was no ocean, only a solid dark unmoving mass as far as the horizon, absolutely still and silent. *Seabird II* was stuck in the middle of it like a fly in molasses.

Elaine yelled for her husband, filling her mouth and nostrils with the evil smell. As he stumbled onto the small square afterdeck Jay stubbed his toe and cursed; as with his wife's reaction, the expletive died the death, smothered in silence as he took his first foul breath and saw the motionless quagmire surrounding them.

Under the purple dome of the night sky the silence and stillness were eerie.

'It's some kind of weed,' Jay grunted, leaning over the stern and scooping up a soggy handful. 'Jesus, what a smell!'

'But where's it come from?' Elaine wanted to know. 'It goes on for ever.'

Jay squatted on his haunches, sun-bleached hair silvery in the moonlight. 'Could be dead kelp,' he said thoughtfully, 'just drifting along with the current. The Sargasso Sea is supposed to be like this, though I've never seen it.'

'That's in the Atlantic, isn't it?'

'There's nothing marked on the charts, no banks of weed. I'd have noticed it. And they didn't warn us about anything like this back at Honiara. Must have just . . . appeared, I guess.'

'Isn't there something stuck in it?' Elaine said, peering closer. 'Just under the surface – look-see, pale-coloured? There's more of them. They're everywhere!'

Jay unslung the gaff from its cradle. Swinging the 14-foot varnished pole around so that he was holding the business end with the brass hook attached to it, he leaned over the transom rail and jabbed at the scummy surface with the smooth wooden end. There was a hollow clunk. He jabbed again. This time it sounded tinny, like striking metal. A third time, the sharper sound of glass. More jabbing and probing, hitting plastic, glass, metal. Using the hook, Jay lifted out an empty two-gallon white plastic container. They could easily read the label in the moonlight. Gro-Fast Lawn Liquidiser.

Finally it dawned on them: *Seabird II* was in the middle of a floating garbage dump, extending mile after mile – maybe for hundreds of square miles, who knew?

. . . drinks bottles, dog food cans, milk containers, face-cream jars, tuna cans, medicine bottles, margarine tubs, salad-dressing bottles, diesel oil containers, beer cans, pickled beetroot jars, shampoo containers, ketchup bottles . . . millions, billions, maybe trillions of discarded items were embedded in a tangled mat of dead kelp, the result of squandering civilisation.

'What are we going to do?' Elaine asked, a slight tremor in her voice. Her old fear of the mysterious, unknown sea came back: the fear she thought had been conquered and left far behind. They were in the middle of nowhere, helpless and alone. The realisation made her shiver, in spite of the heat, and a spasm of dizziness swept over her.

'Elaine, what is it?' Jay was by her side, supporting her. He moved some equipment and helped her sit down.

'A bit faint, that's all.' She managed a weak smile. 'Phew! Thought I was going to pass out. There's no air. It's so oppressive.' Jay too, she noticed, was panting slightly, as if he couldn't quite catch his breath. What was happening to them? Her throat felt tight and small.

'It's probably the smell,' Jay said. 'All that rotting vegetation.' His bare body was running with sweat. He gazed around at the solid carpet stretching away on every side. 'We daren't risk the engine; the propeller would be fouled in seconds. I guess there's nothing we can do except wait until daylight. Maybe it'll have drifted on by then.'

'But if we're drifting with it . . .' Elaine said.

'Yeah, well, nothing for it, honey, but to wait and see.' He put his arm around her, but his skin felt clammy, like the physical manifestation of her own fear, and Elaine didn't feel at all comforted.

Jay found a grin to cheer her. 'Don't worry, it'll be okay. You'll see.' But when he tried to laugh it came out a hoarse choking sound, like the gasp of a dying man.

Oxygen Balance Sheet: Profit & Loss

Estimated population increase to 11.4 billion by year 2036 will mean greater consumption of oxygen and place additional strain on world resources.

Burning of fossil fuels in power plants, industrial and domestic furnaces, automobiles and aircraft consumes 20% of annual biological oxygen production and gives off excess of carbon dioxide.

Increase in carbon dioxide level in atmosphere leads to warming of biosphere.

Greenhouse effect warms polar regions and equatorial currents, creating conditions in which phytoplankton are unable to thrive, and gradually die out.

Burning and felling of world's major forests in South America, South-east Asia, Borneo and New Zealand reduces oxygen production and makes these areas net producers of carbon dioxide.

Waste industrial and domestic gases such as sulphur dioxide, carbon monoxide, nitrogen oxides and carbon dioxide pollute oxygen content of atmosphere.

Thermal pollution from hot industrial wastes and nuclear power plants raises temperature in rivers and oceans, reducing oxygen-carrying capacity of water and suffocating marine life.

Nitrogen and phosphate run-off from farm fertilisers creates eutrophication in lakes, rivers and oceans, leading to algae blooms which consume all available oxygen.

Domestic and industrial effluent consume oxygen in rivers and lakes, killing off marine animal and plant life.

OXYGEN DEPLETION

2025

I

It was a baking-hot Sunday morning, and still early April. The black stretch limo moved sedately along Old Dominion Drive and turned onto Hampton Hill Circle where it joined the procession of custom-built, armour-cased vehicles, none costing less than half-a-million dollars, waiting in line to enter the parking lot of the 2,600-seater church. The service of the 23rd Chapter of the Charmed Baptist Brethren in McLean, Virginia, a few miles northwest of Washington, DC, was more a political edict than social pleasure or religious obligation. Members of the Senate and Congress – both sides of the aisle – were in dutiful attendance. As were the shoals of sucker-fish that circled them, attended them, serviced and guided and fed off them: the corporate lawyers, think-tank gurus and high-pressure lobbying clans situated between 17th and 22nd on the capital's K Street.

But today there was an added attraction, for sure.

Pastor Eldritch.

He took the service perhaps three or four times a year, which always guaranteed a full house. On selected other occasions the Pastor was available to certain elite for personal consultation and private contemplation. The man was an inspiration to the high-powered congregation, many of whom came over from Georgetown for his sermon – and to be seen there of course, by their peers, superiors and rivals.

Reclining on a red-leather divan in the back of the black limo, wafted by the cool breeze of the air-con, Chesney Lea Poulton gazed through the blue-tinted windows, carefully checking out the people alighting from their chauffeured cars. There was a sprinkling of military here today, most in civvies, though he recognised the senior echelons. Many of them had confidential contracts with him; either they received a regular stipend from the organisation he headed – AAAV: the Alliance for the Advancement of American Values – or they had roles as 'technical advisors' to the public face of AAAV's media arm, BlackHawk Public Relations Operations Project, known to key Washington players as Black/PROP.

The real mystery to outsiders was where the AAAV's multi-billion-dollar annual budget came from; that and the reason it should lavish several million in donations to the Charmed Baptist Brethren here in McLean.

Chesney Poulton leaned forward on the divan. He'd spied a new face, fresh young meat, in uniform, an aide to a high-ranker. The guy was lean and blond, with a handsome profile.

He spoke into the intercom, his breath husky in his throat. 'Who's the single-bar lieutenant, three o'clock? Looks to be with General Bryant.'

Inside the driver's compartment behind the screen, the peaked cap swung to the right, broad jowls overhanging the crisp white collar and tailored uniform lapels. 'Nossir, don't recognise him. He's got ribbons up.'

'Make them out from here?'

'One of them's Cuba, I guess, could be. Red pennant, blue stripes.'

'I think you're right, Danny.'

So he'd seen active duty, young and fresh as he was. Maybe the kid had been with a garrison command, one of a score of prisons dotted around the island, which oversaw the incarceration gulag known as Cuba PDF – Prime Detention Facility. Chesney Poulton wasn't up to speed on the total prison population; the last figure he'd seen was getting on four million. He'd heard talk in the back corridors of the State Department that the building programme was being speeded up to handle the increasing flow of militants arrested for social order offences.

For just a few moments he indulged himself in the fantasy of lying beside the handsome blond lieutenant on the afterdeck of his motor vessel, their naked bodies stretched out under a balmy blue sky. The twenty-five-million-dollar MV *Icarus* was berthed at Roanoke Island, just off Cape Hatteras in North Carolina. Poulton took regular cruises into the coastal Atlantic, Bermuda being a favourite port of call, usually with a young male companion or two.

Minutes later he was out of the limo and straight into the pressurised airlock that connected the parking lot to the main entrance. Outside in these temperatures you'd be baked to a crisp in five minutes. The interior of the church was vast and cool and airy, smooth white curved shapes leading the eye up to the Rapture skylight set in the vast domed roof. Many of the 23rd Chapter's congregation were devout believers in the power and prophecy of the Rapture: that one day soon they would be summoned to ascend through the skylight to sit at the left hand of God. Poulton wasn't one of them; he was dismissive, indeed contemptuous of such infantile fancies. His belief was in transcendent states of OBE (Out of Body Experience) and Quantum Jumping; he was a devout disciple of Pastor Eldritch.

A string quartet was playing Haydn as Poulton made his way down the central aisle to his numbered place. He met glances, nods and smiles from all sides, mostly from the men, a few more discreetly from their wives. He could have his pick of these women, if he chose, had he been interested. His physical presence was attractive to the opposite sex, tall and barrel-chested, with a tsunami-wave of chestnut-brown hair (the result of several hundred hours' of painful grafts and implants) matched by a heavy moustache (genuine) of the same chestnut-brown hue (out of the same bottle), as straight and neat as if trimmed by laser.

As Poulton reached his place his wristband vibrated and he touched the dial-screen. It was a message from Burt Mueller, his chief of staff, telling him of yet another leak from a clandestine group which called itself Midnite-Net. Poulton hated these anarchist-pinko rat-finks so bad he could taste it like retched-up bile. Whoever they were, they'd been plaguing AAAV for more than two years now; they'd blown sensitive research and development data on a major American corporation, JEG International, revealing a secret project they were involved in with the Pentagon.

It was worse for Chesney Poulton because he was a friend – a *very* old friend – of Joe Gelstrom, founder and CEO of the company, and Joe had made his displeasure known in spades.

'How bad is it on a ten?' Poulton asked.

'Pretty bad. Maybe a seven or eight.'

'Sheeee-it,' Poulton said softly. 'Tell me.'

'It concerns the environmental activists killed or vanished – their terminology is "disappeared" – in recent years. Somehow they've got hold of the numbers.'

'Huh? What are we talking about here – thirty or forty of these nut-jobs? They could've just died of natural hazards – bitten by snakes or caught malaria or eaten by piranhas in the Amazon. It's dangerous, for fuckin' chrissakes, out there in the jungle—'

'It's more than seven hundred,' Mueller cut in.

There was a pause. 'Seven *hundred*?'

'Point of fact, nearer eight hundred, Chief. In six, seven different countries.'

'Uh-*huh* . . .' Poulton needed a moment to link up his thoughts. 'They're not all ours, are they, Burt? We didn't dispose of that many?'

'I guess around half. The rest were mining corporations, landowners, banking—'

'You're not telling me JEG Corp was involved or implicated! Are they named?'

'Negative, sir. On both counts.'

'Okay, okay . . .' Poulton eased off a little. Did he need one of his little yellow calming-down pills? Maybe not right this minute. 'Do what you have to, Burt. I've got to get my hands on these fink bastards and put them away for good.'

'Yes, sir. Er – just one more item.'

Poulton waited, breathing heavily.

'There's an interview going out live on TV as we speak.' Poulton could hear voices behind Burt Mueller. 'It's with an individual called Bill Inchcape from Boulder, Colorado. He's a climate scientist we've monitored and got on file. I think you should see it.'

'Somebody else who's crapped and won't get off the pot?'

'I'll record it, sir, and remind you later.'

Chesney Poulton broke off the connection, his mood and the morning shot to hell.

2

'Here in our Baltimore studio,' the *Newsline* anchor was saying, 'we are very privileged to have the distinguished emeritus professor from Sefton Metropolitan University, Professor Martin C. Stringer. Martin is a regular guest on the programme, and a popular expert with our viewing audience. And we're also pleased to welcome Dr William Inchcape, senior technical advisor to the National Climate Prediction Foundation, who joins us from his department in Boulder, Colorado. How're things doin' out there, doc? Any severe weather events to report?'

The jaunty presentational style should have warned Binch from the start what to expect. He hated taking part in these interviews – he didn't like speaking in public at all. But he felt a crippling responsibility, a millstone of obligation to report on the latest projections DELFI was forecasting from climate data received on a daily, almost hourly, basis.

The TV monitor directly in front of Binch had a split screen so he could see the other guests sitting in a semi-circle around the host. That half of the screen had a close-up of Martin Stringer, his elaborate dyed comb-over failing to hide his scalp, pink as a baby's smacked bottom. Binch was calm and in control. Knowing he was on camera and they might cut to him at any moment, the scientist repressed any violent facial expression. But he smelled a big fat dirty rat. The researcher had briefed him on who was taking part but had failed to mention Stringer. Was that deliberate or an oversight? What was this, an ambush? Binch had a pretty good guess now what the agenda was, and how the debate would be framed; it was too late to pull out.

After introducing the two other participants, one of them a journalist with a news bureau, the other a freelance technology correspondent, the anchor focused the dazzling glare of his charisma at the camera.

'Controversy seems to be the watchword for climate alarmists. But are we being sold a fake bill of goods by the so-called experts? Bottom line, folks: are these real hard facts we're being fed, or is the motive more underhand and sinister? Not to mince words: scaremongering propaganda to boost tax-dollar spending on "environmental" research?'

He didn't actually qualify 'environmental' with *spurious* or *bogus*, but his intonation left no doubt what he thought; even a sceptical raised eyebrow or sly wink at the camera couldn't have made it more blatantly obvious.

Binch felt a tremendous weariness stealing over him. At fifty-nine he still had to undergo these glib journalistic clichés and threadbare arguments – and for what reward? So he could put himself front and centre in order to get knocked down time after time? And sticking his neck out wasn't the smartest move he could ever make. His bosses at the NCPF – his immediate superior, Si Musso, in particular – took a dim view of one of their most senior physicists appearing in television debates, though Binch was past caring what rattled their cages.

'. . . not that I doubt their sincerity – after all, the best of us can be misled and misguided – it's their loyalty to our way of life, to our American ethos, I have a problem with.'

Binch had missed the first part of Martin Stringer's response because he was inwardly seething. Stella was always cautioning him about his blood pressure; with great effort, and his wife's help, he'd managed to quit smoking, but his weight was still a problem and that and the constant stress didn't help.

'Is it a factor you consider or take into account, Dr Inchcape?' the anchorman asked.

'Is what a factor?'

'Well, uh, your loyalty, your patriotism I guess you could call it.'

'I don't see where you're going with this,' Binch said, sounding and looking puzzled. 'I'm a scientist. My job is to collect and collate as much global climate data as I possibly can. At NCPF we have the most advanced computer modelling programme anywhere in the world. Its forecasts and predictions have been proved accurate again and again. DELFI tells us that within five years – certainly within ten, by 2035 – there will be climate breakdown on a cataclysmic scale. How in tarnation did we get into loyalty and patriotism?'

On the split screen Binch saw Martin Stringer lean forward, his pink dome gleaming through the carefully arranged strands.

'But that's a genuine concern for the hard-working taxpayers of this country, Dr Inchcape. The ones who fund your programme and pay your salary. How can they be reassured you're not creating scare stories and sensational headlines simply to boost your funding instead of sticking to hard facts?'

'So what are you accusing me of, exactly? Lying? Making things up?'

'No one is accusing you of anything, Dr Inchcape,' said Professor Stringer smoothly. 'These are legitimate questions the public has a right to ask. No call to get upset or work yourself into a lather. We can have an intelligent, adult discourse I hope, without any dramatics or inflammatory language.'

'Yeah, sure we can,' Binch agreed amicably. With an effort he steadied his breathing and unclenched his fists. 'You're retired but still under tenure at Sefton, am I right, Professor?'

'Yes, that is correct. And still lecturing, for my sins.' Stringer allowed himself a fleeting, modest smile. 'Two or three keynote lectures a year.'

Binch knew all this. He and Martin Stringer had a lively, chequered history of combative debate, both on TV and public platforms for the past decade or so. Stringer had a much higher media profile, of course, appearing on late-night discussion shows and writing opinion pieces for national magazines. He'd been a guest at the White House on numerous occasions.

'Curse this memory of mine,' Binch said, 'but it's slipped my mind for the minute. What is it you lecture on, Professor?'

Stringer blinked rapidly. 'Excuse me?'

'Your subject. What is it?'

'Well, naturally, it isn't your field of atmospheric physics, if that's what you're getting at.' Stringer had spotted the booby-trap and was sidling cautiously round it.

'If not that, then . . . which scientific field is it?' Binch persisted.

'Political ethics and comparative religion,' Stringer said testily, 'although the fact I'm not a scientist in your sense doesn't invalidate my concern or my views—'

'You're not a scientist in my sense, or *any* sense, Professor Stringer. You don't see the raw data I have to deal with every day. You don't analyse or interpret these information streams, you wouldn't know how to or where to begin.' Binch reached forward and plucked a sheet from the pile on his desk. It was one of twenty or thirty he could have chosen. He held it up to the camera. 'This is one item of today's input, came in at 9.45 a.m. Weather station in southwest Australia reports: temperature maximums of 54°C over a *continuous period of twenty-four days*, which has broken every record in the book—'

'Whoa, hold on, I'm gonna cut in here for a second!' the anchor said, holding up both hands but with a placatory smile. 'Let's not go over the top with some geeky science lesson. Folks at home want to be informed *and* entertained, not bored out of their skulls. And hey'– he looked round the semi-circle of guests, chin on his chest with a *what-the-fuck-is-this-shit?* expression – 'meaning no disrespect, but let's get real here. Australia's a long way away. In the southern hemisphere if I'm not mistaken.'

Binch said, 'If you want plenty more like that relating to the US, I've got 'em.'

'No, don't believe we do,' the anchor said quickly, turning to the freelance journalist. 'Al Nemeth, you cover a wide range of science topics. What's your take on this?'

'If you want a realistic down-to-earth view, the first thing you have to understand is that there always have been extreme climate events. Nothing new there. The history of the planet is one endless roll-call of temperature variants from heatwaves to ice ages. Floods, earthquakes, typhoons, droughts, you name it. Question is, are these events any more extreme than all the stuff that's gone before.'

'And are they?' the anchor asked.

'Jury's still out on that, I guess. Mainly a matter of interpretation.'

Stringer jumped in. 'And more importantly, *who* is doing the interpretation – that's the crucial point. This is where Dr Inchcape and I part company, I suspect. Bombarding the public continually, day in, day out, with dubious stories of freak weather events and natural disasters, usually thousands of miles away on the other side of the world, is not helpful or productive. These are scare tactics aimed at spreading alarm and fear and uncertainty' – his finger was jabbing at the camera – 'in fact this whole campaign undermines us as a nation, sapping our faith, trust and morale . . .'

Jesus wept, Binch thought, *any second now he's going to snap to attention, hand on heart, and start singing the Star-Spangled Banner.*

'. . . we each of us have a duty to behave responsibly. As scientists and academics we must think of our fellow citizens and provide guidance . . .'

On the edge of his seat now, Binch was trying to interrupt this flow of populist windbaggery, but it sounded like his mike was turned off. On the monitor screen he could see himself mouthing emptily and idiotically like a gasping fish. He'd known the debate would be skewed and spun to fit a certain agenda; it always was. But this was worse: this was personal. This was a vindictive attack on his professional competence and integrity.

All he could do, chest tight, was listen to Professor Stringer in full flight, spewing out garbage with no one to stop him.

'. . . feeding the American public false or misleading information could be seen as an act of treason against the state. It's as dangerous as the dissemination of communist propaganda in the forties and fifties. It seeps like poison into the bloodstream of the nation. It saps our moral fibre and corrupts our sense of right and wrong. There were sound reasons why the bill to enact the UnPatriot Act, now passing through Congress, was greeted unanimously, with no abstentions.'

'"Treason" is a pretty strong word, Professor . . .' The anchor inclined his neck and touched his earpiece as if straining to listen. 'Glitch?' he said, frowning, and turned to the camera. 'Apologies, folks. We were hoping to get a reaction from Dr Inchcape but it appears we've lost the audio connection to Boulder, Colorado; sorry about that.'

Binch subsided in his chair, head resting against the padded support. His throat was dry and rasping as sandpaper and he could feel himself trembling. The image of him on the split screen had been replaced, he saw with relief, by a long shot of the group in the studio. If Stella was watching, and she probably was, and happened to have glimpsed the state he was in, there would have been hell to pay. Pray God she hadn't. Her warning still chimed in his ear—

And remember, don't let them bait you, just say your piece and leave it at that. Above everything, Binch, please don't get riled up, not with your blood pressure. I'd much sooner be in my own bed at two a.m. than a hospital waiting room.

On the screen, Professor Stringer was again in finger-jabbing mode. His emphatic, cocksure, high-pitched voice was issuing through the speaker, though Binch wasn't taking in any of the words. He was instead thinking of the one word Stringer had used, quite deliberately.

The word had been "treason".

For *treason* to take place required a perpetrator.

And to commit *treason* meant you were a *traitor*.

3

The cool amphitheatre interior of the 23rd Chapter of the Charmed Baptist Brethren was soothing to the spirit. At the still centre of this everlasting peace and quiet was the figure which seemed to draw out from the assembly and focus its life force, as a prism concentrates the sun's energy.

Pastor Eldritch.

His was an imposing but also a disturbing presence; he was only a couple of inches over six feet, so it wasn't his height that transfixed the attention, but his raw-boned gauntness, as if the stark musculature and bony planes of his skull were on display like those of a medical specimen. His face had the wind-blasted look and deep-etched crevices of an old-time Western hero, a deep-hued red the colour of sandstone. From the sleeves of his black robe his skeletal hands protruded, long splayed fingers twitching with nervous intensity.

Standing thus, tall and impressive, it was impossible to discern that any movement he made was restricted to a shambling, lurching parody of a walk, almost crab-like, due to a shattered left leg, injured in a fall and never regained strength or flexibility.

Arms raised towards the assembly, he intoned, 'Give me your faith, give me your belief, give me your trust, and I will take you on a journey to the sacred zone of inner consciousness . . .'

The voice wasn't charged with hellfire and brimstone and Bible-Belt ranting; it was soft and sibilant. Amplified and relayed by hidden speakers, the soft voice seemed to fill every corner and crook and cranny of the space like a cosmic whisper.

'. . . where everything is possible and permissible for the chosen ones among you. There we will rise, you and I, up above and leave behind this earthbound realm and come to a place where our dreams and desires are fulfilled and made real by the greatest force in the universe.'

Pastor Eldritch paused. His arms were raised higher, embracing the heavens. *The Power of Mind*. Will you come with me and enter the sacred zone?'

There were murmurs of assent from the congregation. Pastor Eldritch now spread his arms wide, palms uppermost, in a gesture of welcome and blessing. His head fell back and his eyes gazed up to the high dome above. There was an audible gasp from the assembly – almost a shudder of ecstasy mingled with revulsion – as the Pastor's eyeballs deep within their sockets rolled upwards to reveal spheres of pure white.

It was brilliantly done, and genuinely chilling; as a piece of theatre for the naïve and the gullible it couldn't be faulted. Next on the bill came an even more dramatic performance. In the front rows of the assembly were twenty young men soberly dressed in black suits and button-down black shirts, known collectively as MOG – 'Messengers of God'. These were the close disciples of the Pastor, chosen for their single-minded devotion and loyalty to be his personal entourage and security guard. Now they were called forward to perform what was known to the 23rd Chapter of the Charmed Baptist Brethren as 'the ritual of sublime ascendancy' or 'Pillar of Fire'.

One in particular caught Poulton's eye: a tall slender young man with blond hair that was almost white, like the others, shorn close in a buzz-cut. A chat afterwards with coffee and cake might be arranged.

Moving robotically, the group of disciples formed a circle, facing inwards, making up a solid wall. At a signal from the Pastor they raised one arm in the manner of a salute, pointing at an angle towards the oval skylight high up in the domed ceiling. The Pastor stood before the congregation and raised both his arms. He brought his palms smartly together above his head and at the sound of the sharp slap of flesh striking flesh there was a sudden *whoosh* and a blinding flash of light. The effect was shocking and mesmerising. Above the circle of bodies there appeared a column of fire, fed by tongues of flame from the outstretched arms.

Members of the assembly shielded their eyes from the intense brightness and those nearest the spectacle felt the prickle of heat on their faces.

It lasted perhaps five seconds, the rush of incandescence with a shimmering outer halo of blue surging upwards. Then it was gone, leaving behind the acrid taste and smell of scorched air. For several moments there was total silence – followed at last by a long drawn-out sigh as the congregation regained its breath and the tension was released.

Even though Chesney Poulton had witnessed the sublime ascendancy before, the visceral impact never lost its power to shock. First-timers were known to have fainted.

The effect was simply achieved: small cylinders of propane were strapped in a harness under the Messengers' black suits. A flexible tube inside the sleeve led to a nozzle attached to a pressure jet held in the palm of the raised hand, manipulated and directed by thumb and forefinger. An electric spark from a concealed lighter ignited the pressurised gas—

And *whoosh!* The result was spectacular.

The Pastor's public performance, as he told Poulton, relied on the visual rather than oratory; it was his belief that images had the greater impact. Although he relied on what was basically a cheap gimmick to impress the crowd (does no harm and they enjoy the show, he assured Poulton) Pastor Eldritch was utterly sincere when it came to his belief in the *Power of Mind* and altered states of consciousness: Out of Body Experiences (OBEs) and Quantum Jumping were his core beliefs.

Poulton too was a devout believer. With the Pastor's guidance he had achieved an OBE on several occasions. In this state it was possible to transcend the mundane physical world, passing through the portal into the realm of higher consciousness. Here there were fewer constraints and greater freedoms than in the physical world; here Chesney Poulton inhabited a probable future he was able to influence and change by his will and his desire.

Now the MOG had returned to their places and there was an air almost of anti-climax among the hushed assembly. Poulton was anxious for it to be over; he was still bothered by Burt Mueller's call and he wished to consult with the Pastor and ask his advice. When certain individuals and groups (environmental activists and climate scientists, for instance) became a nuisance and got in the way of progress, there were several options for dealing with them. One was to enlist the Messengers of God – with the Pastor's permission – to enact 'the ritual of sublime ascendancy', in its secondary meaning, on the selected target. This meant that the person or group achieved 'ascendant status' – vanishing upwards into the stratosphere or downwards into the bowels of the earth – it didn't really matter which, so long as they ceased any longer to be a nuisance.

Chesney Poulton hoped that Pastor Eldritch would give his blessing to solving his latest problem.

4

Binch didn't see or hear the white panel truck closing rapidly until it was suddenly abreast of him and edging towards his side of the two-way blacktop.

His thoughts had been anywhere but on his driving. It was a few minutes after five. The day was clear and fine and he should have seen the truck coming – no reason not to, except he was quietly and monotonously cursing Stringer while gripping the wheel as if to throttle it. Then it was right there alongside and drifting over, the truck's tailgate a few inches from the Dodge pickup's hood.

With nowhere else to go, the pickup was being forced off the hardtop towards the edge of the rainwater gully, its nearside wheels gouging through the sandy gravel. Binch stamped on the brake but he hadn't reacted fast enough; there was a thud and a grinding noise, the impact powerful enough to sheer off the pickup's side-mirror, which fell to the road in pieces. Moments later he felt the pickup tipping as it sloughed side-on into the gully. He was flung with crushing force against his seatbelt, knocking the wind out of him, then rebounding back against the seat as the pickup finally ground to a halt.

In a daze, gasping for breath, Binch couldn't tell if he was hurt or not. His chest felt tight and his heart was pounding as if about to burst.

He closed his eyes and made an effort to breathe deeply and evenly. With luck he might not be injured, just shook up, but he was going to need hospital treatment all the same.

He wiped spittle and snot from his chin and craned his neck to look up at the highway from his slanted position. The truck had gone. Who the hell was that maniac? That hadn't been just reckless driving or some hopped-up kid; it could have almost been deliberate. The crazy notion that it had something to do with the TV broadcast popped into his head and he couldn't shake it. The left side of the hood, he could see, was crumpled, raw metal sticking up from where the side-mirror had been. Binch went into a cold sweat at how close he'd come to being killed.

Damn and blast it, it looked like Stella's woeful warning about spending the early hours of the night in a hospital waiting room was going to come true after all.

5

His gnarled left hand on the deadman's handle, Eddie Barton leaned forward in the bucket seat and stared through his wraparound shades at the glinting shapes directly ahead. Across the cab's wide double windows, the green concertina blinds were pulled low to ward off the hammering rays of the sun. Eddie squinted hard. What in fartin' 'ellfire could that be? Something on the tracks? It was something shiny, gleaming in the hard, direct light, so not an animal . . . then what?

Sticking to the rule-book, especially when faced by the unknown, Eddie gently applied the vacuum brakes of the massive 750-ton diesel-electric engine. This wasn't an operation taken lightly with a train that was half a mile long. And as well as freight there were people on board too: between Eddie in the locomotive cab and Eric Salt in the guards van were fifty-four container flatbeds, boxcars, fuel tankers, granite hoppers – plus three passenger coaches, including a wedding party and twelve members of a school choir: so forty-seven people in all.

In times long gone it had been known as the Tea and Sugar Train, bringing necessities to the isolated farmsteads and cattle stations of the vast and desolate Nullarbor Plain in the great outback of Southern

Australia. Starting out in Port Augusta, it took three days travelling due west to reach Kalgoorlie, 1,050 miles away. Its central section, passing through Tarcoola, Watson, Hughes, Reid, Loongana – flyblown specks between the endless flatlands of fine red dust, sparsely covered with acacia trees and dry bush – was the longest stretch of straight railway track in the world: 310 miles, like a pencil line drawn on a map. In a good year the average rainfall across this region of 100,000 square miles was six inches; but they hadn't had a good one for the past ten years; the average now was a perfect zero.

In the air-conditioned cab, Eddie Barton had a sweat on. The train took nearly a mile to stop, and he had a gut feeling of slowly mounting panic when he realised they might not achieve it in time. The cab was starting to roll, then it began jolting more violently, with thudding noises coming from underneath. Eddie was an experienced driver and knew always to expect the unexpected, but this had never happened before in his nine years on the Nullarbor run. Peering ahead, he got the shock of his life. The gleaming shapes he'd seen from a distance were the solid steel rails themselves; but instead of running straight and level to the far horizon, they were buckled and twisted out of true like liquorice sticks melted in the sun—

Instinctively he glanced up at the gauge on the cab bulkhead, which showed the outside temperature: 52° C. Eddie's brain did the automatic calculation into old money: 126°F.

But even before he could take in this astonishing fact, the engine lurched to the left as if jumping a gap and an almighty screeching of metal against metal set up a deafening clangour that made the fillings in his teeth ache.

The train shuddered three times more and came to a dead stop.

A second later the rear door to the cab opened and the engineer Harry Rourke stood there blinking sleep from his eyes. He'd been in the crew berth behind the kitchen alcove getting forty winks. He rubbed his hand over his grey stubbled cranium and stared out of the wide double windows before meeting Eddie's blank gaze and mouthing, *WHAT IN HOLY FUCK?*

Both railwaymen knew what had to be done, and braced themselves:

it was like opening the door of an oven. Harry Rourke climbed down first, hands encased in heavy gauntlets as protection against the scorching grab-rails. Eddie followed, and as soon as their feet hit the track-bed both men were heaving for breath.

It wasn't just the tremendous oppressive heat, more like having your chest compressed by a huge boulder – as if all the oxygen had been sucked out of the atmosphere.

On his haunches, half-blinded by sweat, Harry inspected the buckled rails. The leading bogie-wheel assembly had slid clean off the track and ploughed up to its axles in the heaped granite ballast. It was damn near a miracle the engine and leading cars hadn't keeled over and toppled down the embankment – anything more than the four m.p.h. they'd been travelling at would have been enough. Driver Eddie Barton's prompt action had saved them after all.

'What d'ya – what d'ya reckon – caused this—?' Eddie was gulping in air between the words. His head felt swimmy. 'Earth tremor maybe?' – gasp – 'disturbance down—' He ran out of breath and jabbed his finger at the ground.

For an answer the kneeling engineer pointed to a foot-long iguana, spread out flat on the buckled rail, sizzling and charring nicely as if on a barbecue.

'Just the heat – alone – did it – you mean?' Eddie said.

Harry looked up at him, sweat running off his nose. '*Just* the heat?'

Median temperatures in South Australia hadn't fallen below 50° C in more than five continuous weeks; of course it was *just* the heat.

The engineer climbed slowly to his feet and leaned closer to Eddie as if the proximity would make up for his lack of breath. 'Get on the blower – now – to Spencer Junction – shit my Aunt Mary, Ed – we're fuckin' – trapped out here!'

As the driver turned back to the engine ladder he was stopped dead by the piercing scream of a child: a girl of nine or ten, one of the school choir group, had touched the blistering-hot guard-rail while being helped down from the passenger car; she'd no doubt burned the flesh clean off. Eddie stumbled forward but could manage only a few steps, feebly raising his hand as a warning, but other people were climbing down out onto the track and yelling in agony as their own fingers touched the guardrails.

What were these idiots doing?

A woman was clutching her throat. 'Can't breathe – inside the train – no air—'

'Worse out here—' Harry Rourke shouted back. 'No air – plus the *heat* – get back inside!'

More desperate people had disembarked and spilled out onto the track. Some were kneeling or on all fours in a state of collapse as not only the unbearable heat but the low oxygen count sapped their energy. The engineer turned to look despairingly at Eddie Barton, but Eddie was in no great shape himself, bent forward with chest heaving, both gloved hands on his knees. *This is a total shit cock-up mess*, Harry thought. They needed help urgently, immediately, and the rescue team base was the rail depot at Spencer Junction in Port Augusta, the better part of five hundred miles away. Harry looked around at the boundless sandstone and scrub. There was no feasible spot for a plane to land out here, and how long would it take a fleet of helicopters to be scrambled and reach them? A few moments ago he'd told Eddie they were trapped.

And that was the God's own brutal truth.

6

He'd been at his desk less than five minutes when his section supervisor passed by his workstation and spoke to him over the barrier. Howard, who was still eating his bagel and sipping a double latte, swallowed and dabbed at his lips with a napkin.

'You nearly done there, Nevison?'

'Yes, sir.'

'You've been summoned by the high and mighty, fifth floor, soon as. Don't stop by the men's room on your way up. Someone will be waiting for you at exec reception.'

'Should I take something with me—? What I mean is do I need anything?'

'Yep! – your brain. Might come in handy.'

'If I can remember where I left it.' The response fell flat. His supervisor's heavy-lidded eyes gazed at him without warmth. Joe Quarles had never taken to Howard since the day he was seconded to AAAV from the research unit at Black/PROP, and with the best will in the world, Howard couldn't stand to breathe the same air as Joe Quarles. What was his problem? The fact that section supervisor was the highest up the slippery vine he was ever going to get? Or that fresh-faced Howard Nevison, twenty-five years his junior, had been fast-tracked to senior intelligence analyst even though he was still wet behind the ears? And – sin of sins – he had never been out in the field.

'Yuh, well,' Joe Quarles said, 'good luck with that.'

Howard hesitated. 'Any idea what it's about?' He left off the 'sir' and it hung in the void, conspicuous by its absence.

Joe Quarles did a swift stealthy glance left and right. 'Could be that CLP wants to shaft that soft white ass of yours over his big desk. That'd be another sure-fire promotion for you, Nevison. Or you could get down on your knees. He's very partial to mouth pussy, I hear.'

Howard nodded, as if considering. 'I'll pass your thoughts along to the director-in-chief personally. I'm told he likes his subordinates well-briefed. Thank you.' Cheesy grin. 'Sir.'

Going up to the fifth floor in the elevator, staring at his blurred silvery reflection in the brushed aluminium doors, Howard Nevison was cursing himself. For the sake of a clever-dick remark he'd only succeeded in riling his immediate boss, which wasn't a smart thing to do; payback time would come around sooner or later.

Howard knew it wasn't just his youth and relative inexperience that rubbed Joe Quarles up the wrong way. The real reason was that Howard had been marked out as something special and given favourable attention while still a second-year undergrad at MIT. All the major players – the Pentagon, the US Army, the big corporations – went head-hunting at the Massachusetts Institute of Technology, the most prestigious recruiting ground in the country. Students there were guaranteed high-calibre offers and enticements; that was understood – but to be cherry-picked so early, as Howard Nevison had been, and by Black/PROP, an outfit regarded as the gold standard in Washington public relations, meant you were carrying heavy baggage from the start. Colleagues, especially the older ones stuck somewhere in the middle grades, watched you with jealous, spiteful eyes, hoping for a slip-up, praying for a spectacular failure.

So to antagonise an already embittered and resentful Joe Quarles was just about the dumbest strategy Howard could have employed.

But there was an additional factor that Howard could hardly bring himself to acknowledge, much less accept: though tall, just over six feet, he was no super-jock. Descriptions of himself he'd overheard ranged from 'that thin lanky geek' to 'willowy' to 'tall glass of weak beer'. Into the bargain he was ash-blond, almost white, the hair covering his ears, with a low fringe almost obscuring his pale-blue eyes. Joe Quarles' remarks about the director-in-chief finding him sexually attractive touched a raw nerve; many times he'd been taken for gay, by both sexes. In truth, Howard wasn't strongly drawn to either gender; he wasn't even vaguely in the middle, more somewhere on the outer fringes of androgynous. But he hated it when people made assumptions.

A young woman with a laser-like gaze, hollow cheeks and auburn hair drawn severely back awaited him in reception, just beyond the elevator doors. She waved an electronic wand at his credentials tag and indicated he was to follow her. There was a sepulchral hush up here, in contrast to the incessant bustle of activity below. Office doors were firmly shut; there was no ganging around the water-cooler, no continual warbling of phones.

The young woman halted by a door and held up a finger. Howard stopped and waited. She was back in a couple of minutes and mimed he was to go ahead without a hint of expression. If her brusque, silent manner was designed to unnerve visitors, it was effective. Howard took a deep breath and stepped through into the huge corner office suite feeling as if he were being ushered into the presence of royalty.

Some might have thought that appropriate for Chesney Lea Poulton, royalty in the American sense at least. Most people who took an interest in politics and international affairs knew what Chesney looked like. His was the public face of the Alliance for the Advancement of American

Values, and its principal spokesman in the media, which usually described AAAV benignly, if misleadingly, as a 'Brain Tank'.

Having only ever seen him on TV, Howard Nevison knew his boss was physically on the big side but he was surprised at the height, width and formidable bulk of the guy. When he rose in greeting, his extended hand seemed to Howard to be the size of a shovel.

'How long you been with us, Nevison?' More growl than bark, no-nonsense.

'Coming up to three months, sir.'

'We seconded you from Black/PROP, that correct?'

'Yes, sir.'

'I've asked around and people tell me you're the hot one on tracking leaks to their source. That, and putting up a smokescreen to kill a viral story or turn it around – what do you call it? You have a name for it . . .'

'Flak,' Howard said.

'Tell me how that works,' Poulton said, leaning back and folding his arms. There was a rich gleam of gold which came from a chunky bracelet on his hairy wrist. As Howard began to recite the standard PR manual guff, he was mesmerised by Chesney Poulton's majestic coiffure sweeping like a bow-wave from its widow's peak: a vibrant shade of deepest brown, with the straight-bristled moustache the perfect colour match. Was he bald as a coot or was this an expensive astro-turf job?

Trying to re-focus, the core stratagem of 'flak', Howard explained, was a method known as the Four Ds. These were, in order of application, Deny, Denigrate, Degrade and Deceive.

By and large it was unnecessary to apply any of these to the corporate press or mainstream broadcast media because the stories they produced and the angles they took were pre-vetted and conformist-friendly; any 'dissent' or 'deviation' that appeared was stage-managed and safely within proscribed boundaries. No, the real targets of the Four Ds were what were termed 'citizen and social media platforms': personal blogs, video-streaming, online discussion forums and the like – that were outside official control. The Black/PROP technique, as used by Howard, was to hire covert hit squads to infiltrate these spaces and infect them with disinformation and misleading assertions. Then the hired trolls would whip up fake disagreements and controversies among the subscribers, which would divert attention and dissipate their energies with endless internal squabbling.

So any 'thread' or 'theme' (as the jargon went) that was deemed unwelcome or off-message would first encounter a flat *Denial*. Whether this was credible, or even believed by the audience, was unimportant; it was there simply to set up the next stage: to *Denigrate* any material facts or scientific evidence by pointing to contradictions, mostly spurious and invented, which cast doubt on their veracity. This led directly to *Degrading* the thread/theme by associating it with something totally unrelated – the more ridiculous and far-fetched the better – but which nonetheless left its taint: the idea being that mud sticks. A textbook example was implanting the notion that global warming was caused by UFOs from the planet Venus, seeding the Earth's atmosphere with pollutants. In some minds, this suggestion, once made, would linger on and never entirely disappear, so that legitimate climate science came to be corrupted in the process.

Of course the goal of the first three of the Four Ds was to achieve the fourth.

At this final stage the plan was to introduce complete distortions – total contradictions preferably – of the truth: in other words, blatant bare-faced lies, which the preceding steps had paved the way for and softened the brain to accept. By then it was judged that the audience would be in such a muddled state of doubt, confusion, disbelief, suspicion, uncertainty, boredom and sheer mental fatigue that they would be unable any longer to separate fact from fantasy, remember their own name or make an educated guess about which way was up.

In which event: Mission Accomplished.

7

When the intelligence analyst had finished his spiel, the director-in-chief of AAAV wore a faint smile. In his eyes was an expression of warmth that made Howard Nevison squirm in his seat a little. Such a look – approval? admiration? – made him distinctly uncomfortable.

'I see now why we poached you from Black/PROP,' Poulton said. 'You're a bright young feller, on top of your brief, sure enough. I take it you implemented this technique personally, on several projects . . . ?'

'Yes, sir. We used it on operations against the Occupy movement, the anti-nuclear weapons lobby, human rights organisations and various groups campaigning for action on global warming. Some of these are ongoing, pretty much on a permanent basis, and there's a whole raft of new ones in the pipeline.'

'That all sounds fine to me,' Poulton said, 'though the problem I have at the minute is more in the nature of an investigative issue.' He reached for a thick binder of material and extracted a file, which he passed across the desk. 'Take a look at the first report.'

Howard opened the file on his knees and took up the top sheet, which read:

AAAV – CLASSIFIED DOCUMENT
SUBJECT: UNAUTHORISED LEAK FROM 'MIDNITE-NET'
VERBATIM TRANSCRIPT:

Environmental Activists murdered or 'disappeared' 2022-2024 after protesting about land clearance for logging, mining (gold, copper, potassium), cattle ranching and grain and soya crops:

Brazil	448
Honduras	109
Philippines	67
Mozambique	61
Peru	58
Thailand	16
Sudan	9

'You appreciate my concern,' Poulton said, 'and why this leak has been given Priority Red. What I need from you, Nevison, is to use your skills to locate this shithouse scumbag, wherever he or she is, which will then enable us to set termination procedures in motion. What I don't wish to hear you say is that you'll give it your best shot. What I do wish to hear you say is, "Yes, I can do that for you, Ches. No problem".'

'Yes, I can do that for you, sir.'

'"Ches".'

Howard held up his curled hands in a slightly defensive gesture. 'To be honest, sir, I don't feel comfortable with the informality . . . you *are* the most senior person in the building.'

'Well, I guess we'll have to work on that, won't we,' Chesney Poulton remarked, leaving Howard unsure exactly what the two of them were going to have to work on.

He was unsure about several other things too. 'These figures of murdered and disappeared activists – are they accurate, sir? Are they correct?'

'In what sense of correct do you mean, son?'

'What I mean is, are they true?'

'If they weren't true, why would their release and exposure by this shithead motherfucker douche-bag be of any concern to us? That's clear, ain't it?'

'I guess so, sir. What I'm not clear about . . .' Howard hesitated, '. . . is who murdered them or had them disappeared.'

'Not important. Just certain anonymous groups, regional factions. Friends of the US who have our best interests at heart.' Poulton waved his paddle-like paw, which created air turbulence. 'In any case, you don't need to know; it's outside your brief, Nevison. Trace the scumbags who're behind this Midnite-Net website or blog or whatever you call it and let us take care of them. Concentrate on that.'

'Take care of them as in "termination procedures" sir? By which I understand you to mean shut the site down—'

'That's also outside your brief. Keep your mind set on what I've asked you to do. Anything else is not your concern, understood?'

Howard nodded. 'Yes, sir. I just need to know a couple more things. When was this transcript posted on the net?'

'The 19th. Sunday last. Check the file.'

'And you've identified the poster as Midnite-Net. Is this a confirmed ident or an educated guess, sir?'

'That's in the file too. We have a long history with these cocksuckers. Their entertainment value is wearing mighty thin. They leaked secret material on field trials JEG Chemicals were conducting – and they're also active in climate disinformation programmes, posting what they call Climate Alerts. The last one was about the decline of oxygen in the atmosphere.' Poulton consulted a list on a clipboard. 'It was titled "Oxygen Balance Sheet: Profit & Loss". Whoever's behind this crap are nothing but a bunch of criminal shit-stirrers who should be serving ten life sentences for treasonous activities against the state. We catch 'em and toss 'em in a dark hole somewhere and we throw away the key.' Poulton lumbered to his feet, a looming shadow. 'You play your part in helping us achieve our goal, Nevison, and there's a bright future for you with AAAV. Come with me.'

Howard had also risen. Now he involuntarily backed towards the door. 'Beg your pardon, sir?'

'You haven't been up to the fifth floor before, have you? There's a great view of downtown from this vantage point. Come, let me show you.'

Clutching the file to his chest, Howard moved round the desk and went towards Chesney Poulton's outstretched arm, welcoming him to stand alongside the director-in-chief at the apex of the corner office suite.

'Down there you have K Street, and this intersection right here is 20th.' As the arm, massive and heavy as a ton weight, fell across Howard's shoulders, every muscle within him tensed. 'You're at the epicentre of the matrix, son. Don't get any bigger or any better. How does it feel, huh?'

Howard's mouth was as dry as a Mexican sandpit. He managed to croak, 'It feels great, sir. I hope I can justify your faith in my abilities . . .'

'So do I,' Poulton said, 'but that's up to you, ain't it, son?' The arm was almost cradling him, the huge hand gripping his shoulder. 'You deliver on your promises, don't you? When people go out of their way to be helpful, you're grateful, I hope.'

Howard nodded dumbly.

'Well for now,' Poulton said, and in a more intimate tone, moving his head with its chestnut-brown mane closer to Howard's, 'I'm happy with that.' His moustache was practically tickling Howard's cheek. This forced Howard to lower his gaze, which made it impossible not to see the impressive erection straining the material of the director-in-chief's clothing.

Poulton was well aware he'd seen it, and he must have felt the quiver run through Howard's body for he said, 'Run along and start justifying my faith in your abilities, son. We'll save that pleasure for another day. Off you go.'

The arm lifted from his shoulders, the pressure lessened and he was able to breathe again.

Howard was free to go. He went without a word.

8

Going down on one knee, hands clasped to his chest, forehead resting against the edge of the desk, Chesney Poulton closed his eyes and sought to enter the Zone. It was here he gained peace and clarity and could see the way ahead. Sometimes it was too easy, in the hurly-burly of everyday living, to lose sight of the true path, not to know where his destiny lay.

Pastor Eldritch had instructed him in the technique. The idea was to focus the mind on its inner core, to withdraw into one's ultimate self, to cast the world and all its turmoil into outer darkness. Chesney Poulton breathed slowly, waiting for it to happen. The Pastor had taught him to be patient. It would come.

One instant there was nothing there, the sensation he was seeking, and the next instant it was.

The sense of falling.

Slowly falling, in between the molecules of his own body, then falling further down in between the individual atoms, then sliding deeper still until all around was nothing but void. Time and space lost their meaning. He alone became the master of this inner, unique place, the creator of all probable futures, with the power to choose the future he desired.

Once you arrive there, in the Zone, the Pastor had said, you are the arbiter of your own fate. Nothing can change that. Other people, circumstances, events, accidents, disasters, the laws of nature – all of the sham reality that holds us back don't amount to a hill of beans.

And according to the Pastor, the sweetest thing about this whole deal? *There was no one to fucking answer to!*

That was the clincher! Sweet Mother of Mercy, what was not to like?

How the Pastor had entered Chesney Poulton's life was strange in itself. About five years ago Pastor Eldritch had appeared at the Charmed Baptist Brethren with a small band of followers, no more than five or six – all male. Since that day he had anointed several others to make up the inner circle numbering around twenty. In addition, the sect had recruited upwards of a hundred 'adepts' whose purpose was to serve the core group of Messengers, and who one day hoped to join the sacred inner brethren.

From the start Chesney Poulton had been intrigued. Something about Pastor Eldritch gripped his imagination. Even when he discovered the astonishing 'Power of Mind' performances in front of a packed congregation were clever theatrical stunts, he became more, not less fascinated. Part of the lure was the way the Pastor mixed ancient mystical beliefs with modern science and elements of parapsychology such as Quantum Jumping, Out of Body Experience and Kinetic Transference, moving objects at a distance by willpower.

The Pastor even had his own special form of communication, which echoed astronauts' jargon from years gone by: A-OK, Optimum Escape Velocity, Final Ascent Trajectory . . .

Where Pastor Eldritch had come from and how he had acquired this profound wisdom, Poulton had no idea, and had never dared ask. His background and personal journey to enlightenment were shrouded in mystery.

The director-in-chief of the Alliance for the Advancement of American Values straightened his shoulders and raised his head from the edge of the desk. He felt replenished and re-energised.

A ruby light was pulsing on the screen, which meant the incoming communication was urgent and important. Coming from Joe Gelstrom, it was both. The message was short, sweet, and cryptic: 'Professor G. Lautner, MIT. Nominate for ascendancy status. Expedite soonest – JEG.'

2

I

Stella Inchcape carried the tray with the pitcher of iced tea and two tumblers out onto the rear deck where Binch was listening to a local station playing popular classical music. The piece happened to be one of Binch's favourites, the third movement of Rimsky-Korsakov's *Scheherazade*.

'How's it feeling?' Stella asked, pouring the iced tea. 'Need some more painkillers?'

Binch was contemplating the spectacular view along the eastern flank of the Medicine Bow Mountain range, lost in thought. His brightly patterned sports shirt was open to the waist, revealing the strapping across his chest and extending partly over the bulge of his stomach. Nothing broken, just a few bruised ribs and a wrenched right shoulder. He had been very lucky, and he knew it.

The verdict as to whether the incident had been accidental or deliberate was still out. There had been nothing else on the road: the other vehicle had acres of room. So what else could it have been but malicious intent? Which left another perplexing mystery. What was the motive? A warning of some kind?

'I'm fine at the minute, thanks.' Binch eased himself forward in the recliner, reaching for his tea. 'It definitely feels better than yesterday. I guess a good night's sleep did the trick.'

Stella was still concerned. She had known him for thirty-seven years and she could see something was troubling him. Something fundamental to his sense of himself and what he believed in had been broken.

As for Binch himself, he was currently immersed in a wish-fulfilment fantasy about how he would like to encircle the throat of the project director of NCPF, his immediate boss, in both hands and squeeze every particle of the life force out of the rat. Just when he needed Si Musso's support, the bastard had betrayed him. Binch didn't fool himself: this had been coming for some time. The rot had set in with Si Musso's appointment just over three years ago. Even at the time, Binch had been suspicious about why Musso was given the post. He was an administrator, not a scientist, and from the start his priorities for the department were completely wrong.

In the past eighteen months his 'revised corporate strategy' had really cut to the bone. First, funding was to be 'rationalised' and 'curtailed' – weasel words for slashing the department's budget. In scientific research circles it was known as 'salami-slicing', which meant death by a thousand cuts.

Binch had fought tooth and nail against it. How could you cut funding to the DELFI forecasting programmes at the precise moment its predictions were so vitally important and desperately needed?

It was, quite literally, insane.

And then, two days ago, Binch had received a call from Si Musso that, thinking about it even now, left him blank-eyed and incredulous. Instead of recieving sympathy or concern over his accident, Binch had listened dumbstruck as Musso started a furious tirade about bringing the NCPF into disrepute.

'There's been a shitstorm coming down on me since that TV disaster went out,' Musso ranted. '*Plus* – not obtaining clearance for the interview is a breach of the department's rule book and code of ethics. Have you been online or looked at social media? Your face and your fucking crackpot opinions, Binch, are plastered all over. You've dragged all of us, the NCPF, me, our reputation, our credibility through the mud. I've even had people in Washington accusing us of subversion and undermining the nation's morale. Ever heard of a body called AAAV? They're gung-ho about promoting American Values, and yesterday they sent out a press release demanding our tax-dollar funding is cut-off and the department disbanded. We're stone-dead in the water, and it's all thanks to your big mouth and sneaking behind my back.'

Binch felt winded. He tried to get his breath back, breathing deeply, but his ribs hurt.

'No surprise you've run out of excuses,' Musso went on. 'Can't even muster a few words in your own defence? I must be stupid; I saw from day one you were a liability and I did nothing about it. But you're not taking me down with you, oh no, I'm not laying my career on the line for you—'

'What the hell are you talking about?' Binch finally said. 'I wouldn't ask you for the time of day. You're a pen-pusher, a paper-shuffler, otherwise a waste of space. Why would I ask for your support?'

'You might need it when they throw the book at you,' Musso said, almost gloating. 'Take a look online. The word is out you've been faking climate data and massaging the figures to fit your own agenda.'

'*What* agenda?'

'There's talk of money changing hands, kickbacks. I'm not accusing you of taking bribes; I'm telling you what the rumour mill's saying. And more serious stuff than that even—'

'The rumour mill can go fuck itself and all who sail in her,' Binch said.

'I advise you to listen and pay attention. This isn't a joke. Big people in Washington are mooting possible indictments on charges of treason with the intent of entering into a conspiracy against the US government . . . you're being accused of being unpatriotic and un-American.'

Treason? Conspiracy? Un-American? What madness was this?

Binch was now, at this moment in time, struggling for breath again. He could feel his heart hammering in his chest. He opened his eyes and thankfully the Medicine Bow Mountain range was right there in front of him, a soothing balm to his tormented spirit.

He then startled his wife by suddenly sitting upright. His fists were clenched in his lap. 'Why doesn't he get in touch? Where the fuck is he?'

'Who?'

'Where is he when I need his help?'

Stella's lips tightened. 'Binch, honey, for goodness' sake, stop banging on about it! You've been trying for months to contact him. Maybe he's gone back to England, or – I don't know – some far-flung part of the world.'

'So how should that stop me getting through to him, no matter where he is?'

'Maybe the famous science writer has outgrown you,' Stella said with a thin smile. 'You played your part, supplied background research for his book, and you're no longer of any use.'

'I don't believe that of him for a second. Aside from the work I did on the book, Gav's always been more a friend than a colleague.' He brushed a hand through his thinning hair sighing. 'There's some other explanation, gotta be.'

'Anyhow,' Stella said, practical as ever, 'what kind of help can he offer? How is Gavin Chase, famous author or not, supposed to do anything about the funding cutbacks? Or that Musso is a joke as head of department? Or you even, getting more irascible with every day that passes. He's an outsider. What can he do?'

'Well, nothing about the last one,' Binch agreed sourly. 'I'm a lost cause.' He finished off his iced tea, lay back in the recliner and gazed at the mountain range.

2

There had been death-threats – ten at the last count. Why 'they' were sending them was pretty obvious, Chase thought – not much doubt there; it was who *they* were that was the tough question. Also knowing how to protect yourself from an anonymous death-threat was fraught with imponderables. So Micki and the Midniters had taken it upon themselves to carry out a patrol of the perimeter at random intervals round the clock, just to feel reasonably comfortable that there were no suspicious parties lurking nearby.

Micki and the Midniters.

Chase was amused by the name. It reminded him of a doo-wop group from his father's era; Owen had grown up listening to the original rock'n'roll stars of the 1950s. Whereas this was a savvy crowd of techno-libertarians with a social conscience.

So far – *touch wood* – the Midniters hadn't encountered anything suspicious. No black SUVs with new plates and a whip aerial (a dead giveaway for an FBI transmitter). No unmarked panel vans with a mysterious bulge on the roof (urban surveillance radar) parked to the rear of the timberyard. Of course there might have been individuals, dressed as vagrants or druggies, with a tracker in the heel of their worn-down sports shoes. But in fact they would probably have been easier to spot. The business park was too far off the beaten track for any downtown dropouts to have been convincing. Situated northwest of Pittsburgh, off Interstate I-79, next to the Perry Highway, it was one of the reasons why Chase and Cheryl had chosen the location in the first place.

There were still other ways *they* might have infiltrated the group. You could never, should never, Chase had learned, underestimate *them* or what they were capable of.

Just two weeks ago a young couple had presented themselves at the Trade Only counter and asked if they could have a view of the bathroom fittings they'd seen advertised online. Alarm bells sounded: En-Suite Dremes didn't have a website. The bogus company had never issued a catalogue and wasn't listed on any trade database; there wasn't anything resembling a washbasin, toilet-bowl, shower cubicle, bathroom fitting, plumbing appliance, faucet, pipe or spigot in the building.

Well, apart from the facilities the staff used, that was.

The young couple had gone away most disgruntled that they had driven out all this way and it was a wasted journey.

Chase had almost felt some sympathy for them – but not quite enough; the cute young couple might have been FBI agents or working undercover for Homeland Security – or more sinisterly, enforcement officers for the UnPatriot Act, the tough law coming into force any day now. Transgress the latter and you could be plucked up and whisked off (most likely to Cuba PDF) before you had time to blow the steam off your coffee.

3

'I'm getting a mite pissed with that guy, Burt. Can't we keep him quiet? Who's his boss?'

Burt Mueller, Chesney Poulton's chief of staff, consulted the dossier on his lap. 'The head of the Climate Prediction outfit in Boulder is called Si Musso. We've talked to him already.'

'And has he talked to Inchcape?'

Mueller confirmed he had.

'Hasn't done much fuckin' good, Burt.'

'Inchcape's a loose cannon.'

'Is he now? Then if he can't keep his goddamn trap shut, we'll have to shut it for him.'

Poulton gazed into the middle distance while he lit a cigar. 'Invoke the UnPatriot Act,' he said eventually, trailing smoke from his broad nostrils.

'Yes, sir.' Burt Mueller made a notation. 'Is it a special operation?'

Poulton nodded. 'We'll call it "Silent Witness",' he said, and then smiled to himself, pleased at his inspiration. 'That'll shut the fat fucker up.'

4

It was so bloody slanted and outright biased that Gavin Chase sat there feeling slightly sick to his stomach. A real hatchet job. And the smirking tanned gigolo with too many teeth whose job it was to be chairing the debate was an abject disgrace.

'. . . feeding the American public false or misleading information could be seen as an act of treason against the state.'

Chase shook his head in disbelief. They weren't going to let Stringer get away with that, were they? Accusing a reputable scientist of treason on national television!

'. . . It seeps like poison into the bloodstream of the nation. It saps our moral fibre and corrupts our sense of right and wrong. There were sound reasons why the bill to enact the UnPatriot Act, now passing through Congress, was greeted unanimously, with no abstentions.'

'Treason is a pretty strong word, Professor . . .'

Chase was so revolted by what he was seeing, there was a sour taste of betrayal in his mouth. And the look of distress on Binch's face, glimpsed for a split second before the camera cut away . . . as if he'd been about to have a heart attack. Those bastards didn't give a damn; and Professor Martin C. Stringer, with that ridiculous stuck-down comb-over, was the biggest bastard of them all. Clearly he had been put up to it, possibly by a department of the US government working hand-in-glove with one of the big corporate sponsors.

Chase couldn't stand to watch any more. He waved his hand to indicate as much, and Micki Vargas killed the picture. They were in the corner office, which had an uninspiring view of twenty other industrial units – gigantic shed-like aluminium structures – shimmering in the heat rising off the baking concrete of the business park. Other units housed a timber supply company, a truck tyres and accessories distributor, a dumpster hire firm, house removals and storage, and several for general warehousing.

Inside, the large open area was divided by framed partitions into dedicated sectors: racks of computer servers in one, data storage consoles in another, and in the main open-plan area an entire battalion of computer consoles, vid and TV screens, watched by thirty or more young volunteers who gave their time and expertise for free. Along the rear wall were offices and quiet rooms, and in the far corner there was an enclosed soundproofed structure like a gigantic shipping crate swathed in bubble-wrap which contained the broadcast studio and control booths.

In charge of the operation was Michaelmas (or Micki as everyone called her) Vargas, a graduate in computer coding and cyber-intel evaluation. The group's task was to monitor and record – filtered with expert discretion – at least some of the vast electronic output that poured from national media, official websites and the blogging community. That was a part – in fact, the lesser part – of their raison d'être. Their main function was to compile and release the latest scientific research and forecasts that were either ignored or actively suppressed by government and the mainstream media.

This was where the studio played its key role. From 'the Crate' in the corner, as someone had sarcastically named it, live radio and webcast transmissions were beamed several times a week; within each twenty-four-hour cycle, upwards of a dozen or more bulletins and updates were circulated via email and online forums by the team in the main arena working in shifts. All this activity was carried out under the collective rubric Midnite-Net.

These 'Climate Alerts' as they were known went out to millions of subscribers. One such Alert, 'Oxygen Balance Sheet: Profit & Loss', had caused a stink to high heaven, and the odour was still floating around a year after its release. It showed, indisputably, how a series of man-made actions formed a chain reaction to reduce oxygen levels and threaten the existence of the human species. Big Government and Big Business, aided by clandestine institutions such as the Bilderberg Group, the AAAV and the Global Warming Foundation, had fought tooth and nail to prevent this knowledge being disseminated to the public at large – and failed.

'When was this broadcast?' Chase asked Micki.

'Sunday last. It's a weekly show, goes out live from Baltimore.'

'You knew, I guess, Bill Inchcape is a friend of mine from way back. He helped with—'

'Everybody who's read your book knows it,' Micki said with a slightly pained expression, as if he'd told her the sun usually comes up in the east. 'Binch gets plenty of thanks, plus the major acknowledgement for his contribution. Ya no stint the man one jot, Gav.'

This quaint sing-song phrase was a touch of the patois she sometimes dropped into the conversation. Having an Afro-Caribbean mother and a Peruvian father, Micki Vargas was physically overwhelming, with a vibrant presence and sexual aura to match. With her exotic looks and statuesque physique – she was practically the same height as Chase – she could cause a traffic snarl-up.

Cheryl always rolled her eyes in mock-alarm whenever Chase mentioned he and Micki were working together. It was a running gag between them that it would take a man of granite not to feel the heatwave Micki generated. Just as well they both shared a sense of humour, Chase thought, because right this minute Cheryl was more than four thousand miles away, out in the middle of the Pacific Ocean.

'And this other guy, the professor?' Micki enquired. 'You know that scumbag too?'

'Unfortunately yes. We've been on public debating panels together, done TV shows in the past. That's what I don't understand – Binch agreeing to take part in the first place, knowing that Martin Stringer is a bought-and-paid-for slimeball mouthpiece for the denial lobby. But even to mention that word . . . ?' Chase stood up. 'To talk openly about treason, for chrissakes – and not only that, he drags the UnPatriot Act into it too, which amounts to the same thing as issuing a direct threat. This is a new tactic, Micki, more threatening, more aggressive. They've upped the ante.'

Micki looked puzzled. 'But why now? What your friend Binch has been saying in public and the climate data he's released . . . well, none of it is exactly *new*.' Leaning back in the swivel chair, she spread her arms wide as if to say, *I just don't get it.*

That was certainly true, Chase reflected. His glance took in several of the screens. Reports of extreme climatic anomalies were there for all to see, and coming in at greater frequency: here they were being monitored on a twenty-four-hour rolling cycle. So what was happening now that hadn't happened before? What had made the difference? Answer: Nothing.

'Asking "Why now?" is asking the wrong question,' he told her. 'These people do what they do. It's that simple. Their *modus operandi* is a continuous escalation of pressure to force the rest of us to see the world as they see it. And for us to accept it and shut-the-fuck-up. That's their mission. They won't stop – they will never stop.'

'To them it's just another tactic,' Micki Vargas said, studying him closely. 'One more weapon.'

'Exactly so. You sent out a Climate Alert last week about the activists who've been killed or gone missing in South America and Africa. It's terrible and it's criminal, but it's not surprising or even shocking news any longer. Think about that: hundreds, maybe thousands of activists get murdered and "disappeared" year after year. The situation never gets any better – in truth it gets worse; the deaths and the disappearances increase. But even that has lost its shock value. The only really shocking thing—'

'—is the fact we're *not* shocked by it,' Micki said. Her large dark eyes were shining, on the edge of tears; whether from pain, or anger or furious impotence, Chase couldn't tell. Maybe a cauldron of them all, with a dose of screaming despair thrown in for good measure.

'What we do 'bout it?' she said. 'What we do 'bout it we're not already doing? *What the fuck more can we do?*'

'I don't know,' Chase said. 'Any ideas?' He was tired, and it came out as facetious.

'You're the leader. You're supposed to tell us.' Micki wasn't even pretending to be facetious; it sounded more like an accusation.

'Keep at it, I suppose. Keep pushing forward. That's all we can do.'

'With Midnite-Net you mean.'

Chase was looking at the screens again. He merely nodded.

'And with the Midniters,' Micki said, almost defiantly, as if she were challenging him. 'That's one way of stopping 'em. That's *our* weapon, agreed?'

Chase didn't answer her. He thought Micki could be right. But he couldn't and wouldn't admit it to her, much less to himself.

5

It was amazing. Ten years ago even the gloomiest of doom-laden prophecies hadn't prepared any of them for the catastrophic decline they were now experiencing. It was as if the environment had driven off a cliff-edge. Maybe Bill Inchcape had known, based on DELFI's predictions, but even that was doubtful. One person who probably *had* known, though Chase had never met him, was the ex-astronaut Bradley E. Zittel.

And now that Binch himself was coming under intolerable pressure, Chase felt alarm and guilt in pretty well equal measure. How long had it been since last they'd spoken? Round about the time of his book launch, he guessed, which would make it a couple of years ago. Binch had supplied the vast bulk of technical data on variable climate conditions for every continent and ocean. His expertise with analysis and projection modelling had been invaluable too, using the computing power at the National Climate Prediction Foundation to do the number-crunching. Doubtful if *One Minute to Midnight* would have ever been completed if not for Binch's contribution and support.

There was, too, a certain bleak irony in the fact that Theo Detrick's prognosis from all those years ago had been vindicated by events. Ignored or derided by so many, the man himself had now achieved the status of prophet in the popular imagination. Never was the saying 'Stranger in a Strange Land' more apt.

Chase bore some of the responsibility for his posthumous reputation: Theo had been the inspiration behind the book, published in 2023, which had drawn extensively on his quarter-century of research, quoting whole chunks from his treatise 'Back to the Precambrian'. In a way, Theo Detrick was the central character.

To this day Chase didn't know the identity of the person who had sent the dossier on Operation Download to Cheryl; but rumour was rife that heads had rolled like ninepins in the Defense Department. General 'Blindeye' Wolfe had taken the brunt of it; stripped of his rank and dishonourably discharged, he committed suicide a year to the day following the book's publication, which, symbolic gesture or pure happenstance, nobody knew, fanned speculation to white heat and did nothing to harm sales of the book either.

The theme of *One Minute to Midnight*, encapsulated in its title, was the utter madness of all-out environmental war, with the superpowers deliberately engineering global catastrophe by means of WCD – Weapons of Climate Degradation. This wanton, reckless tampering with the forces of nature had brought the planet to within sixty seconds – following Chase's analogy of a hand sweeping around a twelve-hour clock-face – of ultimate disaster. Then he hit them with the killer punch: crazy and criminal as this military strategy was, the planet had beaten the superpowers to it and was already, thanks to man's two centuries of unchecked industrial growth, on a steep downwards slope, and possibly already past the point of no return.

The factory furnace and the automobile had already accomplished what the military had been seeking to bring about.

The book polarised opinion and was hotly, even aggressively, disputed. It was accused of being 'paranoid fantasy'. Other critics dismissed it as a piece of trashy sensationalism – panic-mongering at its worst to get a number one spot on the bestseller lists – and the author's cheap bid to become the 'ecology guru' of the twenty-first century. Chase had expected this. He had been less prepared for the abuse and vilification heaped upon his head by many leading scientists.

The success of the book had another unforeseen consequence too – it saved his life.

On his return from New York, there was no shred of doubt in his mind that powerful vested interests were determined to silence him. They had succeeded with Theo Detrick, and Chase had of course been an eye-witness to the threats Cheryl had faced. Precisely who or what these 'interests' were remained speculation, though it wasn't hard to make an educated guess: vast transnational corporations such as JEG were the obvious candidates, based simply on the evidence that they had the most to lose with the book's revelations. It was a dead-certain fact that the would-be assassin who had stalked him at JFK (Chase had belatedly recognised him as the same man who had threatened Cheryl in Geneva) was in the pay of a company or companies, or a government agency, or a military-intelligence group – tick any box. Or a combination of all three; it was immaterial which one, to Chase at least, because their aim was the same in all cases: to shut him up at all costs.

Dead journalists tell no tales.

For ten months Chase worked solidly on the book, living with Dan in a remote croft near the small town of Dornoch on the east coast of Scotland. There they settled down in the tiny two-room dwelling with its whitewashed walls and red corrugated iron roof, with not a neighbour in view. There was no electricity, patchy phone reception and slow-motion internet; they used oil lamps, a portable generator, a camping gas stove and a log fire for when the long dark nights of the northern winter closed in.

By the spring the book was finished. Prior to the official launch, the political and world affairs publication *Sentinel* had featured three long excerpts; almost immediately the internet was abuzz with opinion and debate, most of it ill-informed, but keeping the publicity pot boiling furiously. By then it was evident that Chase's fame – or notoriety, depending on which camp you belonged to – was as good as life insurance. In any event, silencing the author when the material was openly available and the book universally in print would have been closing the stable door after a whole herd of horses had gone galloping off over the horizon.

Gavin Chase looked back on those months in the Scottish croft, just the two of them together, father and seven-year-old son leading a life that was basic, simple, and wholly rewarding, with an aching nostalgia that brought a stab to the heart.

Since the book's publication two years ago, Chase had spent more and more of his time travelling abroad, much of it in America. It was part and parcel of his professional life now and couldn't be avoided. The question of Dan's upbringing and providing a stable background, keeping disruption to a minimum, was a constant worry, which was when Marcus Barrett came up with a solution. His own son, Titus, was enrolled at the Elyot Grange Academy on the outskirts of Sunbury-on-Thames in Surrey. The two boys, just a few months apart in age, had got on well together during a summer vacation spent at Barrett's villa in Portugal; if Dan liked the look of Elyot Grange, this could provide the perfect answer.

Marcus Barrett had even generously offered to pay the fees. Chase appreciated the gesture, but with his journalism, lecture tours and book royalties, he was now well able to manage. After three terms, Dan had settled in; he was happy, doing well academically and had a host of new friends.

For Chase – and Cheryl too – the boy's contentment with his new life had been a relief and a blessing. It meant they'd been able to focus their energies and commit fully to the online climate research network they had created, based on the outskirts of Pittsburgh. The name chosen, Midnite-Net, was a homage and hat-tip to the book – though the link to *Midnight* was never acknowledged or even hinted at, and none of their online webcast audience ever made the connection.

6

At 26,000 feet, the Hilgard Depths is one of the deepest trenches in the Pacific Ocean. Precisely why, Cheryl Detrick knew, her father Theo had chosen this remote location as the base for his almost quarter of a century of research into phytoplankton. Here, just below the equator, the upwelling of colder water brought this rich soup of micro-organisms from the ocean depths in their countless billions – until a lethal combination of pollutants and an increase in median temperatures had triggered a sharp decline.

And with the decline of these tiny free-floating plants, there'd been a sharp reduction in the supply of oxygen to replenish the world's ravenous demand.

It had taken Cheryl four days to get here from the States. The final leg had been a two-thousand-mile jaunt from Hawaii to the Phoenix Islands. The field trip had been part-sponsored by the UN Climate Agency with the object of assessing the distribution and extent of agri-chemical run-off thousands of miles from any sizeable land mass. When planning the six-week expedition, Cheryl had been thrilled to discover that her itinerary would bring her within the neighbourhood – a trifling 140 miles away from Canton Island, the very spot where Theo had lived alone for so many years.

It was too good an opportunity to miss. She had seen photos her father had taken of the island, the lagoon he swam twice round every morning before breakfast, the clear placid water, the white beach and pink and magenta coral, the conical hill rising to the island's highest point of three metres, the few scattered palm trees and meagre vegetation of scrub and thorny bush. Would there be any trace of him left behind? One of his old pipe tobacco pouches, abandoned sunglasses with cracked lenses, maybe a pair of discarded leather sandals with broken straps?

From her stopover on Phoenix Island itself, she had hired a small fishing vessel to make the twelve-hour journey to Canton Island. The weatherbeaten captain, Jonny Royle, had decent charts of the region, and more importantly, a GPS scanner. He was the first to admit he hadn't sailed there in years. But he seemed capable, and confident enough. Visibility on the morning they arrived was excellent, the ocean a gentle rolling swell. Sitting on the prow, Cheryl scanned the horizon through binoculars, her eyes shielded under a broad straw hat. It reminded her of the time she'd spent on the Marine Research vessel *Melville* as a post-grad student at Scripps.

In the wheelhouse, Jonny had the charts spread out and was keeping track with the scanner. Cheryl could hear the beeps getting more frequent as they neared the set co-ordinates. She called, 'What've you got, Jonny? Give me an approx reading. 1000 yards? 1500?'

'Not even close, Missus.' Jonny stuck his head through the hatch window. 'This is it. Under your nose.' The beeps became more insistent, almost an unbroken sound. 'Bang on the button.'

'Here?' Cheryl said, scrambling to her feet and looking in every direction. '*Where?*'

'We's on top of it,' Jonny said. 'The machine don't lie.'

The GPS, Cheryl well knew, was accurate to within half the length of a football field. Yet there was nothing: not a single palm tree or patch of thorny scrub or hint of coral reef. Jonny Royle was wrong, or the scanner was faulty – except Jonny Royle was right: there *was* something there after all, which Cheryl had seen and not noticed. It had looked like a tangle of brushwood floating on the surface, wafting to and fro with the current, but in fact, it was the peak of the conical hill: the highest point of Canton Island, now a majestic half-metre above the waves as the melting Antarctic ice-sheet at the bottom of the planet raised the levels of all the world's oceans.

Cheryl peered down through the water to what had been the white sand beach her father had walked on. Her hopes and expectations of what she had longed to find down there were so stupidly ridiculous she began to laugh. And then she began to cry.

3

I

The crack of the rifle rolled across the valley and was heard as a distant reverberation among the wrinkled folds of scrub and rock that girdled Mount Grafton like a piece of old brown sackcloth.

'Did you hit it?' Steve Fazioli pushed back his grey Stetson with his thumb and leaned forward, dark hairy forearms draped over the steering wheel of the Jeep.

'Bastard was too quick.' Chuck Brant ejected the spent cartridge and kicked it viciously in a spinning arc. He was beginning to suspect that he and his brother-in-law had chosen just about the worst part of Nevada for their hunting trip. It was just too damn dry and bleak. That pathetic damp patch below them – the so-called White River – wouldn't bring the game down from the hills. They should have tried further north, up near Sacramento Pass, near the old copper mines.

'That's the first buck we've seen all day,' Chuck complained. He slid the large-bore hunting rifle into its sheath, dropped into the passenger seat and reached behind into the insulated box and pulled out a can of Schlitz. 'Want one?' He tossed the can to Steve and got another for himself.

Steve tipped his head back and let the cold amber liquid gurgle into his mouth. Drops sparkled on his black moustache. 'What else can you expect? In a coupla years there won't be a fucking gopher left, never mind anything big enough to shoot at.'

Chuck wiped the dust from his visor with his neckerchief. 'Let's get rolling, for chrissakes!'

Three miles on they came to another trail, wider than the one they were on, which led steeply up in the general direction of Mount Grafton, whose highest point was about seven miles away.

Chuck studied the deep tracks in the compacted soil and frowned. 'We're not on military property, are we?' he asked, scratching a damp armpit.

'I didn't see nothing posted. No fences or nothing. The Nellis Missile Range is a good thirty miles from here. That's the only government property I know of in this part of the state. Which way?'

Chuck jerked his thumb towards the mountain and Steve rammed the shift into first. The ride was rough, the trail considerably steeper than they had expected, winding upwards in a series of perilous S-bends. They passed overgrown trails disappearing into shadowy gullies, with indications here and there that they led to disused mine workings.

After twenty minutes of hard climbing the Jeep rounded a bend between two massive shoulders of rock. The trail levelled out on to a small enclosed plateau of baked red earth. At first sight it led nowhere. Dead end. Yet the tracks carried on, and as Steve swung the Jeep around to face the way they had come, both men saw an imposing barrier of timber, tall as a house, inset with solid oak gates twenty feet high.

It might have been an army stockade, complete with horizontal slit-holes for observation, except there were no military insignia anywhere; no signboards, no flags; in fact nothing to indicate what it might be.

'This is screwy,' Chuck Brant said as he gazed around. 'Hey, look – what the hell is that?'

Some of the boulders, either side of the stockade-structure, had dark scorch marks on them. Steve switched off the engine. He got his phone out and took a picture of the smoke-streaked rocks and then swivelled round to take a couple of the stockade. Nothing moved. The silence was unnerving.

'Wait a sec now.' Chuck's forehead was creased in concentration. 'Could it be a storage facility up here? Or a dump, say, for old equipment maybe?'

'Oh, sure,' Steve said caustically. He didn't regard his wife's brother as the greatest intellect since Einstein. 'They drove loaded trucks three miles straight up a narrow track to dump stuff two thousand feet high on the side of a mountain. Yeah, sure, that makes a *whole* lot of sense.' His expressive gestures showed his Italian ancestry.

'So you tell me, Dick-Brain, what the fuck does?' Chuck said, flushing.

'How the hell should I know? A new site for Disneyland.'

Chuck twisted around in his seat and got himself another beer; he didn't offer to get Steve one. His face had gone sullen. Steve didn't notice; he was staring at the ground, still puzzling over the tracks and the scorch marks.

The spidery bushes that grew from the cracks in the rocks were perfectly still, the thin covering of dust on their leaves undisturbed. There wasn't a breath of wind.

Into the silence intruded a sound, hard and metallic, like a hollow musical note.

Chuck heard it and finished his beer in two gulping swallows. He crumpled the can in his fist and tossed it away. He glanced over his shoulder towards the stockade. 'Let's get out of here,' he said in a low voice.

Steve started up the Jeep. He didn't care to admit it, certainly not to his dumb brother-in-law, but this place gave him the creeps.

He pushed the stick into first and was about to drive off when he saw something that made his hands tighten clammily on the wheel. The figure of a young man, dressed in black, white shirt, thin black tie, erect and motionless on a rock. He was cradling a slim metal cylinder under his left arm. From it came a tube, looping to the young man's right hand, in which he was holding some kind of jet nozzle with a trigger attachment, which must have been the source of the metallic sound as it bumped against the cylinder. The young man raised his hand and sighted along a straight arm, as if aiming.

He was positioned, Steve realised, directly above the point where the trail sloped down, in-between the two shoulders of rock standing there like guardians. But guardians of what exactly? *Jesus, there was more than one!* Steve flinched as he spotted another figure, dressed the same, and then three more appeared, moving into position on either side of the trail. Each of them carried a cylinder. They raised their arms and pointed.

In that same moment the image of the scorch marks on the rocks popped into Steve's head and he knew without the least inkling of doubt what they meant, and what the black-clad figures intended; after that he didn't bother thinking any more, he was too busy pumping the accelerator. Dirt spurted from under the tyres as the Jeep lunged forward. Chuck grabbed the metal frame of the windshield for support and hung on.

Foot flat to the floor, Steve was aware of the figures on either side pointing, arms extended; he tried his best to ignore them and mentally push them aside as he drove straight for the gap between the rocks. But he couldn't ignore what happened next. It was like a scene from a Biblical epic as converging tongues of fire shot out and consumed the vehicle in a fireball of highly inflammable propane gas.

This was Steve's last conscious thought.

Taking the shortest and fastest route down the mountain, the Jeep sailed through the air like a fiery comet, bits of flaming debris scattering off it. The two brothers-in-law were flung out like blazing rag dolls before it hit bottom.

An arc of oily black smoke hung lazily in the warm still air. From their vantage point high above, the figures in black looked down on their handiwork. They began to dissemble their equipment and purge the jet nozzle vents, as per the manual, ready for the next time.

Turning away, one of them said, 'That's a first, Karl.'

'What's a first?' Karl said. He stood out from the others, taller, with cropped blond hair, while they were dark-haired.

The first one choked a little as he sniggered, 'Them two achieving ascendancy by rapidly descending.' He mimed the Jeep flying on its death trajectory to the canyon floor. 'Ker-Pow!'

It wasn't much of a joke, though the others snorted; Karl stayed stony-faced.

'I guess they shouldn't have taken photos,' somebody remarked.

'That makes no difference,' Karl said. 'We had to ascend them. We had no choice. They had no right being here and seeing what they saw. We gotta protect Mothership, no matter what.'

The Messengers of God carried their cylinders across the compound and in through the side door carved into the canyon wall.

2

The tables buzzed with the news of the day's event: two foolish intruders had achieved ascendant status – in a very spectacular manner! The joke about 'achieving ascendancy by rapidly descending' rocked the dining hall, Owen taking the credit for the off-the-cuff quip.

Karl listened to the excited chatter in the mess hall but didn't get involved. Such frivolous behaviour was degrading, in his view, to the spirit and aims of the group. How could one attain proper Fitness for Mission without iron discipline and rigid self-control? What he observed around him was not 'the right stuff' at all.

Karl had been fifteen when he first came to the Mothership, two years ago. Then he had been Harry Turlington, shy and withdrawn, given to dark moods. Everyone on induction was assigned the name of an astronaut – American, Russian, Chinese – who had completed a mission. Harry's was Karl Henize, a crew-member of 1967 NASA Group Six. The afternoon's jokester was named after Owen Garriott, 1965 NASA Group Four. Karl didn't know his real name; no one, whether inside or outside the stockade, ever divulged them.

One of the earliest to arrive, Karl had been among scores of young people who started out on the pilgrimage, in his case from Kettering, near Dayton, Ohio. He had been six weeks on the road, sleeping rough, begging for food, when he met up with three other guys in a Buick Century that was falling apart at the seams. Two of the guys had decided – even before they reached the state line – that the Messengers of God wasn't for them. Very few of those who embarked on the trek to Nevada, disillusioned with modern life and inspired by a dream, actually made it . . .

Karl had been glad to see them go. Anyone who didn't possess the qualities and total dedication, *the right stuff*, as they were instructed, had no place here. The MOG had no room for them. Cast them out as weak and unworthy. Let them perish along with the rest.

3

The stockade halfway up a mountain was perfect in its location: a self-contained environment hidden from the outside world, with secure perimeters and views of surrounding roads, trails and tracks for miles around. Any living thing approaching could be seen ten miles away. Bad news for Steve and Chuck that stupid curiosity had made them take the wrong trail.

Behind the twenty-feet-high timber walls, a central compound was enclosed on three sides by separate two-storey lodges. On the upper floors were the sleeping quarters: dormitories for the adepts and a dozen single rooms for senior members; the adepts were never permitted to be alone, at any time, day or night. Presently there were around ninety of them. Below were larger open areas for workshops and meeting rooms, and spaces set aside for private study, recreation and meditation. The large mess hall and kitchen had their own block. Another block housed the generator and four huge vats of oil and liquid gas, providing electric power. Natural springs deep underground had been tapped for fresh water.

There was a general rule maintaining quietness and calm. From a few hundred yards beyond the bend in the trail, not a whisper could be heard. More than thirty miles from any human habitation, there was no sign or sound to disturb the scrub and rocks encircling the bare granite peak of Mount Grafton.

Sitting opposite him, Val (Valentin Varlamov: 1960 USSR Air Force Group One) said with a leering grin, 'I bet it gave you a boost . . . go on, admit it, Karl. It just had to, didn't it? You know . . .' He made the fist clenched, pumping-iron motion which to all men signifies hot sex.

'It was a task with a specific objective,' Karl said, 'and I carried it out as I have been trained to do, to the best of my ability.' He was almost quoting from the Mission manual. 'And as for getting some kind of twisted kick out it, Val, you're letting emotion get in the way of purpose and duty. At this late stage I'm shocked you haven't ironed that bug out of your system.'

Val was taken aback and started to bluster in self-defence, 'You saying I don't know my duty? I've done the work, I've got the grades. I could've handled that situation today just as well as you did.'

'I'm not questioning your ability, Val.'

Heads on either side of the table craned forward, anxious to hear the answer from an adept such as Karl who had achieved Crew Selection, which was the first important step towards the goal of Mission Status. Almost as impressive was that he'd been to the 23rd Chapter of the Charmed Baptist Brethren in McLean, Virginia. Only twenty adepts were chosen by the Pastor for each trip.

'It's your attitude and the seriousness of intent I have doubts about. You're treating it like it was some kind of frat gig or kids' dirty joke we should snigger over. Achieving ascendancy for heathens and non-believers is both an honour and a responsibility. That's why we're here – to help destroy the corrupt pit of sin that humankind has fallen into. You should remember that.'

'I know why we're here as well as you do,' Val protested, though he was slightly shamefaced. 'And you've got me wrong if you think I was making a joke about it. Hell's bells, Karl, lighten up.'

He looked along the table, seeking support, but it was in short supply. You could never be entirely sure about Karl; that he wouldn't report up the chain some innocent remark and you'd find yourself on a demerit or facing discipline charges.

'Maybe when Val does his first OBE he'll see things differently,' volunteered a gawky lad with a fierce red buzz-cut, like a spiky bristled brush, whose assigned name was Vance (Vance Brand: 1966 NASA Group Five).

'Why, you done yours yet?' Val responded. 'Where's your badge? I don't happen to see it.'

Vance said mildly, 'No, I haven't; you know as much. But I don't have your casual approach either. The manual is very explicit: "Get with the programme or get the hell out".'

Several of them along the table glanced covertly at the triangular silver badge in the narrow lapel of Karl's black jacket. This was unde-niable proof of his superior status. He had accomplished not one but two Out of Body Experiences, which he'd written up and were used as case-studies. Not everybody was convinced. There were stories of adepts faking it, though Pastor Eldritch was reputed to have a very reliable BBD (built-in bullshit detector).

Val was simmering, and Karl cut in to defuse the situation. Tempers running high could lead – not often but sometimes – to fistfights, and as one of the senior and longest-serving members of the community he didn't want the blame laid at his door.

'Stop thinking of this as a competition. Every single one of you will get his chance to enter an OBE as well as Quantum Jumping when the appropriate moment arrives. That's the purpose of study and meditation and application, as a path towards understanding and achievement. You'll get there if you keep at it.'

'Is Quantum Jumping better or the same as OBE?' asked Fang (Fang Guojun: 1971 Chinese Shuguang Group One), a boy of fourteen who was small for his age and wore spectacles, one of only three who did – poor eyesight was usually an automatic bar to induction into the MOG; he was one of the rare exceptions.

Karl said, 'It's impossible to compare them. And anyway, it's the wrong question.'

He'd seen before the look of eagerness in the eyes of the younger ones whenever Quantum Jumping was mentioned; it had an exotic, even dangerous, ring to it that drew them like moths to a flame.

'Wrong? How come?' Fang asked.

'Because ego should never be part of the equation. It's wrong, Fang, and I'm disappointed you don't already know it, to ask a question that is centred on self – is it "better", implying will I enjoy this experience more than that?' Karl was speaking kindly, trying to impart a simple truth rather than sound harsh or critical. 'What you feel is of no importance. The ideal state – the "quantum" state, if you like – is to be neutral and impersonal. You're human and can't escape the sensations of pain or fear, and you can't avoid suffering, but such things will no longer matter. Emotional and physical distress have been put in their rightful place, the servant of the self rather than its master.'

'What you're telling us, then,' Val said, staring at him, unsmiling, 'is one day an inner voice will say, "No more pain, no more fear".' He snapped his fingers. 'Just like that.'

Karl shook his head. 'No, it doesn't happen in just one day,' he said slowly. 'It happens every day. Every day the battle is fought anew. The struggle is never-ending.'

Half-turning away, Val was heard to mumble sceptically, 'That's easy to say. Talk is cheap. And it still doesn't answer the question.'

'You're absolutely right,' Karl agreed, surprising them all. 'Talk is cheap.'

Taking the silver badge from his lapel, he opened the fastening pin and with a swift steady movement pushed it through the fleshy part of his extended tongue. He curled his tongue so that everyone could see the steel point had penetrated to the underside. After a moment he removed the pin and calmly re-fastened the badge to his lapel.

4

As they were filing out of the mess hall one of the base controllers touched Karl's shoulder and gestured that he should stand aside. Karl waited, arms folded. He guessed what was coming. He'd made an idiot of himself by breaking the rule of self-aggrandisement. Such pathetic posturing should be beneath an adept with his training and experience. He might even lose status.

Karl followed the base controller from the mess hall to a covered walkway linking the lodges. He feared the worst because they were heading towards the C+C (Command and Control) block, essentially the nerve-centre of the operation. This was 'access restricted' to all adepts. Once inside, they went along a short passageway and through a heavy wooden door which led, to Karl's shock and amazement, to a steep flight of steps cut into the rock. They were going *down*. Karl had never realised there was anything below ground level. It occurred to him that the stockade might have been built on top of an old mine – there were scores of abandoned mines in the eastern part of Nevada.

Hewn out of solid rock, the narrow tunnel was lit by globes in wire cages. The air was cool and fresh, wafted against their faces by hidden fans. Finally they came to a door made of split logs. The base controller pushed it open and indicated that Karl should enter. The space was confined, a small gloomy cell, and once the door was shut he was left alone in darkness and silence.

Was this his punishment, to be put into isolation? Karl didn't mind. Hours or days, or even weeks – the length of time was unimportant – providing his status wasn't degraded; that was his greatest fear.

But he wasn't alone. His senses detected a presence. Had he been locked away with another wrongdoer and rule-breaker?

'Sit down, son.'

Karl's heart hammered in his chest. So it really was this serious, because he recognised the voice straight away, and now that his eyes were adjusting to the gloom he could make out the concave planes of the gaunt face with its deep shadowy eye sockets and the taut ligatures of the neck emerging from the black robes.

Supreme Commander and Mission Leader of the MOG.

'Sit down, Karl. Relax,' Pastor Eldritch said, and it was as if a huge weight had been lifted from Karl's shoulders because he knew by the welcoming words and casual tone that he was not going to be punished or degraded; everything was going to be all right.

Feeling behind him, Karl found a plastic chair and sat down. He tried to calm his breathing. He'd seen Pastor Eldritch often before but this was the first time he had been alone in his revered presence.

'We were impressed with your performance today, Karl. I liked what I saw. You were very calm and cool in the way you accomplished the operation. Straight out of the book. Impressive also that it was your first shot at carrying out an ascendancy.'

There was a pause, and Karl filled it by saying, 'Thank you, Mission Leader.'

He understood now what the Pastor must have seen in him from the beginning, and he exulted in the faith placed in him, that the shy, intense kid who rarely smiled had fulfilled that promise and was ready.

'You've achieved OBEs and have become a fine example to others in the community, even some older than yourself. So I think the time has come to upgrade you to Mission Status.'

Karl's throat was dry and he was trembling.

'You're one of the youngest, if not *the* youngest, to be selected, Karl, which means that we expect more of you. Your sense of purpose must be keener, your desire sharper, your resolve stronger. Age brings disillusionment and the prospect of failure, but at seventeen such doubts lie in the future. You copy?'

'I copy,' Karl answered.

'The briefing plan hasn't yet been finalised,' Pastor Eldritch went on in his droning voice. 'It will be ready in four or five days. As of now, future time and place and movement of the prospective ascendant are being monitored. The likely location will be Boston, Massachusetts. An optimum point for ascendancy has yet to be decided on. Follow the mission brief as closely as you possibly can – but not slavishly. You've been trained to obey orders but also to use your own initiative should circumstances dictate otherwise. You're out there on your own, as if you were in space, so the final decisions to achieve success rest with you and you alone. We at Mission Control can't make them for you. Is that clear?'

'Affirmative.'

Karl could now make out Pastor Eldritch's face in more detail. It resembled a skull more than anything living, deep black holes instead of eyes, the skin shiny and tight like vellum. Karl had never been able to study him so closely before. He had never known that Pastor Eldritch reeked of death.

'This mission is one of many, but each is vital to our ultimate goal. I know you won't fail us, Karl.'

'"To be reborn it is necessary to die first,"' Karl intoned, repeating from the manual.

'One final word of caution.' The Pastor's voice sank to a whisper. 'The Mothership and our community here must be protected, whatever the cost. If you find yourself in a no-go situation, there is only one option – abort. You know what that means. You know the procedure. You have been well-trained. Do I need to say more?'

'Negative.'

'You will receive travel documentation, pyro-equipment, expense vouchers and termination pack twenty-four hours before departure. Questions?'

Karl was too excited to think straight. He shook his head dumbly. His own mission at last!

'Prepare yourself in the time remaining. Meditate on rising and give your thoughts to achieving a perfect ascension. I won't see you again before you leave, so I'll wish you good luck and success, Karl. A-OK?'

'A-OK, Mission Leader.'

When Karl had departed, the Pastor sat quietly and mulled over the interview. The boy was a good candidate, and the decision to award him Mission Status was the correct one. Keen, competent, loyal, determined. Made of the right stuff. The Pastor couldn't remember without aid which particular Karl he had been named after and did a quick check on the database.

Karl Henize: 1967 NASA Group Six.

It had been the Pastor's idea that everyone in the community should take the name of an astronaut who had actually flown, and he had obeyed his own instruction: in his case using his middle name to become Pastor Eldritch, from a lost and forgotten lifetime: Bradley E. Zittel: 1984 NASA Group Ten (*The Maggots*).

5

It had been tough at first, trying to shed his old identity. In those early days and months he still thought of himself as Brad Zittel. He carried with him the emotional baggage of his previous life: not just the memories of wife and children but the years of rigorous training and preparation, the comradeship and pride in being a member of an elite corps. The weight of the past was too great, too personal, too damn *near* if he stayed in the US.

So he began the long journey that would become a pilgrimage, stretching over years and continents. He walked many thousands of miles, wearing simple garments and leather sandals, carrying an old canvas NASA holdall for the absolute basic necessities. He had no money and he did no work, yet in all that time he had rarely been hungry. The people he moved amongst were poor and had little, but he had nothing, and it was the simple custom of goodness and brotherhood to provide for those less fortunate than oneself. A handful of brown rice. A hunk of maize bread. On good days a small portion of goat's meat, sometimes with mashed beans. Perhaps even small fish, cooked underneath flat stones in the glowing embers until the skin was crisp and brittle. Each meal was a feast.

His body erupted in sores, which festered and became succulent feeding places for parasites and flies. He almost died of malaria and lay for days in a burning, shaking stupor, tended by two old women who starved the fever out of him. Twice he was bitten by venomous snakes, which had curled close to share his body heat while he slept. He became thin, almost to the point of emaciation, with stringy arms and lean flanks; yet harder, tougher and more resilient, able to withstand the heat, cold and the hardships of travel over long distances, always on foot.

One accident damaged him permanently; he had fallen down a steep rocky ravine and smashed his left knee. The healing took many months, leaving the limb misshapen, and thereafter his walk was lurching and ungainly and caused him much pain.

His face changed beyond recognition; burned and cracked by the sun and blistered by the wind, the flesh tautened on his cheekbones, leaving deep hollows beneath. His chin became a jutting knob of bone. In this prematurely aged mask his eyes appeared uncommonly large, the white tinged with blue so that they looked even whiter, the brown irises clear and brilliant like convex mirrors. His stare was daunting in its naked, uncompromising directness.

The complete transfiguration took place in the middle of a single night when he was least expecting it and ill-prepared for the consequences. He was living in a dwelling made of straw- and mud-bricks, in a community of fewer than twenty people. The people around him were outcasts and he sensed that they feared and respected him in about equal measure.

Fasting sharpened his awareness while meditation focused his mind.

The outer world faded away as he slid into a state of trance. Even so, every fibre of his being seemed alive and receptive, as if all his senses were sharpened and heightened to a pitch that was above and beyond human reach:

Listening.

Watching.

Touching.

Tasting.

Experiencing.

He was alive and aware of the present, of his surroundings, and at the same time his consciousness expanded until it transcended time and space. Later, he could only describe it to himself as floating away from his physical shell and looking down on the reality of existence. His inner eye conjured up the blue-white bowling ball swinging through the void. Only it was not as he himself had seen it, and remembered it, from space: clear and sparkling and pristine. In this new reality it was wreathed in a grey miasma. The atmosphere was turbid and choking, a dense impenetrable blanket. The once-sweet rainwater that flooded from the skies scorched the flesh. The oceans moved sluggishly, clogged with dying plants and fish. Every breath was a painful gasp.

He was seeing the future.

His inner eye probed further and saw the horror of what was to come. The planet, the home he had seen from space, the Mothership, was dying. It was too late for change. The human species had been give its chance to care for the habitat, and failed – and fouled its own nest.

For the planet to survive, to be re-born, it must be purged of mankind. There was no other course. He saw now with piercing clarity what his destiny should be, and what he must strive to accomplish. With this revelation came the idea of recruiting others to help him with the task of wiping out the deadly spawn that was corrupting and polluting the Mothership. Even those striving to save the habitat should not be spared – if anything, they were more to blame, for they were prolonging mankind's tenancy and delaying the day of renewal and rebirth. Wipe the slate clean and let nature start anew: it was the only way.

This was how it would be. This was how it *must* be. He would bring it about.

The walls of matted straw and mud-brick swam back into focus. The oil lamp, turned low, burned with a smoky orange light, making a steady dim circle on the earthen floor. In this circle, at his feet, he saw the scorpion.

It was the colour of pale amber, its translucent body relaxed, not curled in the stinging position. The claws twitched and opened towards him, wavering slightly as if preparing for a courtship dance. Possibly it sensed the heat of his body.

He waited, motionless, his senses quiescent.

One of the creature's claws touched the big toe of his left foot and immediately went still. This was the damaged leg, misshapen and incapable of being straightened. But he could feel the creature. After a moment the claws opened and tentatively gripped his toe, as if testing it. The creature had to decide between three options. Food. Friend. Enemy.

Which was it to be?

Perhaps two out of three: Enemy *and* Food.

Then he lost sight of the creature as it crawled beneath his bent right knee. He was being tickled on the sole of his left foot. The claws appeared, like blind insects, over the curve of his thigh. Up it came, labouring to gain a purchase, its segmented body gleaming faintly in the lamplight.

His right hand was spread on the crown of his knee and the scorpion used his fingers as the rungs of a ladder to haul itself on to the back of his hand. There it rested, claws raised in the attitude of a boxer wearing outsize gloves, prepared to defend itself.

It was so light he could hardly feel the faintest sensation: just a few grams on delicate jointed legs – yet the bulbous gland with its pointed sting at the end of the coiled tail contained enough venom to kill a giant several thousand times its size and weight. Including a man.

A mosquito whined in the stillness. The oil lamp unfurled its dark ribbon of smoke to a blackened spot on the domed roof.

He raised his hand and brought the scorpion level with his eyes and looked at it. The creature was alerted. Its tail sprang up and coiled stiffly over its head, the glistening sting extended and poised to attack. The man and creature looked eye-to-eye at one another. There could be no communication or point of understanding between them, except both were sentient beings and imbued with some mysterious form of life-force. Nothing interrupted this communion of silence except for the faint spluttering of the oil lamp.

Slowly and carefully he placed his hand flat on the earthen floor. After a moment, the sting retracted and the tail folded back on itself and the scorpion crawled off into the shadows.

The appearance of the scorpion (his friend and companion, as he thought of it) was a test. Had he felt fear, he would have failed. It would have shown that his ego, his identity, was intact. In its place there was instead the concept, vast and impersonal, of a cosmic ocean into which selfhood was merged. Ultimate reality, he at last realised, could be attained by any method the disciple wished, providing he had dispensed with ego.

And he had felt no fear.

His ego was dead.

And without ego there could be no fear of death of self, since that impostor no longer existed.

He had passed the test A-OK.

6

Soon after that night – the Night of the Scorpion, as he now thought of it – he discarded the sense of who he had been and took his middle name to become Pastor Eldritch; with this change of identity the transformation was complete.

On his return to the States, Pastor Eldritch spent three months in New York. During this period he shared living space in an ashram, which was a converted loft in what had been a warehouse on Cleveland Street in the SoHo district. He was a generation older than any of the others, and in these young people he saw signs of spiritual malaise and a deep-rooted disillusionment. Whenever approached by the initiates who had heard of his pilgrimage, it strengthened his own belief, because they were invigorated and fired by the same passion to sweep away the rotten corruptness which surrounded them. They desired, as did he, a fresh new beginning; some prayed for the dropping of the bomb to purify the way ahead, which the Pastor was smart enough to adopt as a tenet of the new faith; he named it the Scorched Earth Doctrine.

All those years ago he had been alone on his journey; now there were others, younger and stronger, who would follow him if he was prepared to lead them. But lead them where? There was an answer, and Pastor Eldritch knew he would find it – or it would find him.

It was the 23rd Chapter of Charmed Baptist Brethren that found him first. Some of the Pastor's messages (he didn't call them sermons) were online, under the sobriquet MOG, and these were passed around by members of the 23rd Chapter e-Congregation. Very soon he was asked to present himself to the administrative board of the church at their headquarters in McLean, not far from DC.

That was nearly five years ago, and since then the relationship had grown into a permanent bond – though not everyone of the Charmed Baptist Brethren approved of Pastor Eldritch, or of MOG either.

Pastor Eldritch had first been introduced to Chesney Lea Poulton through the church, and the contact had proved heaven-sent. It was Poulton, as a member of the admin board, who had arranged to provide the funding which enabled the Messengers of God to construct their community base in Nevada, on top of what had been an abandoned mine—

The Mothership.

The tax-exempt 'donation' was indeed generous: more than six million dollars had been transferred to an undercover business account in Carson City, and that was just a one-off contribution to get the project underway, finagle state planning laws and to provide lumber, building materials, transportation costs.

Everything was done strictly by the book: in other words, concealment by means of fiscal instruments. The purchase of land, for instance, had been arranged by an attorney who was a member of the 23rd Chapter. He had filtered the financial package through a series of holding companies to disguise the ultimate buyer. The continued funding by the Charmed Baptist Brethren was unceasing and as bountiful as ever: $3.5 million a year via holding companies and charities.

This meant that the Pastor and those adepts who had achieved Mission Status were able to travel anywhere in the country while carrying out their ascendancy programme. Roughly half of the recipients were selected by the Messengers of God (in reality Pastor Eldritch), the rest by Chesney Poulton, who called it his 'kill list' – though only in private to Burt Mueller, his chief of staff at AAAV; never to anyone outside. Definitely not to the Pastor.

The latest candidate for ascendant status – Lautner, a professor at MIT – had been nominated by Chesney Poulton. The Pastor accepted this nomination without demur. He had never heard of Professor Lautner, but so what? Part of the deal for receiving the funding from the Charmed Baptist Brethren was that the MOG plan, prepare and carry out these ascensions, discreetly, professionally, no questions asked.

For this one – his very first mission – he had chosen Karl. He would carry it out superbly well, of that, Pastor Eldritch had no doubt.

4

I

Though the bruising on his chest and upper arm had faded, Binch still didn't have full articulation in that arm. But he was determined to go back to the office, even if Si Musso started fussing up a storm yet again about the TV spat with that charlatan academic Martin Stringer.

Binch eased himself out of the pickup and slammed the door shut with his good hand. There had been no serious damage sustained, and once it had been hauled out of the drainage gully and checked over by the garage, the mechanic had said it was okay to drive.

By nature Binch wasn't a confrontational person; he much preferred to settle disputes by talking things over calmly, in a civilised manner; and so as he went up the steps to the entrance of the Atmospheric Lab building he felt leaden inside, dreading yet another unpleasant scene with Musso.

'Dr Inchcape, do you have a moment?' a voice said as he passed through the sliding doors into the lobby.

Binch half-turned to see a tall, broad-shouldered figure in a dark grey suit, crisp white shirt with narrow tie, looming over him. He was bald on top with both sides shaved close to the scalp, and the first thing Binch noticed was that he had rather large ears, and in one of them he wore an earpiece.

Not more damn security. It must be costing the NCPF a small fortune, Binch thought irritably. *They're slashing our budget and yet they're hiring—*

Then he noticed there were two more of them, a white guy and a black guy, both as tall and powerfully built as the first, both with an earpiece. One of them was even wearing impenetrable black aviator shades, indoors.

'Can you confirm you are Dr William Inchcape,' the first man said.

Binch was in the middle as they formed a tight group. He craned his neck. 'Yes, I'm Dr Inchcape. And who are you? What do you want?'

The three men exchanged glances. The first man said, 'We are acting under federal authority. Come along with us, please.'

'Come along where? What are you talking about? No, I certainly will not!' Binch tried to edge out of the group. The black guy grasped him by the arm – the injured one as it happened – and Binch yelped and sucked in a sharp breath of pain. 'Hey! Leave off, don't do that – who the hell are you?'

He tried to see past them into the lobby itself to the reception station at the central desk, but instead felt cool air swirling around his legs as he was hustled out, back through the doors, and almost frog-marched down the steps to the parking lot. Binch tried to protest again, but he was winded by the speed and surprise of it all. As far as he could tell there was no one around to see what was happening; even if there had been it would have looked no more remarkable than a tight-knit group of men walking quickly to a long-axle black SUV with a sliding side door and tinted windows.

As they approached the vehicle the door slid open and Binch was hoisted inside onto the bench seat.

'Dr Inchcape . . .' At the far end of the seat, an older, grizzled man with square-framed spectacles and cropped white hair was holding something up. In the muted daylight of the interior it was hard to make out what exactly – a badge? ID card?

'Under the power granted to me as an officer of the US Federal Court, you are subpoenaed to enter a plea on a charge of Treasonous Subversion as defined under the emergent UnPatriot Act, now passing into law. These are your rights.'

'My *rights*?' Binch said in shock and disbelief. 'I demand to know what right you have, you and your goons—'

The older man held up a finger to his lips and slowly shook his head.

'And if I don't, so what can you do?' Binch said. He'd got his breath back and his anger was notching ten. 'You think I'm gonna just stay quiet and let—'

The older man sighed and at his gesture the black guy's hand shot out and his fingers dug deep into the discoloured and tender shoulder. Binch almost passed out.

'Don't go easy, Bryce,' the older man said. 'And every time he opens his mouth, do it again.'

The black agent slid onto the bench seat alongside Binch. The door slammed shut.

2

The Feni River Delta, the largest on the planet, was in trouble on a catastrophic scale. Fed by the mighty Ganges, the delta was the heartbeat and the lifeblood of Bangladesh, a country of only 56,000 square miles – less than the size of Wisconsin – but with more than 160 million inhabitants, one of the most densely populated in the world. Hemmed in on three sides by the Indian sub-continent, with the Bay of Bengal at its feet, Bangladesh and the sea had a love-hate relationship – or to be more exact, a life-death relationship.

Forty years before, they had constructed a massive dam by the sweat of manpower alone to keep the ocean at bay, but with the unstoppable rise in sea-levels, the dam was finally breached and overcome and the waters were now creeping remorselessly up-country. The delta and its people were drowning.

The head of the field mission for the Médecins Sans Frontières emergency team in the eastern province of Chittagong surveyed an expanse of the Feni River Delta. The mingled river current and seawater were in ferment, stretching from horizon to horizon. Pierre Boutin lowered the binoculars and called to his medical coordinator.

The young woman rose from the trestle table, pushing a hand through her mop of curly dark hair as she joined him at the observation window. She fanned herself with a sealed field-dressing pack.

'Take a look over there, Ruth.' Boutin pointed to the northwest. 'I don't know, maybe my eyes they play tricks. Your eyes are not so old. Tell me what you see.'

Ruth Brosnan took the binoculars from him, fine-tuned the calibration and did a broad sweep of where he had indicated. Then she carried out a series of narrower sweeps, homing in on what looked like an uprooted mango tree being carried along on the surge.

'What do you think?' Boutin asked. 'Any people there? Crazy, I know, but I thought I saw an arm raised . . .'

He shrugged again; more a shrug of weariness and despondency than resignation. He pushed his spectacles up with thumb and forefinger and massaged his eye sockets. A tall, loose-limbed man in his sixties, with elegant greying hair swept behind his ears, tiredness was etched into every pore.

'Difficult to tell, Pierre. It's a tangle of brush and what looks like palm fronds.' Ruth frowned with the effort of concentration. 'I can't see anything moving.'

They were both of them nearly dead on their feet. In the past forty-eight hours they had barely managed a few snatched minutes of rest. They were existing on distilled water, instant coffee and a supply of toasted almonds and peanuts Ruth had in her backpack.

Arching his spine, Boutin pressed the heels of his hands into the small of his back and then slumped into a canvas chair. Ruth continued her sweep of the turbulent waters. This observation platform, with its thatched roof, was the last remaining structure on what had been the Dhaka-Chittagong Dam; the rest of the ten-metre high revetment had been lost to the sea.

'Wait a minute!'

Boutin started, shaken from his doze.

'Pierre, I think you're right. It's a raised arm, somebody waving, I'm almost certain. Looks to be caked in mud . . .'

The mango tree was moving in a wide arc towards them, driven by the swirling current. If it also had a human passenger – or passengers – it would have been no more miraculous than what Ruth and the head of mission had witnessed in the past week or so.

The humanitarian effort, of which the Médecins Sans Frontières' thirty-strong team was a part, had been mounted in response to a gigantic mudflow further up the delta. With the breaching of the dam, a 120-feet-high wall of mud had been forced through a narrow gorge and spread over sixteen square miles of rice fields and village communities, displacing tens of thousands. Near the town of Muhuri, 23,000 people had been swept away by the mudflow – more than half of them engulfed and lost; the rest survived, by some miracle or other, rescued by hundreds of volunteers. Pierre and Ruth, alongside the others in their team, had worked nonstop to provide medical aid as the wretched survivors were brought in.

The last ones had been treated and evacuated by boat around 2 a.m., six hours ago.

Ruth lowered the binoculars to rest her eyes and took a sip of water. Her phone beeped softly on the trestle table. When she answered it, no one spoke and there was no voicemail either, but the display said MESSAGE INTERRUPTED. A flashing icon told her it was an international call. Ruth guessed who it might be. It was the third call from Stella Inchcape, Bill's wife, that had failed to get through. Ruth had tried a couple of times to call her back and failed too, thanks to the remoteness and the poor signal.

If Ruth had been unsettled by the first failed call, now she was the wrong side of worried sick. Stella knew she was working abroad and wouldn't have bothered her unless it was urgent. Binch had been under stress in his job and had a heart condition. Had something happened to him?

She took up the binoculars and adjusted the focus: the tree was now much nearer.

Pierre had been right: there was indeed a human being entangled in the roots of the mango tree . . . or something that had once been human. Her stomach churned and Ruth wished now she hadn't looked.

It was as if the raised arm and cupped hand, covered in mud baked hard by the sun, had been arrested in the act of swimming. The rest of the person was inside a large solid glob of oil and mud and vegetation and what looked like a market awning, its bright colours streaked dark. The man was literally entombed, frozen even as he struggled to survive.

With a sadness that was almost exhausted, Ruth turned to tell Pierre his eyes were still pretty good, and he could trust what they told him – unfortunately.

Her boss was snoring in the canvas chair behind her, chin on his chest, a lock of grey hair across his forehead. She didn't disturb him.

3

It was 8.30 p.m. when Micki Vargas put her head round the door of Chase's corner office. He was standing at the window lost in thought.

'No home to go to, boy? No place to rest your weary head?'

Chase came back to himself and turned to face her. 'Cheryl's not back from her trip yet. She's heading for an overnight in Hawaii and then onto Los Angeles. Two, three days and . . .' He caught Micki's expression. 'Something up?'

'Not sure yet, boss. Glad you're still here though. Come see.'

He followed her through into the open-plan area with its rows of screens and softly humming consoles, skeins of multi-coloured cabling snaking across the floor. Most of the stations were unattended; just four people remained.

Micki leaned over the hunched shoulders of a black kid in a wrinkled T-shirt, peach-fuzz on his upper lip and chin. 'Still gettin' it, Jervis? Stronger or not?'

Jervis mumbled something which Chase didn't catch, though evidently Micki understood. 'Have you tried a wider sweep? It might be weak because it's long distance, maybe. What you think?'

The kid was scanning three screens simultaneously. Each screen showed a solid block of numbers and symbols. Chase couldn't have deciphered a single line if his son's life depended on it. As he watched, Jervis did something with his thumb and the screens divided into four sectors, each one whizzing upwards so fast the digits blurred.

'Jervis thinks we're under cyber-attack,' Micki said. 'Or anyway, they're probing around, searching for a weak spot. We've switched servers to see if Caliban is following us.'

'Caliban?'

'Jervis's codename for the raider.'

'How will Jervis know?'

'Know what?'

'If Caliban is trying to attack or . . . what's the buzzword? Penetrate.'

Micki slowly doubled over, hugging herself. She was biting her lip and there were tears in her eyes. '*Infiltrate.*'

'Yeah. I get it. Highly amusing, Ms Vargas. I knew it was a phallic reference of some description.'

When Micki had partially recovered, still dabbing her eyes, she explained to him that Jervis was playing Caliban as an expert fly-fisherman plays and feints a catch; the difference was that it was *two* fly-fishermen, and they were both experts, both cunning, each one as devious and wily as the other.

'Okay,' Chase said, 'I see that. Nice analogy. But if and when Jervis locates Caliban, can he identify the person or organisation that's making these attacks? NSA? CIA?'

'Or it could be Fut/COE I guess – Future Crisis Operations Executive.'

'Never heard of them.'

'They used to be called ASP – changed their name for some reason.'

'I've heard of them all right,' Chase said. 'And I've met the guy who ran the outfit.'

'You know that douche-bag Colonel Malden?'

'I met him, can't say I knew him. But he was a lieutenant then.' Chase was astonished. Not so much that Malden was alive and breathing, but that he hadn't advanced further up the greasy pole than a lowly colonel.

'How'd you meet such an evil twat as him?'

'I used to move in better social circles. I'll tell you about it someday.' Chase was worried and impatient: he gestured to the screens and the whizzing digits. 'If Caliban breaks into our system could he identify our location – the business park, I mean, specifically this building?'

'It would narrow the search to a region or possibly a city,' Micki said. 'That's as close as he could get. No fear a detachment of marines is going to come busting in through the window any time soon.'

'You think it's a government probe? Or military?'

'We won't know unless Jervis can isolate and identify Caliban before Caliban does the same to us. All depends who's fastest on the trigger.'

Chase wasn't reassured. 'Not only who, but why is the question. Are they trying to block us or just searching for information?'

'There's another possibility.'

'Which is?'

'They're attempting to infect the system without us knowing it.'

'With a virus?'

Micki nodded. 'If they're very smart and have the latest tech they could lurk in there, snug as a bug, steal our codes, monitor our traffic, see and hear everything that goes in, out, or through. Now you're on a safe bet the Seals *would* come busting in through the window.'

'Hell's bells,' Chase said softly. 'That would be end-game.'

'Set and match.'

'We'd better hope Jervis's quick on the trigger then.'

'He's the fastest draw in Deadwood,' Micki said.

Chase jerked his thumb towards the kid hunched over, eyes flicking from screen to screen, and mouthed, *How old is he?* and when Micki answered *Fourteen*, Chase rolled his eyes to heaven. He said aloud, 'How long will it take, tracking Caliban to his lair?'

'Ten minutes,' Micki said.

'Oh . . . right!'

'Or ten hours.'

'Ah . . . you mean all night.'

'And another ten on top of that – maybe. We just don't know, Gav.'

Chase looked at his watch. 'What do we do? Hang around till morning?'

'Not much point,' Micki said. 'We're as much use here as a fart in a wind-tunnel. Listen, seeing as you've no home to go to, let me buy you a drink. The minute Jervis cracks it, he'll get on the phone. We can always come back.' She gave him a brilliant flashing smile. 'What say, boss-man?'

Chase couldn't see any flaw in having a drink with a beautiful woman whose company he enjoyed and who made him laugh. No harm in that, no harm at all.

While Micki went to collect her things he returned to his office and was locking the file cabinet when his phone buzzed on the desk. Seeing there was no caller listed he wasn't going to answer, then changed his mind. The line was atrocious, like listening to a hailstorm. A man's voice with a strong foreign accent asked to speak with Dr Gavin Chase. When

Chase confirmed it, a woman came on, faint and distorted through the crackles, yet clearly distressed.

'Gav, is that you? This is Ruth Brosnan. I've just picked up a message from Stella Inchcape. Binch has been arrested or detained, or something, I'm not sure. Stella doesn't even know who by or what the reason is. It's very confusing. She's been trying to reach you but gets no reply. Gav, can you hear me? Gav—?'

4

Newly promoted intel/anal Howard Nevison wasn't happy about his first assignment for AAAV on two counts.

One: tracking down some two-bit activist website leaking low-level classified material was way below his skill set and pay-grade. There must be thousands – hell, *tens* of thousands – of these anarchist shit-stirring sites such as Midnite-Net; as far as he could tell this one was no different, no more subversive or more of a threat than any of the others.

Howard was beginning to regret leaving his previous job at Black/ PROP, which had been absorbing and challenging, for what he had mistakenly assumed was a step-up to Extreme Top Secret work of national importance.

Two: the prime-echelon Level Five files he'd been ploughing through for the past week made distinctly queasy reading, as far as he was concerned. He'd probably dug a little deeper than his brief required, or Chesney Poulton had anticipated. But the environmental activists dossier had piqued his curiosity as well as giving him a nasty jolt . . . 768 murdered or 'disappeared' in just two years! On top of which Howard had come across another cache of recent reports for Venezuela and Ecuador, listing more deaths and disappearances – 132 of them – which brought the grand total to a neatly rounded-off 900.

These were brutal and ugly facts it was hard to stomach: 900 people disposed of for protecting their land and rivers and lakes from encroachment and exploitation. The stark figures on the page didn't paint a pretty picture.

And how many locals and native inhabitants had perished in the cause, too, not worth even the anonymous memorial of a number in a file . . .

'Mr Nevison? Sir?'

Howard swivelled round from his workstation. The two Tech-Bots (as they were unflatteringly called, though never to their faces) were at an adjacent bench. It was their tedious task to do the mind-numbing graft, then feed the results to Howard.

The sub-basement of the AAAV building on K Street was the sweetest spot in the entire complex, thanks to the air-conditioning installed at vast expense to soothe and pamper the banks of computers, servers and quantum-memory grids, and stop them from going into a meltdown. Concern for the precious hardware came first, naturally, but their human slaves also gleaned the benefit of a fresh cool atmosphere.

'What have you got?'

The jaws of the Tech-Bot who'd claimed his attention were moving like a cow's chewing the cud on a wad of gum. It was slovenly and disrespectful, and Howard wasn't amused.

'That trace-route you wanted on Midnite-Net. At the latest count we've upwards of' – the masticating Tech-Bot glanced back at the screen – 'forty-one network paths involving at least twenty random servers located in as many countries from China through Uzbekistan to New Zealand to Argentina to—'

'Anywhere near locating the geophysical host?'

'Not yet.'

'Is it Stateside?'

The Tech-Bot shrugged. 'Couldn't say.'

'So your question is?'

The Tech-Bot swapped the wad to the other side of his mouth before answering. 'Well, I guess . . . what d'ya want we should try next? This might take for ever. We could engage a proxy encryption search. Or check for a spoofing source maybe . . . ?'

He raised his eyebrows, waiting for a response, and when none came, glanced across to his colleague. Howard saw they were both making an effort to keep a straight face.

'Unless it's in the DarkNet,' the other Tech-Bot chimed in, pinching his nose hard to stifle his sniggering.

Plain what they were up to: the age-old game of using geek jargon to demonstrate their superior technical expertise.

'What do you suggest we do?'

The Tech-Bot paused, chewing sloppily with his mouth half-open. 'I guess it's your call,' he said, staring at Howard. 'Sir.'

'Don't you know what you need to do?'

The Tech-Bot grinned. 'Sure.'

'Well, in that case,' Howard said in a sweet and reasonable tone, 'I suggest you stop jerking off and fucking get down to it, unless you want to pull a 48-hour load this weekend including a double night-shift.'

The second Tech-Bot was nettled. 'The primary source keeps re-routing through all these domains. Every time we get close he gives us the finger and he's gone.'

'Is that the answer you'd like me to take to the director-in-chief?' Howard was mad because he was the one who'd carry the can if they failed to deliver; and Poulton wasn't the understanding type. 'You've got state-of-the-art global surveillance sweep and enough computing power to fly us to Mars and back. What do I tell him? You couldn't find your ass in a darkened room with a flashlight?'

The Tech-Bots swivelled their chairs and went back to work, one of them muttering something with a lot of hard consonants.

Howard let it go. Eyes on the screen, he took a swig of root beer from a cardboard cup while he perused the Level Five database. It crossed his mind to wonder if the Tech-Bots had clearance for this material. Maybe he shouldn't even be looking at it with them in the same room. Much of what he read was deeply strange stuff for an organisation such as the Alliance for the Advancement of American Values to be involved in; there was almost a quasi-religious ring to it.

For instance, a lot of communication between the director-in-chief and the Church of Charmed Baptist Brethren at McLean, north of DC. Money transfers were mentioned – some of the sums were eye-watering, in the tens of millions of dollars – flowing from AAAV into church coffers. The source of all this cash was a mystery. Most of it, as far as

Howard could make out, came from somewhere in the Middle East and from there found its way into various foundations and trusts based in the Virgin Islands and the Bahamas. The AAAV had bank accounts in both places and it was a simple matter to transfer the money – maybe as simple as walking across the street with a suitcase stuffed with $100 bills from one bank to the other.

The real screwy thing was why a religious institution should receive financial support in the first place. The aim and purpose of the AAAV, as its name proclaimed, was to spread the American ideals of freedom and democracy and justice to the rest of the globe, not to evangelise for a particular creed.

None of this had anything to do with his assignment, but Howard couldn't help being both puzzled and intrigued; his curiosity was aroused, and he wanted to get to the bottom of the mystery. He swiped the screen and followed a link to open a sub-menu. Evidently he'd crossed a no-go line because the screen went black. Then up popped a caption:

SECURITY CODE REQUIRED:
CBF/90081-12-074

Fortunately he had clearance and been vouchsafed the cyphers. Howard punched in the appropriate pass-code from a list in his pocket and was granted access. The first item from the new menu that caught his eye read: MOG. He opened the file to learn that MOG stood for 'Messengers of God' and that it was a group affiliated with the Charmed Baptists . . . back on the religious kick again!

Why information on a religious group should require Level Five security clearance baffled him. What was buried down here, the secrets of the Holy Grail?

The deeper he went into it, the less Howard felt he understood. There were jargon words and arcane phrases he couldn't make sense of, such as 'Ascendancy Status (To Be Confirmed)'. He clicked open the file to find a list of about twenty names. One name sprang out at him.

Professor Gerald Lautner.

This could be no other than Gerry Lautner, who held the chair of humanities and ethics at MIT, the academic Howard revered above all others. In his final two years there, Howard had forged a close bond of friendship with Gerry, who might have been in his early fifties, but had the same outlook and verve of a guy thirty years younger. Howard thought of him almost as he might an older brother.

Ascendancy Status? What the fuck was that all about? Ascending where?

If there was an answer to that question, Howard couldn't find it. Hardly surprising with the vast amount of data in the classified cache. He could sit here 24/7 for the next six months and be no nearer.

But none of this was helping resolve the assignment Poulton had handed him. The lack of progress was making Howard anxious. If the Tech-Bots were hopelessly blocked in effecting a trace, there had to be other means of achieving it, other avenues to explore. Feeling frustrated, he shut down the Level Five programme and spent the next hour or so sifting through the Climate Alert blogs Midnite-Net had been issuing over the previous two years. You only had to read a handful of alerts before realising why major international corporations hated the Midnite crowd like poison. The information they'd leaked and made public on the numbers of environmental activists murdered or 'disappeared' was pretty tame compared to the revelations about the secret polluting record and illegal exploitation of natural resources by oil and gas companies, mining syndicates, chemical companies and pharmaceutical giants – aided by the willing collusion of politicians of every stripe.

If there was a theme running through all Midnite activity it was focusing awareness on the degradation and despoilment of the natural world: who was causing the damage and what the long-term effects might be.

This was confirmed by an info-chart Howard found on their site that summed up many of their concerns. It was titled 'Oxygen Balance Sheet: Profit & Loss' and showed in simple diagrammatic form the strains the planet's oxygen budget was under from the progress of civilisation. Howard had no idea if the science behind it was accurate or exaggerated, credible or far-fetched. But he could understand why the Alliance for the Advancement of American Values would see it as dangerous, subversive propaganda, its message a threat to the national interests.

The Tech-Bot with the sloppy chewing habit broke Howard's thread of concentration by cursing under his breath.

Howard took a sip of root beer and asked, not expecting any miracles, what he'd found.

'Not a fuckin' thing – they've found us, the sneaky bastards!'

'What do you mean?'

'They've deployed an anti-probe screen and they know we're operating a trace-route search for their signal ID.' He was shaking his head in bafflement. 'Would you believe it? They've actually designated us a codename!' He wrote something down on his pad.

'When you say "found us", can they identify who we are?' Howard asked, his anxiety rising.

'No, we're too well protected. They just know there's A Prowler out there . . . unidentified.' The Tech-Bot picked up his pad and frowned at it. 'Our prowler tag, for your information, is "Caliban". Whatever the fuck that means.'

'It's from *The Tempest*,' Howard said. He turned back to his own bank of screens, almost in despair. Just what in hell would he have to put in his report to the director-in-chief in twenty-four hours' time that wouldn't make Chesney Poulton bite so hard on his Cuban cigar that it exploded? Nothing, except the wonderful news that his hunters had just become the hunted.

5

Probably the worse thing was not knowing if it was day or night. Night or day. The result of being hooded while on the move. Time soon lost its meaning. Hands pinioned in plastic bracelets, ankles constrained in chain-linked shackles.

Binch knew it had been early morning when they picked him up, but blindness, movement, being roughly transferred from a vehicle to an aircraft, still hooded, then hours in the air made everything a meaningless blur. The shock he felt didn't help: the suddenness of his arrest, this claustrophobic dense blackness in which it was difficult to breathe, the rough material tightly enclosing his head, all contributed to a rising sense of panic making his heart beat madly.

That was another cause for worry – they'd emptied his pockets and taken his medication. When Binch had asked for it he'd received no answer, and for good measure a sharp blow (it felt like someone's elbow) to the side of the head. He got the message. Then his mouth became raspy and dry and soon the dread of not having his medication was replaced by the torture of raging thirst. It became an obsessive need. He tried to gather a little spit to moisten his throat. Not even a smear. His tongue felt bloated, as if covered in sand.

His croak of pleading received the same treatment as before. It jarred his skull and set off a buzzing in his brain.

Then Binch must have dozed off, or gone into a stupor. It might have been for minutes or for hours. When he came back to himself, on top of the throat-crawling thirst he was bursting for a piss. How could that be? Parched at one extremity, too much liquid at the other?

The pain became so intense he thought his bladder would rupture. It was a steady *throb-throb-throb*, like a pumping heart. Binch was in such dire agony that he felt he must pass out any second, when suddenly a blessed warmth spread through his loins. His bladder had released itself, involuntarily, and the relief was exquisite.

Then a voice did speak. 'Did no one think to use a diaper? Jesus, look at the mess. Find a waterproof. Pennell, get me the scissors.'

Binch felt air circulating on his legs and then on his thighs. They were cutting his clothing off. He felt a swift clean motion of a blade slicing the length of the arms of his jacket, and then straight up the back to the collar. The jacket came off in four pieces. They cut through his underwear and removed it entirely. Somebody sponged his privates with tepid water and roughly dried them. The same pairs of hands yanked him into what felt like baggy pyjama bottoms with an elasticated waistband and a loose top with a zipper down the back. Binch wondered if the outfit was bright orange, like the ones they used at Guantánamo.

Now was his opportunity to slake his thirst. They were taking notice of him at last, instead of belting him on the side of the head. Through the hood he managed to croak, 'Please, I need some water. I'm dying in here. Please.'

'Do we give him some water?'

'Could make him drink his own piss; that'd teach the traitor a lesson.'

'Good idea, Pennell. You volunteering to put his dick in a cup next time and feed it back to him? All right, let him drink. He's an old geezer, don't want him to croak before we deliver him to Uncle Sam.'

The hood was loosened and taken off, to be immediately replaced by a blindfold that was so tight it made his eyeballs ache under the pressure.

Binch gulped at the bottle of water, pausing to draw breath, and gulping again. It tasted so sweet and good he could have wept. He drew another breath and said, panting fast, 'Let me speak to my wife. She has to know what's happened to me. I'm a scientist and I have the right to—'

A stinging smack across the mouth shut him up.

'You're a traitor-bastard piece of shit, Mr Scientist, that's what you are, a crust of dried turd on the ass of freedom-loving USA. Did I give you permission to speak? Did anyone hear me give him permission to speak?'

'No, sir.'

'No, *sir!*'

'*So keep your fucking traitor-mouth shut, Mr Scientist! Not a peep. Not one fucking word, traitor scum.*'

The hood was put back on, the cord tightened around his neck, the suffocating blackness returned. Binch slumped against the seat, feeling the sideways motion of the aircraft as it dipped to lose height, coming in towards its destination. And where was that to be?

Quantico in Virginia, Fort Leavenworth in Kansas? Could even be the Cuba Prime Detention Facility. He swallowed, the salty taste of blood burning the back of his throat, more mortally afraid than he had ever been in his life before.

6

Smoking a Havana Cohiba Behike 56 as he stood by the window and gazed down on K Street, Chesney Poulton was in a much brighter mood than he had been for days. Various problems, large and small, that had vexed him were either solved or . . . well, there were solutions in the offing.

The first piece of good news had delighted him: the renegade traitor Inchcape had been detained and transferred to a secret location, charged with transgressing and violating the UnPatriot Act. The shoot-his-mouth-off scientist was by this point shackled to an iron-frame bunk and sweating it out in a sweltering twelve foot by six foot concrete box somewhere in the Midwest. Poulton couldn't help but chuckle at the picture. Let the fat bastard have a first-hand reality-based experience of the heated-up climate he was always blabbing on about.

How d'ya like *them* global warming apples, blabbermouth?

There had been a news blackout so the story hadn't made the airwaves. Poulton knew they couldn't keep it under wraps for very long before one of the subversive websites picked it up and started blasting it everywhere. Not that it mattered. Inchcape was no longer visible and no longer able to spout his bullshit propaganda on national TV. It would serve as a warning to others not to alarm the citizenry and run down the economy by spreading treasonous lies.

Poulton had also ticked the box for Joe Gelstrom. He had been able to assure his old friend that matters were in hand to deal with Gerald Lautner at MIT. Poulton hadn't gone into detail, nor mentioned the ascendancy programme; Gelstrom didn't need to know the how, just that Lautner would be taken care of and would shortly cease to be an irritant.

And he had a trip planned: a four-day visit to London, staying at the Savoy, all expenses paid. The reason was a fairly routine get-together with Lord Derker, an influential voice in the House of Lords who spoke on climate policy as it affected industry. The association between Poulton's AAAV and Derker's Common Sense Coalition went back ten years or more. There was no formal connection, and they didn't publicise the link, but their aims were identical: debunking the climate fanatics, supporting trade and commercial interests in their challenge to environmental legislation and green taxes, lobbying governments all over the world to relax regulation and free up natural resources for development.

Lord Derker was a very welcoming host – as he should be. A founding member of the Common Sense Coalition, he received more than eighty per cent of CSC's budget – around $30 million – from the Alliance for the Advancement of American Values.

On this trip Chesney Poulton was taking Martin Stringer along with him. He planned to fix Stringer up with an interview on the BBC debating climate change with a bunch of the 'Save the Planet' weirdos they had over there. And the trip was also a thank-you to the professor for the superb demolition job he'd done on Inchcape.

So life was looking good at the minute, and Poulton was enjoying it.

The intercom warbled discreetly. His private secretary would only disturb him for a matter that was urgent or, she deemed, important.

'Do you have five minutes for Howard Nevison, sir? He's an analyst in Sector—'

'I know who he is. Send him in.'

This better not be bad news, Poulton thought. His relaxed and benign mood was akin to floating in a warm and tranquil lagoon; he didn't want it threatened by a shark-fin. On the other hand . . . he took in a deep lungful of aromatic smoke, feeling the stirrings of an erection at the thought of Nevison's slender blondness. He could visualise him stretched out naked on the MV *Icarus* as they cruised to Bermuda. His body would be pale, his stomach soft and flat (no six-pack, Chesney Poulton didn't go for the muscle-bound type) sloping down to a nest of fair-coloured wispy pubes. The erection was reinforced.

Poulton sat down and re-arranged his crotch into a more comfortable assembly as Howard entered the room.

'What have you got for me?'

Howard Nevison hovered nervously until Poulton waved him to a chair. The young man cleared his throat before speaking. He sounded short of breath. 'Thank you for seeing me – I mean personally, sir. I could have—'

'How else could I see you except personally, Howard? By hologram? Come to the point. Spit it out.'

Howard plunged in. 'What I meant to say was, sir, I could have submitted the report through the usual channels' – he held up a memory clip – 'but I wanted to tell you, personally, that we've achieved a result on the Midnite-Net tracking operation.'

'That's great,' Poulton said. 'For a moment there I thought you were the bearer of bad tidings. Who are these bastards? You found 'em yet?'

Howard hesitated. 'We're pretty certain it's an activist group led by an English marine biologist, Gavin Chase. They go by the name Midniters. Chase wrote a book – *One Minute to Midnight* – that exposed some top-secret projects; the title is how they came by their name, we believe.'

'I remember that fucking book.' Poulton took a deep pull on his cigar and let smoke drift from his fleshy nostrils. 'Some Pentagon pointy-heads rolled because of it.' He chuckled to himself, as if secretly amused. 'An outfit called ASP got its fingers burned. I seem to recall that traitor Inchcape was also involved, wasn't he? Well, sir, Operation "Silent Witness" fixed his hash. We'll fix Chase's too, the same way, when we get our hands on him.' Poulton eyed the young analyst shrewdly. 'Pretty smart work, tying in Chase with the Midnite group. How'd you make the connection?'

'Through a basic error. Sloppy procedure, you could say. There was an info-chart circulated by Midnite-Net with the title "Oxygen Balance Sheet: Profit & Loss"; it was almost identical to the one used in Chase's book. That and the "Midnight-Midnite" link . . . tied it up, I guess.'

'If this guy Chase is the prime mover, does that mean they're based in the UK? In London?'

'Hard to say.' Howard cleared his throat. 'We're not at that particular juncture just yet.'

'What juncture's that?' Poulton asked, his smile freezing slightly.

'The tech boys are still searching. The trace-route goes through as many as twenty-five countries, back and forth—'

'Now you're making weak excuses, Howard. Which I don't like.' Poulton's happy demeanour had vanished altogether. 'Negative vibes anywhere in my vicinity upset me. Here' – he touched his temple – 'and also here' – he patted his heart. He then pointed to his stomach bulging out of his jacket. 'On top of which my digestion suffers. I don't want ulcers. You understand what I'm saying?'

'I do, sir. Yes, sir. Taken on board. We'll re-double our efforts.'

'We need the location, Howard.'

'I'll do my damnedest, sir.'

'I hope you will. It's important. We gotta nail this guy.'

'Oh but we—' Howard blinked. 'I misunderstood, sir. I thought you were referring to the Midnite network base, which we're still working on. But if you mean Chase, we know he spends part of the year in the States. He has an apartment in Manhattan.'

'You know where? You have a street address?'

'In the SoHo district.'

'Well, well. That certainly makes a difference.' Poulton leaned back, gazing out onto K Street while moving the moist end of the cigar in and out of his mouth. 'If he's resident in the US we can nab him under the UnPatriot Act, the same as we did with Inchcape. Although if he's a British citizen, it might be better to keep it lowkey. Maybe there's another way . . . a quicker way.'

He was obviously following a private train of thought, so Howard thought it best to let him get on with it.

'Okay, listen up.' Poulton roused himself and gazed hard at Howard through the smoke. 'I'm taking a trip later this week and I'll be away four days. When I get back I want to hear you tell me you've located the Midnite base – wherever the hell it is, in New Jersey or Timbuktu or the backside of the moon. That gives you and your tech boys one week from today, Howard. And I want a positive result. You understand me.'

It wasn't a question or a request.

'Yes, sir.'

As Nevison was leaving, Poulton called to him, 'I'm having a little drinks party at the Chambers the evening before I fly out. A few friends, nothing official. You're invited.'

The Chambers was the exclusive drinking hole for top people and VIPs – easier to gatecrash the White House than sneak in uninvited. The unexpected offer threw Howard into a spin. He didn't want to attend and couldn't figure out why he'd been asked, but daren't refuse.

'I'll look forward to it. Thank you, sir.'

7

The driver kept looking in his mirror to make sure. Thin guy with the cropped blond hair in the black suit, white shirt and black tie sitting at the back of the bus hadn't moved a muscle in at least a hundred miles. Not since they left the New York state line two hours ago; he'd lay bets on it. He was just sitting there, straight-backed, eyes shut, as if he were meditating.

What might he be with that sober outfit, a Mormon? Did Mormons meditate?

Couldn't be dead, could he, sitting up stiff like that?

But this guy was young, still a teenager by the look of him. Hopefully not dead then . . . or maybe he was stoned. Just as long as he didn't die, the driver didn't mind.

He sighed and looked at his watch. Another forty-five minutes and they'd be off I-84 and onto I-90 for the final leg into Boston. He'd turned off the air-filtration unit after passing through Hartford. Passengers travelling further south into New Jersey and New York State had to transfer to sealed transportation. The bus was equipped with air-filtration, but it wasn't re-oxygenated. At least up here the air was breathable, more or less, whereas on the other side of Allentown you choked your goddamn lungs up.

Come to think of it, hadn't the kid boarded the bus carrying a cylinder, supported in some sort of harness? He'd been cradling it like a baby, as if it were as delicate and as precious too.

What was the disease that television documentary had said was on the increase? Anorexia? Naw, that was teenage girls starving themselves to death . . .

Anoxia. That was the one. Maybe the kid suffered from anoxia and needed his own oxygen supply.

On the back seat Karl sat with folded arms, oblivious to the jolting motion of the bus, oblivious to everything. The small grey metal cylinder in its webbing carrier was tucked in beside him so it couldn't roll off the seat. The other necessary equipment, sheathed in bubble-wrap, was in a canvas carryall at his feet.

Karl was submerged deep inside himself. He was dimly aware of his heartbeat, like a steady muffled drumbeat. By force of will, his respiratory system was slowed right down. The passage of time didn't exist for him. In its place, at the centre of his consciousness, there was a cold, immutable, implacable sense of purpose. Nothing else mattered or had any meaning.

No need even to think.

He had his instructions. He knew what had to be done and precisely how it was to be carried out. In the litany of the MOG he was approaching 'Optimum Orbital Trajectory'. Everything he had imbibed and been trained for was about to reach the apogee of fulfilment, according to the teachings and prophecy of Pastor Eldritch.

5

I

'Dr William Pemberton Inchcape of Forest Avenue, Newlands, Boulder, Colorado, this document in my left hand is an indictment issued by the State Department, charging you with transgression and violation of the UnPatriot (Emergency Powers) Act, under Statute 419/DF. You have been duly served and notified. At this time you are not required to say anything. You will be given an opportunity at the appropriate time within the next thirty days.'

The brig stockade sergeant, six feet five inches in his bare feet, with the shoulders of an ox and hands the size of shovels, folded the document and passed it behind him to a female private first class. The sergeant looked down on the hooded, manacled and shackled figure in front of him, who wore the standard brig uniform of drab green jerkin, fastened down the front with Velcro, and baggy bloomers, the sagging crotch somewhere below his knees.

Hunched over, as if bearing a great weight, paunchy and bow-legged, Binch was a tragic sight. His voice came almost inaudibly from beneath the hood.

'Say again so's I can hear or shut the fuck up,' the brig sergeant said.

'I need' – tried again, louder – 'I need my medication! I have a heart condition. Please.'

'The medic will check you out. That's next on the schedule.'

'I want to call my wife—'

'WHAT? Can't hear you.'

'My wife will be worried sick. You have to let me call her.'

'That's being attended to.'

'I have a right to an attorney—'

'Your rights have been revoked. Under the provision of the UnPatriot (Emergency Powers) Act, Statute 419/DF, you no longer have full citizenship of the United States of America. You're in limbo, Grandpa. Technically you're a residential displaced person. Take him down.'

Two guards stepped forward, hooked the prisoner under the armpits and propelled him backwards into an adult-sized buggy with straps for the wrists and restraints for the ankles. They didn't bother with the straps and restraints. Swivelling the chair on its fat rubber wheels smartly about, they ran with it from the room and down a concrete ramp to the detention block.

The brig sergeant's voice boomed and echoed behind them, 'Jose Carlos Martino of Saratoga Apartments, West 37th Street, Hialeah, Miami, Florida, this document in my left hand is an indictment issued by the State Department, charging you with transgression and violation of the UnPatriot (Emergency Powers) Act, under Statute 419/DF. You have been duly served . . .'

The cell they arrived at was midway along the detention block. It was to be Binch's home while charges were processed through the system, which would decide whether he was to go forward to trial immediately or if psychiatric evaluation was deemed necessary. During that same period a decision would be made to transfer the prisoner either to another maximum-security facility within mainland US or to Cuba Prime Detention Facility. Conditions in such places on the mainland were horrendous; at Cuba PDF they were ten times worse, mainly because the temperatures down there were higher and there was no air-conditioning.

The guards removed the hood and unlocked the manacles and shackles. Completing their task in total silence, they slid the barred door shut behind them and departed, leaving Binch alone. The cell was a windowless box with just enough room for a thin mattress on a concrete shelf, steel washbasin with faucet, steel toilet bowl. There was a recess above the washbasin containing a metal cup.

Binch slowly sank onto the mattress. No matter how hard he tried, it was impossible to believe what had happened to him.

Why had they done this to him? And who were *They*? Was there no one to help him? But how could anyone help him when not a single living soul except those who had perpetrated the act knew what had happened to him and where he was? Binch himself didn't know where he was. Had the people who abducted him communicated with his wife? Had Si Musso, his boss at NCPF, been informed?

Suddenly, out of nowhere, a huge sob of anguish and self-pity forced itself up from his chest and erupted in a long, low moan of dread. He was so utterly alone. He might drop dead any second and the world beyond these walls wouldn't know and wouldn't care.

He lay sideways on the mattress with his legs tucked up in a foetal ball and wept quietly for twenty minutes, before dropping into a shallow doze. He awoke and knew instantly where he was; everything was exactly the same. The harsh strip light behind its protective mesh glared down from above. Distantly he could hear the sliding clatter and clang of cell doors being slammed shut. Binch wasn't hungry, had no appetite at all, but he wondered if the prisoners here were ever fed. Were they just left to rot, wasting away to an empty sack of skin and bone?

Even in his despair, he couldn't accept that the Government, the US State Department, the prison authorities would be so callous and uncaring as to abandon their citizens and let them starve to death. But he was forgetting. He was no longer a citizen but a 'residential displaced person'. He had no rights. *They* could do with him whatever *They* liked. And who was to know? Who was to stop them?

Food in plastic containers sealed with clingfilm eventually arrived, pushed through a rectangular slot in the bars. There was tepid weak coffee in a cardboard cup. The eating utensils were restricted to two white plastic spoons, one large, one small, not even a plastic knife and fork allowed. Because he didn't know the hour of day, Binch had no idea if the meal was lunch, dinner, or maybe supper. It was meatballs in gravy with mashed potatoes and green beans. The dessert was a square of flaky pastry with a dried smear of unidentifiable fruit inside. He still wasn't hungry, but ate a few mouthfuls anyway to give him some energy.

The small ritual of this meal was the start of what was to become, over days and weeks, a rigid, unvarying regime.

Lights were never extinguished, which made it impossible to tell day from night. Sleeping or even lying full-length on the mattress was not permitted during the 'day'. Binch managed to work out that this period was roughly between 5 a.m. and 9 p.m. Breakfast was delivered at around 6 a.m. Thereafter for fifteen hours at a stretch he had to sit upright or pace up and down in the narrow space between bed and wall, as far as the toilet bowl and back.

The green jerkin and baggy bloomers were exchanged for shorts and T-shirt. He was given a pair of grubby canvas shoes that had obviously been worn before. Twice a week, for one hour, he was permitted an exercise period in an inner courtyard which had an opaque glass roof hiding the sky; for this he had to don the jerkin and bloomers and wear shackles. There was no TV and no newspapers. The rule was one book at a time from a prescribed list. The books were largely thrillers, detective stories, fantasy and horror. Binch didn't choose the horror: anything would be tame to the point of laughable compared to this.

He was given a brief – ten minute – physical check-up by a female medic who asked him two questions, one about his heart, the other about his motions. His heart tablets then came twice a day with his meals. There were cell inspections four times every twenty-four hours at random intervals, so Binch couldn't use them as any kind of timing device. Sometimes, though rarely, he would be roused in the middle of the night and have to stand to attention facing the duty officer in shadow behind the barred door.

After one such inspection, churning inside and practically weeping, Binch requested to see someone in authority. He knew he was reaching his limit. When asked why, he said he wished to pass a message to his wife because she would be worried about him.

'Why should your wife be worried?' asked the duty officer. 'You're in safe hands. You're dry and warm and fed.'

'It could be she has a message for me . . .'

'What kind of message?'

'Well, that's just it. How can I know?'

'Has she a message for you or hasn't she?'

'I don't know! That's the point.' His throat was aching with suppressed emotion.

'If you don't know, why are you worrying about it? Non-logical.'

'Listen—' Binch took half a step forward and the duty officer halted him with the raised palm of his hand. 'I have to see, I *demand* to see someone – a captain or lieutenant, somebody in authority.'

'Do you now, Gram-chops. Straighten up and look at me while I say it. You're here on a very serious charge. Do you think we're playing games? You reckon this is some kind of tax-dollar-funded jaunt you're on? Well, DO YOU?'

Binch shook his head dumbly.

'Any more demands and complaints, Grandpa, and your privileges will be rescinded forthwith.'

Binch thought, *Privileges? What stinking privileges?*

He knew one thing for certain. This was calculated, deliberate punishment. *They* were inflicting psychological torture to break him down. And it was working.

2

There was almost a full contingent of the Midniters group gathered in the open-plan workspace. Chase, perched on the corner of a desk, looked round at them, rubbing his chin. He hated this feeling of being ill at ease and helpless. He preferred to have a goal in sight, achievable by direct action, but this situation offered no such option. He searched their faces. 'Anyone with a viable plan or idea, speak up. I'm listening. We're all listening.'

'What facts do we have?' Micki Vargas said. 'The Doc's been nabbed by persons unknown. Where do we even begin to start with this, huh?'

'It's fucking outrageous, Binch being arrested and detained,' Cheryl said. 'A respected scientist with an international reputation, held without due process? It's a flagrant violation of his constitutional rights.' There were spots of high colour in her cheeks.

Somebody laughed. '*Rights?* What are them? Something out of Harry Potter?'

'What did his wife say when you spoke to her?' asked another of the group.

'Not much,' Chase admitted. 'She's been trying to get answers from everyone she can, from the state governor down. But Micki's right: the only fact we have comes from Stella – Dr Inchcape's wife – and all she knows is that federal agents were waiting for Binch in his office building and escorted him away.'

'Was anyone a witness to this?' somebody asked.

'The receptionist in the lobby; she reported to Binch's boss, Si Musso, and he called Stella.'

'Federal agents? How does the receptionist know who they were? Did they introduce themselves? Leave business cards?'

Chase spread his hands. 'Look, I'm telling you what Stella told me. I didn't give her the third-degree. She was in no fit state.'

'The idea that they can grab a person practically off the street and get away with it,' Cheryl said, 'it's just . . .' She fell silent, fists clenched.

'Whoever *they* are,' Micki said.

'We can make a pretty shrewd guess,' Chase said. 'The State Department or Homeland Security or some other bunch of government goons.' He turned to Micki. 'The television debate you recorded with Binch and that so-called expert, Professor Stringer? I can't help feeling that has something to do with what's happened. Remember how Stringer kept banging away at one topic, one theme, all the way through, accusing Binch of being a traitor. *Treason. Treason. Treason.* That was a set-up if ever I saw one. Stringer also brought up the UnPatriot Act as a "This is your Final Warning" card, didn't he.'

'Then maybe Stringer is the target we should be aiming at,' said one of the Midniters, a slender, diminutive Taiwanese woman scarcely an inch over five feet. 'If we probe his background, his associations, we might discover who is behind him. It's clear to me there is a campaign to publicly discredit Dr Inchcape. Stringer must be the link.'

'We know that Stringer is emeritus professor at Sefton University,' somebody volunteered.

'He is, but that's too obvious a link,' Chase said. 'He's also an advisor and a paid consultant to numerous think-tanks and lobbying groups. That's the place to start digging.'

'One of them being the AAAV,' Micki said.

Chase turned to her. 'What's the AAAV when it's at home?'

'I started some digging already, boss. Professor Stringer is on the advisory committee of the Alliance for the Advancement of American Values.'

'They sound like a cosy bunch of progressives,' Chase said. 'Who's their patron saint, Chuck Heston? What do we know about them?'

Micki shook her head. 'We don't, so far, but I'll get right to it.'

As the impromptu meeting broke up, Chase called Micki back. He was concerned that she hadn't updated him on the cyber-attack in more than forty-eight hours.

'That's because there's nothing new. If something breaks, Jervis'll tell me at once. Any kind of a threat I'll let you know.'

3

As he stepped out of the elevator onto the third floor of his apartment building, Gerry Lautner had only one thing on his mind: ash-blonde, five feet seven, twenty-nine years of age, and her name was Samantha-Rose Clarkson, known fondly and intimately to Gerry as Sam.

They had met by chance at a faculty welcoming party hosted by Lautner in his capacity as head of the Humanities Department at MIT, based in the Human Resources complex on the Cambridge campus. Gerry Lautner considered himself extremely lucky to have attracted such a woman – certainly young to his fifty-four; and himself not much of a catch to be honest, divorced, immersed in his academic and journalistic work, short-sighted and thinning on top, hardly any woman's romantic dream. Might be that Sam begged to differ.

He was even beginning to believe he might be in love with her. And Sam didn't seem averse to the idea of a long-term relationship herself.

Humming under his breath, Lautner entered his duplex apartment and dumped his overstuffed attaché case on the bureau before throwing open the French windows. Warren Avenue was in a quiet, select neighbourhood of Revere, home to many of the faculty staff, with the university a convenient thirty minutes away if you could beat the rush on Revere Beach Parkway. Lautner hated air-conditioning so always had the windows open; this evening the cool breeze felt pretty damn good. Like his mood.

He was taking Sam to dinner in a small and not ostentatiously expensive restaurant where they could dine by candlelight. Afterwards they might go to her place, or come back here.

Almost as a reflex, Lautner glanced along the darkening avenue from his tiny balcony. It was all because of the crank calls and vituperative social media some of the faculty were subjected to, and unfortunately he was a prime target, with his high profile as a commentator on social and ethical issues. Not many academics were prepared to speak out about government corruption and corporate malfeasance – chill thoughts of blighted careers or revoked tenure were powerful deterrents – but Lautner was. He'd written articles and led campaigns, was regarded as an abrasive and controversial spokesman in televised debates.

Which in some eyes made him a hero, in others a dangerous subversive who should keep his goddamn lefty trap shut before somebody shut it for him.

So the advice from the university security unit was to be vigilant at all times. Take sensible precautions and keep your wits about you: if you see anyone suspicious lurking near your residence, inform university security at once and let them handle it. They'll either alert the local police or send someone to check it out.

The other aspect to all this security malarkey was the internet generally and social media in particular. Members of staff were warned to disengage with any social feeds that brought the cranks and nut-jobs out of the woodwork. Nothing was more likely to do this than anything touching, however tangentially, on climate change. Lautner knew this to his cost, after speaking out in support of an activist group protesting about the treatment of communities in Africa, and against the activities of a huge corporation, JEG Industries, stealing and exploiting their natural resources. The reaction and feedback had been ugly and way over the top – so vehement and personally threatening, in fact, that he suspected corporate trolls had been hired to wage this vicious war.

The avenue was deserted, not even a couple strolling in the twilight. Looked like the cranks and nut-jobs were taking a night off.

In the bedroom, Lautner undressed and put on his silk robe. Catching sight of himself in the full-length mirror of the open closet door, he sucked in his stomach and pressed it flat with both hands. *That* would have to go, no two ways about it. He had to start thinking seriously about his appearance and the shape he was in if he wanted to keep Sam interested.

Otherwise, not so bad, he decided. Fifty-odd years' worth of lines on his forehead, but his jaw line was still firm; hair he wore long, brushed back behind his ears, fairly obvious bald spot notwithstanding, still dark. Taller than average, decent shoulders, good bearing.

His jaunty out-of-tune whistle was cut short when he found that the bathroom light wasn't working. The apartment was fully serviced and maintained by an on-call super and cleaning maid, at a hefty premium. He detested inefficiency, especially when it was anything mechanical, and he flipped the switch uselessly several times. Then he tried the concealed fluorescent strip above the mirror, which, thankfully, was still functional. By its light he hung up his robe and stepped inside the shower cubicle.

He set the controls at thirty degrees, medium jet, and pushed the stainless-steel lever to the right.

The fourth note of 'Hey Jude' became a startled gasp as the needle-spray stung his scalp and streamed down his goose-fleshed body. His eyes smarted terribly. The taste on his lips was bitter, the smell making his nostrils pinch and wrinkle it was so vile.

What the hell was this? Drainage? Sewer water?

Cursing, Lautner fumbled blindly for the handle of the door. The dense propane vapour now filling the bathroom ignited on the exposed live wires in the overhead lighting fixture, from which the pearled glass globe and plastic cover had been removed. A blue-edged sheet of flame streaked into the cubicle just as Lautner was emerging and transformed him into a human torch. His mouth yawned to its fullest extent in a scream of agony that never came out because the fierce heat instantly consumed the air in his lungs. Suffocating, he fell raking the air with flaming fingers, constituting his own funeral pyre on the tiled floor of the bathroom, immersed in a spreading pool of fat dancing with little flames of orange and blue.

4

At first Howard Nevison thought it was a gunshot that had woken him, ricocheting inside his tender skull like a cannon. When he came fully to his senses he realised it must have been a car backfiring. He tried to sit up in his single bed and that's when pain stabbed through him. It was excruciating, and not confined to just one spot, one area. It was everywhere. From his throbbing head to his raw throat, to the nausea bubbling in his chest, his bilious stomach, and still onwards and downwards . . . all the way down to his ass.

Howard felt like he'd been hit by a truck, head-on and from the rear.

Had he been in an accident for real last night and forgotten about it? Had he been knocked unconscious and lost his memory? He lay there, swallowing the sour dryness in his throat, trying to remember. Fuzzy pictures spun round on a carousel in his head. Just as an image sharpened into focus, it whirled on again, lost from view.

Gleams of rich mahogany and plush red velvet in the subdued glow of small shaded lamps, pools of light reflected in cut-glass mirrors, shadowy intimate recesses, the low murmur of modulated voices . . .

. . . *one of the bright new stars in our firmament . . .*

Howard lay flat on his back, staring upwards, the image taking form on the ceiling. That's where he was the previous evening, a guest of Chesney Poulton at Chambers private club, enjoying a twenty-five-dollar Flaming Baghdad cocktail and rubbing shoulders with the great and the good, the power-brokers of DC and their coterie of chums, all sharing the same exclusive tastes and the wealth and privilege to indulge them. Now it was coming back to him.

The vision, the oppressive ambience, evolved before Howard's eyes as he lay there, feeling like death warmed up. One incident triggered the next, which led to another, then another, like a batch of photographs flicked by a thumb.

. . . take it easy and don't be greedy . . .

The club had been divided into alcoves and small discreet spaces. Poulton's group numbered about nine, though it changed occasionally throughout the evening as one or two disappeared, others arriving to take their place. The company was all male; in fact Howard couldn't recall seeing a single woman, either as staff or guest. At 8 p.m. buffet food was served.

Howard wasn't a big wine drinker, though he'd accepted two or three glasses of what he'd been informed was 'a very fine Burgundy' with his food, before Irish whiskey, French brandy and Italian absinthe were offered. It was hard to remember after the cocktails and the wine. Did he drink some of that too? Maybe a snifter of one of them, or all three, or none at all . . .

Howard didn't know. He did know that Chesney Poulton had winked at him. 'Gentlemen, let me introduce our latest recruit to the American Alliance . . .'

He was beginning to recall voices and words, disjointed fragments of conversation.

Flushed beefy faces closing in, his hand gripped in fleshy palms.

'. . . he's been with us just a few short weeks . . .'

His shoulder being pummelled, his back slapped.

'. . . brilliant intelligence analyst, one of the bright new stars in our firmament . . .'

Introductions all round, smiles on every face, winks and nods.

'. . . good-looking lad, Ches. You can pick 'em . . .'

Surrounded by such goodwill and bonhomie, Howard had relaxed and lost the nervous flutter in his chest. He had been dreading the occasion, fearing the conversation would be filled with political jargon and Washington tittle-tattle, to which he could contribute very little. To his relief the talk had been empty chatter. They didn't discuss books or movies or world affairs. Jokes and scurrilous remarks about well-known personalities seemed to be the favourite. That was fine with him. Howard could laugh at dirty wisecracks as well as the next guy.

. . . he's gonna enjoy getting it both ways at once . . .

Then came a blank: a black hole in his memory.

Lying there, watching the shifting patterns of reflected sunlight on the ceiling, he had no idea what had happened next.

But *something* must have happened to make him feel so bad, so fucking awful. He'd had hangovers before, pretty severe ones; this was nothing like even the worst hangover he'd suffered in his life.

Howard rolled onto his side to get himself out of bed. He was desperate to pee and he badly needed a drink of water. As he did so the pain down below came back, fiercer than before, as if someone had stabbed him up the rectum with a dagger. He was wearing just a T-shirt, no underpants. When he put his hand round the back to explore, he encountered wetness. His fingers felt hot and sticky. He brought them in front of his eyes and they were covered in blood.

'. . . he's so tight he must be a virgin . . .'

'. . . take it easy and don't be greedy . . .'

Through the pain Howard heard the words, as clear and distinct as if the speakers were in the room. Who had said them? He had no idea.

'. . . his eyes are open, that's not good . . .'

'. . . it's what they call a zombie state . . .'

'. . . when it wears off he won't remember a thing . . .'

'. . . open his mouth and hold it there . . .'

Howard opened his mouth wide and vomit poured out onto the rug by the side of his bed. He lay there weakly, panting, strings of drool trailing down. His mouth had been held open and something forced inside. It was smooth and hard. He was being jolted back and forth at the same time. They were pounding him from behind. Flushed beefy faces pressing up close. Three of them at least, maybe four, or even more.

Chesney Poulton was one of them, his fleshy lips stretched in a grin that resembled a snarl. He was sweating profusely. He winked again, not at Howard, a sly one to the others.

What was this secret they all shared, everyone except him?

'. . . he's gonna enjoy getting it both ways at once . . .'

'. . . his eyes are open . . .'

'. . . he won't remember a thing . . .'

Howard gagged and heaved over the side of the bed, but there was nothing left to heave up except bitter watery bile.

With a desperate effort he made it to his feet and staggered across to the bathroom, avoiding the splattered mess on the rug. He leaned into the washbasin and sluiced his face with cold water. He filled a glass three times and gulped every drop.

As he stepped back from the washbasin something smacked warmly onto his left foot.

It was a large spot of blood, and two others joined it as he looked down. Some part of him inside had been ripped and torn apart. His body had been violated.

He unspooled a long length of toilet paper, folded it several times to form a thick wad and gingerly pressed it up inside as far as he dared. How the hell did you explain something like this to a medic at the hospital? Tell them you'd fallen backwards and there just happened to be a broom handle in the way? He'd heard plenty of jokes about such situations; Howard didn't find this one funny and he wasn't laughing.

He stuck his tongue out and examined it in the cabinet mirror. It was caked with a thick layer of white paste. Even three glassfuls of water hadn't flushed the vile taste from his mouth. The sick feeling in his chest and his bilious rumbling stomach hadn't been caused by alcohol alone, Howard knew for sure. And although he couldn't remember the name of the stuff (Rhinopol?) he'd been fed a substance . . . he'd been drugged. Drugged, and then raped.

He returned to the bedroom, intending to lie down until he saw the state of the bed. Right in the middle was a large area of dark brownish dried blood. He must have lain there bleeding for hours.

A wide black face and shiny-peaked cap.

What the hell—?

Powerful black hands reaching towards him.

With small tentative steps Howard got as far as the door to the living room. He rested a minute or two before making a final effort to reach the nearest armchair, next to the bookshelves, and lowered himself into it, taking the weight with his elbows. He wanted coffee and aspirin badly, but right now he just needed to rest and gather his disordered emotions together.

He felt drained and exhausted. He let his head slump back against the chair and almost immediately drifted off into shallow sleep. When he opened his eyes the light from the window seemed different. He had no idea whether it was morning or afternoon, or even which day it was.

His wristwatch was on the bedside table in the bedroom, a million miles away. The TV remote was within reach, so he flipped it on to a news channel, which happened to be CNN, and had the remarkable and unsettling experience of seeing a face he knew well in the box next to the newsreader's right shoulder. Howard turned up the sound.

'. . . tributes to Professor Lautner have poured in from across the world. His magazine articles and frequent television appearances in support of radical causes made him a controversial figure, both at home and internationally.'

'. . . *made* him a controversial figure'. Past tense. Had Gerry Lautner died? He must have if 'tributes' were being paid to him. Howard could actually feel himself go pale as the blood left his face. The most dedicated and principled teacher – and the most supportive to Howard personally – he had ever known. No question.

'The Boston Police Department have released few details except to confirm that the cause of Professor Lautner's demise was death by incineration. On the face of it, this bears a clear resemblance to other deaths by similar methods, dubbed "pyro-assassinations" in some quarters. There have been at least seven occurrences of a like nature in the past two years, though investigators say that so far no group or faction has claimed responsibility . . .'

Howard stared numbly at the screen, which was misty and streaked through his tears. They rolled unceasingly and dripped off his chin onto his soiled T-shirt.

6

I

The red-eye out of Pittsburgh to New York departed at four-thirty and arrived at JFK a few minutes after six o'clock in the morning. The flight to London Heathrow was scheduled to leave at 9.15 a.m., giving Chase a leisurely period in which to have breakfast and read a magazine. For some odd reason he'd never worked out, he only bought *The New Yorker* at airports, though he always enjoyed it when he did.

This morning the articles distracted him but refused to hold his attention. He'd received a call the previous evening from a member of staff at the Elyot Grange Academy with the distressing news that Dan was in hospital, suffering a broken arm and fractured ribs. Cycling near Sunbury-on-Thames with his best friend, Titus, and two classmates, Dan had been knocked off his bike by somebody driving like a maniac along the narrow country lanes. His wounds had been attended to and his son was in recovery, Chase was relieved to hear. Apparently the medical staff wanted to keep Dan in there for at least forty-eight hours, under observation, and to do more x-rays.

While she was telling him this, Chase made up his mind to be on the first available flight. He requested details of the hospital, the West Middlesex at Isleworth, thanked her for the call and asked her to forewarn the staff of his arrival. It took just a few minutes on the phone to fix up the red-eye to New York and secure a seat in Business Class on an Airbus 330.

The London flight left on schedule and ten minutes later Chase was asleep, wrapped in a soft blanket.

When he woke somewhere over the mid-Atlantic, they were serving lunch. As he ate, his thoughts were on Dan; as always, there was a shadow of guilt. Had he neglected his son? Chase was painfully aware that the book and the Midnite campaign had taken over his life, to the detriment of practically everything else. He couldn't escape the guilty feeling, nor the doubts; yet in his calm, rational moments Chase recognised that his son was in the most advantageous environment he could be, under the circumstances – the circumstances being that he, father, author, public speaker and campaigner, was perpetually on the move. And that was not to make light of the risks and dangers involved either: members of the group, including Chase personally, had received death threats. Bizarrely, some folk blamed the Midniters, in their honest desire to inform and warn the public of looming climate disruption, for causing the catastrophe in the first place . . . by warning about it.

This crazy *Alice-Through-the-Looking-Glass* attitude made no sense whatsoever to Chase, however hard he struggled to understand it.

After lunch was cleared away, he scrolled through the recent vidgrams Dan had sent him. There was a longish clip of his ninth birthday party, surrounded by schoolmates – and three girls – at a Thai restaurant. Titus was there, and Chase caught a glimpse of his dad, Marcus Barrett.

'One of your kids?' his friendly neighbour interjected, catching a glimpse of the party scene.

Chase's nod was polite. He didn't speak, just added a faint smile. Not in the mood for conversation, he closed the device and slipped it away.

The Airbus was two hours from touchdown at Heathrow. In the forward Premier Class cabin, Chesney Poulton was watching an alien-zombie movie while Martin Stringer was listening through headphones, eyes closed, to a string quartet playing Bach. Professor Stringer was looking forward to his first stay at the seven-star Savoy Hotel on the Strand. Poulton's mind was only half on the movie; he was pleasurably recalling the evening spent with his svelte young blond analyst, and wondering what special treats his friend Lord Derker, head of the Common Sense Coalition, had in store for him.

2

'Dad!'

There he was, propped up against the pillows, freckled and blond, grinning broadly. It was wonderful to see him looking the picture of health despite the cast on his left arm and the tube of bandages affixed with surgical tape round his torso.

Chase couldn't hug his son; he could only grip his right hand, kiss him on the forehead and ruffle his hair. Dan's face, remarkably, was without a blemish.

'Tell me you were wearing your helmet, Dan.'

'I was, Dad, honest. I always do.'

'Good lad.' Chase reached into his bag and brought out a wrapped present. The package was slim and square, about the size of a large paperback. 'Can you manage to open this, or do you need help?'

'If you hold it, I'll have a try.'

When the wrapping and final layer of protective film was peeled off, a black shiny square was revealed. No buttons or keys – no controls whatsoever. Dan looked at the blank reflective surface with a quizzical expression. 'How does it start?' he asked. 'And what is it?'

'Remember Dornoch?' Chase said.

'Where you wrote the *Midnight* book.'

'Log fires, oil lamps. Crap signal which scrambled everything. Remember what we found to do most evenings? The game I taught you . . . ?'

'And I got to beat you at it?' Dan's face lit up. 'Electronic chessboard!' He touched the surface and at once a holographic chessboard with all the pieces in place sprang into 3D life. The pieces could be 'grasped' by hand and moved to another square. When a piece was taken it vanished. Dan beamed broadly, delighted with the gift.

'Can we play a game, Dad? Have you time?'

Chase shrugged. 'Maybe not,' he said with a note of regret, 'they told me I could have twenty minutes at most.'

With the five-hour time difference, the flight had landed at 6.30 p.m.

UK time and it was now almost nine o'clock in the evening. Seeing the disappointment on Dan's face, he said, 'But I'll make time for a proper visit before I fly back. That's a promise.' He gently punched his son on his good arm and aimed a finger at him. 'Can't leave before I take my revenge. And look, you have an opponent right here – you can play against the board too.'

Before he left the hospital, Chase spoke to one of the medical staff. There was no cause for concern, he was assured: his son was being kept in purely as a precautionary measure. All being well, he would back at Elyot Grange within a day or so.

It was nearly dark as he went down the steps. Standing next to his hired Subaru Coupe parked in the grounds of West Middlesex hospital, he called Marcus Barrett. Earlier that day, as Chase was waiting for his luggage at Heathrow, he had left a message for Marcus, saying he would call him after visiting his son in hospital. The publisher was preparing to bring out a revised and updated edition of *One Minute to Midnight* and here was a golden opportunity, with the author in the country, for some pre-publication media interviews.

There was another reason Chase's flying visit couldn't have been better timed.

'Might be difficult to wangle it at such short notice,' Marcus drawled in his upper class accent, 'but the Edinburgh Book Festival is in full swing this week. If I can arrange it, will you put in an appearance?'

Chase gave Marcus a provisional yes and said he'd discuss it further in the morning, after a decent night's sleep. Then he drove towards Isleworth, looking for a place to stay.

3

Whenever he stayed at the Savoy, Chesney Poulton always had the same suite of rooms: third floor rear, with its superb view across the Embankment of the River Thames. It had been Judy Garland's favourite suite, which was why Poulton had chosen it. He'd also heard a rumour that when Laurence Olivier met Vivien Leigh for the first time, next door in the adjoining Savoy Theatre, this was where they'd spent the night together. He was fond of the story; it appealed to the romantic in him.

Professor Stringer was nervous and excited, smiling his bland smile to show how relaxed and unintimidated he was. The Savoy had opened its doors in 1889; it was the first luxury hotel in the country. It was the first public building to have electric lighting throughout, and to have electric lifts to all floors. The list of famous names who had stayed there was endless, from Caruso to Bob Dylan, Errol Flynn to George Clooney. Although his smaller room was on the unfashionable eastern side of the hotel, to Martin Stringer it was perfect. He was happy as a clam.

The professor and his patron had a late supper in the Savoy Grill, which was almost empty. Stringer was forever looking around, and the disappointment was evident on his face that there were no celebrities present – or no one he recognised as such.

'What time's your train in the morning?' Poulton asked, finishing off his crème brûlée. He took a sip of his Irish coffee and beckoned to the waiter.

'Eleven-thirty. The event isn't till the evening, so I thought I'd make it a leisurely journey.'

'You can do that of course,' Poulton said, 'but there's plenty to see and do in Edinburgh. Art galleries. Visit the Castle. The Royal Mile, even if you don't agree with all that royalty crap—'

He broke off as the waiter approached. 'I want a large brandy. Armagnac. And bring me a selection of cigars. Havana. Can I smoke in here?'

'I'm afraid you can't, sir.' The waiter indicated with a deferential sweep of his hand an area overlooking the river. 'I can serve you your brandy and a selection of cigars on the terrace, sir. There you are permitted to smoke.'

As the waiter was leaving, almost as an afterthought, Poulton said, 'Stringer – you want anything? Something to drink? Smoke?'

Martin Stringer shook his head.

'Mine's being recorded in the afternoon,' Poulton said. He had an interview on a BBC flagship current affairs programme. He smacked his lips and thwacked his fleshy palms together. 'Then later I shall be having dinner with Lord Derker, and afterwards an interlude of R&R at his club.' He was in reflective mood. 'Gotta've known Bob Pemberton – as he then was, before becoming his Lordship – I guess, what, twenty-five years. Came up from nothing, like me. Swell guy. He spent a week with me on *Icarus* last fall, sailed from Cape Hatteras to Bermuda with some juvenile company. Bob is an actual lord but he's a regular fella, no bullshit. Take my word for it.'

Not only reflective, but sentimental and nostalgic too. Professor Stringer saw the signs and decided a quick retreat and an early night were called for. After a large Armagnac and a fat cigar, Ches would be on an unstoppable roll till the early hours.

Stringer bade his patron a polite good night and scuttled off to bed.

4

The rhythmic churning sound and the whirl of whites interspersed with blue and dark green (his boxer shorts and T-shirt were in the machine as well as the bed-sheets) had a soporific effect that almost rocked Howard Nevison into slumber. He sat on the slatted bench in the basement utility room of his apartment block, eyeballs pleasantly rotating, watching the fabrics through the porthole as they tumbled and writhed. Watching the evil stains of shame and guilt being washed away. Feeling numbed – not even outraged yet, or heartbrokenly sad – by the horrible death of his friend and mentor, and mumbling to himself, *Why Gerry Lautner? Why him? Why would they do it? Why would they choose Gerry? Why him?*

One thing Howard didn't need to ask was *Who did it?* because he already knew that.

Everything had been made plain in the Top Secret archives of AAAV he had been ploughing through. There had been enough references to the 'ascendancy' programme – and an actual list, if there were any lingering doubts – of people targeted, all carried out by the cult of religious nut-jobs Chesney Poulton used for his own devious ends – the fucking Messengers of God. So which god was that exactly? The god of setting innocent people on fire in their own bathrooms? The god of eliminating environmental activists in Ecuador and Brazil?

The more he thought about it, the greater the realisation of how naïve, how *gullible*, he had been. He'd truly believed in the aims and philosophy of AAAV, in spreading American ideals and values throughout the world. To have been singled out and promoted from the ranks of Black/PROP and favoured with the personal attention of the director-in-chief had been beyond his wildest ambitions. Had Poulton's predatory sexual urges been the sole reason behind his promotion all along?

That aside, how could he not have known sooner what AAAV's real agenda was? The signs were all there, if only he'd bothered to look for them. The conclusion was that he hadn't bothered to look because he hadn't wanted to discover the truth. He *wanted* to believe that it was bringing freedom and democracy and enlightened American values to the dark places of the world. That had seemed to Howard to be a noble aim; in his heart of hearts he still subscribed to it. But not the way Chesney Poulton and his organisation were pursuing it. They were acting in their own self-interests whatever the cost to anyone else, they were just as bad if not worse than any terrorist group in single-minded pursuit of their own selfish goals.

Sitting there, watching the soiled sheets churn away, Howard felt the rising clutch of nausea in his throat. The dreadful experience he had endured was still only real and remembered in hallucinatory flashes.

It was his horrifying experiences, he now realised, that had awoken him to the true nature of AAAV. Otherwise he might have carried on living in denial, been content to accept without too much thought or conscious agitation the moral depravity of what Poulton was about. But what had been done to him changed everything – and not only the sheer callous brutality of the act itself, but the presumption by Poulton and his circle that they could do as they pleased, that Howard Nevison counted for naught. They believed they had the licence to do whatever they wished, with total impunity.

Of course, precautions had been taken. He had been given a powerful drug with the drink, which they'd obviously assumed would wipe out or distort the memory, leaving blankness, or at least a turmoil of confusion. Indeed, he couldn't remember most of what had taken place, just glimpses and fragments, vague cloudy images. Not much of real substance.

But that little was enough to remember, and never forget.

Howard eased himself forward on the slatted wooden seat. The discomfort was bearable now. He had applied antiseptic gel and padded the area with strips of torn-up pillowcase. He wasn't going far; he had decided not to move outside the apartment for forty-eight hours at least. He needed time to think. Time to plan.

5

Chase had been to Edinburgh three times before, but never to the Festival. He was pleasantly surprised to find it wasn't held in bleak academic halls; instead it was outside in the open air – or nearly so – in Charlotte Square Gardens at the end of Princes Street, in the heart of the city. Several marquees lined the perimeter, each with a capacity of a hundred or so, leaving a wide green space in the middle for visitors to lounge in deckchairs or have afternoon tea at the refreshment stands.

Marcus Barrett had done as he had promised – with minimum effort. As soon as he contacted the festival director and mentioned *One Minute to Midnight*, it was as if he'd uttered a magical spell. The director hadn't just been obliging, he'd been enthusiastic when the publisher told him the author was unexpectedly here from the States and willing to make a personal appearance, should there be a suitable spot in the programme.

'It's better than perfect,' Marcus had informed Chase, when they spoke on the phone. 'A panel discussion focusing on the environment, with questions invited from the audience. Get in a plug for the book as often as you can, Gavin. We're bringing publication of the new edition forward by a couple of months, so you can announce it as forthcoming.' Marcus rarely gave way to excitement, but a slight quickening of the usual laconic inflection told Chase he was at a heightened pitch.

The setting was delightful. In the morning it had rained heavily, but by late afternoon the venue was thronged, basking in hot sunshine. After checking in at the hotel, Chase wandered over to get a taste of the ambience. He'd attended dozens of literary festivals in the three years since the book first came out and this had to be one of the most welcoming and relaxed of them all. He was looking forward to the discussion in the main venue, which was due to start at eight o'clock.

After a large gin and tonic to calm his nerves, Chase presented himself there and was greeted by the festival director and his staff. Then he was escorted through to the green room, where the other four panel guests were making polite conversation. As Chase was introduced and shook hands, a sudden hair-raising sensation swept from his scalp and down the full length of his back to his buttocks, as visceral and shocking as being doused in a bucket of ice-water.

It was immediately obvious from Martin C. Stringer's insipid smile and extended hand that the name 'Gavin Chase' hadn't registered with him. There was no reason for him to have recognised Chase, and apparently he hadn't. But the moment the festival director identified the new arrival as the author of *One Minute to Midnight*, Stringer made the connection. He visibly stiffened. His hand wavered and limply fell back. Which solved the problem of whether to shake it or not.

The numbing shock lasted with Chase as the five panel members, three men and two women, were led onto the stage and introduced to the packed audience. For at least ten minutes he didn't really know where he was – his head was teeming and tumbling with angry, contradictory emotions. It was so surreal that he couldn't get his mind in shape to deal with it: that he had just come face to face with the slimy slug of a bastard who carried out the hatchet job – the deliberate smearing of a reputable scientist of unimpeachable integrity; a truly despicable act that had blighted his career and ruined his life.

And Binch – his collaborator on the book, and more importantly his friend. That shouldn't be forgotten, and Chase would not forget.

What he hadn't anticipated – though on reflection it was stupid of him not to have foreseen it – was that the proceedings were being televised. From the platform Chase could see the unblinking ruby eye of a TV camera at the back of the marquee – was this going out live or being recorded for later transmission?

After the introductions, each of the five was asked to give a summary of where he or she stood on the environment and the challenges ahead. Were scientific predictions soundly based and to be trusted, or were they misleading and alarmist? It came as no surprise when Professor Stringer launched into his standard spiel that far from being exceptional or unexpected, variations in climate were the norm, and therefore nothing to get excited about. Ever since records were kept – and even before, based on geological evidence – the climate had swung from one extreme to the other.

Look around us, folks – and guess what? We're still here, and we're doing just fine!

'What you have to always keep in mind,' said Stringer, his finger-jabbing already in hyper-active mode, 'is the huge subsidies certain academics and research institutions are receiving, year in, year out. And guess who shells out those billions and billions of dollars – excuse me, pounds – and has no say at all in how they're spent? Or should I say *wasted*? You got it the first time. No prizes for guessing. It's you' – finger-jabbing the audience – 'and you. And you. All of you.'

Jab-jab-jab.

'And why would any scientist want to jeopardise his career and livelihood by refusing to take those wodges of cash? Of course he wouldn't. But the devil's pact that goes with it is he has to keep up the pretence, the sham – the wall of mistruth, if you will – that we're all going to fry or end up choking to death or some other Hollywood doomsday movie epic.'

He bowed forward and gave a sad little shake of the head, his pink scalp visible through the gossamer-thin comb-over from one ear to the other. With a wee pained smile, Martin Stringer spread his hands in an appeal to common sense. 'None of it is true. Believe me – and you can, because I've studied the data – it ain't gonna happen. Don't get taken in by these guys. Don't be chumps. Can't you see you're being had?'

For a second or so there was complete silence, and then the applause came, loud and sustained. Several of the audience were actually on their feet, cheering. Still wearing his faint smile, Stringer waved his hand modestly in acknowledgement of their approbation.

The chairman waited, letting the applause die away. He was a Scot, for many years he had been a political pundit in the UK, making regular appearances on TV and writing opinion pieces for the right-wing press. He turned to Chase, yet at the same time spoke in an amused aside to the audience, 'What's the betting we won't get much agreement on Professor Stringer's views from the author of *One Minute to Midnight*.' He cocked a sardonic eyebrow and gave a throaty chuckle, as if the remark had been amusing or even witty.

'But perhaps I'm maligning him, so I'll ask Gavin Chase to respond for himself.'

'Thank you.' Chase faced the audience. Somehow he got the rage boiling inside under control. With a tremendous effort he spoke quietly and calmly – even reasonably, though punching Stringer in his smug, condescending, smirking face would have felt more than reasonable. 'I intend to drop his academic title of professor and address him as Martin Stringer. This might seem to some of you rude and insulting, so I'll explain why.'

Already there were a few mutterings from the audience, and one or two were shaking their heads at this show of bad manners.

'Martin Stringer's views on quantum-physics and the amount of dark matter in the universe hold no interest for me personally, or scientific validity generally, because Martin Stringer is neither a particle physicist or a cosmologist. He isn't an atmospheric physicist and nor is he a marine biologist. Or an ecologist – behavioural, cognitive, social, molecular or human.

'The actual truth is that he isn't a scientist *at all* – of any description. That's why I address him as Martin Stringer instead of using his title. His views on the environment and climate change, therefore, are no more relevant than somebody you might meet in the street who's read one or two popular science books. In other words, he isn't qualified to speak on the subject—'

Catching sight of the veins throbbing in Professor Stringer's temples and the fixed stare, the chairman tried to butt in. 'That's all well and good, Mr Chase, but you're making a personal attack instead of—'

'Dr Chase.'

'—ah, yes. Well, then . . . Dr Chase, if you'd respond directly to the points Professor Stringer has made.'

'I'm coming to that next,' Chase said ominously. 'And I have to say, Martin Stringer raises the key question . . . he's bang on the money, you might say.'

Instead of appearing relieved or gratified, Stringer had the look of a rabbit frozen in the headlights of a truck bearing down at sixty miles an hour.

'And that is—?' the chairman asked hopefully.

'The professor raises a very important point – and I choose to use that title, since we're talking now about funding. Where does all the money come from? The billions of dollars required to support all this research? It's an excellent question! Perhaps the professor will tell us where the funding comes from to support his tenure at Sefton Metropolitan University? Not only today, as we speak, but for the past – fifteen years, is it? Twenty? Or even longer.'

The chairman half-turned to Stringer as if seeking a response, but quickly turned away again when he saw that the professor's face seemed to have transformed itself into a mute wooden mask with bulging eyeballs. Instead, the chairman focused on Chase once again, but Chase said nothing. It was already warm inside the tented space, but now the atmosphere had become stifling, the silence oppressive. Somebody cleared his throat noisily, then there were a few coughs and shuffling sounds. If this was going out live on TV, these few seconds of 'dead' airtime would seem endless to the audience at home.

On the edge of panic, the chairman said abruptly, almost gabbling, 'Well, I'm not sure, we might be intruding into a matter of commercial confidentiality . . .'

'Then if he's so sensitive about it,' Chase said, 'perhaps Professor Stringer shouldn't have raised the question in the first place. But if he's shy at revealing where his money comes from, I'm happy to tell him where mine comes from. The funding for my research and the group I run is earned through book sales and media interviews, and public appearances like this one. Not one penny of it comes from corporate donors or academic sources.'

'You're avoiding Professor Stringer's question.' A shrill female voice from the audience. 'Typical evasion from the doom-merchants, of which you're a prime example, Dr Chase.'

Before the chairman could step in, Chase said, 'Specify the question please, and I'll try to answer it.'

From the second row, the woman spoke out. 'There have *always* been climate variations – some of them quite extreme. That's the nature of the planet we live on. It never stays still, it never stays the same. Professor Stringer has made this point time and time again, and you fearmongers will simply not accept it. Frankly, it's perverse. The human race has adapted to climate changes throughout its history, and, as he says, "We're still here, and we're doing just fine!" Why can't you see that when it's as plain as a pikestaff?'

The woman's intervention seemed to put fresh heart into Martin Stringer. He stirred himself from his numbed stupor and bulbous-eyed trance and raised his index-jabbing finger. 'Thanks, ma'am, you're absolutely right. You see, these alarmists rely to a large extent on climate computer models such as the facility in Colorado, known as DELFI, which has been totally discredited in scientific circles. For gosh-sakes – it's a computer! We all know how computers can go haywire and get things wrong. What's the old saying from fifty years ago? GIGO: Garbage In, Garbage Out. And you're telling me that they can predict what's gonna happen to the climate in ten, twenty, fifty years from now, when they can't even say what the weather is gonna be like in the next forty-eight hours? Are they serious? Or are they just plain stupid?'

'You can't compare climate and weather,' someone called out. 'They're two different things entirely.'

The chairman raised both palms to forestall any further intervention from the audience. 'Ladies and gentlemen, please, no interruptions from the floor. Let the members of the panel have their say. Dr Chase, climate predictions based on computer modelling is the topic raised. Garbage In, Garbage Out, according to Professor Stringer. How do you respond to that?'

Chase could not credit that Stringer had the brazen nerve to mention DELFI by name. This was the man who had publicly accused Binch of treason; there could be little or no doubt that he had, in some fashion, been a party to Binch's detention by a federal agency. It was almost as if he were taunting Chase with the sly secret knowledge of what had happened to his friend and colleague, was in fact revelling in Chase's ignorance and impotent rage.

As he hesitated, striving to contain his feelings, the same woman in the audience spoke out loudly to those around her. 'You see how it is? When these people are asked a direct question they are totally incapable of providing an answer. This chap's more a charlatan than a genuine scientist. Shouldn't surprise me if his doctorate is bogus.'

Chase didn't reply to the slur. Instead he took a folded sheet of paper from his inside pocket and opened it up. 'Here's a prediction for you,' he said, and began to read.

6

From the BBC studio in central London, Lord Derker's chauffeur-driven Mercedes carried Chesney Poulton to a private members' club in Hampstead. The interview of just under fifteen minutes would be edited down to about six or seven minutes and broadcast later that evening on the BBC's flagship current affairs programme. Poulton stared out through the tinted windows, not really seeing the lines of traffic. He was considering, and reviewing with hindsight, whether the five essential questions had been asked and adequately answered. These had been submitted to the programme's editor prior to the recording, on the understanding that the items would be covered in the order of priority, as specified. On reflection, Poulton reckoned they had. And he was confident his answers had been both concise and comprehensive; he'd rehearsed them often enough.

Number one priority, of course, was the need to maintain close cooperation between the UK and the USA on matters of global security. 'The world is a dark and dangerous place, filled with men of evil intent,' Poulton had pontificated. 'We in the United States need a friend and ally such as Britain to help us hold aloft the torch of freedom and peace. To banish the shadows of hatred and envy that would engulf us.'

He was especially fond of the *dark/dangerous/torch/shadows* analogy.

He'd thought it up himself and was modestly proud of his literary accomplishment.

The final item on the list, though coming last, was actually the most important.

Having finished the 'serious' part of the interview, the programme's female presenter was required to lighten the mood by asking what Poulton did to relax and ease the tremendous burden of being the head of such a prestigious international body as the Alliance for the Advancement of American Values. She was good at her job and phrased the question with a coquettish lift of the eyebrow, as if the temerity of inquiring into the personal life of this major public figure was rather provocative.

With a show of reluctance, Poulton did concede he was the patron of a charity, SOS, whose aim was summed up in its title: Save Our Species. He had a passion, Poulton admitted, to do something to help the endangered wildlife of the planet. Indeed, he felt driven. The group was run by volunteers and relied on donations from the ordinary Joe and Janet in the street. As well as feeling passionate and driven, the great man explained, he felt humbled to be involved in so worthy a project.

'Species are dying every day, almost one every minute, all around us. I feel a responsibility, as a human being, to reach out a helping hand and rescue them. We are here such a brief time, you know, Alison, and life itself is so fleeting, that we can't just turn our backs on our suffering fellow creatures.'

'That's a very noble sentiment,' Alison said. (In his briefing, Poulton had indicated the required response as 'generous gesture' but 'noble sentiment' was better.) 'And also an endearing one, Mr Poulton, if I might say so.' (Better still. He must make that addition to the script.)

The money pitch had come from her, not him; that was the beauty of it. Alison herself had pledged to make a regular donation to the charity, and asked how one went about it.

'Go to the SOS website. The payment details are there. Send what you can. No amount is too small – or too large,' Poulton quipped, smiling to show his impish sense of humour as he stroked his luxuriant chestnut-brown moustache. 'And remember, your pounds and pence are not coming to us. They're going to our fellow creatures, and on their behalf, a sincere and very humble thank-you . . .'

Alison was grateful to him for being so frank and forthcoming on matters close to his heart, and hoped he hadn't been offended by her probing into the private life behind the public façade.

Not at all, Poulton replied, still smiling. He almost winked at her, but held back. Mission accomplished.

His old friend Lord Derker – Bob Pemberton – was waiting in the club's lobby to greet him. Both men weighed roughly the same, but whereas Poulton topped six feet by several inches, Derker was five feet five in built-up shoes. Derker had a swarthy complexion and very thick, suspiciously black eyebrows, which were in stark contrast to his wings of swept-back greying hair separated by a thinning patch over mottled skin.

Poulton looked round appreciatively as Derker led him through to the bar. He'd been to various private clubs as Derker's guest on previous visits, but this was his first time here. It was early, and the bar was nearly empty. In a corner two middle-aged men were in quiet conversation with a fair-haired boy dressed up in school uniform, shorts and knee-high socks. The boy's face was unnaturally vivid, and as Poulton looked more closely he saw the boy's cheeks were rouged, his lips painted over and his naturally blond eyelashes coated in mascara.

At once Poulton's cock swelled until it chafed against his boxers, feeling uncomfortable. His preference might be for teenage boys and young men of Howard Nevison's age but he could definitely see the merit in such virginal youth. The breath expanded in his chest and his head went tight with giddiness.

'Jesus-Fuck-Christ, Bob, where've you brung me to, you old devil?'

'A garden of heavenly delights, dear boy. Take your pick from these tempting charmers' – and he threw down a pack of glossy photographs which fanned out over the bar. The boys were all between eight or nine and about thirteen. They were mostly pretty, some wearing make-up, all naked.

'Are they here . . . on the premises?' Poulton asked, dry-mouthed.

Derker nodded. 'Some of them might be otherwise engaged; you can choose whoever is available. But you can always have three or four in a romp, if you like.'

Lord Derker ordered drinks and they wandered through, sipping them, to the main lounge. It was quiet in here too, with only a few armchairs occupied by middle-aged and elderly men. One of them was nodding off in front of a silent TV wall-screen near the French windows, and for a couple of seconds Poulton was taken aback to see Martin Stringer poking holes in the air, until he checked the time and it clicked: Stringer's appearance at the Edinburgh Book Festival was on some arts channel or another.

'I want to watch this, Bob, if you don't mind.'

They settled themselves on a brocade divan and Derker turned up the volume. Stringer seemed to be going down a storm. The audience were keenly attentive, many of them nodding in agreement, and there was even a burst of applause at one point. Poulton didn't recognise anyone else on the panel. There was a young guy, dark-haired and intense, English judging by his accent, who seemed to be Stringer's chief adversary.

When Poulton asked Derker if he knew who the man was, his lordship's face darkened. 'I certainly do know,' he said grimly, staring at the screen from beneath beetling brows. 'He's a muckraker – a marine scientist called Chase. Two years ago we slapped a lawsuit on him – he claimed in a magazine article that the Common Sense Coalition was putting out false information on climate data, when in fact we were simply providing a more balanced picture of the figures.'

Chesney Poulton leaned back on the divan and folded his arms. Outwardly calm, he felt a surge of anger quickening his pulse-rate, as if venom was coursing through his veins. This was the one Howard had identified as leader of the group giving them such a Grade A balls-ache. So now the enemy was in plain sight.

Poulton said, 'Did you recoup substantial damages off of him, Bob? I hope!'

'Well, no, didn't work out that way,' Derker admitted. He sniffed and took a sip of his brandy. 'We lost the case, ordered to pay damages plus costs. Lost it on a technicality, you understand,' he added.

'Couldn't you offer the judge a private inducement?'

'We tried that,' Derker said heavily, 'but there were three of them and we were out-voted two to one.'

Poulton was absorbed in the debate. He was glad to see that Chase wasn't having it easy: a severe-looking woman in the audience was making her opinions known, accusing him of being a charlatan, not a genuine scientist.

'. . . shouldn't surprise me if his doctorate is bogus,' she said in a loud, penetrating voice.

Chase ignored her outburst. Instead, he unfolded a sheet of paper. 'Here's a prediction for you,' he said, looking at Professor Stringer. He began to read aloud: '"There is no doubt, from the records, that atmospheric carbon dioxide is increasing. Early observations suggest that before man's industrial activities began to make themselves felt, its concentration was about 280 parts per million, about fifteen per cent lower than today's. The most striking results are a twenty-year series of observations from the top of Mauna Loa Mountain in Hawaii, which, if the trend recorded there continues, shows that the level of carbon dioxide in the atmosphere will double in the next forty to fifty years. According to computer models, this doubling up of CO_2 will lead to a further $3°$ C rise in Earth's average temperature, making it between $4°$ C and $6°$ C higher than today's. This is on top of an average increase in temperatures of some $6°$ C since the last Ice Age was at its height, 18,000 years ago. Added together, these increases would make the Earth warmer than it has been since the days of the dinosaurs."'

Stringer was already shaking his head in disparagement. 'Typical scaremongering,' he declared. 'Cherry-pick your facts from the latest academic research paper and present them as the results of an authentic scientific study – when they are nothing of the kind. Tomorrow morning, Dr Chase, I could just as easily find a set of climate statistics that would refute every so-called fact and figure you've just read out to us. Ten minutes' search online is all it takes to come up with that sort of garbage, then cobble it together and call it a "prediction". It's pure nonsense, and I suspect you know it to be so.'

'So you don't believe it's accurate?' Chase said.

'Of course not!' Stringer shot back. 'The figures you quoted are based on somebody's guesswork, so as a prediction of what will actually happen in twenty or thirty years' time, they're worthless.'

Easing back in the armchair, Poulton was smiling to himself, though quietly surprised that Martin Stringer was making such a trenchant and convincing rebuttal. He tipped back the brandy and felt its glorious warmth swirling below.

'However,' Chase told the audience, holding up the paper, 'this doesn't happen to be a prediction of twenty or thirty years in the future.' On camera it was even clearer that he was holding a copy of a newspaper clipping – a long article, accompanied by an illustration: a cartoon-style image of a perspiring planet Earth inside a greenhouse, with sunglasses and fan, mopping its brow. 'The article appeared in the *Sunday Times* in 1981. Forty-four years ago.'

'Is any of this significant?' the chairman asked, obviously floundering. He looked towards Professor Stringer, who was biting his lip.

'That all depends on how accurate the predictions are from 1981,' said one of the other panellists. 'It did seem odd to me that Dr Chase was quoting a figure of 280 parts per million of carbon dioxide in the atmosphere when the most recent number is well above 430 parts per million.'

Stringer had been tricked. He was keenly aware of it, and he was still smarting. 'Well of course I knew *that*,' he said sharply, trying to regain his composure. 'It was just too obvious to comment on. But the figures are wrong anyway, and misleading. The article predicts a doubling of CO_2, which is 560 parts per million. We're only at 430 parts per million.'

'You're forgetting something, Professor.' Chase used the paper to fan himself. 'The final prediction is fifty years into the future; it still has six years to run. At the rate the planet is warming, we could be very close to that higher figure by 2032. And that means an average global increase of at least 4° C. The danger threshold for unstoppable heating and oxygen deprivation has a timeframe of 2036–2046.'

'But these are only *predictions*.' Stringer almost spat the word out.

'Yes they are,' Chase agreed, 'predictions from 1981, which have turned out to be astonishingly accurate today. And they were based on computer climate models such as DELFI – the ones you seem to think are worse than useless.'

Poulton waited, brandy glass in hand, for Stringer to resume the attack and blow Chase's argument out of the water, but the idiot was strangely quiet, as if bereft of words. As was the woman in the audience, whose loud, penetrating voice was notable for its absence.

Startled, Lord Derker jumped, spilling his own drink, at the sound of shattering glass: the remnants of Poulton's brandy glass lay on the parquet floor, the stain of brandy marking the spot on the wall where he had flung it.

'I guess now you're beginning to understand what a bloody pain in the arse he is,' Derker said. He turned the sound off. 'There must be a way to deal with him.'

'No, no, my friend,' Poulton said, breathing heavily, 'I knew it already. But it'll be easier to find a way when I'm back in the States. I need to consult with my spiritual advisor.'

7

As they were leaving the platform – in the out-of-doors space between the marquee and the green room where the festival's guest-speakers were gathered – Martin Stringer made the catastrophic error of seeking to have the last word. He tapped Chase on the shoulder, not gently, and said he had a good mind to report him to the international body for academic sciences on a charge of unprofessional conduct to a fellow academic.

It was a very rash mistake.

The next instant his lapels were seized and he was being shaken so violently that his lower denture came loose and nearly choked him. He held up both hands, gurgling in alarm, his pale cheeks suddenly turning deep crimson.

The chairman and the other members of the panel stood rooted in shock as Chase yanked the man forward and thrust his face into Stringer's. 'I know what you did, you disgusting scumbag. It was you who set it up. For what you did to Bill Inchcape, I'd have every right to beat the living shit out of you, you piece of dried-up dog-turd—'

'Somebody, please . . . ' Stringer was spluttering and choking. 'Stop him. Get him off me. Save me . . .'

One of the festival officials tried to intervene, and Chase elbowed him hard enough to make him stand back and reconsider.

'The most despicable thing, the worst thing one human being can do to another—' In his rage Chase almost lifted Stringer off his feet. He gripped him tighter and shook him harder. 'You've destroyed a decent man – and a scientist of real integrity – which is something you're not – not a scientist, not even a man, decent or otherwise.'

Shaken loose, Stringer's comb-over became unstuck and flopped onto his forehead. He opened his mouth to protest, his watery, panic-stricken eyes pitiful. This vision of him was so pathetic, so ludicrous, that Chase felt a choking sense of revulsion and with a shudder he flung him off.

'I have never witnessed behaviour like this in all my life,' the Scottish chairman muttered to no one in particular. 'It's utterly disgraceful, assaulting a fellow guest . . .'

'You think so?' Chase was trembling. He was white to the lips. 'You want to know the truth, I've let him off lightly. If I thought this bag of shite had the slightest notion where they've taken Bill Inchcape I'd beat him to a pulp to make him tell me. But he's not high enough up the food chain to be given that information. Professor Stringer is no more than an underling, a paid-for shill hired to smear reputable scientists and destroy their careers.' Chase turned back to Stringer, who shrank away. 'I'd say he's less a man of science, more of a whore. If that wasn't an insult to whores.'

After that, Chase decided the hospitality of the green room was probably not going to be that enjoyable for him.

The fresh air and the walk back to the Caledonian were just what he needed to calm down. That, and a large malt whisky in the hotel bar to settle his nerves.

He turned his phone on to check for messages. There was a red flag from Micki Vargas. He ordered a second whisky before returning her call.

'Somethin' kinda odd has happened,' she reported in her sing-song lilt, 'and we can't figure it out. Caliban has made contact – and from a non-encrypted trace-route.'

'Caliban.' Chase had to focus. 'That's the source trying to penetrate our security.'

'Yeh, the codename we gave to the cyber-shadow.'

'Is it genuine or a trick? What does Jervis think?'

'Neither of us is sure. If it's a ploy or a come-on, he's still left himself vulnerable. The message was open-source. I wanted to run it by you before we respond.'

'Do you think we should?'

'My gut says yes.'

'And your head?'

Only a slight hesitation. 'I think so.'

'Then go with it.'

Micki clicked off and Chase sank back in his chair and drank his malt. He was feeling more relaxed already.

8

The toxic dump at Turtle Grove had been off the radar for twenty years. Upwards of 50,000 drums of waste product were stored on the thirteen-acre site, including solvents, napthalene, heavy metals, cyanide, arsenic and a lethal stew of oily sludge containing PCBs (polychlorinated bi-phenyls) which in earlier decades had been used in everything from hydraulic fluid to coolant for power transformers. The facility had also been utilised by the US Army to dispose of the most dangerous compound of the lot: highly unstable stocks of the class of chemicals known as dioxins. Records had gone missing or been falsified by successive administrations. The original (classified) tally for dioxin storage on this site was 35,000 barrels, identifiable by labels with the logo 'JEG Haz-Dox' (Hazardous Dioxin) in red and white, which had long since peeled off most of them. These were in addition to the drums containing chemical waste.

Turtle Grove is southeast of Pittsburgh; three miles west is the Allegheny River, a major tributary of the Ohio River, which after several hundred miles joins the Mississippi in Illinois.

On the northern side of Pittsburgh, thirty-nine miles away from the toxic dump, was the business park location chosen by Gavin Chase and Cheryl Detrick for the Midnite-Net climate alert group.

The populations living along the banks of these rivers were not in imminent danger of contamination by chemical and dioxin pollutants – not, that is, if 'imminent' could be arbitrarily defined as three to ten years in the future. The steel drums had already begun deteriorating and starting to leak before 2025; the substances they contained were so virulently corrosive that the chemical processes could no longer be controlled or sustainably stored in the longer term.

The 35,000 drums of dioxin compounds, originally produced for Operation Download, were stored in circular concrete silos with composite asphalt bases. As the metal corroded and the contents started to seep out, the floors turned to a sea of toxic black sludge. Beneath this was the land: the natural geological strata of sand and gravel, sandstone, shale, sandstone again and finally a deep bed of limestone which served as the aquifer, soaking up groundwater and transporting it by force of gravity to the nearest lake or river. As the dioxin sludge seeped into the ground and passed through the different strata, the limestone aquifer acted as a channel to convey it to the nearest watercourse: which in the case of the Turtle Grove site was the Allegheny River, a major tributary of the Ohio River.

From Pittsburgh the Ohio takes a northwesterly direction before heading south. 981 miles in length, it flows through or along the borders of six states, and its drainage basin covers fourteen states. The Ohio River is the source of drinking water for 4.7 million people.

None of whom had ever heard of Turtle Grove or the 35,000 barrels of dioxin compounds which were slowly but surely leeching into the water table and thence to the Allegheny, less than three miles away.

I

Ruth Brosnan drove the hire car from Rocky Mountain Metropolitan Airport the nineteen miles to Bill and Stella Inchcape's house north of Boulder. One of the last times she'd visited their home had been four years ago, when she and Jeff Henshaw had been invited to dinner. Ruth and Jeff had been an item at the time, until she'd rumbled what an overbearing, ignorant prick he was. The relationship hadn't lasted long after that particular evening, which was the same evening she first met Gavin Chase, Ruth recalled.

During her residency at the hospital in nearby Denver, Ruth and Stella had become good friends. It was a relief to find that Stella was more composed than Ruth had feared. Perhaps she was holding most of the trauma within, keeping the raw reality at bay, because to confront it every minute of every day would be just too searingly painful and emotionally destructive.

'I can't thank you enough for making this trip.' Stella was sitting, dry-eyed and calm, in the living room. The TV was on, tuned to CNN, though with the sound turned off, just in case there was a mention – a rolling news caption, a scrap of information, anything at all; so far Bill Inchcape's detainment had merely been reported as a 'matter of state security,' an explanation the media seemed pretty sanguine about.

'I couldn't *not* come,' Ruth said, meaning it. 'It's so dreadful, so awful, they can act in this way, abducting innocent people without any reason or explanation. Did Binch have no indication at all that something like this was going to happen? No threats or warnings—?'

'There might have been, but he never said anything. He was like that – I mean, he *is* like that—' For a split second Stella's control wavered;

she swallowed and blinked a couple of times. Then she bore down. 'When something is worrying him he goes quiet, sort of distant, and I know not to bother him. Just like after the accident. But I should have said something, I know that now, at least asked him what was wrong—'

'What accident?'

Stella told Ruth about the panel truck forcing Binch's pick-up into the ditch. She said they hadn't made up their minds whether it was an accident or deliberate. Only now, of course, in hindsight, the incident fitted a pattern of intimidation; same with the personal attack Professor Stringer had made during the television debate.

Ruth, having been out of the country, was again struggling to catch up. When Stella told her about it, Ruth's eyes rounded in shock and amazement. 'Did Stringer actually use the word "treason" on live TV?'

'I'm pretty sure he did, yes. He kept harping on about a new Emergency Act passing through Congress. It's aimed at anyone making unpatriotic statements that might harm the United States. The inference was clear as daylight: Binch is a traitor because he's a scientist spreading alarm about climate change, according to Stringer. So I guess he's been accused of damaging some commercial interest or other, undermining confidence, aiding our competitors. It always comes down to business in the end, doesn't it?' she said bitterly. 'The bottom line. Every time.'

'TCB,' Ruth said.

'Sorry—?'

'"Taking Care of Business". It was a slogan Elvis and Colonel Parker used to justify anything and everything they felt like doing. Elvis had the initials cast in solid gold and wore it as a necklace. He had dozens made up and handed them out to his buddies.'

'I used to have the hots for Elvis,' Stella said. 'And then Binch came along.'

The two women caught one another's gaze. They couldn't help themselves; both burst out laughing. But a moment later they were both weeping, the laughter turned to tears. Ruth moved to sit beside Stella on the couch, comforting her as best she could.

Later, becalmed and numb, they sat watching the news on the silent screen. An image of a mild-looking middle-aged man came up, identified by a caption as Professor Gerald Lautner of MIT. On a diagonal banner across one corner of the photograph it said in flaming red capitals: 'PYRO-ASSASSINATION?'

Ruth sat up. The breath seemed to leave her body. 'Oh my God. Not Gerry Lautner . . .'

'Did you know him?'

'I met him, yes, a couple of times.' Ruth sounded dazed. 'He gave a talk to a group I was involved with in New York. When did this happen?'

'About a week ago. Of course they can't leave it alone, the TV news shows. It's just a horror movie to them, with a mystery as another added twist.'

'Do they know who did this? Or why?'

'They're calling it a ritual carried out by a religious group.'

'Which group?'

Stella shook her head.

'I've seen reports of occurrences like this before,' Ruth said. 'Of people being incinerated . . . at least two or three.'

'It's the ninth.'

They watched the item, involving the anchor and two talking heads, play itself out, to be replaced by another in the relentlessly never-ending, endlessly repeating news cycle.

'I'm sick to the stomach of waiting for something to happen,' Stella said. She switched off the TV and stood up. 'Come into the kitchen and I'll make us some lunch. Is a sandwich all right? And maybe a little soup?'

Ruth followed Stella from the living room. 'I finally managed to contact Gavin,' she said.

Stella looked up from where she was taking salad from the fridge. Her expression was stiff and resentful. 'I tried to reach him, but every number I had, both here and in England, was unobtainable.'

'He's had to cover his tracks.' The explanation sounded feeble, though Ruth didn't elaborate further.

They ate lunch in the kitchen. While the two women were drinking coffee on the rear deck and contemplating the unspoiled splendour of the Medicine Bow range, Stella's husband was being escorted, blindfolded and wearing leg shackles, from his cell in the holding block and assisted down a flight of concrete steps to an armoured Humvee.

Dr Bill Inchcape's status under the UnPatriot (Emergency Powers) Act as a dangerous and subversive influence, acting against the public interest, had been upgraded from 'high risk' to 'severe threat'. Orders had come directly from the State Department that he was to be transferred immediately from mainland prison to the Cuba Prime Detention Facility. He was to be held there indefinitely, or until a trial date was set.

Once again Binch was given no prior warning of his transfer. He had no concept that the request to the State Department had come from the office of the director-in-chief of AAAV, nor would he have understood why.

For Chesney Poulton, it was partly a tactical move and partly one of spite. On their journey home from England, Martin Stringer had spelled out the links between Bill Inchcape and the 'scheming, underhand, lying bastard' who had been the thorn in his flesh at the Edinburgh Festival. It was Inchcape who had supplied much of the data which underpinned Chase's book *One Minute to Midnight*. From then on, it all became clear to Poulton; the web of connections fell into place. Howard Nevison had identified Chase as the man behind the Midnite-Net organisation. Chase and Inchcape were colleagues. As yet, it hadn't been possible to get their hands on Chase, whose current whereabouts were unknown.

But if Chase was proving elusive, no matter – for the moment at least – because they had his collaborator and fellow-traitor Inchcape under lock and key.

And if they made the bastard's life as uncomfortable as they possibly could, it might enrage and galvanise Chase into making an incautious and rash move that would flush him out of hiding. Then he would join Inchcape and the two buddies could sweat it out together.

2

The USA had taken Cuba in a bloodless coup in 2021. Soon afterwards, the prison facility at the tiny naval base at Guantánamo, which had housed foreign detainees following the invasion of Afghanistan, had been extended to include the whole of the eastern sector of the island, including the provinces of Camagüey, Las Tunas, Holguín, Granma, Santiago de Cuba and Guantánamo itself.

The death of Fidel Castro had marked a total reversal of US policy. After sixty-odd years of fierce, implacable hostility, the US did a complete turnaround and made available low-interest unconditional loans to rebuild the economy. It was an offer the communist government couldn't refuse. Massive injections of cash flowed in from Wall Street and the major European banks. The IMF and the World Bank poured in billions to fund and underwrite the construction of highways, airports, power plants, water and sewerage utilities, hospitals, schools, factories, apartment complexes, hotels, holiday resorts and a chain of casinos. There was a frenzied period of growth during which the economy was boosted by nearly one thousand per cent. Unemployment was practically zero. The population of Cuba was enjoying unprecedented growth and prosperity. Tourism was booming and the future was golden – until April 21, 2021, when disaster struck.

A busload of US tourists was ambushed and massacred at Santa Clara, a small town in the centre of the country. This atrocity had, according to the media, been orchestrated by a band of rebels who opposed the capitalist influx of money and influence. In the days after the Tourist Bus Massacre, there was a public outcry in the States demanding retribution. Why, politicians and media wanted to know, was the US supporting and funding a terrorist state? Under pressure from Washington, global financial institutions pulled the plug, cut off credit and cancelled extended loans. At once all building projects ceased. The multi-billion-dollar construction boom and infrastructure renewal programme was dead in the water; the economy stalled and became stagnant, leaving behind a gigantic black hole of debt.

Most of it was owed to the US government, the IMF and the World Bank, and as a single consortium they moved in to recover the debt, which in effect meant taking ownership of state assets and land – the entire island – and Cuba's sixty years of freedom and independence were over.

Even in the higher echelons of the State Department and intelligence services, only a handful of people were aware that the Tourist Bus Massacre, codenamed 'Bulldozer', was an operation conceived by the Alliance for the Advancement of American Values, under Chesney Poulton's leadership.

Part of the same plan was to transform the island into a gulag for political prisoners and dissidents in general. Construction had been frantic and relentless. From a dead start, and after only three years, Cuba PDF was half-completed, presently holding a fraction under four million inmates in seventeen locations, mainly in the open air.

In the latter years of the last century, average June and July temperatures for Cuba were 32° C. In line with soaring global temperatures, they were now averaging 45° C and nudging into the fifties for weeks on end. The bulk of the prisoners were kept in open compounds, housed under plastic sheet roofing, and water was strictly rationed to two pints per inmate a day. The result was that thousands died through heat exhaustion, dehydration and disease.

This was the destination Binch was bound for in the double-deck cargo bay of a C-133 Gladiator, along with six hundred fellow prisoners, some convicted, the rest, like Binch, awaiting a distant if not indefinite date for trial.

3

Even here in the foul canyons of New York City, Karl had no need of a mask. Many of the residents and commuters wore them, especially downtown. But Karl's strict training regime to effect a low metabolic rate, and his application of mind control to enter the Zone – an enhanced level of Out of Body Experience – meant that he was able to perform his task effectively where others might struggle to function – or might even collapse – in the tainted and impoverished air.

He had been here only a matter of hours and his preparation time was limited. To be granted the privilege of achieving another ascendancy so soon after his first mission to Boston was a rare accolade; maybe even a unique one. That Pastor Eldritch had such faith in his ability was a source of tremendous pride, or it would have been had pride been a permissible concept in the brotherhood of the Messengers. The Lautner ascendancy had gone perfectly; even now it was being held up as a textbook exemplar of accomplishing the mission cleanly and effectively, with zero blowback. Law enforcement agencies, local, state and federal, had been unable to come up with even a ghost of a theory about the perpetrator, the motive or the reason behind the method of pyro-assassination.

The location he had been given for his next assignment was somewhere to the west of Broadway.

His briefing had not specified a time, or provided a means of access to the building. It was up to him to select the optimum moment, taking into account the prime factors involved: location, access, concealment, withdrawal and anonymity.

Karl walked slowly along the streets of lower Manhattan. It was strange territory to him, and he was mindful not to waste energy. The harness chafed his shoulders. The cylinder of liquid propylene it contained gave him the deformed appearance of a hunchback.

At the traffic signal he crossed Canal Street and headed west towards Mercer Street.

Had there been anyone concerned enough to observe this awkward, lurching figure they might have thought of him as one of life's unfortunate victims, whereas in fact Karl thought of himself as precisely the opposite.

4

It wasn't until after Chase had been detained at JFK passport control on his return to the US that his own stupidity and lack of foresight hit him with the impact of walking into a brick wall.

What the hell was the matter with him? Bloody fool!

Obviously he should have realised that his appearance and outspoken remarks at the book festival would rile the authorities and lead directly to this kind of heavy-handed, punitive reaction. Stringer himself – if no one else – would have brought it to the authorities' attention. How had he not seen it coming?

After his eye-scan he was directed out of the line to a waiting immigration officer who must have weighed 250 pounds. She wore her cap on the back of her head, and her black forearms emerging from the uniform shirtsleeves were folded across her enormous bosom. She raised one arm and beckoned by lazily curling two fingers in a follow-me gesture.

Chase complied. Carrying the leather attaché case which contained his laptop, with his raincoat flung over one shoulder, he followed her splay-footed trudge behind a frosted panel and along a corridor with interview rooms either side. Some of the doors were open, with individuals or family groups being questioned by stern-looking officials. Chase was thinking fast – or trying to, anyway. His travel documents and residency permit were in order and up to date, he was certain of that. What other discrepancy might they find?

He was under no illusions that the authorities would discover – or manufacture – a reason for holding him if a legitimate reason couldn't be found. They hadn't even gone to the trouble of finding a reason in Binch's case; they'd just executed an extra-judicial order without regard to legal consequences. Idiotically, in a fit of paranoid guilt, Chase found himself dreaming up some kind of story to explain why he'd flown to Europe, as if to justify himself for what was a perfectly genuine family trip to see his poorly son. The State Department wouldn't be interested in that, of course; they would want to know what he'd been doing in Edinburgh, participating in a controversial debate with a respected American academic. Gaining credence by the minute in his mind, Chase was convinced that Stringer was behind this – maybe not personally, hands-on – but certainly the organisation he worked for or who sponsored him. The situation just had the unmistakable whiff of state conspiracy to it.

At least he hadn't been snatched at the arrivals gate, Chase reflected, frog-marched off by armed guards and bundled straight into a prison vehicle.

The official he faced across the table was an attractive young Hispanic woman. The name tag on her crisp uniform shirt was S. Machado.

She held his passport in front of her and was tapping away at a screen-pad. After a couple of minutes, and hardly looking at him directly, she said, 'Dr Gavin Chase, dual UK-US citizenship. Born Bolton, England, 1989. Is that you?'

Chase said it was.

'Have you ever been to Babuyan Island, and if so, when?'

If he could have chosen one question in the world *not* to have been asked, this came pretty close to winning the prize. He blinked at her in bewilderment, shaking his head.

'You've never been there?'

'I don't even know where Babuyan Island is.'

'Not even on a stopover?'

'If you tell me where this is on the globe, ma'am, maybe there's a remote chance . . .'

'Babuyan Island is in the Luzon Strait, off the northern coast of the Philippines. Is your answer no or you don't know?'

'Then it's definitely no. The nearest I've been to the Philippines is Hong Kong. Or is Vietnam nearer? I've been there too.'

Her expression unchanged, the young woman tapped away for a minute or so.

'What month is your birthday?' she eventually asked.

'February. It's in the passport.'

Some more tapping and then she looked up and actually smiled, handing him his passport. 'You are free to go, Dr Chase. Apologies for any inconvenience. The officer will show you the way out. Have a pleasant onward journey.'

Chase stood. He wasn't going to argue, but his curiosity was aroused.

'You pulled me aside because you thought I'd been to some obscure island in the South China Sea?'

'There's a US naval base there. It's not all that obscure.'

'Why did you think I had?'

'Your name flagged up a match. But this person is ten years younger, his birthday is in July, he's six foot four inches tall and an African-American. So we kinda guessed you weren't the one. But procedures had to be followed.' She deadpanned him, though Chase saw a glint of humour in her dark eyes.

His bag had already been taken off the carousel and was waiting for him at the retrieval point. He was in two minds whether to catch the connecting flight back to Pittsburgh or spend the night in the fourth-floor loft apartment on the edge of SoHo, just north of Canal Street. Staying in Manhattan, even for just a few hours, was his least favoured option these days: the air was stale, used up, with a metallic, almost acidic tang to it that stung the nostrils. Most New Yorkers wore plastic facemasks reinforced with medical gauze or sanitary pads. Banning all except electric-powered vehicles from downtown had only marginally improved air quality. It wasn't only the all-pervasive chemical pollutants drifting over the city in a bluish-grey haze; the real problem was the lowered oxygen content, so that you were continually running out of breath – not even because of running around, just by standing still or sitting down.

Chase didn't know the prevailing oxygen level in the city. The quality and content were monitored on a daily basis, although he suspected the actual figures made available to the public were massaged if not actively distorted to hide the truth.

The delay caused by that stupid Babuyan Island business meant he'd have to wait more than two hours for a flight. Forget it. He'd take the shuttle into town, get a drink in a bar in the Village and pick up some Chinese food to take back to the loft.

On the shuttle he called Cheryl and told her of his change of plan. Her voice was guarded and he knew it was down to their distrust of all forms of electronic communication. Micki Vargas and her team had done their utmost to encrypt calls to and from the Midnite base in Pittsburgh, while stressing that it was all but impossible to guarantee total security. So Chase and Cheryl had formulated their own personal code – pretty crude yet effective – to indicate certain levels of urgent priority or imminent danger. In the midst of a fairly inconsequential chat about his trip to Europe, Cheryl used the phrase 'so much to learn, so little time' – the 'Peter Sellers' code, a line taken at random from a 1960s recording, *Songs for Swinging Sellers*. They both knew every routine by heart and could immediately recognise any line quoted; the code meant 'priority' rather than 'danger'.

Over the next couple of sentences Chase dropped in a phrase from another sketch – 'the awkward age' – to confirm he had picked up the reference; Cheryl responded with 'I wouldn't go on TV looking like that' – the line came from the same sketch as her first quote, indicating that the priority was near the top of the scale. Chase closed their conversation by mentioning a friend who 'was hawking his brat around'– it might not have made much sense to anyone else, but it did to Cheryl: she understood.

By the time he reached Manhattan he was too tired and fractious to bother going for a drink. Anyway, there was liquor and wine in the apartment, including a bottle of Laphroaig single malt if he remembered right. He picked up a Chinese meal from a block away and let himself into the third-floor loft apartment, chest heaving from the climb up the iron stairwell. There was a freight elevator at the rear of the building which – foolishly perhaps – he rarely used. The apartment itself was something of an indulgence, he had to admit, since he and Cheryl stayed overnight in the city only when they had to.

He poured himself a large Scotch and carried it into the bathroom. There was always plenty of hot water in the system, fed from the communal boiler, and right now, that's what he needed most: a long hot shower followed by whisky, food, more whisky, and then several hours' uninterrupted slumber. Chase dumped his sweaty underclothes and socks in a heap and stepped into the cubicle. It was as his hand gripped the grooved knob and twisted it to full jet that a terrifying thought – and an even more terrifying image – entered his head: the naked form of a man, sheathed in flames, clawing for air and screaming soundlessly as the heat sucked his lungs dry – the professor from MIT incinerated in his own shower, a 'pyro-assassination' described in graphic detail on all the news networks. Lautner had been branded an activist, a left-wing agitator, by the media. Somebody from a shadowy organisation wanted him eliminated, and they had achieved it.

And he was as much an irritant to the established order as Lautner was – maybe even more so.

What was to stop them getting to him?

What if they had already succeeded?

Looking up, Chase saw bubbles form in the shower-head; involuntarily he held his breath and screwed his eyes tight shut as the globules burst out and cascaded towards him. A moment later he released his pent-up breath as the water flowed down his body, bringing with it a delicious feeling of being caressed by hot silk.

5

'It's a trap; anyone can see that.' There was a note of impatience tinged with pleading in Cheryl's tone. 'They want to draw you out into the open and blow your cover. For God's sake, don't be a fool, Micki!'

Micki Vargas shook her head defiantly. 'I'm too smart to play the fool. I've given it a lot of thought. I wanna do this and you've given me no reason why not.'

It was after 11 p.m. and they were still at the Midnite base, drinking strong black coffee in the corner office, probably a mistake because the last thing their inflamed tempers needed was an injection of caffeine.

'Listen, it isn't just you I'm concerned about. You've got to consider the entire operation.' With an effort Cheryl lowered her voice and tried to take the sting out of her tone. 'This isn't about any single one of us – you, me, Gavin, Jervis, none of us individually. If you go out on a limb you're putting us all, and everything we've worked for, in jeopardy. I can't allow that, Micki. It's too risky.'

'What do you mean, "allow" it?' Micki stood with her back against the window ledge, arms folded, her eyes glittering dangerously. 'I came here as a volunteer. According to my own free will. I don't take no orders from you, Cheryl. This is a golden opportunity, we can't lose it or turn it down. So there's a risk involved, so what? There always is *some* risk. Comes with the deal.' She shrugged. 'If we can't handle it we should choose some other line of work.'

Cheryl had almost literally to bite her tongue not to respond. She admired this woman in many ways, appreciated her formidable skills and dedication. But on the flipside, Micki Vargas was too headstrong, too much the maverick. And the inference that Cheryl didn't have the stomach for the fight was way below the belt.

Swallowing hard, she said, 'You're right, I'm not your boss. I'm just trying to take a reasonable position here, Micki, and not land any of us – you included – in hot water, or worse. Have you checked up on this Nevison guy? Is he genuine? I mean, is he who he says he is?'

Micki unfolded her arms as if in a gesture of conciliation. 'Far as I can tell: he's an analyst at this Washington political outfit, AAAV. They advise the government behind the scenes. He made the first approach – gave us info and contact details he didn't have to—'

'Which could be bogus. He might be fishing, dangling a line to tempt you to reveal yourself.'

'Cheryl,' Micki said with a hint of asperity, 'I wasn't born yesterday; you must know I've considered that already. And before you ask, no, I told him nothin' about us, no contact info – what we do or where we are. He knows zilch about us.'

'But he wants to set up a meeting,' Cheryl said. She picked up her paper cup of coffee, hesitated a second and put it down without drinking.

'No, he don't. He's blowin' the whistle and we're the party he's chosen. This all started, remember, when Jervis caught somebody snoopin' and codenamed him Caliban. This guy – if it is a guy – is offering us information for free, no conditions, no stipulations.'

'Without meeting face-to-face . . .'

'Right.' Micki moved to the chair across the desk from Cheryl. 'The goods are on a data-drive, which we collect from a dead drop. We waltz in, do the pick-up and we're away free.'

'Unless somebody's waiting and waltzes you off first,' Cheryl said stonily.

'We can't pass this up. I have to go.'

'Or they could watch you make the pick-up and follow you back here. Next thing, we're surrounded by helicopter gunships and a Special Forces squad armed with grenade-launchers. And you can say goodnight to the Midnite operation. Everything, the whole works' – she swiped her hand through the air – 'finished.'

'You think it's a set-up.' Micki's face had grown sullen, her dark eyes hooded.

'I honestly don't know. The point is, neither do you. Nevison could be the real deal and we'd be missing a great opportunity to get hold of classified data, really important stuff. But the question I'm asking, Micki, is it worth risking everything? Well? Is it?'

Micki stared past Cheryl's head to the darkened window and the night outside and didn't answer.

6

The onboard computer calculated that it was 177 miles from the Midnite base near Warrendale on the outskirts of Pittsburgh to Hagerstown, Maryland, which was the destination point Micki had been given. Somewhere near there was a Sheetz gas station and rest stop – in fact there were at least three Sheetzes in the general vicinity, though she didn't yet know which one to aim for, and she wouldn't know until the Dodge Ram had completed its three-hour journey.

The clock in the soft green glow of the dash showed a few minutes before six a.m. An hour, maybe a little longer, and they would be there.

On the map there was a place not far from the rendezvous named Funkstown, which somehow appealed to Micki. Is that why Nevison had chosen this particular area? Did he have the same warped sense of humour as she did? Another reason for this choice, she surmised, was because it wasn't very far from Washington, DC, not much more than an hour away on a traffic-sparse I-270 in the early hours. She had checked up on Nevison's employer, the Alliance for the Advancement of American Values, and found its address was in the capital, which was presumably where Nevison was based.

The more Micki learned about the AAAV, the more she was growing to detest it. They were pretty frugal with their information. Most of it was opaque corporate-speak, employing marketing jargon such as 'sharpening business focus to achieve political concordance' and 'enhancing funding opportunities by progressive legislation'. Loosely translated, that meant something like 'grease our palms with billions of dollars and your company can do as it pleases, no questions asked'. In fact, you were less informed and more confused after reading their prospectus than you were before starting it. What AAAV actually *did* and what services it provided was akin to solving a conundrum wrapped in a mystery on a foggy night.

And yet as Micki had to remind herself, however impenetrable their purpose, this was the same organisation using people like Nevison to seek out and infiltrate online entities such as Midnite-Net for as yet unspecified reasons. And whatever the reasons, they weren't friendly and they weren't benign, you could bet your last red cent on that.

The sky was starting to brighten on the undulating horizon. By the time they reached the turn-off to Hagerstown it would be fully light. Then she would have to locate the Sheetz gas station next to a Sunoco Food Mart, where she would buy ten dollars' worth of gas and proffer a \$100-bill in payment. The attendant would ask if she had anything less, and Micki would produce two fives. The attendant would then hand a sealed envelope containing the rest of the directions to what Micki hoped would be the meeting place with Nevison.

The brightening sky was making Micki Vargas fretful, and on two counts. Both door panels of the Dodge Ram had been painted over, obliterating the Midnite-Net logo, but the job had been botched, or the paint had weathered and faded, and if you looked at it for more than ten seconds, the symbol was still faintly discernible.

The decision to hide the logo had been made when the death threats had started multiplying. In the early weeks and months after Gavin Chase had achieved celebrity with the publication of *One Minute to Midnight* he had been hailed as a brave new voice by environmentalists and the media alike, but it hadn't lasted long. The fundamentalist cranks and right-wing nut-jobs soon came out of the woodwork and denounced him and his book as an assault on democracy and the free market. It got nasty and then nastier still, and the vehicles that had been proudly emblazoned with the Midnite symbol became a target for anyone with a grudge, a frontal lobotomy and a firearm.

Micki's other reason for her mounting anxiety was whether Nevison, with the benefit of broad daylight, would see that she hadn't arrived at the meeting place unaccompanied, contrary to his specific instruction. In the rear seat of the extended Dodge Ram cab were two of her Midnite crew: Bud Keiser and Jon Pineda. Both had been chosen, Micki freely admitted, because they were hefty guys who could handle themselves and would be useful in getting her out of a tight spot. Also, both were expert shots – and Keiser was an ace marksman with a telescopic sight.

Not that Micki was expecting gunplay, or even a physical confrontation, but she felt much safer and more confident with their backup. The pair of them would have to hunker down near the floor so they wouldn't be seen; she had to just hope that Nevison wouldn't be inclined to carry out a closer inspection of the vehicle.

She jumped slightly when a hand reached out and touched her shoulder. It was Bud Keiser. He was in his mid-forties and had served fourteen years with the 82nd Airborne Division stationed at Fort Bragg. What he had seen and experienced had transformed him from a hardened combat soldier into a committed pacifist and environmental campaigner.

'Sorry. Didn't mean to startle you.'

'No problem. I was miles away. You boys bored back there?'

'Not at all. Had a snooze. Jonny's still in dreamland. We anywhere near?'

'Fifteen, twenty minutes. I need to find a gas station somewhere between Hagerstown and Funkstown, near a Sunoco. We come off the interstate onto Beaver Creek Road and head north. You spot a Comfort Inn, shout out. It's a marker.'

'Roger that.'

Micki concentrated on her driving now that the traffic was getting heavier. She was willing herself not to think about it, but couldn't stop wondering how long it would take Cheryl to register her absence and put two and two together. She had told Cheryl a monster fib – that there was to be no human interaction; that the deal involved a data-drive and a dead drop, with no actual contact with Nevison. Micki had gambled that Cheryl would regard it as less of a risk and be willing to let her go. Wrong. So what would be Cheryl's reaction when she found out there had been an actual meeting and that Micki had flouted her trust by going against Cheryl's express wish?

The words 'shit' and 'fan' came readily to mind.

The next sign came up: HAGERSTOWN – Beaver Creek Road – 1/2 Mile.

Micki eased the Dodge Ram to the exit lane.

7

Up at 6.30 a.m., a perfunctory shave in the strip-lighted bathroom mirror, then showered and dressed in sweater and jeans. By 6.50 a.m. Howard Nevison was sitting on the edge of the bed in room 44 of the Dormez-Bon Motel.

The cellphone he'd bought for fifteen bucks the day before was on the bedside table. It would be used only once – to take an incoming call – and then tossed into a dumpster after being crushed under his heel. He felt he'd covered everything; he was just waiting for the call from the heavily tipped gas attendant to let him know that the Midnite contact had departed and describe the vehicle he was driving; that way Howard would know the exact time to expect him and be able to identify him by his vehicle.

He would have dearly loved a cup of coffee, but he daren't venture outside in case the call came through earlier than expected. It was only five minutes from the gas station to the motel and he wanted to watch his Midnite contact arrive in the parking lot and enter the coffee shop – that was why he'd requested a room on the second floor with a decent view.

This involved the next part of the plan; he'd wait at least thirty minutes before going down there himself, keeping his eyes peeled from room 44 for any other vehicles pulling in off Oak Ridge Drive. There shouldn't be any, not at this early hour; no one but an overnight guest who wanted a quick getaway would want to eat breakfast here; Howard was confident he'd thought of everything.

. . . Except for one small, niggling, yet very important, detail. Should he carry the data-drive on his person, or leave it in the room? Or hide it in the trunk of his car, which was parked at the rear of the Dormez-Bon? He couldn't decide what was best. Leave it till the last moment, that's what he'd do, then make a snap decision. But his mind wouldn't stay calm and he had to grip his knee to stop the twitching and the foot that was tap-tap-tapping on the thin carpet.

To distract himself and occupy his thoughts he went to the window and surveyed the uninspiring vista of the dozen or so cars parked in bays, and the side-on view of the coffee shop. It was a grey day, with mist or maybe a fine drizzle hanging in the air. Craning left and then right, he looked as far along Oak Ridge Drive as he could in both directions. It wasn't a commuter route, apparently, because traffic was light. He breathed a circle of condensation on the glass and wiped it off with his elbow sleeve. He discovered he couldn't quite manage a full breath. He got so far and then his chest went tight and backed up, as if there was an impediment—

Jeez, he could murder for a cup of coffee.

Smacking a fist into his palm, he turned away and picked up the phone. *Come on you sonofabitch, ring!*

Had the deal fallen through? Was all this planning and waiting and torment for nothing? Howard glared at the phone and then realised something that made him go numb with shock and anguish. The fucking thing wasn't fucking switched on! He'd made sure the device was fully charged and somehow forgotten to turn it on. No evidence of smart planning there, you pathetic useless dickbrain . . .

When the screen lit up he went straight to messages, but it was empty, and there were no missed calls either, which made him release his long-held breath. He plucked a tissue from the pack on the bedside cabinet to wipe his forehead. As he did so, the phone played the opening guitar riff from *Pretty Woman.*

Howard listened, said one word – 'Thanks!' – and switched off.

There must have been an instant rush of adrenalin, because at once his mind became clear, his nerves were steady and he felt calm and in control. Back at the window, he watched the second hand sweep round the dial, waiting patiently for the five minutes to pass. The plan was in operation; now, his confidence renewed, he felt certain it was going to work.

Howard allowed himself a small smile of self-congratulation as the dark grey Dodge Ram swung in off Oak Ridge Drive and headed for the bays nearest the coffee shop. Moments later he felt the smile go stiff, more surprised than shocked when the driver emerged and it was a woman. No reason it shouldn't be, though it had never entered his head. And even from this distance, through the misty murk, he could see she was striking: tall and statuesque, wearing a hip-length tan jacket and dark blue jeans, a silk scarf furled loosely over her shoulders, long black curly hair framing strong, dark features.

She was carrying a blue leather attaché case, Howard saw, and he noticed something else: as she strode away from the truck the woman looked back over her shoulder, as if checking it out. What could that mean? His view of the vehicle was from the tail-end so what he could see inside the cab was restricted to the rear window. A worm of suspicion entered Howard's mind. Was there someone else in there, in spite of his demand that the meeting was to be strictly one-to-one?

After ten minutes, when no other vehicle had entered the parking lot, Howard was chafing at the bit, his nerves once again starting to get the better of him, so he decided to abandon the 'wait-thirty-minutes' part of the plan and get the damn thing over and done with, then maybe he could relax.

Pulling the door shut, he went along the landing in the opposite direction and took the stairs round the corner, hidden from the coffee shop. The idea was to confuse anyone seeing him appear in the parking lot and make it hard to locate where he'd come from. Arriving at the bottom of the stairs, Howard suddenly realised that the data-drive was in the inside pocket of the jacket he was wearing. So that was decided then. No going back.

There were fewer than a dozen people eating breakfast: three at the counter, the rest occupying tables. The person he'd come to see was in a side booth facing the entrance. Howard felt intimidated. First, he had been expecting a guy, and second, he'd had little experience of interacting and conversing with such a stunning creature as this. She was looking at him as he approached, her eyes slowly widening, and her mouth broke into a perfect smile, quite dazzling against her coffee complexion.

'Caliban, I presume, right?'

Howard nodded.

'Why don't you sit and I'll order you something.' She raised a slender hand to summon the waitress, and then offered it to him. 'I'm Micki Vargas. And you I guess are Howard Nevison. You were open about divulging your identity, Howard. That's one of the reasons I feel I can trust you.'

'But can I trust you?' Howard ventured to ask.

While Micki just asked for a refill, Howard ordered ham with scrambled eggs, hash browns and wheat toast, plus a large mug of coffee. He realised he was ravenous. She let him eat, with enough of the usual chitchat not to leave an awkward silence.

'To be honest,' Howard said, 'I never imagined they'd send a woman.'

'Any particular reason?'

'No. It didn't occur to me, I guess.'

'Women are capable of lots of things. You'd be surprised.'

'Don't think I would. Not with you. But I knew it wouldn't be your leader.'

'My leader? An' who would that be?' Micki Vargas said with a small crooked smile.

'The one who started the Midnite group,' Howard said. 'Gavin Chase.'

It was a calculated bombshell, and it worked. He wanted to show her he was a serious player, not just a geek, and gain her respect (and to be honest, impress her a little bit too). But Micki's most notable reaction was that of suspicion, which was not what he'd intended.

Micki was no longer smiling when she said, 'You know where we're based as well? Where we operate from?'

Howard shook his head.

'Can I believe that?'

'I've no reason to lie to you, Ms Vargas. I don't know where you operate from, that's the truth.'

'But you was fishin' for our location, you admit it?'

'Of course – that's how we first made contact. You knew Caliban was lurking around, trying to infiltrate the firewall, and I knew you were blocking us.'

'Us?'

'The AAAV tracking team: that's how I was able to get a message through.' Howard gestured round. 'And why we're here having this meeting.'

'So tell me then. How'd you find out Gavin was linked to the Midniters?'

'Is that what you call yourselves?' Howard asked. He was becoming interested in this operation, and more and more intrigued by it.

'Some of the time, Mr Nevison. Other times we call ourselves somethin' different.'

Howard said, 'I made the connection through your Climate Alerts. The one about the Oxygen Balance Sheet? A similar chart was in the book, *One Minute to Midnight*. It wasn't much of a stretch to join the dots between the author and Midnite-Net.'

Micki's eyes narrowed. 'Who else knows? Your tracking team? Your boss?'

'No one else.'

'Why should I believe you?'

'Why should you believe anything?' Howard reached into his inside pocket and took out the data-drive. He placed the small matt-grey rectangular object on the table between them. 'Maybe this is what you need to show you I'm telling the truth. Not all of it, not everything, but a substantial chunk of the AAAV classified archive is in here.' He tapped it with his index finger. 'Their elimination operations in South America and Asia. Where the funding comes from and who it goes to. Files listing more than three thousand corporate sponsors and affiliated organisations. Their political contacts in the US and overseas. The ascendancy programme they operate with a religious cult called the Messengers of God . . .'

Howard held up both hands, palms facing her. 'In point of fact, Ms Vargas, this could well be—'

'I'm not used to that, bein' called Ms Vargas. It's Micki.' She picked up the data-drive. 'You was sayin', Howard?'

'That this might convince you. The leader of your group, Gavin Chase, he has an apartment in New York, right?'

Micki's nod was guarded.

'Let's see if I remember . . . a fourth-storey loft converted from a warehouse, north of Canal Street on the edge of SoHo. Between Broadway and Mercer, if memory serves.'

'So what if he has? The point you tryin' to make?'

'The point I *am* making – Micki – is this. You've heard of pyro-assassinations, I suppose, seen reports in the media?'

'Sure. There was one just recently in . . . Boston?'

'Yes.' Howard was stony-faced. 'Gerald Lautner. A professor at MIT. He happened to be someone I knew – a friend. He was a victim of this so-called ascendancy programme, which is a cover name for these pyro-assassinations. The director-in-chief of the AAAV, Chesney Poulton, personally selects the targets and a cult of religious fanatics called Messengers of God carries them out.' Howard put his elbows on the table and leaned forward. 'Gavin Chase is a target of the ascendancy programme. The information, all the details, are contained in that drive.'

Micki was struggling to take this in. 'You tellin' me the Messenger cult – they got his New York address?' The note of anxiety in her voice was rising to one of panic.

'They were given *an* address in New York,' Howard told her, 'but it happens to be a Chinese restaurant on the West Side.'

Micki's eyes were fixed on him. 'How come?'

Howard smiled. 'I switched them. But it was close. The dossier I compiled had the genuine address – fortunately for us, Chesney Poulton can't be bothered reading dossiers. So I changed it and substituted the restaurant for the real address; I just hope the Messengers like egg noodles.'

'And what about the digital copy? The archive backup?'

Howard nodded appreciatively. 'You think like an analyst. I deleted some of them, corrupted a lot more. They're in one helluva mess.'

'What about a trace? Will they know it was you?'

'Not straight off the bat, but eventually, I guess, by a process of elimination.' He clasped his hands together and stared at her. 'That's part of the price I'm asking . . .'

'You mean you want money for this?' Micki said. She was still holding the data-drive.

'Not money, no. I'll need some place to go, a secret location. A safe house. Can you help me find one? You've got resources – your group, I mean. You work as a clandestine operation, evading detection. That's what I'm going to need. Will you talk to Gavin Chase? I'm serious about this – Micki. I'm asking for your help.'

'Okay. Maybe. But I don't understand somethin' you said just now. You first gave your boss the address of Gavin's place – the real one. Then later you switched it. What made you change your mind?'

Through tightened lips Howard said, 'I can't tell you. I can't say.'

'You mean you can say but you don't want to.'

Howard looked away. He could feel himself going red.

'The reason bad enough for you to spill the goods,' Micki said. 'That bad, huh?' And when Howard didn't answer, she went on, 'Us findin' a secret place for you might be a cute way of you findin' where our base is. I lead you there and then what happens? You tell your boss-man Poulton, next thing – bingo! – the National Guard or the Marines bust in. And Howard Nevison is the new wonder kid on the block, gets all the kudos and medals for bein' such a smart spook.' She pointed to the ceiling. 'Up the ladder you go. Top boy.'

'If that's your answer, what can I do to convince you?' Howard said, nettled. 'I hand you one hundred gigabytes of classified data with no preconditions, without demanding a cent off you . . . not asked where your base is and I don't want to know. What else can I say? It's a no-win situation.'

Micki considered him for a long moment. 'Okay. Tell you what I do. I will see Gavin and I will ask how we can help, finding you someplace safe. I promise you that much. But you understand, Howard, why I gotta be careful. I *have* to be certain you bein' straight with me, tellin' me the truth.'

'As straight as you're being with me, you mean?' Howard said.

'Huh? Don't get'cha,' Micki said, tilting her head back and wrinkling her nose. 'Not bein' straight?'

'I think you do get me. We made an arrangement. The deal was a one-to-one meeting.'

'This is one-to-one far as I can see.' Micki swivelled her head from left to right and back again in an exaggerated fashion. 'You spy somebody else?'

'Now who's being cute?' Howard leaned back against the padded seat and half-glanced towards the parking lot. 'Bet you ten bucks there's someone else in your vehicle out there.'

After a pause, Micki admitted, 'Okay, there is somebody. I felt I needed backup.'

'And I came alone, as we arranged, in good faith. So which one of us is being straight with the other?' Howard swiped his hand as if wiping a board clean. 'Don't bother. No need to answer. I want to go ahead with this. How 'bout you?'

A shadow fell across the table and Howard flinched at the sight of a grizzled, thickset man with cropped grey hair holding a Glock .45 semi-automatic across his paunch, the trigger-finger pointing along the barrel in the approved military safe-mode.

Micki said, 'Bud! What in hell's happenin'?'

'Jonny picked up a signal on the drone sensor. It could be nothing, or it could be the perfect shit-storm about to drop on us. We're out of here. As of now.' Bud Keiser stared hard at Howard. 'This guy kosher?'

'You seriously asking?' Howard said. 'You think I led somebody here?'

'Did you?'

'I'm risking my—' Howard broke off, incensed. He plucked the data-drive from Micki's fingers and brandished it in Bud Keiser's face. 'I risked every fucking thing I have to give you this!'

Bud Keiser raised his hand as if to slap him; instead he snatched the drive and slipped it into a breast pocket. 'On your feet.' He motioned to Howard with the muzzle of the semi-automatic. 'You're coming with us. If and when the shit-storm descends, I want you close as fleas on a hound dog, son.'

Before he could protest, Howard was dragged by the arm from the booth and hustled towards the exit. Two of the men eating breakfast at the counter and a waitress appeared to be the only ones to notice what was happening. Micki had the presence of mind to toss down a twenty onto the table before she grabbed her blue leather attaché case and followed.

8

Out in the parking lot the misty drizzle had cleared and the sky was brightening. Jon Pineda had reversed the Dodge Ram from its bay and was about to swing it towards the coffee shop when two black unmarked SUVs appeared from Oak Ridge Drive and screeched to a halt across both exits, blocking them.

Bud Keiser let go a string of obscenities. He grabbed Howard roughly by the shoulder and yanked him backwards towards Micki. He held up his left hand in a signal to tell her to stay where she was, in the entrance porch of the coffee shop. Shielding his eyes with the hand holding the gun, Keiser looked towards the skies. After five seconds he saw it – the tiny black speck of a drone – and released another fruity string of ripe expletives.

Howard was standing out in the open, beyond the entrance porch, not sure what to do. He made up his mind fast when a single high-calibre rifle shot, and then three more rapidly following, cracked and echoed across the parking lot. Both sets of side windows of the Dodge Ram exploded into fragments. Ducking, Howard scuttled into the porch behind Micki, who reached into the blue leather attaché case and withdrew a Walther PPK 9mm handgun. She thumbed off the safety, going into a crouch and signalling Howard to follow suit.

Employing the vehicle as cover, Bud Keiser ran to the driver's side of the Dodge truck. One knee on the tarmac, he reached up and opened the door. Jon Pineda had taken a direct hit; the high-calibre round had made a mess of his upper rib-cage, blowing most of it and the accompanying soft tissue across the steering wheel and the inside of the door Bud Keiser was holding. A lot of Pineda's blood was running down the door panel and dripping onto the tarmac. He pushed Pineda across to the passenger seat, lifting his legs over the central control column.

Micki Vargas had no clear view of what was going on. The windshield had become opaque, a muddy red colour – it must be coated on the inside with blood. It had to be Jonny's blood, because Bud had moved after the shots were fired. She turned her head to look behind her, but the glass doors revealed nothing except her and Howard's reflections.

Taking a deep breath, Micki was trying to slow her thought processes down, to figure things out rationally and logically – even in the heat of the moment – as Bud Keiser would have done.

She spoke to Howard over her shoulder. 'Where's your car?' It took an agonisingly long moment for him to gather his wits. 'It's out back in the parking lot.'

'You have the keys on you?'

It took the pale-faced boy another couple of moments before he felt his pockets and nodded.

'If Bud can't get the truck here, we go that-away' – pointing behind her – 'through the kitchen. Could be our one chance, boy – our only chance.'

With Bud Keiser behind the wheel, the Dodge Ram was moving towards them. She could see Bud's open palm wiping clear a bloody circle to see through. If he could use the vehicle to shield them, Micki thought, they might have a chance of scrambling into the back seat. But that hope proved forlorn the instant it entered her mind as a fusillade of rifle-fire erupted from both directions. If Keiser stopped now, even for a matter of seconds, he was a sitting duck. He had to keep going, and he did, swinging the Dodge round so that all four tyres shrieked and smoked.

Only one way out now, Micki Vargas knew. With the attaché case in her left hand and the gun in the other, she kicked Howard on the shin to make him stand up, which activated the sliding doors. Going back through the kitchen and into the rear lot was their only option, but as the doors slid apart she realised it wasn't: two of the men at the breakfast counter she had paid little attention to now had their weapons levelled and aimed not at Howard but at her. Micki fired instinctively and she was bang on target: the bullet hit one of them full in the chest before he had time to fire. There was no chance for her to see the outcome because a 9mm round gouged a hole the size of a coaster, ragged and red round the edges, through her own windpipe. It also took with it most of her lower jaw.

Frozen in shock, unaware he had voided both his bladder and his bowels and was standing in the result, Howard looked down at the woman he had known for less than twenty minutes lying dead at his feet with half her face blown away.

Out in the parking lot, the Dodge Ram performed three complete rubber-shrieking pirouettes before Bud Keiser brought it to a halt, slammed into reverse and put his combat boot hard down on the pedal. The vehicle accelerated backwards fast and, true to its name, rammed its tail-gate into one of the SUVs blocking the exit, forcing it sideways and nearly overturning it, before heading off at high speed down Oak Ridge Drive in a haze of blue exhaust smoke.

9

It was the third item in the routine daily bulletin from the North Las Vegas Police Department that snagged Russ Trambo's attention. The news editor of WNRB-TV read it through twice and got that tell-tale prickly feeling on the back of the neck that forty years of print and TV news gathering had bestowed on him. He wasn't always right, but he was rarely wrong.

#03
OCTOBER 09, 2025
UPDATE ON INVESTIGATION: (MNF/T2834/25) OFFICER P CLAYTON (DET)
SUBJECT: DISAPPEARANCE OF — STEVEN BRANDO FAZIOLI (AGE 34)
CHARLES (CHUCK) STOCKTON BRANT (AGE 31)

Investigation renewed when two (2) horse-riders [see Appendix 1a] reported finding the burnt-out shell of a Jeep Renegade in a dry creek along the Valley of Fire, situated approx. seven (7) miles southeast of Mount Grafton, on the lower elevation of the Muddy Mountains Wilderness Range.

Officer Clayton attended the scene with forensic support and identified several human body parts in an advanced state of incineration. These have been sent to Fulmar Biopsy Solutions for lab analysis and possible identification.

This discovery has led to renewed investigation into the disappearance of Fazioli and Brant (brothers-in-law) who were reported missing after failing to return from a hunting trip in the Wilderness Range, which covers more than nine (9) thousand square miles, making it a formidable task for search teams.

Police request circulation of above details to facilitate eye-witnesses to come forward with information re sightings of named individuals and their vehicle. Further reports to follow.

A faint bell kept ringing insistently that he couldn't ignore. The only route that went anywhere near Mount Grafton was Highway 604, which passed by the Nellis Missile Range. Beyond the base was nothing but the Wilderness the godforsaken terrain was named after. As it stood, there was hardly anything in the police report to qualify it as a bona fide news item. Should he run it anyway, as a goodwill gesture to the North Las Vegas Police Department?

Pouring himself a glass of ice tea, the editor had a light-bulb moment when he suddenly remembered what was niggling him: it was the young reporter, Jack Chang, who was the connection. Chang had been gone three years now, so it must have been that length of time – at least four years, nearer five perhaps – since he tried to interest Trambo in the Jesus freaks story. Groups of soberly dressed young men had arrived in town and been trucked out up Highway 604 to . . . well, where exactly?

Chang had speculated that they were members of a doomsday cult – End-of-the-Worlders. Russ himself had wondered if they were anti-war protesters picketing the missile range. They definitely weren't the latter, because he would have heard about it. But the real mystery of where they were heading for had never been solved.

Sitting at his desk, gazing out through the venetian blinds at the downtown Strip, Russ let his mind idle at its own pace. Something in the report, bland as it was, had bothered him. Was it the fact that the

Jeep and its occupants had gone up in flames? If the driver had lost control and swerved off the trail, plunging them down the hillside, then the vehicle catching fire as it hit bottom would be the expected outcome, certainly no surprise.

So the fire of itself wasn't the niggling prickly thing.

But in an open Jeep, why would the two occupants also be incinerated? They'd have been flung out, wouldn't they, on the way down? Unless, Russ qualified to himself, they were wearing seatbelts and couldn't release themselves in time.

Finishing his ice tea, he moved to the whiteboard and took up the magic marker. Under the general heading '5 p.m. Digest' he added the item to the end of the running order, giving it the title 'Blazing Jeep Puzzle'.

It would make an intriguing little story, and folks liked to mull over a mystery.

IO

CLIMATE ALERT
Issued by MIDNITE-NET [September 2025]
Subject: **"The Tipping Point"**
The dramatic shrinking of the Antarctic Ice Cap became known in climate science as the Rignot Effect, named after Eric Rignot, a glaciologist at the University of California. The retreat of the ice was unstoppable, and as early as 2013 Rignot concluded that its melting into the warming ocean 'has passed the point of no return'.

Rignot and other climatologists found the most severe effects were taking place on the West Antarctic Ice Sheet. Should this vast body of ice melt entirely, it would increase global sea levels by ten to twelve feet.

Since the beginning of the twentieth century, the oceans of the planet have risen by eight inches. They continue to rise in this century, monitored daily by satellites, which bounce radio waves off the ocean surface. Because seawater expands as it warms up, higher temperature increase the volume, leading to rising levels.

It was predicted that very soon we would arrive at 'the tipping point'

Many scientists believe this took place when a NASA surveillance aircraft spotted a twenty mile-long crack across the Pine Island Glacier, which widened at an alarming rate. The glacier split apart and gave birth ('calving' as it's called) to a giant iceberg of 450 square miles: eight times larger than New York's Isle of Manhattan. This gave Pine Island the unique distinction of being the most rapidly shrinking glacier on record, causing sea levels to rise faster than any other glacier on the planet.

This wasn't the only bad news. There are dozens of glaciers, some smaller than Pine Island, some larger, along the West Atlantic Ice Sheet. Could the same Rignot Effect be happening to them? Nearby lies the truly massive Larsen Ice Shelf. Measurements and calculations showed the rates of ice depletion to be increasing there also. An American-led scientific team recorded the disintegration of Larsen B, an ice plateau measuring 1,250 square miles (bigger than Rhode Island). They were the last human beings to see it intact: two months later, satellite images showed Larsen B had collapsed – 'shattering like the safety glass of a car's windshield' as one team member described it.

In the nine years since then (2016), the process has accelerated to the point where the entire Riiser-Larsen Ice Shelf is in danger of disintegrating and sliding into the sea. Should this happen, the volume of water released would raise sea levels by at least fifteen feet.

This aftermath of this process has brought unstable weather patterns and violent storm surges – dubbed 'Superstorms' by the media. Storms of such ferocity are classified by scientists as 'century events', meaning the odds of them happening are once every hundred years. These are now occurring seven times more frequently than before – Florida averaging a Superstorm every two years instead of once a century.

Florida happens to be at the highest risk of any state in the US due to rapid climate change. Eight of the top ten US cities likely to suffer flooding are in Florida. When accompanied by tidal surges, most of the southeast of the state will be three feet underwater, with Miami-Dade having the most homes at risk: thirty billion dollars' worth of taxable property.

Florida might be under threat, but it's not alone.

States on the eastern and western seaboards are also vulnerable to rising sea levels: California on the west coast, New York State, New Jersey, Virginia, North Carolina and Georgia on the east coast, all the way down to the Florida Keys, which will vanish beneath the waves.

Across the country, nearly five million people live in 2.6 million homes at less than four feet above high tide. Forecasts based on climate records and future trends show rises in sea level between seven and fifteen feet by 2036 to be conservative estimates.

Eleven years from now.

8

I

Chesney Poulton studied the photograph of the woman lying naked on the stainless steel trough. Even in death, and with her head attached to her body by just a few tattered threads of pale tissue and torn bloodless ligatures, it was evident that she was – or had been – an example of womanhood in its prime. Even Poulton could see as much. He tossed the print aside. 'Who was the fucking bitch?'

'We haven't I-Deed her as yet,' Burt Mueller, his chief of staff, admitted.

'*What?*' Poulton hunched himself forward over his desk. 'Goddamnit, Nevison must know! He fixed the fucking meeting with her. Make him spill his fucking guts.' There was a purplish tinge in his jowls and his wide neck was throbbing and red.

'He's doing that as we speak with Specials Ops,' Mueller said. 'The minute they have a coherent narrative, Mitchell will call me.'

'Mitchell?'

'Conrad Mitchell, in charge of interrogation. He and his team are specialists. They worked on Julian Assange.' Burt Mueller checked the time. 'I'm expecting his call within the hour.'

Poulton lit up a Cohiba Behike. His hands were trembling. He blew out a vast cloud of smoke.

'Makes my fucking blood boil when I think of it – the future I had planned for that boy. I thought he was a real prospect, genuine talent, that he'd go far. I was even prepared to help and nurture him, invest in him *personally*. And then this cheating and treachery.' He leaned his head back on the leather rest, plumes of smoke issuing from his nostrils. 'To think – for chrissakes! – I *trusted* the fucking deceitful bastard!'

'I didn't,' Joe Quarles put in quietly.

Burt Mueller shot a warning look at him which said, *Now is not the time to score points and big yourself up . . .*

'You were his head of section,' Poulton said, taking out the cigar and glaring at Quarles. 'If you knew he was unreliable, gonna leak like a fucking sieve, why didn't you say something? Bragging about it after the event is not a smart career move.'

'Excuse me, sir, but I didn't know it for a verifiable fact. I didn't have proof.' The whining note in his voice made plain how suddenly anxious Joe Quarles had become. 'It was just a feeling I had, he was so stuck-up and superior. But then he was assigned to the Midnite investigation, which meant he had Level Five security clearance. So I kinda assumed . . .'

Burt Mueller closed his eyes in quiet desperation. That particular decision had been made by the director-in-chief personally; to remind him of the fact, with the implication that it was he who had made a fatal error of judgement, was not a wise course to take.

But Chesney Poulton was sidetracked by something Joe Quarles had said. He jabbed his cigar at the print on the desk. 'Burt, this bitch on the slab: could she be connected with the Midnite operation? Quarles is right about that – Nevison was on special assignment to track them and close them down. How far did he get?'

This was Joe Quarles' domain. Burt Mueller looked to him for a response.

'There's no indication of a Midnite connection at this time,' Joe Quarles said carefully. 'What we do know is that Nevison extracted a large cache of data and then tried to cover his tracks by corrupting a number of files.' The director-in-chief was seated at his desk, with his chief of staff seated opposite him, while Quarles was left standing in no-man's land, like a servant grovelling before his superiors.

'Which files specifically?' Burt Mueller asked.

Joe Quarles sorted through a dozen or so sheets of paper, swapping them from hand to hand. 'Er, yeah, uh . . .' He shuffled his feet uneasily. 'Environmental activists death toll in South America and southeast Asia is one. Financial transactions with the Church of Charmed Baptist Brethren. Something called the ascendancy programme, which is new to me. Donations and pledges to Common Sense Coalition UK. Register of social meetings with members of the Senate and Congress—'

Chesney Poulton whipped out his cigar and held it above his head. 'Wait. Stop. *Hold it*. Are those pages you're holding a list of all the files that've gone missing and been corrupted?'

'Not all of them, sir. We're still in the process of checking and verifying them—'

'So how many so far? How many you got there, for instance?'

Joe Quarles riffled through the sheets once more. Finally he found the one he was searching for. 'Um . . . 284,366.' He sounded quite pleased to have produced so exact a number. He looked up and smiled helpfully at Poulton and Mueller. 'That's as of . . . oh, about one hour forty minutes ago, say two hours.'

'Holy Shite and Corruption.' The words were muffled because Poulton had laid the cigar in the ashtray and was speaking through his large hands, which covered most of his face. To no one in particular he mumbled, 'That's just fine and dandy . . . the ascendancy programme, the Messengers, the Brethren. Fish in a barrel.' He removed his hands. 'And at the end of the line there's us, wrapped up neatly with a fucking pink bow and blue ribbons.'

He drummed his fingers. 'Burt. Talk to Mitchell. We need to know – I mean this minute, *now* – who this data was leaked to. We have to come up with a counter-revelation strategy before any one of us leaves this office.'

Mueller spoke on his phone. Poulton beckoned Joe Quarles to step nearer the desk. 'Which tech operatives worked with Nevison on the Midnite project?'

'I don't know right off the bat, sir. I'll have to check.'

'It never occurred to you that these highly qualified operatives might have just the tiniest clue what this scumbag was up to? Which direction the investigation was heading in? What kind of progress he'd made? Tell me, Quarles, I'm interested in exactly what you do all day. Stare out the window and play with yourself?'

'Allow me a moment to look into it, sir. I'll have the answer immediately.'

He started to move away when Burt Mueller said, 'Mitchell's ready. He's on the CC link, sir.'

Chesney Poulton touched a button and swung his chair round to face the large screen suspended from the oak-panelled ceiling. A middle-aged man in black-framed spectacles with a heavily lined forehead and thinning grey hair was standing in front of a white ceramic-tiled wall. In the background could be heard the dry crackle and faint hum of electricity.

'We have you, Conrad,' Burt Mueller sang out.

Mitchell nodded to show he'd heard and consulted a clipboard. 'Nevison is being co-operative,' he began. 'I think it's genuine. But he's not contrite – he doesn't regret what he's done.'

'And what *has* he done?' Poulton broke in impatiently.

'Nevison made contact with a media activist outfit called Midnite-Net,' the head of interrogation carried on in the same clipped, unhurried tone. 'His idea. Arranged to meet an unnamed person at the Dormez-Bon Motel in Hagerstown. He was expecting a guy, but a woman showed up. The name she gave was Micki Vargas. That's the person terminated during armed interaction with our agent. We have her corpse in storage. Nevison handed over a data-drive containing one hundred gig of classified information from AAAV digital storage and archives. He also included the encryption codes. That's the equivalent of two million pages, or 75,000 volumes of printed material. The files he selected—'

Poulton interrupted, his voice a peremptory bark. 'Was the data-drive recovered?'

'Not with the Vargas corpse, no sir,' Mitchell said.

'Then where the fuck is it? Who the fuck has it?' Poulton looked from the screen to Burt Mueller, who shook his head to signify he had no idea. Poulton addressed Conrad Mitchell again. 'What does Nevison have to say? Chrissakes, man, he was there! He must know what happened to it.'

Mitchell was unfazed, his tone and delivery no different than before. 'Nevison claims he was confused at this point. According to Nevison, a male accomplice of Vargas' entered the coffee shop. Nevison believes

– but he can't accurately recall – that the accomplice took possession of the data-drive. We surmise that this is the same man who drove the Dodge truck and absconded the scene. As the data-drive hasn't been retrieved, we must conclude that the accomplice took it with him.'

'The vehicle was found abandoned,' Poulton said. 'No sign of it there either?'

'Outside my field. I'm not forensics,' Mitchell said.

'No, sir,' Mueller answered, 'the Dodge had been set on fire. There was a corpse inside, male, unidentified as yet. He was the guy first seen driving the Dodge in the parking lot, we reckon. Well, we know for a fact. He was dispatched by three high-calibre rounds compatible with the firearms deployed.'

Poulton sat in thought for a while, then looked to the screen. 'Mitchell, two questions. Both vitally important. Does Nevison know the geographical location of the Midnite operation?'

'No.'

'You've asked him?'

'We have, yes sir. He says not.'

'Apply more pressure, Mitchell. More coercion. My guess is he does know and the bastard won't say unless we force it out of him.'

Mitchell raised his eyebrows, slowly, almost wearily, as he did everything. 'Nevison is wired up for respiratory and glandular function, hyper-medicated and under continuous MRSI brain-mapping. We know from neurological and physiological scans when a subject is lying and when he's telling the truth. Nevison is telling the truth.'

'You believe him?'

'I have just stated so, yes, sir. In my professional opinion. Second question?'

'You've already answered it.'

'Good. Thank you, sir—'

Chesney Poulton snapped off the link and the image vanished. With his big hands curled into fists on the desk in front of him, he sat and stared straight ahead at nothing. A pulse was beating in his temples. Burt Mueller and Joe Quarles exchanged looks. Neither one was going to break the silence.

At last, a growl, almost a rumbling grunt, came out. 'How're we gonna stop 'em, Burt? How *can* we stop 'em?'

Mueller squinted at him. 'The Midnite organisation?'

The director-in-chief was frowning, muttering to himself. 'I don't understand it. Chase was on the list – by rights he ought to be a puddle of grease and a hank of burnt hair by now. There's been no report of it . . . so what the fuck happened? He should be dead. *Dead*.'

'That wouldn't help any. They can release the files Nevison purloined with or without him,' Mueller pointed out – 'if the accomplice has the drive and makes it back to wherever their base is. Our number one priority is still the same, sir: somehow we have to identify the location and nullify the threat by physical force of arms.'

'And the Vargas woman could have told us that,' Poulton said, 'if she hadn't been killed. That was a bungled operation, Burt, from start to finish.'

'Hold on, sir. Wait a sec. If we hadn't tracked Nevison he would've got clean away. The procedure worked. The execution was flawed, I grant you.'

Quarles was keen to agree on something he felt safe about. 'Mr Mueller is correct, sir. The covert surveillance period for people new to the department came up aces. As soon as Nevison went beyond the DC boundary line he couldn't take a pee or fart without it being monitored. With respect, sir, the procedure was vindicated.'

Slowly, Poulton turned his head and directed the full-on beam of his laser-like attention at Joe Quarles.

'You pea-brained nincompoop. You chunter on like a mindless moron about some procedure or other being "vindicated". Don't you get it? This organisation, the organisation *I* created' – he banged the desk so hard the smouldering cigar was jolted out of its ashtray – 'the Alliance of American Values is facing possibly the greatest threat to its viable existence. Don't you have the slightest grasp of what's happened? What we're dealing with here? The vast bulk of our classified material has been compromised. The analyst responsible – somebody, I might add, under *your* direct authority – is about to be launched on the world as a brave and principled whistleblower. Some wonderful fucking paragon of virtue and integrity who's sacrificed his own freedom and security, and his personal life, for the greater good. In some eyes Howard Nevison will become a hero. He'll be on the cover as *Time*'s Man of the Year. Procedures, vindicated or not, don't matter a goddam fuck when we're heading up shit creek without a paddle, or even a boat.'

His chief of staff had rescued the Cohiba Behike and set it back in the ashtray. Poulton picked up the cigar and feverishly puffed it back to life.

Quarles had a flush in his cheeks, of shame, perhaps, or humiliation. He said quietly, 'I don't see how Nevison can be viewed as any kind of hero when he sexually abuses little children.'

Poulton glanced at Burt Mueller and leaned back in his chair, his eyes hooded. His mouth moved around the cigar. 'Is that a cotton-pickin' fact?'

Joe Quarles shook his head. 'Not yet it isn't. But we could make it one.' He kept his eyes fixed on the director-in-chief and refused to look away.

'Let me tell you something, son. That's a very interesting perspective . . .' He indicated a chair. 'You think of that all on your own?' Poulton enquired.

Quarles sat down. 'It was when you mentioned Nevison being turned into a hero, sir. I started to wonder what was the opposite of hero, and paedophile was the first thing that popped into my head.'

Chesney Poulton drew in a lungful of smoke and took all the time in the world as he contemplated the aromatic blue plume ascending to the ceiling.

2

'Do you know if she made it out of there or not?'

'No.'

'So you don't know if Micki is alive or dead?'

'No,' Bud Keiser said again.

Cheryl shut her eyes. She was robbed of speech. There was silence then. Chase couldn't think what to say, so he said nothing, watching the news channel on mute, the ribbon headlines scrolling across the screen.

The three of them were in the corner office, trying to gather the pieces together and make some sort of sense of them. But there were too many unknowns, blanks and half-guesses to form a coherent picture. It had taken Bud Keiser nearly twenty-four hours – deliberately – to return to the business park near Warrendale, north of Pittsburgh. He could have driven there in less than three in his stolen wheels, even via the circuitous route he had chosen, heading north and then west. But uppermost in his mind had been the absolute necessity of making sure the trail was stone-cold dead, which had meant spending a night in a motel; after the events at Hagerstown he couldn't afford even the remote possibility of jeopardising the Midnite location.

For the same reason he purposely hadn't made contact with Chase or Cheryl, by phone or any other means. Besides, he had to face the music in person.

'I guess Micki told you I asked her not to make the rendezvous,' Cheryl said finally. 'Or maybe she didn't and you weren't to know.'

'Not specifically, in so many words.' Keiser's body language revealed how desperately uncomfortable he was. 'But Jon and I knew, I guess . . . when Micki straight off told us not to say anything to anyone else. And leaving in the middle of the night . . .' He scratched the back of his neck. 'Well, yeah, I have to admit it: we knew it wasn't a sanctioned mission, Cheryl. Of course we knew.'

'But still you went ahead.' Cheryl was sitting at the desk, in Chase's office chair, her face stony. 'What happened to discipline, Bud? What happened to loyalty?'

Keiser looked like he wanted the earth to open up and swallow him. 'Micki convinced us that we had a bona fide whistleblower and it was worth the risk. The info he had to offer was just too good to pass on. But that's no excuse, Cheryl. I'm not offering it as one.'

'And was it worth the risk?' Cheryl said. She picked up the piece of rectangular grey plastic from the desk blotter. 'Was *this* worth the risk?'

'We won't know until we check out the content,' Keiser said, reasonably enough.

'And suppose it turns out to be a pile of junk you and Micki risked your lives for and Jon paid with his? Nothing but a trick to draw us out into the open? We don't know a single damn thing about this Nevison guy that hasn't come from him. He could be just a stooge for all we know.' Cheryl pushed both hands through her cropped hair. 'Jesus, Bud . . . that's what I tried to tell Micki – what I was trying to warn her about! And what happens? You guys ignore all the rules and precautions we've put in place and risk every—'

Chase cut in. 'Okay, Cheryl, you've made your point. I don't think Bud can feel any worse than how he's feeling right now. So stop trying to make him. You don't suppose he feels happy about what happened to Micki?'

'But that's the point, Gav – *we don't know what happened to her*. And if she is alive, if she was arrested or detained, the psy-ops witch-doctors will go to work on her and she won't be able to hold out. Nobody can. The network, our location – the entire operation – it'll all be blown wide open. That's what most concerns me. Frankly, I don't give a shit what Bud feels happy or unhappy about.'

Chase held up his hands, palms outwards, placatingly. He knew better than to argue, what with Cheryl in this inflamed mood. He didn't condemn her for it – he actually agreed with her – but starting on the blame game would get them exactly nowhere. All they could do was make the best of what this sorry farrago had presented to them: the rectangular piece of plastic on the blotter.

He said, 'First things first. We'll have Jervis take a trawl through the drive and get an overview of what's on there and an evaluation of the content.' He looked at Bud Keiser, who was sitting disconsolately with his elbows on his knees, head hung low. 'Did Micki give any hint at all what kind of material this is? Did she have any prior knowledge before she talked to Nevison?'

'If she had, she never said so. But I don't think she did.' Keiser raised his head. 'And there was no time to tell me anything when I barged in on them. I was in too much of a hurry. We had to get outta there kinda fast. *Holy*' – he sat up straight, eyes wide – '*fuck*. That's him, that's the guy.' He was staring at the TV screen in the corner. Alongside the newsreader's silent mouthing there was an insert of Howard Nevison's boyish blond head.

The rolling caption read: BREAKING NEWS – GOVERNMENT SYSTEMS ANALYST ARRESTED ON CHILD PORN CHARGES.

Cheryl turned up the volume.

'". . . a truly shocking revelation," said a spokesperson for the State Department. Nevison had only been in place a matter of months, working as an analyst on agricultural statistics, when a routine check of his office laptop turned up thousands of indecent images, stills and movies. These involved minors of both sexes, and children as young as eight years old. Many of these feature Nevison in a participatory role. When not taking part himself, Nevison is behind the camera, issuing instructions to the unwilling participants, some of whom appear drugged.'

Pausing dramatically, the newsreader cast a look of dreadful foreboding, combined with a high magnitude of moral concern at the camera.

'For obvious reasons we can't disclose to our audience any of these images, which a spokesperson for the investigating team has described as utterly repellant. More on this breaking story in our later bulletins . . . and now to Kip, for tomorrow's weather-word. How's it lookin', Kip?'

Cheryl flicked it off. She said calmly, 'Okay, so that answers one question. They wouldn't go to all that trouble of smearing Howard Nevison if he wasn't who he says he is.'

'It answers a bigger question than that,' Chase said, picking up the data-drive between thumb and forefinger, as if handling a precious artefact. 'Whatever Nevison put on here, it definitely ain't no pile of junk.'

3

It was fiendishly clever. The labs had done a brilliant job, Poulton thought, absolutely fucking brilliant. Watching it again and again, he was fascinated at how they'd digitally incorporated Howard Nevison's head into the actual frames of a real-life video with real-life children. The rest of the adult's body, representing Nevison, matched Nevison's own body perfectly, as Chesney Poulton could attest to from memory.

He defied anyone but a technical expert to spot even the tiniest discrepancy between fake and reality.

And to imagine that Joe Quarles, that total vacuum of intellect and gumption and personality, had come up with this brainwave. Very soon –

if not now, this instant – Nevison's name would be such anathema to the public, so tainted by the sickening depravity of what he had done to those innocent sweet kids, that any leaks for whom he was the source would be worthless. Not only that, anyone giving them credence or wider dissemination would be tainted by association.

The Nevison disclosures were just too searingly hot to handle. *Might as well juggle balls of uranium-235*, Poulton thought, chuckling aloud to himself.

The green line burbled: his chief of staff.

'Burt, you don't know how much I'm enjoying this. Fact is, I'm feeling so magnanimous I got a notion to give that dickwit Quarles a raise or a promotion, or something anyways. Kick up the ass maybe.' Poulton couldn't stop chuckling. 'He's turned the Nevison débâcle completely around, 180 degrees. He deserves something, you think?'

There was an absence of sound on the line, which was more than annoying, it was unnerving.

Poulton said, 'Burt? You there?'

'I'm here.' It was no consolation that Burt Mueller sounded calm, because he always sounded calm, no matter what. Burt Mueller would have sounded calm as he slid down the deck of the *Titanic*, saluting as he thanked the band for playing 'Nearer My God to Thee'.

'This isn't good news, no matter how—'

'Are you going to destroy my beneficent mood, Burt?'

'Afraid I am, sir. I've this minute put down the phone speaking to a CIA contact of mine. He's picked up a report that a television station in Nevada has run a story about two guys on a hunting trip who went missing. A burnt-out Jeep and two incinerated bodies were located and retrieved by the North Las Vegas Police. They've been biopsied and there is now a full-scale homicide investigation under way.'

'Join the dots for me, Burt. What's that to us?'

'The location is in the Muddy Mountain Wilderness, not far from Mount Grafton. I think you can figure out what this is—'

'I can now.' The images on the screen were distracting him, so Poulton switched it off. 'The police have been up there, you say?'

'Yes, sir. To recover the vehicle and bodies.'

'What about the stockade? They found it?'

'Not that we can ascertain. But the problem isn't the police alone. There's been a TV crew nosing around, the same station that ran the report: WNRB, based in North Las Vegas. They must think there's a news angle and they've started running it as a story. Some of the national wires and press agencies have picked it up.'

'Did you really have to ruin this perfect fucking day for me?'

'Sorry, sir.' The voice was still calm, stolid.

Poulton slid open a drawer and poured himself a handsome shot of Laphroaig. He added one cube of ice. It lit a molten path right down to his gut. The liquor was supposed to steady his nerves; instead its ravaging heat made him furious.

He said tersely, 'What in hell's name were they doing? Practising the ascendancy programme as a weekend pastime? Letting off steam after a few beers? I can't believe they'd ascend a couple of rednecks so close to home. It's beyond comprehension. I just don't get it.' He took another slug to put a blurred edge to his jittery nerve-ends.

'Me neither. Crazy.'

'What do we do? We have to contain it, Burt.'

'Off the top of my head, I don't know. I have to process it.'

'Homicide investigation or not, we can't let the local police dig their claws into this; there are records kept up there, and witnesses with connections to the Charmed Baptists in McLean . . .'

'The Nevison leaks might also have a bearing on how it plays out,' Burt Mueller said. There was a quality to his tone – unease? wariness? – that Poulton hadn't heard before.

'How can that be? Nevison is dead in the water.' Chesney Poulton gestured to the blank screen. 'That paedophile turd's showcase with his dick in a kid's mouth has gone viral. Any information with him as its source is discredited. You're not making sense, Burt.'

'I hope I'm not. I hope I'm up a gumtree with my thumb up my ass. But let's examine the facts, sir. The data-cache Nevison extracted will most likely contain files on the MOG ascendancy programme and their links to the Charmed Baptists. It might also, in addition, have chapter and verse on the financing channels, and where the Charmed Baptists get their revenue from.'

'It comes from us,' Poulton said, as mystified as ever. 'Why is that important?'

'Because I know what the next question will be.'

Chesney Poulton took a sip of Scotch and closed his eyes. What was that saying? *The elephant in the room?* A big uncomfortable fact that everyone can see and yet all pretend isn't there . . . that's what Burt Mueller was driving at. This particular elephant took the form of a plant that grew about thirty inches high and had a large bulbous seedpod on top, similar in size and shape to a lamp-bulb. The plant thrived in barren tracts of desert plains and mountain ranges. It required continual irrigation to help it grow and a cheap plentiful labour force to harvest it. The proceeds of such cultivation made it the most valuable cash crop on the planet. In the last year alone, Poulton knew, the yield of hashish poppies in those hot dusty empty places had increased by 4,000 per cent, producing more than two-thirds of the world's supply of heroin . . . which in turn brought in the bulk of the AAAV revenue.

'You really believe they'll dig that deep? Follow all those links?'

'I'm just speculating, sir, on the possible eventualities.'

'All the way back to Afghanistan?'

'If it explains the money, yes.'

'But they're taking the word of a fucking paedophile!' Poulton broke out savagely. 'They'll have witnessed these depraved acts with their own eyes. What kind of conscience could they have, believing a single word from a man who has committed such despicable . . . terrible . . . bestial . . .'

Poulton was almost choking in his outrage, while Burt Mueller was doing his level best to stay focused and rational.

'I guess the truth is, they won't care. If the Nevada state police follow the link from the Messengers of God and arrive at the conclusion that the Charmed Baptist Church is a conduit for laundering drug money, they'll overlook whether Howard Nevison has been discredited or not. He could be Jack the Ripper. He could be the resurrection of Adolf

Hitler. It won't matter one damn. They'll follow the trail until the footprints come to a stop at our door.'

'I think you mean my door,' Poulton said. 'And they'll be elephant-size.'

Not knowing what that meant, or how to respond, Mueller let it pass.

Without further ado, the director-in-chief broke the connection. Reflexively, eyes lost in thought, he reached for the tumbler of single malt, then stopped himself. If he was going to resolve this crisis he needed his brains intact, not floating away in a mellow haze, no matter how enticing the prospect.

CRISIS.

The word flashed in his head like a neon sign. If this didn't qualify as such, Poulton thought, he didn't know what the word meant. This time he allowed himself a tiny sip of the malt before he picked up the phone. At first he asked for the security branch by its acronym – 'Fut/COE' – but when the intern didn't comprehend, Poulton gave the full title: 'Future Crisis Operations Executive. And I want to speak directly to Colonel Malden.'

Colonel Malden couldn't be immediately located, a competent-sounding female voice informed him. Would he care to hold, or should the Commanding Officer of Fut/COE return the call as soon as he was available? Poulton decided to hold.

Whenever he thought of Lloyd Malden – which wasn't all that often – Poulton's senses retrieved a faint whiff of rosewater. He didn't know if it was the after-shave Malden preferred, or maybe the body lotion or his favourite shampoo; the unmistakable scent had been there when their paths had crossed for the second or third time, an occasion Poulton vividly remembered, five years previously at the Pentagon.

The two men had met face to face in one of the labyrinthine basement corridors. Both were surrounded by a phalanx of retainers: personal aides, security detail, Pentagon junior officers. Poulton was a couple of inches taller than Colonel Malden, but they were still virtually eyeball-to-eyeball. Neither offered to shake hands. The tension was obvious and palpable; their retinues remained silent and unmoving. Poulton had indicated with an almost imperceptible motion of the head that Malden should follow him, and moved off. After a slight hesitation Malden did so. Poulton led the way into a gents' washroom a few steps along the corridor. There was no one at the basins. Poulton pushed open the doors of the toilet stalls to check they were empty. He chose the toilet stall furthest from the door and stood just inside. With the same small motion of the head, he bade Malden to enter; in the small space the two men were squeezed close together, touching, chest to chest: the director-in-chief of AAAV in his Fifth Avenue bespoke charcoal three-piece, the CO of Fut/COE in his light tan crisply pressed summer uniform. That's the moment Poulton remembered breathing in a waft of rosewater, as he gazed into Malden's eyes. Then Poulton's eyes, with no hint of warmth, looked downwards. He looked back up, cold and pitiless, then downwards again. To give himself room to kneel, Malden turned sideways, and Poulton did the same, unhooking the zip at the top of his fly and allowing Malden to do the rest. He then waited, in calm and patient anticipation. Nothing had been said, not a word uttered, during the encounter, until it was over.

Then Poulton said, 'You understand now? That's our relationship basis. I tell you to suck dick, you suck dick.' Malden got to his feet, wiping his mouth.

'Understand me?'

Malden nodded. His eyes were downcast. These were the only words spoken, their one and only exchange, until today, this minute—

'Colonel Malden, this is Chesney Poulton. I have a request.'

'I'm listening.'

Poulton explained what was required. The matter was urgent, the timing critical, the outcome vital. So as to leave no room for error or doubt, he employed official security service nomenclature: the phrases 'Total Coverage' and 'Elimination to the Max' – meaning no one was to be excluded, without exception, and there were to be zero survivors.

'Understand?'

'Yes,' Malden said.

'My chief of staff Burt Mueller will send you the co-ordinates. When can you initiate the action?'

'What will accommodate your requirement?'

'Noon tomorrow, latest.'

'I'll see to it. Any other request?'

Poulton had none. They said their goodbyes and rang off.

4

The 'trawl through the drive' Chase had asked Jervis to carry out was a tall order, even for a geek like him. Four of them were crowded round an array of screens while Jervis demonstrated the extent of the task. 'There's a year's work here, at least. And that's just to identify and classify what we got . . . never mind *read* the stuff. More than a million individual files, Gav.'

Crouched forward, bony elbows resting on the desk, Jervis tapped a sidebar on one of the screens, which flashed a row of digits. 'See that? One hundred gigs. That's a big slice of the archive he took.'

'Any doubt in your mind this isn't genuine?' Bud Keiser queried. 'Does it look the real McCoy to you?'

'Far as I can tell. Any reason to believe it ain't?'

Keiser shook his head. 'No,' he said, and looked relieved.

'I have no doubts whatsoever,' Cheryl said. 'The slimy bastards at AAAV wouldn't mount a smear campaign this quick, and be so malicious with it, if they weren't desperate to poison the well.' She glanced at Chase, who nodded his agreement.

'I can see there's a huge mass of data to sieve through, Jervis,' Chase told him, 'but hasn't Nevison flagged anything up? He's gone to such enormous risk extracting it; why hasn't he provided a few clues to help us?' To his untrained eye the screens were filled with endless streams of numbers and symbols that might have been in Serbo-Croat for all the sense they made; in fact they probably *did* look the same in Serbo-Croat.

Jervis' long lean fingers tap-danced over the keypad. Menus appeared from the top of the screens and slid out of sight again. Option boxes were summoned and dismissed. Finally he opened a file with intelligible words that Chase could actually read:

Cuba PDF

'What've you got, Jerv?'

'Come to it ass-backwards, so to speak. This thing with AAAV all started when they tried to hack into our system, so what I did was a random search to find out what they picked up on Midnite-Net. One thing they tabbed was a Climate Alert we did about Bill Inchcape of the NCPF in Boulder, Colorado. See there.' Jervis indicated another screen. 'This was linked to an operation codenamed "Silent Witness" up there' – he pointed – 'and then from that we get to the Cuba file.'

'From Binch at the NCPF to Cuba,' Chase said, frowning. 'I don't see the connection.'

'That's where they took him.'

Chase was both shocked and incredulous. 'Are you sure about this? The Cuba Prime Detention Facility?'

'See for yourself. That's what "Silent Witness" was for: detain the Doc and lose him where he couldn't be found.'

'The bastards didn't even bother with a show trial,' Cheryl said. She turned to Chase. 'Stella's half out of her mind not knowing what's happened to him; the least we can do is pass this on to her.'

'You think it will bring any comfort?'

'We have to tell her, Gav. She's sick with worry.'

'Knowing her husband is being held in the Cuba PDF won't make her worry any less,' Chase said.

Jervis was still busying away with the keys. 'Seems the AAAV make donations to charity. Jeez, and how! – *big* donations to religious institutions. Ever hear of a church called the 23rd Chapter of Charmed Baptist Brethren?' Nobody had. 'They gave it more than fifty-four million dollars last year for' – he read from a screen – '*charitable donations and endowments for religious education and "evangelisation programmes"*. Mighty generous of 'em.'

'I don't see why the AAAV giving money to charity really matters,' Cheryl said.

'Money always matters,' Chase said. 'Who gives it, and especially who gets it.'

'Gav, let's grab a coffee. I need to talk to you.'

She sounded fretful and distracted, and Chase knew her thoughts were with Stella Inchcape. Cheryl wanted to help, that was natural. Though what reassurance they could provide, giving his wife the horrendous news that Binch was in a tropical prison outside the boundaries of law and legal jurisdiction, was highly contentious.

He patted Jervis on the shoulder. 'Jerv, keep following the money trail. I'll look at what you come up with later.'

'Yeah, yeah, okay . . .' Jervis was only half-listening. '*Wow* – and a nice piece of change goes to a religious cult way out in the badlands of Nevada. I guess a name like that guarantees you a big fat slice of the pie,' he chortled, wagging his head back and forth.

'Who?' Chase had been drawn back and was lingering at the desk. 'What are they called?'

'The Messengers of God.'

'Check it out, Jerv. See if they've got their own file.'

'Give me a coupla minutes,' Jervis said, fingers flying over the keys.

'Gavin, please—!' Cheryl called.

Chase patted Jervis' shoulder once again and reluctantly left him to it.

5

Two or three hours' sleep was the best that Binch could hope for. The lumpy straw mattress was prickly and uncomfortable, constantly undulating under his back because the lumps happened to be rats eating the insects and lugworms living in the straw. A night didn't go by when he wasn't awakened by a rat crawling across his face. The other factor that made it impossible to rest was the stifling heat. Cuba had once been a semi-tropical country with a healthy climate whose average temperature in recent years had inexorably crept up the scale. Now it was in the high-forties, which meant peaks of 55° C. Sleeping out in the open, at night, under a rough timber construction of plastic sheets and thatched roofing, the sensation was one of being submerged in hot glutinous syrup; ideal conditions for the variety of mosquitoes, hornets, ticks and the termite-spiders which liked to make a nest in human hair.

Since arrival, his weight had dropped by forty pounds. The diet was basic and unappealing, and it didn't encourage the appetite when there was something alive and wriggling in his food, which turned out to be weevils and maggots. He had developed erupting sores on his shoulders and arms and both his feet had become infected. Binch was in abject terror that they were gangrenous.

To supplement the diet, inmates caught rodents and snakes, which they roasted on a piece of tin over an open fire. Despite his hunger, Binch couldn't bring himself to eat even a morsel. Once, having taken a small bite, he started heaving uncontrollably and ended up retching his stomach dry.

This Prime Detention Facility in Holguín province, on the east of the island, held a current inmate population of 138,000; it was a specially segregated community for 'political insurgents'. The majority of the people here were activists in some shape or form: community and civil rights leaders, radical journalists, dissident writers, labour organisers and assorted social militants. The most recent arrivals, like Bill Inchcape, had fallen foul of the draconian UnPatriot (Emergency Powers) Act. No one he had spoken to had been through a courtroom trial, or anything remotely resembling the judicial process. Legally, they were all 'under review', which meant they were awaiting a date when they would be formally charged. So far, no one had been.

Although the conditions here were primitive and barbaric – herded in behind wreathes of razor-wire and watched from observation towers bristling with machine-guns – Binch almost preferred this living hell to the regime in the induction cellblock. There he had come within a hair's breadth of total psychological meltdown – which was the purpose: to break the morale and spirit of anyone harbouring idealistic tendencies dangerous to the state.

The regime had been similar to what he had endured in the military brig, only harsher. Eye-wateringly bright strip-lighting was never switched off. The cell was barely big enough for the concrete shelf with a mattress on top and the hole in the corner that was his toilet. He was awakened every hour, on the hour, day and night, and made to stand to attention. Food came on a paper plate through a slot in the door. Binch never saw another living soul; before anyone came into the cell he had to place a heavy canvas bag with ventilation holes over his head and stand facing the wall. Mostly there was dead silence, so he was aware of his own breathing and bodily sounds. Then a head-splitting noise would suddenly erupt through the speakers, loud as an explosion; it might sound like a sledgehammer striking an anvil, or the mechanical screeching of raw metal being dragged across a concrete floor. It might last for a few minutes or go on for what felt like hours.

The worst aspect of this treatment was that nothing was ever demanded as a condition to make it stop. It wasn't possible to plead with the authorities, or to beg forgiveness, or promise never to do again what had brought him here in the first place. They asked nothing of him. They didn't insist he recant his views. They didn't demand he name colleagues and associates who shared his concerns . . .

Binch would have eagerly agreed never to engage in climate research again. He would have faithfully promised to suppress any scientific findings that might have a negative impact on the national interest. It was as if they were indifferent to what he believed; Dr Bill Inchcape's idealistic convictions were of zero interest to them.

So there was no way out.

The sky above the Holguín facility was a flawless blue except for a puffy grey cloud to the east, like a ball of dirty cotton wool. This was the direction hurricanes and tornadoes came from. Sprawled on the piece of sacking, his back against a wooden crate, Binch was oblivious to any portents in the stratosphere, even though he had predicted and plotted such weather events a thousand times. In his mind's eye he was relaxing in the recliner on his own back porch with a splendid view of the Medicine Bow range. His darling Stella was bringing out a pitcher of iced tea.

A flash of light to the southeast did capture his attention: the sunlight flaring off the wings of an aircraft as it banked to make the final approach to the naval base at Guantánamo on the south coast. Another six hundred-strong cargo of wretched bastards shitting themselves . . .

Welcome to Tropical Paradise, Binch thought grimly.

For at least one of the six hundred pitiful wretches in the upper hold of the C-133 Gladiator military transport, this was literally the case, because Howard Nevison was indeed mired in his own ordure.

6

Photo-recon revealed nothing, which was infuriating, but Major Sam Coogan had been given precise geo-sat co-ordinates by his Brigade HQ and told that the terrorist hideout was slap-bang where they said it was. In Coogan's Order of Combat the location was specified as being northeast along Highway 604 leading to the Valley of Fire, situated in the Muddy Mountains Wilderness, 7.3 miles south of Mount Grafton.

All of which – plus the geo-sat – was pretty exact. Not much of an excuse for not finding the fucking target, Major Coogan reckoned. He could only surmise that the compound was so well camouflaged as to blend seamlessly into the surrounding drab terrain of bleached rocky scrub and fifty shades of ochre.

This was one helluva rushed mission. Less than twenty-four hours had elapsed since he was first alerted that two companies of the 92nd Marine Corps were to be flown from Fort Bragg, North Carolina, to the landing strip at the Nellis Missile Range in eastern Nevada. Once there, they would assemble their convoy of Humvees, troop-carriers and armoured gun-platforms into a task-force.

As well as the location, Coogan's Order was explicit in its Mission Task, the essence contained in two key phrases, highlighted for emphasis: After infiltration of the compound, ensure 'Total Coverage' of terrorist suspects with the aim of 'Elimination to the Max'. In layman's terms, this meant to carry out a thorough sweep, to exclude no one; and there were to be zero survivors. Not even wounded and disabled combatants. Coogan had been given this Mission Task only twice before, in Iraq and Syria, and had never dreamed of being ordered to carry it out within the United States.

Soon after first light, Coogan and his second-in-command, Captain Hance, were in the leading Humvee as the column departed Highway 604 and began the climb through the steep-sided canyon that was designated the Valley of Fire. According to the geo-sat, the single shale track zigzagged higher and higher via a series of hairpin loops, leading nowhere until it eventually petered out amongst boulders and scattered rockfall.

One aspect that Coogan fretted about was 'Total Coverage'. Road-blocks had been set up on Highway 604, but undoubtably there were minor roads and backwoods trails unmarked on any map. Possibly there were scores, maybe hundreds of mining trails crisscrossing the lower slopes around Mount Grafton; it was impossible to seal off such a vast area to prevent loners and even small groups sneaking through the cordon.

It also occurred to him that the 'fortified base' (as it was termed in his orders) might have been built on top of an old mine-working. In this part of Nevada there were countless abandoned mines with tunnels extending for miles: achieving 'Total Coverage' would be a damn sight easier said than done.

A few minutes after 6 a.m., after a painfully slow ascent lasting nearly an hour, Major Coogan told his driver to stop. Behind them the column crept to a halt. With his second-in-command, Coogan climbed down to take stock of the terrain. They were at elevation 2,950 feet. On the geo-sat, the summit on this shoulder of the range was 3,410 feet. They were possibly less than half a mile away from the top, travelling vertically, but maybe three to four miles off labouring up the treacherous hairpins.

Major Coogan flipped open the e-map scanner and circled the target area with a gloved finger. 'Let's deploy a couple of advance ground units both sides, Gene. They can pick off any absconders and get close without causing a fuss. With the racket this caboodle makes we might as well send up flares.'

Captain Hance went down the line to get it organised. Coogan gazed around at the scrub-dotted hillside. At this early hour it was cool and the sky was darkening from the southeast. Seven miles away the peak of Mount Grafton wore a cap of purple thundery-looking clouds.

'Storm coming on, sir,' Hance observed, returning. 'Damn, if we had a couple of choppers we could wrap this up in under an hour.'

'Not sure about that, Gene. Even if we'd had time to bring 'em, the intel says between two and three hundred insurgents: a bunch that strong could make one tidy mess before our boys got their boots dirty. This way we can blow their fuckin' brains out before they have sight of us.'

Hance was frowning. 'Why are we doing this in such a damn flat spin anyway?' he wanted to know. 'Forty-eight hours pre-op planning would've made all the difference. Do we even know who they are?' he asked, warming to his discontent. 'I've never heard of a terrorist group called the MOG before, have you?'

Coogan admitted he hadn't. 'No sweat to us. All we need to know is that they're the bad guys, Gene, and we're the good—'

His attention was caught by a staff sergeant further down the column who was standing on the lip of the trail and staring down intently at something in the dry creek below. The two officers went to look. There wasn't much to see, but it was odd: an area of some dark grey oily sludge on the sandy bed with bits of what looked like charred and twisted metal scattered about. Some of the surrounding brush, Coogan noticed, had been scorched to blackened stumps.

Major Coogan raised his eyebrows quizzically and looked at Captain Hance. Together they turned to look up the sheer hillside behind them. The Mission Task assigned to 92nd Marine Corps at such short notice had just taken on a more daunting prospect than either expected.

7

A wick floating in a bowl of oil provided a dim flickering glow, illuminating the crudely carved walls that sloped up to the conical roof. In the centre of his cell, Pastor Eldritch sat crosslegged on the sandy floor. From outside, in the tunnels hewn out of rock, came the low drone of chanted litany: the inner circle of adepts now preparing themselves, waiting for the Final Ascent. The Pastor knew it was bound to come one day, so when he was awakened shortly after daybreak and received the report from Vance (US) and Owen (US), relayed to them from the observation post, it came as no revelation. It would not be long now. Soon men with weapons would come to destroy, in the same way they had with their blind stupidity destroyed the earth. Let the earth perish, and let the species that had destroyed its own habitat perish with it. Pastor Eldritch had no fear for his own fate; he rejoiced in the certainty of what was to be. His own mortal body, the selfish ego that was 'I', had no meaning for him. It was merely a transient vessel composed of random uncountable atoms that would continue after 'death' to circulate endlessly throughout the universe, and – eventually, inevitably – form part of another consciousness.

From somewhere out there, dispersed across a billion light-years of space, the ghost of his atoms would witness the end of the breathing planet.

In the meanwhile, everything had been prepared and was ready and waiting for Optimum Orbital Trajectory. He was the one to lead the way to destruction.

I am become death, the shatterer of worlds . . .

The chanting died away as he appeared in the doorway.

Pastor Eldritch gave no word or sign. He moved slowly past them with his crippled, lurching walk, the chosen eleven of his most faithful and devout disciples. There had been twelve, until his favourite son Karl had failed in his mission and never returned to the Mothership.

Led by Fang (China) and Val (Russia), they followed the Pastor along the tunnel lit by caged wall-lights. These eleven had been specially chosen and trained to participate in the final act: a secret ritual unknown to those still asleep in the dormitories above them at ground level, their fellow adepts, oblivious of what was to take place and blissfully ignorant of their future. Which didn't exist.

When the inner disciples were gathered together, silent and kneeling, Pastor Eldritch spoke softly, reminding them that very few were as fortunate as they, in having been given a purpose and the heaven-sent opportunity to achieve it.

'We do not fear death,' he told them, 'because death is merely a passing phase; exchanging one form of existence for another. The stuff of our being cannot be destroyed, only that which is the selfish ego. So when we renounce the self, the ego, our identity, death has no meaning for us. Instead it is the gateway to everlasting life.'

A gateway they were about to enter.

Ascendant!

After his blessing, the disciples assembled in the main chamber directly above the abandoned mineshaft. The chamber had once housed the winding-gear which raised and lowered the cages. In this space were nine large spherical tanks containing liquefied propane gas under extreme pressure; the walls were seven inches of solid steel to guard against explosion.

Propane was the gas used by the Messengers to carry out the ascendancy programme of pyro-assassination. Highly flammable and volatile, liquefied gas has an auto-ignition temperature of 480° C, but under full pressure, the combustion level of the inner flame reaches temperatures of 1,480° C.

Four of the adepts had donned harnesses with portable cylinders. At a signal from Pastor Eldritch, they opened the valves and lit the nozzles. Jets of searing fire with a white core spewed across the chamber. Two of the adepts spun the exit valve on one of the large spherical tanks, emitting a blast of pure liquid propane. In less than a second, this had been ignited by the fiery jets and the chamber was filled with a billowing cloud of incandescent gas and white-hot flame, consuming everyone there in a single scorching blast.

The process, once begun, was unstoppable. The fireball of heat trapped in the chamber raised the temperature of the propane inside the remaining eight tanks. As the temperature rose, so did the pressure. When both pressure and temperature reached the critical point of auto-ignition, the tanks would erupt, and not even seven inches of solid steel could contain it.

In the dormitories above, the first thing the sleepers knew about it was a distant rumble and a vague shudder from below. There was no time to get out of bed, no time to even think as a *whoosh* of heat like a giant blowtorch swept along the corridors and blew the doors off their hinges.

Then the eight tanks went critical—

—and erupted—

Instantaneously, the temperature inside the underground chamber exceeded 1,000° C. The chamber itself acted as the casing of a bomb, confining and concentrating the extreme forces of heat and pressure. Iron girders supporting the tunnels turned white and writhed in the heat. The hewn walls ran with molten threads of silver and copper.

And still the temperature continued to rise until it reached its peak of almost 1,500° C.

Rocks became incandescent. Cracks appeared and split into jagged fissures. The walls of the chamber gave way as the pressure and heat surged upward. In a matter of seconds the eruption broke through, taking with it the stockade and its wooden buildings, the compound, blasting everything in an angry funnel of flame and smoke into the overcast sky.

Half a mile below the summit, grinding slowly up the narrow hairpin trail, it seemed to Major Coogan that a volcano was erupting. The ground beneath the Humvee started shaking and suddenly rocks were showering down from out of the sky. Coogan stared through the windshield, craning upwards to see a halo of blood-red fire and curling black smoke outlined against the massing storm clouds.

Jesusholymaryjoseph.

It was an image of the end of the world: a vision Major Sam Coogan would never forget to his dying day.

8

It was Eliot, the Weavers' cute little cross-breed terrier, which sounded the alarm. Marian and Don Weaver were finishing a late Sunday breakfast at a few minutes after ten-thirty. Don was looking forward to watching the game on television later in the afternoon, his team Miami Marlins against the Atlanta Braves. Marian, who had recently had knee surgery, would be happy with her puzzle books, in between clipping saver and bargain coupons out of the magazines stacked by her recliner.

On retirement they had moved to this quieter gated community for over fifty-fives in Tamarac, East Broward County, a mile or so north of the Sawgrass Expressway – only a ten-minute drive from their former home. Both enjoyed living in southern Florida; they were acclimatised to – and prepared to put up with – the extreme summer heat, although Marian came to dread the onset of the hurricane season more with each passing year.

Eliot was usually a quiet, well-behaved dog. As soon as he was settled down with his blanket and bowl of water in the shaded area of the screened-off porch overlooking the front lawn there wouldn't be a peep out of him. So his agitated yelping brought Don hurrying to the door, wondering if the animal was distressed, or maybe even hurt.

Goshdarn it! Somebody's crashed into my car—!

Straight away Don realised it couldn't be, because surely he would have heard the smash, the crump of tortured metal. So why was the car tilting sideways, front and rear wheels on the passenger side sinking into the ground?

Don raised his hand to quieten Eliot down, and the yelps subsided into a mournful whimpering. Sliding open the screen door, Don saw what had happened. He froze and drew in a sharp, shocked breath. Where once there had been a neat rectangle of trimmed lawn, there was now a gaping hole. The edge of the asphalt driveway was crumbling and falling into it, as was the low picket fence, and the sidewalk beyond, and so was his Chevy Malibu.

All of it was being sucked underground.

Don thought about stepping through the screen door, and then wisely decided against it. The paving slabs bordering the lawn were buckling and tilting, and even as he watched, a whole section of the path he would have set foot on a minute ago vanished. The hole was creeping – no, faster than creeping, *surging* – towards the house, like a hungry monster with an insatiable appetite, gulping everything down into its black maw.

Next item on the menu was the Chevy Malibu, which rolled onto its roof and disappeared. What was left of the driveway followed it. The rapidly widening chasm was now so near that Don could see into it, and he knew he was staring down into a sink-hole. Hurricanes apart, this was every Floridian's worst nightmare. In the past, whole streets had been swallowed up; one minute, people had been sitting at their kitchen tables, or in their living rooms watching television, sleeping in their beds; the next they had vanished through a hole in the earth's crust, never to be seen again.

Large tracts of land in the state – thousands and thousands of square miles – comprised a thin layer of soil on a bed of calcium carbonate limestone. When attacked by erosion from sulphuric and nitric acids in rainwater, the limestone was dissolved away, leaving cavernous underground chambers half a mile or more deep. Over time, this process would leave a few slender columns supporting a tenuous crust of soil and plant life. Under the weight of buildings, concrete roadworks and sewerage systems, the fragile limestone columns would eventually fracture and give way, resulting in voracious sinkholes like the one that had appeared in Marian and Don Weaver's front lawn.

Luckily for the Weavers, Eliot had warned them in the nick of time – lucky for Eliot too. Don grabbed him from his blanket, ran indoors and through to the kitchen where Marian was loading up the dishwasher. Opening the back door and pointing with his free hand, Don cried, 'Outside, honey. *Now!*'

Together they went through the rear screened-off porch and out onto the sloping lawn, Marian with her two artificial knees leaning on her husband for support. They could feel the earth shuddering under their feet. Halfway up the lawn, Don looked over his shoulder. His and Marian's house was diminishing, becoming physically smaller even as he watched. The windowsills were now at ground level. Then the windows themselves slid out of sight. Next, the guttering sank lower until it was level with Don's eye-line. In a few minutes that too vanished, and all that remained of his house above-ground was the roof. Like the upper bridge of a ship sinking beneath the waves, the roof was the last to go, and in no time at all it too was gone.

Don and Marian stood hand in hand looking through the thin air at where their home had been, to their neighbour's house across the quiet suburban street. Don was seventy-two, Marian was seventy-four, and suddenly they were homeless.

9

The sinkhole that opened up in the front lawn of the Weavers' home at 4139 East 45th Street, Tamarac, in November 2025 was not the first to have occurred; but it was the beginning of what was to become an ecological disaster on a scale and severity never seen before in the state of Florida.

It would also have a devastating effect on the Florida Keys, the chain of atolls stretching from Key Largo to Key West, as the toxic seawater ate them away to little more than corroding lumps of coral, like tiny stumps of rotten teeth.

But this was yet to happen, sometime in the future.

2030

I

I

Sometime in the future had arrived.

The man, woman and boy strolled along the broad strip of dazzling white sand. They wore facemasks and protective PVC coveralls, with bright orange compressed-air cylinders slung on their backs. The line of empty-eyed concrete towers had once been busy tourist hotels; they were now derelict and vandalised, had been ever since the southern half of Florida collapsed and Miami Beach was evacuated.

The ocean to their right was a toxic cocktail of high acidic saltwater, with methane and sulphur belching from its surface. It was this lethal combination that formed the unbreathable atmosphere at the tip of southern Florida.

Chase stepped over one of the heaps of decaying seaweed that straggled along the beach as far as the eye could see and held out his hand to steady Cheryl. Following on, the slim fifteen-year-old boy, almost as tall as his father, leaped it and bounded up the shallow slope of sand, not even breathing hard. 'You've been here before, haven't you,' Dan asked, 'when it was a holiday resort?'

'Couple of years before you were born. Your mother and I drove down from New York and stayed for three days.' Chase studied the row of concrete hulks through his curved faceplate. He pointed one out. 'I think that could be it: Holiday Inn, Collins and 22nd Street.'

He linked arms with Cheryl as they walked towards the low wall separating beach from road, their coveralls crackling as they moved.

'You think anyone still lives here?' Dan asked curiously. His thick black hair sprouted in clumps through the mask's nylon webbing.

'I don't think they're allowed to any more. This far south of Florida and to the west are designated Official Devastated Areas. They say the pollution in the Gulf is even worse than on this coast.'

'It would have been great to visit New Orleans.' Dan sighed. 'I've seen old movies of the French Quarter. It looked fantastic.'

'About five years too late, sorry to report,' Cheryl said. 'Downtown New Orleans is solid algae bloom feeding off industrial sludge; the rest of Louisiana is buried in protozoic slime. You can forget Basin Street, Dan.'

'Everything I want to see isn't there any more,' the boy complained. 'I suppose the Grand Canyon has been filled up with junked cars and Yellowstone Park is a refugee camp!'

Chase and Cheryl failed to crack a smile; Dan's sarcastic observation might be closer to the truth than he realised.

It was only thanks to an odd geophysical quirk that Miami Beach was still here at all. It was essentially a deep spit of sand, impervious to the assault by acid corrosion that had devastated much of the state. Across the intracoastal waterway which divided Miami Beach from what had formerly been the 'mainland', the underlying limestone structure had been eaten away – first by acid rain, a combination of sulphuric and nitric acids – and then the encroachment of seawater, its acidity boosted by twenty-five per cent since the Industrial Revolution. The problems with both rain and seawater were caused by the same villain responsible for the planet warming up: the burning of fossil fuels.

The thin crust on which most of Florida was built literally melted away, leaving vast empty caverns and tenuous pillars of limestone which were unable to support the highways and buildings above them. Everything below Lake Okeechobee, from Fort Myers on the Gulf Coast to Boca Raton on the Atlantic Seaboard, had gone, dissolved in acid soup.

Further south, what used to be the Everglades was now a toxic swamp comprising two- or three-mile-long low-lying mounds of rotting vegetation with mangrove trees and diseased palms sprouting out of them.

The native freshwater alligators which had populated the Everglades had been all but wiped out, and in their place a mutant breed of giant alligator was evolving. These 35-foot-long beasts were not just adapting to but thriving in this new harsh environment. As the climate warmed and humidity increased, anacondas from Central America had migrated north to the swampland, relishing the 50-plus degrees centigrade all-year temperatures.

Miami itself had been wiped off the map. Its population of 2.3 million residents had fled north to the parts of Florida still habitable. Many of them weren't welcome, being of Cuban descent; they had migrated unwillingly into Alabama, Georgia and Tennessee.

From the highest point on the beach, Chase, Cheryl and Dan paused and looked out to sea. There was no horizon, just a thick milky mist through which the blurred disc of the sun could be dimly perceived. Chase shaded his eyes and wondered which presented the greater menace: the acidic ocean, the toxic atmosphere or the raw sunlight. As the oxygen content thinned, so too did the ozone layer in the ionosphere, allowing deadly cosmic rays and ultraviolet radiation through. *Quite a range of options*, Chase thought. You had the choice of being poisoned, fried, getting skin cancer or suffering genetic damage – or maybe go for broke and get the lot.

Back on Collins Avenue they walked past the broken shop windows and through the looted debris covering the pavements. Grass and weeds flourished in the crumbling concrete. Their yellow half-track with the faded MIDNITE-NET logo on its doors was in the parking lot of a shopping mall on 29th Street. The vehicle was powered using solar panels – this far south, and in the new subtropical atmosphere, the internal combustion engine couldn't be relied on; it had also become necessary to use chemically fuelled aircraft because of the number of jet- and piston-engined aircraft that had started crashing on take-off and landing, starved of oxygen.

As Chase reached up to the recessed handle of the cab a shiny crease appeared in the body panel, inches away from his hand. The reverberating crack of a rifle shot echoed back and forth between the buildings.

Another shot gouged up a chunk of asphalt as they scuttled into the protective cover of the half-track. Chase released the safety on his eight-cylinder Glock automatic and peered cautiously over the vehicle's streamlined nacelle.

'Anybody see where the shots came from?' *One sniper or two?* Or maybe even more . . . they might be in the middle of a war-zone. Oh *fuck*.

'Sorry, sweetheart,' Cheryl said laconically. 'I was too busy to notice.'

'Why didn't they take the half-track while we were on the beach?' Dan said. 'We were gone nearly an hour.'

Chase wondered about that too. He could only suppose their attackers hadn't spotted it before now. Maybe they'd spied the three of them on the beach, been watching and seen them returning to the vehicle. Even so, there was an even more puzzling question: who could possibly survive in such a harsh environment?

Of course, it was possible that a few crazed loners, off their heads on skunk and pills, were living in the ruined hotels, taking potshots at anything that moved, human or animal. There were also vigilante gangs roaming around, he'd heard: private militias, in effect, defending their own turf and sending out marauding parties to neighbouring territories to scavenge for supplies – food, weaponry, ammunition, vehicles, gasoline and women, in that order.

Another possibility occurred to him: a squad of state troopers whose mission was supposedly to prevent looting and maintain law and order. As everything disintegrated into anarchy and their task became hopeless, these had also turned into rogue outfits, and the result was that southern Florida had been abandoned by both Federal authorities and law enforcement agencies, just as New Orleans had been after the floods of 2005.

Chase was angry with himself; he ought never to have exposed Cheryl and Dan to this danger. Cursing his own stupidity, he glanced behind and was taken aback to find his son grinning behind his mask. 'I'm glad you think it's funny.'

'You kept promising me an interesting trip, Dad. This is the best bit so far.'

'Getting your head blown off is *interesting*? I see. Pity they haven't a nuke warhead handy and then we could really enjoy ourselves.' Chase tapped the metal bodywork with the barrel of the automatic. 'You do realise this isn't armour-plated. If they hit something vital we could be here for quite some time. Like for ever.'

Cheryl had another fear. She was examining the gauge on the end of the rubber tube that was clipped to her harness. 'We've got twenty minutes' supply left, Gavin. Do we climb in and take the chance we can get far enough away before getting hit?'

The half-track was equipped with a regeneration system that filtered the outside air and extracted the low-yield oxygen from it; this artificial air-supply could sustain them indefinitely – but first they had to get inside and seal the doors under the eyes of at least one marksman with a high-powered rifle.

Chase said, 'You two climb in while I draw their fire. I'm going to run for that corner – there, by the bank. As soon as I get there, be ready to move. I'll keep them occupied while you drive the half-track up the avenue. Take one of the streets off to the left, out of their line of sight.'

'Where do we pick you up?' Cheryl said, watching him steadily through the curved faceplate.

'Sound the horn every thirty seconds. I'll cut down the side streets as soon as you're clear.'

'If we sound the horn they'll know where we are,' Dan pointed out.

'Then let's hope I get there first,' Chase said grimly. To Cheryl he said, 'Give Dan your gun. He can ride shotgun while you drive.'

Cheryl unbuttoned the holster flap and handed him the automatic. 'Keep it on safety until – unless – we need it,' she ordered.

Dan's dark eyebrows arched. 'Don't you trust me?'

'Do as Cheryl says and don't play the bloody hero!' Chase saw Dan drop his eyes and for a moment thought perhaps he'd been too severe – but no, dammit, this wasn't a schoolboy game.

'I thought the National Guard was supposed to keep law and order in the Official Devastated Areas,' Cheryl said, craning around the vehicle to get a view of the upper windows on the opposite side of the street.

Chase smiled bleakly. 'That's the government line, but it's pure propaganda. Look around. What is there worth protecting?'

'Who do you think they are?' Dan asked.

'No idea.' Chase checked the magazine and practised sighting along the burnished barrel. 'How they manage to survive is the bigger mystery.' He looked up. 'All right, you two?'

Cheryl touched his arm with her gloved hand. 'Please don't get shot.'

'That's odd,' Chase said. 'I was thinking exactly the same thing.'

He crawled on all fours to the rear of the vehicle and crouched next to the links of the half-track. Taking a few deep breaths, he prepared himself to leap and run. The distance was about twenty yards. He glanced over his shoulder. 'Get ready.'

Cheryl reached up at arm's length and gripped the handle. She nodded. Chase sprang out and ran as swiftly as he could, encumbered as he was by the one-piece coverall and the air-tank as he went swerving and ducking, leaping piles of rotting garbage. He was thankful he couldn't smell the stench; the air was probably rife with typhus and a cocktail of any number of deadly germs.

Two shots boomed out and reverberated along the street. He thanked God he didn't feel either of them. The decomposing corpse of an unidentifiable animal lay in the gutter. He saw a staring yellow eyeball filled with maggots, almost lost his footing as he skidded around the corpse and staggered the last few yards before flattening himself against the rough stucco wall. The rifle barked again and the plate-glass window on the front of the bank, miraculously preserved until now, shattered and fell with a tremendous crash.

One sniper, or more? He still didn't know. Looking back, he saw that Cheryl had opened the cab door. Once she and Dan were inside, the sniper would have a clear shot through the windshield, so now it was up to him to act as decoy. The upper-storey windows were his best bet, Chase decided, and he stepped into full view, both arms extended, left hand gripping his right wrist to steady his hand, and fired twice. Keep the bastard occupied and he wouldn't be able to concentrate on the vehicle. Cheryl and Dan needed those few vital minutes to start up and drive away.

Chase ducked back out of sight. There had been no return of fire and it occurred to him that the sniper wasn't all that hot. Four – five? – shots and he'd been wide of the mark every time. Of course, could be his weapon was old and in poor condition.

Even so, an imbecile with a blunderbuss would have the corner of the bank fixed in his sights by now. He'd be waiting, finger curled lightly on the trigger, for Chase's next appearance. Time for the old B-movie routine.

He scoured around and found a splintered strut of timber and a piece of checkered material that might once have been a tablecloth in a trendy café. He draped the cloth over the end and poked it out. The bastard was ready and waiting, all right – the strut jerked in his hand as a bullet ripped through the cloth and whined away.

Chase dropped to his knees, braced his right shoulder against the wall and fired twice, then whipped his arm back. As he did so he heard the rattle and clank of the half-track moving away. The electric motor was virtually silent, just a soft pulsing hum. Picking up speed, the vehicle trundled up Collins Avenue, and the sniper reacted with a fusillade of shots. Chase had been expecting it, and this time he saw the flare of the rifle in the darkened window directly above the curly x in Roxy's 101 Varieties Pizza Parlour.

With deliberation he took aim and fired, three times. The cry brought him out in gooseflesh. Not human surely? More like the screech of a wounded animal.

Sweating and yet cold, Chase flattened himself against the wall and watched the half-track, now a good thirty yards away, turn off at an intersection and disappear from view. He moved off along the side street, staying close to the protective lee of the buildings in case taking potshots at vistors was a popular pastime in the district. Crossing the street at a brisk jog, he turned right into the one parallel with Collins Avenue, glancing into every doorway and shattered shop-front. That strange guttural cry had made him additionally cautious. What the hell had he shot?

He didn't have fond memories of Miami from his previous visit and this trip had done nothing to modify his opinion.

Distantly the horn sounded and he ran gratefully towards it. His heart hammered in his chest and his rapid breathing fogged the faceplate. He wasn't in shape, Chase realised, even for someone in his mid-forties.

Nearing the corner he slowed to a walk and buckled the automatic into its holster. Glass crunched underfoot, making him stop dead in his tracks. There was a queer dragging sound. He spun round, coming face-to-face with a childhood terror made real: some undead-looking thing lurching towards him from a doorway with reaching arms and sightless staring eyes. The outer layer of the thing's flesh had peeled away, leaving a drab pasty white. There were eyes but no eyelids. There was a gash of a mouth and two raw holes in place of nostrils. The bone of the skull showed through the peeling strips of skin, and in his stricken terror, when the mind seizes on irrelevant details, Chase saw that the fingernails on the outstretched hands had fallen off leaving red tatters of flesh.

If this thing had once been human it was human no more.

Then the most remarkable thing about it struck him like a blow. *It wasn't wearing a mask!* It was breathing the denuded atmosphere and surviving.

Chase's hand fumbled with the holster flap and gripped the butt of the automatic. He stepped backwards as the non-human thing shambled towards him. A moment later Chase dropped through a trapdoor as his foot slid from beneath him and he hit the slimy pavement with a jarring thump that dug the air tank into the small of his back as if he'd been rabbit-punched.

Chase gasped with pain. Frantically he tried to squirm away as the creature stooped over him, its face looming nearer like a rotting skull. The mouth opened. A few jagged pegs of black teeth remained in the red weeping gums. A string of brackish brown saliva leaked from its mouth and dribbled on to his faceplate.

The groping hands reached for him, grabbing hold of his mask. One quick wrench and he was as good as dead: the toxic mix of gases would kill him even if oxygen starvation didn't.

In his panic Chase thought he was blacking out. The thing's head had vanished. Huge dark spots obscured his vision. It was blood. He hadn't heard the explosion as Dan's shot smashed the thing between the eyes and scattered shards of bone and red-speckled brain matter ten yards across the street.

Cheryl helped Dan pull the headless body from Chase, but even without its weight he was unable to stand. They got him to his feet, one supporting each arm. His mouth was clamped shut. He gagged and vomit spurted from his nostrils.

'Hurry, for God's sake!' Cheryl started dragging him along the street. 'If he's sick inside the mask he'll suffocate!'

Chase was bent forward, gagging and choking, the mask filling up. Drowning in his own vomit, he was led blindly up the street.

2

A few miles north of Fort Pierce they encountered civilisation again: the pitted and pockmarked two-lane blacktop that was all that remained of the Florida turnpike. Regular patrols by the National Guard made the road reasonably safe.

Above the old fifty-five miles per hour speed limit signs a warning had been added in large red capitals: DON'T BREATHE THE AIR!

Some people still lived this far south, surviving in isolated communities. Like bacteria and insects, it seemed, the human race could adapt to the most adverse and hostile conditions. Chilling to think, Chase brooded, that in time they might adapt to the point of actual mutation – was the creature he'd encountered in Miami Beach the portent of things to come?

It was a murky yellow dusk by the time they reached the outskirts of Orlando. Atmospherics down here produced sometimes weird, sometimes beautiful, effects.

At the National Guard checkpoint where the turnpike intersected the Bee Line Expressway, he asked the young guardsman for a secure overnight place to stay. He was dressed like a worker from an atomic reactor; enclosed from head-to-foot in a black protective cocoon and linked by umbilical airline to the guardhouse. Through the transparent faceplate they could see he wore a white helmet and had a throat mike taped just below his thyroid cartilage.

He was genial and helpful. 'Take the next exit on to Highway 27. About fifteen miles west of here you'll come to a transit camp for immigrants heading north. I guess you could stay there. Follow the signs to Disney World and you can't miss it.'

Dan's face lit up. 'Is it near Disney World?' he asked, nose pressed against the cab window.

The guardsman gave a wry grin through the faceplate. 'Hell, son, it *is* Disney World. But you won't find any rides or amusements any more.' He spoke to Chase. 'They've set up the camp there, accommodation for ten thousand people. That's your best bet within fifty miles of here.' He stepped back to survey the door panel with its MIDNITE-NET symbol, which had been painted over, but was still faintly legible.

'What are you, some kinda survey outfit?' the guardsman asked.

It would take too long to explain, so Chase merely said, 'Social media survey. It stands for Midnite-Net.'

To his surprise, the guardsman perked up at once.

'I remember that! I saw the guy on TV once – who wrote the *Midnight* book. I thought what he had to say made a lotta sense. I mean, I agreed with his aims and everything. I was even gonna send a donation, except it ain't permitted for service personnel to support political causes.' Under the black shroud, his head waggled to and fro. 'That's the Defense Department for you!'

Chase said, 'We appreciate your support all the same.'

The guardsman waved them off. 'Keep up the good work,' he called out as they pulled away.

'Another convert,' Cheryl said, smiling across the cab. 'You should have given him your autograph. He'd have been thrilled, Famous TV Personality.'

'So famous he didn't even recognise me.'

'Maybe this is the reason why.' Cheryl leaned across and tugged at his beard, which was showing a few flecks of grey. 'I know now why you grew it,' she teased him. 'So you wouldn't be recognised by your legion of fans.'

Chase laughed. He was glad to be with someone who could

unfailingly prick the bubble of his own pomposity. Cynical and yet tolerant, Cheryl possessed an incisive mind coupled with homespun common sense. Six years together (and counting) hadn't dulled the edge of their relationship, though there had been a couple of occasions when heated rows had nearly led to a final breakdown.

It was sad to see what had befallen Disney World.

The pronged dome of Space Mountain housed the reception centre, and other buildings on the sprawling site had been converted into dining halls, dormitories, and general living quarters. Remembering what it had been like when the huge entertainment complex catered to thousands of visitors every single day and seeing it now, pressed into such cheerless, austere service, depressed him intensely.

The International Hotel, connected by monorail to the Magic Kingdom, billeted a division of the National Guard. In days past the monorail had transported millions of visitors to and from the parking lots, and it was still in working order. The EPCOT Center nearby, 'city of the future', was now the National Guard HQ for central Florida.

The air-conditioning plant had been adapted to make each building a sealed enclosure, filtering the outside air and supplying an enriched oxygen mixture up to the required twenty per cent by volume.

'You must have been about nine or ten when they shut it down,' Chase told Dan. 'That's the perfect age to experience something like this. I'm sorry now I didn't bring you. The Haunted Mansion, Starflight to Saturn, Pirates of the Caribbean, Space Mountain, the Rocky Mountain Railroad . . .'

'I used to go to the one in Los Angeles,' Cheryl said. 'The sky over Disneyland always looked different from everywhere else; a deeper kind of blue. The sun was always shining. When I was a kid it was a make-believe world at the end of the rainbow.'

'Thanks for that, folks. Knowing I've missed out, I feel tons better,' Dan said lugubriously. 'I knew I'd been born twenty years too late.'

The picture-book colours on the towers and turrets had faded, the once sparkling gilt on the rides peeling and dull. There was a tragic sadness about the place. It was a ghost town still echoing faintly with long-ago music and fireworks and children's laughter.

They lined up at the steel counter in one of the crowded dining halls. Chase thought it looked familiar, and then knew why. It had housed the 360-degree cinema, a continuous screen surrounding the audience. Broken ceiling panels hung from the aluminium framework. Many of the people in line, he noted, looked haggard and pale. There were the unmistakable signs of cardiovascular and respiratory illness. The survival of the fittest wasn't just an abstract phrase any more.

Chase looked at his son, mopping up gravy with a piece of bread. Thank God he was healthy. His skin was tanned and his hair black and glossy. Skin and hair usually showed the symptoms of anoxia first, when the body's tissues were receiving an insufficient supply of oxygen.

'How long are we staying?' Dan wanted to know.

'Overnight, that's all,' Cheryl said. 'Tomorrow we'll start the drive up into Georgia, to a place south of Atlanta.'

'Is it breathable up there?'

'Oh, sure,' Cheryl smiled. 'It's outside the Official Devastated Area. There's a Midnite-Net group in a small town called Griffin. We can leave the half-track and carry on to Washington by train.'

'We'll probably stay a couple of days in Griffin,' Chase said. 'They've started a small community farm and they want to get as many Midnite volunteers as possible.'

Dan pulled a face. 'What's that entail – speeches and stuff?'

Chase nodded and Dan rolled his eyes. The boy saw the ordinary man, not the person with a worldwide media reputation as an ecology campaigner. He still couldn't come to terms with his father's role as a cross between guru, whistleblower and crusader. To tell the truth, Chase had the same difficulty.

As they ate their meal, Chase became aware of being watched. This was always happening nowadays – beard or no beard. So when the man called out from a nearby table, he was half-prepared for it.

'I got the right fella, yeah? Your name's Chase, ain't it?'

Several heads turned. Chase nodded and looked at Cheryl. Their eyes exchanged a coded message. They both knew what was coming. And Cheryl knew how uncomfortable he was, genuinely, with being recognised.

The man raised his voice. 'Thought so. I seen you on TV and read the book you wrote.' He had a broad red face, in fiery contrast to his white hair cut so close that the pinkness of his scalp showed through. Next to him sat a frail hollow-cheeked woman of about fifty with lank mousy hair trailing to thin shoulders.

'I wanna tell you somethin', friend.' The man leaned forward, hairy forearms flat on the table, face thrust out like a challenge. 'Tell you what I think, yeah? I think what you wrote was a Grade-A load of bullshit. Bull. Shit. You invented it, dreamed up the whole shebang – every goddamn last fuckin' word.'

'Harry, please.' The woman spoke down at the table. 'So it ain't true, so what? Leave it be. Please.'

Her tone was a plaintive whine which seemed to incense her husband. He blurted out, 'All that crap about the United States dumping poison in the oceans and the Russkies burnin' off gas to kill us all.' He jabbed and kept on jabbing a blunt forefinger. 'I wanna tell *you* something, smart-ass dick-brain. You're the one who started this whole fuckin' mess in the first place. You're the one responsible. There wasn't no eco-logi-cal or whatever-you-call-it crisis until that goddamn book came out and you started spoutin' off on TV and in the newspapers. We was getting along swell. Then you come along and started everybody panicking and running around in circles and shittin' themselves. And for what, I ask? *For what?* We all know. For the big bucks, that's what. You can't deny it because it's true.'

His reasoning was too illogical to debate, reasonably and sensibly. Chase had faced it so many times in the past, and found it useless to even try. He picked up his fork and carried on eating.

'Hey!' the man suddenly yelled, livid at being ignored, so he thought. 'See her – see my wife?' The circle of quiet had spread along the trestle tables. Heads were turned, rows of them, impassive faces, resentful eyes. He was speaking for all of them, it seemed. 'This woman is forty-four years old and she's dying. Her lungs is rotted away. The doctors say she can't take it no more.' The man's face was pulsing redly and his eyes were moist. His voice died away to near choking. 'You sure as hell started something with that goddamn trash. You fuckin' Limey cock-sucker.'

'Harry, don't,' the woman pleaded. 'Come on now, please, hush up.'

Chase pitied the man in his impotent rage and bewilderment. But what answer could he give? In some twisted way the man had got the notion into his head that the changes taking place over the last ten years were to be blamed on what Chase had written – even the changes happening *before* it was written. By the same strange logic, Chase supposed, had he never written the book at all, such changes would never have occurred. The book had created its own reality. Craziness.

'Gavin,' Cheryl said under her breath, 'let's get out of here . . .'

She was too late. There was a collective indrawn breath of apprehension from the crowded tables. The red-faced man's wife was shrieking, 'No – No – No!'

Chase ducked. The knife passed inches away from his ear and embedded itself in the wall. The red-faced man had risen and was clambering over the table. People reached out to restrain him. He swatted them away, his eyes never leaving Chase's face. 'You fuckin' sonofabitch. You started all this—'

'No, Harry, no,' the woman was wailing. 'Harry, no, *please!*'

Chase moved his chair aside and stepped backwards into the aisle. He didn't unfasten his holster flap but rested his hand on it. There was complete silence. The wretched man was crouched on the table, eyes enraged and bloodshot in the sweating red face. Chase waited, his stomach aching with tension. The man sat back on his haunches. He put one hand across his eyes and covered it with the other. He slowly curled up, shoulders bowed, and began to shake soundlessly.

Chase wiped his hand on his thigh. His fingertips were quivering. Three attacks in twenty-four hours? At this rate he might begin to believe he really was to blame for the whole miserable mess.

At his side, Cheryl said softly, 'The poor man's deranged.'

'The way things are going he won't be the only one,' Chase said.

3

They had crossed the state line into North Carolina and were heading for Charlotte when the blizzard struck. After the torpid, airless climate of Florida and Georgia, the contrast in plummeting temperatures was a shock to the system: like being dragged out of a sauna and slammed into an industrial deep-freeze.

Dan suffered more than his dad and Cheryl. Coming from the temperate European zone, he wasn't accustomed to such violent extremes; in a matter of hours and over a short distance, just a couple of hundred miles, the thermometer plunged from 42° C to a bone-numbing -35° C. It was welcome relief that the half-track coped well in such conditions. Traffic was light on the freeways, most people sensibly staying at home; some of those who hadn't been sensible had paid the price, their cars humps of snow along the hard shoulder. Chase hoped the drivers had been rescued, though he felt no inclination to stop and investigate.

As they approached the outskirts of Charlotte the flurries of snow became too heavy for the wipers to deal with. Their only option was to find overnight accommodation, no matter how basic.

'Will this mean we can't swing by Pittsburgh?' Cheryl said. She sounded worried. 'This delay's gonna wreck the schedule.'

Chase, sitting beside her in the passenger seat, knew why she was worried. What had once been the former Midniters' base near Warrendale, northwest of Pittsburgh, was now reduced to three or four volunteers. Bud Keiser was still there, and so was their technical whiz, Jerv Cooper, who had recently turned twenty. But the loss of Micki Vargas had been a demoralising blow to the group's morale and after her murder, many of the crew lost heart and drifted away. Chase and Cheryl had felt her loss as keenly as anyone. For the past five years they had kept on the move, travelling around the US and spending part of the year in Europe. On their most recent visit to England Dan had urged Chase to let him spend more time with him.

Their schedule wasn't set in stone, but even so, a delay of more than a couple of days would be seriously disruptive. She didn't want to break their promise to Bud, Jerv and the others by postponing this visit.

Chase's nose was nearly touching the windscreen and his eyes were screwed up as he tried to see through the onslaught of wind-blasted snow. Even their full-beam headlights and the rack of four halogen spotlights on the roof illuminated little. He and Cheryl had been spelling each other, changing drivers in a two-hourly rota, and it was coming up to his turn – but if they didn't get off the highway soon and find a haven for the night, the half-track would become just another humped shape like those he could just make out in the fading light.

Dan had been quiet for a while. Glancing back, Chase saw that he was soundly asleep. 'We'll come off at the next exit,' he said. 'That's if we can find it.'

'That's just where I'm headed,' Cheryl said grimly. She'd brought their speed down to fifteen miles an hour and steered the vehicle into the nearside lane. 'Where's global warming when it's needed?'

'Hey, don't grouse! You can be fried, frozen, asphyxiated or drowned – you're almost spoilt for choice.'

His feeble attempt at humour fell flat. It contained too much painful truth, way beyond irony, to be funny. Chase and his Climate Alerts had made a significant contribution to spreading awareness about climate change and what its impact would be. More importantly, they had exposed the covert efforts by organisations such as the Alliance for the Advancement of American Values to suppress the facts and silence those people trying to reveal them. Howard Nevison had made an even greater contribution: that huge cache of classified material leaked by the analyst and disseminated by Midnite-Net to media outlets the world over had blown the lid off AAAV and its nefarious operations. Its head, Chesney Poulton, hadn't escaped scrutiny either, but as they used to say about the banks, he was too big to fail. Poulton was too well-connected with the top hierarchy of politicians and corporate chiefs to suffer any real consequences; his influence ran too deep and would have involved (and implicated) too many powerful people. So, naturally and understandably, Poulton had never been brought to book or made to pay for his crimes. He simply vanished off the radar.

Whereas Howard Nevison paid the price in full, or so Chase assumed. Despite his best efforts, he had been unable to discover Nevison's fate after he'd been detained by the security services. He too had vanished off the radar, but in a far more sinister fashion. Maybe he was dead, or perhaps he'd been transferred to the Cuba PDF, which was where Bill Inchcape had ended up. This fragment of intelligence, concerning

Binch, had come from Howard's data-cache and another informant, a one-time comrade-in-arms of Bud Keiser had confirmed it. The informant still had many links to the Marine Corps, and through them he discovered that the scientist had been interred at the Prime Detention Facility in 2025; according to the most recent report he was still alive, though in failing health.

For Gavin Chase, this was the most shocking – the most *sickening* – development of all: how could the human rights of US citizens such as Binch and Howard Nevison be utterly disregarded, how could they be simply dumped in the trash? There had been no due process; no charges were brought, no trial took place. The authorities were so brazen in their brutal use of power that there was no need for even a fig-leaf of pretence: the UnPatriot (Emergency Powers) Act trumped every other consideration. People who were troublesome or a nuisance or held contrary opinions could be 'disappeared' at will, no questions asked.

'Is that it? The exit sign?'

Cheryl's eyes were sharper than his; she'd spotted it first, even though his nose was pressed to the curved glass.

They came off the highway down a gentle slope and the fierce blast of snow eased off in the lee of a natural windbreak. Cheryl stopped the vehicle and Chase cleared the windscreen. They had to find shelter for the night. It was practically certain now that they wouldn't make their promised visit to the Pittsburgh base, no matter how much Cheryl wanted to.

2

I

They arrived in Washington, DC, during what they called a freak electrical storm, 'freak' implying uncommon, although these spectacularly ferocious storms now occurred two or three times a month.

The white cupola of the Capitol, bathed in a purplish glow, resembled a brain from a science fiction movie. The great thunderheads of cloud were rent by razor-toothed lightning flashes that flickered around the stone spear of the Washington Monument, blackening its bevelled tip. The air had the acrid stink of ozone molecules energised by millions of volts.

Thus far no one had come up with a satisfactory explanation for this vicious heavenly onslaught, though a number of quasi-religious groups claimed that it was the wrath of God – in each case, their own particular god – and paraded up and down Constitution Avenue bearing banners, always on the theme of 'The Day of Judgement Is Nigh – Repent Before It's Too Late'.

This was Dan's first visit to Washington and he objected to spending even a small portion of it in a television studio. Cheryl came up with the answer: she would take him on a tour of the Smithsonian Institution and the Air-Space Museum on Jefferson Drive while Chase did his live interview for the news and current affairs programme *Crossfire*. Dan was most keen to see the animated Red Planet exhibition: working models of the 2022 Russian-China mission to Mars, the joint team who had set up a colony and lived there for seven months before returning to Earth.

The storm clouds were clearing as Chase stepped out of the courtesy car. Two armed security guards escorted him to the hospitality suite where Claudia Kane, the show's famous host, came forward lithely to greet him. She had the professional interviewer's cosmetic smile and laid-back manner. This was to be a discussion rather than a straight interview, Claudia Kane informed him, leading him forward to meet his fellow guests: Professor Gene Lucas, head of atmospheric physics at Princeton, and Dr Frank Hanamura of Jonan University, Tokyo.

Chase knew of Lucas, though they'd never met. A small, round-shouldered man with neatly parted grey hair and a neat grey moustache to match, it was Lucas, Chase recalled, who'd abruptly resigned – or been dismissed from, it was never made clear – the position of the president's senior scientific advisor eight or nine years ago.

Hanamura, still a young man, had already established a brilliant reputation for his work on the biosphere, with specific reference to the effects of urban and industrial pollution. He was of mixed parentage, born in Kyoto of a Japanese father and an American mother. His father had died when Frank was thirteen after collapsing in a Tokyo street, stricken by the pollution that a few years later would make world headlines as the 'Tokyo Alert', when thousands choked to death; this had inspired his career. Tall and slender, with glossy jet-black hair, he had inherited the best physical attributes of both races, with dark expressive eyes in a strong, intelligent face. He was almost too perfectly handsome.

After outlining the programme's format, Claudia Kane led them into the studio and seated them in comfortable armchairs. She herself was centre stage on a revolving chair that could be spun around by remote control to face any of the participants. In the trade this was known as a 'media interrogative debate'.

True to her breed, Claudia Kane astutely picked up a point of contention between Lucas and Hanamura: she zeroed in on it like a shark scenting blood.

Gene Lucas was given first crack. 'We're paying the price for two hundred and fifty years of indiscriminate growth brought about by greed, selfishness and crass stupidity,' he expounded gloomily. 'And the truly frightening thing is, we refuse to learn from past mistakes and mend our ways. You can't save the world from what I see as inevitable destruction without changing human nature, and let's face it, you're never going to change human nature.'

'But you speak as though we're helpless, Professor.'

Claudia Kane whirled round to take in Frank Hanamura's contribution.

'I don't think we are,' Frank said, addressing Gene Lucas, 'I also think, with respect, that you are underestimating the regenerative capacity of our planet. There have been literally *thousands* of catastrophic natural disasters – volcanic eruptions, earthquakes on a colossal scale, floods, meteor strikes, ice ages – all of which make what man has done look puny in comparison.'

'But you do believe there *is* a problem?' Claudia Kane pressed him.

The handsome Japanese spread lean brown hands. 'Sure I do, most definitely. Everyone can see that the biosphere is undergoing a fundamental change. Where I part company with Professor Lucas is in believing that we can do something about it.'

The camera picked up Lucas' gentle smile. He was hearing an echo of his former self. At sixty-three he didn't consider himself old, but he wondered, with hardening of the arteries, did advancing age also stiffen hope into despair?

'And what about you, Dr Chase?' Claudia Kane spun around, flashing him her wide, bright smile. Frank Hanamura might be conventionally handsome, but Chase's saturnine looks, set off by a close dark beard touched with grey, had a far stronger appeal to a woman of her age. 'Which side are you on?'

'Is it a contest?' Chase enquired mildly.

'The two views we've heard expressed are diametrically opposed, I would have thought.'

The camera featured Chase full-frame in close-up as he said, 'It's easy to score points and engage in a slugging match. The three of us could do that all night, because no one knows for certain what the future holds. But if you want a serious debate—'

'Yes, of course I do,' said Claudia Kane, completely unruffled. She flicked back a stray lock of silver-tinted hair with a red-clawed hand. 'So what I'd like to ask *you*, Dr Chase, is what you see as the prime motivation behind the Midnite-Net movement. Is it basically a plea to common sense?'

Chase smiled. 'We don't aim for the impossible. No, the idea originally was to unite those people who share a common belief, a common hope. Perhaps "unite" is too forceful a word, because the movement doesn't exist in any formal or organised sense. It's more a commitment to a philosophy – to the feeling, the *emotion*, if you like – of what it is to be just one form of life coexisting peacefully and in harmony with all the other forms of life that share this planet with us.'

Claudia Kane nodded, watching his mouth. 'That has almost the sound of a religious belief.'

Chase said lightly, 'If it is, it's pantheistic.'

'In the sense that you identify God with the universe, as one and the same thing,' said Claudia Kane, quick to demonstrate that she hadn't got the job on the strength of her pearly smile and chest measurement. 'Though we don't visit Stonehenge in robes and sandals at the summer solstice, predict the future from chicken entrails or read fortunes in teacups.'

'Is it true that the movement has more than two million followers throughout the world?'

'Not followers,' Chase corrected her. 'Two million people who subscribe to the beliefs I've just mentioned.'

'More than one hundred thousand of them in Japan,' Hanamura put in. 'My country has sound historical reasons for wishing to foster those ideals.'

'So anyone and everyone is free to join,' Claudia Kane said, keeping the focus on Chase.

'Yes, if they share our beliefs.'

'I think a great many people do. And I'm sure many more will in the future.'

Chase had lost count of the TV and radio shows he'd taken part in. Sometimes it was just like a mad, mindless merry-go-round: endless talk and very little action. Not that he undervalued the concern shown by people wherever he went – Europe, Africa, the Middle East, Asia, South America, the United States – not at all. But more and more he was beginning to wonder what good it did for 'experts' like Lucas, Hanamura and himself to sit around endlessly discussing the environmental crisis.

The form was always the same: they agreed that things were getting worse. They disagreed about what could – *should* – be done to put them right. They agreed that something *ought* to be done, because in five, ten, twenty or fifty years from now it would be too late.

There were many times when he brooded about what, ultimately, his book had achieved. When it was published there had been extravagant claims that it had actually averted an all-out environmental war. Chase didn't think so, not for an instant. No, he'd merely blown the whistle when the game was already over. By the time the book appeared it was transparently clear to everyone – even the American and Russian military – that the atmosphere and oceans were already rapidly deteriorating and that for the superpowers to continue with their environmental war plans was akin to putting a pillow over a sick man's face when he was gasping for breath and didn't have long to live anyway.

In the section of the book entitled 'The Suicide Pact', Chase had revealed these secret war plans, based on the Operation Download dossier and the information supplied by Boris Stanovnik. It had been this revelation rather than the broader (and, to Chase, the more important) theme of global decline that had assured *One Minute to Midnight* of its international bestseller status.

The truth was that most people still had a naïve and misplaced faith in mankind's immortality. They refused to accept that during the earth's 4.5-billion-year evolution something like eighty per cent of the species had been wiped out, and that man had no God-given right to survive when so many other life-forms had failed. There was now a distinct possibility that man would become just one more failed biological experiment to add to the list.

And now, almost eight years after the book came out, what were its achievements? Or more to the point, its failings? Official Devastated Areas girdled the equator, widening, spreading outwards like a poisonous belt choking the planet. The acidity of the oceans had increased by twenty-five per cent, as he had seen for himself off Miami Beach. Vast swathes of the Pacific Ocean were turning into stagnant weed-choked dead zones. Starvation had wiped out millions in India, Africa, Asia and South America. And perhaps more ominously, measurements with sensitive instruments were beginning to show a fall in the oxygen of the atmosphere, just as old Theo Detrick had predicted all those years ago.

And while all this was going on, what was he doing? Sitting in an air-conditioned television studio in Washington, DC, talking. Talking . . .

Endlessly talking.

2

After a hard day's work there was nothing the UN Special Rapporteur on Global Environment enjoyed more than to linger in a sumptuous hot bath liberally sprinkled with Esprit de Lavande from Penhaligon's of Covent Garden, London. The small round bottle with the ground-glass stopper travelled in the UN transatlantic diplomatic pouch, a little privilege Ingrid Van Dorn allowed herself.

She was tall and straight-limbed, with long silvery-blonde hair and classic Nordic features clearly evident in her wide, pale forehead and icy blue eyes. Rather angular perhaps, though she measured the same now as she had twenty-five years ago when a strikingly beautiful twenty-two-year-old girl from Örebro in Sweden. That had been before two marriages, two divorces and two children, both girls, now at boarding school in Vermont.

Floating in the sunken oval bath and breathing in the perfumed mist, Ingrid Van Dorn watched the large screen inset into the wall. A crystal carafe of iced sangria was within reach of her slender white arm and a tall glass, beaded with condensation, stood on the tiled shelf by her elbow.

'In the studio tonight,' Claudia Kane was saying, making the introductions, 'we're delighted to welcome Dr Gavin Chase, a British marine biologist, better known to us as the author of that hugely successful and influential book *One Minute to Midnight*. Several years after publication, it continues to sell many thousands of copies a year. Also with us we have Professor Gene Lucas of the Geophysical—'

'Is this live or recorded?' she asked. Her husky voice still had a trace of accent, though less pronounced than when she gave interviews; the media loved it.

The man seated in the upholstered recess took off his horn-rimmed glasses and wiped away the steam with the hem of his bathrobe. 'Live. Claudia Kane thinks it gives her programme a dangerous edge.'

Kenneth J. Prothero – 'Pro' to his friends, and some of his close enemies – Senator for Rhode Island, slipped his glasses back on and leaned forward, hands clasped above his long, tanned, hairy legs. 'You know, this guy has a lot to—'

'Sssshhhh!' Ingrid held up a finger. She glanced towards him, looking like a goddess with her gleaming hair coiled on top of her head. 'Are we recording this?'

Prothero nodded and topped up his glass with sangria. He chewed on a piece of orange peel, cursing under his breath. Bath-time for Ingrid was a sacred ritual; this damned steam meant he had to keep wiping his specs every two minutes.

As commanded, he remained obediently silent until the programme was over. There was the gentle swish of water as Ingrid moved languorously in the tub, accompanied by the creaking of ice melting in the carafe. Prothero stood looking down at her. He couldn't look enough at this fabulous woman: that she was his was a stroke of wondrous good fortune.

'Well, what do you think?'

'Yes, I'm impressed. What do we know about him, Pro?'

'I've had him checked out, every last detail. In my opinion we'll never find anyone better qualified.'

'But if he's as committed to Midnite-Net as he makes out, perhaps he won't want to.'

'All the more reason for him to accept, I'd say.'

'Why? Because of the "challenge"?' She used the word with scorn. 'A man like Chase has more challenges than he can cope with already.'

Prothero reached into the water and took her hand. It was like a pale water-lily in his broad palm. 'If Chase is the kind of guy I think he is, he'll *want* to do it. An opportunity like this? Sure, he'll jump at it.'

She gave him a quick sideways smile. 'I guess I'm scared.' An uncharacteristic admission for her. 'We've talked about it for so long, and now we have to make the decision. We're burning our bridges . . . or at least you are. If your government finds out—'

Prothero's face tightened. 'My government is up to its neck in bacteriological herbicides. The old, old games – like a kid fooling around with matches in a house that's burning to the ground.' It spilled out of him like venom: 'I've had all that, Ingrid. Fut/COE can go screw itself, *and* the generals, *and* the Joint Chiefs of Staff! They all have a vested interest in keeping the billions of dollars flooding in to perpetuate global conflict and they'll never change. They can't. It's like asking a blind man to paint a sunset. We have to do it without them – *against* them. It's the only way.'

'Screw them before they screw up the world,' Ingrid said. She pouted at him through the rising steam. 'What are you smiling at?'

Prothero couldn't stop grinning. 'It sounds funny, an expression like "screw up" in a Swedish accent.'

'So! You think I'm funny, huh?' She pulled her hand free with ladylike hauteur and slid down until the water lapped her chin.

'That's right, madam, I do,' Prothero said, wetting the sleeves of his bathrobe up to the elbows, and pulled her up under the arms until they were both standing, his bathrobe open, her wet breasts pressing spongily against his hairy chest. He stooped and picked her up in his arms, a hot, wet, desirable woman, faintly steaming.

Prothero frowned. 'Just one logistical handicap.'

'Oh?'

'Glasses. Fogged. Can't see my way to the bedroom.'

'No logistical handicap at all,' said the UN Special Rapporteur on Global Environment huskily. She unhooked his glasses and flipped them over her shoulder. They landed in the lavender-scented water with a plop.

3

Afterwards, in the green room, Claudia Kane thanked her guests for a 'splendid' programme. She laid her hand on Chase's sleeve and purred in his ear, 'I just love that English accent of yours, Gavin. Where are you from?'

'Bolton,' Chase said.

'Is that near London?'

'About two hundred miles away.'

'Oh,' Claudia Kane said, 'pretty close then.'

Lucas turned to him. 'I read your piece on Calcutta in the *Herald-Tribune*. Five hundred suicides a day? That's terrible.'

'The situation's even worse in Bangkok,' Chase said. 'Twenty-five million people, more than half of them living without water or adequate sanitation. It's one huge refugee camp.'

'No sealed enclosures?' Hanamura said.

'Government buildings and the business sector are sealed, but the streets are open to the air. People drop down on the pavement and literally choke to death.'

Claudia Kane shuddered and swirled the whisky in her glass. 'That's my idea of hell on earth.'

'That's exactly what it is,' Chase said gravely. 'If you can imagine an updated version of Dante's *Inferno*, that's it all right.'

'Do you have any plans to visit Japan?' Hanamura asked.

'Not at the moment. I was there last year for six weeks on a lecture tour. Those new measures you've introduced appear to be having an effect, which is an encouraging sign.'

Hanamura nodded agreement. 'At long last our politicians are waking up. They've passed legislation to limit population and the decentralisation policy is being implemented. The big stumbling block is industry. Trying to break down the tradition of paternalism is very difficult.'

'At least we don't have that problem in Britain,' Chase remarked, with a touch of gallows humour.

'Ah,' said Hanamura sagely, 'but Britain has reverted to cottage industry.'

Whether he regarded this as being to Japan's advantage or not, Chase couldn't tell. 'You mean souvenir rubbish suppliers to the world – cardboard Big Bens and plastic busts of the king and queen. It's turning into a bargain-basement historical joke shop.'

Lucas was interested to know what Frank Hanamura was working on, and the tall, elegant Japanese gave an enigmatic smile. 'A pet project of mine. I've been trying to get it funded for the last five years, but I suspect they think it's crazy, an impossible scheme. I want to give the world its oxygen back, that's all.'

'How do you propose to do that?' asked Lucas with a half-smile, half-frown.

'By using a process that every schoolboy learns in the first grade: the electrolysis of seawater.'

'On what kind of scale?' Chase asked.

'Well, yes, that really is the crux of the problem,' Hanamura admitted wryly. 'As you know, it's easy enough in the laboratory, and the process has been used to a limited extent for industrial purposes. But producing the tonnage of oxygen that would make any appreciable difference to the biosphere is one hell of a problem, and so far unresolved.' He sounded quite cheerful about it.

'My first-grade science isn't all that hot,' Claudia Kane said. 'What process is that again?'

Chase said, 'Electrolysis of seawater. You split H_2O into its component parts of hydrogen and oxygen by passing an electrical current through brine. As Frank says, nothing is easier in theory, and we've been doing it for years on a small scale. But for the amounts he's talking about there are problems of corrosion and—' He stopped, realising he was getting technical, and said, 'Well, there *are* problems, and pretty daunting ones.'

'It's the obvious solution when you think about it,' Hanamura enthused. 'Seven-tenths of the earth's surface is seawater: there's a virtually unlimited supply from which we can obtain the oxygen we need to replenish the atmosphere. It's never been done before because we've never needed to do it. And also, of course, because electrolysis has one major drawback.' He glanced keenly at the two men.

'Power,' Lucas said.

Hanamura nodded briskly, his sallow face becoming more animated. 'I've done some preliminary computer studies and I'm convinced it's technically feasible, given—'

There was a distracting flurry of movement as a bald-headed man in a bowtie came in. He was flushed and agitated. He spoke to a group near the door, whose faces registered numbed disbelief. The word spread. Associated Press had filed a report that Joan Weinert, head of research at the World Meteorological Organisation, had been assassinated while on a fact-finding trip to Venezuela. She was the third high-ranking climate official to have been murdered in the past eight months. The perpetrators and their motives were unknown.

For Chase, this made an immediate connection with the series of murders and disappearances of environmentalists planned by the AAAV and executed by its proxy thugs and mercenaries. The disclosure by Howard Nevison that the JEG Corporation had also been implicated – which Chase and Midnite-Net had made public – forced Chesney Poulton and the Alliance for the Advancement of American Values to assume a low profile. Their activities had become even more clandestine.

So were these killings the first signs that Poulton and the AAAV were renewing their campaign of violence and intimidation? Chase would have dearly loved to know who was behind them. Unfortunately, his prime source of classified information, Howard Nevison, had, or so it was rumoured, spent the past five years rotting away in the Cuba Prime Detention Facility. As had Bill Inchcape. All efforts to secure their release had been met with a blank wall of denial: the authorities would neither confirm nor deny that the two men were being held.

The strain of not knowing her husband's fate and state of health – even if he were alive or dead – had finally been too much for Binch's wife Stella, who had died of a stroke two years ago.

Claudia Kane thanked her guests for coming and departed.

'I worked with Joan,' Gene Lucas recalled sombrely. 'We served together on a World Climate Research committee two or three years

ago. What in God's name is happening? Why? What's the purpose?'
He shook his head, mystified.

It was time for Chase to get back to the hotel. Cheryl and Dan should
have returned from their sightseeing trip by now and he was looking
forward to a relaxed family dinner at a restaurant, and hearing Dan's
opinions of the capital.

As they were shaking hands Lucas said, 'Give my regards to Cheryl.'

Chase was surprised. 'I will, Gene. I didn't know you two were
acquainted.'

'We've never met,' Lucas said, a secretive smile lurking at the corner
of his mouth, 'but I once sent her some information.' His smile broad-
ened; he was quite obviously tickled pink. 'Which she made excellent
use of, I might add.'

This left Chase with a mystified frown. 'What information was that?'

'About a certain project called Operation Download – I think you've
probably heard of it.'

After a stunned moment, Chase grasped Lucas' hand and shook it
again, this time more warmly than ever.

3

I

For reasons Dr Ruth Brosnan had never been able to figure out, from 6 p.m. onwards was the busiest admissions period of the twenty-four-hour cycle. People collapsing on the streets were ferried in by ambulance, or staggered in themselves to receive treatment at the Manhattan Emergency Hospital in the dilapidated eight-storey building on East 68th Street that had once housed the Cornell School of Medicine.

The admissions department resembled a battlefield casualty clearing station. Anoxia and pollution cases were sprawled on chairs or laid out on stretchers on the floor, so tightly packed that there was barely enough room to move among them. There was little more she could do except make a quick diagnosis, classifying them as terminal – requiring hospitalisation – or short-stay. The latter were given a whiff of oxygen, drugs to clear their bronchial tubes and sent on their way. Orderlies followed her, sorting out the patients according to the red or blue stickers on the soles of their shoes.

Then it was on to the wards.

The unwritten policy of the hospital was not to give anyone over the age of fifty-five a bed – better to save the life of a younger person than waste drugs and space on someone whose life expectancy was only a few years at best. Ruth hated the policy; more than once she had been reprimanded for admitting a patient above the 'death line'. She had even falsified the records, subtracting five and sometimes ten years from the patient's age to slip them though the net.

Fred Walsh, aged sixty-three, was one such. He lay shrouded in a plastic oxygen tent, a small, wiry man with spiky grey hair and watery brown eyes who, from the day he'd arrived, had not uttered one word of complaint. He had the native New Yorker's caustically laconic wit, honed to a fine art by a lifetime spent as a cutter in the Manhattan rag trade. Ruth didn't know why she had admitted Fred when she had rejected hundreds of others, some just as bad as he, some younger. Yet a week ago she had written 'Walsh, Frederick Charles; Male; Caucasian; age fifty-two' on the pink admissions sheet after an examination lasting no more than a minute.

In her heart of hearts she suspected it was Fred reminded her of Grandpa Brosnan; he had the same slight body that was nevertheless as tough as old boots. She remembered her grandfather with so much affection; he had taught her to ride in the summer vacations back in Columbus, Ohio, a million years ago.

Ethically it was wrong, of course she knew that – but was it any less ethical than turning people out on to the streets on the basis of some arbitrary death-line? Didn't Fred Walsh deserve at least the same chance as the thousands of others who were seeking refuge in these hopelessly overcrowded wards staffed by doctors and nurses working ceaselessly to save as many lives as possible?

'Hey, you're looking better today,' she told him brightly, which wasn't an outright lie. Indeed there was a spot of colour in his sagging cheeks, and his lips were noticeably less blue. 'How're you feeling, Fred?'

'Reminds . . . me . . . of . . . my . . . honey . . . moon.' Even with oxygen he had to draw a deep breath between each word.

Ruth smiled. 'How's that, Fred?'

'Flat . . . on . . . my . . . back . . . and . . . shorta . . . breath.' He winked at her through the plastic sheet, his narrow chest rising and falling, the air wheezing and bubbling through his furred tubes. Second-stage anoxia with pneumogastric complications. An operation was out of the question; anyway, it was too late. In one respect Fred was lucky. Many anoxic patients suffered a sharp decline in their mental processes, becoming confused and incoherent because of the reduction in oxygen-rich blood circulating through the brain; that's when premature senile dementia set in.

Ruth inserted her arms into the plastic sleeves that gave access into the tent; self-sealing collars gripped her wrists. 'Tell me when you feel anything,' she said, pricking his toes and the soles of his feet with a surgical needle. Loss of sensation in the extremities was one of the first indications that the anoxia was getting worse.

Fred lay passively, not responding. The needle had reached his lower calf before he twitched.

'You feel that?'

He nodded. 'Try . . . lower . . . down. My . . . feet . . . are . . . cold.'

'We'll do that tomorrow,' Ruth said cheerfully. 'Around here we take our time.' She took hold of his hand, which felt like clammy wax, and pricked his fingers and palm.

'My . . . old . . . lady . . . came . . . yester . . . day.' He paused, wheezing. 'Asks . . . how . . . long . . . this . . . vacation . . . lasts.'

'Well, it'll be some time yet, Fred. Why, what's she planning to do, run off with the mailman?' Ruth tried his other hand. No response there either. She pulled her arms free and dropped the needle into the bin. 'Say, how do you feel about being moved to another hospital? There's a clinic in Maryland where they could take better care of you. It's a special treatment centre with all the latest facilities. I think I can fix you up with a place. How about it?'

'Hopeless . . . case . . . huh?' His moist brown eyes were fixed intently on her face.

'Hell, no, I wouldn't bullshit you, Fred.' Ruth lowered her voice conspiratorially. 'The temptation's getting to be too strong for me. You're driving me crazy with lust. I've got to get you out of here before I disgrace myself. This thing is bigger than both of us.'

'Not . . . at . . . the . . . moment . . . it . . . ain't.'

'I'll give you some time to think it over, okay?' Ruth said, writing on the chart. 'Talk it through with your wife. Let me know in a day or two.'

Fred Walsh nodded and closed his eyes. Ruth replaced the chart at the foot of the bed and went on with her rounds.

An hour later it was blessed relief to put her feet up and relax with a cup of strong black coffee in the staffroom. She'd take ten and then finish off the wards. No pathology lab tonight, unfortunately. Her duty didn't end till midnight; by then she'd be dog-tired.

The door swung open and Dr Grant McGowan breezed in and

helped himself to iced tea. McGowan was head of surgery, in his forties, and happily married with three children. He had a sympathetic ear for Ruth's grouses against Valentine, the chief pathologist, and the hospital at large.

'You still here?' she said, surprised.

McGowan scowled up at the clock. 'I was on my way out when they caught me. Why do people choose such inconsiderate times to have cardiac arrests? I was all set to watch the fights on TV and I get paged at the damn door.'

'Couldn't agree more,' Ruth said fervently. 'All sickness and disease should stop at 6 p.m. on the dot: germs and viruses knock off for the day and come back tomorrow.'

McGowan sat down in the armchair opposite and eyed her critically. 'You look beat, Ruth. What is it? Too much work, not enough sleep, or both?'

'Old age.'

'Are you still working in the path lab after hours?' At her nod he shook his head and sighed. 'You know you're asking for trouble, don't you? Being a resident on the wards is a full-time job without waging a one-woman crusade in the name of medical science. We don't have the staff, the resources or the back-up for that.'

'You sound like Valentine,' Ruth replied testily.

'Christ, I hope not,' said McGowan with feeling. 'Look, Ruth, I *know* the work is important and that somebody ought to be doing it – but why you? It isn't as if you were getting *paid* to do it.'

'It isn't a question of money; it's what I want to do. What I *must* do.'

'I didn't mean to imply—'

'You didn't imply anything, Grant.' Ruth smiled at him. 'I'm just thankful – really and truly – that you're around to talk to. Valentine thinks the diagnostic work I did in Denver isn't worth shit. At least you recognise it's worthwhile.' She arched back in the chair, massaging the nape of her neck with her fingertips. She was aware that McGowan's eyes were upon her. The head surgeon had never made any advances, and Ruth was glad about that; she preferred him as friend and colleague than a more intimate relationship.

With a guilty start, as if she had read his mind, McGowan swivelled around to look at the clock, then hurriedly finished off his iced tea. 'Better get along before they start without me. See you tomorrow.' He strode to the door and paused there. 'And listen, Dr Brosnan, get a good night's rest. Forget Manhattan Emergency even exists.'

'Yes, sir, Dr McGowan.' Ruth wrinkled her nose at him as he went out. Easier to forget you had a raging toothache.

2

From the fifth-storey window Ruth gazed down into the tunnel of smog that was East 68th Street. She recalled her first visit to New York as a teenager, the thrill and excitement of the electric city. Just to stroll down Fifth Avenue was in itself a magical experience. The tall buildings gleaming in the sunlight, the *haute couture* shops and bustling department stores, the vendors on every street corner assailing the senses with mouth-watering smells – the crazy mad whirl of big-city life that was like a shot of pure adrenaline into the blood-stream.

And the people!

Elegant women who had stepped straight out of a *Vogue* fashion plate, slender-hipped black dudes in soft wide hats and dazzling striped suits lounging behind the tinted windows of long limousines; old women in threadbare fur wraps; goggled-eyed tourists trying not to look battered and bewildered; poets, prophets and cretins addressing the passing parade from the gutters.

The smile of fond remembrance faded. Nobody strolled down Fifth Avenue any more. If you tried it without a respirator you could manage maybe fifty paces before collapsing facedown on the sidewalk and coughing up shreds of pink lung tissue. She'd seen that happen, and more than once. From the safety of a sealed car she'd observed a couple of down-and-outs, a man and a woman, slumped against the granite base of the Rockefeller Center: their grey, exhausted faces, eyes blood-red and streaming from the photochemical irritants in the air, lips drawn back in a ghastly snarl of abortive inhalation.

That had been during her first week in New York, almost three years ago, following her stint with Médecins Sans Frontières on the Indian sub-continent.

Every day now, several times a day, she searched her thirty-five-year-old face in the mirror for a hint of the ravages to come. Inevitably they would; everyone who stayed in the city was affected sooner or later.

Emphysema. Anoxia. Pollution: together they were a lethal combination. But that was only the start of the story. What now seemed to be happening was that a new range of viral infections and diseases was taking over from the age-old diseases such as polio, smallpox, malaria, typhoid and yellow fever, which medical science had conquered. Medical theory said that environmental changes during the past quarter century had triggered off new and mysterious strains of illness. There was Reye's syndrome, which attacked children between the ages of five and eleven, and killed nearly a third of all those who contracted the disease, cause unknown. Lyme disease gave patients skin lesions and painfully swollen joints, caused by bites from the tiny parasite *Ixodes dammini*, which until recent years had been a harmless pest. Infant botulism, a highly toxic bacterium in the form of spores found in the dust on fruit and vegetables produced a nerve poison in the intestines of babies up to a year old. There were haemorrhagic fevers, the generic term for a group of virus-related illnesses from which up to ninety per cent of the victims died.

Somehow, in ways not yet properly understood, chemical changes in the environment had created conditions that were ripe and ready for new plagues to replace the old.

Ruth's experience with the Diagnostic Research Unit in Denver had hardly been adequate to cope with this. And so far she'd received scant support in setting up a clinical investigative facility here in New York.

Although quite a lot was known about emphysema, the fusing together of the air sacs in the lungs, which reduces the total area of efficient oxygen-carbon dioxide interchange, anoxia, in effect 'an insufficient supply of oxygen to the tissues', had never until now been thought of as a chronic condition. The only people known to suffer from it in the past were airmen, mountaineers and deep-sea divers. Ruth had read up on the subject, combed through textbooks and medical journals and talked with Air Force doctors and physiologists in an effort to understand the nature of the condition. The Air Force had found in tests that if the oxygen supply was cut off and then turned back on, pilots would black out within seconds and just as quickly regain consciousness, without being aware of what had happened: they would have absolutely no knowledge of the incident, not even a blank space in their memories.

More crucially, Ruth needed to understand at what point anoxia began to have a permanent debilitating effect on the brain and the body. She had learned that the maximum altitude at which human beings could survive for long periods of time was around three miles up. At that height the pressure was forty per cent lower than at sea level. Mountain climbers had scaled higher peaks without oxygen, but by God-like coincidence Everest, at 29,141 feet – more than five miles – was the highest man could reach unaided, even had there been a higher peak to climb.

Here in Manhattan, although the air pressure was normal, the oxygen content was several points down. Ruth had calculated that it was similar to that at twelve thousand feet. Pollutants in the atmosphere reduced the body's ability to assimilate oxygen still further. Carbon monoxide, for example, displaced oxygen in the lungs by combining with the blood's haemoglobin, which normally transported oxygen to the system. Sulphur dioxide had the nasty habit of forming sulphuric acid in the lungs, which burned holes in the delicate alveoli tissue. Nitrogen oxides had much the same effect as carbon monoxide, reducing the blood's oxygen-bearing capacity.

Ruth had obtained much of her data from patients suffering these complaints, and it was the reason why she had decided to come east, to examine the problem at its most acute.

So far she had been able to pinpoint two major effects caused by pro-longed exposure to an atmosphere low in oxygen and high in pollutants. One, it accelerated the ageing process, bringing on premature senile dementia, as was evident from the physical condition and behaviour of the people admitted to Casualty. Two, it attacked the nervous system, giving rise to a number of mental abnormalities, from hallucinatory hysteria to paranoia to violent psychotic disturbance.

As to why – she didn't know. Thus far in her lone campaign she had concentrated on observing her patients and hadn't ventured into diagnostic speculation.

One thing she did know for an absolute certainty: these aberrations were the result of living in an atmosphere with a reduced oxygen content and a high pollution factor – and all the signs were that the atmosphere was getting worse.

3

At 2:17 a.m. on a bleak moonless night the XXL-class *Gagarin*, the largest and most powerful nuclear submarine ever built, surfaced in the Bering Sea, 375 miles off the coast of Kamchatka, the desolate and most easterly peninsula of the Russian Federation. The commander's map-reading was excellent; the sub came up alongside the missile destroyer USS *Nebraska*.

For twenty minutes the two vessels precariously held station on the treacherous black swell while a breeches buoy transfer was carried out. Then the darkened destroyer turned to starboard and steered a course due east, leaving the long featureless hull to slide silently into the inky depths. On one-third propulsion the *Gagarin* proceeded north-northwest at a depth of forty-five metres. In the communications room on the middle deck the radio operator tapped out an apparently random sequence of letters and numerals, which were picked up by satellite and beamed to Moscow.

At 3:00 a.m. precisely Commander Lev Yepanchin led the way to the executive stateroom, ushered the two men inside, touched the peak of his cap and departed.

The stateroom was spacious, thickly carpeted, and lined with illuminated map panels, now conspicuously blank. A long glass-topped table had been centrally positioned, with four walnut-and-leather chairs on one side, two on the opposite side. A metal water-jug and three plastic-wrapped tumblers had been placed with military exactness, a set of each on plastic trays at either end of the table. A large plain pad and two sharpened pencils were arranged in the centre of each leather-trimmed blotter, embossed with the insignia of the Russian Federation Third Fleet.

In the low-ceilinged room the only sound was the just-audible hum of the humidifier. The *Gagarin's* nuclear power plant and progress through the water were both utterly silent.

Colonel Gavril Burdovsky came forward, his stubby hand outstretched, while his three fellow officers waited in a respectful semicircle. What he lacked in height – five-feet-four in thick-soled shoes – Burdovsky made up for in girth. His dark blue tunic with its ribbons and gold-thread epaulettes strained to contain his meaty bulk. His face too was broad and smooth, the pink flesh packed tight so that what should have been wrinkles became folds, and with a thick dark moustache that did nothing to camouflage his prissy belly-button of a mouth.

That he had chosen to wear full-dress uniform seemed to the two Americans more personal vanity than a matter of military protocol. They were wearing forage caps and plain army greatcoats over zipped quilted blousons, displaying the minimum of rank designation and decoration.

Colonel Burdovsky introduced his colleagues, a blizzard of Russian names, and then stood with his hands on the place where his hips should have been and said in good though halting English, 'We will drink, yes? To keep out this dreadful Siberian cold. We will have five-star French cognac.'

Brandies were brought forth on a tray. Major Jermain Dukes, a tall slim black man with the shoulder flash of Fut/COE on his pale green tunic, glanced circumspectly at his superior as if worried that this might constitute a breach of regulations, but Colonel Malden unhesitatingly took two glasses from the tray – not the ones nearest him – and handed one to Major Dukes. After a curt salute with his glass, Malden threw the brandy down, and everyone else did likewise. No one proposed a toast.

At Burdovsky's invitation the two Americans removed their greatcoats and all six seated themselves at the table. Malden raised his finger to the Russian captain with a pad on his knee, pen poised above it.

'There will be no official transcript of these proceedings.'

He was pointing to the captain but speaking to the colonel, and after a slight shrug Burdovsky nodded and waved his flabby pink hand. The captain closed the pad and placed it on the blotter.

Malden smiled inwardly. It probably made little difference; the stateroom would be wired, just as Major Dukes was digitally wired – the metallic-thread audio pickup was woven into the green-and-gold cravat at his throat.

'We appreciate your act of good faith,' said Burdovsky, 'in permitting us to see your computer predictions. They are from your facility in Colorado, yes?'

'That's right, DELFI. As we were at pains to point out, Colonel, this material has hitherto been on the Pentagon's classified list.' Malden's pale blue eyes were fixed on Burdovsky's fat round moon of a face. He might have been observing an inanimate object. 'The material remains highly confidential, to be divulged only to senior staff officers of our respective defense departments. I trust that is clearly understood.'

Colonel Burdovsky raised his sparse eyebrows. 'Of course, of course,' he said jovially, though there was a harder glint in the slitted eyes. 'You Americans: you imagine the rest of the world is backwards. We have very advanced computers also, capable of similar calculations. The information was not entirely new to us, Colonel Malden. It is not the information itself we appreciate, you must understand, so much as the act of releasing it.'

'You're telling me you knew of our WCD strategy before we divulged it?' Malden's eyes were narrowed, his tone sceptical.

'If you are speaking of Operation Download, then of course.'

Malden smiled thinly. He had learned it was the best way to counter a thrust that had struck home. Also, it gave him time to think. 'Do you wish to review our respective defence strategies, Colonel, or shall we get closer to the ball?'

'Closer to the ball?' Burdovsky repeated with a frown. He glanced right and left at the stolid faces on either side, and then at Malden across the table. 'What is that?'

'It means shall we get down to business.' Malden turned his wrist to look at his watch. 'We have two hours and forty-one minutes. I'd like to accomplish something in the time left to us.'

Colonel Burdovsky said something in Russian and clicked his blunt fingers. The captain got up and brought a japanned box of Davidoff No. 1 cigars to the table. He put down four large glass ashtrays and felt mats, which he went to some pains to space equidistantly.

Malden refused a cigar, but Burdovsky selected one for himself and accepted a light from the captain. He smoked the fat cigar through pursed lips, as a schoolboy might puff at his first cigarette. 'Please,' he waved, expansive now. 'Let us get closer to the ball.'

Malden said, 'Major Dukes is scientific liaison officer attached to Fut/ COE. He has a doctorate in climatology. I take it you have a scientific officer present?'

Burdovsky gestured with the cigar to the two men on his left. 'Major Ivolgin and Lieutenant-Colonel Salazkin. Both are members of the Academy of Sciences. I think that between us' – he drew on the cigar and released a curling blue ball of smoke – 'we shall understand whatever you have to say.'

Malden leaned forward, his nicely shaped hands clasped together on the blotter. He began to speak in a flat, clipped voice, having rehearsed until word-perfect.

4

Both their countries faced a new threat. In the last ten years an urgent factor had arisen. Even the most cautious scientists agreed that man's activities had altered the natural dynamic forces that powered the biosphere.

Although the causes of this were complex, the principal effect was a substantial reduction in the amount of oxygen produced by photosynthesis in the oceans. The most up-to-date estimates showed that between sixty and seventy-five per cent of phytoplankton growth had been killed off. Taking the most conservative figure, this meant that the oceans were at present supplying only forty per cent of their previous oxygen yield. Added to that, the equatorial forests which had once supplied one quarter of the earth's oxygen requirement were now virtually defunct.

The conclusions were inescapable: the remaining forty per cent supplied by the oceans was insufficient to meet current rates of consumption. Mankind was existing on the stock of oxygen presently in the atmosphere, which wasn't being replenished quickly enough.

'Our studies have shown that there isn't an adequate supply to continue to support the present world population of 9.4 billion people,' Malden concluded, his voice quiet and unemotional in the softly purring stateroom. 'Someday the oxygen will run out, and that day is soon. It is also inevitable.'

Colonel Burdovsky had been leaning back in the chair and smoking his cigar like an aristocrat. Now he turned his head sideways so that the two Americans could see the fleshy pouch that sagged from his chin to where it was trapped by the high collar of his tunic. His jowls shook as he spoke for some time with the scientists. Malden's Russian was scant and he only managed to pick out the odd word here and there: *climate, oxygen, threat.*

The rest passed him by; not that it mattered.

'Can I get you a glass of water, sir?' Major Dukes asked him, reaching out. Malden shook his head. Major Dukes took one of the tumblers and began to peel off the plastic wrapper.

'What do you think you're doing?'

'Getting myself some water, sir.'

A muscle rippled in Malden's lean cheek. 'Not unless they drink first,' he said through clenched teeth.

Major Dukes blinked and swallowed and replaced the partly unwrapped tumbler on the tray.

Colonel Burdovsky turned back. 'Our findings are in accordance with yours,' he said complacently.

Like hell they are, thought Malden.

'But there is a question I should like to ask. You say in your study that DELFI predicts fifteen to twenty years before this effect takes place – before the oxygen is finished, yes?'

'The most accurate forecast we've been able to obtain with existing data is 2045 to 2050. That's assuming the deterioration in the climate doesn't get any worse than what we've allowed for.' Malden added deliberately, 'If it does, the prediction could be ten years out – on the wrong side.'

'Ten years!' Colonel Burdovsky removed his cigar and stared. 'You say a possible miscalculation of *ten* years?'

'We've had to make certain assumptions as to the rate of decline, but there's no guarantee that the rate will stay as plotted. It could become more acute – in other words speed up – or it could level out.'

Malden was enjoying the expressions on the faces of the Russians. They had to put on the paltry show of being abreast – or even one step ahead – of their great rival. Yet he doubted whether they had an inkling of the real situation. It was rather pathetic. Take Burdovsky, for instance. No matter how much he tried to hide his feelings, acting out the charade of the man of authority and decision, the tiny eyes under the puffy lids were restless, shifting, furtive. Human beings were so predictable, even more so than the climate. They could be manipulated with ease because they were at the mercy of the supreme traitor: emotion. Malden had proved it time and time again, to his own intense satisfaction.

He said glibly, 'Major Dukes has the detailed projections if you'd care to see them, gentlemen.' Amused at the alacrity with which Lieutenant-Colonel Salazkin leaned across to take the file.

'We shall examine these later,' said Burdovsky, nodding to himself. 'No doubt they will be similar to the figures we have obtained.'

'No doubt,' Malden said without a flicker.

'Good. Now we are nearer to the ball, yes?'

'Yes.'

'Which is, Colonel . . . ?'

'Which is, Colonel, our mutual problem: some of our major American cities, especially in the southern states, are already experiencing severe depletion problems, as are other cities around the world in the tropical regions.'

'That is hardly *our* problem,' Burdovsky contradicted him. 'The vast proportion of the Soviet Union lies north of forty degrees latitude.' He spread his hands and grinned fatly. 'Our country is not affected.'

'No?' Malden said. 'Major Dukes.'

'In the region surrounding Lake Balkhash in Kazakhskaya you've had to evacuate two million people,' said Major Dukes crisply. 'In 2026 there were fifty thousand deaths attributed to atmospheric pollution. By spring of last year an area of forty-six thousand square miles had been designated as unfit for human habitation. Emergency plans were put in place for mass evacuation of the region.'

Burdovsky's chins were quivering and the other Russians were sitting as if turned to salt.

'. . . contamination in the Nizmennost region due to the indiscriminate use of chemicals reached crisis point in 2028. Evacuation was carried out over a three-month period beginning in September of that year; since then all freshwater lakes in the region have remained biologically dead. There has been total decimation of all flora and marine life. The atmospheric oxygen count is four per cent below normal and falling.'

'It's your problem too, Colonel,' Malden said, studying his finger-nails. 'Even discounting these local and relatively minor effects, which in themselves are unimportant. But we know for a fact that oxygen depletion in the equatorial belt is widening, spreading north and south. In ten years, fifteen at the most, both our countries will be largely inside the depletion belt.'

Colonel Burdovsky sucked on his cigar and blew smoke down at the blotter. 'This rests on the assumption that DELFI is correct, does it not?' He raised his eyes to catch Malden's nod. 'So tell me, what precisely is our "mutual" problem, Colonel Malden?'

'Too many people using up too much oxygen.'

Furrows appeared on Burdovsky's broad forehead as his consternation transformed into a smirk. 'So what are you proposing?' he asked with droll humour, 'that we exterminate half the world's population?'

'Not half,' Malden softly corrected him. 'Three-quarters.'

Burdovsky's hand twitched and a neat cylinder of grey ash fell to the table and disintegrated in a powdery explosion on the glass surface.

'Seven billion as a guesstimate,' Malden went on, as if discussing a golf handicap. 'We calculate that the biosphere can comfortably support about two and a half billion human beings. The combined population of the Russian Federation and the United States is around one billion – or a fraction over. So that leaves breathing space for another billion spread across the rest of the globe.' As if stating a fact that was so obvious it hardly needed mentioning, he added, 'Of course China will have to go. India too. Africa and most of Indonesia. But China is the major culprit driving oxygen depletion; already its population is nearly two billion and they're breeding like lice. In ten years, at current rates of growth, China will constitute one third of all the human beings on the planet. We can't permit that to happen, Colonel. It's self-evident.'

Major Ivolgin was staring at Malden with bulging eyes. 'Is this meant to be taken as a serious proposal by your government?' he asked.

'Serious, yes. But not from government; the plan has been formulated by the Secret Planning Group – of which Major Dukes is lead military liaison – which is part of Future Crisis Operations Executive, which is my creation within the Pentagon, and responsible solely to the Joint Chiefs of Staff.'

'The Joint Chiefs know of this proposal?' Burdovsky said incredulously.

'Yes.'

'But not your government?'

'No.'

Burdovsky placed his cigar carefully in an ashtray and looked at it for several moments. 'How can you be sure your government will grant approval of such a scheme?' He raised his eyes. 'Is it possible?'

'As of now – this minute – the answer is no. Which is why we need your cooperation.' Malden held his left hand, palm uppermost, in front of him and pressed back the forefinger. 'The depletion problem is worsening year by year. Right now both our governments are unwilling to face up to the facts of the situation. But very soon they'll have no choice.' He pressed back the index finger. 'When they *have* to face it they're going to want a solution pretty desperately. One that's quick and effective.' He pressed back the ring finger. 'That's our moment to put forward this proposal. Speaking for my government I know they'll react negatively to the idea – I can hear the whimpering of the bleeding-heart socialists and Holy-Rollers already.'

Malden pressed back the little finger. 'Then we play our trump card. We tell our government that the Russian Federation is already in the process of implementing an identical or similar scheme. You tell your government the same thing about us.'

Malden curled his right hand into a fist, which he smacked firmly into his left palm. 'That leaves both governments no way out, Colonel. The only feasible course left to them will be to reach a joint agreement, our two nations acting in unison to implement the plan. There will be *no alternative* if they wish to survive.'

'A plan which already exists. Secretly,' mused Burdovsky.

'At the military level, yes. Politically off the radar.'

'I understand now why you insisted that this meeting take place under such extreme circumstances, Colonel,' said Burdovsky with a knowing smile. 'The usual diplomatic channels would be out of the question.'

'And with zero chance of success,' Malden remarked.

Burdovsky thought for a moment. 'You realise, of course, that I can give no immediate response. Until I have reported to my superiors and the proposal has been discussed.'

'I didn't expect one,' Malden said briskly, looking at his watch.

Lieutenant-Colonel Salazkin had a question. His voice was nasal and high-pitched. 'You predict that climatic conditions will become very bad – much worse – in ten to fifteen years. If that is so, why not let depletion do the work of extermination? People will die in any case.'

'True,' Malden conceded, 'but unfortunately not fast enough or in sufficient numbers. And there's another factor to consider: in the meantime, while we're waiting for their demise, these useless billions are using up the available stock of oxygen that the rest of us needs in order to survive. The equation is very simple: us or them.'

Colonel Burdovsky was gazing at Malden as if at a rare and dangerous species of jungle animal. He said, 'I must tell you, Colonel Malden, that never in my lifetime have I heard of an idea so fantastic. To exterminate three-quarters of the human race?' He breathed gustily. 'Incredible.'

'But entirely necessary,' said Malden flatly, 'as I'm sure you'll agree.'

'How is this plan to be implemented?' asked Major Ivolgin. 'You have a method?'

'Several.' A playfully sly expression came into Malden's eyes. 'One might be to utilise our laser-weapon and killer-beam space platforms. Used on a joint basis, we can put them to some practical purpose instead of floating around up there playing catch-as-catch-can. Finally, Colonel Burdovsky, a return on all those billions of dollars and roubles invested!'

'Perhaps,' Burdovsky said cautiously. 'It requires further thought.'

'The final solution will have to be decided at a senior scientific level,' Malden went on, 'and with the utmost secrecy. To this end, Major Dukes here has come up with a code name. He suggests "Longfellow". The major is a student of poetry,' Malden added drily.

'I know of the poet Longfellow,' Burdovsky said. 'But I do not see—'

'What's the piece, Major?' Malden prompted.

Major Dukes straightened up and recited solemnly:

> 'Sail on, O Ship of State!
> Sail on, O Union, strong and great!
> Humanity with all its fears,
> With all the hopes of future years
> Is hanging breathless on thy fate!'

'From a poem entitled "The Building of the Ship",' Dukes informed them.

4

I

WASHINGTON – CHICAGO – KANSAS CITY

Everywhere they went there were questions, the same questions, over and over again.

Why hadn't Chase been more vocal about the government's broken promises in enforcing environmental legislation?

What were the Russians up to in climate-tampering?

What about the Australian Big Drought situation?

When was Midnite-Net going to move into the political arena?

What was it really like in the Deep South? The state authorities had clammed up about the Official Devastated Areas; were conditions as bad as the rumours had it?

This last question was top of the list and uppermost in most people's minds, and the mounting concern was brought home to Chase when their cab from the airport to the hotel was held up by a demonstration: a procession of several hundred people bearing placards with the slogans OKIES NOT OK HERE and KEEP KANSAS KLEAN – KILL A TEXAN TODAY.

It was in protest against the migration from the south, their cab-driver told them, which over the past fourteen months had swelled from a trickle to a flood. The Federal Resettlement Programme wasn't able to cope with the problem, so citizen militia groups had set up roadblocks along the southern state line to stop the 'illegals' spreading north.

ACROSS THE PLAINS TO NEBRASKA

There was a Midnite-Net outpost of volunteers on the shores of Lake McConaughy. Since the shift in climatic patterns the temperature for late September was an appreciable 10° C warmer than usual. Many people were taking a late vacation – boating, fishing, water-skiing, and swimming along the banks of the North Platte.

Dan couldn't get over it. Never before had he seen people bathing in inland 'fresh' water – and the fish being caught were *edible*!

They sat under a striped awning and watched him splash about, his body flashing in the sunlight. In pleasant contrast to the sultry south and muggy Washington, the climate was mild, the air clear and refreshing. Chase was wistful, seeing his son's face losing its soft boyish roundness, his features hardening and becoming more defined as the genetic template moulded them into adulthood.

What went through Cheryl's mind when she looked at the boy? Even had the miscarriage three years ago not made the possibility remote, the likelihood that she might have a child of her own as she approached forty was fast receding. She had been as good and as caring a mother to Dan since he came to live with them as it was possible to be. Leaning back in his chair and studying her profile against the glittering water, Chase still wondered if she yearned for a child of her own . . .

Cheryl turned her head, caught him watching her and stuck her tongue out.

He loved the woman.

EAST OF THE ROCKY MOUNTAINS

Over Wyoming the twelve-seater turbojet was twirled in the grand-daddy of all thunderstorms and they had to make a forced landing near a spot in the wilderness called Muddy Gap.

They sat on the single runway gazing out as hailstones as big as golf balls clanged and bounced off the wings. The pilot told them that he was quite seriously thinking of quitting. Sure, the pay was good, but three forced landings in two months were one hell of a strain on the nervous system. Besides, he had a wife, two kids and a girlfriend to consider.

BREAKFAST IN IDAHO

In the hotel coffee shop Cheryl thought Dan looked sickly. 'How are you feeling? You okay, Dan?'

He shrugged listlessly, scooping up cereal. 'I just wish we could stop somewhere for a few days.'

'I thought you wanted to see America?'

'You call this seeing it? It's just a blur. Can't we *stay* somewhere?'

Cheryl looked at Chase over her waffles and syrup. Then she said to Dan, 'We do have a lot of people to see, and to thank: groups and communities that have supported us and made donations. Your dad has meetings and interviews lined up all the way to California. It's a vacation for you, Dan, work for us.'

'Some fucking vacation.'

'Dan!' his dad said.

'Sorry.'

But Chase sympathised. To an exuberant fifteen-year-old, this continual moving from one hotel to another, rarely staying more than twenty-four hours in any one place, must feel more like just changing prison cells. But the itinerary was fixed and he couldn't alter or cancel it.

He said, 'We'll stop for a few days when we reach the coast, fair enough?'

'The Pacific?' Dan said, brightening.

Chase nodded, avoiding Cheryl's eye. The great and glorious and boundless Pacific. He prayed that it wasn't clogged up with Coke cans and dead kelp, that a few of the waves still moved.

PORTLAND, OREGON

Phone calls from out of the blue always made him suspicious; even if they came from bona fide organisations, on the face of it, such as the United Nations, Chase entertained a healthy level of paranoia. As the saying went, just because you're paranoid doesn't mean they're not out to get you. He recalled the time, a few years back, when Cheryl had taken a call from somebody purporting to be from the American Press Association. In all innocence, and to be helpful, she had given details to a stranger of Chase's travel plans, which had led to a nasty incident at JFK when a blond-haired thug hired by JEG Corp had tried to kill him. Some poor Asian kid had died instead – a stiff price to pay for stealing Chase's bag in the men's restroom.

This call came as he was about to do a lunchtime Q&A session at Annie Bloom's bookstore on Southwest Capitol Highway. He was sitting with Cheryl and Dan in an anteroom, going over his introduction with a member of the bookshop staff. Chase excused himself for a moment, moving to a quiet corner as he listened to the caller identify herself as personal assistant to Ms Ingrid Van Dorn, UN Special Rapporteur on Global Environment.

This meant nothing to him – the name or the position, but what came next was such a shock, and so unexpected, that it somehow disarmed his suspicion. Would he be on the next available flight to New York? No, she was sorry, she couldn't give reasons. She would like him to understand that the UN Special Rapporteur's office considered the matter to be urgent, and also highly confidential. On arrival in New York he was to call the number she gave him and further instructions would follow.

Was this a request, Chase wanted to know, or an order? Was he being politely asked or peremptorily summoned? The edge of sarcasm in his voice cut no ice with her. He could take it as he pleased – but be sure to be on the next available flight.

'It's gotta be important, Gavin. Don't you think? You must go.' When he looked undecided, Cheryl smiled and said, 'Leave the rest of the schedule to me. I can handle it. And here's an idea: it's Dan's birthday on Wednesday. Why not take him with you, let him visit New York as a birthday treat.'

'A final chance to see it before they close the city down, you mean,' Chase said, still in sarcastic vein. 'Some treat.'

The connecting flight to Salt Lake City left two hours later, at 3.30 p.m. Pacific time, with father and son on board. Chase was bemused, Dan ecstatic.

2

Chase was searched three times even before he got to the reception hall at the UN. When he finally made it, his ID was scrutinised by an operative behind a bulletproof glass shield while a red-capped guard stood nearby cradling a snub-nosed automatic pistol in the crook of his arm.

The operative fed the serial index into the terminal and read off the instant dossier that flashed on to the screen. Carefully he compared the two mug shots – the one on the ID with the one on the screen – then punched a button, and in seconds a facsimile photograph was spat through the slot. This he affixed to a green-bordered security pass and ran it through a magnetised coder before handing him the pass and the ID and waving Chase through the electronic barrier.

There must have been several hundred people milling about in the hall with its gigantic mosaic murals, marble columns and spotlit fountain as its centrepiece. The continual movement of feet on the marble floor was a sibilant sound that scraped at the nerves.

'Are you lost, Dr Chase?'

He swung around and looked down into the brown eyes of a woman with dark curly hair. It was years since they'd met, but he knew her at once. 'Ruth!'

They shook hands and Chase said, 'You recognised me after all this time?'

'Of course.'

'Even with this . . .' Chase tugged at his beard.

'You're not exactly unknown, are you?' Ruth Brosnan smiled. 'Best-selling author, interviews on TV, profile in *The New Yorker*.'

Foolishly he almost blushed. He couldn't get used to fame. The Gavin Chase in the media was some other famous guy, definitely not Gav Chase, the scruffy urchin with the bruised knees from Bolton, Lancashire.

He was genuinely pleased to see Ruth. 'You were working in . . . India, was it?'

'With Médecins Sans Frontières in Bangladesh.'

'Where are you now?'

'I actually live and work here.'

Chase was astonished. 'In New York?'

'Yes!' Ruth told him about Manhattan Emergency on 68th Street and her research there. 'I have just spent a frustrating and totally fruitless two hours with the medical attaché of the Chinese delegation. I heard that they'd introduced a new respiratory drug in China and I've been trying to get hold of a sample to test.' Her lips tightened. 'Oh, they're exceedingly polite – yes, madam . . . of course, madam . . . leave it to us, madam. That makes the third "positive assurance" in three months.'

'And still nothing?'

Ruth shook her head. 'You know, we send them our new stuff *and* the formulae. Clinical research shouldn't have ideological barriers! For Christ's sake, we're all living on the same planet—' She threw up her hands and tapped her heel on the marble floor. 'Okay, Ruth, take it easy. I tend to get carried away – and will be one day, literally. So what are you doing here?'

It was Chase's turn to shake his head. 'Wish I knew,' he said. 'I've been summoned by the Office of the UN Special Rapporteur on Global Environment. But beyond that . . .'

'Ingrid Van Dorn?' Ruth was obviously impressed.

'You know her?'

'I know *of* her. Powerful woman. I only wish I had your kind of clout, Gavin.' Ruth's face clouded. 'Did you hear that Stella Inchcape had died?'

'I did hear, Ruth. It was very sad – and what happened to Binch was an outrage. He was deliberately targeted in a covert operation, "Silent Witness", and made a scapegoat . . .'

His voice trailed off as he took in the bewilderment in Ruth's eyes. 'What is it?'

'Stella never received one word about him from the day he disappeared. She was never officially told anything. How do you know all that?'

'Through an intelligence analyst who blew the whistle on a DC lobbying group, the American Alliance. They went after Binch and had him arrested under the UnPatriot Act on a trumped-up charge of "subversive treason". A sick man with a bad heart, the bastards.'

'But Gavin, if you knew what had happened to him, why didn't you tell Stella? She was *desperate* for news of her husband. Why the hell didn't you tell her?'

She was staring at him now, almost accusing.

For a moment Chase couldn't meet her eyes. Then he did. 'Some of my people in the Midnite group traced his whereabouts.'

'And?'

'He was interred in Cuba.'

'*Cuba?*' Ruth looked distraught. 'You mean that filthy, diseased concentration camp?'

Chase let go a sigh. 'That's why I didn't tell her, Ruth. I *couldn't.*'

'Is he still alive?'

'I don't know.'

'How old is he?'

'Sixty-four or five. If he's survived . . .' Chase glanced at his watch. 'I'm sorry, Ruth, I have to go. When can I see you again?'

'If you're in New York for a few days why don't we have dinner one evening?' Ruth proposed.

'A few days is all I can stand, to be honest. You can meet my son, Dan. It's his birthday tomorrow – he's sixteen.' They exchanged numbers and Chase said he'd give Ruth a call as soon as he knew what his plans were.

'Better not keep the lady waiting,' Ruth Brosnan called out. 'Put in a good word for me!' and with a wave was gone in the surging tide of people.

3

It was Chase, not the lady, who was kept waiting.

He sat in an outer office on the twenty-second floor browsing through a stack of glossy UN pamphlets that ranged from famine relief in Indochina to the annual report of the International Union of Pure and Applied Physics.

Through the high narrow windows the sun was a drab orange smear, seen diffusely through the murky haze that covered the city to a height of two thousand feet. Even at this hour there was hardly any natural daylight; the lights in the offices were kept burning all day long. It was eerie, like being underwater, submerged in a viscous ocean.

When the UN Special Rapporteur did appear, emerging from her office to greet him personally, Chase recalled having seen her before, on the cover of *Time*, possibly, though she was far more striking in the flesh than as an image in a magazine. Her silvery-blonde hair was parted at the side and brushed back in a burnished curve that enhanced strong bone structure and widely spaced blue eyes. She wore six-inch heels, which with her proud bearing meant Ingrid Van Dorn was fractionally taller than Chase: altogether a stunningly impressive woman.

She led him through into a large softly lit room that was more like a luxury apartment than an office – except the windows were crisscrossed by triangular metal rods. 'In case of rocket attacks,' she explained casually. 'And there isn't much to see out there, is there? One might as well stare at a blank wall.'

Carpeted steps led down to a circular depression in which fat armchairs and two squat sofas were grouped around a low chrome-and-glass table. In the centre of the table a large ceramic sculpture posed in frozen animation.

Ingrid Van Dorn introduced Ken Prothero, Democratic Senator for Rhode Island. The senator uncoiled from an armchair, dwarfing Chase by five or six inches. Deeply tanned and beautifully dressed, Prothero had a full head of hair streaked with grey that might have been trimmed and razored not five minutes ago. Thick horn-rimmed glasses lent him an air of thoughtful academic or earnest newscaster.

A secretary appeared, poured fragrant coffee from a silver pot, and silently glided away. Whatever this was all about, it had better be worth it, Chase thought: worth breaking an itinerary planned months in advance, not to mention adding a three-thousand-mile flight. He sipped the delicious coffee and waited.

Prothero took time adjusting the crease in his trousers before crossing his long legs. As if imparting a tidbit of gossip that had reached his ears, he said, 'Would it surprise you to learn that the President, the entire administration and the Pentagon are, as we speak, making contingency plans to leave Washington and set up political and military headquarters elsewhere? Does that alarm you, Dr Chase?'

'No.'

'It doesn't surprise you? Or it doesn't alarm you?'

'It does neither. My alarm threshold is pretty high, Senator, and has been for the past twenty years. I'm surprised it's taken them so long to wake up to what's happening.'

The glance between Prothero and Ingrid Van Dorn was laden with coded information.

Prothero said, 'It's our belief that the government is abandoning its federal responsibility. Instead of facing the situation and tackling it – and being open and honest about what's really happening – they're moving their fat hides as quickly as possible to a place of safety. All they've done up to now is to declare six states Official Devastated Areas and send in the National Guard to shoot looters. As a member of the Senate, I find that reprehensible and cowardly beyond words. Both of us – Madam Van Dorn and myself – believe it is time for independent action. Above all else we need practical solutions and not empty rhetoric.'

Prothero clasped his long brown hands and rested his chin on his extended index fingers; this was the musing academic. 'You'll be familiar, Dr Chase, with the legislation we've tried to push through in recent years – and, I hardly need add, failed on nearly every count. Too many vested interests; commerce and industry closing ranks and screaming "regressive" at the tops of their voices. Anything we've managed to push through – and precious damn little it's been – is merely a sop to the environmentalists, and anyway, doesn't make one iota of difference because the government turns a blind eye to breaches of federal law and point-blank refuses to enforce it.'

Chase had been slow. Kenneth J. Prothero had been, for years, chief administrator of the EPA, the Environmental Protection Agency, before it was disbanded. He remembered Prothero had been highly active: speeches, articles, campaigning for radical change in government attitudes.

'So what happens?' Prothero said, spreading his hands. 'Everybody sees the problem as being somebody else's, and so it ends up being nobody's.'

'You tried to make it everyone's concern when you were with the EPA,' said Chase. 'It didn't come off.'

'Made me damned unpopular into the bargain,' Prothero said with feeling. 'You wouldn't believe the crank calls, the hate mail, the abuse, the threats. Anyone would think I was trying to destroy the environment, not save it.'

Chase smiled grimly. 'I know. People get the strange notion you're somehow personally to blame. If only you'd shut up the threat would go away.'

'Of course, you get all that crap too.' The eyes behind the thick lenses softened a little, as if the shared experience had forged a common bond between them. 'Well, that probably makes it easier for you to understand our feeling, Dr Chase. As concerned citizens we have to act – independently of government – and try to find a way out of this mess. We have no choice, because if *somebody* doesn't we might just as well walk out on to the street down there, take a couple of deep breaths, lie down in the gutter, and wait for the meat wagon.'

'You have a teenage son, Daniel,' said Ingrid Van Dorn. She was watching him closely. When Chase looked at her without responding, her lips twitched in a smile. 'We have investigated you in depth, Dr Chase – background, career, family, everything. We had to.'

Chase didn't respond to her smile. 'Would you mind explaining what my son has to do with this?'

'I mention him simply to make the point that the only hope of survival for future generations is if people like us are prepared to take upon ourselves the responsibility that the governments of the world have abdicated. It is *we* who must act.'

This sounded to Chase like part of a speech she had prepared for the UN General Assembly. It began to dawn on him that all this, including the informal atmosphere, had been deliberately engineered. His being here was the culmination of a long process whose aim was to achieve . . . what?

'We greatly admire the work you've been doing,' Prothero told him. 'Your book and journalism, and the Midnite-Net group you set up. However, the time for words alone is over. We need action before it's too late. Specifically, a concerted effort by a group of dedicated specialists – scientists, ecologists, engineers – and yes, even though the coinage has been debased: politicians too. People with a common goal who will do what must be done.'

'Are you planning a world revolution?' Chase said. 'Or is it something simple like overthrowing the government of the United States?'

'This isn't a joking matter,' Ingrid Van Dorn rebuked him, showing more of the Nordic iceberg that resided below the surface.

'It isn't? Then let me get this straight.' Chase pointed to each of them in turn. 'You're proposing that a group of private individuals – specialists in their own fields – should band together to halt the slide towards ecological disaster that all the world's governments are unable or unwilling to achieve. Is that it? Have I got it right?' The scepticism in his voice was thinly veiled.

Prothero nodded gravely. 'It's possible, Dr Chase. It can be done.'

'How?'

'You're the scientist, you tell us. Surely it isn't beyond the wit of man to devise the means of saving this planet from extinction? The misuse of technology has brought us to this state; therefore technology, properly applied, can rescue us. You must believe that.'

Chase had heard, and debated, this argument many times before. He said curtly, 'There's no "must" about it, senator. Maybe it can, but there's the very real possibility that it can't. It could already be too late.'

Prothero plucked at his crisp white cuffs through force of habit. 'Then we shall all perish,' he said calmly, 'if what you say is true. But I believe, quite passionately, Dr Chase, that we at least have to try. We *have* to find a solution.'

'A scientific solution.'

'Yes.'

'Without government aid.'

Prothero nodded, his long tanned face stiff and without expression.

Chase was silent. Was this any more crazy than what was already happening to the world? In the face of governmental inertia and political funk it was clear that *something* had to be done. For if nothing was done, what was the alternative? He said quietly, 'Have you the remotest idea of the cost of such an undertaking? The top line is a hundred million dollars, and I could go on adding noughts until you got dizzy. Have you considered that?'

'Funding is available.' Ingrid Van Dorn smoothed her skirt and laced her slender white fingers around her knee. 'We have obtained pledges and offers of support from wealthy individuals, trusts and organisations. Money is not the problem.'

'Then what is?'

'You're a scientist,' Prothero said, 'and you also have proven organisational ability. More important, from our point of view, you are known and respected, and you have an international standing. You could find and recruit the right people. They'll listen to you.'

'You want me to head this thing?'

They looked at him without answering.

Did this preposterous scheme have a chance of succeeding?

'You do realise why it would be a serious mistake to make this public knowledge,' Ingrid Van Dorn said. 'The United States government would not look kindly on such an independent research project on its own soil. For that reason we must proceed cautiously, and in the utmost secrecy. For obvious reasons, neither the senator nor myself can be overtly involved because of our roles as prominent public servants.'

'Very properly you raised the matter of funding,' Prothero said. 'One of the biggest items of expenditure will be a research base large enough to accommodate several hundred personnel and all the necessary facilities. Also, it will have to be isolated, hidden away somewhere. That's a pretty formidable specification,' Prothero said, though he was smiling. 'It so happens we already have such a facility, courtesy of the Defense Department.'

'They're going to rent it out by the month?' Chase said tartly.

'No, it's entirely free of charge: the Desert Range Station at Wah Wah Springs in southwestern Utah. It's part of the MX missile silo complex that was abandoned more than a decade ago when the Defense Department decided to phase out nuclear weapons—'

'—in favour of Weapons of Climate Degradation,' Chase interjected.

'Quite so. What you might not know, Dr Chase, is that the total cost of the MX missile system amounted to eighty-six billion dollars – but it was outmoded before it was even completed. They left behind workshops, maintenance bays, living quarters and plenty of room for laboratories and other facilities. What's more, the entire installation is buried under millions of tons of reinforced concrete in the middle of the Utah desert. The nearest town of any size is nearly a hundred miles away.'

'You say it was abandoned – but wouldn't they leave a small military unit behind to keep guard?'

'As a representative of a Senate committee I toured the area in 2024,' Prothero said. 'It's an empty shell. There isn't a soul there.'

Ingrid Van Dorn said, 'We've mentioned the need for secrecy, and I'm sure you appreciate the necessity. But there's another reason, one that might not have occurred to you.'

'Which is?'

'You heard no doubt of the assassination of Joan Weinert? She was head of research at the World Meteorological Organisation.'

Chase nodded.

'This is the third such murder in as many months,' Ingrid Van Dorn said. 'Every target has been someone – scientist, politician, administrator – working to improve the environment in some way. They are too well planned and executed to be the work of lone individuals. The pattern is too systematic to be random homicides.'

Neither the UN Special Rapporteur or the senator would be aware of the attempts on his own life, Chase knew, and he decided this wasn't the moment to enlighten them. He had more than theories to fuel his suspicions of who was responsible. The classified files leaked by Howard Nevison had made a direct connection between the Alliance for the Advancement of American Values and the JEG Corporation, but without evidence it was impossible to know if the AAAV and Joseph Earl Gelstrom were also behind these more recent deaths.

'You're suggesting there's an organisation of some sort behind them,' Chase said. 'Who might it be?'

'My money is on one of the intelligence agencies,' Prothero said. 'Take your pick. The US, Russia, China, Israel, Saudi Arabia – it's a wide field.'

'I could go along with that,' Chase said, 'except you've failed to provide a vital element: motive.'

'That's true, we don't have one,' Prothero conceded. 'But you and

I both know, Dr Chase, that with intelligence agencies screwball ideas are a dime a dozen – the screwier the better.'

'What you're driving at, I guess, is that anyone known to be involved in a project such as this is a prime target.'

'Yes.'

'As a former head of the EPA, your views are well known, Senator. You're already at risk.'

'As are you,' Prothero said. 'And I already take precautions.' He took off his spectacles, flicked out a snowy white monogrammed handkerchief and began to polish them. His eyes were watery, but no less piercing without the thick lenses. 'And if I were you, I'd do the same.'

'Even if I decide not to accept your proposition?'

'Even so.'

'Though one can take too many precautions in this life.' Ingrid Van Dorn's glacial blue gaze was fixed on the ceramic sculpture, yet her remark was addressed to Chase as forcefully as if she had taken hold of his lapels. 'Sometimes we have to take risks to make it worth the living. For ourselves and for our children.'

I

Beaming like a child on Christmas morning, Cheryl followed Boris Stanovnik through the pine-floored hallway and into the long sunny room that was more like a cluttered study than a living room. Bookshelves lined three entire walls and there were books scattered everywhere, some sprouting markers made out of folded typing paper. Piles of magazines, scientific and technical journals, newspapers and files of different colours were stacked on every flat surface. In a recess next to the window was a massive stripped-pine chest, reaching almost to the ceiling. In place of the usual ten drawers there must have been fifty, some quite small, others the size of shoeboxes.

'This is wonderful!' Boris hugged Cheryl to him and then held her at arm's length for a long searching scrutiny. 'Wonderful to see you! After all this time!' He beamed at her delightedly.

Shafts of sunlight made slanting pillars at the far end of the room, but even so a log fire blazed in the rough-hewn stone fireplace. Oregon in the fall could be decidedly chilly.

Cheryl smiled, trying to get her breath back after the bear hug. 'It has been a long time. Five years. Gavin was really disappointed at not being able to see you, Boris, but he was called away on urgent business.'

'As you said when we spoke yesterday. I'm so glad *you* were able to come.' Boris lifted his close-cropped grey head and called out to his wife in Russian.

Amazing how little he's changed, thought Cheryl. Still the same broad powerful physique and vigour, the same alert-eyed intelligence, and he was well into his seventies. Nina appeared, and to Cheryl it seemed the reverse had taken place. She was small and frail and she now walked with a stick. There was the pinched, harrowed look on her face that those who live constantly with pain acquire; she suffered badly with arthritis.

Cheryl expressed her sympathy, but Boris had to translate; after ten years in America his wife's English was still limited to a few phrases.

They sat cosily around the log fire drinking the strong tea that Boris had made in the samovar. Cheryl explained about their trip, and after every two or three sentences Boris would dutifully translate. He shook his head when he heard that Gavin and Dan had gone to New York.

'We know what's happening there; we watch the reports on TV. They named it now the Rotten Apple . . .' He grimaced. 'Very bad there, the East Coast, and the South. It's like a cancer, eating away the country bit by bit. Every day it creeps nearer.'

Cheryl looked towards the sunlit window. 'You seem to be all right here. The air smells good.'

'Yes, the air is mostly good and clear,' Boris agreed, sipping his tea. 'There are forests and relatively few people. On some days we see dark clouds, industrial smog, but it blows' – he pushed his large hand through the air – 'away to the ocean. Thank God.'

'Don't you miss your own country at all?' Cheryl asked.

'At certain times of the year perhaps. When all the leaves turn brown and fall like pieces of burned paper. Yes, we feel sad then.' Deep vertical creases appeared in his cheeks as he smiled. 'But it is beautiful here too! Mountains, lakes, forests. And it has one tremendous advantage over Russia.'

'Oh? What's that?'

'No Federal Russian Security Bureau. At least here we are not spied on and followed everywhere. Vida is a good place to live and work. We feel safe and protected – look, let me show you!'

He wanted her to see the unbroken range of peaks to the north and east. Their slopes were thickly wooded and dusted lightly with the first snow of the season. It looked like they formed an impregnable barrier, shutting out the rest of the world – but no barrier was impregnable to the climate.

'Mount Jefferson, South Sister, Huckleberry, Diamond Peak, Bohemia Mountain.' Boris sounded them off proudly like favourite grandchildren.

'What work are you doing?' Cheryl asked him.

Boris stood with his thumbs hooked into his belt, his chest swelling under a dark brown woollen shirt with embroidered pockets. 'I write and study and do research. I've been cataloguing the plant life along the McKenzie River, collecting specimens. There are hundreds; it's so fertile and varied.' He leaned towards her. 'Up to now I have classified one hundred and twenty-six different species.'

'I didn't know you were a botanist,' Cheryl said in surprise.

'No, I'm not, strictly speaking. I was a microbiologist. Much of my work for the Hydro-Meteorological Service was concerned with the conditions in rivers and lakes, how a change in climate might affect them and vice versa. That meant examining the soil, fauna and flora in order to understand the interaction between them and the natural water supply; my particular study was the process of eutrophication.'

'Is there any sign of eutrophication in the McKenzie River?' Cheryl asked, vaguely uneasy.

But the big Russian shook his head unhesitatingly. 'None. No trace at all.'

That was something to be thankful for. Eutrophication indicated that the biological oxygen demand of underwater plants and animal life was exceeding the water's capacity to provide it. This led eventually to stagnation – the lake or river turning into a foul-smelling swamp, which is what had happened in the Gulf of Mexico.

Regretfully, Cheryl had to refuse the invitation to stay for dinner. She had to drive back to Eugene and prepare for an early start in the morning. There were two Midnite-Net groups in the general area to visit: one at a place called Goose Lake in southern Oregon, the other across the border in California.

A soft, mellow dusk was falling as she was preparing to leave. The firelight threw dancing shadows along the crammed bookshelves as Boris went across to the large pine chest in the corner, its row upon row of brass handles winking like fireflies. He beckoned to her, and Cheryl sensed a certain reluctance or indecision, as if he couldn't make up his mind about something.

'Do you know what this is?' he asked, sliding open one of the drawers and taking out a rigid sheet of plastic. She saw that it consisted of two wafer-thin sheets pressed together and held by metal clips. Between them the stem and leaves of a plant were spread out on display, sealed from the air.

Boris switched on the desk lamp so that she could see better. Cheryl held the plastic sheet in her spread fingertips and bent forward into the light. The leaves were about two inches in length, heart-shaped, with a fine tracery of darkish-green veins.

'I'm not sure. It looks a bit like knotweed. The generic species *Polygonum convolvulus* is very similar to this, only much smaller, about one third this size.' Cheryl looked up. 'What is it?'

'Right first time: *Polygonum convolvulus*,' Boris said.

'You mean it *is* knotweed?' Cheryl found herself gazing at the embroidered breast pocket of his shirt. Tiny pink hearts on twined green stems. 'You actually found this along the McKenzie River?'

'Also many other species that are three, four, even five times bigger than normal.'

Boris took the plastic sheet from her fingers. Its surface caught the reflected glare of lamplight, illuminating his face from below and giving him the appearance of a giant in a fairy tale. He carefully replaced it and slid the drawer shut. Cheryl was reminded of Jack, with a rampant *Polygonum convolvulus* beanstalk leading up to the giant's lair. The difference was: this was no fairy tale.

2

They had seen all the sights and visited the tourist attractions: the Statue of Liberty inside its transparent protective dome, like an ornate green cake under a glass cover; the Empire State Building, where they'd hired masks and strolled blindly around the now purposeless observation deck on the one hundred and second floor; Central Park with its hellish landscape of stunted trees, grey grass, searchlight towers and graffiti scrawled in blood on Wollman Rink; the eternal guitar-shaped holographic flame of the John Lennon Memorial on the Upper West

Side; Checkpoint X, which marked the entrance into the electrified perimeter fence surrounding Harlem; the shattered stump of the seventy-storey GE skyscraper at the Rockefeller Center near Times Square, whose top thirty floors had burned out and collapsed in the week-long hostage stand-off in 2027.

Dan was eager to see everything, although Chase suspected this was more so that he could boast afterward of having been to New York, which was considered daring and dangerous, like penetrating a forbidden zone, a dark continent, than enjoying the experience itself.

They dined with Ruth at a small restaurant on Third Avenue. All that day Dan had been chirpy and in high spirits, and so the change in him was apparent straightaway. He hardly touched his *ragout de boeuf bourguignon*. He looked pale and said he felt sick. Chase wanted to get him to the hospital, but Ruth advised against it; hospitals in New York were no places for sick people. Her apartment was three blocks away and they managed to get him there in a sealed cab. In the bathroom he heaved up some stringy black bile and complained of dizziness and buzzing in the ears. Ruth examined him and said he had a touch of 'Manhattan Lung', prescribed aspirin and rest, and insisted on putting him in her own bed.

Chase felt guilty at this imposition, though Ruth told him she had two days off owed to her and could catch up on her sleep later.

'It isn't anything serious?' he asked when they had tucked Dan in and closed the bedroom door.

'Most out-of-towners feel the effects: streaming eyes, nausea, dizziness and so forth. You can't help breathing in some of the foul stuff that passes for air in this city.' Ruth poured out two glasses of bourbon. 'Were you outside for any length of time today?'

'A few minutes, here and there, that's all, between cars and enclosures. What did you call it? "Manhattan Lung"?'

'Some people are more sensitive than others. Don't worry, Gavin, he'll be fine in the morning. He's young and strong.' She gave him a reassuring smile and sat back in the chunky armchair. The living room was furnished with period pieces and bric-à-brac in the style known as mid-century kitsch. There was a half-moon coffee table inlaid with tiles of antique cars. The three-pronged tubular light fitting had inverted pink plastic shades. In an alcove were a circular dining table and four chairs in matching blond wood.

'Why does anyone stay in New York?' Chase asked with genuine consternation. 'Why do you, for God's sake?'

'I guess people just come to accept things. Conditions get worse year by year and you learn to live with them.' The pallor of Ruth's face was softened by its frame of dark curly hair. She wore a simple grey silk blouse and a dark blue skirt of fine weave. 'Think of the really terrible conditions people have endured in the past. New York isn't the first city to choke its inhabitants to death. It's been going on for centuries.'

'Is it safe for Dan to travel? The sooner I get him out of this place, the better.'

'Let him rest for a couple of days, then he should be okay. Are you ready to leave right away? What about your business at the UN?'

'Good question.' Chase sipped his drink. 'Wish I knew the answer.'

Chase told her about his meeting with Ingrid Van Dorn and the Senator for Rhode Island. As he spoke he could see Ruth's interest quickening, and soon she was absorbed as Chase outlined the proposal. At one point he said, 'Maybe I shouldn't be telling you any of this, Ruth.'

'Were you sworn to secrecy?'

'Not in so many words – but knowing about it could be dangerous if the wrong people get to hear of it. And the last thing I want is to jeopardise your safety.'

'I won't breathe a word to anyone – and I wouldn't have anyway – without your permission. To be honest, Gavin, I don't see the dilemma. If it's technically feasible, then you must go ahead. If not your duty, it's a heaven-sent opportunity.'

'But Ruth, what you've just said – that *is* the dilemma.'

'What did I say?'

'Is it even possible? I don't know, and I doubt anyone does. Take any ten scientists and you'll get three who'll say yes, three who'll say no, and the other four wouldn't care to express an opinion either way.'

'Then suppose we just leave the environment alone,' Ruth said. 'Does it have the ability to restore the natural balance without our interference? Perhaps in a few years' time the biosphere will revert back to normal.'

'There's no such thing as a "normal" biosphere,' Chase said. When she looked confused he said, 'Life creates the conditions for its own existence. Before life appeared on Earth, the planet was incapable of supporting life. What's happened now is that we've come full circle and the converse is true: life has created the conditions for its own extinction.'

'You mean conditions will get steadily worse and there's nothing we can do about them?'

Chase said wearily, 'I truly don't know. Nature has no ethics; it's not bound by moral considerations. It simply obeys the fundamental laws of cause and effect, of supply and demand. It doesn't concern itself with whether conditions are suitable for life or not. Species are created and become extinct while nature looks on indifferently.'

'Ingrid Van Dorn and the senator seem to think we can alter things positively.'

'They're not scientists. It's hope, blind faith, maybe wishful thinking, nothing more.'

Ruth watched him closely. 'And do you think it's futile?'

'If I thought it was futile there would be no dilemma, would there? I wouldn't need to think twice.' Chase pressed his fingertips to his eyelids, rubbing the tiredness away. He looked up at her. 'You think I'm making excuses?'

'Yes, I do,' Ruth said bluntly.

'But why me, for Christ's sake? I'm not a climatologist or an atmospheric physicist—'

'You're a scientist! Gavin, one minute you're saying that none of the so-called experts can agree; the next you're complaining you're not up to the task. But just think what someone with your reputation and influence could achieve! That's why they approached *you* – you must see that.'

A trio of sirens wailed somewhere in the city, sounding like birds crying mournfully in the wilderness.

Ruth went to the kitchen to make a pot of coffee. She came back and knelt down next to the half-moon table to pour. Chase saw that it was nearly midnight.

'What shall I do about Sleeping Beauty in there?' he asked.

'Best leave Dan where he is and come back for him in the morning. He'll be fine, I'm sure. I've got a couch in my study. When do you have to give them your answer?' Ruth asked, handing him his coffee.

'Give who—?' Chase was confused for a moment. 'Oh – before I leave town. In a couple of days.'

'That isn't much time for such a big decision.'

'You're right, it isn't,' Chase agreed. 'But it's enough, because I've already made it.'

He was rewarded with Ruth's wide smile.

3

A man of medium height with a slight paunch, a reddish beard and a bald head fringed by curly gingerish hair strode straight up to him through the crowd and stuck out his hand. 'What-ho, Fortescue, old bean!'

Chase stared at him in utter astonishment. 'Carruthers!' Then he burst out involuntarily, 'What the fuck are you doing here?'

'I'm the welcoming committee,' said Nick Power with a grin, pumping his hand. 'Didn't Gene mention I worked in his department? Gav, it's great to see you again!'

Nick chattered on as they walked across the concourse of the Princeton monorail terminal and down the steps into a large glass-enclosed parking lot. A winking LED display cautioned ELECTRIC VEHICLES ONLY!

'Came over in '26 and spent a year with a government outfit in Washington. Bloody awful! Then I applied for a post at the Geophysical Fluid Dynamics Lab, been here ever since. Gene didn't know you and I knew each other, but then I saw the TV thing you did together with the gorgeous Claudia Kane.' Nick Power became lost in wistful reverie.

Chase said, 'There's more Claudia Kane left behind in the make-up department than there is your actual Claudia Kane.'

'Don't spoil a middle-aged man's fantasy, Gav, you swine. So anyway, when Gene said you were coming down I volunteered to meet you. You're looking well, you old bastard! Too bloody well!'

Chase stashed his carryall and laptop case on the rear seat of the small battery-powered runabout. 'What about you, you old lech?'

'I object to that! *Old?*'

'Still working in glaciology?'

'Yep, and fifty other things,' Nick replied cheerfully, climbing behind the wheel. 'We all pitch in here. Climatology, meteorology, palaeontology, Scientology—' He let out a bark of amusement at Chase's reaction. 'Joke.' He swung the little car around in a tight circle and coasted down the tunnel ramp to the street. 'How long are you staying?'

'I have to get back to New York later today. My son's there and I want to get him away as soon as I can.'

'That's a pity. If you were staying you could have met Jen, my wife.' Nick's face contorted hideously. 'Can you believe it – me marrying somebody called "Jennifer"? Shit and Corruption.'

Chase smiled to himself. He hadn't heard the phrase *Shit and Corruption* for fifteen years, not since he and Nick were at Halley Bay together.

'You seem to be thriving on it,' Chase said. He grinned, genuinely pleased to have run across Nick after all this time. Perhaps it was a good omen.

'Jen's the one who's thriving, I'm losing my hair,' Nick said, patting the top of his head. 'But she's a truly *wunnerful* person and we have a *wunnerful* daughter.'

'Still smoking the Moroccan Blue?'

Nick sighed. 'It was Lebanese Red, you dildo!' He pursed his lips in misty remembrance. 'Wow, that was prime stuff, m'boy. You can't get hold of natural health-giving weed like that nowadays; it's all chemical shit now. After a couple of trips you start to smell like a photographer's rubber apron.'

Chase laughed, his spirits lifting. After New York's doom and gloom, Nick's company was as bracing as a breath of pure clean air.

The white modular construction of the Geophysical Fluid Dynamics Laboratory reminded Chase of a cubist painting. Nick showed his pass and they went up to Gene Lucas' office on the second floor. Like the man himself, it was neat and tidy to the point of prim fastidiousness. A blackboard took up all of one wall. Even the equations were written in a carefully rounded hand in chalk of different colours. Diagrams, flow charts and memoranda were pinned in precise patterns to the corkboards along two walls. The window looked out on to a deserted campus, wraiths of mist draping the trees.

The Peterson pipe Gene Lucas was smoking looked several sizes too big for him. Chase hadn't seen anyone smoking in a public building – much less a pipe – in years. Such was his revered status, Chase surmised, that no one dared complain.

Lucas rose to greet him; he was just a fraction over five feet tall, so that wasn't saying much. They shook hands as Chase said, 'I really appreciate your finding the time to see me, Professor, and at such short notice.'

'More than glad to, Gavin. And what's this "professor" bullshit?' He laid the pipe in a glass ashtray and pointed to his laptop on the corner of the desk. 'Either of you caught this today?'

The three of them stood in a group, leaning towards the screen.

What they were seeing looked like a disaster movie: blurred, jumbled footage of stupendous crashing waves and palm trees bending at forty-five degrees, cars and trucks disappearing under a vertical wall of water. Another shot showed a Delta passenger aircraft about to land on what appeared to be a lake, but was in fact an airport runway; the plane veered away at the last moment.

'What's going on?' Nick wondered, puzzled. 'Hurricane season isn't till the end of the year . . .'

Gene Lucas folded his arms, his expression grim. 'I've been watching it for the past half hour.'

'Where is this?' Chase asked.

'A storm front off the coast of Venezuela, heading towards the Caribbean. These are live pictures from Barbados and Trinidad.'

'Jesus wept,' Nick muttered. 'Looks bad.'

To Chase, what he was seeing, and at this precise moment in time, seemed like an omen of the most prescient, chilling kind. It made his trip to Princeton to see Gene Lucas even more urgent and vital – if that were possible. Now that he'd made up his mind to head the project, he was anxious to get started – as if a few hours and days would make a difference, ultimately, to something that should have been done decades ago.

In less than twenty minutes he had told Professor Lucas and Nick Power as much as he knew, though as he spoke, it seemed to be precious damn little.

'Who's funding this grandiose enterprise?' Nick enquired, picking idly at a loose thread in his striped pullover. 'The estate of Howard Hughes?'

'They've assured me – Van Dorn and Prothero, that is – they can raise the money,' Chase said, stroking his beard. He looked across the desk to where Gene Lucas, pipe clenched between his teeth, was leaning back in an aluminium chair with a padded headrest. 'I told them straight off that this was a multi-million-dollar undertaking and it didn't faze them one bit. I suppose there are wealthy people around who feel their money isn't much use if there isn't a world to spend it in.'

Lucas wafted smoke away. 'This is quite some project you've landed yourself, Gavin,' he said. 'One helluva job.'

Chase opened his briefcase and took out three photocopied sheets stapled together. He passed them across the desk. 'That's why I'm here, Gene. This is a list of the people I intend to approach. Seventy-four names.' He had another thought, asked for the sheets back and added another name. 'Seventy-five.' To Nick Power he said, 'Sorry about that. If I'd known you were here I'd have put you top of the list.'

Nick groaned. 'Please, Gav, just forget we ever knew each other. That kind of favour I can do without.'

Lucas glanced up. 'You've put Frank Hanamura down.'

'He's one of the top people in his field. That electrolysis idea of his might be the answer – or one of them.'

Lucas went back to the list with a noncommittal grunt. He didn't look impressed. After a few moments he laid it aside. 'You want my input, Gavin? Your nucleus of scientists sounds all right: atmospheric physicists, oceanographers, climatologists, all good research people, strong on theory. But you're going to need a lot of practical help too:

engineers, lab technicians, computer staff, people with hands-on, can-do skills. The backup is essential if this project isn't just going to turn into a seminar of abstract theories that never get off the blackboard. It's workable solutions you want, right?'

'If they don't work, forget it,' Chase said. 'Any names you feel ought to be on the list, go ahead and put them down, Gene. That's the reason I'm here.'

Lucas nodded. 'Leave it with me and I'll get back to you. Where are you planning to be, the next couple of weeks?'

'I spoke to Prothero yesterday and he wants me to look at the Desert Range site at Wah Wah Springs. First I intend to get my son away from New York and then I'll fly out there.'

Nick's face lit up. 'Hey, listen now. He can stay at our place. It's out of town, in the country, and the air is clean by New York standards. Send him to us, Gav. Jen and my daughter Jo will like that.'

Chase thanked him and turned to Lucas. 'There's something else you could help me with: a second opinion on the Desert Range site. If it's suitable, Prothero believes we can take it over without the Defense Department being any the wiser. Anyone you could spare for a day or two?'

'Oh sure, we can fix that,' Lucas said promptly. 'Can't we, Nick?'

Nick Power gave Lucas the steely eye, then his head drooped back and he stared disconsolately at the ceiling. 'I *knew* it wasn't going to be my day when I couldn't find the Mars Explorer kit in the cornflakes packet this morning at breakfast.' He sighed heavily. 'I guess everyone ought to visit Utah once before they die. Then they'll know the difference.'

Chase reached out and gripped Nick's shoulder. 'That's the stuff, Carruthers! The old team back together again. Bet you're glad I came, aren't you?'

'Absolutely, Fortescue, old bean. Over the fucking moon.'

In the act of rekindling his pipe, Lucas looked at Chase over the curling blue bowl. 'If I'm being up front about this, Gavin, you're not sounding like you're exactly brimming over with enthusiasm yourself. Do you honestly believe there's a chance of this working?'

'Honestly, Gene, I don't know. What's your guess?'

Lucas blew smoke through a small tight smile. 'I'd say it has the ghost of a chance. Which is a helluva lot better than no chance at all.'

Chase said soberly, 'I can't get rid of the nasty feeling we're thirty years too late. We should've been doing this at the turn of the millennium.'

Gene Lucas looked towards the muted newscast, now showing a satellite image of a huge ominous swirl of writhing dark clouds, like a vicious, tightening spiral. 'Damn pity we didn't,' he said. He wasn't smiling any more.

4

The storm surges on the satellite display had been predicted to happen by 2036 at the latest, so they were six years early, and their ferocity and devastating impact seriously underestimated. Rising sea levels had been expected along the Eastern Seaboard of the US and the states bordering the Gulf of Mexico, somewhere conservatively between seven feet and a frankly ridiculous fifteen feet. It was believed that upwards of five million people would be displaced. Many of these predictions had been thought exaggerated at the time, or blatant scaremongering.

Instead, Florida was hit by a triple whammy. Already the most vulnerable state in the country thanks to its low-lying terrain, the erosion caused by encroaching acidic seawater had dissolved the limestone sub-structure, resulting in total, catastrophic collapse. Florida fell in on itself.

That was whammy number one.

This combined with the rising sea level brought about the submerging of the state from the Atlantic Seaboard to the Gulf, on a line roughly from Boca Raton to Fort Myers. Everything below Lake Okeechobee was now permanently underwater. In the few months since Chase, Cheryl and Dan had visited Miami Beach, breathing compressed air from tanks on their backs, the spit of land they had walked on had been reclaimed by the ocean.

That was whammy number two.

The third part of the deadly equation hadn't been foreseen. When rising global temperatures exceeded 4° C (as they had by late 2029), it set in motion what was known to scientists as the 'Tipping Point': from now on, every severe climatic event would reinforce the next event, which would become even more severe; this in turn would speed up and deepen the next climatic event, like an icy slide down a mountain that gets steeper and steeper, faster and faster, until it becomes unstoppable. This part the scientists *had* foreseen.

Then the third whammy came along, straight out of left field: a complete shock to the system.

The 4° C rise in temperature speeding up the melting of the Western Antarctic Ice Shelf had also been expected. What *hadn't* been was that this sudden surge of extra heat would interfere with the deep ocean currents welling up from the Antarctic and pushing north along the eastern coast of South America. These acted as the planet's thermostat, keeping the atmosphere and oceans in thermal equilibrium; now they'd been disturbed and the equilibrium upset, driving the global weather system into a frenzy and triggering storms and double cyclone-strength winds of 250 miles per hour, sweeping up past Venezuela and across the Caribbean:

Welcome to whammy number three.

The chain of tiny islands, known as the Lesser Antilles, stretching from Trinidad to Puerto Rico, and then onwards to Haiti and Jamaica, never stood a chance. Hurricane force winds blasted everything in their path and blew it all away; next came tidal waves, whipped up by the winds, which deluged the islands and finished off the job. The 'frankly ridiculous fifteen feet' rise had been surpassed by the unprecedented storm surges. Nothing could withstand their sheer overwhelming power, and nothing did.

Next in line and directly in the path of destruction was Cuba.

The island has a rocky backbone, the Sierra Maestra, rising to a height of 6000 feet, which was the only visible feature remaining above the waves after the storm had passed on. This superior elevation was of no help to the 9.2 million prisoners incarcerated in the Cuba Prime Detention Facility: all the camps were purposely sited and built in the fetid lowlands, on the edges of swamps and forests. Some of the camps were below sea level. For the inmates, trapped inside the razor-wire enclosures, there was no escape. The winds blew their flimsy shelters to smithereens and the waters engulfed them.

Within twenty-four hours, it was over and done with. There were no survivors.

6

I

From nine thousand feet Starbuck Island resembled a pink coral necklace on plush blue velvet. The pilot of the USAF K-113 *Aurora* strato-shuttle banked to starboard and raised the lead-lined shutters from the tiny saucer-size windows to give his passengers their first view.

'One-third power and full flaps,' he rapped out to the flight engineer. 'Check yaw and drift stabilisation.'

The engineer acknowledged, throwing levers, watching gauges.

The stubby silver craft with its embryonic wings and steeply raked tail plane was ungainly at this height and speed, dominated as it was by the huge rocket engines that protruded aft from the rectangular fuselage like the gaping maw of a deep-sea predator.

The *Aurora* had arced across the Pacific at a height of one hundred twenty thousand feet. Because exposure to ultraviolet and cosmic radiation at this altitude could cause skin cancer and total hair loss, the entire craft was encased in lead shielding. The passengers saw daylight only when the shutters were raised below ten thousand feet.

Strapped into a padded reclining seat, Lieutenant Cy Sprote stared rigidly at the curved ceiling panel directly above him. The muscles on his thin freckled neck were corded and covered in perspiration. He'd never liked flying, but he absolutely hated rocket-booster flights. The high g-forces on lift-off and re-entry made him fear he might lose control of his bodily functions.

In the seat next to his, nearest the window, Major Jermain Dukes was leaning forward against the straps, straining to see outside, a hand cupped to his eyes to reduce glare. Nothing got to him, thought Sprote. Made out of rock.

Yet if Dukes was rock, what in hell was Colonel Malden in the seat in front? He had spent the two-and-a-half-hour six-thousand-mile flight with an electronic slate-file across his knees. Sprote guessed that for him it was simply the quickest way of getting from A to B over long distances, end of story.

Sprote instinctively gripped the arms of his seat as the pitch of the engines deepened. The rapid deceleration was making his eyeballs bulge. Luckily for him, the pilot was experienced and brought the *Aurora* in on the first pass, lining her up dead-centre on the twelve-thousand-foot floating concrete runway anchored two miles off the island. Fifteen minutes later the three Fut/COE officers could taste salt on their lips as the launch cut a creamy swathe through the glittering blue ocean.

'I never expected this!' Sprote shouted. The warm wind snatched his words away. He gestured all around with one hand, holding on to his peaked cap with the other.

'The oxygen level is only one per cent below normal in this area,' Malden called back. He pointed. 'Two thousand miles southwest of here, on the other side of the Kermadec Trench, it's solid weed. New Zealand is completely surrounded. They'll have to evacuate soon.'

Cy Sprote nodded. Marine ecology wasn't his subject.

From the jetty they were taken to Zone Two, the bacteriological research centre where the director, Dr Jeremiah Rolsom, and members of his staff were waiting to greet them. Everyone donned protective white suits and technicians adjusted the air supply to the bulky fishbowl helmets. Then the party lumbered out like spacemen on their tour of the sterile bays.

'The problem is twofold,' Rolsom explained over the intercom. 'Deployment and containment. If that sounds contradictory, that's because it is. TCDD has extreme toxicity and we don't want to spread the stuff around indiscriminately. Somehow we've got to keep it away from the protected territories, namely the United States, Russia, and parts of Europe. So you'll understand it's a matter of precise selectivity.'

Sprote understood very well indeed. Tetrachlorodibenzo-para-dioxin was the most virulent poison known to man. Spray Africa from cruise missiles, for example, and there was the danger of wiping out the populations of Spain, Portugal and most of southern Europe as well.

The party moved on to the animal experimentation area. Rabbits, guinea pigs and hamsters were drinking water laced with a few parts per million of TCDD. Contaminating the water supply held promise, the director informed them. Minute concentrations caused changes in the blood cells and enzymes and led to liver damage, cancer and severe foetal deformities.

Lloyd Malden paused by a row of cages and fondled one of the rabbits. Even though the colonel was wearing thick rubber gloves, Sprote couldn't repress a shudder. He turned in the cumbersome suit and looked at Major Dukes, but the dark face in the fishbowl was impassive, quite unperturbed.

It was irrational for him to react in this way, Sprote knew. Safety precautions on Starbuck were rigorous and strictly enforced. He could only put it down to his experience in genetics, which made him edgy.

Colonel Malden had a question: why not employ the techniques already developed for Operation Download? 'We had some very effective methods of deploying 2,4,5-T, which contains dioxin,' he said to Rolsom. The only difference here, as I see it, is that we need to disseminate TCDD in its pure form rather than as part of a weaker mix. Am I right?'

'You're right, Colonel, but that difference is crucial. In the past we wanted to achieve maximum spread and penetration in the shortest time possible.' Rolsom pushed through a pair of rubber doors and held one aside for the others to follow. 'But now we have to set precise limits and *know* we can confine the spread of TCDD within them. If we don't, it's going to get out of hand and kill our people too.'

'Including the Russians,' said Major Dukes.

'Yes.'

'Maybe that can't be helped anyway.' Malden's laconic remark seemed to hold a number of veiled meanings.

In the next bay the party stood on a yellow gantry while Rolsom went on about 'contaminatory media', which Sprote understood to mean air, water and food.

'Drop a litre of TCDD in the Mumbai water system and we can

guarantee a wipeout of eighty to eighty-five per cent of the population within a fifteen-mile radius. Unfortunately the rest of the city-dwellers drink collected rainwater. With food we can spray grain crops and rice fields, but again, we can't be certain of total wipeout. There's the question of toxic run-off into the oceans too, which could spread the contaminant globally. However . . .'

Rolsom beckoned and the group clustered around an angled observation panel. Inside the garishly lit chamber was a family of chimpanzees, two adults and five offspring. All were slumped or sprawled, eyes dull, patches of fur missing, the flesh raw underneath. Some of their fingernails had dropped off.

The director pointed out one of the small males, marked with a circle of red dye on its back. 'That's Chappaquiddick. We injected him with a ten-ppm solution about a week ago. Look closely and you'll see that he's gone blind. But more interesting, from our point of view, he's transmitted it to the others. Now they're all starting to show symptoms.'

Sprote was surprised. 'I didn't know genetic damage caused by TCDD was contagious.'

'In the normal course of events it isn't,' Rolsom replied. 'All previous outbreaks, from Seveso onwards, were air- or waterborne.' A quiet note of pride crept into his voice. 'One of our toxicologists injected hamsters to test for its effect on enzymes. Purely by accident he discovered that above a certain concentration – roughly seven parts per million – the disease is transferable by means of infected bacteria, depending, that is, on a specific behavioural pattern. Can you guess what?' he asked, turning to them.

Nobody could.

Rolsom pursed his thick lips and over the intercom came a metallic kissing sound. 'Hamsters and chimps are both very affectionate creatures. They kiss and cuddle a lot. And that's how the disease is transmitted.'

Rolsom wore a triumphant grin, like a conjurer pulling a rabbit out of a hat.

'Animal carriers,' Colonel Malden mused. 'Deployment and containment in one neat simple package.'

'Somebody here gave it the name of the "Kissing Plague",' said Rolsom, still grinning. 'We've hopes for humans too.'

'You've tried it on humans?' Malden asked.

'Not yet, but the physiology of chimps and humans is very similar – their DNA is ninety-nine per cent the same.' Rolsom winked at them through the fishbowl. 'And humans also kiss a lot.'

2

After lunch they were shown the special area known as Zone Four on the far side of the lagoon. The laboratories and medical wards were outwardly unimpressive: an untidy jumble of single- and two-storey white stucco buildings surrounded by a double perimeter electrified fence. The only odd thing about it, for a research establishment, was that the windows were very small and barred, like those of a prison.

On the short ride across the lagoon Rolsom jokingly remarked that the electrified fence wasn't to keep intruders out; it was to keep the patients in. If any of them escaped and managed to interbreed, Starbuck might become – in his phrase – 'an island of freaks.'

Even with his experience in genetic engineering Sprote had never seen anything like it. The director hadn't been joking after all; it really was like a fairground freak show.

First they were shown the anoxia and pollution victims, grey shrivelled wrecks in oxygen tents living on borrowed time. In answer to Sprote's enquiry, Rolsom said, 'We use these to study the effects on body tissue resulting from drastic oxygen depletion. Very little medical research has been done on the subject till recently. We also need them as guinea pigs to find out if TCDD can be transferred as effectively in humans as in chimps. We'll be starting on that in about a month from now.'

'What do you intend to do?' asked Major Dukes sardonically. 'Force them to kiss one another?'

Rolsom smiled and shook his head. 'You'd be surprised – or maybe you wouldn't – at the strength and persistence of the human sexual impulse. Even in cases like these.' He nodded down the wards at the rows of oxygen tents. 'Perhaps you've noticed that the wards are mixed. At night we turn out the lights and let them get on with it.'

He led the way down the central aisle, the muted hiss and rumble of oxygen being piped into the tents the only sound. It was like a mortuary, keeping alive the undead. A technician in a white smock was injecting an old man. The party stopped to observe.

'New arrival,' Rolsom said, after glancing at the chart. 'We're pepping him up a bit – he's no good to us dead. It's a hormone extraction that dramatically improves their condition, for a short time, at least. After a couple of months they have a relapse.'

'What happens then?' Sprote asked.

Rolsom looked at him, puzzled, as if it were a trick question. 'They die,' he said. He leaned over the rail at the foot of the bed, raising his voice. 'How are you feeling today, Mr Walsh? Not a thing to worry about. You're in good hands.'

The old man gazed up at them dully with brown watery eyes. His face was the same colour as the pillow, except that his lips were purple.

As they were moving away Sprote said, 'Where do these people come from?'

'You mean how do we get hold of them?' Rolsom said. 'Our main source of supply is the Pryce-Darc Clinic in Maryland. As you probably know it's funded and administered by Fut/COE through an intermediary organisation. In effect, the clinic is a staging post. They send us anoxia and pollution cases referred to them by hospitals.'

'They come here willingly?'

'Sure.' Rolsom held the door into the corridor open and caught Malden's eye as if the two of them shared a private joke. 'The patients are told they've been fortunate to be selected for special treatment – very expensive treatment – which is free of charge. Naturally they're only too happy to participate. They think Starbuck is a highly advanced medical research unit with miracle cures galore.' He chuckled gruffly. 'Once we get them here it's too late to change their minds.'

Major Dukes said, 'How many of them will you inject with TCDD?'

They were approaching a large riveted-iron sliding door with a red M in a white circle on it.

'We intend to isolate six to begin with, three males, three females. We'll inject just one of them and see how quickly it spreads. What we're really hoping for is a chain reaction: a male infects a female and carries on infecting other females, while the females infect the other males. We also want to find out whether males or females make the best carriers.' They were climbing concrete steps now, whitewashed walls on all sides.

'You know,' Rolsom added, as if anxious that the full implication of this shouldn't escape them, 'in quite a short space of time it ought to be possible to infect a city of twenty million people, starting off with just a handful of carriers.'

'I like the sound of it.' Malden patted the director's arm. 'I think you're on the right track.'

Rolsom was obviously pleased by this rare praise and led on with renewed enthusiasm. Sprote followed behind Colonel Malden and Major Dukes; he couldn't help wondering how they disposed of the corpses of the infected patients. Straightforward burial would be too dangerous. Incineration seemed the best way and certainly the safest – but it was risky. If the infection were ever to break free of its quarantine and be let loose on the island . . .

This section of Zone Four – behind the iron door with the red M – reminded him of a modern and sophisticated version of Bedlam, the old Victorian lunatic asylum. Padded cells, barred windows, heavy metal doors, everything monitored and controlled by an all-seeing electronic surveillance system. Now they were entering Cy Sprote's territory, that of genetic manipulation. Sprote was a theorist; this was where the theories found practical expression.

They passed through a complicated series of checkpoints and entered a darkened control gallery in which twenty or so people sat wearing headsets, presiding from a semicircular instrumentation console over a huge bank of screens.

Sprote stood between Malden and Dukes, all three silent. The reason was all three weren't sure what they were looking at until Rolsom took them through it, screen by screen. These were the so-called 'natural' mutants: creatures misshapen in their mothers' wombs by the genetic damage of the deteriorating environment. Many of them were so grotesquely deformed as to be incapable of movement. Others were maniacally strong and dangerously homicidal – hence the need for the high-level security and the constant electronic vigilance.

To Sprote it looked as if each screen showed a separate section of the human anatomy – as if all the screens together would make up one complete human being. It finally dawned on him what in fact he was looking at. On each screen there was a human being, though not necessarily a complete one. He stared, sickened and fascinated and frightened . . .

A body without a rib cage, lungs exposed. A smooth head with blank depressions for eyes. A trunk with four legs, two where the arms should have been. A head and torso narrowing down to a bifurcated stump. A child with liver, pancreas, kidneys and bowels growing externally. Another child (he couldn't be sure) with two tiny hands sprouting from its neck. A hairless woman with a vagina-like slit up to her navel. A skeletal figure with transparent flesh, the organs visible inside (like a medical student's anatomy model). A gargantuan head, all the features squashed into the lower left side. Hands with no thumbs and seven, eight, nine fingers. Arms and legs jointed the wrong way. Feet attached heel to heel and joined in a single limb. Bodies with both sets of sexual organs. A man (he assumed it was male) with membranes of pink translucent flesh attaching elbows to chest. A fish-like creature with bulbous eyes and what appeared to be gills on its neck. A baby without a face, with apertures in its chest and stomach for breathing and eating.

Rolsom braced his hands on the backs of two chairs, leaning forward. 'What you're seeing is natural selection at work: the human species adapting genetically to changes in the environment. Their parents have been exposed to conditions that have affected the chromosomal structure of their offspring: such extremes as solar and cosmic radiation, pollutants in the air and water, nuclear fallout, herbicidal and pesticidal contamination, carcinogenic agents in food, tobacco, vehicle exhaust, industrial waste, so on and so on.

'In recent years the declining O_2 levels have contributed significantly to the numbers and varying types of genetic mutation. The ones you see here represent the tip of the iceberg. Nature has many ways of dealing with aberrations from the norm, of course: infertility, abortions, still births.' Rolsom gestured at the screens. 'Those that survive probably account for less than fifteen per cent of the total.'

'It must be one hell of an operation just keeping them alive,' Major Dukes marvelled. He sounded awestruck.

'This control room is manned round the clock,' Rolsom said. 'We keep an audio-visual check on them and they're wired up to alert us of any primary malfunction. We do lose some,' he admitted, 'but not many.'

'What do you think?'

Malden's question caught Sprote off guard. He had to clear his throat before he could find his voice. 'I've never in my life seen anything like it,' he managed to say, which was the gospel truth.

'I'm damn sure of that,' Malden replied crisply. 'This is the only research facility of its kind in the world.' He turned to Rolsom. 'How are the breeding experiments coming along?'

'It's too soon to know, Colonel. We've taken sperm and ovum samples and at the moment we're trying – hoping – to induce conception in the laboratory. You'll appreciate that the patients here in Section M aren't capable of normal sexual activity, and in any case the females lack the equipment for childbearing. That's why we're trying for mechanical conception. But if that doesn't work out we'll go for insemination of mutant sperm using normal healthy women as incubators.'

'That's where Lieutenant Sprote should be useful,' said Malden. 'He was trained in genetics at the Front Royal Military Hospital in Virginia. He's been seconded to Fut/COE as scientific-medical liaison officer. I know he'll be happy to give what assistance he can.'

Sprote nodded rapidly in the flickering room. He was obviously expected to be agreeable. 'Yes, of course. Though I should point out, Dr Rolsom, that I was concerned mainly with the theoretical aspects of genetic engineering. This side of the coin, so to speak, is new to me. Completely. Absolutely.'

'That's what we need,' Rolsom was quick to assure him. 'We're light on theory. I'll be glad of any contribution you feel you can make, Lieutenant. Don't hesitate to pitch right in.'

'Thank you, sir. I'll do that.'

He turned his head jerkily to the bank of screens. A myriad of tiny rectangles of Frankensteinian horror reflected in his slightly bulging eyes. Over the headsets he could hear a faint mad gabble of discordant noises, like the tape of a creature in pain played backwards.

3

The dramatic shrinking of the Antarctic Ice Cap had rung serious alarm bells as far back as 2011.

Now, nineteen years later, things were warming up nicely on the West Antarctic Ice Sheet. The Rignot Effect was kicking in with a vengeance. In late April of 2030 a huge mass sheared off the Riiser-Larsen Ice Shelf – including what was left of Halley Bay Station, where Gavin Chase and Nick Power had carried out their underwater research. The base had been abandoned several years earlier; the living quarters and labs, the mess hall and R&R areas, the stairways and passages, were still there but now thirty feet below the surface, diminishing and disappearing as they were slowly crushed in the vice-like pressure.

This massive chunk of ice, containing a deep sub-stratum of permafrost several million years old, dwarfed the 2011 Pine Island breakaway. It was twice its size: forty-five miles long by thirty-three miles wide, as large as Rhode Island, the single largest free-floating iceberg the planet had ever known – more than 1,200 square miles – weighing approximately 2.9 trillion tonnes.

As with any large mass, it moved slowly and ponderously, heading northwards across the Weddell Sea towards the South Atlantic. At the start of its journey, it was travelling no more than a dozen feet every twenty-four hours. With the surrounding waters being only a degree or so above freezing, the Riiser-Larsen Calving Berg retained much of its bulk; its drifting speed would increase as it lost mass and thickness in the gradually warming currents.

And the speed would gain appreciably when it was caught up in the South Atlantic Polar Vortex and carried up the eastern coast of South America towards the much warmer waters of the Caribbean.

4

Waiting for the motor launch to take them back across the lagoon, Lieutenant Sprote was convinced he must be living in a dream. The swaying palm trees and the white sandy beaches and the little dancing waves gilded with sunlight seemed unreal, like a movie set. The actual reality, strangely enough, had been left behind in those innocuous white buildings with the rows of tiny barred windows behind the electrified fences.

He didn't seem to be here; not on Starbuck Island in the middle of the Pacific Ocean. Sprote listened numbly to Colonel Malden's voice.

'If we can develop new mutant strains . . . it will be a fantastic achievement . . .'

Which only compounded the unreality.

'. . . a new breed of human being that can survive in the most hostile environmental conditions. Something with twice the normal lung capacity and inbuilt resistance to chemical pollution.' The colonel's voice became harsher, more emphatic. 'It should be possible. It *will* be possible.'

'Starbuck Man,' said the musing voice of Major Dukes. 'Heir to the New Earth. Two hundred years from now it could be the only species left.'

Rolsom was more cautious. 'Can we be certain the Russians or the Chinese aren't working along the same lines? They could have advanced even more than we have—'

'No.' Colonel Malden refused to entertain the faintest doubt. 'The Chinese don't have the scientific expertise. The Russians are concentrating on the extermination plan.' He addressed Rolsom directly. 'That's why the work you're doing in Zone Two with TCDD is just as important as the work here in genetic manipulation. The "Longfellow" extermination plan is a vitally important element in our overall strategy. On that we cooperate *fully* with the Russians; we even invite them to look over Zone Two if necessary to demonstrate our total commitment and cooperation.'

'Zone Two.' Major Dukes' voice. 'Not Zone Four.'

'Not Zone Four,' Malden's voice repeated.

'That's our baby.' Rolsom's voice.

'So it is.' Dukes' voice. 'Literally.'

5

The Desert Range missile silo complex straddled the state line dividing Utah and Nevada. Although sited geographically in Utah, part of the labyrinthine network of tunnels actually extended across the border.

Chase and Nick Power arrived at Wah Wah Springs after a seventeen-hour journey by aircraft, bus and finally diesel-engined Jeep. As Prothero had said, the nearest towns were considerable distances away: Richfield was a hundred miles due east and Cedar City about eighty miles southwest of the complex. There were a few small settlements – Black Rock, Milford, Lund, Beryl – but none of them nearer than forty miles. Chase had to admit that it was the perfect location.

With Nick at the wheel they drove along a crumbling concrete road with weeds and sagebrush growing in the cracks and gutters. The terrain was bleak. Undulating desert scrub as far as the eye could see, the ground compacted and fissured through lack of rain. There were no signposts – no visible evidence at all, in fact, that this had once been a restricted military area.

'How much did you say the MX system cost?' asked Nick, lolling back and steering with one hand. The road went straight as an arrow into the far distance.

'Eighty billion dollars, give or take the odd billion.' Chase shaded his eyes. 'Altogether they constructed forty-four hundred silos connected by ten thousand miles of roads and two thousand miles of railway track spread across southern Nevada and southwest Utah. They planned to have two hundred missiles with nuclear warheads constantly moving on five-hundred-ton transporters. The idea behind it was to give each missile the option of twenty-two available silos. It was a crazy scheme and it never worked. They hoped to keep the Russians and Chinese guessing at which silo any one missile was at any given moment.'

'Christ, a bloody expensive permutation if you ask me,' Nick commented with a weary shake of the head.

'Bloody futile as well,' Chase said. 'By the time the system was completed and operational, it was already obsolete. You know, it cost three hundred dollars for every man, woman and child in the United States. And this' – he swept his arm out to indicate the barren landscape – 'is what they got for their money.'

'Hey, come on now,' Nick chided him. 'You're forgetting the four thousand six hundred holes in the ground. I bet the gophers were extremely grateful.'

Fifteen minutes later they passed a concrete blockhouse almost completely buried in windblown sand. Chase unfolded the army map supplied by Prothero. The main installations were marked as broken red lines, indicating that they were below ground. The blockhouse was shown as a solid black dot, with the designation GP5.

'Guard Post Five,' Chase said, putting the map away. 'Not far now. About six miles to the complex itself.'

'How many silos in this one?'

'One hundred and fourteen over a grid of two hundred square miles.'

'Hey, Gav' – Nick glanced quickly at him, struck by an uncomfortable thought – 'you don't suppose they left any missiles behind, do you?'

Chase shook his head, stern-faced. 'Oh no. Just the one I asked for.'

'Just the one . . . you fucking *what*?' Nick blew out his cheeks and let the air explode. 'You bastard.'

Six miles further on there was only a radio communications tower to be seen above ground. The antennae and microwave dish had been stripped off, the structure held by taut steel guy wires that sang in the wind. Because of the dry desert air the tower and wires were untarnished, without a speck of rust.

Finding the entrance wasn't easy. They wandered around for several minutes trying to locate it, until Chase happened to come upon a sloping gully that was partly filled with sand, rocks and sagebrush. He hardly gave it a look and almost passed on before noticing that the shallow bank of sand followed a regular descending pattern. It was a flight of steps leading down to a studded metal door that was silted three-quarters of the way up. After scooping the sand away they were at last able, with a little forceful persuasion, to slide the door open.

Chase led the way with an iodine halogen lamp into the musty passages of slabbed concrete. The bright beam showed the tunnels were strung with skeins of thick multicoloured cables secured by aluminium cladding. The cladding was brightly polished, proving that Prothero had been right about the installation: it was still in pristine, unblemished condition.

He swung the circle of light around and picked out arrows painted in varying colours where the passage branched in different directions. Beneath the arrows, in corresponding colours, they saw:

COMPLEX 88-B
RED DOCK
GREEN DOCK
BLUE DOCK
LAUNCH CONTROL
MASTER ENGINEER
ELECTRICAL STORES

The beam roved higher. 'Buggeration,' Nick said gloomily. 'Don't like the sound of that, one tiny cotton-pickin' bit.'

Above the arrows somebody had scrawled a message in chalk.

WELCOME TO THE TOMB

'You and me neither, old chap,' Chase said, swinging the lamp away and moving on.

Taking one of the wider passages they came upon three enormous freight elevators with their doors yawning wide, big enough to take a truck apiece. Further on, a wide concrete stairway with the edges of the steps painted yellow led downwards. As they descended Chase took a careful note of each turning and the number of levels; he didn't have a plan of the complex and he didn't fancy getting lost in several hundred miles of tunnels.

Three levels down and ninety feet underground they came to the launch control room. Here they found row upon row of empty metal racks and faceless consoles, the equipment and instrumentation ripped out. One panel remained intact, its fascia protected by a solidly bolted stainless-steel cover two inches thick. Nick read out the inscription.

'"Silo Door Release Mechanism".' He fingered one of the bolts. 'Pity we can't find out if it still works.'

At the bottom of the missile silo they were able to gaze up the circular shaft lined with black ceramic heat-deflector tiles to the silo dome itself, two hundred feet above them, dimly reflecting the beam of the flashlight.

Chase's ghostly voice echoed upwards. 'They had to keep the missiles at a constant $16°$ C and thirty per cent humidity. The air-conditioning plant in just one of these silos is enough for a one hundred and twenty room hotel.'

Nick said, 'And if it's radiation-proof, which it must be, it's got to be airtight as well. It could have been custom-built.'

They looked at each other, their faces bathed in the penumbra of the upturned beam, the same thought in both their minds: the silo and adjoining control rooms were a self-contained sealed enclosure. They could provide protection and life support, irrespective of the conditions outside. And there were more than a hundred such silos in this complex alone, connected by two to three hundred miles of tunnels. Desert Range was perfect.

On the way back up, pausing for breath on one of the landings, Nick said, 'Has it occurred to you that the joker who named this hole in the ground might have been a prophet as well as a cynic?'

Chase frowned at him. 'Named it?'

Nick gestured upward, his expression lugubrious. 'The Tomb.'

6

Twenty minutes later they were climbing over the sand and windblown debris that had spilled through the door. Chase switched off the lamp, squinting in the raw sunlight. A shadow rippled down the sand-covered steps. Chase stared up at the figure of a man silhouetted against the clear blue sky, his face a dark featureless blur. All that Chase could make out was spiky blond hair: recognition happened instantaneously, the time and place and circumstance of their last encounter telescoped so that it might have been yesterday. Chase's throat was parched dry. He was thirsty and he was also very afraid.

Sturges turned and disappeared from view. Nick stumbled up the shallow slope behind Chase. 'Who is that?'

A six-wheeled square-bodied hummer, painted silver, with large rectangular smoke-blue windows was parked not far away. Attached to it was a long streamlined silver trailer, rounded at both ends like a bullet. Vehicle and trailer bore an embossed motif in the shape of a golden conch shell.

Sturges stood by the open door of the trailer. He wore black shades with wraparound lenses, the sun glaring off them in splinters of light. His forehead was tanned and deeply lined, shaggy blond eyebrows peeping over the glasses.

He waited impassively, a glint of gold at his throat and wrist.

'What's going on?' Nick murmured in Chase's ear. 'I don't get it, Gav. What's happening?'

'I think we're about to find out.'

Chase walked across, past Sturges and up the three open-mesh aluminium steps into the silver-bullet trailer. Close behind, Nick gave Sturges a malevolent stare as if he might be the devil incarnate.

After the harsh desert light the interior was pitch-black, and it took several moments before they were able to discern a sheen of greenish light reflecting off curved metal. There was a row of green dials set in stainless steel casings and a panel of touch-screens showing red and black calibrated displays. It reminded Chase of a medical laboratory, or maybe an operating theatre. Taking up most of the space, right in the middle of the trailer, a coffin-shaped shell with a curved transparent cover at the end nearest them; the whole arrangement was connected by thermoplastic tubes to a coil in which cascades of bubbles were swirling.

From the apparatus came soft gurgling and swishing sounds, rhythmical and sinister.

Now accustomed to the subdued lighting, Chase and Nick could see a human form beneath the transparent cover. It appeared to be the foreshortened shape of a man. He looked ancient: bald and gaunt-cheeked, his rib cage clearly outlined in the emaciated torso.

Behind them, the door of the trailer clicked shut. Sturges unhooked a pencil microphone from the wall and thumbed the button. 'I have them, Mr Gelstrom. They're here.'

Inside the transparent shell Chase saw white skeletal fingers trembling towards a keypad; it was so positioned to allow Gelstrom to view it without lifting his head. It would have been impossible, anyway, on such a thin stalk of neck, to raise it from the foam pillow.

The fingers hovered and trembled and tapped and on a screen above the sarcophagus shell a green blip spelled out:

Is Desert Range suitable, Dr Chase?

Sturges handed the microphone to Chase. The pump gave a long, drawn-out *aaaaaahhhhh* as it evacuated the spent air.

Chase realised his jaw was aching from the clamped pressure. When he managed to speak, his voice was unnatural, strained and quivering. 'Nobody told me you were involved in this project. Or said anything about the JEG Corporation.'

The white fingers touched the keys.

My stipulation to Senator Prothero. I knew you would refuse outright: emotion over rational behaviour. But you have accepted thus far. I am funding the project personally. If you decide to go ahead I must know your verdict. Suitable or not?

The trailer was air-conditioned and yet Chase could feel rivulets of sweat between his shoulder blades. 'Yes, it's suitable.'

Good. Are you willing to accept the funding and proceed?

The pump churned and sighed *aaaaaahhhhh*.

Chase had trouble holding the microphone, which felt cold and slippery. His mind couldn't grasp any of his slippery thoughts either, which were swirling around like the bubbles in those damn gurgling tubes. Somehow the past was all mixed up with the present moment, and the unreal present with the unknown future.

When he didn't answer, Sturges said from behind him, 'Eight

months ago Mr Gelstrom suffered an attack that left him dependent on medication and this respirator lung. The condition was diagnosed as acute anoxia. It is a malignant condition and there is no cure, which Mr Gelstrom accepts. He has decided to back this project with all the resources at his disposal, personal, financial and corporate.'

Chase didn't know whether to laugh or to cry. What wonderful, rich irony that Gelstrom had been snared in a trap of his own making. The wealthy tycoon had made his billions by inflicting damage on the environment and now he was trying to buy his way out. Fifty million dollars for the promise of . . . what? Redemption? Salvation? No, make that two hundred million. No, wait – better make it five hundred million. A billion. Two billion. Ten billion. Whatever it takes. As much as you need. Just name your price.

But there was a catch, a flaw, and Chase almost felt exuberant. He was torn between triumphant anger and hysterical, gloating laughter.

'It's too late. You've made all those profits without thinking of the consequences; and the laugh is you've reaped your own destruction as well. What did you think, Gelstrom? That if we succeeded with this project you'd get your life back?'

The white fingers moved across the keypad, but Chase didn't wait. He couldn't. It was like a surge of adrenalin through his bloodstream, purging, purifying.

'Gelstrom, you are going to die and there's nothing you can do about it. Your disease is terminal. You are finished. You must know that – not even if you spent every last cent you possess.'

The big blond man at his shoulder said, 'You don't understand – that isn't—'

Chase cut him short. 'It's too late, *too fucking late!* This project, even if it succeeds, is a lifetime too late for him! He's got a couple of years at most and this will take decades, perhaps centuries.'

But it seemed that he was wrong and Sturges was right; Chase hadn't understood. He stood looking into the transparent shell, at the deep eye sockets in the shrivelled face. The trembling hand moved to the keypad, tapped, and as the green blip danced across the screen he read the words:

I expect nothing for myself. My end is near. But like you, Dr Chase, I have a son. Twelve years old. I want him to survive, to have a future and somewhere to live. You want the same for your son. I have money. You have knowledge. Together we can save them.

Chase finally did understand.

7

I

'You don't feel sick or dizzy or anything? Sure?'

'I'm all right now. Honestly.'

Cheryl ruffled Dan's hair and he squirmed away, embarrassed.

'Don't! I'm all *right*.'

'I certainly hope so.' Cheryl frowned at Chase accusingly.

Nick chipped in, 'He was perfectly okay in Princeton. Jen said he ate like a horse.' He winked at Dan. 'Must have been all that female cosseting.'

The four of them were in Chase's hotel room on West 110th Street, overlooking Central Park. This side of town, and further east to Park Avenue, had once been the most expensive and exclusive real estate in New York. The big apartment blocks had housed the wealthiest, most successful and most famous residents of Manhattan. It was still high-price, even though many had given up and moved out – way out – some as far as Oregon and Washington State, where the air was still breathable.

Here in the city the apartment complexes and larger hotels, such as this one, had been made into sealed enclosures, with clean, oxygen-enriched air pumped through the guest suites and public reception rooms.

Chase stood looking out at the murk over Central Park; even if there'd been something to see he wouldn't have seen it. He felt restless and nervous.

'Is Madam Van Dorn expecting you?' Cheryl asked him, the 'Madam' sounding distinctly frosty.

'Yes, but she's got a heavy schedule today. She's giving her annual Special Rapporteur report to the General Assembly.'

'I still don't understand, Gavin.' Cheryl wished he'd turn around to face her; he'd been staring out at nothing for the last ten minutes. 'You've always insisted that we have to change people's attitudes first: that unless we achieve that, no real progress is possible, politically or scientifically. That was the whole idea behind your book and Midnite-Net, wasn't it?'

After a moment, Chase nodded.

'And yet you've agreed to this.' Cheryl shook her head, puzzled and frustrated. Not only did she *not* understand it, she was baffled also by his reluctance to discuss it. This wasn't a bit like Gavin. 'We've got our hands full already with Midnite-Net and the media campaign and the national tour and your speaking dates – some of which you've had to give up on.' There was resentment in her tone.

'There's no reason why Midnite-Net shouldn't carry on as before,' Chase said. 'But I happen to believe that this could succeed, or at least has a chance of succeeding. It could make a positive difference.'

'You mean a practical solution? But you've always said that unless we can change *people*, change the way they think, nothing else is worth a damn. Don't you believe that any more?'

'I also believe that as scientists we have a duty to sort out this mess – if it can be sorted out.'

At last he turned to her. 'Why do you think your father spent years of his life on a lump of rock in the middle of the Pacific? Because he wanted to use his gifts, his talents, whatever, in the service of mankind. That's what he was best fitted for. So was he wrong? Was his life wasted?'

Their eyes met and locked, yet it seemed to Cheryl that this time – and it had never happened before – she couldn't see *inside* him.

It was Chase who broke away, turning back to the dismal view, and Cheryl said, 'What do you think, Nick?'

'To be honest, I'm not really sure.' Nick leaned back, hands clasped behind his balding head. He gnawed his lip above the frizzy fringe of beard. 'In theory there's no reason why we couldn't undo the harm we've done. That's point number one. Point number two is how do we do it. Point number three – assuming we find the answer to point number two – is do we have the urge and the will to change things?'

'What do you mean, the urge?' Dan asked. He was hunched forward on the arm of the couch, chin propped in his hand.

'I mean that the human race seems to have a collective death wish. It's like somebody who accepts that cigarettes cause lung cancer and still carries on smoking. We've known for decades we were damaging the environment, and look what we do: the response of a supposedly intelligent species.' His elbows lifted in a shrug. 'Just keep right on doing the same.'

'But is there any chance? What do you think?' Cheryl said.

'What, of finding a scientific solution?' Nick nodded slowly. 'I think there is. I hope there is. Providing it's organised properly and the funds are available.'

Cheryl was studying the back of Chase's head. 'Well, they've got the organiser lined up, haven't they,' she said, a small frown on her lightly freckled face. 'That only leaves the money.'

There was a further silence, and then Chase said, 'The money has been guaranteed. Ingrid Van Dorn and Senator Prothero have arranged it.'

'The UN is funding it?' Cheryl said in plain disbelief.

Chase turned finally and met her gaze. 'No, not the UN. Other sources. Corporate finance. Trust funds. Wealthy private individuals. That's one of the matters I want to discuss with them.' He looked at his watch. 'In fact I'd better go; I'll try and catch Ingrid before her speech.'

Cheryl didn't say anything.

There was an expression on her face that Chase couldn't read, and wasn't sure he wanted to.

2

The luminous dial of his watch read 4:17 a.m. Chase squinted at it and lay back on the pillow. He stared up at the shadowed ceiling, knowing that sleep would never come. There was too much on his mind. Cheryl knew he was holding something back – her silence told him that.

Slipping out of bed, taking care not to disturb her, he put on his dressing gown and went into the living room. He didn't switch on the light. The bottles on the cabinet gleamed temptingly, but instead he fumbled his way to an armchair and sat down.

Sooner or later he would have to tell her. The inevitable was near; in fact it was here and now, he realised, when he saw her pale form in the bedroom doorway.

'I couldn't sleep,' Chase said unnecessarily. 'Sorry if I woke you.'

'You didn't.' Cheryl came into the room. 'Do you want some coffee?'

Chase shook his head before it occurred to him that she wasn't able to see him properly. 'No thanks.'

He heard a rustle as she settled herself on the couch and arranged her robe to cover her legs. Neither of them spoke for a minute.

'Why didn't you tell me?'

'Tell you?' Chase said obtusely.

'Yes, tell *me*,' Cheryl said deliberately, 'instead of me having to drag it out of Nick.'

'You asked him?'

'Of course I did. It was obvious there was something wrong. I was waiting – hoping you'd tell me yourself.'

'I had to get it straight in my own mind first.'

'Get it straight?' Cheryl said in outrage and astonishment. 'What the fuck is there to get *straight*? Gelstrom is funding the project and you didn't have the guts to tell me.'

'It isn't that simple.'

'It couldn't be more simple,' Cheryl contradicted him. Her voice was suddenly quiet and calm. It was a serious sign. 'Do I really have to remind you? A man who made a fortune supplying toxic chemicals to the army; who for years was in collusion with the Pentagon, hatching a cosy little plan to kill every living thing on this planet. And now – sweet Jesus, talk about poetic justice – because he's been stricken with the disease he wanted to inflict on everyone else, this guy has a change of heart. Well, well – and get this for a sick joke – all at once he decides to switch sides, to become the saviour of mankind instead of its executioner. Does that cover everything? I think it does.'

'Nothing can save him,' Chase said patiently. 'Gelstrom is dying. He's beyond hope. He's not doing this for himself.'

'So what is it? Some kind of "grand final gesture"?' Cheryl exclaimed with ponderous sarcasm. 'Well, sure, of course, that changes everything. Forget what's happened before and welcome him back into the fold. Hey! – I bet he's really a great guy at heart, fond of his grey-haired old mother, had a tough upbringing—'

'Cheryl, please listen.' Chase leaned towards her. 'Gelstrom isn't behind this project; can't you understand that?' His voice had risen. He glanced at Dan's door, then went on in a lowered tone, 'He's not involved in any way.'

'Except for the small matter of – what, two, three billion dollars.'

'Does it matter where the money comes from? Money is money.' Chase said it without knowing if he believed it.

'I can't accept that. I can't even begin to understand what you're saying. How can you, of all people . . . knowing what that man has done? For God's sake—' She broke off, fighting down emotion. 'My God, Gav, it *does* matter about the money – of course it does!'

Cheryl stood up and he heard her rummaging about in the darkened room. A moment later something solid and heavy with sharp corners hit him on the chest and winded him.

'Read your own goddamn book!' Cheryl stood next to the armchair, breathing hard. 'It's all there: how companies made fortunes by raping the world and quietly disposing of anyone who got in their way. How a few scientists tried to warn people what was happening and ended up dead for their trouble. One of them was a marine biologist called Theo Detrick, you might remember. You ought to read the book, Gav. It might jog your memory about a few things you've obviously forgotten.'

Chase placed the book on the table. There wasn't anything Cheryl could say that he hadn't already thought about and agonised over. He was even prepared to concede that she was right; morally right, at any rate. But moral rightness or wrongness wasn't the issue. He had to work on the project; it was a compulsive feeling as strong as any he'd ever felt in his life. Right or wrong didn't stand a chance.

Chase said, 'You've discussed this with Nick. How does he feel about it?'

'He thinks you've taken leave of your senses.'

'Then he must have changed his mind within forty-eight hours,' Chase said. 'I told him about Gelstrom – everything, the whole story – on the way back from Desert Range. His exact words were, "Money is the means to an end, not an end in itself. If the guy wants to pay for his sins, why try to stop him?"'

'You didn't tell him that Gelstrom murdered my father.'

'No,' Chase said, 'that's true. I didn't. The reason is simple. We don't know for sure if Gelstrom was responsible. It could have been an accident, Cheryl, a heart attack—'

Cheryl laughed, an ugly, harsh sound. She said, 'What the fuck is this? A gathering of the Joseph Earl Gelstrom Appreciation Society?'

Chase couldn't see her face but he knew its expression. She spoke with a virulence he'd never heard before. 'At least Nick has principles. At least he believes in them and sticks to them.'

Well, well, well. A true-confession therapy session had been going on here while he was seeing Ingrid Van Dorn, it appeared. No wonder when he got back to the hotel he'd walked into an atmosphere you could have cut with a blunt shovel.

'All right,' Chase said consolingly. 'I hear what you say. So where do we go from here?'

'I guess that's up to you.'

'I've given them my answer.' Chase was firm. 'I can't go back on it.'

'Then I guess you have my answer too.'

A horrible sickening chill swept through him, right to his stomach.

Chase took a deep final breath and said, 'I'm not doing this for Prothero or Van Dorn, for Gelstrom or for myself. If you can't see why I'm doing this, Cheryl, if you won't understand – then you and I have nothing more to say to each other.'

'No,' Cheryl said. She was tight-lipped and dry-eyed. 'I didn't think we had.'

2036

I

I

In the opinion of Colonel Gavril Burdovsky, the woman was perfect. He had chosen her himself and therefore had cause to feel smug and self-congratulatory. He was also aroused by her – one of the reasons he thought her ideally suited for this assignment. Unfortunately this left him with a gnawing ache that could only be assuaged by Natassya Pavlovitch's smooth firm body. The fact that he was an obese, balding man of fifty-seven and she a beautiful young woman of twenty-four was a trivial incompatibility.

'I trust you have everything you require,' said the colonel, sitting on the corner of the desk and swinging a short bulbous leg in an attempt to make this final briefing casual, friendly – and dare he hope? – intimate. 'The black silk underwear is satisfactory?' There was a slight tremor in his voice at the mention of this item.

'Yes. Thank you, sir.' Natassya Pavlovitch was brisk, impersonal. She had been too well trained to display emotion in front of a superior.

Colonel Burdovsky nodded and stroked his pencil-thin moustache. The moustache was real, but it looked artificial, as if a strip of black paper had been stuck to his broad wax-like face with its hanging jowls.

'Good. Excellent,' murmured Burdovsky, for a moment lost in contemplation of the pale curve of her neck at the point where it disappeared into the enticing shadow beneath the collar of her dark grey woollen suit. That the rest of her should be so soft and warm and pliable . . .

He cleared his throat and said gruffly, 'You have all you need. Excellent.'

'I do have a question, if the colonel will permit.'

'Yes, of course.' Burdovsky slid down awkwardly from the desk, straightened the tail flap of his uniform with an abrupt tug and strolled behind her chair, hands clasped behind his plump buttocks.

Natassya looked straight ahead, speaking to the desk. 'Do we have no intelligence at all, Colonel, regarding Zone Four? The reports give no indication whatsoever of the research being carried out there.'

'There are a number of speculations, but nothing definite. The Americans thought they were being very clever in allowing our scientific people to inspect their facilities at Starbuck Island. Of course it was to satisfy us that the research was solely in connection with the Final Solution programme.'

He came to stand close behind her, breathing in her perfume. 'We are not that stupid, Leytenánt Pavlovitch. It was noted that parts of the island were off-limits to our inspection teams, and therefore it was necessary to instigate this series of operations.' Burdovsky unclasped his hands and placed them lightly on her shoulders, experiencing a sensation that was at once stimulating and extremely uncomfortable in his tight uniform. 'From the reports we know that the operatives who preceded you met with considerable difficulty in obtaining intelligence on Zone Four, which has led, as you know, to this new type of approach . . .' His stubby fingers touched her neck. Her skin felt cool, and yet his fingertips burned. 'And to you, Leytenánt, being personally selected by me to undertake the assignment.'

'I understand that, Colonel.' Her voice was totally without expression. She might have been carved out of stone. His fingers roamed lower, feeling for the hollows formed by her collarbones.

Natassya said crisply, 'The reports are quite explicit in having discovered nothing at all about the activities in Zone Four.'

Explicit they were, thought Burdovsky, with one crucial omission: that of the three operatives sent to Starbuck as members of the scientific inspection teams, two had failed to return. Their reports had been culled from notes and tapes left with their colleagues. As for the third operative, he had returned, but had no information to add to the sketchy findings thus far.

'We are satisfied that the Americans have cooperated fully in their research into various techniques of mass extermination.' Burdovsky's fingers strayed down inside the woollen collar. 'But Starbuck Island is being used for some other purpose, which they do not wish to reveal.' He could feel the gentle slopes of her breasts, rising and falling with each steady breath. 'And it is vital that we learn what that is. Absolutely vital.' His voice sank to a throaty whisper. 'I know you will not fail me . . .'

In a calm, unhurried movement Natassya Pavlovitch removed his chubby paws and rose to her feet, towering statuesquely above him like an Amazon confronting a Pygmy. 'You may have every confidence that I will do my duty, Colonel Burdovsky. I thank you for this opportunity to be of service.'

With trembling regret, he watched her leave, the fleshy palms of his hands damp.

2

The lip of the sun crept over the straight edge of the horizon: a sharply defined and perfectly symmetrical arc of vivid orange that widened and deepened until the entire glowing orb stood precariously balanced on the rim of the world. At this hour it was possible to stare it full in the face. But not for long; for in minutes the first faint rays lanced through the cool air, bathing the onlooker in a virulent wash of solar radiation unchecked by the tenuously thin ozone layer.

For Chase, unable to sleep, it brought back poignant memories. He was reminded of that other sunrise, nearly a quarter of a century ago on a bitterly cold, inhospitable continent, when as a young man he had been filled with unbounded optimism and the promise of all the years stretching ahead into the golden future. Then it had seemed as if nothing would be denied him, that anything and everything was possible.

But the possibilities had dwindled one by one, the options had been annulled – until he was left with only the bleak reality of the inescapable present.

Below the desert scrub, secure beneath thick slabs of concrete and steel, another day was beginning. Not for the first time, nor probably the last, Chase wondered at the purpose of this ceaseless activity. Every day for the past four years, ever since the scientists and technical staff had assembled here in the refurbished silo complex, work had gone ahead to solve a problem so vast that it numbed the imagination. Was it all just a grand illusion, or more aptly, delusion? What folly to think that their puny efforts could achieve anything – what arrogance! Cheryl had been right, maybe for the wrong reasons, but she had been right all the same.

Now he could feel the heat of the sun on his face, feel it gaining in strength by the minute. Time to go below.

High above yet invisible, the wreath of carbon dioxide formed a barrier blocking off the escaping heat. Temperature medians had gone haywire. While some parts of the globe had increased by $10°$ C and more, others had drastically cooled. Parts of Africa that had never seen a snowflake now had blizzards. Siberia was turning into jungle. The equatorial belt was a steamy, airless no man's land, mimicking the conditions of five million years ago. Flooding of coastal areas had shrunk western Europe drastically, so that many cities – London, Amsterdam, Copenhagen – were gradually being abandoned.

In the early years of the twenty-first century Mexico City, with a population of thirty-two million, was the largest city on Earth. Now it was virtually abandoned. Chase had seen documentary footage of conditions there that reminded him of the Nazi death camps in World War II. The film showed rotting bodies in the streets, the city dumps piled hundreds deep. Public utilities and services had collapsed completely and untreated sewage ran in the gutters and formed huge stinking lakes in the plazas and marketplaces. Plague had swept through the city and there were packs of huge rats roaming through the shops.

From the faces of those who managed to survive it was apparent that they were suffering from the early stages of anoxia. Pinched, their lips blue-black, they slumped in total exhaustion, mouths sucking in the depleted air. Oxygen content was nearly forty per cent lower than normal, equivalent to an altitude of fifteen thousand feet.

Chase recalled the profound shock felt by the scientific community. It had always been assumed that such a decline would take decades, but Mexico City had slid into ecological nightmare in just a few years, becoming a poisonous and decaying wasteland, a memorial as well as a dreadful warning of things to come.

At the entrance to the Tomb he was met by one of the guard corps, a tall loose-limbed boy with a drawling southern accent whose breast patch identified him as 'Buchan'. Although Chase had been loath to employ armed guards, the threat of attack left little choice.

'Morning, sir.' Buchan touched the steel rim of his camouflaged helmet. 'How's it look topside?'

His concrete cubbyhole contained a chair, table, a few tattered magazines, and on the crude walls an even cruder patchwork of naked women in bizarre contortions. From the ceiling extended the polished tube of a periscope, through which Buchan surveyed the surrounding terrain. Aboveground had been left completely undisturbed, so that the site, even from fifty yards away, was virtually undetectable. This was their greatest defence.

'All quiet on the western front,' Chase reported. He nodded towards the periscope. 'Don't you get eye strain peering through that all day?'

'Naw, ain't too bad.' Buchan gave him a gap-toothed grin. 'Standing orders say you gotta do a sweep every fifteen minutes. Reckon nothing could get near inside of that without being spotted.'

'Except a helicopter.'

'Yeah, I guess so,' Buchan conceded with a shrug. 'But we'd pick 'em up on radar, wouldn't we? I think we're pretty safe from a sneak attack,' he said confidently.

Chase went down in one of the freight elevators to the mess hall. Seventy feet underground he passed the large board listing the various departments on the different levels.

Marine Geology. Marine Chemistry. Geochemistry. Meteorology. Physical Oceanography. Botany. Biology. Atmospheric Physics. Microbiology. Biological Oceanography. Physiological Research. Marine Ecology. Geophysics and Planetary Physics. Neurobiology. Physiological Psychology. Altogether, counting technical and laboratory staff, there were about eight hundred people. There was space in the Tomb to accommodate many more – twenty miles of tunnels in this section alone. The complex actually stretched much further, two hundred miles of tunnels in all, though the rest of it had been sealed off from the Tomb itself.

As he ate his scrambled eggs and toast and sipped his coffee, Chase found himself hoping fervently that Buchan's confidence was justified. There were nine access points, each one closely guarded, but even so, the fear of discovery was never far from his mind.

Over his second cup he read the online editions of the *New York Times* and *Washington Post*. The complex also had its own twice-weekly newsletter, *The Tomb*, which consisted of relevant items from international news agencies as well as internal gossip.

By 8 a.m. he was at his desk. As director he had to coordinate the efforts of the multi-disciplined research groups, keeping the climatologists informed about what the marine biologists were up to, the oceanographers in the picture about any progress made by the atmospheric physicists, the microbiologists up to date on what the meteorologists were doing. It was a daunting and time-consuming responsibility. He also had to arbitrate between them: there was still an element of rivalry that he had tried unsuccessfully to eradicate in the early days. Then he had come to the conclusion that perhaps it was necessary, this competitive spirit, to keep everyone keen and on their intellectual toes. Later in the day there was to be a monthly update meeting, when Chase's patience and diplomacy met their sternest test.

3

Shortly after eleven Prothero called him from New York. The news was more of the same: another rash of emergency committees to deal with the social consequences of the deteriorating climate. It was common knowledge that the government apparatus had been set up in Des Moines, Iowa, well away from the steadily creeping Devastated Areas. Official pronouncements continued to insist that this was a temporary measure 'in the interests of administrative convenience', which naturally fooled no one. The rats were always the first to abandon a sinking ship.

'What's the weather like?' Chase asked facetiously.

'If I could see out the window I'd tell you.' Prothero's face was more lined these days, pouchier, his eyes hollow and haunted. 'I thought I'd better speak to you before you had your update. It is today, isn't it?'

Chase nodded warily. Something was up.

'It's about Gelstrom,' Prothero said. 'He's got a matter of days.'

Chase gazed at the screen. He felt nothing. 'So what happens now?'

'It all depends on whether he's made provision for the financial support after his death. I'm checking out the legalities.'

'I never expected him to last this long,' Chase said. To give him his due, Gelstrom hadn't quibbled over a single penny of the cost of setting up and maintaining the project, a figure that must now be approaching a quarter of a billion dollars.

'How near are you to carrying out field trials?' Prothero wanted to know.

'On which process?'

'Dammit, how do I know? Which is the best bet? You're the scientist.'

'If I could answer that there'd be no need to be working on twenty different solutions to the problem. Maybe there isn't any one single answer.'

'What's your best shot?' Prothero demanded. 'Come on, Gavin, you must have an idea. A hunch even.'

'The microbiologists are trying to develop a new algae strain with a high oxygen yield that is super-resistant to chemical pollution. Long-term, I think that's the one. But at the moment it's still at the lab stage.'

'How long is long-term?'

'Optimistically, ten years.'

'Jesus Christ,' Prothero said faintly.

'And then there's Hanamura's approach, splitting seawater by electrolysis and releasing the stored oxygen into the atmosphere. He's got a pilot plant in operation that's producing good results.'

'You'll have to push him. Time's running out. You've seen the reports in the papers recently?'

'You mean the northern latitudes?' Over the past months it had been found that oxygen levels were decreasing as far north as latitude fifty degrees, which placed most of Europe within the threatened zone. Even more alarming were the stories from Africa and the Indian subcontinent that millions of people were dying from a mysterious sickness. Here at Desert Range debate had raged fiercely. Some believed that it was due to oxygen deficiency, or possibly genetic damage caused by ultraviolet radiation, while others blamed another, unknown factor. Whatever the cause, it was wiping out entire populations, laying waste to whole regions.

'I've got some figures you won't have seen,' Prothero said gravely. 'The NOAA estimates that within two years New York will be another Mexico City. We need some answers, Gavin, and we need them now!'

'I'll do what I can,' Chase said stiffly. 'I'll get back to you after the update.'

'What are conditions like there?'

'Atmospherically still pretty good. We haven't got around to selling oxygen on the black market yet. What's the going rate these days?'

'Fifty dollars a tank. Last week they had to turn out the National Guard to control a mob that attacked one of the food distribution centres. More than a hundred killed. You'll get back to me?'

Chase promised he would. The screen faded to grey. Even an intelligent and sympathetic layman like Prothero failed to understand why such a 'simple' thing as replenishing the atmosphere should prove so immensely difficult. Hadn't oxygen been produced commercially for a hundred years or more? Surely all that was required was to increase the size of existing plants and mass-produce them. What could be more straightforward?

4

From April 2030, when it sheared away from the western edge of the Antarctic Ice Shelf, to late 2033, the Riiser-Larsen Calving Berg had travelled barely past the South Sandwich Islands and the rocky outcrop of South Georgia on the northern limit of the Weddell Sea; in more than three years it had covered fewer than fifteen hundred nautical miles.

This was mainly due to its size: 1,200 square miles and a mass of more than 2.9 trillion tons – the largest free-floating iceberg on Earth.

Leaving these near-freezing waters, however, its geographical disposition changed drastically. Now caught up and swept along by the warmer currents of the South Atlantic Polar Vortex, the berg was carried northwards along the eastern coast of South America at a rapidly increasing rate of knots. It also began to lose weight, and as its mass decreased, its speed increased. By mid-2034, when it crossed the Tropic of Capricorn, on the same latitude as Rio de Janeiro, the slimmed-down chunk of ice and permafrost was moving faster by the day.

Though 'slimmed-down', the Riiser-Larsen Calving Berg, still at more than two trillion tonnes and almost a thousand square miles, was still a massive object. Because of the obvious threat to shipping, satellites tracked its progress day by day, hour by hour. Schemes were proposed to plant a series of nuclear devices deep inside the permafrost stratum and blow it apart; these were practicable ideas and might have worked, given the iceberg was half a mile thick at its deepest point. Then a major snag was spotted; instead of tracking one giant iceberg, there would be hundreds, perhaps thousands, still massive and very dangerous, drifting randomly across the shipping lanes. Tracking them all was clearly going to be an impossible task, making the situation worse.

There were hopes that it might veer westward towards the Mid-Atlantic Ridge, away from the cargo and tanker routes, but it didn't. Nor could it be diverted, slowed down or halted. Direction of travel and speed were dictated solely by the South Atlantic Polar Vortex: nothing could resist this dominant current which followed a course 700 miles from land, roughly following the coastal outline of Brazil.

Five years later and 4,900 miles further on from when, in 2030, it broke away from the Antarctic Ice Sheet, it crossed the equator, and at this point the powerful Polar Vortex current began to disperse and ebb in strength as it encountered the warmer waters of the Caribbean and the depths of the Puerto Rico Trench.

Rapidly – in just a few months – the iceberg began to lose volume, density and mass. The warm acidic waters ate away at the underside layers of permafrost, and huge chunks the size of mountains broke off and slid into the ocean. Now caught in the gentler drift of the North Atlantic, the iceberg began to slow down; by the spring of 2036 it was six hundred miles off the coast of Florida and moving northwards at a sluggish pace of three to four knots, heading in the general direction of Bermuda and its little group of islands.

Six years since its birth, the Riiser-Larsen Calving Berg was less than half the size since the day it sheared away from its parent Antarctica: reduced to a mere 1.2 trillion tonnes.

5

The logistical difficulties became starkly apparent when he sat through an update meeting, as Chase did that afternoon. More than thirty scientists – the heads of the research groups – assembled in the main conference room with its greenboards and work-in-progress charts, graphs and blueprints. Chase took up his usual position on a small wooden platform, sitting with arms folded, a clipboard balanced on his knee.

First they listened to Dr George Franklin, a biochemist, who voiced his concern about a new virulent strain of bacteria, one that might thrive in a heavily polluted atmosphere and against which mankind would have no genetically inherited defence.

'A form of bacterium that would thrive in conditions hostile to us, you mean?' someone said.

Franklin nodded, hunched forward with an elbow resting on his crossed knee, spectacles dangling from his long bony fingers. 'Such strains already exist, of course, and have ever since life evolved on this planet. They've always been with us – they've preceded us, in evolutionary terms. Whereas man can't survive without an adequate supply of oxygen, some bacteria are suited to such conditions. And – this is the point – an atmosphere rich in pollutants might positively encourage them to evolve further, develop new strains. The planet could be slowly reverting to the protozoic, with bacteria as the dominant species.'

'Is this just a theory or do you have evidence?' asked Carter Reid, a marine chemist.

'Well, not directly,' Franklin hedged, 'though there's some circumstantial evidence to support it. We've noticed that dead animals are decomposing at a much faster rate than is normally the case. We're not sure that bacteria *are* responsible, but I can't think of another explanation.'

'So we inherited the earth from the dinosaurs,' someone remarked, 'and the bacteria will inherit it from us.'

'There is a kind of poetic justice to it,' said Franklin with a small smile. 'After all, the bacteria were here first. It's come full circle.'

'Makes me feel a whole lot better to know that,' muttered a sardonic voice from the back of the room. There was some muted laughter, and a few rueful grins.

'Could this be what's happening in Africa and Asia?' said Faulkner, one of the oceanographers. 'No one's been able to identify the cause yet, have they?'

'That occurred to me too,' Franklin said. 'As far as we know they've eliminated the most likely scenarios – virus infection, oxygen deficiency, malnutrition – and yet millions are being wiped out with the efficiency of bubonic plague. A new form of killer bacterium would fill the bill.'

'I'm sure this is all very fascinating, Director,' interposed a balding, thin-faced man named Lasker, addressing Chase. His tone implied quite the reverse. 'But I fail to see what it has to do with our function here at Desert Range. Do we really have time for such speculation, particularly in view of the rapidly deteriorating situation? A new species of bacterium is the least of our worries, I would have thought.'

'The purpose of this meeting is to exchange information,' Chase reminded him, in his role of judge and jury. 'We can hardly decide what's of value or relevant until we've heard it.'

Privately, Chase conceded that Lasker might have a point, though he didn't like the way the engineer had made it. Lasker was one of the technical support staff, a man who dealt in hard practicalities and eschewed random speculation. It was essential, however, that all viewpoints receive a fair hearing, no matter how wild or pie in the sky.

Lasker sat back and folded his arms with a show of churlish indifference. After four years it wasn't surprising that tempers should be on short fuse; perhaps it was remarkable that only occasionally they flared into irritation or outright anger.

Next it was Frank Hanamura's turn. He spent twenty minutes at the board outlining a problem with the electrolysis pilot plant, which at the moment was undergoing laboratory trials. Although the principle of splitting seawater into its component parts was established and understood – the lab model was in fact producing oxygen at 99.5 per cent purity – the trouble arose when the process was scaled up to supply the enormous quantities that would be required, measured in tons rather than cubic feet: 'tonnage oxygen', as it was called.

The problem was to find an electrode material that wouldn't dissolve in the solution and at the same time would resist the build-up of oxide deposits, which reduced the effectiveness of the process. Even the purest metal, such as platinum, formed a film of oxide one or two molecules thick, which after a very short period of time brought a drop in electrical efficiency leading to a loss of production.

The process was potentially hazardous too. Certain combinations of hydrogen and chlorine and hydrogen and oxygen were explosive, so it was crucially important that none of the gases be allowed to mix within the cell. On the scale proposed, such a mixing would not only destroy the plant but also cause widespread devastation. Yet another problem was that the hydrogen film formed on the anode was corrosive and poisonous, endangering the plant personnel.

To be globally effective it would be necessary to build thousands of large-scale electrolysis plants on coastlines throughout the world where seawater would be processed in billions of gallons, releasing its precious store of oxygen into the atmosphere. Millions of tons annually would have to be produced if they were to achieve a significant change in boosting the oxygen content to the level capable of supporting life.

When Hanamura had finished, dusted the chalk from his hands, and resumed his seat, Chase broached the thorny question: how long before marine trials could commence? He didn't add to the pressure by mentioning Prothero's call; as director it was his duty to shield his people from external hassles and financial headaches. What he had to have was a positive commitment: if the money were to run out then the whole enterprise would be a complete and utter waste.

'We've yet to decide on the most efficient cell voltage. At the moment we're testing a range of power requirements.' Hanamura stared into space, his high fine cheekbones catching the light. 'I'd say a year to eighteen months, providing there are no unforeseen problems.'

'But you already have a lab model operating successfully,' Chase said, doing his best to sound reasonable. 'How do you know that marine trials won't actually help you select the optimum cell voltage? You can carry on the work here in any case while we test the process at sea.'

Hanamura glanced towards Carter Reid, his number two, who shook his head dubiously. Hanamura looked at Chase.

'Does that mean you can't or won't?' Chase said.

'It means we're not ready.'

'Is there any technical obstacle to prevent us from building a pilot plant and installing it in an oceangoing vessel?'

'No,' Hanamura admitted slowly, his handsome face puckered in a frown. 'I just don't like the idea of running marine trials until we've ironed out all the bugs.'

'I don't like it either, Frank, but we don't have the luxury of time. How soon?' Chase asked bluntly.

'Maybe six months, and that's working double shifts.' Hanamura swept a lock of glossy black hair from his forehead. He was being rushed and didn't like it. 'It would mean building one from scratch.'

'What about the lab model you already have? Couldn't you adapt that one for marine trials?'

'Come on now, Gavin,' Hanamura protested, 'be reasonable. We need the lab model here. Anyway, it's too small. The pilot plant would have to be at least four times the capacity.'

'Okay, starting tomorrow, what's the absolute minimum, given all the resources we can muster?'

'Cutting it to the bone? I'd say three months.'

'Right, that gives you till September fifteenth,' Chase said briskly. He was satisfied, but he didn't intend to show it. He'd succeeded in bringing Hanamura down from a year to six months to three months, but it would have been a tactical error to ease off now. 'What about location? I can have one of the Scripps' research fleet standing by – choose anywhere within a week's cruising from San Diego.'

Hanamura looked at Carter Reid, then turned to Chase. 'Providing it's well clear of the algae blooms, anywhere in the Pacific will do.' His dark eyes sparkled angrily for a moment, as if he'd suddenly realised he'd been backed into a corner. But it was too late. He jabbed a finger. 'And I want to be there, Gavin, directing the operation personally. If we have to meet this September fifteenth deadline I'm going to make damn sure the trials are conducted properly. Any objections?'

Chase shook his head, smiling sweetly. 'None whatsoever.'

6

Cheryl coughed up more of the evil-smelling black stuff and wiped her streaming eyes. She raised her head and caught sight of herself in the bathroom mirror. Her face was deathly pale and covered in beads of sweat, a faint bluish tinge to her lips. She knew the signs and symptoms, had seen them in others, so there was no point in fooling herself.

Dan hadn't noticed anything, she was certain; he would have come straight out and said something. A lump came into her throat, whether at the thought of Dan or out of self-pity she didn't know. But this wouldn't do, she told herself sternly. He'd know in an instant something was wrong if he saw her like this. She doused her face in cold water and pinched her cheeks to bring the colour back.

Outside the cabin in the fresh air she felt better. The grandeur of the Oregon landscape with its thickly wooded slopes rising steeply to bare granite peaks had a healing effect, and the sky, a brilliant translucent blue, was unsullied by any trace of industrial fouling.

That was the odd and remarkable thing, Cheryl thought – that while some parts of the globe turned into uninhabitable wastelands, other areas benefitted, indeed, thrived under the new conditions. It was all due to the complex, unpredictable interfusion of gases in the biosphere which no one properly understood and never had. At these latitudes, for instance, the oxygen level was only a fraction below par and the ozone cover was still pretty much intact. Some fried while others thrived. Luck of the draw.

This was a good place to build a settlement. She had been right to bring Dan here, to start anew. They had been warmly welcomed by the locals, who had made them part of the small community in what had been the Willow Valley Reservation a few miles from the California border on the northern shore of Goose Lake. Yet in the last two years there had been changes, disturbing changes, mainly caused by the exodus from the south. First it had been a trickle of refugees, increasing to a steady stream, seeping northwards like an insidious stain. Now this part of Oregon was dotted with tiny isolated communities and what had once been the little townships of Beatty, Bly, Adel, Plush and Valley Falls were in danger of being swamped.

There had been other changes too, even more disturbing to Cheryl. She found it hard to define, to be precise about, but it was as if the attitude, the temper of the people was undergoing some kind of transformation: a kind of nervous, brooding suspicion where previously there had been tolerance and a feeling of fellowship. The change was more psychological than anything else, she felt, convinced that it wasn't her imagination playing tricks. She likened it to a kind of subversive paranoia, slowly infiltrating the community and corrupting people's minds.

And why, for God's sake, was she sick? Surely this beautiful place, with its mountains and lakes and thousands of square miles of forests, was as healthy an environment as you could wish for? If you couldn't survive here, then nowhere on the planet was safe.

Dan was with some of the other young people over at the community centre, discussing an extension to the school. By the time he returned Cheryl felt much better and had regained her colour and composure. To her relief Dan gave her a casual wave, apparently noticing nothing out of the ordinary.

Watching him, she felt the stab of a familiar poignancy. He was perhaps a fraction taller than his father and not quite as broad, but it might have been the young Gavin Chase: the same shock of black hair hanging over his forehead, the same intelligent blue-grey eyes and the firm, rather stubborn mouth. Though he never raised the matter, Cheryl often wondered if Dan harboured any resentment against his father for insisting that his son travel with Cheryl to the settlement in Oregon rather than move to the Desert Range site in Utah. While she understood his reasoning – a desire to place Dan in the most benign, most protective, environment – Cheryl still doubted that while the motive was right, the decision was wrong. There had been no great family rows at the time, three years ago, about where Dan should reside; the boy had seemed shell-shocked, Cheryl recalled, following the estrangement between her and Gavin. When Chase had set out his plans and explained his reasons, Dan had quietly gone along with them without demur. What deeper psychological distress it might have caused, Cheryl could only guess at.

'What are you doing this afternoon?' Cheryl asked him. 'Like to row across the lake?'

Dan looked at her oddly, then shook his head. 'Sorry, Cheryl, I've already promised to go riding with Jo, up by Drews Gap. We're going to have a picnic and collect some herbs.'

'Just the two of you, you mean?'

'Sure,' Dan said, flashing her a wide grin. 'You don't mind, do you?'

'It isn't up to me to mind. I take it her parents know?'

'Yeah, they said okay.' He'd lost the crisp correctness of his English accent and now spoke without the reserve that many Americans took to be standoffishness in the British character. 'Anyway, I thought you had things to do this afternoon – didn't you say Tom Brannigan had called a council confab?'

'That's not until four. Never mind, you go off and enjoy yourself.' Cheryl patted his shoulder and went ahead of him on to the porch. It had been a mistake to suggest a change in the routine, she realised, but she was afraid that time was slipping by too fast and she needed his company to reassure her that all was well.

All wasn't well though. She felt queasy again at the thought and had to make a wilful effort to control her panic.

They stood together looking across the little square around which were grouped the rough timber buildings of the community centre, the surgery and dispensary, and the three cooperative stores that served the needs of the three-hundred-strong settlement. Outwardly primitive, the sturdy pine-clad buildings were fitted out with all modern amenities, including electricity and non-freeze plumbing. It was a tenet of the community's philosophy that technology was the friend and not the enemy; there was no reason not to take full advantage of man's inventiveness and enterprise if used sensibly and with due consideration for the environment. No one here subscribed to the back-to-nature fallacy: that was simply a stupid and shortsighted return to the Stone Age. They were far from the masochists and martyrs who felt conscience-stricken at the thought of killing a rabbit or burning a log. The important thing was to live in harmony with their surroundings and not to plunder or despoil out of sheer greed, indifference or asinine thoughtlessness.

Above all, they determined to indoctrinate those same beliefs in the rising generation. Theirs was the earth to inherit – providing their forebears hadn't already squandered the inheritance.

'Are you serious about Jo?' Cheryl asked, surprising herself with the question. She didn't want to pry.

'Do I have to be?'

'I just wondered.'

'What's up, afraid she'll get pregnant?'

'Dan!' Cheryl said, disapproving more of his directness than scandalised by the sentiment itself. 'I didn't think that for a moment. She's only seventeen and I wondered how you felt about her.'

'She's okay. We have fun together.' Dan folded his arms, his brown work-hardened biceps bunching and stretching the short sleeves of his T-shirt. He was full of the confidence of a healthy and good-looking young man, delighting in his own appeal. *And why not?* Cheryl thought. If you didn't feel good about yourself at twenty, you'd never have a better opportunity.

She said, 'I guess you're old enough to know what you're doing.'

'I guess so,' he agreed, the same grin lurking at the corners of his mouth.

Was he making fun of her? Maybe she was losing her sense of humour, which was hardly surprising under the circumstances.

7

The trail was steep and rocky leading up to Drews Gap, and the horses were jittery, sensing the danger of a slip or a stumble, their eyes white and rolling as they shied away from the drop. Thick vegetation and the spiky tops of pine trees dropped away steeply below.

Jo led the way, neat and trim in check shirt and jodhpurs, the set and balance of her slim body just right on the grey's broad back. Dan got a lot of pleasure from just watching her. Her long blonde hair, pulled back and tied at the nape of the neck, gleamed like a silver scarf in the clear sunlight. When she'd arrived at Goose Lake with her parents two years ago she'd been an awkward, gangling kid with long skinny legs, pretty much as he remembered her from their last meeting. He'd teased her and unkindly nicknamed her 'Stilts'.

The teasing had lasted about a year, until shortly after her sixteenth birthday when (almost overnight it seemed to Dan) the proverbial swan had appeared. From then on he'd started to take notice in an entirely different way.

The trail levelled out and Jo coaxed the grey towards a small clearing girdled by a circle of slender pines, the breeze whispering in their branches. Jo slid down and the horse immediately began cropping the luxuriant grass. Steam rose from its flanks and hung in the sunlight, which lanced like pencil beams through the overhead cover.

'What was all that with Cheryl?' Jo asked, unfastening the straps on her saddlebag and pulling out a small bundle swathed in white cloth.

'She was worried that we might be sneaking away for a spot of afternoon delight. You know how they are.'

Jo looked at him sideways from under long fair lashes, her expression mildly scathing rather than coquettish.

'Naturally I told her the thought had never entered our heads,' Dan said with a perfectly sincere face that still managed to seem devilish.

'I'm glad about that,' Jo said, 'because it never entered mine. From what I hear there's no shortage of that on Saturday nights with Baz Brannigan and his cronies.'

Jo didn't miss much, though Dan hadn't realised it was common knowledge what Baz – Tom Brannigan's son – and some of the others got up to on Saturday nights. In truth, he didn't know how to take Baz – whether he liked him, despised him or even secretly feared him. Baz was a braggart, and cocky, a natural leader (or bully), and yet there was an intense, almost mesmerising quality to his character that made him popular. The way he'd suddenly switch from being lethargic to hyperactive for no apparent reason kept people on edge. Maybe the pill-popping caused that.

From the saddlebag, Dan took the food wrapped in silver foil, green salad in a plastic container and the Thermos of chilled white wine and laid everything on the sun-dappled cloth Jo had spread on the ground. The day couldn't have been more perfect. Propped on one elbow, tearing off strips from a chicken leg, Jo gazed around at the dense proliferation of vegetation. From her expression, Dan could guess what was chafing her, because it was a topic they'd discussed before: if the flora world-wide was struggling to survive in the strange new atmosphere, how come the greenery hereabouts was flourishing like mad? He said, 'Still can't get your head around it, can you?'

'I know!' Jo said, sounding vexed. 'Still bothers me. Explain it again.'

'It's Cheryl's explanation, not mine. She's the scientist. The super-growth is caused by the abundance of carbon dioxide, which means the plants are being hyperventilated, speeding up their metabolic rate. There's a friend of Cheryl's who lives north of here – Boris Stanovnik. He says the trend will continue, and it'll accelerate the growth as the carbon dioxide builds up.'

Jo tossed the chicken leg aside and licked her fingers. She looked puzzled. 'Still doesn't add up to me. If the plants are growing faster and becoming more lush, they ought to be giving off more oxygen – it's a two-way deal, isn't it?'

'That's true, here, where we are. The problem is, according to Cheryl, that we wiped out most of the equatorial forests in the last century, which drastically reduced the oxygen supply. The stuff that's left' – Dan waved his hand at the encroaching greenery – 'isn't enough to make a whole lotta difference. What we've left ourselves with are huge tracts of desert and small areas with superabundant growth. The balance has been upset, so the whole thing's out of kilter.'

'So what's going to happen next, do you think?' Jo asked, nibbling on a slice of cucumber.

'Do you mean world-wide?' Dan said. 'Or just here, to us?'

'There's no difference that I can see. If the global situation gets worse, which it is doing, I don't see how we're going to survive in our little Garden of Eden. Or are we somehow immune—'

She broke off and they both looked round at the pulsing growl of engines in the distance. The sound was coming from below the ridge, on the opposite side to the trail they'd ridden up. Their two grazing horses also looked round, swishing their tails.

Jo sat up. 'Is that a helicopter?'

'No.' Dan went still. 'They're quad bikes.' His eyes narrowed. 'Only one family I know has them.'

'The Brannigans?'

The noise had broken the spell of the peaceful summer day. Dan was hoping and praying that Baz Brannigan would give them a wide berth. This area of forest and lower meadows, crisscrossed by rocky spines, with Goose Lake its focal point, was big enough for everyone. They sat listening on the grass while the engines boomed and reverberated, trying to gauge if they were getting louder or growing fainter. A minute or so later they were left in no doubt when, with a sudden roar, two quad bikes crested the ridge and bounced on their fat tyres into the clearing, startling the horses. It was Brannigan sure enough, Dan saw, immediately recognisable with his shock of fair hair and thick white eyebrows standing out against his ruddy skin. Brannigan was riding with a companion, two more on the other bike, none of the four young men wearing helmets.

Dan was cursing them all under his breath as he tried to calm the animals. When he had time to look, the two bikes were coasting round in circles as they approached the picnic spread, Jo sitting on her haunches with her arms tightly folded. In a show of brazen provocation, Baz Brannigan had a kind of leering smirk on his face. His attitude seemed to say, *What have we here, two little lambs, lost in the wood . . .*

'Found yourselves a nice quiet little spot, heh?' Brannigan gunned the motor before turning it off. Scratching his chin, and with a studied thoughtful look, he glanced round at his companions. 'Here's a little lesson for you guys. Look-ee here now. Whoever said the Brits can't get horny?'

They all cackled as if their leader had made a really funny remark.

Looking directly at Jo, Baz Brannigan then prissily folded his arms and pursed his lips, as if mocking her body posture and expression, which set the three others off into more cackles of hilarity.

They seriously needed to get a life, Dan thought, while forcing himself, with painful effort, to remain silent. In Brannigan's present mood of aggressive showing-off, Dan knew that he'd seize on anything, on the smallest thing, to take offence at and be riled by. And Dan could see where Brannigan's gaze was lingering, on Jo's breasts under the checked shirt. The top three buttons were undone, showing a vee of smooth tanned skin.

Jo, also wisely, was saying nothing. Just give them a few more minutes, let them have their juvenile fun, Dan thought, and they'd be on their way.

Brannigan took out a slim silver flask, took a gulp and handed it round. He sucked the moisture off his lips, which in contrast to his face were an almost raw-looking red. He then swung his right leg over the handlebars so he was sitting side-saddle. When Brannigan turned his head, Dan noticed that his pupils were dilated, his nostrils flaring and closing with each breath.

'Seen you around the place. You're a cute little kid, what's your name?' When Jo didn't answer, Brannigan said, 'I'm Tom Brannigan's son. Everyone calls me Baz.'

'I know who you are,' Jo said quietly. 'Thanks for spooking the horses and ruining our picnic. Only sorry you couldn't have arrived sooner and ruined the entire day.'

Brannigan bent his head forward. 'Is that the famous English Sar-Cas-Um I've heard so much about? Why, cute little girl, it's Hil-Air-I-Us. We're all in stitches.'

'That can be arranged,' Jo said.

Dan gritted his teeth. *No, Jo, please no. Don't rile the bastard, please*.

Baz Brannigan signalled for the flask and took another pull, emptying it to the last drop. When he stood up he was unsteady on his feet. Just that small amount of whisky, or whatever it was, wouldn't have done that to him, Dan knew; this was the chaser to some form of chemical stimulant.

'What's she like, a hot fuck?' Brannigan said, addressing Dan. 'She any good at blowjobs?'

Dan moved forward a couple of paces to the edge of the spread-out picnic cloth. 'This is stupid, Baz, and you know it. Move on now and we'll forget this.' He gestured to the others, an appeal to their better judgement, but all he got back was one sullen stare and a couple of snide grins.

'Why keep her all to yourself?' Baz Brannigan asked. 'Thas jus greedy, when there's plenty for everyone.'

Jo got to her feet. She was staring hard at Brannigan now. Brannigan took his time looking at her breasts and down along the length of her thighs and legs moulded tightly in jodhpurs and boots. There was a pulse beating in the centre of his forehead. Dan let his eyes drift towards the ground. On the picnic cloth was the boning knife he had used to carve the chicken. The serrated blade was about four inches long. He shuffled another half-step nearer to it as Baz Brannigan moved clumsily forward as well. He stumbled, and in a cold clear voice Jo said: 'You can't even take your liquor.'

Jo, don't! Please please don't provoke him . . .

'I can take you,' Baz Brannigan said, throaty and ragged.

Oh Christ . . .

'What are you trying to do, you and your brave posse? Scare me?'

'Are you scared, or just a liddle bit excited? Which is it?' Baz Brannigan licked his fleshy lips and came for her with both hands, as if to grab Jo by the shoulders. She stepped away, caught the heel of her boot in the cloth and tripped over backwards. Trying to scramble to her feet, Jo's boots skidded on the cloth and Brannigan clamped his hand round her ankle and with brute force dragged her full length across the white cloth, through the remnants of chicken and salad and untasted chocolate cake.

Dan lost sight of the knife in the struggle, and then he found it again. He got a firm grip on the knife and from a stooping position drove the blade towards Baz Brannigan's stomach. He felt the knife strike something soft, but felt nothing much afterwards except a numbing crash to the side of the head which exploded into a roaring red inferno.

Very far away a girl's voice was screaming, 'Get off me, you bastard, let go of me!' before pleading, 'Oh, God no, don't! No, please don't! No! No! No—!'

The pounding of a piston in Dan's head obliterated the sound until the pounding piston went silent too, before everything turned black.

8

'It's like a disease or a virus, infecting us,' Nick Power said. 'Don't ask me whether it's physical or psychological because I don't know – but something's happening, especially to the young people.'

'What in hell are you talking about, for God's sake? Jesus, you damn English are all the same,' Tom Brannigan complained. 'Nothing but high spirits. Kids just being kids is all.'

Brannigan was playing dumb, Cheryl thought, or he *was* dumb – probably the latter. Nick was right, she knew it, as did a lot of others in the community. And she trusted Brannigan about as far as she could have thrown his sway-bellied 210-pound frame. There was a crafty slyness about him hiding behind his honest-as-the-day-is-long blue-eyed stare. The down-to-earth all-American patriot, that was Tom Brannigan, or so he liked to make out.

Nick looked around at the other council members, nine in all, who carefully avoided his and one another's eyes; none of them were prepared to support him – or more likely, were afraid of disagreeing with Brannigan.

'Nick is right and we all know it, or most of us do,' Cheryl said. 'The rest must be walking around with their eyes shut. It isn't only the climate and vegetation that's gone haywire – there's something else, something more fundamental that's affecting this community.'

'Hey now, let's not get too hysterical,' Brannigan snorted with laughter, and gazed at Cheryl indulgently. It was only to be expected, his manner suggested, that nervous and highly-strung females were prone to such outbursts.

Cheryl recognised the ploy and choked back any riposte.

'I'm no psychologist, I'd be the first to admit,' Brannigan went on reasonably. 'I'm just a simple guy, you all know that. The last thing Tom Brannigan is, thank the Lord, is some kind of intellectual. Sure, I've read a book or two, but I believe at bottom in good old-fashioned common sense. Isn't that why we joined the community in the first place, to get back to the simple, basic issues and not get mixed up with all that nonsense outside? Look, set me straight if I'm wrong, but we have a good life here at Goose Lake. We've built it up from nothing and make it work by the sweat of our brow. We grow our own food and see to our own needs.' His blue eyes in their brown crinkles were so sincere it hurt. 'Is anybody seriously telling me that something is wrong with us? Because, to be honest, I don't see it. What I *do* see is a community with – yeah, okay – one or two problems, but you're always gonna get that. It's only to be expected.'

Nick was staring at the wall. His eyes didn't flicker when Brannigan said, 'Now Dr Power here, who we all know ain't a medical doctor – and Dr Detrick likewise – in my opinion are getting uptight over nothing at all. And judging from the rest of you I'd say you go along with me. Am I right? Or am I right?'

'You're not only blind, Tom,' Cheryl said, 'you're stupid as well—'

Nick held up both hands. 'Tom, listen to me. If you don't wake up to what's happening you're heading for trouble – and you're going to drag the rest of us with you, whether we like it or not.'

'Aw bullshit – this is a load of crap and you know it. Goddamnit, we're *safe* here. Nothing can touch us.'

'What about your son, Tom?' Nick said quietly. 'Are he and some of the other young men behaving normally in your opinion?'

If someone had stabbed a pin into Brannigan he couldn't have reacted more furiously. 'My son? What're you getting at? What the hell d'you mean?'

'You haven't noticed his influence over the others and the way they've been acting?'

Brannigan's crinkly blue eyes had turned to Arctic ice. His breathing became audible.

Nick glanced at Cheryl, then turned to Brannigan and looked him straight in the face. 'I didn't want this to get personal, Tom, but it has to be said. Baz leads the other kids into all kinds of troublemaking, and everyone but you seems to know it. I hate saying this—'

'Then don't fucking say it!' Brannigan's voice was flat as a whip-crack. 'I don't make remarks about your kid, so don't start on mine. It's none of your concern.'

'It is if it disrupts the life of the community.'

'Jesus,' Brannigan snorted, 'you goddamn English.' He'd flushed a darker brick-red. 'Like to think of yourselves as everybody's conscience, don't you, you and your prissy high-minded ways.' He pointed a thick forefinger like the barrel of a gun. 'Let me tell you, what Baz does is my affair, and none of yours. Do you think I need you to tell me about my own son? Go to hell!'

'That means you don't know,' Nick said in the same quiet voice.

Brannigan's square jaw jutted. 'Know what?'

'Baz and his friends are on a big drug kick. They're eating them like jelly beans.'

A pulse throbbed visibly in Brannigan's temple. He swayed forward in his chair, a fist half-raised.

But it was Cheryl who said blankly, 'The kids are on drugs? Nick, are you certain?'

Nick nodded without speaking, watching Brannigan.

'How many of the kids? All of them, or just a few?' Cheryl said. She really wanted to come straight out and ask if Dan was one of them, but daren't.

'I'm warning you, Power.' Brannigan's voice was low and dangerous. 'Don't you come making accusations about my boy. I see your game all right. You're out to cause trouble. Well I'm telling you here and now for the first and last time to keep your fucking nose—'

The door crashed open and Nick's wife stood wilting against the light. Her face was in silhouetted shadow, but they didn't need to see it to know that something was badly wrong. Cheryl felt the nausea churn in her stomach.

Nick was on his feet, staring at his wife. 'What is it, Jen?'

Her voice sounded like a faulty recording, indistinct and periodically fading so that some of the words were lost.

'It's Jo . . . please come, she's been . . . horrible and I can't believe . . . please come now . . . oh God, help her, please . . .'

She would have fallen to the floor if Nick hadn't caught her in time.

2

I

The genetically adapted virus containing TCDD (tetrachlorodibenzo-para-dioxin), developed in the Zone Two laboratories on Starbuck Island, had been spectacularly effective in contaminating the most densely populated areas of Africa, Asia, the subcontinent of India, China and the Far East. Burrowing its way into the gut of animals, from small rodents to man, the virus attacked the cellular structure of its host, causing cancer, disruption of blood-cell function, deformation of the liver and other organs, leading eventually and inevitably to death.

It had been deployed via the water supply and thence by the con-taminated hosts themselves, which passed it on to other animals and humans by means of direct contact, infected faeces and by the rotting corpses, each of which was a bacteriological factory in miniature. A single contaminated corpse, for instance, could wipe out a village or small town. It was the modern version of the Black Death, which swept Europe in the Middle Ages, only this time the plague was man-made, scientifically deployed and a hundred times more virulent.

No one had been forewarned. No one – not politicians, scientists, business leaders nor even military personnel – could be trusted not to reveal the existence of the Primary Plan before its inception, and there-fore everyone without exception in the Designated Areas was included.

Contamination squads – specially trained units operating under orders from Future Crisis Operations Executive – dumped canisters of the TCDD virus in streams, rivers and reservoirs – only a few parts per million were required. Even had the authorities suspected that some form of toxic contaminant was being added to the water supply they would have needed highly sophisticated detection equipment, which they didn't have, to verify the act. As it was, they were in total ignorance that the covert operation had been mounted and put into effect.

Once ingested by the population, it went immediately to work.

C-Day + 7 (one week after Contamination Day) nearly fifty per cent of those in the Designated Areas had been infected.

C-Day + 12 and the first deaths were being reported, and thereafter the red line on the graph rose steeply to the vertical as millions perished in writhing agony.

Once begun, the process was self-perpetuating. The mounds of rotting corpses, left where they fell because there was no one to bury them, spread the contamination to the soil. Rainwater washed it into sewers, streams and rivers. A black stain spread across continents, killing every form of animal life it encountered. The numbers of dead and dying went rapidly from hundreds to thousands to millions, to tens of millions and then to hundreds of millions. Statistics were meaningless; megadeaths became the standard term of measurement.

It was the Chinese who tried most desperately to find an answer. They were successful in isolating the virus, but its rapid spread left no time to deal with a chemical substance that hadn't existed until man invented it. The Chinese were frantically seeking an antidote to the most deadly poison on earth, and no such antidote existed.

Three weeks after C-Day it was estimated that more than one and a half billion people had died. This was still a long way short of the projected target of 4.3 billion, but it was an encouraging start. The poison would carry on doing its work because there was no way it could be stopped. Even the most remote regions with their own independent water supply weren't safe, thanks to cloud seeding: God's rain falling from the skies brought death in parts per million.

The scientists at Starbuck had warned that this technique should be used only as a back-up to the main operation; clouds were at the beck and call of winds and winds were no respecters of national boundaries. A cloud bearing its deadly load of TCDD might cross an ocean and drip creeping black death on friend instead of foe – or, worse still, on the land of its perpetrators. Great care had to be taken to confine the cloud-borne contamination to specific geographical localities whose meteorological patterns and trade winds could be plotted with a high degree of certainty.

As the weeks went by and the death toll mounted and entire cities, regions, states, countries and continents were progressively laid waste, the decaying carcases were subjected to the gradual yet ineluctable processes of nature.

Still alive and thriving inside the cellular structure of the dead, the virus increased in concentration and began to infect the soil. Sewers became biological fermentation tanks. Rivers were log-jammed with sodden, decomposing corpses adding their toxic load to the already bacteriologically fertile water. On the seaboards of every affected continent mighty rivers and small streams alike discharged their quota of chemical-bearing virus into the oceans.

The black stain spread from the landmasses and began to seep outwards in ever-widening circles, carried by the mingling currents into every ocean of the world. In relation to the volume of water it was an exceedingly minute concentration, but it had been genetically adapted to survive in conditions that otherwise would have dissipated and destroyed it.

To the scientists at Starbuck, who had accomplished the task set them, their pride and jubilation was unclouded by any fears of what might happen now that the Primary Plan had been implemented and successfully concluded. They reasoned that the amount of TCDD in global terms was infinitesimal, hardly enough to be measured even with the most sensitive instruments.

Literally, a drop in the ocean.

2

The film was all the more horrific because it was silent: mute, dreamlike images of death.

Continuous movement and fast disjointed cutting engendered in the viewer the impression that this was the work of an insane director who'd abandoned the conventional technique of moviemaking and instead pointed his camera randomly at bodies erupting with cancerous growths and babies decaying in gutters. As a horror film it was brilliant in its totally objective non-involvement: a clinical record in lurid, disgusting Technicolor.

Shot by telephoto lens from a helicopter, whose shadow flitted brokenly over buildings and raced along streets, this was official Fut/COE footage of the results of the Primary Plan – proof of its success for the politicians and military brass.

'I'm impressed, Lloyd,' hissed Wayne Hansom, the secretary of state, into General Malden's ear. 'Not a sign of life, and yet all facilities left intact. We couldn't have achieved this even with our neutron bomb capability.'

'Aside from which, the expense would have been prohibitive on this scale. The cost effectiveness of a bacteriological strike can't be matched by any other method.' Malden's voice was soft and measured as usual, yet with an undercurrent of excitement, of nervous glee. 'We're talking about a few cents per hundred thousand, Wayne. Plus we made use of the army's existing delivery technology – no fancy systems had to be developed. It was all the usual hardware manned by crews specially trained in handling contaminants.'

They lapsed into engrossed silence, watching the film, an aide replenishing their glasses when they ran dry. Malden had seen it perhaps a dozen times already but wasn't bored. The close-ups were fascinating. The Primary Plan had fulfilled all their expectations and the secretary of state would have no hesitation in commending Fut/COE's role to the President when he made his report.

One of the State Department officials had a question. How soon before the target figure of 4.3 billion was met? At this moment in time, he pointed out, there was a considerable shortfall.

Malden delegated that one to Major Dukes, whose stolid black features concealed a brain bulging with data. 'Our original projection was C-Day plus four months for virtual wipeout of the Designated Areas, but it now appears more realistic to think in terms of C-Day plus six months. Right this minute we're approaching two billion, which means that all cities and large towns have been zilched. Obviously the dense urban populations were easiest to hit. The rural and less-populated regions will take longer for precisely that reason. But the virus will get to them eventually because nothing can stop it. By C-Day plus six' – he turned down both thumbs – 'total wipeout.'

Hansom and Malden exchanged looks, smiling into each other's eyes.

'As I understand it, you're completely happy about containment.' This was neither statement nor query, but rather a nervous plea for reassurance from Jim Devanney, the assistant secretary of state. Fingers drumming the arm of his chair, eyes behind gold-rimmed bifocals swivelling from face to face.

Malden's faint smile snapped off like a light. 'Completely. Isn't that right, Lutz?'

'TCDD in the form of the virus as developed at Starbuck is highly contagious and is transmitted either by person-to-person contact or through the water supply,' intoned the scientific officer. 'It can't be transmitted any other way. There is no risk of spreading the infection to landmasses many thousands of miles away, absolutely none whatsoever.'

'Supposing an infected person were to carry the disease to the United States,' Devanney proposed. 'That's possible, isn't it, if they take days or even weeks to die after being infected?'

Lutz smiled, amused by the naïveté of the layman. 'If an infected person managed to reach the United States – highly unlikely because the symptoms are debilitating in the extreme – we should know at once. One of the first signs of infection is chloracne, a particularly unpleasant and very noticeable skin complaint. Such a person would be handed over to the military and quietly and effectively disposed of.'

'And what about the people he travelled with – those on the same aircraft or ship?' Devanney persisted.

'They would be quarantined until such time as we were satisfied beyond any doubt that they were free of the disease.' Lutz leaned forward, eyebrows raised, his neck thin and veined like an ostrich's. 'I can categorically assure the Assistant Secretary that we have provided for all eventualities, unlikely as they may be. Believe me, sir, anyone infected with the virus will be in no fit state to travel.'

Devanney gnawed his lip, still uneasy. 'It can't travel by air? I mean, carried by the trade winds?'

Eyes closed, Lutz shook his head.

One of the State Department officials said, 'But it can travel by water – presumably there's a considerable runoff from the infected bodies that will find its way into the oceans eventually? What happens to it then?'

It was Malden who said brusquely, 'Nothing happens to it. The concentration is minute to begin with – only a few parts per million. In the oceans it will simply dissipate until it's ineffective.'

'You've carried out tests to show this,' Hansom said.

'Of course.' Malden reached for his crystal glass and took a sip of Perrier. 'The matter of containment has received the most careful and thorough investigation at Starbuck. I can give you gentlemen an absolute assurance. You need have no qualms.'

Whatever qualms Jim Devanney might still have entertained he kept to himself. He listened to Major Dukes, who went on to talk about the Secondary Plan. The Russians had cooperated fully in the Primary Plan, while knowing nothing about the Secondary. They had helped in the extermination of three-quarters of the global population by taking care of China, their traditional adversary, but would play no part in the recolonisation of the Designated Areas by the mutant breeds now being developed in Zone Four. Though as Major Dukes was at pains to make clear, whereas the Primary Plan had taken five years to come to fruition, the Secondary might take fifty years or even longer. Genetic experimentation on pollution and anoxia victims was not only difficult and highly complex, but by its very nature long-term.

'There is no way of speeding up the breeding cycle of the human species,' Dukes explained regretfully. 'Even mutants take the usual span of time to reach adulthood. Unless we can adapt our present stock so that it can exist in a redundant atmosphere – that is, with less than five per cent oxygen content – we have no choice but to wait for their offspring to reach maturity. Or at least puberty,' he added with a wry smile.

'How close are you to producing a mutant breed that can survive in these conditions?' asked one of the State Department officials, a middle-aged woman with dyed red hair and eyebrows shaped like seagull's wings.

Major Dukes looked apologetic. 'I'm afraid that that information is under strict security classification, ma'am. I'm not at liberty to divulge it, even to the present company, with respect.'

Malden didn't miss the look of outrage creeping into the woman's eyes. He said smoothly, 'For obvious reasons all material relating to Zone Four has to be restricted, as I'm sure you'll appreciate.' He glanced in Hansom's direction. 'But I don't see why we couldn't stretch a point in this instance. Mr Secretary?'

Hansom waved a condescending hand.

'I won't go into the technicalities, but we are making excellent progress,' Malden informed them. 'After working on this for the past seven years, we're getting to the point where we can breed suitable specimens in the laboratory using sperm and ova from anoxia victims, and then genetically manipulate the DNA structure to encourage certain characteristics and eliminate others. The main problem, as Major Dukes has already indicated, is generational – it will take at least a couple of generations before we can start to breed in bulk. Starbuck's director, Dr Rolsom, has also been conducting experiments in surgical adaptation, but we don't yet know whether this will be successful. It could possibly be a shortcut to producing the mutes we need for our recolonisation programme.'

'Mutes?' queried Devanney with a frown.

'The Starbuck term for mutants,' Malden elucidated. 'Molecular biologists have their own slang, like all closed communities.'

'The TCDD virus was created by genetic means, isn't that so?' asked the red-haired woman. When Malden nodded she said, 'Then why not use the same technique to produce these mutes of yours? Isn't the process similar?'

Malden called on Lutz, the expert, who nodded briskly and explained, 'You're quite right, ma'am. Gene splicing – in other words chopping up DNA to obtain the pieces you want and then growing multiple copies – is the same basic technique used in all genetic manipulation experiments. But the order of complexity alters dramatically with different organisms. Let us take, say, a simple laboratory strain of Escherichia coli, or E. coli, as it's known. This is the bacterium that lives in the human gut and has a single chromosome. Incidentally, the TCDD-bearing virus is even more primitive in terms of cell structure. Anyway, when we come to deal with human cells, which are roughly six hundred times the size of *E. coli*, these have not just one chromosome but forty-six. Each human cell contains a thousand times more DNA than a single cell of *E. coli*, so perhaps you can gain some idea of how much more complex it becomes when you're dealing with the human cell, even though we're employing the same gene-splicing techniques of restriction enzymes and a plasmid cloning vehicle to—'

'Yes, yes, yes.' The red-haired woman raised a hand in self-defence. 'I take your point – or rather, I don't. But never mind.'

'And when you've perfected this mutant technique, or process, or whatever it is,' said Jim Devanney, 'how many of these creatures can be produced?'

Malden said, 'Once we have the genetic blueprint, as many as we need. A million. Ten million. A billion.' He shrugged. 'There's literally no limit. We can recolonise all of Africa, India, the Far East, China – everywhere – with our own people.'

'People?' Devanney said, staring. *'You call them people?'*

'Whatever you care to call them, they'll be ours,' Wayne Hansom said, his upper lip slightly curled where a fine scar tugged at it. 'Ten years from now the Russians will be gasping for breath themselves; they'll be in no fit state to offer any kind of challenge. At least half their population will be on the verge of extinction. In my opinion we're very fortunate that General Malden was perceptive enough to foresee this several years ago and to lay his plans accordingly. Fut/COE has proved itself of inestimable benefit to the United States, as I'm sure everyone here today acknowledges.'

'You mentioned something about surgical experiments,' Devanney said to Malden. He was like a man with a loose tooth who couldn't stop probing it with his tongue. 'On whom are you experimenting?'

'Children,' Malden said, smiling at him. If the whining son of a bitch wanted it, he could have it straight between the eyes. 'The Pryce-Darc Clinic sends us kids with pollution sickness and genetic deformities. Dr Rolsom came up with the idea that we could make use of their defects and surgically adapt them for our own purposes. Grafting tissues and transplanting organs and so on.'

'You're using *children*?' Devanney said faintly. 'In God's name, why?'

'Research,' Malden said, as if he'd been asked a stupid question. 'Maybe we can construct the perfect model for the next generation of Americans. I find that a pretty exciting prospect, don't you?'

3

The rasping siren was part of his dream, warning him not to step into the minefield. Chase sat bolt-upright, the sound real and all around him as the dream faded into the warm black air.

Switching on the bedside lamp, he reached for the telephone just as the red light began to wink in time to the urgent bleeping. He snatched up the handset and threw back the sheets.

'Duty Officer, sir, somebody trying to gain entry through Access Five.'

He recognised Drew's voice. 'How many, Sam?'

'We're not sure. Eight, ten, maybe more.'

'Are all other access points secure?'

'So far, though Eight and Nine have yet to report.'

The attack hadn't been unexpected. Even though the Tomb was hidden below ground and even though the supply trucks approached Desert Range from the Nevada side, keeping a hundred miles clear of Baker, Garrison, Mitford and Lund, the movement of supplies could have been spotted by somebody with a curious mind and a suspicious nature. Probably they thought it was a top-secret government establishment – as it had been once – which in these fraught times would be enough to provoke hostility.

None of that surprised Chase. Nobody was sure any more who controlled what. The location of the political and military seat of power – still referred to as Washington – was a mystery to the population at large. For a while 'Washington' had been in Des Moines, then moved, so rumour had it, to Minneapolis. When the president appeared on television, speaking from a replica of the Oval Office, he might have been on the far side of the moon as far as anyone knew.

The general public had the certain conviction that their esteemed leaders had folded their tents and stolen softly into the night. In fact they'd stolen, according to Prothero, to the Strategic Air Command headquarters near Omaha, Nebraska: an impregnable underground installation that had been constructed to protect SAC from nuclear attack and which might have been custom-built to serve as a command and communications centre for 'Washington' and the Pentagon. The air in Nebraska was still breathable, with the additional safeguard that SAC HQ was a sealed enclosure with its own self-contained oxygen plant.

The siren's harsh blare would have woken the dead, so Chase was prepared for the bleary-eyed faces peering out of the rooms as he ran for the elevator. He didn't waste breath with explanations; everyone had been drilled in the emergency procedure. He thumbed the button, fretting as the huge elevator rose with ponderous slowness to the upper level. If the attackers were from one of the nearby townships they might be merely a bunch of guys filled with liquor and frustrations who'd decided to find out what was going on at the old Desert Range MX missile site. That was his hope, because their security force was more than adequate to deal with what might be a straightforward policing situation.

And then again, maybe they weren't just curious, and that could be bad.

All year long there'd been a steadily growing exodus from the south. This corner of Nevada, mostly desert scrub and dried-up water holes, wasn't exactly hospitable, and so the stream of immigrants kept right on heading north, looking for a better place to settle. Chase hadn't seen any of them with his own eyes, but he'd seen the reports. Among the dispossessed families and the anoxia and pollution victims were looters, drug-crazed youngsters and, worst of all, tribes of 'O-zoes' – those who had suffered genetic damage to the brain cells due to ozone depletion in the upper atmosphere. He'd heard tales of bloody battles on the road and of small towns terrorised by demented mobs. His fear was that some of these had accidentally stumbled across the site, in which case they could be in for real trouble.

The grain of comfort he clung to was that even at this moment

Frank Hanamura was setting up the pilot plant on the Scripps' research vessel in San Diego. At least Hanamura and his team were well out of it and able to carry on the work.

Sam Drew looked up from the map table as Chase entered the operations room. Drew was ex-Army, like most of the others in the security force, all of whom had been carefully screened and chosen for their commitment to the project. A guard in dun-coloured camouflage gear stood at his elbow and there were three radio operators wearing headsets at the communications console, receiving reports and issuing instructions to the other command posts, nine in all, throughout the complex.

Drew brought Chase up to date on the situation. He was a compact, stocky man with a frizz of prematurely greying hair. They sometimes played chess together, with Drew invariably the winner. 'All other access points are secure – no signs of attack,' he said, circumscribing the layout of the Tomb with an outspread hand. 'Either they don't know about the other entrances or they've decided to concentrate on this sector.' He suddenly raised his hand. 'Listen!'

From thirty feet above their heads came the muted rattle of small-arms fire. The operations room was on the topmost level, yet still protected by a thick slab of reinforced concrete and a series of lead-lined steel shutters.

'Any chance of them getting in through the silo door?' Chase asked worriedly.

'Not a snowflake in hell.' Drew shook his head. 'Not unless they've got a nuke warhead handy. The retracting cover weighs more than seven hundred tons. No, their only hope is through the Personnel entrance, and I've posted six extra men there. We can pick 'em off like wood pigeons as they come through. That's if they can break down the door – which is about as likely as a cow giving processed cheese.'

'It's like being a rat in a trap.'

'A pretty damn secure rat.' Drew didn't seem too concerned, which Chase found reassuring.

'Any idea who they are? O-zoes, maybe?'

'Buchan got a peek at them through the scope, but the light wasn't good enough to make out any detail.' Drew nodded towards the clock on the slabbed wall, which read four forty-seven. 'Still dark up there.'

'How long before dawn?'

'About an hour. But it should be light enough to identify them before then if you want to risk putting the scope up.'

'Is that their gunfire or ours?' Chase asked.

Drew grimaced. 'Them, the crazy bastards. They're taking potshots at the door. I wouldn't worry about it; they're going to need more than a 9-millimetre shell to even put a dent in it.'

Chase studied the site layout in the cone of light. The complex was in no immediate danger. Each access point was secure and under guard. Desert Range had been built to withstand all but a direct nuclear strike . . . so why was he uneasy? What was bothering him?

What was bothering him, he realised, was that the location of the site had been discovered. This particular group mightn't pose much of a threat, but suppose they sent for reinforcements or spread the word around? The Tomb would become a sitting target for every gun-happy loon within a hundred miles. In no time at all they would be under siege – and it didn't take a tactical genius to realise that this was their one weak point. With their supplies cut off, sooner or later the moles would have to push their snouts aboveground and get their heads blown off.

'Access Six in Blue Sector,' Chase said, tapping the layout with his finger. 'That's about a mile away, right?' He looked at Drew, who nodded slowly, frowning. 'I want you to put as many men as you can spare on the surface and have them circle around to cut off the attackers' retreat.' He described an arc on the map. 'Our men open fire at the same time as we come up through Access Five. If we time it for daybreak we should be sure of getting them all.'

Drew blinked and gazed at Chase, dumbfounded. His Adam's apple bobbed above the white triangle of sweat shirt at the open collar of his dark brown tunic. 'You want to wipe 'em out?'

'Every single one. No survivors.'

'You think that's necessary?'

'Listen, Sam, if word gets out, they'll come back with every piece of heavy armament they can lay their hands on. We've got to stop that

before it starts.' Chase glanced at the clock. 'It's nearly five. How long
will it take to get your men in position?'

'Fifty, sixty minutes.' Drew stroked his chin with hairy fingers. 'That
should be plenty of time to deploy before full light.'

'Let's make it dead on 6 a.m. to make sure.'

'"Dead" being the operative word,' said Drew, looking at Chase as
if he'd never seen him before. In a sense he never had.

4

Forty minutes later they were standing tensely in the concrete cubicle
next to the ramp leading up to Access Five. Now and then shots could
be heard ricocheting off the steel door and whining into the desert air
like demented wasps. In the corridor outside six men in combat gear
were squatting with their backs to the wall, smoking and quietly talking,
automatic weapons propped between their jutting knees.

Buchan was waiting nervously by the periscope control box mounted
on the wall. 'Beats me what the fuck they want.' He gestured vaguely.
'None of this scientific stuff can be of any use. What are they *after?*'

'Perhaps it's the idea of people hiding underground they don't like,'
Chase said. 'Makes them feel insecure. Vulnerable. And when things get
really bad out there they'll want somewhere safe to run to. This is it.'

'How bad are things gonna get, sir?' Buchan asked. He was sweating
profusely.

'Don't you listen to the news bulletins?'

'What, you mean all that stuff in Africa and India and those places? I
thought that was a plague of some kind, spread by bad drinking water.
Nothin' to do with the climate.'

'We don't know for sure what caused it,' Chase said. 'If anybody
does they're keeping quiet.' He was about to go on and then found he
couldn't. All of a sudden he felt very weary, and it had nothing to do
with being hauled from his bed in the early hours of the morning. His
fatigue was rooted in every fibre of his being, much like the effect of
for ever climbing a slippery slope that got steeper and slipperier, and
however hard you struggled you kept sliding down into unimaginable

depths. In the absence of Cheryl and Dan, his one, tenuous lifeline was somewhere out in the Pacific. But if the trials failed and the lifeline broke, the slope would become a vertical plunge into oblivion for himself and all mankind.

'Five minutes,' Drew said, swivelling his black-haired wrist to look at his watch. 'Want to take a gander topside?' he asked Chase.

Buchan cleared his throat explosively and blurted out to Drew, 'Sir, I gotta tell you: there's two of our guys out there somewhere – Rubiera and Monteith.' He gulped, staring at the floor with stricken eyes. 'They went up before the alarm, hunting for fresh meat. The guys do that, pick up a rabbit or a prairie fox and get the cook to put it in the pot. I mean I know it's against regulations . . .' His hoarse voice died miserably.

Drew was standing rigidly, fists bunched at his sides, the cords on his neck sticking out. 'The stupid bastards! Did you see either of them when you looked through the scope? Was there any *sign* of them?'

'Like I told you before, there were shapes but that was all. It was too dark. Maybe they came in through another entrance?' Buchan said hopefully. 'They might have seen the attack coming and couldn't make it back there—'

'All access points are sealed,' Drew told him harshly. 'Nobody has entered the complex. Nobody. If Rubiera and Monteith went out, they're still out!'

Chase stepped forward, pointing to the control box. 'Hit it!'

Buchan pressed the green button with the heel of his hand and the periscope slid upwards, accompanied by the whine of hydraulics. Buchan flipped down the ribbed rubber handgrips, then stood aside for Chase to look through the moulded rubber eye-piece. He adjusted the focus. There was nothing much to see at first except a thin grey mist. Against the flat colourless backdrop he could just make out a group of shadowy figures. Chase turned the calibrated setting to greater magnification and faces loomed in close-up. The skin on the back of his neck crawled. He swallowed a nasty taste in his throat.

There were eight or nine of the O-zoes, as near as he could tell. Pitted and scarred like lepers, dressed in rags, they were huddled around a pathetic fire from which a thin trickle of smoke ascended into the whitening sky. He hadn't expected this; hadn't been prepared for kids. The oldest couldn't have been more than thirteen. Some of the others were aged nine or ten, maybe, and one of them, a girl, was possibly younger still.

It was too late to look away; his eye had taken in too much detail. A head with the flesh hanging off it like strips of yellow tissue paper. A boy with milky-white eyeballs staring emptily into the distance. A girl with scabrous patches of raw flesh on her back and buttocks. Some had a black fungal growth obliterating their face. At least four that he could see had fingers or hands or complete limbs missing, leaving only raw stumps through which the pale bone gleamed.

And in every eye – even the blind boy – was a kind of bloodlust dementia that made Chase break out in a cold sweat and caused his testicles to shrivel.

The bloodlust was actual, not his imagination. Near the fire lay two corpses, crudely dismembered. They still had heads, but the tatters of their brown tunics swathed shoulders without arms, and the empty legless trousers were torn wide open. The children had divided the spoils; they held their portions on pointed sticks to the smoky flames, crunching and chewing with rapt concentration and ravenous enjoyment.

Chase turned away and leaned weakly against the wall. Pearls of sweat covered his face and neck. He didn't say anything, merely shook his head as Drew gripped the handles and looked into the eyepiece.

5

The three men in the concrete cubicle with its garish contorting nudes stood without moving. Distantly, like snapping twigs, they heard the spasmodic stutter of automatic weapons, followed by the fading reverberations across the flat landscape. They heard the screams, too; muffled by the steel and concrete surrounding them, they reminded Chase of seagulls whooping and crying in a parody of human pain. Then the screams were not muffled but loud – much louder – as the guards in the corridor slid open the heavy steel door and charged up the sand-blown steps, rifles and machine-pistols spitting death.

No one in the cubicle wanted to witness the carnage thirty feet above his head. Imagining it was as bad, perhaps worse. Chase and Drew still felt sickened by the images of those grotesque children, which Buchan had refused to look upon.

Moments later the firing ceased.

Chase wiped his face and neck with his wadded handkerchief. Would he have experienced less guilt, less responsibility, if they had been adults and not children, common looters or a drunken mob?

But there were no comfortable or comforting rules any more, no genteel morality. The only rules, the only morality, concerned survival at all costs. The freakish children had lost their claim to humanity when the sulphur dioxide had corroded their tissues and the needles of ultraviolet radiation had lanced through the depleted ozone layer into their brains, corrupting each cell with cancerous madness. Given the chance, Chase knew, the children would have ravaged everyone they encountered, and the Tomb would have lived up to its name.

He followed Drew into the corridor and up the concrete steps. The air was cool and would have been refreshing, had it not been for the heavy taint of roasting flesh.

'Where do you suppose they came from?' Drew asked in a low voice. He was pale, his thick eyebrows like an unbroken dark bar.

Chase shrugged. 'No idea. Down south somewhere. You can't trust government reports any more. They say the official Devastated Areas don't extend north of Little Rock, but for all we know they could be twenty miles away, right on our doorstep.'

Behind him, Buchan said gloomily, 'You hear of them mobs all the time on Highway 15. Most of 'em are stoned out of their skulls on all kinds of shit. They don't have a notion which planet—'

Buchan turned his head suddenly, catching a whiff of roasting meat as he emerged above the concrete emplacement. His face contorted into a series of horizontal lines, as if the muscles were attached to drawstrings that had been suddenly yanked taut. Then he clutched himself and bent over, moaning, and brought up the contents of his stomach.

6

Two days later Prothero called again from New York. He wanted to know the word on Hanamura. Chase said it was too early to expect a result, encouraging or otherwise. 'I'll get through to you as soon as I hear anything,' he added.

'You may not have to.' Prothero's face was grey, the pouches underneath his eyes a livid purple. 'They're evacuating the city. It isn't official yet, and when it is there'll be a wholesale panic. I'm leaving right away. Is there room for one more in the Tomb?' he asked with gallows humour.

They'd often discussed the possibility – indeed the certainty – that one day New York would be evacuated, but now that it was actually here it still came as a blow. Another nail in the coffin. 'What about Ingrid?' asked Chase.

'She's gone back to Sweden. Her parents are there and she wants to be with them.'

'When are you planning to leave?' Prothero's wife had left him four years ago, Chase recalled, and his sons were married.

'Day after tomorrow.'

'I want you to do me a favour,' Chase said. 'I have a friend in New York, Dr Ruth Brosnan, who works at Manhattan Emergency on East 68th Street. Will you tell her what's happening, Pro? I wouldn't like to think of her being trapped there when they blow the whistle.'

'Sure, I'll tell her.'

'If she decides to come with you, can you arrange transportation?'

'Sure. There's a convoy of trucks and buses leaving at midnight on Thursday. I'll find her a place if she wants to leave.' He looked old and haggard. 'She'd be wise to, Gavin. One week from today this town will go berserk.'

7

The deteriorating conditions that had made Ken Prothero realise the game was finally up extended far beyond New York. The blight had affected a huge swathe of the eastern states, causing widespread panic and mass migration from the densely populated urban areas. Washington, DC had largely been abandoned, except for the poorest of the poor who hadn't the wherewithal to flee and no place to flee to.

Chesney Poulton, among the first to leave, had found refuge in the nearest of his three vacation homes, in the small fishing port of Engelhard, North Carolina, overlooking Pamlico Sound. The gated community had the reassuring presence of armed militia, funded by local residents, which had been reinforced by the deployment of National Guards to make the area ultra-secure. Poulton's pine lodge right on the water also had the advantage of being a short boat-ride away from Roanoke Island where his yacht, MV *Icarus*, was berthed.

Poulton had taken only one brief ocean trip so far this year. For three days he had cruised the Diamond Shoals off Cape Hatteras. It hadn't been a pleasant or relaxing outing. The air at sea was good, but the storms sweeping down from Greenland across the North Atlantic had brought ice blizzards (*in May, for chrissakes!*), plunging the temperature below zero.

There had been no lounging on the after-deck with his young companions of the moment. How far, he wondered, would he have to voyage to find decent weather? Poulton was badly in need of a few balmy weeks with the sun on his back while he sipped a chilled margarita and contemplated a slender toned physique. A couple of the Guardsmen on dock-patrol had caught his eye. He might suggest they accompany him, as his security detail, on his next trip. Two days' sail away was Bermuda, where hitherto he'd always enjoyed fantastic weather; the more he thought about it, the more enticing it sounded.

3

I

Cy Sprote lay spread-eagled in the warm liquid darkness with the woman kneeling over him, her hair brushing the insides of his thighs. His right hand moved across the soft swell of her buttocks and he heard her tremulous moan of rapture to the stealthy infiltration of his fingers. Sprote was himself in rapture. Never had he desired a woman so much in his life, and never had he received such pleasure from one.

Sprote had never rated so much as a second glance before. This had never surprised him. His unprepossessing appearance – a pale skin that the sun brought out in blotches, narrow chest, thin arms and spindly legs and his drooping, heavy-lidded eyes were not attractive features. Knowing the feeble figure he presented to the world had made him retire inside himself, obeying a natural impulse to protect himself.

He wasn't appealing to the opposite sex, and that was that.

Then from out of nowhere this magical experience had grabbed him by the scruff of the neck and tossed him over the moon, and Cy Sprote was still reeling from it.

She had been at Starbuck for several weeks before they struck up an acquaintance. He'd noticed her of course (there wasn't a man on the base who hadn't), but she'd been so utterly out of reach that he hadn't even fantasised about her, as he often did with desirable women seen at a distance. Sprote didn't even know her name; only that she was one of the scientific observers sent by the Russians as part of the reciprocal inspection pact. They were granted access to the research in Zone Two, while a team of American observers was allowed the same freedom at the Russian research centre in Kazakhstan.

Not himself employed in Zone Two, Sprote only chanced upon her in off-duty hours when he and his colleagues went across the lagoon to the clubhouse in the main complex. He wasn't a heavy drinker but liked to sit nursing a weak gin and tonic and watching the spectacular green and purple sunset while the conversation ebbed and flowed around him. Sometimes he might play pool or, if pressed, sit in on a poker game. But that particular evening he happened to be alone (the others had gone off to the squash court) and his thoughts were several thousand miles away in Portland, Maine, where his childhood still existed, it seemed to him, intact, untouched. Nothing could have been further from his mind than what, by a wonderful coincidence, then took place.

2

It started with a jammed cigarette machine.

Sprote was on his way back from the restroom when he saw the woman thumping and glaring at it with the kind of baffled, impotent rage that human beings reserve for machines that stubbornly refuse to perform the function for which they were designed. Sprote paused in the corridor. He would have carried on if the woman hadn't happened to catch his eye and thrown up her hands in a gesture of defeat. Even then he was reluctant to go to her aid, mainly because he was intimidated by a vision of beauty that seemed to him then, and still did, sheer perfection. She was tall for a woman – in low heels about the same height as he – and Sprote gazed into her green-flecked eyes for a full five seconds, mesmerised, before nervously touching the thinning patch on the crown of his head and performing an awkward shuffling dance of indecision.

Her first words to him were, 'These machines must have been invented by someone with a sadistic sense of humour. Or someone who wishes to destroy Russian-American relations, don't you think?'

'I'm afraid I don't smoke,' Sprote responded, immediately struck by the irrelevance of the remark. He moved hesitantly forward. 'Have you tried the coin refund?'

She shook her head, dark polished ringlets bouncing against the white sweep of her neck. 'I wanted cigarettes, not my own money back.' Her English was faultless, with only the trace of an accent that her low, husky voice made infinitely seductive to Sprote's burning ears.

He yanked the lever and coins clattered into the metal cup. One of the quarters was old and worn smooth, and after exchanging it for one of his own, he reinserted the money and asked her to try again. This time a pack of menthol Kools plopped into the tray. Sprote handed it to her, feeling ridiculously pleased, and she leaned forward and impetuously kissed his cheek.

If he'd been teetering on the brink before, Sprote now fell head over heels in love.

They drank and talked the rest of the evening, Sprote doing his fair share without any of his usual blushing, tongue-tied embarrassment. He was quietly amazed at himself. He'd never been so forthcoming, so relaxed, so witty. Natassya laughed at his jokes and became rapt when he spoke of his childhood and thoughtful whenever he ventured an opinion. His confidence grew. It was as if his personality, until now bound tightly in a straitjacket, had been miraculously released, and he experienced a giddy starburst of freedom that was as intoxicating as champagne.

As for Natassya, she staggered him by confessing that she was lonely. She'd been at Starbuck for six weeks, and apart from her Russian colleagues, she had no real friends. And as for male company – her wide sensuous mouth was pulled down at the corners – well, they turned out to be either boring scientists without any topics of conversation outside of their specialised fields or service personnel with but a single thought in their tiny grubby minds. Sprote would never believe, Natassya told him, how clumsy and boorish they could be in their sexual advances. One drink, a bit of chat and they expected her to fall into bed. Not only was it insulting but also extremely immature.

Sprote sympathised totally, almost vehemently, shaking his head at such oafish behaviour. Secretly he resolved to be a paragon of all the opposite virtues: polite, caring, interesting, amusing, sophisticated and above all, not too pushy.

Maybe he had taken this to extremes, because eight days later, while strolling along the beach in the tropical twilight, Natassya had enquired why he didn't find her physically attractive.

Sprote was struck dumb. He gaped at her in the mellow golden light, stricken by an unbearable and overpowering yearning. Minutes later they were in each other's arms and Natassya was smothering his thin face in kisses and whispering endearments in husky Russian. Minutes after that they were making love on a bed of ferns beneath the dry, rustling fronds of a palm tree, the gentle lisp of the waves synchronised to their movements, a tempo they soon left behind . . .

They had made love every night since that first night two weeks ago. It was dangerous, and they had to be careful. As scientific liaison officer for Zone Four, Sprote had been expressly warned against becoming involved with any member of the Russian team, male or female. At a conservative reckoning, about a quarter of the so-called Russian scientists would be working for the Federal Russian Security Bureau. For the American personnel attached to Zone Four, the cover story was that they were engaged in research into the long-term effects of TCDD using human guinea pigs and that this was too hazardous to allow the Russians free access. In the early days some of the Russian military brass *had* been taken on a conducted tour, but everything they had been shown had been rigged, stage-managed. The real research into genetic manipulation and breeding experiments had been out of sight behind locked doors.

And Sprote wasn't without his own suspicions. For wasn't it, being brutally realistic, such fantastic good fortune that it just *had* to be a Russian intelligence ploy? He detested the thought (and hated himself for thinking it), but it had to be faced and somehow resolved, one way or the other.

So he faced it by devising a ploy of his own. He pretended to get drunk.

As Natassya knew by now that he wasn't a heavy drinker and therefore accustomed to it, this would have been the perfect opportunity for her, had she wished, to pump him for information. Sprote made it even easier by raising the subject himself. Hoping his slurred speech was convincing, he hinted that Zone Four wasn't all that it pretended to be, that some aspects of the research being carried out there were of a highly classified nature. To his delight, which he disguised by a fit of supposedly drunken giggles, Natassya told him pretty quickly that he was acting like a boring scientist and would he please shut up and make love to her at once? Scientific lectures she could do without; what she really wanted was to feel him hard inside her.

He obliged the lady, ever more deeply, hopelessly, in love. He was as certain as he'd ever been about anything in his life that her feelings for him were genuine and not part of a devious conspiracy. Natassya Pavlovitch had passed the test with flying colours.

In a curious and perverse way, this made Sprote want to unburden himself to her. Disgust was too feeble a word for what he felt about his work in Zone Four. It made him sick to the stomach. He despised himself for his involvement over the past five years. Five years! How on earth had he stood it? And, more to the point, why? It was a catalogue of horror that ranked with the medical experiments in the Nazi concentration camps, and he, God help him, had played a part, been a leading character in this barbarity. He jerked and trembled and felt himself go as Natassya worked him fluidly with her soft mouth, her cool firm hands aiding the spasm of release. He moaned and went slack, his body quivering as the urgent ecstasy died out of it.

She snuggled close, smearing his chest with a burning kiss, her warm breasts and hard dark nipples flattening against his stomach. Her hair clung to her neck like seaweed. 'Was that good, Cy?' Natassya pressed her damp face to him. 'Do you like it in my mouth?'

'It was beautiful, fantastic. God, I can't tell you. I'm not very experienced with women.'

'Now, Cy, you've told me that before and I don't believe it. You know how to give a woman pleasure. You must have pleasured hundreds of women.'

'Hundreds . . .' He laughed weakly. 'If that was true, which it isn't, none of them could have compared with you, Natassya.'

He stroked her hair, feeling relaxed and at peace, yet his mind was singing with exhilaration. He hadn't the words to express his gratitude. To be loved was incredible enough in itself, but that it should be this woman who loved him, the most perfect dream-image he could possibly have imagined! His happiness filled up, overflowing.

As if sharing his thoughts, Natassya said, 'You've made me so very happy, Cy. I want us always to be together. I never want to leave you.'

He thought he detected a strained note of pleading in her voice. There were other emotions buried there, and she was holding on to him fiercely. Sprote felt a convulsive shudder pass through her body.

'You don't have to leave me,' he comforted her. 'There's no reason why—'

But to his alarm and mystification she was sobbing now, dry, heart-broken sobs that were muffled against his chest. He tried to lift her head, peering at her in the dim light that filtered in through the slatted blinds; but she resisted, turning her face away from him. 'Please don't, Cy. Don't look at me like this.'

'Darling, what is it? What's upset you?' To Sprote, female psychology was as deep and impenetrable a mystery as the Pyramids. He knew that women cried when they were happy, but these without doubt were tears of sadness, of anguish. 'Come on, honey, tell me!' he pleaded. 'Let me share it, let me help you!'

Natassya raised her head and wiped her eyes with the heel of her hand.

'I'm being stupid. It's nothing.' She tried to smile. 'While we are together we'll be happy. If it lasts for only a few weeks . . . well, we have that. It's better than nothing. Let's take our happiness while it lasts and forget about the future. I'm just being stupid, darling. Forgive me.'

'What are you talking about, Natassya?' Sprote held her shoulders and stared at her, his heart thudding painfully. 'Are they sending you back to Russia? Is that what you're trying to tell me?'

Natassya freed herself and sat up, slender and pale in the darkness, and leaned against her raised knees. 'Cy, dearest, I don't see how it *can* last much longer. When the work here is finished we'll both be sent home, you to America, me to Russia. There isn't much left to do now that the Primary Plan has been concluded, for either of us. Starbuck will be shut down and that will be the end – for it and for us.'

What she said was true – in a sense. Now that the work in Zone Two was winding to a close there would be no need of the Russian presence on the island. But in another sense she was quite wrong. The Primary Plan was indeed finished, whereas the Secondary Plan was in its infancy, with decades of research ahead. In ten or twenty years' time he would still be here, Sprote realised bleakly, alone, Natassya gone with the rest of the Russian observers. He breathed in and out slowly, his head whirling with ideas, notions, plans, a chain reaction of thought like a lightning bolt through his brain.

'Would you be willing to stay here – with me – if it could be arranged?'

'Yes, of course,' she answered dully, 'but how is that possible when the research will be finished in a few months? We shall have to leave. We will be sent home—'

Sprote smoothed her hair from her forehead and shaped his hands to her face, a pallid oval with rudimentary eyes and lips. 'We're not through here,' he mouthed softly. 'The research goes on – and if you're prepared to defect, I can arrange for you to stay here, on Starbuck.'

'Stay here? There is more work to be done on the Primary Plan?'

'No, my darling, not the Primary Plan,' Sprote said with infinite tenderness and undying love.

3

The trip from New York had left its mark in the lines of strain around Ruth's eyes and mouth. Her smile of greeting was perfunctory, her handshake limp. It seemed to Chase as if a vital part of her had been left behind, and this, the dark-haired woman seated across the desk, was a faded facsimile.

Chase had invited them down to his office, which Prothero viewed with a faint air of disgruntlement. It was austere and windowless, corkboard-lined walls pinned with graphs, data sheets and flow charts. Silver-coated pipes were fixed to the ceiling and coloured ribbons fluttered from the air-conditioning vent.

'Okay to smoke down here?' he asked, in the act of lighting a cheroot.

'Go ahead,' Chase said with a smile. 'The Pentagon spent billions of dollars on this place and at least half of it must have gone on air-conditioning.'

'Where's the vessel stationed?' Prothero asked.

Chase got up and pointed it out on the large wall map crisscrossed with red, blue and green tape. 'She's called the *Nierenberg*, one of the Scripps' fleet, at present here, two hundred miles out on latitude thirty-five degrees, roughly midway between San Diego and San Francisco.' He sat down and held up a yellow flimsy – a radio message not two hours old. 'First report from Hanamura says they've been operating the pilot plant for forty-eight hours nonstop. So far no hitches.' Chase tapped the plastic woodgrain desktop for luck. 'It's too soon to know for sure, but at least it looks encouraging.'

'Just as well,' Prothero said and didn't trouble to soften the blow. 'Gelstrom's dead. The financial situation is as yet unresolved. I can't get a straight answer from the JEG Corporation, which I guess means there's a major hitch. The funding might stop.' He gestured with his cheroot at the map. 'Does he say what tonnage they're producing?'

Chase read from the flimsy. 'Throughput of brine ten thousand gallons an hour. Oxygen yield of ninety-two per cent purity at fifteen plus tons an hour.'

'*Fifteen* tons an hour?' Prothero was aghast. 'Is that all? I understood that the existing industrial plant could produce ten times that amount?'

'That's right, it does,' Chase said. 'The Linde double-fractioning process extracts oxygen from the atmosphere and compresses it to ninety-eight per cent purity. But there isn't much point in taking oxygen from the depleted atmosphere only to put it back again. Splitting seawater is a totally different technical proposition. You've got to keep the gases separated so that they don't mingle and form an explosive vapour inside the cell. You've got to watch for corrosion and the build-up of hydrogen film on the anode, which can give off poisonous fumes. Don't forget, Pro, that this is an experimental plant. Output isn't significant. If Hanamura can overcome these problems we can scale up to a hundred times the size with a thousand times the tonnage for every plant we build.'

'How many plants will be needed?' Ruth asked. It was the first time she'd shown any interest.

'We estimate between fifty and sixty thousand spread around the world, with a greater number in the equatorial regions. Computer studies have shown that the oxygen shortfall in the atmosphere is currently running at about five hundred trillion tons. That's going to take a lot of making up.'

'How many's a trillion?' Prothero asked.

'A million million.'

Prothero's lined pouchy face looked glum.

Ruth said, 'Surely sixty thousand plants that size will take years to build. Decades.' She sounded sceptical, yet prepared, even desperate, to be convinced.

'Five to ten years,' Chase said. He saw the look of disbelief in her eyes and went on. 'Once we have the basic proved design there's no technical reason why we couldn't meet that deadline, given the resources.'

'You mean the money.'

'Yes.'

'Will you get it?'

Chase tugged at his beard. 'We have to get it. Ten years from now – say by 2050 at the very latest – we'll be fast running out of time. If we haven't achieved at least seventy per cent of our construction programme by then we might as well crawl away and count the seconds till our final breath.'

Ruth was watching him intently. 'If you get the money and you build enough of these oxygen plants by the deadline, will it be enough? What I'm asking is, can it actually be done? Will it *work*?'

She reminded Chase of a shipwrecked sailor clinging to a piece of driftwood who, having given himself up for dead, sights a desert island and can't accept the evidence of his own eyes.

'If we can replenish the atmosphere with oxygen instead of depleting it, we can restore the balance. But it all depends on Hanamura and whether the field trials deliver the goods. If they're successful, then yes, it can be done.' Chase smiled, seeing the faint gleam of renewed hope in her eyes. After the foul, miasmic canyons Ruth Brosnan had left behind, this must have seemed like a breath of fresh air.

'Something called "The Island Option" ring any bells?' Prothero asked Chase.

'Never heard of it.'

Prothero shook his head with a weary smile. 'It's the usual madness, Gavin. The government is *still* spending billions of dollars on harebrained secret projects when they ought to be concentrating on saving what's left of the environment. Won't they ever learn?'

'So what are they planning to do? Make Washington into an island and tow it out to sea?'

But Prothero didn't find Chase's facetiousness funny. 'Even that wouldn't surprise me,' he said gloomily. 'All I know is that one of their technical advisors is a US Air Force scientist, Major Gary Zittel. He's pushing the idea for all it's worth, apparently.'

Chase frowned. 'I've heard that name somewhere,' he said, trying to remember. 'Zittel . . .'

'Most likely his father you've heard of: Brad Zittel. He was one of the last Skylab astronauts back in the nineties.'

'That's right, I do remember. I never met him, but he worked for a time with Bill Inchcape at the National Climate Prediction Foundation in Colorado. So his son's following in his footsteps.'

'And up to his neck in some tomfoolery or other,' Prothero said darkly.

There was a knock at the door and a messenger came in with a yellow flimsy from the communications shack. Another message from the *Nierenberg*, Chase supposed, scanning the three lines. Prothero and Ruth saw the colour drain from his face. They waited silently as he digested it, brows knitted together. At last he said, 'It's from Goose Lake,' which meant nothing to either of them.

Part of Chase's mind registered their incomprehension. 'One of the Midnite-Net settlements in Oregon. Cheryl and Dan are living there,' he told them. 'Cheryl is ill. They think she's dying. They want me to go right away.'

4

Drew had provisioned the Jeep for a trip lasting five days, which was three more than Chase planned to take. The most direct route to Goose Lake – due west across Nevada then cutting through a corner of California – was about eight hundred miles, and that was assuming that the roads over mountains, through forests and across deserts were passable, without the need for detours.

He was reluctant to ask Ruth to accompany him, but her years of experience in treating anoxia and pollution victims might prove crucial. When asked, she readily agreed. She had brought a quantity of drugs used to treat anoxia patients from New York, though as she was at pains to point out, 'I can't promise anything, Gavin. A lot depends on how long she's been suffering from oxygen deficiency – if that's what it is.'

'I understand that. What I don't understand is how this could have happened to Cheryl when she's been in Oregon for the past five years. Dammit, there's hardly any pollution there, and the oxygen level is only a fraction below normal. It doesn't make sense!'

'It doesn't make sense that people who've smoked for forty years don't get lung cancer while some who've never smoked a cigarette in their life do. Some people are more susceptible to certain diseases.'

'Is anoxia always fatal?'

'I won't pretend that the death rate isn't high, but I have treated patients who would have died and managed to keep them alive. Drugs can help.'

They departed an hour after dawn the following day. Chase had asked the meteorology section for a detailed forecast for the northwestern sector of the country, though conditions at the moment were so unstable that it was about as reliable as consulting a mystic. Nonetheless, it was reassurance of a sort to be told that no major climatic anomalies were expected. The temperature medians, however, weren't so comforting. For this time of year, late September, they averaged an increase across the United States of $4°$ C – the result of the build-up of carbon dioxide in the atmosphere.

The greenhouse effect here at last, with a vengeance.

By 8 a.m. they had crossed the border into Nevada on Highway 73. The two-lane blacktop zigzagged up through Sacramento Pass, skirting the flanks of Wheeler Peak to their left, its thirteen-thousand-feet summit outlined raggedly against the bottomless blue of the sky. There wasn't a trace of snow up there, Chase saw, and no hint of any to come.

Ruth sat with a bolt-action hunting rifle across her knees, her black curly hair ruffled by the warm slipstream. She wore a loose plaid shirt, faded blue denims, and green leather ankle boots with white socks folded over the tops. The rifle was not merely a precaution; it was absolutely essential. Chase himself carried a Browning .32 in the zippered pocket of his windbreaker. The Jeep was stocked with food, water, cooking equipment, sleeping bags and a large canvas sheet for temporary shelter. They also carried three twelve-gallon jerry cans of gasoline, sufficient, he hoped, to get them to Goose Lake. Ruth's medical supplies were in an aluminium case stowed away underneath the other stuff. Those drugs were worth a small fortune.

There was still a blankness to Ruth's eyes, as if she were somewhere else, reliving a bad dream. Chase asked her about New York, hoping perhaps to purge the memory.

When she spoke, her lips were curved in something resembling a smile of despair. 'You can't imagine what it was like. In some ways it was a relief, knowing it finally had to finish. But the really hard part was in having failed; at last to admit defeat.'

'The situation was hopeless, and you did the best you could,' Chase said ineffectually. 'Christ, you did far more than that – you chose to stay when it would have been so easy to leave.'

'I can't forget the children; they were the worst,' Ruth said, unravelling a thread that trailed endlessly through her mind. 'At least the older ones had lived some sort of life before it ended. But those kids never stood a chance from the day they were born – from *before* they were born, because they were damaged in the womb.' She looked across at him. 'Have you ever seen a child suffering from pollution sickness?'

'Photographs and on film, that's all.'

'Pray to God you never see one in the flesh,' Ruth said. 'The symptoms are most evident in children under five – sore throat, slight temperature, nausea – what you'd think of as the usual children's complaints, nothing too serious. In the early days many doctors diagnosed scarlet fever, because the symptoms are very similar. Then it was found that the kids didn't respond to penicillin, which is the standard treatment for scarlet fever.

'In the next stage their temperature shoots up to 40° C and the lymph glands in the child's neck swell to the size of golf balls. The lips and tongue turn bright scarlet and red blotches appear on the chest, back and buttocks. After about a week, during which the high fever persists, the blood vessels in the eyes become congested and burst, rashes break out all over the body and the skin starts to peel from the fingers and toes.

'The damage isn't only external. They develop aneurysms – that's an irregular thickening of the coronary arteries, which weakens them – which leads to abnormalities in the heart rhythm and the rupture of the coronary artery itself. When that happens it's invariably fatal.'

'Is there no treatment?'

'We can lower the fever, which reduces inflammation and prevents the blood from clotting, but there's no real cure. The death rate is between fifty and sixty per cent, most of them under five.'

'And the cause is pollution in one form or another?'

Ruth nodded, watching the blur of road through the windshield. 'We still don't know precisely how or why. It could be a hereditary factor, some weakness or deficiency that's triggered by the deterioration in the environment. It's probable that these kids were genetically damaged to begin with and lacked the normal defence mechanisms to withstand pollutants in the air and water. We know from studies as far back as the eighties that environmental factors can cause abnormalities – the white blood cells contain broken fragments of chromosomes that jumble up the genetic message. This can cause cancer, spontaneous abortions, miscarriages and birth defects. The miscarriage rate over the past fifteen years has jumped up from a national average of 8.5 per cent to more than thirty per cent. The women who don't abort or miscarry produce offspring who are ripe candidates for pollution sickness. The poor little bastards can't win,' Ruth added without emotion. 'They're either aborted or born damaged.'

'What about anoxia?' Chase asked, thinking of Cheryl. 'Is it as common as pollution sickness?'

'Less so in people below the age of twenty-five.' Ruth propped the rifle between her knees and eased back in the bucket seat. 'It tends to affect the older age groups, presumably because they've been exposed to oxygen deficiency over a longer period and their tissues aren't as flexible and can't cope with the additional strain. It's a far more complex problem than pollution sickness and the medical background is sketchy. For one thing, we don't have any reliable figures on the number of people affected, or how many survive.' Her mouth twisted sourly. 'That's what I've devoted the last seven years of my life to finding out. Or maybe it's more accurate to say *wasted* the last seven years.'

'You did all you could. You're not to blame.'

'Oh, no, I don't blame myself,' Ruth corrected him. 'I just feel so fucking angry. How could we do this to ourselves? How could we have been so stupid and shortsighted?' She shook her head, gripped by a kind of impotent amazement. 'You know, it was all in your book, every last damn word of it – not just the stuff about environmental war, as if that weren't bad enough, but how we've crapped in our own nest, polluted the air we breathe with chemicals and turned the oceans into toxic soup. And Christ, we've known for nearly a century what we were doing and we kept right on doing it! What kind of species are we, for God's sake? Are we crazy or just plain stupid?'

'There are no votes in sewage,' Chase muttered.

'What?'

'Something Theo Detrick once said. He meant you can't blame the politicians, because they'd never get elected to office on an ecology ticket. Cleaning up the environment, much less protecting it, doesn't have the instant easy appeal the public demands. More production, more growth, more cash in the pocket, more goodies – those are what people vote for, certainly not for some earnest do-gooder preaching the doctrine that consumption is bad and will lead to ruin.'

'So who is to blame? Is it us, each one of us individually? Is that what you're going to say?'

Chase looked across at her grim pale face. He smiled and shrugged. 'Hey, don't get angry with me, Ruth. I've done my share of preaching – and consuming, if it comes to that. If I knew the answer I'd have spat it out long ago.'

Wheeler Peak was behind them now, the road curling down in a series of spirals to Connors Pass. Forest stretched on either side, lush, thick and green. At certain points along the road there were shaded recreation areas with wooden tables and benches set in concrete.

On a day such as this, not many years ago, Chase reflected, cars would have been parked between the diagonal yellow lines and families would have been eating at the tables and kids pitching baseballs and chasing one another on the neat smooth grass. No families today. No kids. No baseball. The scene was eerily empty, like a vast, lavishly expensive sound stage complete with cyclorama of mountains, forests and sky waiting for shooting to begin. But Equity was on strike. There were no actors. All this beautiful setting had been built for no purpose, a complete and utter waste.

Was this how the future would be? Empty? A deserted planet?

In dreams he'd had visions of what the end would be like (it was how he imagined New York had become: steel and glass towers poking out of shit-coloured murk), but this was worse, infinitely worse, because the beauty remained like a mocking taunt.

Yes, the planet had been entrusted to mankind, given into its care, and in just a few thousand years out of a 4.5 billion-year history the species had succeeded brilliantly in transforming a paradise into a cesspool.

5

They were on Highway 50 in the heart of the Humboldt Forest. Up ahead was a white-lettered sign, and Chase pointed it out with a grin. The town was called Ruth.

After studying the route, Chase had provisionally picked out a spot to camp overnight between Austin and Frenchman, somewhere along Railroad Pass. If possible, he wanted to keep clear of towns, in fact, any place of habitation. With the continuing exodus northwards he guessed that the locals would be suspicious and perhaps hostile to strangers. Neither could he rule out the possibility that there'd be shanty settlements of immigrants from the southern states.

But most of all he wanted to avoid Reno, the only place of any size between them and Goose Lake. Apart from its reputation as a vacation resort and one-time divorce capital, he knew nothing about the city, but he mistrusted all cities now, suspecting that that was where the frayed edges of civilisation began to show first. In the backwoods there was only nature in the raw to contend with, whereas cities compressed the madness and hysteria into a volatile mixture that could explode at any moment, with unpredictable results.

Thus far on the journey they had seen only a few other vehicles, so presumably the main interstate highways running due north were carrying the bulk of the traffic.

A couple of miles past Eureka, they ran into the first real sign of trouble. It was mid-afternoon and Chase was silently congratulating himself on their unhindered progress when they came down a long sweeping curve out of the shadow of Pinto Summit into bright sunshine to find a truck, farm tractor and two patched-up cars with smeared windshields strung across the road.

Ruth got a grip on the rifle and was about to hoist it when Chase motioned with the palm of his hand, warning her not to make any sudden moves that might be misinterpreted.

He shifted down into second and brought the Jeep to a halt about ten yards away. There were five men lounging about, all clad in farmers' dungarees, two of them cradling shotguns in their brawny arms, another holding a carbine. One of the others was gripping a thick pine stave, which he thwacked menacingly into his open palm.

As casually as he could Chase unzipped the pocket of his windbreaker. The butt of the automatic was hidden, but within easy reach.

The men were rough-looking, unshaven, their eyes slitted against the sunlight. Hard to tell whether they were God-fearing, public-spirited citizens or mean sons of bitches with something nasty in mind. The two men with shotguns ambled to either side of the road to cover the Jeep while the man with the stave came forward, a grimy Stetson tipped forward so that the curled brim almost rested on his sunburned nose.

'Real pleasant day fer a ride.' The man had stopped a few feet away, his scratched red boots spread in an indolent stance on the blacktop. The greeting might have been innocuous enough, though Chase was uneasily aware of the double meaning it contained. 'What ya got back yonder?' The soiled hat brim nodded towards the back of the Jeep.

'Camping gear.' Chase hesitated and then said, 'We're driving up to Oregon. This lady is a doctor. We're on our way to treat a sick friend.'

The man tapped his palm with the stave jerkily, as if to the beat of a metronome that only he could hear. 'What kind of speech d'ya call that?'

'Speech?'

'That – what ya call it? – ack-cent of your'n. Where ya from, mister?'

'I'm English.'

'An' you're goin' up to Oregon,' the man said in a mocking tone, 'to help a sick friend.'

Chase moved his hands from the wheel and placed them, fingers spread, on his thighs. Ruth was sitting tensely in the seat beside him, her fingers wrapped around the burnished blue gun barrel.

'Would you mind telling us why you've blocked the road?' Chase said.

'Jest passin' the time of day.' The man smiled without opening his lips. 'Never know who'll happen along.'

'Are you from around here?'

The man grinned, revealing a sliver of red gums. 'I really dig that ack-cent. It's right dandy. Ain't that what you English say?'

'No, it's what you Americans say. Listen, we have to move on. What I'm telling you is the—'

But the man ignored him and walked around to Ruth's side of the Jeep and stood looking at her from underneath the brim of his hat. It was difficult to see his eyes properly, but they could tell that he was taking everything in: her dark windblown hair and thickly lashed eyes, the wrinkled open vee of her shirt exposing her white throat and the slopes of her breasts, swelling and falling as she tried to control her breathing, the blue denims moulded to hips and thighs.

After his inspection he moved his eyes lazily up to her face again. 'So you're a lady doctor, huh?'

'That's right. And my friend has just asked you why you're blocking the road. Would you mind telling us why? This isn't some kind of game. Please move those vehicles so that we can drive on.'

The man settled himself more firmly on the blacktop, legs wide apart.

'Well, since you ask so polite, lady, I'll tell ya,' he said conversationally. 'We stop all kinds along this here stretch. Weirdos, acid-heads, crazies, mutes, the halt, the lame, and the blind. An' what we do is this: we take what we find an' have a little fun at the same time – harmless fun, that is, nuthin' to it. But as you can see we're simple folks and we like to enjoy ourselves once in a while with all the human dung that passes by. All them that's used up their own sweet air and fresh water. We reckon as how we've a right to do that, seein' as how they've muddied their own drinkin' hole and want to do the same to our'n. You dig me, lady?'

'You have no right,' Ruth said coldly. 'This is a public highway and everyone is free to use it without hindrance. You're breaking the law.'

To put it at its tamest, Chase felt that Ruth's reading of the situation wasn't the most incisive; this band of roughnecks weren't going to be pushed into an accommodating frame of mind by accusations and threats.

The man cocked his head to one side and squinted at her. 'Where you bin livin' these past five years, lady? Backside of the moon? If you don't already know it – and it sure sounds like you don't – this ball of mud is comin' apart at the seams.' He leaned forward from the waist and held up the stave between his fingertips. 'You talk about rights? *Law?* This thing I'm a-holding is the law and rights is what every man can get for hisself by usin' it. Next you'll be tellin' me that the fine huntin' piece between your knees is jest to get you an' yer friend a rabbit supper.'

Chase said, 'We've only got camping gear with us, nothing of any real value. Nothing that would be of any use to you.'

'Well now,' said the man craftily, 'wouldn't be too sure 'bout that. Not at all sure.' His eyes under the brim glinted with amusement.

The knuckles of Ruth's hands were white. Chase rested his right elbow on the back of the seat, his hand hanging slackly.

Grinning, exposing his red gums, the man reached out with the stave and parted the vee of Ruth's shirt. Her jaw went rigid as the jagged end of the stave snagged her flesh and drew a red line, droplets strung along it like ruby beads.

'Not at *all* sure,' repeated the man softly.

Chase slipped his hand into his pocket.

'You're the best piece of ass I've seen in a long while,' the man remarked, pressing the stave against her breast through the plaid shirt. 'I do reckon Oregon's gonna have ta wait till we've done what has to be done. I guess you can take five of us, lady doctor, an' as you're in such a hurry, we'll make it right quick.'

He lowered the stave and with his other hand rummaged about his baggy groin and pulled out his erect cock, slug-like against his soiled dungarees. He grasped it and began to slowly masturbate, his eyes never leaving Ruth's face. 'Two at a time, how's that?' The grin widened on red gums and black stumps of teeth.

Chase's sweating thumb slipped over the safety catch. He had to keep the gun in his pocket, hidden from the others. The faint click as the catch moved sounded to Chase like a hammer striking an anvil. He curled his finger through the trigger guard.

'If you'll jest give that to me,' the man said, releasing his cock and taking hold of the rifle barrel. Ruth hung on and the man half-raised the stave. 'You heard what I said. Jes' do it and nobody'll get hurt.'

'Let go of the rifle,' Chase said, 'and listen to me very carefully.' The sweat through his shirt made his back stick to the seat. 'I'm pointing a gun straight at you and if you don't do what I tell you right now I'm going to blow a hole in your chest. At this range it'll take your backbone with it. Understand? My English ack-cent clear enough for you?'

The man was standing perfectly still, the stave arrested in midair. He was staring at the outline of the gun in Chase's windbreaker.

'Step up on the running board and tell your friends to move the truck. If *you* don't do as I say – or if *they* don't – I'll kill you first. Whatever happens, you've run out of future.'

The creased, grimy face, burned dark by the sun, was an immobile mask under the sweat-marked Stetson. The man released his hold on Ruth's rifle and tucked his cock away as if it didn't belong to him.

'Step up now. Tell them to move the truck,' Chase ordered, hardly moving his lips. 'If you feel inclined, say that if they try anything, you won't be around to see it.'

The man got on to the running board, still holding the stave in his right hand. 'Move the truck!' he shouted, turning his head, but keeping his eyes on Chase. 'He's got a gun on me, better do as he says. I reckon he means it.'

'I mean it all right. Drop the weapon.'

The man tossed the stave aside and it clattered on the black asphalt. A small dilemma occurred to Chase. As soon as the vehicle started to move, and while he was occupied with steering it, the others had only to raise their own shotguns and pick him off. He was trying to figure out an answer, and damn quick, when Ruth solved it by thrusting the barrel of the hunting rifle into the man's stomach.

'I mean it too, believe me.' She pulled the bolt back and curled her finger around the trigger. 'As you pointed out, this is the law – and I happen to be holding it.'

There was a billowing of blue smoke as the truck roared into life, followed by a hideous grating of gears as it backed off the road, the rear wheels sinking into the dry red soil, the tailboard pushing through the brush.

Chase laid the Browning on the seat between his legs, revved the engine and pulled sharply away, the man holding the metal edge of the windshield for support. The business end of the rifle made an indentation in his dungarees, right between the slanting double-stitched pockets.

Any second now, Chase thought, crouching forward in the seat. His shoulders expected a bullet, or several. *Any second now.* He steered for the gap left by the truck and had a blurred impression of a murderous face in the cab, fleshy lips drawn back in an expression of pure venomous hate. In the rearview mirror he glimpsed the driver scrambling down from the cab and the others running forward to cluster around him. Chase kept his eye on this receding image, distorted by the shimmering waves of heat rising from the blacktop, a tableau which vanished as a bend cut it off from view.

6

Chase drove steadily so that Ruth could keep the rifle pressed in the redneck's gut. But what would happen next? While they held the man hostage they were safe, but at some point soon they'd have to dump him. The others would probably follow at a distance, waiting for him to be released – and once he was free, the pack of them would come after the Jeep, their killer instincts fanned to white heat.

Neither he nor Ruth, Chase acknowledged, could kill the guy in cold blood and dump his body off the road, and in any event, it wouldn't stop the others coming after them with redoubled fury and murderous intent. Ruth, for all her pent-up anger, was incapable of such an act. She was preoccupied with the same problem.

'What are we going to do? The minute we get rid of him—'

'I know,' Chase snapped, irked by the knowledge that they had escaped and yet were still trapped.

The redneck was sure they wouldn't kill him, even with the rifle barrel poking into his belly. He even wore a grin, lips spread wide across his gums. 'I guess you're 'tween the devil and the deep blue sea – you got me sure enough, but they got you. Ha!'

The grin thinned only slightly when Ruth rammed the barrel deeper. 'Don't tempt me, brother,' she said viciously. 'I've seen decent people die, so it wouldn't bother me one bit to get rid of scum like you.'

'Maybe so, lady. But when I go your lives sure as eternal damnation ain't worth bird-spit and you both know it.'

They were now winding upwards towards Hickison Summit. On their left the rockface rose vertically, sheared away in broad swathes like orange-yellow cheese sliced by an uneven hand. On their right, beyond a narrow fringe of grass, the valley dropped steeply away, strewn with large boulders and fragments of rock, remnants of the road's construction. Chase flicked his eyes to left and right. Ruth looked alarmed when he stopped the Jeep, kept the engine running, tucked the gun into the pocket of his windbreaker and swung himself out.

'If he so much as moves an eyelid, Ruth, you have my blessing. Shoot him.'

'I might do it anyway,' Ruth said.

The road, being impassable on either side, had given Chase the idea. He hoisted one of the jerry cans from its rack on the back of the Jeep and sloshed a pale amber stream across the road to both edges, shaking out every last drop, then returned the empty can to its cradle.

Gasoline fumes drifted in a throat-catching mist off the hot blacktop. Pray to God it wouldn't all evaporate before it had a chance to . . .

Whooosh!

The lighted match ignited the fumes and there was a gentle boom as a wall of flames sprang up. Chase retreated slowly to the Jeep, watching anxiously in case the fire should burn itself out too quickly. He smiled, catching a whiff of a gorgeous rich aroma: the tar itself was alight, bubbling and frothing and giving off a blanket of dense black smoke that rose sluggishly to form an impenetrable smoke screen.

'That should hold them long enough,' Chase said, climbing in. He put the Jeep into gear and looked at the redneck. 'And here, my friend, is where we part company.'

The man opened his mouth to say something but never got the chance. Even Chase was taken aback at the savagery with which Ruth thrust the barrel into the man's groin. The guy's gummy mouth opened wide, he shrieked like a banshee and clutched himself with both hands, and fell onto the road, doubled-up and writhing in agony.

His eyes fixed on the road ahead, Chase drove without speaking for several minutes; Ruth was silent also, as if words might break the spell of their getaway. When finally he glanced across at her, she was slumped in her seat. She looked shocked and ashen-faced, her lower lip quivering. She was clutching the rifle in both hands that might have been locked in rigor mortis.

'It's all right, it's okay, Ruth, we're safe,' he tried to reassure and calm her. 'They won't get past that blazing tarmac for at least an hour. You can relax.' When she didn't respond, Chase spoke with heartfelt admiration. 'You were fantastic. You really had me believing you'd have killed the slimy bastard.'

Ruth took a huge breath, as if clearing her throat of a bucket-full of sawdust. 'You know what? I would have – I mean *really* would have shot the sonofabitch,' she said in a high fluttery voice, 'except I forgot to put bullets in the rifle.'

Chase gripped the wheel, staring straight ahead through the windshield. 'You're telling me the motherfucker wasn't even *loaded*?' He held onto the wheel as his shoulders began to shake. His eyes filled with tears so that he could hardly see where he was going. They rolled down his cheeks. His stomach was trembling.

Ruth gazed at him, eyes large and round, before she too succumbed and her distraught face collapsed into helpless hysterical laughter, and for the next twenty miles they were like two giddy kids.

4

I

General Malden listened to the sounds of sex. When the man began to speak in a low, barely audible voice the rage boiled up inside him. His jaw ached from the pressure of his clamped teeth.

Colonel Travis Murch, senior security officer, pressed the tab, pausing the voice. 'I have a transcript you can look at. They met on a number of occasions' – Murch glanced down at the open file – 'eleven that we know of for certain. But I'd say this was the first time he'd passed sensitive information, in my opinion.'

'You didn't record all the meetings. How can you be sure?' Malden asked bluntly.

'I'm not,' Murch admitted, 'but how does it sound to you? He was briefing her from zero. Then when she says, "I can't believe this is happening, not here, not on the island" – doesn't that suggest she was hearing it for the first time? I'd say so.'

'She could have been faking.'

'Possibly,' Murch said, 'but that's not important. Now we *know* for a fact that Sprote has divulged classified material to an agent of a foreign power.'

'What's the woman's name?'

'Natassya Pavlovitch. Biochemist, according to her accreditation. She's almost definitely mid-echelon military. We've had her under surveillance since the day she arrived. The Russians are so simple-minded it's unbelievable. They send this knock-out dame to penetrate our security – and she is *built* – and expect us not to smell a rat.' He shook his head, grinning through a pained expression. 'Amateurs.'

'Amateurs or not, they succeeded,' Malden said coldly. He was infuriated, and yet strangely aroused. He would deal with this personally; there were several intriguing possibilities. 'You haven't broken this to Sprote, of course.'

Murch shook his head. 'I embargoed further action till you arrived.'

'Can we be sure she hasn't already passed on what she knows?'

'All channels are intercepted at source. There's been nothing.'

'Code?'

Murch shook his head again, this time with a faint smile.

'We could infect Sprote or the woman with the virus,' Malden said suddenly. 'It would be transferred during their sexual activity and they could watch each other decay.' He'd like to witness that himself.

Colonel Murch looked away. He cleared his throat and said, 'Wouldn't that be dangerous, allowing TCDD outside the clinical area? It might spread, and if that were to happen . . .'

'Yes,' Malden said absently, 'too risky.' His eyes were blank, his head teeming with serpentine schemes.

'We could use the woman to pass on spurious information,' Murch suggested, thinking like an intelligence officer. 'Wipe out what she already knows and chemically implant something else.' He cast around. 'Something unconnected with genetics. Psychic weaponry, contact with aliens, something like that.'

'Except I don't want to lose her.'

'What use is she otherwise?'

'We'll find a use for her,' Malden said.

'Sprote? Do we pick him up?'

'No.' Malden had thought of something. 'For the moment we do nothing.' It excited him. 'I want the lovers to be together one last time.'

2

The smell of bacon, sausages, beans and coffee flooded Chase's mouth with saliva as he slung the canvas over a low branch and secured it to the mossy ground with steel pegs. They had covered a fair distance despite the hold-up. Frenchman was behind them and Fallon three or four miles ahead – the latter was a town of respectable size, according to the map. With an early start in the morning it was even possible that they might reach Goose Lake by late tomorrow, though this depended on whether they chose the most direct route, which meant going through Reno, or took one of the minor roads heading north past Pyramid Lake.

After the encounter that afternoon Chase was unsure what to do. It was a straight choice between civilisation and backwoods, neither of which had great appeal.

They ate off metal plates sitting cross-legged next to the camping stove. The sultry heat of the day lingered on, so the unlit stove served merely as a symbolic campfire.

Something squawked near at hand in the undergrowth and they both jumped. 'We're a couple of townies and no mistake,' Chase remarked, wiping his mouth.

'Is that what we are?'

'Sure: city people who drive at eighty miles an hour without seat belts and yet turn pale at the sight of a cow. Where were you born?'

'Columbus, Ohio. Though we had a place in the country where I learned to ride.'

'Are your parents still there?'

'Both dead. My father was a druggist. He ran his car into the back of a bus when I was twenty-one. He was drunk at the time. Six months later my mother committed suicide.'

'So you put yourself through medical school?'

'Yes. It wasn't too hard. I didn't have the struggle that is supposed to be character-building. There was money from the sale of the store and two fat insurance policies to collect on.' Ruth smiled mirthlessly. 'I never starved.'

'No brothers or sisters?'

'An older brother, Kevin. He's a chiropodist in Wisconsin Rapids, married with two kids. I haven't seen him in more than three years.'

'You never married?'

Ruth shrugged, a dim blue shape in the darkness. 'I had my chances, I guess. Back in Denver I got involved with a guy called Jeff Henshaw – remember him, at Bill Inchcape's the first time we met?'

'What happened?'

'Jeff was fun to be with at first, and we got on well together. But he was like a one-note tune, same attitude that never changed, and I guess I eventually got bored with it. And after that I started to get involved in other stuff. For which you were largely responsible.'

Chase was genuinely astonished. 'Me? I was?'

'You impressed me no end, that first time at Bill's,' Ruth said. 'And what was worse, you started me thinking. I began to realise what a hell of a mess we were getting ourselves into and I decided I'd better do something about it – Ruth Brosnan, a one-woman crusade to save the world. After Denver I did three years with Médecins Sans Frontières, in India and Bangladesh. Then I came back to the Rotten Apple and dedicated myself to mankind. The rest, as they say, is history.'

Her spiritual desolation was even deeper and more intractable than his. And he had nothing to offer her except empty phrases and meaningless platitudes.

In the middle of the night he was shocked into bleary life by a kick in the ribs. He opened his eyes and everything was dazzling white. The pain seeped through him like syrup as he shielded his eyes from the flashlight shining directly into his face. Ruth wasn't beside him. That fact brought him fully awake. At the same time he was trying to remember where he'd put his windbreaker with the gun in the pocket.

'Take that light out of my eyes, for God's sake!' Chase said, angry with himself. Shit and corruption, he should have known Redneck and his mates would come after them. They'd tracked them to this secluded spot in the trees, and now he and Ruth were at the mercy of those sonofabitch bastards with revenge in their hearts.

And where was she? What had they done with Ruth?

The flashlight swung away and a voice with a peculiar nasal intonation said haltingly, 'Don't bother – looking for rifle – won't do – no good.'

Chase squinted into the darkness, but could only make out a vague humped shape. That wasn't the voice of the man with the Stetson. Must be one of the others. He struggled to sit up, wincing at the pain in his rib cage.

'What have you done with the woman, you bastards?'

The beam flicked across the grass and settled on two figures, one held in the embrace of the other. Chase felt his stomach go rigid. Ruth, transfixed like a rabbit in the light, stared at him, her eyes dark and wide. Something bony and clawlike covered her mouth. Behind her shoulder he saw a white gleaming skull with black eye sockets and two rows of exposed teeth, like the head of a skeleton.

O-zoes – it was worse than he'd thought.

'Woman not harmed,' said the clotted nasal voice behind the flashlight.

Chase knelt up on the canvas groundsheet and the voice said, 'Don't move!' He subsided slowly and felt something digging into his left knee. It was the hard shape of the gun in the zippered pocket of his windbreaker, which he'd rolled up and placed within easy reach.

Now that his eyes had adjusted to the darkness he could make out the owner of the voice, a broad squat figure whose head was sunk into his shoulders. What facial features he could dimly discern were twisted askew beneath a deep sloping forehead. There were dark patches on the hairless cranium, which Chase realised were open, suppurating sores; he could actually smell the sweetish odour of decay. The creature was rotting alive.

And he realised something else that made his heart thud in his chest – they weren't armed. The creature with the flashlight had no weapon because its other arm ended in a stump at the elbow, and the skeleton man was using both arms to hold Ruth in his bony embrace.

Chase cautioned himself to take it slow and easy. First he had to get the gun. He inched his hand downwards, his fingers delving into the wrapped folds of the windbreaker.

'Where you from?' The creature sounded as though it had no roof to its mouth. The light swung back and Chase froze in its glare.

'I'll tell you if you'll take that bloody light off me.'

The beam dropped away.

'A place called Desert Range in Utah. It's a—' He stopped. He'd been about to say 'scientific establishment' when it occurred to him that these two would hardly be kindly disposed towards science of any description – not after what chemicals and the climate had done to them.

He said, 'My companion is a doctor, we're on our way to treat a patient in Oregon. We have nothing of any value – nothing to give you. Just this camping gear you see here and a few personal belongings.'

His fingers touched the metal tab of the zipper. He tugged at it. *Keep on talking, keep them distracted.* 'Why not tell your friend to let the woman go. She can't do you any harm.'

It occurred to Chase that Ruth was effectively shielding the skeleton man. That's if a bullet would have any effect; kill or even harm something that looked more dead than alive. This creature might have transmuted into a bloodless and nerveless entity.

Chase wormed his fingers into the pocket, cutting off further ghoulish speculation. The crosshatched butt was good and solid in his hand. *Now, don't forget the safety . . .*

He was ready with the weapon, about to hoist it and get to his feet when the thing holding the flashlight turned the beam on to Ruth and instructed, 'Let – woman – go.'

The creature's skeletal hand fell away. Ruth tottered forward, wiping her mouth with both hands. She uttered a sob and sucked in air.

Now Chase had his first clear view of the skeleton man. He was bizarrely dressed in a grey pinstripe suit with wide pointed lapels that hung upon him as emptily as on a hanger in a closet. His face was sheathed in a pale membrane, so transparent that the tendons and musculature of the neck were clearly visible. Between the pointed lapels his collarbones shone like ivory, the plate of his breastbone reflecting the flashlight. The creature had wasted away to practically nothing; he was just a walking bag of bones.

'You have drugs?' said the hunched thing with the light.

Chase kept hold of the Browning, still hidden. 'What kind of drugs?'

'For me . . . him . . .' It swivelled the beam to illuminate its own head. 'For this, please.'

Chase flinched at the sight and looked away. He felt his flesh crawl.

The thing with the squat neck emitted a gurgling growl, which might have sounded threatening, but then it began to cry. Tears were squeezing out from beneath the raw peeling eyelids and dripping over the deformed features. 'Need help – my friend, me – we die – help us please.'

Chase grimaced from the dull pain in his side as he stood up. He made no attempt to conceal the gun; there was no point. These wretched husks of human beings were no threat. Fear was driving them, of what was happening to their bodies. Fear of what they were turning into.

He went to Ruth and held her. She was shaking, her skin clammy, her mouth red where she had rubbed away the feel of the skeletal hand.

'Can't we do anything for them?' Chase asked.

'No, it's too late.' Taking in a deep breath, Ruth held his arm tight. 'Too far gone. There's nothing anyone can do.'

3

Daybreak on Interstate 80, twenty miles from Reno. Chase was determined to reach Goose Lake before nightfall. Keeping to the side roads and the backwoods hadn't been such a great idea after all; whatever Reno had to offer, it couldn't be much worse. He kept his foot pressed down hard on the accelerator, willing the Jeep to take off and fly. When daylight came he thought it would somehow diminish the memory of those figures seen by flashlight, bring back a measure of everyday sanity, but the reverse had been true. Seeing for himself the terminal effects of pollution sickness had intensified his feeling of dread and filled him with a desperate panic that Cheryl might be suffering the same fate.

The hard shoulder and inside lane of the highway were strewn with wrecks. People were living in some of them. Small fires burned in front of truck doors hanging off their hinges; cooking utensils and belongings were scattered around, and ragged dirty-faced children played among the dented metal and rusting engines.

They'd fled from the south, got this far and run out of money, gasoline, goods to barter and luck. Now they were stranded in no man's land with nowhere to go. Recently erected signs every quarter mile warned in large red capitals:

ABSOLUTELY NO ADMISSION TO IMMIGRANTS
WITHIN CITY LIMITS!

If conditions were this bad here, what must they be like back east in the densely populated industrial areas of Chicago, Detroit, Cleveland, Pittsburgh and Cincinnati? Chase visualised it as a vast stinking Dickensian slum: skies perpetually black and rivers choked with putrescent sludge, inhabited by grey ghosts who trudged to work and carried out their tasks like automatons. According to the newscasts, goods were still being produced and sold, the service industries still functioned, life went on 'normally' . . . but for how much longer?

'What's happening, can you see?' Ruth asked, craning to look through the windshield.

Chase slowed down as the stream of traffic built up into a solid jam. It was a perimeter checkpoint manned by state militia and city police. Each vehicle and its occupants were being closely scrutinised. The guards were wearing respirators, Chase saw, their visored white helmets gleaming like skulls in the murk that had thickened the nearer they got to the city. He recalled with a small prayer of thanks that Drew had packed respirators and goggles.

'They'll want to see our IDs,' Chase said, fumbling for his own. He noticed that many of the vehicles, the majority in fact, were being directed on to a slip-road. These were the rejected, turned back to swell the tide of flotsam along Interstate 80.

The line crept forward with infuriating sluggishness. The vehicle in front was a clapped-out microbus with taped-over cracks in its tinted windows and a bent TV aerial on the roof. It contained a family with two or three kids and an old woman who stared morosely through the rear window, chin propped in her hand.

A semicircle of militia, weapons drawn, covered all angles. Chase watched a barrel-chested sergeant who topped six feet examining the family's ID cards and papers. His voice sounded hollow and distorted inside the faceplate.

'State your business in Reno.'

'Just passing through.'

Chase couldn't see the driver's face, but he could imagine it from the tone of voice: timid, hopeful, anxious, sweating.

'Destination?' demanded the burly sergeant.

There was a fractional pause. 'San Francisco.' The driver rushed on with a hurried explanation. 'We got relatives there, officer, my wife's parents. They wrote and promised us a place—'

'San Francisco is off limits. Has been for six months.' The sergeant pointed with a gloved hand. 'Pull over to the right. Access denied.'

'But we *have* to get through,' the man whined. 'You see, it's my son, the youngest, he's sick. He needs medical attention. My wife's parents have fixed it for him to be—'

'In that case you've crapped out twice,' the sergeant said indifferently. 'Nobody with an illness or disease of any description is allowed inside city limits. Now move this fucking heap of rust before I have it impounded. That's if you don't want to forfeit everything except the clothes you stand up in.'

The microbus shuddered off to the right and Chase took its place. He handed the documents over. 'We're both doctors. We have a patient who urgently requires—'

'Did I ask you a question?' The sergeant glanced at the ID cards and held them over his shoulder without looking. 'Check these on Memorex.'

Chase couldn't stop blinking. His eyes were starting to sting. He noticed that Ruth's eyes were red-rimmed too. Photochemical smog activated by the sun's rays. Welcome to California.

'State your business in Reno.'

'Passing through.'

'Destination?'

'Goose Lake, Oregon.' Chase could see the trooper inside the glass-walled booth feeding data into a keyboard terminal. What did they expect to find? That he and Ruth were a couple of homicidal maniacs on the run from a mental institution? He gripped the wheel with both hands. There was no reason to turn them back. Not a single one.

'Are the two of you healthy? Pollution sickness?' To judge from the flat gaze behind the faceplate he might have been inspecting a side of beef to see whether it ought to be condemned.

'Yes, we're both healthy.'

'Are you carrying drugs?'

Chase was about to say no when Ruth said, 'Medical supplies. No hard drugs or hallucinogens.'

'Show me.'

She opened the aluminium case and the sergeant looked at the plastic bottles, capsules, and vials in their padded compartments, the syringes in their pouches. Everything was clearly labelled, though whether the sergeant knew the difference between digitoxin and ethyloestrenol was open to doubt, in Chase's view.

The trooper returned with the ID cards. He handed them to the sergeant without a word, who folded the papers he was holding and gave them to Chase.

The sergeant recited: 'You are allowed to remain twelve hours within the Reno City boundary. One minute longer will be considered a violation of the special emergency law, as will the sale or purchase of drugs by trade, barter or any other form of exchange, punishable by imprisonment and confiscation of all possessions and personal effects. Unauthorised purchase of oxygen is also forbidden, subject to the same penalties.'

He stepped back and waved them on, his attention already on the next vehicle in line.

A mile further on visibility was so bad that they had to don the goggles and respirators. 'Twelve hours,' Chase laughed shortly. 'Who in his right mind would want to stay any longer?' He squinted up through the murk. The sun was a diffuse orange blur and it was noticeably warmer, by several degrees: a thermal inversion layer, trapping the heat and fumes in a thick vaporous blanket that hugged the ground. It was like driving through a hot burning mist of sulphuric acid.

Buildings loomed and they realised they were already in the city itself. Beyond knowing that he wanted to head roughly northwest, Chase hadn't a clue where he was going or which direction to take. Headlights came towards them like dim yellow eyes. Several times he had to stamp on the brakes as a glowing red taillight warned him of stalled traffic.

'Like being back in New York,' Ruth said with mordant humour.

Chase peered hopelessly ahead. 'Can you see any signs? Can you see *anything?'* Nightmares were like this, wandering about lost in an eerie blank timelessness. He began to believe that it *was* a dream and would last forever, driving through acid mist for all eternity. It was almost restful, nothing to see, everything distant and muffled and muted—

'Watch out!'

Chase wrenched the wheel and the Jeep missed the tailgate of a truck by less than a foot. Next they hit the kerb, and the bouncing jolt threw them forward, Ruth striking her forehead on the windshield's metal upright, blood spattering the glass like teardrops.

They had stopped with their headlights blazing into a shop window. The world was indeed going crazy. Illuminated like a stage set, the window was filled with inflatable rubber dolls with jutting red nipples and silky vaginas.

Ruth was holding her head in both hands and moaning softly, blood seeping through her fingers and running down her wrists.

4

If there was one part of the procedure that Cy Sprote abhorred, it was this. Bad enough to theorise about it in the sterile atmosphere of the labs or engage in dispassionate debate over coffee with his colleagues, but the surgical blood and guts of it made him physically ill. There was no escape, however; he had to be present in the operating room, gowned and masked, custodian of the refrigerated vacuum flask containing the culture.

The seeds of our own destruction . . . The thought flitted unbidden through his mind like a torn scrap of paper.

Standing three feet away from the operating table he had a ringside view of the surgeon at work. The column of mirror-directed light from above made every last detail clear and sharp. On a stretcher nearby the round grey flask with the chrome handle on the recessed red stirrup release mechanism waited ominously: on its side in stencilled black letters, STERILE CELL CULTURE, and underneath in scrawled graphics, *Experimental Batch MC-D117-92.*

The last two digits indicated that this was the ninety-second strain to be tested. Incubation would take anything from fourteen weeks to the usual nine months, always supposing that the foetus didn't self-abort. The success rate wasn't high. Of the previous ninety-one, forty-eight had been rejected within six weeks, some in less than two weeks.

What had come as a surprise was the fourteen-week pregnancy: not a termination, as had been supposed at first, but the full-term delivery of a perfect specimen: blind, dumb, deaf and mentally retarded, but with lungs three times the normal capacity. Dr Rolsom had congratulated the team, calling it 'an important and encouraging breakthrough'.

Sprote tried not to look as the surgeon's scalpel sliced through the epidermis and the fatty layer of the abdomen. The surgeon made another incision at right angles to the first and a nurse folded back the flap of tissue and swabbed the V-shaped area underneath, already saturated with blood.

'Tie off,' the surgeon instructed. The nurse clamped the pumping arteries and applied ligatures to stanch the flow.

'Young, healthy, good pelvic cavity,' the surgeon said, pleased. 'She should give us a fine bouncing mute or my name's not Sweeney Todd.'

Everyone around the table laughed. It was one of his standard jokes, but it helped break the monotony.

Before going in, the surgeon glanced towards the anaesthesiologist, who was looking down at the woman's face, obscured by a sterile green sheet. 'How is she?'

'Everything okay. She's dreaming of fluffy white lambs in a spring meadow.' The eyes of the anaesthesiologist curved as he grinned behind his gauze mask.

'I'm fond of lambs myself,' the surgeon quipped. 'Especially with mint sauce.'

Everyone laughed again, and one of the younger nurses got the giggles.

'Right boys and girls, in we go.' The surgeon began cutting in earnest, the three assisting nurses standing by with sponges, clamps, plastic tubes and ligatures. It was a perfectly choreographed ballet of gloved hands and shiny steel instruments. As the layers were stripped back and the cords of muscles pushed out of the way, the surgeon became more intent as his work became more intricate. In the centre of the raw gaping hole the narrow end of the Fallopian tube, at the point where it entered the uterus, was now exposed. A tiny snick of an incision in the wall of the Fallopian, high up at the site of fertilisation, and he was ready for the cell culture.

Grasping the red stirrup, Sprote unscrewed the heavy lid from its brass seating and lifted it out. A puff of dry ice floated away. Very carefully he withdrew the stainless-steel core and set it down on the stand alongside the operating table. Now the surgical team would take over; ensuring that the correct culture was delivered safely from lab to operating room was Sprote's task and responsibility, implantation was theirs.

Batch ninety-two was rather special. It comprised the splicing of genes from two patients with different characteristics. Both were severely deformed, yet each possessed certain physical peculiarities that, combined in the right proportions, might produce the ideal specimen. Sprote wasn't too optimistic, however. It was a wild gamble and he had the nagging fear that the 'ideal' specimen might well resemble a monster.

Part of its genetic heritage would enable it to survive in conditions normally hostile to human beings – the lungs would be rudimentary, their function taken over by gill-like growths on either side of the neck and chest. These would give it an appearance not unlike that of a humanoid water-dwelling lizard.

The other fundamental difference was in cranial capacity. Breathing deoxygenated air would rend a normal-size brain comatose, followed quickly by death. So this brain had to be smaller and less complex and yet capable of the basic modes of comprehension and communication. After all, there wasn't much point in breeding a new species that was incapable of understanding commands and carrying them out.

Something between a cretin and an educationally subnormal person was what they were aiming for, with an IQ, say, in the low sixties.

Sprote closed his mind to picturing such a hybrid. Equally distasteful to him was that this creature would receive its sustenance from the body of a normal healthy woman, growing and forming inside her womb like an alien reptile. Suitable female incubators were shipped in from the mainland. Like the woman on the table, they were poor, ignorant, and sadly misinformed. Told that a minor form of pollution sickness they were suffering from (usually a rash that proper treatment could have cured) was a terminal condition, they were invited to participate in an experimental drug programme that, while risky, would give them an excellent chance of survival.

'Right, kiddies. Let's sew the lady up and make everything shipshape!'

With the culture in place, fertilisation would now begin. The newly formed zygote would start to divide into a cluster of sixty-four cells, taking about a week to travel down the Fallopian tube to the uterus. There the young embryo – the blastocyst – would attach itself to the lining of the uterus and – if there were no complications – pregnancy would proceed in the usual way.

Using an interrupted suture, the surgeon was sewing up the sub-cutaneous tissue. One by one the layers were folded back, the wall of the abdomen sealed up, and finally the outer flap of skin and fatty tissue replaced and stitched, leaving a puckered V-shape edged with red against the alabaster white.

Sprote felt relieved that it was over. He thought longingly of a cup of coffee. Even more longingly he thought of his rendezvous with Natassya after dinner that evening. Her text said that she couldn't make it to the bar, their usual meeting place, but that he was to go directly to her room where she would be waiting.

The surgeon called out jovially, 'Next, please!' and the operating-room staff dutifully laughed, if a little wearily this time.

As he turned to leave, Sprote noticed a group of people watching from the observation room, high up in one corner behind the angled glass panel. Dr Rolsom was there – he sometimes liked to look in – but it wasn't usual to see General Malden among them. Malden was gazing down with a rare smile; in fact, he seemed to be actually laughing.

'Excuse me, sir.'

'Sorry.' Sprote stepped aside as the nurse wheeled the gurney to the door, the rubber tyres squealing on the tiled floor. He looked down at the bleached face above the white sheet, the eyebrows like black brush marks on a flawless porcelain vase.

Sprote felt his heart go small and hard as though the blood had been squeezed from it by an angry fist. He watched mutely as Natassya was wheeled out and the doors swung shut behind her.

5

Sierraville. Loyalton. Vinton. Doyle. Milford. Janesville. Standish. Ravendale. Termo. Madeline. Likely.

The small towns on Highway 395 rolled by, their cosy suburban names in stark contrast to what they had become: the refuge and the dumping ground for those fleeing north to escape the stench and decay seeping up from the south. They had escaped, so far, but they were tainted by it. For Chase and Ruth it hung in the air like a sickly odour.

Chase had done the best he could with the nasty gash in Ruth's forehead. It really required medical attention, though Ruth wasn't carrying a stapler or surgical glue, and the idea of looking for a hospital filled them both with wearisome despair. Chase had decided that the sensible course was to reach Goose Lake with all speed; there would surely be somebody at the settlement with medical expertise.

Highway 395 was patrolled by state police and the armoured personnel carriers of the National Guard, their blue-and-gold crest fluttering from the radio masts. Without such protection Chase doubted whether they would have made it past Sierraville.

By late afternoon they were midway between Likely and Alturas, about sixty miles from the settlement. Chase had made room for Ruth in the back of the Jeep where she was wedged into a cubbyhole padded with blankets. She lay back, eyes closed, her face whiter than the bandage around her head.

Without actually thinking about it, he'd made up his mind to take Cheryl and Dan back with him. At the outset, when Desert Range was being planned more than five years ago and the site made ready for occupation, Chase had resolved that Dan would enjoy a far better quality of life amidst the greenery and open spaces of Oregon than in a scientific installation in the middle of the Nevada desert. Even though he missed his son terribly, he had never regretted the decision. Dan deserved the best opportunities and the healthiest environment for a sixteen-year old, and that's what Chase had sought to provide, despite the personal sacrifice of separation.

Everything had changed. What he had witnessed on this journey convinced Chase that social fragmentation was now endemic, growing rapidly, and probably unstoppable. An isolated and vulnerable community like Goose Lake was no safe haven. At this rate, it wouldn't be long before the craziness he'd observed out here arrived there and overwhelmed the community. While he fully recognised that The Tomb wasn't impregnable, it offered more security than being on the outside. And it had the vital advantage of being a sealed enclosure; as the atmosphere continued to deteriorate, such places would be the last remaining refuge in an increasingly hostile environment.

Chase had lost count of the number of checkpoints they'd passed through since Reno. There was another one ahead now. In a sense it was reassuring to know that some form of rule of law was still operating.

The ebbing sun was distended into a flattened brown balloon by the stratified layers of noxious gases in the lower atmosphere. It would soon be dark, and travelling the last fifty or so miles on a pitch-black highway – with or without patrols – was an experience he would much rather avoid. Aside from which he felt ragged with tiredness and his bruised ribs throbbed painfully.

Yet again he went through the rigmarole with documents and IDs, explaining for the umpteenth time what was the matter with Ruth. The young state police trooper on duty, not unsympathetic, advised them, 'Don't go through Alturas after nightfall. There's been some bad trouble there. Even the National Guard had to pull out.'

'What kind of trouble?'

'Riots, looting, arson. A lot of people killed. There's a big refugee camp near Cedarville and raiding parties have been crashing in there and taking whatever they can lay their hands on. You want my advice, find someplace out of town to stay overnight. They're a bunch of crazies, believe me.'

'Is there another route into Oregon?' he asked the trooper.

'Not unless you go back to Standish and take the 139 through Susanville, and even then I couldn't guarantee it.'

Standish was a hundred miles back the way they'd come; plainly out of the question. Chase said, 'It's my injured friend I'm concerned about. I was hoping to make Goose Lake tonight to find her some medical attention.'

The trooper shrugged. 'I can't stop you, mister, but it's at your own risk; hope you realise that.' He looked at the sun dipping behind the trees, casting long spiky shadows across the road and the concrete guardhouse. 'I'd say you've got thirty minutes of real daylight left. Alturas is seventeen miles from here. If you move like a bat out of hell and stop for nothing and nobody, you might just make it. Good luck.'

6

They might just have made it, but for the storm.

It was a weird kind of storm such as Chase had never seen before. Chase saw the ALTURAS 5 MILES sign flash by in the dusk, his body bathed in nervous sweat as he tried to solve the equation of distance versus waning light. It reminded him of a problem in physics, plotting a light-distribution curve: *If 1 mile is equivalent to a reduction of 3.6 lumens, calculate the distance to be travelled before . . .*

Then without any warning, the Jeep was enveloped in a cloud of yellow rain, the colour of piss and smelling even worse. The headlights sliced feebly through the slanting downpour and a sudden gust flung it into Chase's eyes with stinging force. He stopped and fastened down the tarp, which wasn't much use against the driving wind. It certainly did nothing about the smell: the acrid stench of rotten eggs. What the hell had they run into – a cloudburst of industrial waste?

Proceeding with more caution, he had to lean forward to peer through the wipers. A vivid flash of sheet lightning illuminated everything like a sepia print. Road, bushes and trees were stained a muddy yellow, the scene fading at the edges where the gusting rain reduced visibility. As the lightning flickered in and out, the air sparked and crackled with ionised particles. A million electrical fireflies danced in front of Chase's dazzled eyes. The smell tasted like old pennies on his tongue, bitter and metallic, and he feared he might lose control of his stomach.

Ruth's cry of anguish was drowned by the boom of a thunderclap that shook the ground and the Jeep. It would be impossible to survive out in the open. The highly charged air made every breath a searing agony, as if windpipe and lungs were on fire. This stuff would eat into their tissues like acid into copper.

Chase brought the Jeep to a halt. Ruth handed him his goggles and respirator, having already donned hers. Another lightning flash transfixed them in its glare: goggled and masked, they resembled a pair of divers at the bottom of some primordial ocean, caught helplessly in fierce currents that threatened to sweep them away.

As darkness descended, the air around them crackling and spitting, Chase helped Ruth into the passenger seat. A sudden crash of thunder and a huge pressure-wave pushed down on them like a giant hand, making the Jeep rock on its springs.

'You all right?' Chase shouted.

Ruth nodded. Her dark hair was plastered to her scalp, the bandage a sodden strip stuck to her forehead. Chase cursed everything he could think of – the heavens, the universe, eternity, himself included. Dear God, he should have known that this wasn't going to be a joyride. Yet like a bloody fool he'd embarked on this trip as if on a Sunday school picnic!

A mile or so along the road Ruth spotted a building. It was a service station. There were no lights showing, and as they drove into the forecourt it became obvious why: the cantilevered roof slanted at a dangerous angle, every window in the two-storey building was smashed, the fuel pumps had been vandalised and uprooted from their mountings. The concertina doors leading to the repair shop were mangled out of shape, as if rammed several times by a truck driver with a score to settle.

Chase was anxious to get the Jeep under cover. Everything was already soaked and reeking, but he was afraid that prolonged exposure to the acid rain would leave the tyres threadbare and the bodywork looking like Gruyère cheese. Around the back they came to a concrete ramp leading up to a door. Without hesitation he ran the Jeep inside, switched off the engine and slumped back in his seat.

Ruth peeled off her goggles and mask and sucked in air. The smell was still strong, though not quite as pungent as outside. 'Would you believe they used to call Californian rain liquid sunshine?' she panted.

'It's yellow, what more do you want?'

'Yeah, so is horse—'

'I know, I know.' Chase smiled wearily.

They unloaded all the gear and supplies and spread them out to dry. By now it was dark and they worked by the light of a battery lamp, which extended its welcoming circle across the pitted floorboards and along the bare, crumbling plaster walls. An old calendar with scenic views advertised Firestone tyres: the Grand Canyon basking in a pink sunset, the month March, the year 2024.

While Ruth sorted out something to eat, Chase unpacked the gas stove and got it going. Then he took a flashlight and poked around the derelict building. On the ground floor he found an office-cum-shop, stripped bare except for a battered cash register, its empty drawer thrust out like a rude tongue. A worn wooden staircase led up through a trapdoor to three large rooms, two used for storage, the other, apparently, as a bedroom, containing a mildewed mattress and a dresser with a cracked, discoloured mirror. In the storerooms metal racks and shelves, thick with dust, reached almost to the ceiling, and the floor was knee-deep in brown wrapping paper and squashed cardboard boxes. Either the owner had cleared out fast, Chase surmised, grabbing what he could, or the garage had been raided and pillaged.

He switched off the flashlight and stood at the shattered window looking out at the yellow rain spattering the black surface of the highway, lit spasmodically by flickers of lightning moving towards the west.

Something rose up inside, choking him: tomorrow he would see Cheryl and Dan. Had they been the ones to suffer, to endure the sacrifice, for the sake of his noble pursuit of a goal? He was forty-seven years old. Good for you, Gav. Never any doubts. Always in the right. Right to the bitter fucking end.

The storm rumbled on distantly. Outside it was almost too dark to see anything. He and Ruth should be safe here for the night. From the road the building would appear deserted, with the Jeep out of sight and the only light in a back room.

Chase turned to go and went absolutely still. He held his breath, the hairs on the nape of his neck springing erect. There was somebody (or something) up here with him.

Mouth suddenly dry and heart thumping, he switched on the flashlight. Its beam travelled along the floor, over the crumpled boxes and brown paper, and up to the empty metal shelves. Could he hear breathing or was it the beating of blood in his ears?

The broken circle of light moved along the shelves, bending and folding itself around the metal uprights. A triangular fragment of beam struck the far wall and he thought he saw movement there, but when he shone the light, no, nothing. It had been an exhausting trip and they hadn't had much sleep the night before; his nerves were shot, his mind playing tricks.

Chase squatted down on one knee and aimed the beam under the lowest shelf. Scraps of paper, dust, some round dark blobs that looked like mouse-droppings, that was all. Yet he still sensed it, another presence ... watching him from the darkness, lying in wait for the moment to leap out—

'Gavin!'

A spasm like an electric shock went through him and the flashlight made a dull thud as it fell from his hand. It rolled along the dusty floor, its beam diffused and dim through crumpled brown paper. His face and neck were bathed in icy perspiration. He wiped his forehead with his open palm and reached down for the flashlight—

'Gavin, where are you?'

—and that's when he heard the movement. No doubt this time; it was up above. Something up there, near the ceiling. The flashlight was still buried in cardboard and brown paper, so he was straining his eyes in the brownish gloom to see anything at all. What was up there? Watching him. Waiting. Ready to spring. Down on his knees, Chase scrabbled through the litter until his hand found and closed around the metal casing, and then heard footsteps on the wooden stairs, and

Ruth's voice, uneasy at the lack of response, again calling his name.

'Stay there, Ruth! Don't come up!'

She was already a dim figure in the doorway. 'Where are you? What's wrong?'

'Stay where you are. Don't move.' Chase held the flashlight and directed its beam across the crude plaster and lath ceiling, the circle of light changing to an ellipse as the angle became steeper. And then the two of them heard the sound, this time it was unmistakeable – a slow, stealthy scratching.

Chase swung the beam towards the sound. In the cone of light were ten elongated and unblinking yellow eyes.

'Oh, Jesus.' Ruth gasped aloud as if she'd been punched in the stomach.

'Keep still! Don't move a muscle, for God's sake.' Chase kept his voice down. 'Any movement spooks them. The light mesmerises them. Or something.'

'But . . . what are they?' Ruth whispered. She sounded puzzled.

'Rats. Can't you tell?'

'*What?*'

Ruth's reaction was understandable. These were giants, almost as huge as German shepherds; they were crouched together in a tight pack, pointed black snouts between their paws, watching from the jagged hole in the ceiling where it had fallen through, or been gnawed away perhaps. Behind their narrow heads with the slitted eyes and flattened leathery ears, their backs rose fat and smooth under a light covering of grey dust.

This pack must have sunk their razor-sharp teeth into everything, living or dead, to have achieved such a size. But feeding alone wouldn't have done it. Rats breed fast and plentifully over generations; rapid genetic changes had developed this monstrous breed, each generation getting bigger and fatter, more voracious, more audacious, as their chief enemy, man, retreated, forced to fight a rearguard action against the natural world he had perverted and destroyed. The rats, it appeared, were among the first to take advantage, but other species would follow.

As somebody had once said: Nature Bats Last.

One of them was pawing the broken edge of the plaster, sending a fine trickle of dust onto the top shelf of the metal racks. They hadn't altered position since the moment Chase put the light on them. Their yellow lidless eyes simply stared, snouts wrinkling as they scented the air (something moving meant food), mouths salivating as their appetites sharpened.

If they came all together, in a concerted rush, neither he nor Ruth, Chase knew, stood the remotest chance. An average-size rat could leap yards; these monsters could clear the length of the room and take the pair of them without trouble.

Snap. Crunch. Done. Next.

So why were they waiting? A thought occurred to him that turned the marrow in his bones to water: these weren't the only rats in the building. The walls might be full of them. Even now there might be others slithering from the bedroom next door and the rear stock room, creeping up the stairs, coming through the ceilings, slyly cutting off their retreat. Did rats think that way? Weren't they just greedy rodents who wanted everything for themselves and didn't like sharing with their fellows? They were cunning, yes, but he'd never heard of an altruistic rat before.

Chase carefully transferred the flashlight to his left hand, keeping the beam steady. Then with his right he took out the Browning automatic. When they came he might get one or two, possibly three if he was lucky, but not all five. The odds were heavily in their favour.

First priority was to get Ruth out of the way. Practically mouthing the words, he said, 'Step back slowly. Don't make any noise. When you're out of sight go downstairs, get the rifle and wait there.'

From the corner of his eye he saw the pale blur that was Ruth's face drift out of sight. There was the lightest of footfalls on the stairs. Holding both flashlight and gun at arm's length, Chase began to edge sideways towards the door, not for an instant letting his attention waver from the crouching rodents. The elongated yellow eyes swivelled in their sockets, following the light. Yet careful and painstaking as he was, it was impossible to prevent his feet making a rustling noise on the rubbish-strewn floorboards. The rats heard it. Their sleek heads went lower still and their eyes detected the movement of the light . . . their prey was seeking to elude them.

As if on a silent command they bunched together, haunches flattening as they prepared to hurl themselves in a ball of gouging teeth and tearing claws and whipping tails into the beam of light.

Chase was four or five paces from the doorway to his right. A couple of shuffling steps nearer, he decided, and he'd make a leap through the doorway onto the landing and go full-pelt down the stairs. It was a plan, but he was too late. About to take the next step sideways, they came en masse, in a leaping rush of bodies.

The fastest and greediest took the first slug in its snarling mouth. Bits of pink tongue and bloody splinters of teeth exploded as it crashed on to the metal shelving. Chase continued to pull the trigger in a reflex action, pumping shot after shot into the squealing mass of bodies. In the beam of light he saw lumps of flesh fly off, an eyeball vanish into a ragged red hole, a stump of paw whirl away and strike the ceiling, leaving a spattered bloody star. Every detail was sharp and precise in the beam as he emptied the gun and in the next instant was through the door and onto the landing.

At the bottom of the stairs Ruth stood with the rifle at her shoulder, aimed and ready. Scrambling down, Chase flung himself aside to avoid her line of fire. On hands and knees, he rummaged in the canvas carryall that contained their belongings and snapped a fresh clip into the Browning.

Together, side by side, he and Ruth waited for the rats to emerge from the black rectangle at the top of the stairs. Chase was certain he'd killed at least two and wounded a third, maybe. That left two of them, based on the assumption there weren't more in the roof-space or hiding in the walls. The adrenalin and physical exertion had left him light-headed, charged up like a generator running at peak power. Chase knew that later – if there was to be a later – he would collapse into a quivering mound of jelly.

Ruth straightened her head from the rifle stock. She whispered, 'Gavin . . . can you hear that?'

The two of them listened, holding their breath. From the floor above came a medley of tearing, chewing, crunching, grunting, snuffling: the salivatory sounds of animals feeding.

5

I

Knees drawn up, arms laced across his bloated belly, the man in the bunk moaned continuously and monotonously. His mouth was pulled back in an awful grimace of pain. His face was the colour of mouldy cheese.

'Come on, man, you must have some idea!'

Frank Hanamura swung around and glared at the medical orderly, his tolerant good nature sorely tried. This was the third case in the past fourteen hours: stomach cramps, vomiting, fever, swollen abdomen. And would you believe it, not even a qualified doctor on board! He calmed down a little; it wasn't fair taking it out on the kid, and besides it wouldn't do much good. The young orderly was frightened and way out of his depth.

'Are you sure it isn't food poisoning?'

The orderly stuttered, 'I— I don't know. But they've eaten the same food as the rest of us, haven't they? How come we're not affected?'

Hanamura turned back impatiently and leaned over the bunk, his glossy blue-black hair reflecting a sheen of light from the frosted globe on the bulkhead. 'Smithy, can you hear me? Smithy!'

The man moaned, eyes creased shut, rocking himself.

'Smithy, what did you have for your last meal before the pains started? Can you remember?'

A froth of some dark viscous substance had formed on the sick man's lips, like an oily scum. Hanamura drew back sharply at the smell. It stank of putrefaction, as if Smithy's intestines were rotting.

Without a word Hanamura left the cabin and went up to the bridge. According to the chart the *Nierenberg* was 233 miles off the coast of California. At top speed that translated into eleven sailing hours from the Scripps Institution in San Diego. In that time the three men could be dead. Worse, the disease – virus, or whatever it was – might spread and affect other members of the scientific team and the ship's crew.

Even so, he was reluctant to abandon the trials; the results up to now had been promising. Installed in the lowest hold near the stern, the pilot plant was operating at maximum capacity, producing a yield of twenty tons an hour at ninety-five per cent purity. From the bridge, Hanamura could see the huge flexible silver tube snaking over the side, sucking up seawater. After filtration to remove fish, marine plants and all but microscopic sea life, the brine was heated and pumped below, where it passed through a series of electrolysis cells. The constituent gases given off, oxygen and hydrogen, were then analysed and measured before being released into the atmosphere via ducts on the afterdeck.

Hanamura had discussed the men's sickness with Carter Reid, his chief assistant, who held a Ph.D. in marine physics. Their first assumption was that hydrogen film forming on the anodes was the culprit, which if allowed to build up gave off corrosive and poisonous fumes. But Reid's tests had all proved negative: the anodes thus far were clean, no film had formed and the confined space in the hold adjacent to the pilot plant was free of noxious gases.

Additionally, as Reid had pointed out, two of the three men affected weren't on duty anywhere near the plant. They were out on the open deck, supervising the intake tube and venting ducts. So what else did that leave? Food poisoning? A mystery virus? A transmittable disease? What else? He couldn't think; it was pure blind guesswork.

'I'm going to radio for a chopper,' the captain said as they stood together on the port side of the bridge. The vessel rolled gently on the dark green swell. Thin layers of haze lay close to the water, like vaporous ribbons. 'We can have one here within an hour. We'll winch the men off and get them to hospital.'

Hanamura nodded absently, not really listening.

'What's on your mind?' asked the captain, following the scientist's gaze to the jumble of equipment in the stern.

'Three down . . . how many more?'

'Will there be any more?' the captain said, tight-lipped.

Hanamura shook his head thoughtfully. 'There has to be a common factor, but I can't see it. We've checked the plant thoroughly and can't find anything wrong. They've eaten the same food as the rest of us. What else can it be?'

He nearly went on to mention the dark froth on Smithy's lips, the breath that smelled of rotting flesh, but he didn't. Possibly it might make the captain decide to return to port, and Hanamura didn't want the trials jeopardised on account of three men – or fifty, for that matter.

The bridge telephone beeped and the first officer stuck his head through the sliding hatch. 'Dr Reid asks if you'll go down to the stern hold right away, sir,' he said to Hanamura.

Carter Reid was waiting for him at the bottom of the companionway, his bifocals winking dully in the dim light from the overhead caged globes. Beyond, in the darker recesses of the hold, the pounding rush and swirl of seawater could be heard as it was pumped through the banks of cells. The air was heavy and cloying, with a tang of acridity.

'In here, Frank.'

Reid bustled across the steel-plated deck and into a windowless cubicle, its steel walls running with condensation. His agitation was plain, which caused Hanamura to feel a sickly foreboding; usually Carter was bland to the point of fading into the woodwork.

'Well?'

Reid stepped around him and pulled the door shut. His round, pink-cheeked face shone with sweat. He gave Hanamura a grim look and nodded to the gas analyser with its row of tracing pens performing squiggles on the broad band of graph paper. 'Take a look.'

The three main curves were the readings for oxygen, hydrogen, and chlorine. Several other tracings, registering smaller peaks and troughs, indicated other products being given off in minute quantities.

'What are they?' Hanamura asked stonily.

'These are trace elements, hydrogen salts, the usual stuff.' Reid sucked in a shaky breath and pointed. 'This one is tetrachlorodi benzo-para-dioxin. I've taken four samples and checked them independently. There's no mistake. It's TCDD.'

Hanamura looked at the tiny squiggle. His face had drained of colour and his eyes felt hot.

'It's very small, only a fraction of a per cent,' Reid told him, 'but it's definitely there, mixed in with the oxygen product.' He looked bleakly into Hanamura's eyes. 'That's the cause, Frank – Smithy and the others – they were on deck and must have got a whiff from the oxygen duct. Only it's oxygen spiked with a lethal dose of dioxin.'

'But where? Where's it coming from?'

'The ocean, where else?'

Hanamura stared at the one offending line. He couldn't believe it – wouldn't accept it. *Dioxin?* How? Where? Why?

'We have to shut the plant down right away, Frank.'

Hanamura shook his head stubbornly.

'Frank, *we have to!* We can't carry on pumping dioxin into the atmosphere!' Carter Reid clutched his arm. 'We're supposed to be *saving* the human race, not killing it off!'

Hanamura shook him off roughly, reached out, took hold of the broad band of paper, wrenched it from the machine and started tearing it to shreds.

The pens jittered on, aimlessly tracing peaks and troughs, recording the same message on to nothing.

2

Of course they knew the name. His book was their bible. It was Gavin Chase who had started Midnite-Net – but the photograph on the dust jacket and the face on TV bore scant resemblance to the dishevelled middle-aged man with dark circles under his eyes who sat haggard from lack of sleep behind the wheel of the Jeep.

The tall broad-shouldered young man with fair hair and thick white eyebrows had a kind of leering smile on his face, as if secretly amused by something. 'You really Dan's father? No shit?'

It wasn't the most welcoming of arrivals, to be waved down by four young men with weaponry as they approached the settlement along the western shore of Goose Lake. About a mile away they could see a cluster of wooden buildings set among fir trees. Chase held his irritation in check. They were young and excitable, fingering their rifles and handguns as if itching to use them; there was also a feverishness in their eyes that disturbed him.

'Yes, Dan is my son. Are you going to let us through now?'

The one with fair hair glanced at the others, who copied his smirk.

Ruth's patience was even more depleted than Chase's. She exploded. 'Listen, you bunch of pricks! Either let us pass or find somebody with some real authority. We're in no mood to be messed about by fucking dickheads!'

The fair-haired young man didn't take kindly to her attitude. His ruddy face flushed even darker.

'Do you want me to go get your father, Baz?' asked one of his companions.

'Shut up,' Baz Brannigan said to no one in particular.

'I received a message from Nick Power telling me that Cheryl Detrick was ill,' Chase said, doing his best to retrieve what was left of the situation. 'If you want to ride along with us, Nick Power will confirm that, okay?' He smiled tiredly. 'After what we've seen between Utah and here I don't blame you for taking precautions.'

It was enough, it appeared, though only just, to save the young man's face.

He debated for a moment and gave a surly nod, then gestured with his rifle to one of the others, who climbed on to the back of the Jeep. As Chase drove on he could see the fair-haired young man in the mirror, standing in the middle of the road and watching them all the way.

Nick was pleased and relieved to see them. He'd been afraid they wouldn't get through. Over the past year, and the last six months in particular, things had got to be very bad. They'd had trouble with the refugees from the south, many of whom had set up camps in the woods nearby. The morale at Goose Lake was in pretty poor shape.

'We gathered that,' Ruth said curtly, lying back exhausted in the living room of Nick's cabin. It was a pine-clad, single-storey building with a shingled roof, plainly yet comfortably furnished. 'A gang of gun-happy teenage thugs guarding the road is a kind of a hint.'

Nick and his wife, Jen, who was pouring tea, exchanged looks. 'That's Baz Brannigan and his mob. Baz is Tom Brannigan's son. Tom's the council leader – or he was until he got a dose of megalomania and set himself up as dictator.'

'Today Goose Lake, tomorrow . . .' Jen said, handing around the tea, though she wasn't smiling; clearly it wasn't a joke.

'Well, I suppose it's necessary to have someone watching the road,' Chase said.

'You miss the point, Gav. Those kids are Brannigan's personal militia. They're bombed out of their skulls most of the time – and they're there to keep people in as well as out.'

Chase paused with the cup halfway to his lips. 'You mean you're not allowed to leave? What the hell is going on here?'

'Ask the Brannigans,' Nick shrugged. 'Father or son, because I'm not sure who's in charge any more. Come to that, neither are they.' His expression was deadly serious. 'I wasn't kidding about the megalomania. Tom Brannigan's developed a king-size power complex; he sees Goose Lake as his own private empire. And with Baz around, things get kind of complicated because *he* thinks he's running the show.'

On top of their trip and everything else, Chase couldn't take this in. Where he'd expected to find a stable, tightly knit community, there was instead fear, resentment and suspicion: Goose Lake was no refuge, a haven from the crazy world outside; instead it reflected in microcosm the chaos and disintegration that was infecting the rest of the country – as if a potent nerve gas had been piped into their bedrooms while they slept. There was no escape.

'Have you found out what's wrong with Cheryl yet?'

Nick rubbed his hand across the bald dome of his head, surrounded by curly gingerish hair. He glanced at his wife again and said awkwardly, 'I guess I'd better tell you. Apparently – though we didn't know this till recently – Cheryl's been sick for several months. We didn't find out till about two weeks ago, and there was no doctor to carry out a proper examination.'

'There's no doctor?'

'Not any more. There was one, a guy called Middleton, but there was some trouble between him and Tom Brannigan over Brannigan's son. Middleton accused Baz of stealing drugs from the dispensary.

There was an argument – Brannigan senior is a mean-tempered bastard and he pulled a gun. He shot Middleton and killed him. That was four months ago. After that, Tom really went haywire. We don't know how true this is, but the story going around is that the father's been hooked himself on all kinds of pills and whatnot. He was afraid that Middleton would find out that Baz was stealing the drugs for his pa, so he had to shut him up.'

'Which is why we don't have a doctor any more,' Jen added.

'Hasn't Cheryl been treated at all?' Ruth said. She was struggling to keep her drooping eyelids open.

'The old guy in charge of the dispensary gave her some medication,' Nick said. 'And Jen and our daughter have been looking after her.'

'Who's with her now?' Chase asked.

'Jo is.'

'Where's Dan? Isn't he with her?'

It was if his words were pebbles plopping into a placid pool, sending ripples of silence into the corners of the room. 'Where is Dan?' Chase said, feeling so utterly weary that it needed a supreme effort to drag his brain into a semblance of coherent thought.

'Brannigan had him locked away,' Nick said quietly.

'Which Brannigan?' Chase said, more confused than ever.

'The son. Baz. A few weeks ago he attacked Jo while they were out riding—'

'Don't mince words,' his wife said coldly. 'He raped her.'

Nick held up his hand. 'Yes, yes, all right. He was stoned on LSD at the time.'

'That doesn't excuse *anything*.'

'I never said it did.'

'This isn't making sense,' Chase said. 'Are you saying Baz and Jo were out riding and he raped her? How come Dan is involved? Nick, what the hell—?'

'It's a muddle, I'm sorry.' Nick Power clasped his hands together and tried again. 'Jo and Dan were out riding together. Baz and some of his pals turned up on quad bikes, and Jo was molested—'

'Fucking well say it!' Jen snapped. 'She was *raped*. By Baz and at least one of the others. Dan tried to stop them and was knocked unconscious. They left the two of them, Jo and Dan, up on the ridge by Drews Gap.'

'You just said Dan was locked up. What happened?'

'Dan confronted Baz when he got back,' Nick said, 'and the four of them dragged him off and shut him away.'

'Did no one stop them? At least try to help him?'

'I'm sorry, Gav, we did what we could, but Brannigan's got the firepower, and the truth is, we haven't.'

'I'm getting mightily fucking tired of hearing the name Brannigan,' Chase said. 'You mean to tell me that blond kid and those others on the road back there – a bully and three punks – are running this place and nobody has the balls to stop them?'

Nick shook his head wearily. 'Gav, listen, it's not just them. Brannigan senior is in on the act, and he has half a dozen cronies backing him up. If it was just Baz and his pals on their own, we'd have done something.'

'What about Dan? How are they treating him?'

'We don't actually know, to be honest.' Nick looked more than uncomfortable, he was shame-faced. 'As I told you, Brannigan junior's had him locked up since then and . . .' His voice trailed off.

Chase's nostrils were pinched and white. '*And?*'

'He's drugged up to the eyeballs and they won't let anyone near him.'

After their nightmare journey, Chase had entered the world of the madhouse.

3

Ruth carried out her examination at ten the next morning. As she sat at the bedside Chase was struck by the miraculous change that fifteen hours' sleep had achieved. Though pale, her movements were calm and steady, her eyes alert below the fresh dressing that Jen had applied to her forehead.

As for Cheryl, he had prepared himself for the worst and was therefore relieved to find her conscious and able to recognise him, though she had lost a lot of weight. Her cheeks were grey and sunken, her eyes dull and lethargic.

'We're going to take care of you,' he said, smiling down at her. Emotion welled up within him as he took her frail hand and felt the gentle pressure of her fingers responding to his own. Her lips moved as she tried to speak, but all that came out was a dry rasp, like dead leaves blowing in the gutter.

'It's going to be fine. We've brought some special drugs to treat you. Ruth has a lot of experience in dealing with this. You're going to get well, I promise you.'

Cheryl's lips formed a word – a name. She stared up at him beseechingly and her face suddenly convulsed. Her chest heaved and bile-coloured fluid dribbled down her chin.

Chase wiped it away with absorbent cotton. 'It's all right. I know, Nick told me everything. We'll get Dan out of there. Don't worry.' He continued to smile reassuringly and hold her hand, but afterwards in the living room, waiting with the others for the prognosis, the smiling mask fell away.

'It's anoxia at a fairly advanced stage,' Ruth told them bluntly. 'The alveoli in the lungs, where the exchange of oxygen and carbon dioxide takes place, are impaired, which means other cells in the body are not being replenished with oxygen. This leads to a gradual debilitation of the system and eventually . . .' She paused. 'I've treated patients at this stage of anoxia before and some of them have recovered. It all depends on them being in a sealed respiratory enclosure – in other words a pressurised oxygen tent. And an intensive programme of medication.'

'What about the drugs we brought with us?'

'They'll relieve the symptoms, the nausea and so on, but only for a few days. A week at the outside.'

'Can we risk moving her?'

'We can't risk not moving her,' Ruth said. 'We must get her the optimum recuperative environment.' She thought for a moment. 'Maybe your technical people at Desert Range could rig up an oxygen enclosure. With the proper medication and nursing attention, Cheryl stands at least a fighting chance. Here she doesn't stand any chance at all.' Ruth hesitated and said, 'It's just occurred to me: the best place for recovery might be the Pryce-Darc Clinic. It's a specialist unit for anoxia and pollution cases. I sent some of my patients there from New York and they achieved a high success rate, so they claim.'

'Where is this clinic?' Chase asked.

'Used to be in Maryland, but they've had to move the location to Iowa. Not sure where exactly, but I can find out.'

Chase nodded slowly. 'All right, Ruth, thanks. We'll think about that later. After we get Cheryl out of here and back to Desert Range.' He said to Nick, 'Of course, you and your family will come with us. There's nothing to stay here for.'

'That's if we can get out,' Nick said.

'We'll get out. All of us.'

'What about Dan?' Ruth asked, studying him.

'Dan as well,' Chase said. 'Either with the Brannigan clan's consent or over their dead bodies.'

4

The lagoon was a pool of warm black ink, and gliding along on its surface like a smiling yellow coin the perfect simulacrum of the moon moved ahead of the launch.

4 a.m. No better hour for an emergency, Sprote reckoned.

They would come hotfoot at the first shrill siren, befuddled with sleep, stumbling into their shoes, faces still creased. He hadn't formulated yet exactly how it was to happen, but he knew enough about the security system to know how to penetrate it and cause the most confusion, wreak the greatest havoc.

Cy Sprote watched the moon sliding over the still black water and didn't care that he might never see it again, brilliant and beautiful as it was. Madness came with the full moon, though Sprote knew quite lucidly that he was far from mad. He was too sharply, too coldly, too brutally sane. Saner than he'd ever been in his entire life.

The white concrete cubes were like a child's neatly stacked building blocks under the pale anaemic light. Sprote passed through the double perimeter fence showing the ID he had lifted from the locker room and went directly to the control hub. Such was the increase in the number of inmates that Section M had expanded fourfold from its original capacity. The breeding experiments had added considerably to the total: there was now a fifty-cot ward of the little monsters, nurtured under stringently controlled conditions. Some were actually breathing a mixture of methane and nitrogen, with only minimal oxygen content. Known as 'Meeks', the new breed had been named by Dr Rolsom after the saying 'the Meek Shall Inherit the Earth.' Doc Rolsom liked his little quips.

The good doctor will get his too, Sprote vowed. Oh, yes indeed. The Meek would Inherit the Earth with a fucking great V for Vengeance.

Only one duty technician remained in the control hub. His name was Hyman. Sprote knew and liked him; they had swapped books, shared the same taste in classical music, discussed cosmology; it wasn't enough to stop Sprote severing his colleague's jugular with a clean swift slice of the hunting blade. The blood spouted out in gobs and spattered the bank of monitor screens, showing like huge black raindrops against the flickering images.

Sprote allowed himself several seconds' calm reflection. On the screens the grotesqueries twitched and writhed in their padded booths. Limbless torsos. Eyeless faces. Ribless chest cavities. Grafted gills.

On a larger screen the docile ranks of Meeks slept beneath their plastic shrouds, breathing their own special atmosphere. Primordial babes: protozoic prototypes of the brave new world.

Sprote hadn't thought of it before, but he knew now what he must do. The Meeks were the key: Doctor Rolsom's pride and joy – but he must have Malden too. He wanted them both. Yes, of course Malden would come if the Meeks were threatened.

Very calmly, Sprote stepped over the gurgling body and peered at the dim green gauges. He opened the computer safety lock and switched it to manual override. A flashing red light came on. Next he turned to the control console and spun a calibrated dial. The level on the gauge marked METHANE rose. He spun another dial and the OXYGEN level crept towards zero. The panel lit up, became a fairyland of multicoloured lights. Competing buzzes sounded. Distantly a siren howled, splitting the peaceful tropical night with its clamour. The alarm would register in the main complex across the lagoon and Rolsom would be tumbling out in pyjamas and bare feet.

There was only the one door to the control hub, which Sprote now locked. He had eight rounds in his service automatic and a spare clip besides. He would now wait patiently for Malden and Rolsom to cross the lagoon. Wait for them to get inside Zone Four. Wait for the trap to snap shut.

Returning to the main console, feeling relaxed and prepared, he seated himself in Hyman's vacant chair. Every nook and cranny in the building was under close surveillance. The entire complex was riddled with cameras. Every door was electronically controlled from this room.

His hand hovered, decided and touched numbered square white buttons. The screens flickered and changed vantage points: here a corridor, there a stairway, an emergency exit, inner compound, perimeter gate. A screen showed two security guards looking lost and panic-stricken. One of them ran to the main gate, his shadow splaying in all directions from the battery of arc lights. He gestured agitatedly to the guard emerging from his glass cubicle. Rapid mouthing, fierce gesticulation. Arguing, the two guards went into the guard-post.

A moment later a blue light winked on in the centre of the panel and a buzzer rasped urgently.

'Hyman . . . Hyman! Are you there?'

Sprote grunted.

'This is Rimkuss at the main gate. What in hell is happening in Section M? Every fucking goddamn alarm in the place is sounding off!'

'Life-support failure,' said Sprote calmly.

'Holy Mother of shit – where?'

'Meeks' recovery ward.'

There was a fearful stunned silence. 'The Meeks? But what—? How in hell? I don't get it. Why didn't the computer fail-safe come on-line?'

'It failed.'

The fail-safe failed?' This was becoming too much for Rimkuss. 'Have you told the director?'

'Yes,' Sprote lied. 'He's on his way.' Another light on the panel winked for urgent attention. That was him, Doc Rolsom, trying to get through to find out what the fuck was going on. Sprote said to Rimkuss, 'When the director arrives take him immediately to Section M. I'll do what I can from here.'

'Hyman, I think you'd—'

Sprote cut him off but didn't replace the handset. He watched the light on the panel winking futilely. After thirty seconds it ceased. They were on their way. On one of the screens he saw Rimkuss emerge from the guard-post and look anxiously towards the landing jetty. Under the arc lights his tan was the colour of bad meat. On the larger screen the Meeks slept on, probably for ever. The needle on the OXYGEN gauge stood quiescent at zero. They were breathing pure methane.

Sprote flexed his right hand, circled the numbered buttons with outspread fingers, then like a cobra striking, punched up a view of the maternity ward. It looked peaceful. A shaded light burned in the night nurse's station. In one of the nineteen beds in two rows on either side of the ward, under a sheet, lay Natassya Pavlovitch. It didn't matter which bed she occupied. She wasn't his Natassya any more. She was an incubatory receptacle for an experiment in genetics: an experiment he had helped create. Natassya would give birth to his monster-child. Their love would bring forth horror. He had worked for five years in order to destroy the only human being who had meant anything to him in his adult life. Sprote thought he must be mad. There was no other rational explanation.

5

The screens blurred into prismatic fragments and Sprote realised that he was weeping. A momentous revelation made him stop and blink the tears away. He had regained his sanity, after five years of madness, so real and painful that it was like someone twisting a knife in his belly . . . and he came to recognise the long gradual decline that had brought him to accept these obscene experiments as if they were the most natural, logical thing in the world.

How could it have happened? He had never wished ill or harm to another living soul and yet he had obeyed, acquiesced, played his part in a scheme so monstrous it froze the marrow in his bones. Where had he, Cyrus Ingram Sprote, been all those years? An imposter must have been strolling around wearing his face, dressed in his clothes, walking in his shoes, because the real Cy Sprote, the one from Portland, Maine, would never in a million years have participated in such loathsome depravities.

And now that it had become clear and his sanity returned, he felt like screaming.

His throat tightened, but instead of a scream, a throaty animal sound emerged: he could see the hurrying cluster of figures pass through the main gate and enter the brilliantly lit stage set of the inner compound.

Rolsom, because of his height and colour, he spotted at once. After a brief heart-stopping moment of doubt he picked out the slighter frame and sharp features of Malden, even less substantial in a short-sleeved tan shirt and white deck shoes.

Rimkuss, poor bastard, was making a valiant attempt at explaining what he himself plainly didn't understand. There was some insistent questioning and unsatisfactory replies, after which Malden turned and stormed towards the main building, issuing orders that Sprote couldn't hear. The others followed their leader and passed out of sight.

Sprote stabbed a button and picked up the group as it entered the building. What would Malden decide to do? Head for the control hub or go directly to Section M? *Section M, Section M,* Sprote willed them in his mind. *Go to Section M!*

Under Malden's direction, three of the guards peeled off and came towards the stairs leading up to the control hub. General Malden himself, Doc Rolsom, Rimkuss and the two remaining guards turned in the other direction.

Sprote wiped his palms dry, unbuckled his holster and placed the semi-automatic 9-shell Glock on the panel in front of him. He made sure the safety was off. A diagrammatic layout informed him of the location and index number of every CCTV camera throughout the complex and he sat back in the chair, smiling a little, as he observed Malden's progress towards the centre of the web. The group passed through the complicated system of steel doors and sliding shutters into

Section M and Sprote watched as they took the corridor leading to the ward where the Meeks lay gasping their last.

Happy now that his prey was inside Section M, he was happier still when he had flicked shut all electronic circuits, sealing the doors of Section M behind them.

From outside the control hub, boots thumped along the corridor. Without taking his eyes off the screens, Sprote picked up the Glock semi-automatic and curled his finger around the trigger.

Malden, Doc Rolsom and the others, he could see, were approaching the final barrier that led to the Meeks' recovery ward: a steel-barred gate. On the diagram it read MV-43. Sprote punched up the image on the screen and in the same movement closed the electronic circuit. One of the guards inserted a key and turned it. Nothing happened. Malden brusquely shouldered the guard aside and tried it himself. When the gate refused to open he turned in a slow circle, the first pucker of doubt showing on his face. Sprote could read his mind. He remembered how Malden and Rolsom had gloated over him from the booth in the operating theatre, in what had been the bleakest moment of his life; and now, at last, it was his turn to watch and gloat . . .

Fists pounded on the door and a voice shouted *Hyman!* and repeated it several times, yelling louder, baffled and angry.

The smile still lurking, Sprote was looking at Malden's face on the screen, which was pointed and peaky under the strip lights, and the smile didn't even waver when pounding rifle butts smashed through the door panel behind his chair. An arm appeared through the splintered gap, reaching for the handle and quite casually, and for the first time in his life, Sprote aimed a gun at a human being and blew his arm off at the elbow.

There was a horrible choking scream and the bloody stump vanished.

On the screen Malden was debating what to do, and Sprote was enjoying his dilemma. His choices were limited. Further progress to the Meeks' ward was restricted, clearly. He could either retreat along the main corridor to the main entrance or take one of the side passages to an emergency exit. The problem (Sprote could see the uncertainty, the reluctance, working in Malden's face) was that the side passages were lined with confinement cells, which housed all kinds of creatures. Moreover, the security system of Section M was foolproof, designed to keep the inmates locked away. Period. Both Malden and Rolsom had had a hand in making it totally secure, and it surely occurred to them that the system was just as effective at keeping the two of them inside as it did the inmates.

An automatic weapon stuttered like a tractor, filling the control hub with a stupendous racket, and what remained of the door was pulverised in a cloud of flying splinters.

Sprote spun around in the swivel chair, gun at arm's length, and pumped three shots into the first man through. At such close range his ineptitude didn't matter. Two hits and a miss: one passing clean through the man's windpipe and out the other side, the other smashing his rib cage and making a dog's dinner of his innards.

The anatomical destruction was so spectacular that Sprote was surprised, until he remembered that these were dum-dum shells, the percussion type that spread internally on impact, reducing everything to jellied pulp.

One guard dead, the other disabled, which left just one of the three sent to the control hub. No way he was going to try it on his own. The last guy wouldn't dare toss a stun-grenade, Sprote reckoned, because it would cause carnage to the controls and leave everything a smouldering electronic wreck.

For just a few moments, he was safe. He prayed there would be enough time. *Just a few more minutes, that's all I ask. You can't refuse a dying man his last request.*

Malden and the others were moving back along the main corridor, scurrying now, almost running. Panic was setting in. Sprote switched cameras in time to see them arrive at the external steel door, the last barrier to the outside. But that too, they now discovered, was electronically sealed. Options were running out: the ways forward and back were barred, which left only the emergency exits – and to reach those they had to pass the confinement cells.

It was only now that Malden raised stony eyes to the surveillance camera. With an abrupt gesture he led the way to the gate of Block Six.

Rimkuss tried it with his key and of course the gate slid open, because Cy Sprote had allowed it to.

Sprote switched viewpoints and picked them up as they entered the smaller corridor lined with cell doors. He wondered why Malden had chosen Block Six, and then he knew why: the control hub in which he sat was on the floor above, and there was a stairway past the emergency exit leading up to it.

Malden was moving onto the offensive.

At a sound behind his head, Sprote spun round, the Glock ready in his hand. The guard he had cut to pieces was lying like butchered meat, legs splayed, in a lake of blood. Had the last guard summoned reinforcements? Were they grouping for an assault in the corridor? Sprote had been too busy with the other screens to notice. Perhaps he didn't have minutes, only seconds—

Snapping his attention back to the control board, he closed the circuit on the Block Six gate. Malden's range of options had narrowed down to one – he had no other choice now but to pass along the Block Six corridor to reach the emergency exit, which, like every other door in Section M, was electronically controlled.

The banked screens of individual cells were little capsules of deformity, ready to be unleashed. The men guarding Malden and Doc Rolsom would kill some of them, most of them, perhaps, but they couldn't kill them all. There were just too many – and Sprote intended to release every single inmate in the entire complex. Soon there would be several hundred roaming wantonly through Section M. Malden and Doc Rolsom ought to be grateful to him, Sprote told himself, to be given this opportunity to see their handiwork at such close quarters.

Footsteps and muffled whispering in the corridor outside: they were preparing for the next and final assault.

Sprote quickly ran the heel of his hand along the row of switches, then the next row, and the one after, and the one after that until he had released the locking mechanism on every cell door.

Malden and the others couldn't fail to have heard the mechanism operating; Sprote could tell at once by their petrified expressions and frantic mouthings that they knew what was happening. The guards drew their weapons and backed along the corridor, shoulder to shoulder, tightly bunched.

The cell doors began to open.

First to reach the emergency exit at the end of the corridor, Malden banged on the solid steel door with his clenched fist. Rimkuss tried the key, without optimism. He was right to feel hopeless; the door was immoveable. Malden yelled something and the guards clustered around. But instead of firing at the inmates as Sprote had expected, they stupidly aimed at the steel door, wasting ammunition and endangering themselves by the ricochets.

Sprote now released the circuits on the internal barred gates, allowing the inmates from Blocks One to Five to move freely within the complex. His work was done. The trap had been set and sprung. All that was left for him to do was watch and enjoy . . .

Viewing it on the large screen was an eerie experience, like watching a horror movie with the sound turned off. Having at least realised the futility of shooting at two-inch-thick plate steel, the guards were killing inmates. They killed quite a lot of them. The pale green walls were spattered with red and the floor was soon a swamp. After less than three minutes the ammunition ran out.

The sound of gunfire and mayhem of screams and dying cries attracted the inmates in other parts of the complex, who now came lurching, stumbling, slithering and dragging their deformed bodies through the open gate into Block Six. The corridor filled up. The packed deformity surged forward. Many of them had enough glimmerings of comprehension left to recognise the director, and the guards were familiar symbols of oppression.

The five men were ripped apart. Hair was torn out at the roots and eye sockets gouged clean. Those inmates who lacked a limb or two, or functioning arms and hands, used their teeth. Malden and the others were engulfed and disappeared from view, though Sprote caught glimpses of unrecognisable body parts, ragged bloody chunks which had been wrenched off and flung aside. The men's genitalia suffered the same fate, separated from their bodies by force, chewed and spat out. The frenzy on the screens filtered up to Sprote's ears from below;

a cacophony of muted screams and howls, like a soundtrack from the bowels of the underworld.

Sprote didn't even bother turning his head when the guards came through the door: he was preoccupied with releasing the electronic locks on the emergency exits. Once outside the main building, the inmates had the double perimeter fence to scale before losing themselves in the luxuriant flora of Starbuck; maybe a few would survive long enough to contaminate the island with their genetically-adapted bodies, rich in new viruses. Undetected, they might even breed and produce a race of monsters.

Sprote would never know how successful this latest venture – his very own experiment – would turn out to be, because the combined impact of a dozen or more bullets shredded his head and torso and the chair in which he sat, a faint smile and a soundless name on his lips.

6

In the early hours of its second day at sea, MV *Icarus* was 274 nautical miles out from its home berth at Roanoke Island, North Carolina and very nearly halfway to Bermuda.

The trip thus far hadn't been all plain sailing. The Diamond Shoals off Cape Hatteras had been calm enough, with a light easterly breeze and a gentle rolling swell that the curved white prow cut through at a steady seventeen knots. Chesney Poulton ate lunch in the top lounge, aft of the bridge, with wonderful views on three sides through the ten-foot-high windows. He was accompanied by Rik McGlen and Scottie Hench, two husky members of the 14th Army Brigade of the Charlotte National Guard, assigned as his security escort. Poulton wore a dark green Lacoste polo shirt and cream linen slacks, while the Guardsmen wore loose T-shirts and, appropriately enough, Bermuda shorts, with blue canvas deck shoes.

On their first day Poulton hadn't made any overtures; he had plenty of experience and knew how to handle these matters.

His first appraisal was that Rik McGlen was the more likely candidate. There was nothing remotely suspect about either of the Guardsmen, but Poulton sensed that the younger of the two, at nineteen, was the better prospect. Yet it might be that Scottie was up for it also, which would mean he had struck lucky twice over.

Later in the afternoon the cool breeze turned into a chilling wind as it veered on the compass to a more northerly quadrant. The boat started to pitch and toss; spray broke as high as the third deck as it plunged through the foaming white caps. Both Guardsmen were poor sailors and brought up their lunches. Poulton excused them their duties and they went to lie down in their separate cabins. He himself enjoyed rough weather; it was very close to an orgiastic experience.

On the bridge, Poulton checked out the forty-eight-hour forecast with the captain. A few scattered squalls were predicted, with gusts up to forty miles per hour, but nothing too alarming. At twenty-five million dollars, *Icarus* was a streamlined, state-of-the-art craft that could take nearly all marine conditions, except the most catastrophic, in its stride.

Come dinnertime and Scottie Hench was still poorly. Poulton looked in on him, asked if he wanted anything from the galley – soup or a sandwich, maybe – but at the mention of food the Guardsman buried his head in the pillow with a low, muffled groan.

Rik McGlen was in much better shape. He seemed to have found his sea-legs and even accepted one of Chesney Poulton's lethal 'specials' before dinner: a forty per cent proof combination of gin and vermouth with a splash of soda and four ice cubes. During the meal Poulton drank red wine and Rik stuck with beer. Once or twice the plates and dishes slid along the tablecloth, then slid back again as the boat lurched into a solid wave and they felt the deck shudder under their feet.

The Guardsman held onto the arms of his chair.

Poulton reached out and gripped the boy's wrist reassuringly. 'Trust me, Rik, this is nothing. I've been through force eights and nines in this tub. She's sleek as a seal and happy as a clam in all weathers. The rougher it is, the better she likes it.'

'It's not that I'm scared, sir,' the Guardsman said, which he plainly was. 'I just don't wanna lose this delicious steak five minutes after I've swallowed it.'

'Have another beer, son. Or how about a cognac? That'll settle things down.'

After dinner they retired to the main saloon. Poulton proposed watching a movie . . . or if Rik preferred, they could relax and listen to music. The young Guardsman seemed more ill at ease than before. He had a dry cough, as if nervously clearing his throat, and it occurred to Poulton that the guy was starting to wonder what this generous hospitality and cosy fraternisation with such a senior and Very Important Person were leading up to. But no matter; one way or another, Poulton would have his way, like he always did.

Perhaps due to his nervousness, Rik McGlen was on his third cognac in under an hour. Poulton didn't want him too inebriated – he'd be no use passed out, and hardly any fun at all if he couldn't raise a respectable stiffie for the occasion. At a few minutes after 10 p.m. the captain called down from the bridge: radar had picked up a huge object. It was too big for any vessel afloat, even the largest supertanker – it could only be the Antarctic calving berg the US coastguard were tracking.

Poulton was annoyed at the disturbance. 'So why bother me, for chrissakes? If you know what it is and where it's at, steer round the fuckin' thing.'

'We also have a solid weather front heading toward us, all the way from Greenland, sir. It's passing Newfoundland at near cyclone strength and rising—'

Poulton interrupted. 'What are you trying to tell me?'

'I think we ought to turn about and head back to port.'

Poulton took his time with a sip of Courvoisier 5-star from the crystal tumbler. The pads of his fingers were white from the pressure on the glass. 'How much cruise-time have we had this year, Captain? On how many occasions have you taken *Icarus* out of port and put to sea?'

'Just the once, sir.' The captain sounded contrite.

'And how far are we, at this moment in time as we speak, from Bermuda?'

There was a slight pause while the captain presumably checked the digital readout.

'Two-nine-seven nautical miles, sir.'

'Is that halfway?'

'Roughly fifteen miles short of it.'

'Then proceed as planned. If necessary, and you feel you have to, make a detour. I trust your judgement, so use it. And Captain.'

'Sir?'

'Do you value your job?'

'I do, sir. Very much so.'

'Then don't disturb me again.'

By one a.m., Chesney Poulton was a tired and contented man. It had taken a little gentle persuasion, but Guardsman McGlen had come to his senses and acquiesced to what was required of him. They had stayed in the saloon, and the pair of them were now lying naked and partially entangled on the red velvet divan. Rik had a sweet mouth. Was there enough strength left for another grunting, thrusting escapade, perhaps after they had both taken a nap? Poulton was drowsily contemplating this possibility when the floor became the wall and the wall became the ceiling. The entire saloon, it seemed, had turned ninety-degrees onto its side. Poulton was left wondering if he had drunk too much Courvoisier before a solid green wave entered through the bulkhead and instead of brandy he tasted salt water . . .

Scooped up by the cyclone as if it were a piece of flotsam, the MV *Icarus* was lifted and driven into the sheer towering wall of the Riiser-Larsen Calving Berg. The impact broke its back and split the motor yacht in two. The aft section of the vessel, containing the engine room, driving mechanism, turbine house and fuel tanks, went down like a stone. It took less than ten minutes for the seawater to rush in and engulf the staterooms, the main saloon, the dining room, the galley and the crew's quarters, sending Chesney Lea Poulton, Guardsmen Rik McGlen and Scottie Hench, the captain and all nine members of the crew to the bottom of the North Atlantic, which at this point was nearly one thousand fathoms deep.

There wasn't time to send out a Mayday or deploy the satellite-tracking buoy.

The calving berg that had sheared off western Antarctica six years ago, once more moved majestically onwards under the night sky, a floating mountain of granite-hard ice and million-year-old permafrost. Nothing could resist it or stand in its way.

6

I

Baz Brannigan's eyes were wide, blue and mad. His corn-coloured hair was in disarray, as if he'd just that minute woken from a sweating nightmare. The hands gripping the rifle were as tight as claws.

'Sure! Take who you want and get the hell out – only Dan stays here. He stays here for good, whether you like it or not, Dr Chase.' The polite use of his name sounded like a slur.

'Doesn't your father have any say in this?'

'I don't take orders from nobody.' Baz jerked his head to include the group around him. In addition to his usual clan of three, there were several other recruits in their late teens and early twenties, all carrying weapons. 'We run the settlement. We say who goes and who stays. There's a war on, or maybe you hadn't noticed.'

Chase frowned. 'War?'

'You're just plain dumb, jackass. *Survival of the fittest*, dummy, and we're the fittest. The outsiders are scum, vermin. They bring disease from the south and we don't intend to let 'em through. We gotta keep ourselves pure.'

The trouble was, he sounded perfectly serious. Chase looked across the square to the general store and the wooden schoolhouse. Baz had taken the council hall as his headquarters, a self-styled guerrilla leader with delusions of grandeur. He saw the Goose Lake settlement as the last outpost holding out against a tidal wave of corrupt humanity. The irony was that the worm was gnawing away from within. Their 'pure' community was rotten to the core.

Chase tried to tell him as much. 'What's happening in the south is going to happen here. You can't keep it out with guns, Baz. This disease you talk about is in the atmosphere, it isn't caused by the people who are suffering from it. Cheryl caught the disease and she's been here for five years.'

One of the other young men who'd been with Baz on the road eased himself off the porch rail. 'Then the sooner you and her fuck off, the better. And take the woman you came with and get out. Now.' He levered the bolt back and swung the rifle around so that it was pointing at Chase's head.

'Not without my son. You've no right to lock him up.'

Baz sniggered. His eyes were huge and round, the pupils dilated. 'Are you going to take him, Dr Chase? Just you alone?' He made the same nasal snort and glanced around. 'I said he was dumb.'

'Then tell me why you're holding him.'

'That's my business.'

'You must have a reason.'

'Tell the cunt to go screw himself,' said a slurred voice from the group. 'We don't have to take this hassle.'

'Damn right, we don't.' Baz raised his rifle and Chase saw that several small notches had been cut in the polished stock. A tally of animal – or human – kills?

There was no sense to this. Perhaps the only 'sense' resided in the convoluted workings of Baz Brannigan's drugged brain and it was futile to expect a logical explanation.

Baz pointed the rifle. 'Put all your crap in the car and get out. I want you off the settlement by sundown. And take the sick woman spreading the plague with you.'

Chase stood his ground. 'I demand to see my son. I have a right—'

A spasm of insane fury broke across Baz Brannigan's face, which under its ruddy tan had a grey pallor. 'I just *told* you what to do and I'm not going to repeat it. I'm all through with words. From here on we talk in bullets.'

2

'It's impossible; you can't reason with them,' Nick said later in the cabin. 'In the end it all comes down to brute force. What are you going to do?'

'What about you?' Chase said, looking at the majestic sweep of mountains to the north. Was Boris still out there somewhere? 'Are you coming with us?'

Nick leaned against the stone mantel, hands in pockets, and stared down at his shoes. 'This place isn't going to last much longer, not with Baz and his cronies running things.' He glanced up. 'We'll come with you if it's possible. But there's a problem – there's not room enough for all of us in one Jeep.'

'There must be other transport.'

'Yeah, a couple of pickups and an old truck, but that's it. They're parked around the back of the council hall where Baz can keep an eye on them. We'll have to try for one of the pickups; though how we do that without getting our heads blown off I don't know.' Nick added reflectively, 'And I've grown attached to mine.'

'We need something to divert their attention,' Ruth said. 'A disturbance of some kind; anything to keep them occupied.'

Chase nodded, but he was thinking of their other problem. Stealing the pickup would be easy compared with getting Dan out. He looked at his watch. 'Whatever we decide, it'll have to be quick,' he said. 'Baz wants us off the settlement by sundown, which gives us four hours. We'll have to start making preparations right now. How soon could you be ready to leave?' he asked Nick.

Nick surveyed the room and sighed. 'Well, there's not a lot we can take with us. About two hours, I'd say, to get our personal stuff and supplies for the trip together. Jen?' His wife nodded her agreement.

'Have you got a gun?'

'Two rifles. Jo's a crack shot – better than me.'

'Four weapons,' Chase said. He kneaded the bruise on his ribs. 'If they're unprepared for us that might be enough.'

'How are you going to do it?' Ruth asked, her eyes heavy and dark beneath the swathe of white bandage. 'We can't start a gunfight with Cheryl in the middle of it, and she's in no shape to be moved quickly.'

'Cheryl won't be there, and neither will you.' Chase stared into space, thinking it through. 'The three of us will leave in the Jeep before sundown, exactly as Baz wants us to do. We'll find a quiet spot somewhere off the road where you and Cheryl can wait in the Jeep while I double back on foot. Then Nick and I will get Dan out, take the pickup and rendezvous with Jen and Jo down by the lake.' He looked at the others.

After a moment's silence Nick said, 'The first part is easy enough – the three of you leaving in the Jeep. It's the rest of it that worries me. Baz has Dan under guard night and day, and there's probably someone watching the pickup too. If shooting starts we're outnumbered, Gav. Ten, fifteen to one.'

Chase gave a thin smile. 'Baz already made that point and I haven't forgotten it. As Ruth says, we need some kind of diversion to draw them away from the council hall. Do you know which room they're holding Dan in?'

'He was in the library stock room,' Jen said, 'if they haven't moved him.'

'Let's hope they haven't. Has it got windows?'

Jen nodded. 'I used to help out in the library. It's a corner room with two windows.'

'How many doors?'

'Just the one. I'll draw you a plan.' She suddenly banged her fist on the arm of the chair.

'What is it?'

'Next door to the stock room – I've just remembered: there's a small kitchen with a trapdoor into the loft. If you could get into the loft from outside you could get in without being seen. Maybe they're not even guarding the stock room, just the main door.'

'Can we get into the loft from outside?' Chase asked Nick.

'I don't know. There's an outhouse, a kind of lean-to shed at one end, so we should be able to get on to the roof.'

'Okay, that's a possibility we'll have to keep in mind.' Chase paced up and down the small living room.

Jo appeared at the door and said apprehensively, 'Ruth, Cheryl's having trouble breathing and there's that stuff on her lips. Can you come?'

Chase turned anxiously, but Ruth held her hand up. 'I'll see to her. You've got enough to be thinking about.' She moved quickly to the door and followed Jo out.

'Would a fire do as a distraction?' Jen asked, hugging her knees and looking from Chase to her husband and back again.

'It might,' Chase said, racking his brains. 'But it would have to be something that threatened Baz personally, his house, his drugs—'

Nick thumped his palm. 'Christ, Gav, that's it: the dispensary! If that went up, they'd beat the flames out with their bare hands!'

'That would do it all right,' Chase agreed, 'but we'd be hurting everyone else in the community, too, destroying drugs that innocent people need.' He tugged fretfully at his beard. 'No, we can't do that, Nick. It would cause suffering, even death.'

'It's life or death for us, too,' Nick said. 'It's every man for himself.'

Chase looked away, his face drawn and tight. 'That's why the world's in a fucking awful mess right now. The biggest grab the most. "What's yours is mine and what's mine's me own." Old Lancashire saying.'

'I remember you and your bloody conscience at Halley Bay,' Nick said, shaking his head wryly. 'Fretting about the dissolution of carbon dioxide in seawater, and what it might mean.'

'While you and the rest of them were wallowing in lurid sex fantasies,' Chase said.

'Not all that lurid. Pretty tame actually. How about some coffee?' he said to Jen.

'Yes, all right. Do you want something to eat?'

'Not for me. Gav?'

Chase shook his head. Jen went through to the kitchen and Nick took a bottle and glasses from a cupboard. 'Genuine and original Oregon brandy,' he said, pouring out four measures. 'Made from apple cores and caribou droppings. This stuff puts hair on your chest and takes it off everywhere else.'

Jen returned and while they were drinking, Chase told them about the marine trials. 'Up to the time of leaving the Tomb they seemed to be going well. I'm hoping Frank Hanamura's final report will be waiting for me with some optimistic news.'

'What if the trials aren't successful?' Jen asked.

'There are some other methods we've been working on. Problem is it could take another twenty years to develop them sufficiently. Micro-organisms with a high oxygen yield, seeding the deserts to make them net oxygen producers, stuff like that. But I'm not sure we've got twenty years – or even ten, the way things are going.'

'Not even *ten*?' Jen said numbly.

'There's a negative feedback operating now: adverse climatic conditions reinforce themselves to produce even worse conditions, and so on, and so on, turning the spiral even tighter. The climatic deterioration is happening a lot faster than anyone predicted. And there could be other factors we've overlooked or simply know nothing about. In which case we might already be too late to do anything about them.'

'Because you don't know what they are?' Jen said.

Chase nodded. 'Like a man backing away from a rattlesnake and walking deeper into the quicksand he doesn't know is there. He's going to die anyway, and not much consolation to know it won't be by snake venom.'

Ruth and Jo came in and helped themselves to coffee. He searched Ruth's face anxiously. 'Is she all right?'

'I've given Cheryl another injection. It should ease her breathing, but it won't help her condition much. Nothing will help till we get her back to Desert Range. Have you decided what you're going to do?'

'I don't know,' Nick said to Chase. 'Have we?'

Chase told them about Nick's idea for setting fire to the dispensary, which he couldn't agree with, and Jo spoke up. 'There's no need for that. Baz and most of the others will be over at Tom Brannigan's place watching blue movies. They do that every Friday night.'

'Is today Friday?' Chase said. He hadn't the faintest notion.

'They'll leave two or three guys at the council hall,' Jo said, 'but if you time it for about eleven, they'll be drunk, drugged or asleep, or all three. It's the ones at the checkpoint we'll have to watch out for.'

'Are they posted there all through the night?'

Jo nodded. 'Since they set up a refugee camp near Alturas we've had to watch the road all the time. We've always had immigrants from the south, but these are mutes and O-zoes; they'd loot the settlement and wipe it off the map if we didn't keep them out.' She added grudgingly, 'I guess that's one thing we have to be grateful to Baz for.'

Chase found Jo an attractive and spirited girl. He liked her. 'Well, let's just hope Baz and his crowd are too busy watching dirty movies and getting off their heads to bother about us.' He turned to Nick, 'I'll need to know a back trail that will bring me here, to the community, avoiding the road. You be ready to move by eleven. We'll get Dan out, take the pickup, load it up with your stuff and get out fast, roadblock or no roadblock. If they want a fight we'll give them one. We're leaving tonight. All of us.'

Chase looked around at them. His chest felt tight with tension. He hoped he appeared more confident than he felt. 'Right, Carruthers. Let's get organised.'

'Tally-ho, Fortescue,' Nick responded.

3

The lights of the settlement resembled dim glowworms along the black oval curve of the lake. Beyond and all around was the impenetrable forest darkness. Coming down the pale sandy trail, the sky ablaze with stars, Chase was struck by how vulnerable it looked. The possibility of an attack by the mutes and O-zoes Jo had mentioned would leave the place desolate in a couple of hours. And if it became known that a bunch of youngsters, equally crazy in their own way, was in charge, it would be an open invitation, too ripe and juicy to resist.

He and Nick had arranged to meet at the point where the trail dropped steeply through the trees, only a few hundred yards from the settlement. Nick was there already, on his haunches with his back to a tree, a rifle balanced across his knees. He got up and without a word being exchanged they moved in single file down the last gentle slope, seeking the protection of the shadowy trees and bushes.

Chase had left the rifle with Ruth and carried the Browning. The night was warm and he was already perspiring from his three-mile hike. Nervous sweat mixed in with it too, no doubt.

As they approached the first lighted cabin Nick touched his arm and they skirted it, stealthily working their way around to the rear of the meeting hall cum library. There was no sign of activity within, or indeed anywhere; except for the cabin lights, the entire place might have been deserted.

Nick pointed out the vehicles parked in the back lot. There was a Dodge pickup that looked in reasonable shape. They agreed it was the best bet. In the shadow of the building, Nick leaned close and murmured in Chase's ear, 'We'll check the roof first. The outhouse is at the far end.'

A jumble of packing crates made it easy to climb onto the lean-to roof. Stepping like cats, they moved along the lean-to searching with their outspread fingers against the rough timber wall of the main building. Chase strangled an oath as he caught a splinter under his thumbnail. The pain ignited his furious anger. His son was only a few feet away, the thickness of a timber wall separating them; it took a tremendous effort to fight the impulse to smash his fist through the wall, reach inside and pluck his son to freedom.

Nick's hand tightened on his shoulder and in the almost total darkness Chase saw that his companion's bearded mouth was split in a grin. Nick was pointing out a small recessed hatch, access to the loft, at about knee-height, fastened by a bent nail through a hasp. There was no padlock.

Nick put the nail in his pocket, opened the hasp and pushed gently. At first the door resisted and Chase's heart sank that it might be barred on the inside. Nick pushed harder and the small door suddenly gave and sprang open. They both held a collective breath, expecting a crash or loud squeaking of hinges, but there was a creaking of timber and a faint thud, that was all.

Crouching down, Chase clambered through after Nick. Inside it was black and stifling. Chase waited on all fours until the pencil-beam of Nick's flashlight pierced the blackness and then flicked across the massive crossbeams supporting the roof and settled on the floor of the loft. At once they saw the trapdoor. Nick started edging his way towards it along one of the rafters, flashlight in one hand, rifle in the other.

Waiting until he had safely made it, Chase followed, guided by the thin beam of light. They knelt either side of the trapdoor and listened. They were listening for noises, but they were more anxious to hear silence, and after several moments, total beautiful silence was all they could hear.

Chase released the safety-catch on the Browning, then held the flashlight while Nick drew back the bolt on his rifle with slow, infinite care. They listened once more. No sound from below meant there was nothing to be gained by waiting. Nick pried his fingers around the edge of the trapdoor. It took him some time to get a grip, but as soon as the trapdoor began to lift upwards, Chase switched the flashlight off. A square of light appeared, and directly beneath them was the corner of a sink unit, dishes drying in a rack, scuffed pine floor with a plastic bucket and foam mop.

The kitchen was empty.

It was a tight squeeze. Chase lowered himself and hanging at arm's length, dropped as lightly as he could to the floor. He took the rifle and Nick followed on. The kitchen was narrow and rectangular, with a fluorescent light that buzzed like a fly trapped in a jam jar. Chase pointed to a laminate-topped table alongside the wall; at Nick's understanding nod they lifted it together and positioned it under the trapdoor: their quick escape route. Chase was even beginning to hope that Dan's disappearance wouldn't be discovered till morning, by which time they'd be miles away – even if they had to shoot everyone in that road patrol, he thought with grim resolution.

Pressing close to the wall, Chase eased the door open a crack, saw that it was clear and sidled out into the passage, the gun close to his chest. As Nick followed, the floorboards creaked under their combined weight. Chase could feel his shirt clinging to him, and when he stole a glance over his shoulder, he saw that Nick's face, like his own, was running with sweat.

The door of the stock room was at the end of the passage. Opposite was a pair of double doors, which led, presumably, into the library and the main meeting area. Was that where Baz had posted his guards? There was no murmur of voices, no music playing, though of course the silence didn't mean there was no one there.

Chase reached the door to the stock room and was dismayed to find it fastened with a large padlock – recently fitted, judging by the film of grease – and a heavy-duty hasp bolted to the door-frame. This was more than bloody frustrating. It wasn't possible to force it open or lever it from the frame itself, even if they had the tools, because the noise would be enough to wake the dead. For some reason Nick wore his idiotic grin. His whisper was barely audible. 'Look there, Fortescue, old bean.'

On the wall next to the door was a hook, and on the hook hung a key.

The key turned silently and easily and the oiled padlock sprang open. Chase unhooked the padlock from the hasp and placed it on the floor. With a firm, steady pressure he pressed the handle down and eased the door ajar. Nick's breathing was close to his right ear as Chase pushed the door further open and took a step into the room. He knew right away that something was wrong. Why hadn't he sensed that getting in here had been far too easy and straightforward? He and Nick had made a dreadful mistake. It was a trap, and Fortescue and Carruthers had blundered into it.

There was someone strapped to a chair, bound and gagged. The eyes, wide with fear, were Dan's eyes – trying to signal a warning. Even as he took this in, which lasted no more than a couple of seconds, Chase was still too slow in reacting as several hands grabbed him, clamping his shoulders in a vice-like grip and snatching the gun from his hand. From across the corridor there was the sound of the double doors being violently pushed open as more bodies entered from the main hall, and instantly Nick was surrounded by them, held in their grasp as the rifle was wrenched from his hands.

Baz Brannigan stood in the corner of the stock room, beaming triumphantly. 'What did I tell you guys?' he boasted to the others. 'I knew they'd fall for it.'

Laughing out loud, he took a long hunting knife with a curved blade from its sheath and approached the trussed-up figure in the chair. Chase squirmed and struggled, but he was held fast. Baz went behind the chair and slashed with the knife, severing the ropes. Dan sagged forward. With his hands free, he clawed the gag from his mouth, chest heaving as he sucked in a deep breath. Chase couldn't believe his appearance. He had lost so much weight, and was so pale that he looked ill. There were hollows in his cheeks and deep dark shadows round his eyes.

'You fucking shitheads,' Nick said hoarsely. 'You've starved the poor bastard!'

Chase was unable to say a word or even utter a sound. He was in paralysis. There was no rage or anger, no torment or grief, just an icy nothingness.

Baz was holding the knife upright, touching the point with each fingertip. 'What's your problem? He ain't dead.' Baz had an aggrieved tone, as if upset that his compassionate nature hadn't been appreciated. 'We could've let Danny boy die if we'd wanted to. Or finished him off. You ought be grateful we didn't.'

He was looking directly at Chase with eyes that were a bright dreamless blue – drugged, just plain mad or maybe both; it was impossible to say.

Chase found his voice. 'Let me comfort him. Please.'

With a shrug of indifference, Baz nodded his agreement.

Chase pulled himself loose and knelt in front of his son. He couldn't speak because his heart was breaking. He cupped Dan's face in both hands and simply gazed into the dull eyes. Dan weakly held onto his father's wrist and even managed the ghost of a smile.

'I tried to leave . . . I was coming to see you, Dad, trying to get help. But they stopped me. You see, Dad, after what happened to Jo—' Dan choked up. His eyes were red-rimmed.

'They told me what happened to Jo,' Chase said. 'Rest easy. We've come to get you out of here.' He stared up into Baz Brannigan's face, which still had traces of a gloating grin on it. If Baz had heard and understood the reference, it had no meaning or relevance for him. In the stewed soup of his brain perhaps the incident with Jo had vanished into the memory hole of oblivion.

Chase stood up. He looked round at the pack of hotheads crowding in the doorway and finally turned back to Baz. 'Let's keep this neat and simple. Nick and his family already have their gear packed, ready to leave. We're all getting out of here, Dan included. Then you and your pop can carry on to your heart's content, taking turns at playing tin-pot dictator.'

Chase's glance swept over them. 'I guess you realise you're all stark bloody raving mad. You've pumped yourselves to the gills with so much poison that your brain cells have rotted away. And you talk about "survival of the fittest".' Chase said pityingly, 'You're a dead man, Baz. All of you are the walking dead, and nothing can save you now.'

Baz reached out and grabbed Chase by the shoulder and held the knife blade at his throat. The arteries on his forearm stood out, the skin hard and shiny where repeated punctures had formed scar tissue.

'You, my friend, are the fucking dead man!' He leaned forward and Chase felt the tip of the knife penetrate his skin. There was a warm trickle underneath his jaw. 'Because all I have to do is push this a tad deeper,' Baz said, 'and keep on pushing, and you know what? We all stand around and watch you bleed to death like a stuck pig. I told you once before to get out. That was your chance, my friend, your one and only chance.' His fleshy red lips widened in a sneer. 'I knew all along you'd be too dumb to take it.'

'If we leave now, we're out of your way,' Nick said. 'That's what you want, isn't it? Why keep Dan here, or any of us?'

Baz took the knife from Chase's throat and directed the point of the blade at Dan, addressing Nick, 'I couldn't give a flying fuck about you and your wife and your cunt of a daughter, it's him I want. He'd like nothing better than to kill me, wouldn't you, Danny boy? The bastard already tried it once.'

With a snarl, Baz yanked out his shirt to expose a white bubbled scar across his stomach and pelvic bone. 'And nearly fucking did it . . .'

'Just give me another chance,' Dan said, his voice low and trembling. 'Next time I'll finish the job properly. I give you my promise, Baz.'

'That's why you're not going anyplace!' Baz screamed, his eyes glazed wide. 'Not a single fucking one of you!' He wiped his mouth and pushed a shaking hand through his dishevelled blond hair. Something like a seizure came over him and in a fit of rage he pushed Chase violently in the chest and sent him reeling into the wall.

He issued instructions to the others. 'Lock these three in here and guard the room. Two of you come with me; we'll get the wife and daughter and bring them here.'

Hawking up in his throat, Baz spat on Chase, who was crouched over from the impact. Turning away, Baz shouldered through the crush in the doorway, which was when Nick got his chance and went for him. He grabbed a handful of Baz's shirt and tried to head-butt him before he was pounced on and dragged off. One of the crew thought this wasn't punishment enough and swung a rifle butt at Nick's head, and there was a solid thud of wood meeting bone; as Nick fell groaning to his knees, Baz kicked at him viciously.

'Stay here and fucking rot!' He glared round at Chase and Dan, chest heaving, spittle on his chin. 'That's it, none of you leaves. Cheryl and that other woman have gone, good riddance, they can take their chances on the road.' The vacant mad grin reappeared. 'Hey, don't you worry, I'm gonna let your wife and daughter stay,' he told Nick. 'Now that she's been raped once, I bet Jo's got a taste for it.'

Nick struggled to rise, his eyes hooded with pain. 'You touch them, Baz, go anywhere near my family and I'll fucking swing for you.' He got to his feet and stumbled forward, but Baz easily avoided him. He was still holding the hunting knife, and almost casually he swung it in an arc, slicing into Nick's shoulder. Nick cried out and grabbed himself. In a trice the front of his shirt changed from pale green check to a dark plum colour and clung to his chest.

Baz waved the dripping knife in a taunting circle in front of Nick's face. 'What you gonna do, old man? Bleed to death? Yeah, great, like to see that. Go on, bleed, bleed, bleed . . .' He stuck his head forward, grinning, spots of Nick's blood on his forehead and cheeks.

Supporting him, Chase got his friend to a chair. He covered Nick's hand with his own and squeezed hard, attempting to staunch the flow of blood. It was useless, Chase knew, trying any longer to reason with Baz, because there was no reason left. There was only one way to deal with Baz, only one way to stop him – if only they had the means to do so. It wasn't just the three of them here in this room who were in danger; it was the women too.

Baz was standing in the doorway with the others bunched around him. To Chase it looked as if each individual expression was part of a splintered mirror, together forming a single demented face. Under his hand, Chase felt Nick's body stiffen. 'Gav . . . Jesus, Gav—!'

Chase raised his eyes.

The double doors across the passage had swung open, and through them Chase and Nick watched somebody charge from the main hall with a double-bladed axe raised high above his head. The man brought the axe down with maniacal force on the crown of Baz's head, splitting it into two halves.

4

The scene turned red. Through the sticky fountain spouting from Baz's split-wide brain, Chase saw a rush of bodies pawing their way forward clutching knives, hatchets, steel bars, hacksaw blades, scythes, all of them cutting and slashing indiscriminately at whatever was in their path. They were a filthy and wild-eyed rabble, with matted hair and beards, clothed in tattered rags. Some were putrefying, faces and arms covered in scabs, others totally bald with skin a drab pasty white. All of them were demoniacal with bloodlust.

The carnage filled the passage and spilled back into the main hall. With the shock of the assault, the weapons held by Baz and the others were ineffective at such close range. Within minutes all but three of the young men had been frenziedly hacked to pieces, and of these one of them had had the side of his face scythed open, his ear hanging off the open flap. Then from the hall came the rapid fire of a semi-automatic as one of the two survivors found enough space to use his weapon. Chase could hear howls and screams as the attackers were gunned down. Ignoring the cacophony of pain, he scavenged through the hacked bodies on the floor of the stock room and corridor, grabbed a shotgun and found Nick's rifle where it had been dropped. His own Browning automatic was stuck in the belt of a young guy whose neck was almost completely severed, an arm attached by a tattered sleeve of skin.

The double doors had been wedged apart by fallen bodies. From his crouching posture Chase could see into the main hall, the three young guys left alive backed protectively into a corner, two of them toting weapons as if preparing for another attack. The third member, the one with the scythed-open head and hanging ear, was holding the face flap in place with a clamped hand, rivulets of blood running freely between his fingers.

Chase got hold of Nick under his good arm and pulled him to his feet. 'Can you walk okay? Can you make it?'

Nick held out his rifle, 'I can't fire this. Take it and give me the automatic.' He made a rueful grimace. 'Shoulder – caught a packet I'm afraid, old chap.'

Dan could see that Chase was juggling two weapons.

'Dad, I'll take the rifle.'

'You sure?'

'Yeah, if you help me get up.'

The floor of the stock room and corridor was awash with blood. Holding the rifle, Dan was supported by Chase as they stepped over bodies. There was still a stand-off in the main hall. Chase knew he couldn't risk getting out that way; there was as much danger from the guys with guns as the bunch of crazies, however many were left. The other way out, though, via the kitchen and back up through the loft, was near impossible with one wounded and the other weak from hunger. He'd never get Nick and Dan through the ceiling hatch unaided.

'This is a bit of a spot,' Chase said tersely. 'We might have to rush them – if we get trapped in here we've had it.'

'No need for that,' Dan said. 'We can use the side door instead.'

'The side door,' Chase repeated lamely. 'Why didn't I think of that? Which way?'

Dan pointed along the passage, past the kitchen. 'Take a right at the end, straight in front of you is the emergency fire exit.'

Nick was able to walk by himself, holding his shoulder, the Browning tucked into his belt. Dan needed his father's assistance. The three of them made their way as quietly as they could, anxious not to attract attention from the hall, which had fallen silent. But as they reached the corner at the end of the passage there was another outburst of clashing steel and bloodthirsty yells, followed by an explosion of gunfire. It was a good opportunity not to give a rat's ass about making a noise: Chase kicked hard with the heel of his boot at the release bar and the emergency door sprang open. He'd been afraid there might be twenty more of the ragged crazy mob waiting for them outside – O-zoes, or whatever in God's name they were – but the compound to the rear of the building was empty.

They could still hear sporadic gunfire from inside the hall. No better chance than now; nobody was going to spare Chase and the others a second's thought. Nick's wife and daughter would be waiting at the rendezvous on the edge of Goose Lake. This was a small detour, less than half a mile, before it met up with the single-track road leading towards the main highway. The checkpoint set up by Baz and his cronies was no longer a threat, that was certain. The kids there would have been dealt with already, or deserted their post if they had any sense.

With Chase helping Dan, Nick led the way to where the Dodge pickup and other vehicles were parked, next to the chain-link fence. At the back was a shed with a door panelled in metal sheets. Holding his shoulder, Nick raised his foot and kicked at the padlock on the door.

'What's in there?' asked Chase.

'Gasoline.'

Chase took a step forward and sheared the padlock from its mountings with the shotgun butt. In a few minutes, working alone, he had loaded ten large jerry cans into the back of the pickup. With Dan in the middle on the bench seat and Chase at the wheel, the Dodge accelerated across the compound and through the gate, headlights blazing, and roared past the meeting hall.

5

They were between Sulphur and Tungsten when the pickup blew a front tyre. Chase thought the symbolism apt: on one side a bitter, acrid chemical associated with hellfire, on the other a hard grey metallic substance used as an abrasive.

During the night they had switched drivers; Jen took over the Dodge while Chase drove the Jeep, with Ruth and Cheryl cradled in the back seat. He backed the Jeep on to the sandy shoulder, taking extreme care not to jostle his passengers. They had driven nonstop for nine hours and it was now a few minutes after 10 a.m. There was no cloud and no welcoming shade. Already the temperature was climbing into the mid-forties.

Chase climbed down, cramped and stiff, and stretched himself. 'How is she, Ruth? Would it help if we stopped for a while?'

'Her pulse is weak. I can't give her an injection, I'm afraid her system isn't strong enough to take it.' Ruth moved her arm where it had supported Cheryl throughout the night. She winced as the renewed circulation jabbed her with a thousand needles. 'I think we should carry on. Truth is, Gavin, I can't do anything for Cheryl until we get to Desert Range. How long would you say?'

'About fifteen hours, best guess, without stopping or hold-ups. Maybe we should have something to eat now while they're changing the tyre.' It was anguish for him to look at Cheryl. In the shade of the Jeep's tarp her face had the colour and consistency of wax.

Nick and Dan were squatting by the pickup while Jen and her daughter, working together, were trying to loosen the bolts on the wheel. Chase went over to help them. Just then everyone went still, heads lifted to catch the low throbbing of an engine; moments later a small red car loaded down onto the wheel hubs toiled around the bend towards them. The roof rack was piled high with boxes, furniture and household goods. Through the dust-smeared windows it was possible to make out a man and two women, one of them elderly, and two young children with wide curious eyes.

The car laboured past in the direction of Sulphur without any kind of greeting being exchanged.

Chase helped the women fit the jack and began to crank it. 'What condition is the spare in?'

Nick shrugged wearily. 'Let's hope we have a spare.'

'We're in a hell of a mess if there isn't one,' Chase said. 'Dan, take a look, will you?' His son got up and went to check. 'How's the shoulder, Nick?'

'Jo dressed it for me,' Nick said. 'But I'll never be able to play the violin again.'

'Shame . . . were you any good?'

'Couldn't play a note.'

'We're so pleased for you.'

'How's Cheryl holding up?'

Chase was noncommittal. He didn't want to tempt fate by any show of optimism. He gazed around at the baking hills, stunted trees, the grass burned brown. There was a low mountain range ahead topped by Star Peak. 'We're not far from Interstate 80. From there we'll head south as far as Highway 93. Can you make it without a break? Ruth thinks we should press on.'

'Of course, let's keep going,' Nick said lightly, 'but listen to me, Fortescue, old bean. You've driven all night. Get some rest and let Jo take over.'

Dan appeared pushing the spare wheel. His arms in the baggy T-shirt looked incapable of supporting it. Chase hurried to help him. He had to clench his teeth to keep his aching emotions in check. He went back to the Jeep, suddenly concerned about Cheryl. Not only was the heat oppressive, the sun's rays caused a prickly sensation, as if the skin was being bathed in acid. The air tasted tart and coppery.

Chase found a reassuring smile from somewhere. 'They're okay to carry on,' he informed Ruth. 'We'll stop later for something to eat. We're going to make it, kiddo, trust me.'

Ruth returned his smile. 'I know we will, Gavin. I trust you.'

Cheryl was padded with blankets in the back seat. Her eyes opened but there was no expression in them. Chase didn't know whether this was a reflex action or if it was significant; nevertheless he felt a surge of hope. He decided Nick was right. He was totally beat-up. Jo took his place driving the Jeep, and Chase gratefully crawled underneath the canvas in the back of the pickup and stretched out on a sleeping bag. His bones seemed to creak with tiredness. Beside him, cushioned in a cocoon of blankets and baggage, Nick was already fast asleep.

Chase had a vivid dream that Baz Brannigan was trailing them – Baz with an axe buried in his head. The landscape, a bleached sulphurous yellow. Baz pursued them to the edge of a cliff using a giant hypodermic syringe as a crutch. In an instant the Jeep went over the cliff and in slow-motion sailed down and down and down into the canyon. With muscles taut, Chase tensed every fibre in his body, waiting for the expected crash—

As the Jeep hit the ground he sat bolt upright, arms shielding his face. It was nightfall. The pickup had stopped. He was awake.

There was no one in the cab. They had pulled over onto the hard shoulder of, he assumed, Interstate 80. Chase climbed down from the pickup, a foul taste in his mouth, and spat out. What he wouldn't give for a cup of scalding black coffee!

Jen and Dan were standing by the Jeep. As Chase went over he saw Jo collapsed over the steering wheel, her head cradled in her arms. At first he thought there'd been an accident of some kind, and then he knew there hadn't. There was no need to ask, and nothing he wanted to see.

Nick helped his daughter from the driver's seat and held her in his arms. Chase did what he could to comfort Ruth. She clung to him and wept, but he could think of nothing to say.

Afterwards, when Cheryl's body had been wrapped in a blanket and placed in the back of the pickup, they turned onto Highway 93 and drove without stopping until they reached Desert Range at two o'clock the following morning.

2042

2042

I

The war between the prims and the O-zoes was getting closer . . .

There had been fierce and bloody clashes in the hills and forests to the west, but so far Desert Range had remained undetected and unmolested. It was in the middle of an arid plain and well away from the main routes north, on the periphery of the tribal conflicts that raged across California, Nevada and Utah.

Dan had never been able to understand what the fighting was about. Every time he led a reconnaissance party from the furthermost tip of the western network of tunnels he was struck afresh by the sheer mindless lunacy of conducting a war for no conceivable gain. Not territory. Not natural resources. Not plunder, even in the crudest sense of the term. And certainly not patriotism or pride, or any of the other emotional intangibles that had traditionally sent men to war. It was fighting for the sake of it, merely obeying some atavistic impulse as natural and breathing and sleeping.

Below him, in what had once been the verdant Meadow Valley Wash, an antiquated Sherman tank was trundling over the dried-up riverbed, blue smoke rings sputtering from its exhaust. A stone-tipped arrow wavered drunkenly through the air and clunked against the turret. The tank halted and laboriously cranked its gun through ninety degrees in the direction of the aggressor, apparently oblivious to the fact that the barrel was a splintered stub, like a joke cigar that had exploded.

Another arrow clattered harmlessly against the armour plating and snapped in two. From its trajectory Dan was able to pinpoint its source: a screen of bushes concealing a small opening in the riverbank.

Jo, kneeling beside him and watching through binoculars, said,

'You were right. It's a raiding party of O-zoes – but who does the tank belong to?'

'Can you see any markings?'

'Some old army insignia, nothing recent.' She lowered the binoculars and edged behind a rock that had some form of bell-shaped fungus growing on it. There were strange species of flora appearing everywhere, so commonplace now they hardly noticed them. Jo's face was completely hidden behind tinted goggles and a gauze mask, underneath which she was plastered with barrier cream as protection against ultraviolet radiation. The thinness of the air they could do little about, except to become acclimatised to what was the equivalent of being twenty thousand feet up a mountain.

'Where are Fran and the others?' Dan said. 'I hope they know we've got company.'

There were five of them in the reconnaissance party. They had come out the day before and were due back by nightfall – thirty-six hours was the maximum time permitted by the medics. This particular skirmish was the nearest one so far, barely ten miles away from the western access of the Desert Range complex.

'Fran won't move from the camp till she hears from us,' Jo said. Her straw-coloured hair was pulled back under a forage cap, wisps trailing over her upturned collar. 'Where do they find the diesel fuel to run a tank, for God's sake? You'd think they'd find a better use for it – generate power or even to keep a fire going. They must—'

Dan silenced her with a wave of his gloved hand and at the same time ducked down. Somebody shrieked below them, a cry that hardly sounded human at all. The crack and echoing reverberation of a gunshot rolled along the valley.

'What's happening?' Jo said, craning to see.

'The O-zoes decided to rush them, and somebody in the tank opened fire with a rifle. Keep down, we don't want to be spotted.'

Carefully they peered over the rock and saw three men emerging from the turret. They were unshaven and dressed in patched-up army fatigues but otherwise looked normal. The O-zoes – about a dozen of them – were crouched behind rocks and bushes, armed with crude spears, cudgels and bows and arrows. One of them lay sprawled on the bank with half his face missing.

It was such a one-sided contest that Dan was loath to watch: the three men had firearms, rifles and pistols; the O-zoes had primitive homemade weapons. It was the twenty-first century versus the Stone Age. But what were they fighting *for*? Ownership of this barren tract of valley and riverbed that wouldn't have supported a couple of goats?

As they moved forward, dodging the missiles casually, almost indifferently, the three men picked off the O-zoes like plaster ducks in a shooting gallery. Dan gripped his own rifle in a paroxysm of frustration and despair: this was cold-blooded slaughter.

Jo said needlessly, 'There's nothing we can do.' She reached out and he felt her fingers tighten on his arm. 'Come on, Dan, let's go back. We don't have to watch this.'

She moved back, and as he squirmed around on his haunches to follow her, they both froze as a grunting, gibbering snarl tore the air apart. From out of the cave-like opening in the riverbank came a small bundle of fur and teeth that moved in a blur through the rocks and leaped at one of the men before he had time to sight his gun. In seconds the riverbed was swarming with the creatures, all moving so fast that Dan couldn't make out what they were – a kind of rodent, he guessed, but with an insatiable ferocity he'd never seen before.

They systematically tore the three men apart. They went for the throats first, then worked downward. Once he was able to see them properly, Dan realised what they were and his blood chilled. Desert gophers, one of the most timid and reclusive of creatures, feeding off worms and grubs, mutated into aggressive, voracious animals with a ravenous taste for human flesh.

Where the bodies had fallen had turned into writhing mounds of grey fur. The clicking and snapping of tiny teeth could be heard. Four or five of the surviving O-zoes had climbed up on to the tank and were poking their spears into the open hatch. Dan hoped there was no one hiding inside.

After ten minutes of careful retreat, he and Jo descended the hill to their temporary camp, about a mile away. The raw sunlight scoured the bleached landscape and the air tasted metallic. They were reaching the point at which further exposure would be dangerous, though this wasn't the reason Dan was anxious to return to the Tomb. Six months ago there hadn't been an incident within a hundred miles. As the skirmishes got closer, the threat of discovery became more likely and their survival depended on the Tomb being alert, preparations made. It had been safe from attacks by prims and O-zoes, but now somebody – and who the hell *were* they? – had tanks, and tanks meant explosives, even a nuke warhead, perhaps. Dan shrank from the thought.

The tent was still up, he saw. The dozy layabouts were still asleep, or maybe lingering over a late breakfast.

Dan pushed aside the light brush they had piled up as camouflage and raised the tent flap. It was very quiet inside and he felt a twinge of unease – then he saw an outstretched leg wearing a knee-high brown boot, which he recognised as Fran's. The leg wasn't attached to her body. Next to it was a hand, fingers curled, like a discarded glove.

The interior of the tent was dark, but he could make out the canvas walls, obscured by something that *seethed*: the canvas was coated with millions of tiny white grubs. And not just the canvas; they were covering every surface, feasting on the three bodies, devouring them inch by inch. In the middle of Fran's chest was a hole that pulsed whitely as the grubs burrowed inside.

2

Art Hegler was small, bald, and rotund. He sat at the communications desk, headphones around his neck, listening over the desk speaker and making an occasional note. The message was in Morse, very fast, outstripping Chase's rudimentary knowledge; the few words he did catch were jumbled and meaningless.

After a minute or two Hegler threw down the pen and arched back. His straining T-shirt read: *From the womb to the Tomb*.

'Same code?'

Hegler nodded, tossed the headphones onto the desk and waddled across to the coffeepot. 'Want some?'

Chase shook his head. Two cups a day of ersatz caffeine were all his system could take. 'Is it military traffic?'

Hegler shrugged. Their conversations were usually terse and cryptic. Perhaps Hegler resented the fact that while the scientific purpose of Desert Range was defunct, Chase was still nominally in charge. With its empty labs and silent equipment, the lower levels sealed off, the establishment was a shadow of its former bustling activity. Of the eight hundred people who had lived and worked here five years ago, fewer than sixty remained – though less to do with choice than that the options for a secure, hospitable environment were nonexistent now.

Hegler sipped his 'coffee' and paused to belch softly. 'Whatever it is, it goes on night and day,' he said, as if inwardly musing.

'At least it's not alien,' Chase said, trying to lighten the mood. There had been a rash of UFO sightings over previous months, and he'd even heard a few people speak seriously of an 'invasion'.

'The source is southwest,' Hegler said, leaning over the desk and jabbing a stubby finger at the map. 'I can't pinpoint it exactly, but I'd say between two and three hundred miles away.'

'Anything in that area?'

'Yosemite National Park, Death Valley, China Lake Naval Weapons Station, Fort Irwin, Las Vegas – take your pick.'

'So there's a military presence near the source of the signal,' Chase said thoughtfully.

'Is. Was. Who knows what's there any more?'

'And what about Emigrant Junction?' Chase studied the map. 'Is that an actual location, or just a call sign?'

Hegler shrugged again. 'If it exists, I can't find it.'

Chase listened for a moment to the remorseless beeping coming over the speaker. 'Does nothing in the message make sense? I thought I heard the word "island". Did you get that?'

'Comes up pretty often: that's in plain English, but then it's followed by a string of digital noise.' Hegler glanced at him. 'If you think you can crack it, be my guest.'

'I'll leave it to the experts,' Chase said, smiling. 'Anyway, I wouldn't want to deprive you and Ron of hours of harmless amusement.'

Art Hegler reached out to fine-tune the dial. Chase admired his persistence. It had been sheer accident that the signals had been detected at all: Ron Maxwell had picked them up on a random sweep several months ago and, ever since, he and Hegler had spent countless hours monitoring them and trying to crack the code. Why they went to all this time and trouble wasn't clear – even to them, Chase suspected. Like most activity in the Tomb it had taken on the form of a ritual, a way to get through the day.

They were all, himself included, on a journey with no destination. There was a time bomb ticking away inside every brain; the trick was to ignore it, to swamp it with ceaseless activity so that the ticking faded until it was no more intrusive than the background hum of the filtration plant. Of course one day – *one day* – the ticking, like the filtration plant, would stop and the bomb would explode. But he didn't want to think about that. Neither did Hegler nor Maxwell nor any of the others, which was why they carried on obsessively with futile tasks.

'Hear that?' Hegler said suddenly.

Chase paid attention, but the Morse sounded the same as before, garbled and indecipherable. 'What is it?'

'Answering message. They gave the call sign, and then the coded message follows.'

'If we knew who they were talking to . . .'

Hegler waved his pudgy hand impatiently. 'It's a random signal, could be coming from practically anywhere, and we only have one directional fix on it.'

Communication with the outside world had dwindled as everyone withdrew into secrecy and suspicion, as remote and isolated from one another as tribes of headhunters in the depths of the Borneo jungle. The global village was no more. The Tomb itself never transmitted, for fear of hostile outsiders locating their position.

Ron Maxwell came in carrying a stack of magnetic disks. Tall, thin and buzzing with nervous energy, he was Stan to Hegler's Ollie. He wore a brown one-piece coverall with an oxygen counter on the left breast pocket: below a certain percentage it turned blue, then purple, then black. Some also had audio circuits attached that trilled like songbirds.

'When are they due back?' asked Maxwell, stacking the disks onto his half of the console. He peered amiably at Chase through tinted spectacles.

'The deadline is nine o'clock tonight,' Chase replied. Maxwell's daughter Fran was with the reconnaissance party that Dan was leading. 'I should think they'll be back before then. Art's been telling me about your daily soap opera; pity we can't follow the plot.'

'Maybe we can't,' Maxwell said, brandishing one of the disks, 'for the simple reason that it's in another language.'

'What?' Chase bristled. Surely they weren't back to the nonsense about aliens again? And why hadn't Hegler mentioned this? He got the feeling that private lines of research were going on all around him that he knew nothing about.

'Computer-speak.' Ron Maxwell flipped one of the disks and caught it in his bony fingers. 'We dusted off the weather-modelling computer – it hasn't been used for three years – and ran some of the archive. Had to teach it Morse code first, and we're dealing with an unknown programme, but the computer recognised a distant cousin when it heard one – overjoyed to hear a friendly voice. You could almost see its diodes glowing with pleasure.'

'It was able to interpret the binary code?'

'Ah – no,' Maxwell admitted, perching himself on the corner of the desk and swinging a lanky leg.

Hegler said tartly, 'It didn't tell us anything we didn't already know.'

'If it didn't break the code, what did it do?' Chase demanded. He was befuddled by all this, and becoming exasperated.

Maxwell shrugged. 'We don't know, chief. Highly complex technical data for sure, but until we crack the programme we can't say.'

'As I just *said*, we're no nearer interpreting the messages than we were before,' Hegler put in, sounding pained and weary. "They could be military, scientific, or a new recipe for hamburger.'

'Do you think you'll crack it eventually?'

'Bound to,' Maxwell asserted, full of confidence. 'All we need is time and that's one thing we've plenty of. Come back in three months and we'll have the answer.'

'Make that "might have",' Hegler rejoined, eyes down, pressing keys.

3

'I don't see the point, Gavin,' Ruth said. 'What are they hoping to prove?'

'They're not out to *prove* anything. They're investigating a problem – or maybe a mystery; who knows?'

They were sitting in the recreation room they shared with ten others, Nick Power and his family among them. There was no shortage of living space in the complex – in fact, there was too much of it – but sharing communal facilities saved energy. Someone had suggested they depressurise the corridors and stairways, but Chase thought it might be too dangerous. Most of the available energy went towards maintaining a breathable sealed environment; it was their most worrying problem.

'We already know things are getting worse,' Ruth said drily. 'Why use instruments to tell us? Just step outside.'

'You don't think we ought to continue our investigations?'

'To leave as a legacy for those unborn who never will be?' Ruth's complexion had always been fair, but now it was very pale, emphasised by the crooked pink scar on her forehead that intersected with her right eyebrow, giving her a perpetually quizzical expression. The strain of living underground was telling on them all. Everyone was pale because the sunlight was too fierce on unprotected skin; everyone was subdued because of the inevitability of what was to be – what *had* to be. Ruth was not the only one to voice scepticism about the work that still went on regardless.

'Art Hegler's doing the job he was trained for; it occupies his mind,' Chase said, downplaying it.

'I just don't see the purpose, the reason behind it all – and you're almost as bad, scribbling away in that notebook of yours.'

Chase drank his coffee. 'So you're having a go at me now, eh?' He pulled a face, but it was the lousy coffee rather than irritation with Ruth's gentle prying.

'No, simply making an observation. But I am curious – what are they, your memoirs?' There was a hint of humour in her dark eyes. 'They must be pretty racy if you have to keep them under lock and key.'

Chase smiled. 'Nothing as interesting as that. I suppose you could call it a "future diary", for want of anything better.' He immediately regretted his choice of words; his intention had been to make light of it, pass it off, but the explanation backfired because Ruth's curiosity was aroused.

'A *future* diary? How does that work? By definition, Gavin, a diary is a record of *past* events, not things that're yet to happen. Unless you're psychic and can see into the future.'

'Not one of my many talents, I'm afraid,' Chase said. 'Getting back to Art and Ron—'

'Forget Art and Ron. If that's an attempt to change the subject, it's a pretty feeble one.'

'Ruth, you're making a big deal out of nothing, honestly. It's just random jottings, that's all. I don't suppose you'd like other people reading your diary, would you? We all have personal thoughts.'

Ruth folded her arms and leaned back in the chair. 'That's true, you're right. Sorry if I was being a pest.' Her mood had changed and she looked forlorn. Chase could hardly blame her. Maybe her consternation about Maxwell and Hegler beavering away like a pair of mad scientists was justified. When you came down to it, really, what was the point?

He said, 'We don't have to stay. We have the choice to leave, if you want to. The question is—'

'I know what the question is, Gavin. Why leave, when there's nowhere else to go? At least we're safe here.' Ruth gave a short, bitter laugh. 'Safe . . . to rot. Safe to die. Safe from everything but . . .' Her voice sank to a whisper and she closed her eyes.

Chase reached out and took her hand. It felt limp and lifeless. 'What about you,' he said, 'writing up medical research notes from ten years ago?'

'That's to fill the time. Stop me from going mad.'

'What Art and Ron are doing could be for the same reason. And who knows? They might, just possibly, come up with something really important.'

Ruth opened her eyes. 'If they do,' she said, pressing his palm to her breast, 'I hope they won't expect the Nobel Prize.'

4

Night enveloped them with the dramatic abruptness of the desert. Above, the stars wavered and blinked with the rising heat, like a purple sequinned cloth shimmering in the breeze. Except there was no breeze: the desert was inert, silent, pulsating heat in waves so that it was like walking through hot sticky syrup.

They had abandoned everything but their weapons. Hours spent scrambling over rocks and fighting their way through thorny brush in the searing sunlight had sapped their strength and there was none left for anything that didn't contribute directly to their survival.

Dan pretended to drink, merely moistening his lips, and gave Jo the last few drops from the canteen. He estimated that they had crossed the border and were back in Utah. The nearest access point to the tunnels could be only two or three miles away, but that still left an underground walk of perhaps ten miles before they reached the Tomb. Was it better to go underground or continue on the surface? Three hours' steady march would see them back at the Tomb, whereas it could take two, three times longer through the tunnels.

There was, however, a more pressing worry: they were being followed. At Echo Canyon, a few miles back, he thought he'd glimpsed movement behind them. Had the O-zoes picked up their trail? If so, he and Jo were leading them straight back to base, revealing the Tomb's location.

Jo screwed the top on the canteen and slung it around her neck. 'Will they have lights?'

'What?'

'If they're following our trail they'll need lights, won't they? So we should be able to see *them*!'

That hadn't occurred to him. But see what, for God's sake? O-zoes, prims? Men with guns in Sherman tanks? Or somebody else – some*thing* else . . .

They stopped and looked back, straining their eyes to penetrate the dense velvety darkness that seemed almost palpable. 'Can't make anything out, can you?' Jo said, sounding relieved.

'No. They won't need illumination if they've got good night vision.'

'You mean like cats?'

'It's possible.'

Dan looked at her, seeing the polished glint of her eyes in a smudge of pale yellow, the barrier cream caking her face. They had removed their gauze masks and goggles the minute the sun had dipped over the horizon. 'Most of the O-zoes have impaired faculties, but some of them have developed heightened senses to compensate. There was one I came across near Adamsville last year who could actually smell water, you know, like animals can. And somebody else I heard of who had infrared vision. If they've got that they won't need any light.'

'You're great for morale, Dan.'

'Sorry. Thinking out loud.'

'Why not think of something cheerful instead, and keep moving while you're doing it.'

Ten minutes later they heard what sounded like a cry in the distance – but human or animal? They listened intently, but heard nothing more.

Dan flicked on his pencil flashlight and, shielding it with his body, squinted at his wrist compass. They were heading northeast. At this rate they couldn't be more than an hour, perhaps less, from the nearest access point. He'd made up his mind to enter the complex, not to risk being overtaken by whatever was following them. He prayed he could find the concealed entrance in the darkness – it was hard enough searching for the triangular markers in daylight.

He moved on, took a dozen paces, before he realised that Jo wasn't beside him. Dimly he made out her silhouette standing rigid, head raised, and then he saw the reason: plumes of pale fire, like inverted candle-flames, ascending against the starscape. They rose in total silence from somewhere to the northwest, heading into space, and gradually faded to nothing in the region of Draco.

'There they go again,' Jo said in a hushed voice. 'What the hell can they be, do you suppose?' Everyone at Desert Range had seen the UFOs, and no one had a clue what they were. Dan for one hadn't believed in their existence until he saw them for himself. 'Are they terrestrial?' Jo wondered.

'You mean manmade? Some kind of spacecraft?'

'It's possible, isn't it? They look like rocket exhaust flames.'

Jo was right. That's exactly what they did look like.

Again they heard the cry, like a lost bird, nearer now, and Jo clutched his arm. 'Some fucking thing's back there and it's following us! What if you're right and the bastards have infrared vision?'

'I wish I'd never mentioned it,' Dan said gloomily. 'That was an animal, I think. A raccoon maybe, out hunting.'

'I never knew raccoons lived in the desert.'

'It's lost. Satisfied?'

They picked their way carefully across the rocky terrain. The air was stifling and their bodies were running with sweat. It was as frightening as a nightmare: a never-ending journey through a barren alien landscape, pursued by a nameless horror.

Eventually, with immense relief, they came upon the grey squat shape of a blockhouse: the nearest access wasn't too far away now. The steel doors of some of the entrances had been welded shut; Dan hoped and prayed this wasn't one of them. Another fear gnawed at the edge of his reason. Supposing there were other life forms in the abandoned tunnels? Creatures who, like them, had sought shelter and protection underground? There were more than two hundred miles of tunnels beyond the Tomb's sealed enclosure that had never been explored.

The entrance had to be fairly near, within a few yards; all they had to do now was find the bloody thing.

Again the forlorn cry came, this time on their left, this time answered by others from every direction. In the darkness Dan thought he saw ghostly white shapes, floating like wraiths, making no sound. They had form and yet were disembodied: the living dead. *Zombies*.

Perhaps Jo didn't believe in zombies – or maybe her reactions were sharper than his, for she was already down on one knee, rifle levelled, and had fired three times before Dan had unslung his weapon from his shoulder. He fired himself and saw one of the white shapes fold and crumple. Another drifted into view and he fired again, seeing it spin and wobble comically to the ground.

Crouched with her back against his, Jo said through gritted teeth, 'There are more of them than we've got ammunition for. Is that fucking entrance around here or isn't it?'

Jo was right, of course. They had to seek protection underground, quickly. Killing these white blobby shapes was making no difference, for more and more of them were materialising out of nowhere.

'Keep firing while I search around.'

'What happens when I run out of ammo?'

Dan had no answer for that. He went down on his knees, his face inches away from the ground, only too aware that Jo was firing not far over his head. It was so frustrating to think they might be right on top of the entrance – literally, if it was covered with sand. Even if it was as close as ten yards away, he might never find it. Dan circled around like a mole, thinking the whole situation was insanely funny, yet unable to find a grain of humour in it. In minutes his gloves were in shreds, his knees raw and bleeding. Besides the pain, his mind was racing, wondering, *What the fuck are those white things?*

There were three of the blob-like forms directly in front of him, about six or seven yards away, as near as he could judge – and then he got a shock: not *yards* away but only a few feet. In the darkness it was difficult to scale objects and he'd assumed they were approximately human-size, when in reality they were perhaps two feet high – the creatures were almost within touching distance!

Dan scuttled backwards, and cracked his shinbone on a protruding edge. In the middle of a violent curse he paused, and then unslung his rifle. Groping about with bare fingertips through the shredded gloves, he touched a concrete surface: the sloping parapet, almost completely buried in sand, that guarded the entrance. He ducked as a shot whistled over his head and a white shape wobbled and slowly collapsed with a tiny plaintive cry. Jo must be running short of ammo, so he'd better get a move on . . .

He slithered belly-down into a shallow depression. He could feel the edges of the steps under the sand scraping his stomach and thighs. He'd definitely found the entrance – but could he get in? With both hands he began scooping at the windblown sand, and as he burrowed deeper, the soft sand sucked him down until he was half-submerged. *This isn't working.* He was getting desperate. He knelt up and used the butt of his rifle as a paddle, and finally started to make some progress, but it was taking all his strength and he wasn't sure how long he could keep flailing away like this – then the brass strip on the rifle butt struck metal: the iron door. Now he had to get the door open somehow. *Hope to Christ it isn't welded shut.*

He was in an awkward position, it was hard to exert any leverage. Nor was he sure if the door was hinged or sliding. Not sliding, he decided after a moment, because there wasn't enough space either side. He smashed the butt against the door, seeking any slight movement, but the sand acted as a buffer, dulling the blows. He could feel his strength ebbing away; he was breathing in long painful gasps, his lungs straining. All at once the sand cascaded down on top of him and he felt as if he were drowning in it – and then he was sinking deeper still as the iron door gave way, until down he went, in a long slide on a pillow of sand, coughing and choking as he fought to keep his head clear.

He'd forced the door open and was inside. He pulled his rifle free and propped it against the wall. A moment or so later he was crawling back up the steps and cautiously poking his head above the concrete parapet.

'Jo, over here – I've found it!' he called.

Silence.

'Jo, where are you? *Answer me!*'

There was no response. Dan felt petrified with anguish. Had Jo run out of ammunition and been overwhelmed by the amorphous blobs? Again he called out her name, his mouth gritty with sand, and his heart contracted in mortal fear as a pale shape rose up inches in front of his face. A hand fastened around his wrist, tugging at him.

'One of them bit me or stung me, on the leg . . . before I got to him.' Jo's voice was clogged with pain. 'Help me . . . can't walk.'

Dan lifted her around the waist and staggered with her down the steps, disappearing below the parapet as a score of shimmering white things materialised from the darkness, uttering little mewing cries, like babies demanding to be fed.

5

Chase looked up sharply as a siren welled through the peaceful laboratory. For several seconds everyone stood frozen, heads raised, eyes staring. Threats from outside were something that everyone had learned to live with, a fact of existence, yet there was a real tremor of shock whenever the alarm sounded.

Everyone knew the drill: return to living quarters for essential personal belongings, account for members of the family and assemble in the mess on Level Two. On average there were three or four alerts a year, usually false alarms caused by an animal triggering the electronic warning system.

Chase hurried to the operations room, worried because Dan's party was still outside; they might have run into trouble. It wasn't the first time a party had failed to meet the deadline, but the alarm made him doubly anxious.

The duty officer told him that they had an unauthorised entry in one of the sealed tunnels: somebody had located an access point and was approaching the Tomb underground from the west.

'How near are they?'

'The last sensor to be activated was here' – he put his finger on the map – 'about a mile from the enclosure.' He traced the grid to an area shaded in orange. 'If they keep to the same tunnel they'll come up against a sealed entrance down on Level Four.'

That was one of the lower levels no longer used, once living quarters and dormitories, now a warren of empty corridors and rooms.

'Is that entrance permanently sealed or is there access?' Chase asked. Some of the tunnels spreading out into the wider complex had been filled with concrete blocks, while others had steel doors.

'There's access.'

'Have you posted men there?'

'Yes; we'll be ready for them.'

'Tell them to identify the intruder before taking any action. It could be one of our parties.' Chase paced up and down, wringing his hands. The duty officer watched him circumspectly and raised an eyebrow at one of his colleagues; under normal circumstances the director would have left security to the men whose responsibility it was, but now he was clearly agitated.

Chase stopped pacing and said abruptly, 'I think we ought to send somebody out to investigate. If it is the reconnaissance party they might need help.'

The duty officer shifted uneasily to another foot. 'That'll mean opening the doors – they're our last line of defence.'

'Listen, there are five people still outside somewhere. It could be them in the tunnel. Send three men to take a look – if they run into trouble they can get back and seal the doors. It's a risk we have to take.'

Still reluctant, the duty officer relayed the order while Chase brooded in a corner. It wasn't a risk they *had* to take at all, he knew that damn well, not when set against the lives of the sixty or so people in the Tomb. For all anyone knew the tunnels could be swarming with O-zoes or prims – there could be an army of them. Anyway, they'd soon know.

By the early hours of the morning the Tomb was buzzing with rumours. They had been attacked via the underground complex and six men had been killed. There was a huge encampment of prims on the surface, waiting for someone to emerge. The UFOs had landed and they were surrounded by aliens . . . .

It was unusual for an alert to last more than a couple of hours and the atmosphere in the crowded mess was tense and edgy. Nick, Jen and Ruth sat together. Some people were dozing fitfully, some were playing cards, others were queuing for coffee and sandwiches.

'What did Gav say?' Nick asked Ruth. 'Is it an attack?'

'He doesn't know. Somebody or something triggered a sensor in one of the tunnels, which they're investigating. He thinks it might be Dan, Jo and the others.'

Jen looked at her husband. 'Why come back that way? It's easier and faster on the surface. Besides, they could get lost down there, it's a labyrinth – literally.'

Easier and faster, Nick thought, *unless you were hiding from someone, or something*. But he kept that thought to himself.

In the operations room Chase was having to deal with a fraught Ron Maxwell. 'It's been over an hour since we sent three men to check it out, Ron.' Chase tried to sound reassuring. 'We should know something soon.'

'Are they in radio contact?' Maxwell's tall, loose-limbed figure was bowed as if he carried a millstone on his back. He cracked his bony knuckles distractedly.

'Reception is patchy in the tunnels, Ron, you know that. They'll have to return to the Orange Sector access on Level Four first and report on the internal phone.' Chase gripped his shoulder. 'If it *is* our kids in the tunnels, they'll bring them back safe and sound.' He wanted to emphasise that his own son was one of the group as well as Ron's daughter Fran.

'And if it isn't?' said Maxwell bleakly. 'Will you send out a surface party to look for them?'

It was a demand rather than a question.

'As soon as we know,' Chase said quietly.

6

'For Christ's sake, take that light out of my eyes!' Dan held up a shielding hand, his face behind it contorted with irritation and fatigue.

The beam swivelled away, striking blank concrete. Two pairs of hands took the burden of Jo's weight from his shoulder. His knees buckled and he collapsed in a sweating, shaking heap. He'd supported her, sometimes physically carrying her, for almost four hours; sometimes he thought they were staggering into the bowels of the earth.

The man with the flashlight lifted him and asked him a question. The words sounded urgent but he was too weary to decipher them. The man had to repeat the question twice more before he understood.

'Dead,' Dan said at last. 'The others are dead.'

'Are they following?'

'No! I just told you.' Dan's head lolled. 'They're dead . . .'

'Not the people you were with – the ones who killed them. The O-zoes, or whatever they were. Did they come after you? *Did they follow you underground?*' the man asked sharply.

Dan shook his head, befuddled. 'I don't know. I'm not sure. They might have.'

It took forty minutes to make their way back to the safety of the Tomb, and once inside the enclosure, the doors were sealed and barred. The man who had helped Dan unhooked the handset from its wall cradle and reported to the operations room.

As they listened over the speaker, Chase saw Ron Maxwell's face lose colour. The millstone became a crushing load, the lines on his forehead even more deeply etched. The hand covering his eyes was trembling and his Adam's apple jerked convulsively as he swallowed.

Chase leaned over the bed in the sickbay and shook his son into consciousness. 'How many? Twenty? Thirty? How many of them were there?'

Dan struggled to open his eyes. A pleasant, dreamy torpor was pressing him down into the wonderfully soft mattress. His lips moved. The words he spoke sounded in his own ears as if they came from a great distance.

'They were kinda pale and blurry. It was too dark to see anything clearly . . . too dark.'

'Did they come after you into the tunnels?'

'Maybe. I don't know.' Dan opened his eyes. 'We heard them crying.'

'Crying?' Chase stared down at his son. 'You mean these things were actually alive and . . . you heard them *crying*?'

'They sounded like babies. They were white globules . . . vicious things, one of them stung Jo, she said, or bit her . . .' Dan closed his eyes and drifted off, but after a moment he said, 'We killed some of them, ten or more, but they couldn't be stopped. When they fell down, others kept on coming. They didn't bother about dying.'

Chase straightened up. He was torn between deciding whether Dan was delirious or relating what had really happened. White shapeless things that cried? 'Were they armed, did they have weapons of any kind?' he asked.

'Didn't see any,' Dan said, and carried on mumbling. It was too much of an effort; exhaustion defeated him. In seconds he was fully asleep.

Chase turned to the medic. 'There's nothing seriously wrong, is there? Anoxia?'

'Breathing rarefied air over such a long period has sapped all his strength. It's rest he needs. If Dan sleeps undisturbed he should be recovered in the morning.'

'I hope we can let him sleep that long,' Chase fretted. He took a last look at Dan and went into the corridor. Nick Power and his wife came out of the next room, followed by Ruth, who had been attending to Jo. From their expressions Chase could tell that Jo too was going to be all right. Ruth had dressed her wound and she was sleeping peacefully.

The four of them went along to the main mess. Chase was anxious to discuss what their appropriate response should be. Were the steel doors enough to keep these things out (whatever weird bloody form of animal, vegetable or mineral these things were) or was it wiser to go from defensive to offensive and launch a counter-attack?

'Do we know how dangerous they are?' Ruth asked. 'Have they got weapons? Explosives?'

Chase combed his fingers through his beard. 'Dan didn't think they were armed.' He voiced his real and pressing concern. 'What I'm wondering is how many of them came underground. We're safe enough here, where we are, with all access points sealed. But if we don't clear them out, in effect we're as good as trapped. It's also an open invitation to every O-zoe and prim and white fucking blobs, whatever they are, to move downstairs and set up house.'

They halted in the passage and looked at one another. Nick was first to give way, then Ruth, and then there was an outburst of hysterical laughter from all four of them.

'Oh save us, please save us, from the white blobs,' Nick burbled, the tears streaming down his cheeks.

'Never fear, Carruthers! I shall do my bit.' Chase raised both fists triumphantly above his head.

'Hurrah!' Nick exclaimed. 'You can always depend on Fortescue! Good chap!'

Sobering up, they turned a corner and pushed through the double doors into the mess.

Chase said, 'Seriously, how do you feel about living alongside a city of freaks?'

'Think we'd notice any difference?' Nick muttered. This time nobody laughed.

Jen shuddered to herself. 'I hate the idea of sending somebody into the tunnels after them – I know *I* wouldn't go.'

Most of their colleagues were gathered here, too distracted for sleep, waiting for news. Relief took the tension out of their tired faces when Chase reassured everyone that the situation was under control: there had been no breaches or incursions; the Tomb was secure and everyone should go back to bed. Then there was a stirring of unease when somebody asked if it was true that intruders had been detected in the outer network of tunnels. Other voices were raised in alarm. Chase held up his hands for silence. 'Yes, it is true, I won't lie to you. There's been some activity *outside* the sealed enclosure . . .'

He hadn't yet made up his mind what action to take, but he did so in that moment.

'Tomorrow we're sending a recon team, armed of course, into the complex to flush them out and seal off all access points. If anyone wants to volunteer and join the squad, you're welcome; we need you. It's not going to be an easy or pleasant task, but if you're up for it and want to help, report to the operations room at noon tomorrow.'

'You mean today,' somebody called out. 'It's five o'clock in the morning.'

'Yes, right. Noon today.'

There was a general movement towards the exit. Smothering a yawn, Nick turned to Chase. 'You've got your first volunteer. But listen, chum, if the blobs break in before eleven, don't even bother to wake me.' He linked arms with Jen and they joined the rest of the dispersing crowd.

Chase arched his head back, massaging his neck muscles. 'You go to bed,' he said to Ruth. 'I'll stop by the operations room to make sure everything's secure. Won't be long.'

Ruth eyed him critically. 'You need to rest too.' She added with mock severity, 'Doctor's orders.'

'Yes, Doctor.' Chase squeezed her hand and smiled. Outside in the corridor, worming his way through a knot of people, a distraught woman snatched at his sleeve. Her eyes were red and swollen, and for a second he didn't recognise Ava Maxwell, Ron's wife.

'Have you seen him? Is he here?' Ava looked up at Chase, searching his face anxiously.

'You mean Ron? Not since we came down from the ops room.'

'He told me—' Her lower lip quivered as she fought to keep control. '—about Fran . . . he went off somewhere. I haven't seen him in two hours or more.'

'Ava, I'm so sorry about your daughter.' It sounded feeble, this glib phrase of condolence. Instead, Chase tried to reassure her: perhaps Ron wanted some time on his own, maybe he'd gone to the lab?

Ava Maxwell wandered off, shell-shocked with grief.

Chase was glad to escape. He mounted the stairway to the operations room, feeling guilty. His son was alive and Ron and Ava's daughter was dead. The raw emotion scraped at his nerves and distracted him as he walked into a taut silence in the ops room that at first he didn't notice. All eyes were fixed on a winking red light on the huge wallboard plan of the Tomb. The duty officer turned, the phone in his hand, arrested by Chase's appearance. He dropped it back in its cradle. 'I was just about to call you.' He nodded towards the insistent red light. 'The sealed door down on Level Four: it's been opened. I've already sent a couple of men to check it out.'

'Opened – from inside?'

'It had to be. The alarm sensor wasn't tripped. Any incursion would have lit the board like a Christmas tree.'

'Who'd be crazy enough to do that?'

Chase didn't need long to ponder the question; the answer came in practically the same instant: somebody crazy with grief and despair and an urge for revenge that would obscure every other rational impulse. Somebody with an only child now gone for ever. In a dying world the death of a loved one might prove to be the final blasphemy.

Somebody like Ron Maxwell.

'How long has the access door been open?'

'A few minutes, that's all. I got on to it right away. We should have it sealed tight again pretty soon.' The armpits of the duty officer's tan shirt were ringed with sweat. He wiped his mouth with a hand that was visibly trembling. 'Want me to raise a general alarm?'

'It's just broken up in the mess and everyone's on their way back to bed. We'll give the guys down there time to call in. How long should it take?'

The duty officer looked at the wall clock. 'Not more than ten minutes.'

'That's what we'll give them,' Chase said.

For everyone in the operations room it was the longest ten minutes of their life. Chase tried to stand still or sit down but could do neither, so he kept pacing. The duty officer switched his attention from the board to the clock and then to the phone, and round again. After five minutes the tension was so high the room was humming with a high-voltage charge. One of the technical operators began to moan through his hands, which were pressed to his face.

The sweeping red hand reached the vertical: the ten minutes were up and Chase had a decision to make. They'd allowed sufficient time for a report, a call back, an emergency alert, but there'd been nothing but silence. How many intruders could have entered the Tomb during those ten minutes? Could they have made progress in that time up from Level Four to Level Three? Immediately above Level Three were the living quarters, the dormitories and the sickbay. Dan and Ruth and most of the community were down there sleeping.

The duty officer's face was haunted and beaded with sweat. His eyes moved from the clock and settled on Chase. 'What's it to be?'

'Hit it.' Chase was on his way through the door even as the siren started to wail.

7

Dan had been wrong: they were not babies. The correct classification was homunculi: tiny stunted dwarf-like beings with pulpy alabaster flesh and black pinprick eyes like raisins stuck in dough.

Like ants, they blindly followed a trail laid by the one in front, and the one in front of that, and the one in front of that. A few of them, perhaps five or six, had picked up Dan and Jo's scents as they struggled back across the hot barren landscape and more of the creatures had joined the march, which soon became a straggling procession, with dozens, then scores, then hundreds plodding onwards across the desert scrub and disappearing into the tunnels like a long jointed white slug burrowing underground.

Guns could kill them, though it didn't appear to matter to them; instinct and hunger drove them on and death was immaterial. They ate voraciously, like a plague of caterpillars stripping a forest bare, and they were seeking food of any kind, animal or vegetable. Kill one and another climbed over the body to take its place. Kill twenty and fifty more came on with pudgy blank faces and small red gaping mouths. They were mouths on stunted legs, quite mindless, living only to eat and reproduce.

The raw sunlight with its fierce dose of ultraviolet radiation was not just beneficial to this species but essential. It had warped their genetic structure, each successive generation adapting more comfortably to the new conditions. Even the thinning atmosphere with its low oxygen content had been assimilated and was now vital to the development of their metabolic structure.

There was no way they could be stopped, as Chase soon discovered.

They had packed Level Four with their soft squirming bodies and were stumping up the stairway to Level Three, jammed naked shoulder to naked shoulder: Chase hopelessly pumped shot after shot into their midst, but it was like shooting at the tide. The upper levels above him were in turmoil as everyone grabbed the few personal effects they could carry and scurried upwards. Some had spared the time to dress hastily; others were still in nightwear. The siren blare filled the corridors as Chase and the security guards tried to at least delay the inexorable progress of the eighteen-inch-high pulsating white tide.

Now, retreating before it, Chase followed the others up to Level One. Nick was overseeing the evacuation of their two families – Dan was still groggy with exhaustion, and Jo needed help to walk – but they had no other choice, Chase knew, but to evacuate and seek sanctuary elsewhere.

In the operations room he came upon the duty officer, holding his post when the rest had fled. His lips were trembling and his eyes were bloodshot.

'How near are they?'

'Level Two.'

'What in God's name are they after?'

'My guess is food.'

'Food?' The duty officer stared. 'What kind of food?'

'Us.'

'What can we do?'

Chase shook his head.

'Then we abandon?'

'Unless you can come up with the brainwave of the century in the next two minutes. Are the charges primed?'

'They prime automatically during an alert.'

'Is everybody out?'

The duty officer looked at him, grey in the face. 'Do you expect me to check?'

'All right, set the timer and let's go.'

The duty officer lifted the circular stainless-steel plate to reveal a red stirrup handle. Quickly he unscrewed two chromium-plated bolts, turned the stirrup through 180 degrees and pressed it fully down until it locked. A timing device whirred and began to tick away the seconds.

The fifteen-minute countdown before the Tomb erupted had started.

In less than a minute the operations room was empty.

Scrambling up the steep stairway to the outside, Chase realised he'd forgotten something: the notebook he'd spent hour after hour scribbling in, which he'd described to Ruth as a Future Diary, was lying in the locked drawer of his desk. It was too late now to retrieve it, and nothing flammable would survive the final immolation. The handwritten pages would curl and shrivel to blackened fragments, turning to ash in the heat; all his speculations about the future of the species and the planet would perish unread.

The final entry, written only a day or so ago, was still fresh in his mind, the words seared into his memory. It was a short passage from one of the science reference works in his library. As Chase climbed higher, the words came alive in his mind like tongues of flame, dancing in front of his eyes:

There is a goal, one that has the potential to unite every man, woman and child on this planet, which, if reached, will enable them to build that 'land fit for heroes' at last. A home which they can be proud they helped to build, one in which they can live in harmony with the wild things . . .

From the final few steps Chase stumbled into the unprotected sunlight and denuded atmosphere, eyes screwed up against the glare, lungs straining to find oxygen.

The rest of the passage was forgotten. All he could think about now was the matter of survival.

2

1

Sixty feet above the jungle the black helicopter gunship banked left and aligned on the Strip, taking its bearings from the crumbling overgrown tower with the ornate lettering just visible through dense foliage and twining mossy creepers: Caesar's Palace.

Swooping lower, the gunship clattered over the swampy hollow formed by the convergence of roads and side streets between Flamingo Road and Sahara Avenue. Circus-Circus went by on the left, smothered in greenery; directly ahead was Las Vegas Boulevard South, in the downtown casino section.

The only gambling that took place now had to do with survival.

The tropical belt, fed by heat and the abundance of carbon dioxide, was encroaching steadily northwards, taking possession of a wide swathe of desert. Further south the swampland was too hot and stagnant even for amphibians. Deep down in the sludge, new formations of molecules simmered and thrived, stirred into activity by the bombardment of radiation, creating forms of life that had yet to evolve and emerge into the light. Further south still was the bubbling, toxic ocean, a seething cauldron of chemical soup.

Only the reflected gleam of the sun, picking out the muddy Strip like the trail of a slug with a slide-rule sense of direction, gave any hint of man's erstwhile intrusion.

2

Dan shaded his eyes from the intense glare and watched the speck of the black gunship disappear into the hazy distance. His face and neck were caked with yellow cream. He slipped the dark goggles into place and moved slowly, measuring each breath, along the squelchy bank to where the others were stretched out under the giant ferns.

He couldn't help remembering Miami Beach in 2030. In twelve years he hadn't progressed very far – and the only prospect in view was not reaching his twenty-sixth birthday. At least here the air was just about breathable: two or three per cent lower and they would have been floundering about like beached fish.

He stepped over something squirming in the mud and gained the higher, firmer ground. Once out of the direct sunlight he stripped off his goggles and dropped down, chest heaving, by his father's side. Chase tried to smile through his own yellow mask. Though only in his mid-fifties, Dan was afraid that his dad's respiratory system would no longer be able to cope with the thin atmosphere. During the last six days people younger than he had collapsed, frothing, blue-lipped. He tore his mind away from the stark possibility.

'Couldn't you make out any markings?' Ruth asked.

'There weren't any. But it was armed – rocket launchers, big-calibre weaponry.'

'Against whom?' Chase said angrily. His eyeballs were crazed with broken blood vessels. 'Why kill when we're dying anyway?' He sounded dumbfounded.

'The O-zoes aren't dying, they're flourishing,' Jo said. Her finespun hair spilled out from underneath her forage cap. 'And those things back in the Tomb' – her throat muscles worked – 'those white grubs or whatever they were? The conditions seem to suit them.'

'No, they suit the conditions,' Chase said. 'Nature always fills a niche.'

Big brown opaque bubbles formed in the swampy hollow, burst with an explosive farting sound and belched yellowy-brown steam that drifted slowly through the hot turgid air. It smelled of sulphur and methane laced with various oxides and nitrites. Back to the Precambrian, Chase thought, with a sense of almost macabre relish. Theo had seen it coming thirty years ago. Perhaps even then it had been too late to change anything: The balance was already upset; factors beyond anyone's control had conspired to bring the earth to its knees and now the count had reached nine, the referee's hand was raised and there wasn't going to be a bell to save it.

Or them. There was nowhere to go from here.

After evacuating the Tomb they had made for Interstate 15, intending to travel north, but the highway was impassable. It was too dangerous to cross the border into Nevada; all the evidence indicated that the tribal fighting among the prims, O-zoes and other groups had spread across northern Utah, which meant the route was closed to them. So the raggle-taggle column had turned south, splintering into smaller groups and losing people on the way as they encountered the damp fingers of swampland reaching out from Lake Mead.

Other travellers on the road had told them of conditions elsewhere. Arizona was a jungle as dense and impenetrable as any in darkest Africa. In California huge concentration camps covered half the state. Most of the travellers were hoping to find a way north, preparing to risk the tribal wars to get to Idaho and Oregon. The jungle, so it was said, was advancing at the rate of four miles every month, but surely, *surely*, it had to stop somewhere; it had to, hadn't it?

'Is it painful?' Ruth asked, examining Jo's leg. The wound in her thigh was superficial, but Ruth was afraid that with the humidity and insects it might turn gangrenous.

'Not any more. It's kind of numb. Doesn't bother me.'

Ruth tightened her lips. 'Well, that's good,' she said, taking a fresh dressing from the medical pack. 'I'll give you a shot to stop the infection spreading. Not much point in telling you to rest it, I guess. Not until we find somewhere safe.' She glanced at Chase, her eyes clouded.

Nick and two other men appeared through the greenish gloom cast by the tall rubbery plants and swaying ferns. On the far side of the clearing what at first sight was a sheer rock face was in fact the wall of a ten-storey motel. Thick green lichen had gained a purchase in the pitted concrete, partly obscuring a signboard that read in faded Day-Glo: VIDEO GAMBLING IN EVERY ROOM PLUS 9-CHANNEL 3-D PORNO!

'Did you hear it?' Nick squatted down, the breath rasping in his throat. 'I think it was a chopper.'

'We saw it,' Dan nodded. 'It came in very low and flew straight down the river.'

Nick's eyes brightened. 'Did they see you? Any signal?'

'We kept out of sight.'

'You . . .' Nick stared at Dan, then looked slowly around at the others. 'What the hell for? Don't you know it means there's some kind of civilisation around here – *somewhere*!' His shoulders sagged.

'That was a gunship with enough firepower to wipe out a city,' Chase said. 'I want to know who they are and what they're doing here. It's too late to ask questions when you've been napalmed—'

'You're talking as if we had a *choice*. Look around, Gav, open your eyes for Christ's sake!' Nick swept his arm out to indicate the thirty or so people in the clearing, weary, travel-stained, faces streaked with yellow, exuding hopelessness like a bad smell. 'We're down to a few days' rations, we've used up nearly all our medical supplies, we've nowhere to go and you're fretting like a maiden aunt that someone's about to start World War Three.' He shook his head in bewilderment. 'Maybe it might be for the best if they *did* drop a nuke on top of us. At least it would be quick and painless.'

Chase pointed grimly across the muddy water to the buildings choked with vines and foliage on the other side of the Strip. 'If you're so bloody keen to die, Nick, that way's just as quick. I wouldn't give you fifteen minutes.'

'I *don't* want to die, none of us do. But that's precisely what's going to happen unless we can get help. Any kind of help – and soon.' Nick looked around despairingly. 'Stay here and we starve, rot and get eaten, and not necessarily in that order.'

Someone else behind him said, 'I think Nick's right. Even if it was a gunship it must have been American, with our guys in it.'

'Hell, for all we know it could have been a search-and-rescue mission!' Nick said bitterly.

Ruth was staring hard at Chase, her eyes holding a message it took him a moment to decipher. Then he understood: it concerned Jo. Ruth said quietly, 'We've got to find help, Gavin, and very soon.'

3

During the day they had to contend with the airless oven heat, but after nightfall it was worse: insects came out in their millions. Centipedes a foot long undulated across the clearing and had to be beaten to a pulp before they got to the rations. Dan took a group down to the brackish water to see if it was fit for drinking and disturbed a posse of alligators snoozing in the mud.

They decided to seek shelter in one of the ruined buildings along the Strip.

Everything of value, everything portable, had long since been looted. The jungle had crept indoors, transforming the public bars and restaurants, the gaming rooms, the lobbies and passages into dank sweltering caves. By flashlight they explored the labyrinth, hacking through festoons of creepers and climbing stairs where the carpets squelched underfoot like thick moss. They came upon a swimming pool half-filled with green slime, the crusty surface broken here and there by snouts and unblinking eyes reflected in the beams of light. In other rooms the silence was intimidating. Tapestries of foliage clung to the walls, the leaves a dark mottled brown giving off an acrid scent that bit at the throat like ammonia. This vegetation was feeding off the poisoned air and becoming itself poisoned in the process, adding to the toxic fumes that formed the new atmosphere. The spiral of decay was winding tighter and tighter, each malfunction in the biosphere contributing to the next perverted link in the crooked chain. It was evolution, but in the wrong direction.

Dan went ahead with Art Hegler and two of the younger men, leaving the main party in the corner of what had been an electronic amusements room on the third floor of the Stardust Hotel.

Two floors above, the advance group battered down a fire door to find themselves in a corridor stretching the full depth of the building. The jungle hadn't penetrated this far, although the humidity had rotted the carpets and the velvet-flocked wallpaper made a perfect breeding ground for white bell-shaped fungi.

Tentatively pushing open each door and standing well back, they investigated every room, some of which were untouched, the beds still made up, the TV blank-faced in the corner, towels in the bathroom hanging flaccidly from chromium-steel rails. And in one room which showed signs of occupation, Hegler slid back a closet door and goggled in amazement: it was crammed solid from floor to ceiling with cartons of tinned food – somebody's secret hoard, which they hadn't had time to eat.

'Strike starvation off the list,' said Dan gleefully, ripping open a carton and spilling two-pound tins of smoked ham over the floor. 'At least for the time being. This guy was all set for the millennium, by the look of it.'

Wayne Daventry, the twenty-year-old son of a biologist who had died of a heart attack two years ago, started to cry. The other three said nothing, averting their eyes, but they understood his emotion well enough. It was one thing to put up a stoic front in the face of adversity, but it was impossible not to betray real inner feeling when Providence offered a small gift of kindness, the briefest glimmer of hope.

'Now, if we can get a good movie on TV,' Dan said to divert attention and began punching buttons with a conjurer's flourish, 'I reckon the Stardust deserves a five-star rating!'

As the set began to hum, Art Hegler staggered back and tripped over his own feet.

The others stood with hearts pounding as the concave screen lit up and a fuzzy picture appeared, which at first nobody could make any sense of. It was like a surgeon's view of a pumping heart, stark, eye-searing red, being pierced by an enormous black veined torpedo.

Dan smiled forlornly in the artificial flickering twilight thrown by the screen. 'Just what we need: the in-house porn movie. The circuit must be still wired up to the generator.' He shook his head sadly. 'It's true what they say: "The world will end not with a whimper but with a bang".'

One of the others gave a hollow laugh.

Not really believing that it would work – why bother transmitting pictures when there was nobody to receive them? – Dan tried to get another channel. Yet there were – dammit, there *had* to be – other pockets of civilisation, if only on the evidence of the gunship. Where had that come from? What was it looking for? Survivors?

As he expected, nothing more came through, and he switched it off.

Hegler said, 'If there's power on, maybe we can tap it – get some light in this place, if nothing else—'

'I don't think that's wise, Art.' Dan crossed to the window. 'Turn your flashlights off for a minute.'

The four of them stood looking out at the jungle below, just about discernible in the fading light. It stretched away into the murky dusk, an unbroken canopy covering the low-level buildings, with the multi-storey hotels and casinos poking through like concrete piles in an inland Sargasso Sea. Nearest to them was Circus-Circus, then the Sahara, further yet the Hyatt and in the distance the Union Plaza.

'Think about it: up here we'd be like a beacon for anyone or anything down there. I've no idea what's living in the swamp and I'm not keen on finding out. I don't think it's sensible to advertise our presence, do you?'

'It could bring help,' Hegler pointed out.

'It could bring trouble. I think the only help we're going to get is from ourselves. What do you say, Pete?'

Pete Kosinski, who had worked as a technician with Ron Maxwell, stroked his week-old growth of beard, which softened the lower half of his angular jaw. 'This seems to me like a good place for now. We've got a supply of food and we can make the place secure. I don't want to share with *anybody*, least of all those little albinos with the soft handshake and tiny pointed teeth. Let's keep it just for us.'

'What about you, Wayne?'

'I agree – I mean about the lights and everything. If we can rest up for a few days and get ourselves organised, give ourselves time to think, we stand a much better chance.' The young man sounded grateful to have been asked his opinion, anxious to show he'd recovered from his emotional outburst. 'Let's end with a bang, not a whimper.'

Dan arched back, shaking with laughter.

They split up into pairs and searched the rest of the rooms along the corridor, thirty-six in all. Dan didn't want any nasty surprises in the middle of the night and so paid particular attention to the doors at the far end of the corridor and the three fire exits. All were intact, and could be made secure.

Finding this place was the first stroke of luck they'd had since leaving the Tomb. He was still concerned about fresh water, and there was the problem of medical supplies, which were almost gone, but at least from here, in daylight, they'd have an excellent view of the terrain. Tomorrow he'd explore the upper floors. How high was the Stardust? Ten, twelve, fifteen storeys? Despite his fatigue he felt buoyed up, almost cheerful, and he clapped Wayne on the back and told him to go back down to the third floor and bring the others up.

'And tell them we've got vacancies for everyone – king-size beds, first-class food, panoramic views and stimulating entertainment. The Stardust seasonal special, compliments of the management.'

4

It wasn't, as it happened, any of the four children in the party who were responsible for disturbing the blue-speckled spiders in their comfortable nests, but a middle-aged computer technician named Richards who couldn't resist taking a peek inside one of the egg-shaped video booths. Anything electronic drew him like iron filings to a magnet; after taking a careful scrutiny of the padded interior and finding it empty, or so he thought, he clambered in and settled back in the contoured seat.

Of course nothing was working. The angled screen was layered in a thick film of dust and the grooved joystick and control levers swathed in cobwebs, which he batted out of the way. Jesus, they were sticky and tenacious, clinging to his fingers, and damn strong too; it took considerable strength to get rid of them.

He examined the console by the light of two powerful battery lanterns that had been set up in the room, figuring out the object of the various games and tests of skill, from Star Pilot to Extermination Squad, with avid interest. As a youngster he'd been a sucker for electronic games, which had led to his career in computers. If he'd stuck to something simple like this, why, he could have made a fortune. The idea was the thing – the circuitry was dead simple, first-year stuff. All you needed was the basic know-how, a bright idea, and you had a licence to print money, Richards thought as something stirred above his head.

He squinted up, but except for two tiny points of light (like a reflection on something hard and polished, it occurred to him), it was pitch-black. Feeling only a vague tremor of disquiet, Richards was puzzling over this when the door of the egg slammed shut.

How had that happened? He must have moved, rocked the booth slightly, causing the door to swing to under its own weight. But where was the handle? In total blackness now his fingers searched the interior of the padded door. He could feel the edge of the door, but he couldn't find the handle. There had to be one – how else did the players get out of this stupid contraption?

It was then he sensed rather than felt something directly above him and the breath went solid in his chest. He opened his mouth to scream. Something hard and bony and covered in spiny hairs brushed his forehead and the scream expired into a croak of numbing terror.

Other hard, bony, hairy sensations followed as the jointed legs closed around his head and neck in a constricting embrace, the beaked mouth coming down in a swift stabbing bite that gouged a four-inch piece from his scalp clean through to the bone.

Too late for screams or even terrified croaks. Richards was devoured alive. Not having eaten for some time, the blue-speckled spider, grown to a span of some three feet across, finished off the head and sucked out the brains before wrapping the remainder of its unfinished meal in silk for later.

The carpeted staircase felt mushy underfoot. Wayne Daventry shivered, imagining he was treading on Jello. It made him think of a lab culture with a myriad bacteria multiplying, thriving, expanding.

He shook his head, dismissing the unpleasant fancy. The air was close and stifling, his shirt sticking to his back – what he wouldn't give for a long, cold, bracing shower! He came on to the landing of the fourth floor and as he squelched past the four elevators stuck his hand out and thumbed the sensor-touch buttons in their corroded metal plates, a childish habit he had never outgrown – and stopped in mid-stride as the last set of doors slid open. Dan was right, there was still power somewhere in the building.

He shone his flashlight inside the elevator and recoiled. Gleaming whitely in the cone of light was a pile of bones, the skeletons of three, maybe four, people, though it was hard to tell exactly. Shreds of clothing were wrapped around some of the bones, a shirt collar, a cuff. Wayne sucked in his breath and bent forward as a glint of gold caught his eye. A jewel sparkled like a lighthouse beam. He took a step nearer, seeing rings, bracelets, necklaces and watches among the clutter. And on the small finger of one of the skeletons was a diamond ring that flared like a miniature sun, throwing off dazzling highlights.

Wayne placed one foot on the floor of the car, testing it gingerly. A cable above him creaked and there was a dry, sticklike rattle, but the car itself was rock-steady. Down on one knee, the flashlight held in his left hand, he picked out the jewellery without touching the bones. As the diamond ring came off, so did the finger, falling with a bony clatter.

That sound seemed to echo in the shaft above his head, and for one dreadful, heart-pounding moment he thought the cable was about to snap and plunge him a hundred and twenty feet into the basement. The car did teeter fractionally, but it still held firm, and Wayne hurried on with his plundering, his parted lips dry and hot.

Behind him he heard a soft heavy plop and a harsh rasping, like scales being rubbed together. Swinging around, the flashlight slippery in his hand, he stared with bulging eyes at what lay coiled on the floor of the car. The rattlesnake was a monster. Its dark green and grey body was as thick as a man's waist, the massive spade-shaped head raised up and swaying to and fro, the eyes glinting like icy diamond chips. Its bony tail blurred and in the confined space the rattle was earsplitting.

Clutching a fistful of rings, bracelets and watches, Wayne staggered back and crashed against the rear wall of the elevator, scattering the bones.

Now he understood. The skeletons – *of course*. The snake lived in the warm dark recesses of the elevator shaft and whenever it was disturbed slithered down from its lair on to the roof of the car and dropped through the open trapdoor ... and he had disturbed it *for gold*. For worthless metal. For glittering trinkets that wouldn't buy a mouthful of food, a sip of water or a single gulp of pure air.

The elongated eyes in the swaying head watched him unblinkingly. The brain computed the distance across the floor of the car to the millimetre. The tongue flicked out, tasting the air for his body smell. Then the neck drew back upon itself like a tightly coiled spring and the deafening rattling sound suddenly ceased.

A mumbled prayer on his lips, Wayne Daventry saw nothing, it was that fast.

The first strike was good and deep, a clean bite with both fangs in the side of Wayne's neck. The giant reptile shook him, a violent threshing movement and then coiled back upon itself. The tongue flicked out several times as it contemplated its stricken dying prey. And then very slowly the snake uncoiled itself and reared up, tall as a man, and slid back through the trapdoor. The silent rattle vanished into darkness.

3

I

For two days nonstop and well into the third it rained torrentially. They slung sheets on the balconies and collected the rainwater in every kind of receptacle that didn't leak. Pete Kosinski tested it as best he could, and pronounced it drinkable, though he couldn't account for any impurity it might contain, nor whether in the long-term it might prove harmful.

The fifth floor came to resemble a refugee camp.

With careful rationing, Chase reckoned that the food would last them nearly two weeks, and they now had enough water for drinking, even if they had to go without washing. All things considered, they couldn't complain. They hadn't seen the gunship again, probably because of the bad weather, and despite his private fears he was beginning to think that making contact with it really was their only hope.

To the north of the city was hostile territory, overrun by tribes and wandering crazies who wouldn't hesitate to kill either for gain or just for the sheer hell of it. South of Vegas was jungle, which said it all. But the Californian border was less than thirty miles away – was that a possible sanctuary? They had heard rumours about concentration camps, hundreds of square miles surrounded by fences where people were herded in by the thousands. Uneasily, Chase connected such stories with the black gunship. Supposing there was a major war going on somewhere – maybe right here – that they knew nothing about?

He could imagine the scenario well enough: the government in 'Washington' (wherever that was now) overthrown by a military coup, the armed forces split two, three, six different ways, the scramble for those geographic areas least affected by the deteriorating climate, the usual power-plays by the pros and antis, the hawks and doves, all busy clubbing one another into the ground and grabbing what they could.

Yes, he could see it all too clearly. Here and now, though, there were more personal and far more immediate concerns – Jo's condition, for one.

Ruth was blunt about it. 'She's got five days, then she'll either lose that leg or her life.'

'Does she know it's gangrene?'

'I haven't told her, but she isn't stupid.' Ruth sat on the end of the bed and looked at Chase, lying propped up on pillows. His eyes were sunken, his cheeks marked by deep vertical lines above his tangled beard. Despite the use of protective cream his forehead and the bridge of his nose were badly blistered. 'If she doesn't know now she definitely will in a day or two when the wound starts to suppurate. And the smell will leave no one in any doubt.'

'Five days,' Chase said, staring at the wall opposite. 'What can we do in five days? Where can we *go*?' He thumped the bed impotently.

'Take it easy, honey,' Ruth took his fist in both hands and pried open the stiff fingers. 'You've done everything you could. The responsibility isn't yours alone – not any more. It's ours, too. Everyone's.'

Chase was hardly listening. He could see Wayne Daventry, poor kid, his head bloated to three times its normal size, eyes like buttons in a padded cushion of blue-black leather. It was obvious what had killed him from the bite marks – but the width of that jaw! That thing must be a monstrous size, and there might be more than one – perhaps the building was infested with them.

And what about the computer technician, Richards – where had he disappeared to? One minute he'd been with them on the third floor and the next . . . gone.

Five days, Ruth had said: five days in which to get help from somewhere. If any of them lived that long. What else did the famed Stardust Hotel have up its sleeve?

Later that afternoon he, Dan, Nick and Art climbed to the roof of the building, ostensibly to spy out the terrain, but really he needed to talk through the situation and form a plan of action. Printed in his brain like flaring red neon, the words *How?* and *Where?* blocked every thought so that his mind became a circular track endlessly repeating itself.

Before venturing out they plastered their faces with cream and put on dark goggles. The sky had at last cleared and under the hot sun the jungle steamed and shimmered like something alive. It *was* alive, Chase reminded himself, crawling with all manner of creatures and insects.

He stood with the others looking west. Not long ago – ten or fifteen years – this had been sand and scrub. Nature had come back with a vengeance; almost as if it had a personal vendetta: *You asked for it. Here's where you get what's coming to you.*

'Jo hasn't got long, has she?' Nick said. Under the yellow cream it was impossible to read his expression.

'No,' Chase said.

'She was feverish last night, though the leg isn't hurting her. At least she's not in pain.' His chest heaved as he sucked in a thin breath. 'By God, I've never wanted to kill anything, but I'd gladly wipe them out, every single grub . . .'

'The ways things are going, it'll be the other way around. The old law still applies: survival of the fittest.'

'And we're not fit for anything,' Nick said drably.

Art called out from the other side of the roof and when they joined him, he pointed to one of the tall buildings directly across the Strip. 'Do you know what that is?'

'Yes, it's the Riviera Hotel,' Dan said.

'How can you tell?'

'I remember seeing the sign above the entrance. You can see it from our floor—'

He stopped because the sign was no longer there. Chase and Nick searched for it too. The realisation dawned gradually.

'Jesus, it's under the water,' Dan said in a small voice. 'That sign was way up above the entrance – the level must have risen by at least . . . twenty feet?'

'Now we can't leave,' Nick said, spitting the words out, 'even if we had somewhere to go. We can't fucking leave!' He lurched towards the low parapet and Chase grabbed his arm and hauled him back.

'What were you trying for, a gold medal in the swan dive?' he said, keeping a firm grip. The two men held on to each other, each swallowing back emotion. Chase said, 'This is getting to be a habit. I saved your bacon at Halley Bay Station too.'

'Those were the days,' Nick sighed. 'I didn't have a care in the world.'

'Except where to get hold of some Moroccan Blue.'

'Lebanese Red, Carruthers, you stupid bastard.'

'Sorry, Fortescue,' Chase said automatically.

'So what now?' Dan said. 'Build an ark?'

Behind them Art was gazing thoughtfully at the tangle of television antennae sprouting from a concrete box in the middle of the roof. 'Is there any juice in the system? That TV set you tried,' he said to Dan, 'is it still working?'

'I haven't tried it since.'

'What if it is?' Chase said. 'It was a closed-circuit channel feeding off the hotel's emergency supply – there was nothing coming in from the outside.'

'I was thinking of stuff going out, not coming in.'

'You mean transmitting? Is it possible?'

'It's possible,' Art said.

'And we've got hundreds of TV sets we can cannibalise for parts,' Dan said eagerly. He looked around at the others. 'Surely we could build a transmitter of some kind?'

'How do you make a microphone out of a cathode ray tube?' Nick asked caustically.

Art explained, 'I wasn't thinking of anything that advanced. All we need is to transmit a constant signal – not even Morse – that somebody somewhere would pick up. They'd use the signal to get a fix on us.' He scratched his sideburn. 'I don't know, maybe it wouldn't work; it's just an idea.'

'The best one I've heard today, or this year,' Chase said with a grin. 'How about it, Art, will you give it a try? Get Pete Kosinski to help you, and ask around for anyone else with knowledge of electronics or communications.'

'Okay.' He grabbed hold of a tarnished cross-strut with his gloved hand. 'First thing is to find out if the power's still on. If it isn't, this isn't worth scrap.'

They went back down to the fifth floor using the main staircase. On each landing Chase made sure the elevator doors were closed. He knew it was a futile precaution, because the elevator shaft would access other parts of the building – in the spaces between the floors and ceilings, or possibly the ventilation system; he had warned everyone not to go into any of the rooms without first making absolutely certain they were empty, and to take extra care when opening closets and cupboards, anything which might connect to the cavity wall space.

Dan suggested doing a recce of the upper floors. 'There must be five, six hundred rooms above us – there could be food, supplies, all kinds of useful stuff.'

'Not to mention things living up there.' Nick sounded unimpressed. 'If you want to go poking around, count me out. I'd say we've got enough trouble without going looking for it.'

'Let's keep to our own floor, Dan,' Chase said. 'We can barricade the doors and at least have some protection.'

He didn't qualify that by reminding them of the giant snake and the narrow spaces snakes could slide through. But he didn't have to.

2

Chase tossed and turned, the sweat pouring off him until he felt himself to be wallowing in a soggy morass. His feet had swollen with the heat and his hands felt boneless, spongy.

He slid off the bed, rearranged the single sheet over Ruth's sleeping figure and took a drink of tepid water from the jug. Instantly sweat rolled down his face and plopped into the water like raindrops. He tottered in the darkened room as a wave of dizziness swept over him. Was it just the heat or was it something else? At the back of his mind was anoxia, the creeping disease of oxygen deficiency in the tissues. Was this how it started, with fainting spells and nausea?

A tremendous crash shook the building. The uncurtained window suddenly flared with blinding brightness and with it came a boom of thunder of such violence and pressure that Chase feared his eardrums might rupture. He thought for a moment that the hotel had received a direct hit from a missile, but the cause was natural, thank God – like everything else, the desert thunderstorms were built on a gigantic scale.

Awakened by the noise, Ruth sat up and hugged her knees. 'If it keeps on raining we'll have to move to the penthouse suite.'

'And after that grow wings.' Chase turned back to the bed. He doubled up as pain twisted like a knife in his gut, then collapsed across the foot of the bed, groaning through clenched teeth. The sweat was now gushing off him, drenching Ruth's hand as she sought to help him. He was burning up with fever.

Ruth darted across the room to get the medical pack from the closet and as she touched the handle of the sliding door she heard a dry rattling noise from inside. She whipped her hand back, heart palpitating with fear. Step by wooden step she withdrew, eyes straining to see in the darkness. Faintly she heard the closet door creak as if, perhaps, a heavy weight was pressing against it. She waited, fists knotted by her sides, almost unable to hear anything because of the blood pounding in her ears.

CRASH!

Thinking the snake had broken through the door, Ruth almost leaped out of her skin. The room filled with crimson light and there was another deafening drumroll of thunder. Behind her Chase moaned and writhed on the bed. Her mind snapped shut like a steel trap. *Do something!*

Her decision made, she acted calmly and swiftly. Dragging Chase across the floor, she got him into the corridor, returned for the battery lantern and slammed the door shut, making sure it was securely on the catch. She switched the lantern on and by its light saw that his face was white as paper, his hair plastered to his head like a skullcap. She was afraid he was dying.

A footfall behind her jerked her upright, her nerves taut as piano wires.

Dan knelt beside her. 'Is he sick, too?'

It was only then Ruth became aware of stifled groans coming from other rooms along the corridor. Chase wasn't the only one. What could be the cause? Food poisoning? Or the water? *It had to be the water.*

Poisoned water from the skies! Christ, it was impossible: they couldn't win. Unbreathable air and undrinkable water – what hope was there for any of them?

With Dan's help, Ruth moved Chase to another room. Out of thirty-six, nine had the same symptoms: intense stomach cramps, fever and vomiting. And several more were complaining of feeling unwell and Ruth resigned herself to the fact that eventually all of them would succumb. Everyone had drunk the same water, so why not? At Nick's suggestion they carried all the sick into one of the larger apartments, one with two connecting rooms, where it would be easier to keep an eye on them. Mattresses were brought in and arranged around the walls. Some of the others came to join them, obeying the primitive instinct of herding together for mutual protection and companionship.

The storm raged around them with terrifying ferocity, battering at the walls and shaking the windows in their frames.

Nick knelt by Ruth's side as she made one of the children comfortable. 'How are you feeling?' he asked her worriedly.

'All right so far, but I don't think any of us will escape it, Nick. We've all eaten the same rations and drunk—'

A middle-aged man was crying out piteously for water, raising himself on one elbow, mouth gaping. One of the women hurried to him with a plastic cup and Ruth leaped up and knocked it from her hand.

'No water!' She swung around, shouting it at everyone in the room and those through the connecting door. 'The water could be contaminated. Nobody is to drink it!'

'Is it the water?' Nick asked her. 'Are you sure?'

'I don't know anything for sure. It could be the food, the heat, the air —' Ruth made an empty, angry gesture. 'How in hell do I know? How does anyone?'

Nick looked across at Chase whose face was contorted in an awful grimace of pain. He turned slowly, seeing the writhing bodies, hands clutching their stomachs. 'We have to give them something. Have we any painkillers left?'

'Yes,' Ruth said stonily and told him about the medical pack and the noise she had heard.

'Did you actually see anything?'

'I didn't wait for that. Would you?'

'That means you can't treat Jo,' Nick said in a hushed voice. 'You can't give her a shot—'

'I can't treat *anybody*!' Ruth snapped coldly. She shut her eyes. 'I'm sorry, Nick.' She opened them after a moment, took a steadying breath. 'All the drugs we have are in the medical pack in the closet of that room. I'm sorry.'

Ruth turned away. There was nothing more to say, and nothing more she could do. She tried to comfort Chase, who was delirious, babbling something about being lost in Antarctica.

Nick closed his hand around the doorknob and very carefully increased the pressure. As it began to turn he said, 'Is the safety off?' His voice was thick and ragged.

'Yes,' Dan whispered. In the light of the flashlight his face had the appearance of a Halloween mask. The automatic was a burnished blue glint at the level of his hip. He raised it in front of him as the door opened a crack.

At first sight the room was empty.

Dan crouched and shone the light under the bed. Nothing there. He turned the beam on the door of the closet. According to Ruth, it was the double closet furthest from the window. The sliding doors were shut. If there was anything inside, it hadn't come out. He doubted that snakes, even mutated ones, had the ability to close doors behind them.

Nick whispered, 'As soon as I open it, don't wait – fire.' He cleared his throat, trying to muffle the sound. 'Ready?'

Dan went down on one knee, flashlight in his left hand, and sighted along the barrel of the gun held in his right. He nodded. 'Go for it.'

As if in slow motion Nick bent at the knees and reached out at full stretch. He touched the handle with his fingertips and gently pushed and the door slid silently open on polyurethane bearings. Dan's finger tightened on the trigger, but he didn't fire because there was nothing to shoot at. The bulky brown canvas pack, flap unbuckled, stood on the third shelf down with two cartons of cotton swabs beside it, one opened. The rest of the closet remained hidden behind the centre and side panels, an unknown quantity.

'Move to your left,' Nick murmured. 'Shine the light inside.'

Still on one knee, Dan sidled around, angling the beam to probe further inside. He held his breath as he saw Nick craning forward, trying to peer into the shadowy recesses, and wanted to warn him not to go too near, but his throat was so dry he couldn't even swallow, let alone speak. It was as if his tongue was made of dried leather.

Jagged lightning from beyond the window lit everything up like a stage set, followed by a rolling boom of thunder and underneath the thunder, another sound, a dry rattling of scales.

The moment froze when nothing happened – or seemed to happen. Dan saw a shadow move, the rattling sound ceased and simultaneously Dan pressed the trigger as a shape reared up, light reflecting in two elongated black eyes. A splinter of wood spun through the flashlight beam, sheared off by the bullet from the centre panel. Dan fired again and again and the broad diamond-backed body recoiled, curling back upon itself; he fired again into the heavy mass of coils, pumping the gun until it was empty and the hammer clicked metallically in the sudden deathly silence.

'Is it dead? Did I kill it?'

He stood up and in the flashlight's beam saw a quivering mound twitching convulsively. The inside of the closet was spattered with blood. The snake's head had been almost severed from its body, the mouth gaping open, the curved fangs dripping blood . . .

'Christ, it was fast, wasn't—'

Dan stopped. Blood?

Blood!

How could there be blood on the fangs? Where from? He'd fired before the creature could strike. Dan blinked sweat from his eyes and shone the light downwards. In the beam he saw Nick was lying on the floor. His face was obscured by an elephant's trunk with two deep raking marks in it. The trunk ended in a hand. It was Nick's hand, raised across his forehead to protect himself. The trunk was his arm, swelling with poison and turning blue-black.

Dan knelt down and touched him. His flesh was still warm and yet clammy, with a strange mottled pattern forming underneath the skin. There was no pulse he could detect. The venom must have reached Nick's heart in a matter of seconds. If not dead, he was in total paralysis.

In the corridor the dense cloying smell of rotting carpets and fungi growing on the walls made Dan's stomach heave. He shouldered the medical pack, trying not to breathe in the stench of putrefaction. His shoes made squelching sounds as he went along the corridor. In the beam of the flashlight the walls appeared to shimmer whitely, the bell-shaped fungi trembling and exuding tiny white pearls of fluid. He stepped nearer and held the flashlight up close. The pearls were white grubs with rudimentary features and a bifurcated division in the tail. He watched as one of them squirmed over the lip of the bell and dropped to the floor. The floor, he then realised, was seething with them – what his shoes had been squelching through.

Dan swung the light in an arc. The carpet itself seemed to be alive underneath him, a moving white stream filling the corridor with numberless millions. They were dropping from the walls by the hundreds, he saw, eager to move out into the world, their own habitat, seeking nourishment.

Dan remembered the white grubs in the tent feeding off Fran and the others. He knew now what they were – and what they would turn into.

These were the larvae of the homunculi, come to inherit the earth.

He walked through them leaving flattened oozing footprints, entered the suite and shut the door.

3

Chase stirred and moaned in drug-induced slumber. His shirt and trousers were saturated, the foam mattress soaking up perspiration like a giant sponge.

Ruth sat watching him with her back to the wall, knees drawn up. She had administered morphine-based analgesics and was down to the last pack of vials. On half-dose it might go round one more time. With the fever and lack of water there was a danger of salt depletion and dehydration, but there was nothing else she could do.

The room was airless and sweltering and it was getting hard to breathe. Every breath required a conscious effort. She'd never realised how difficult it was when you had to concentrate on the simple act of replenishing your lungs.

Breathe in, breathe out.

In and out.

In. Out.

The storm had faded to a background rumbling, and mingled with it was the sound of weeping from the next room. Jen had wanted to go to him, unable to bear the thought of her husband lying alone, untended, uncared for, but Dan had restrained her. He didn't give a reason, only that it was safer to stay here and not to venture into the corridor.

It was very peaceful now that the storm had abated. Ruth felt comfortably drowsy and relaxed, only dimly aware of the tightness across her chest, drifting into a deep dreamless sleep.

'They're blocking off the air!'

Dan was standing in the middle of the room, staring at the door. She watched him hazily. He seemed to be babbling.

'If they fill the corridor we won't be able to breathe.'

Ruth flinched, then cowered away as he grabbed hold of a chair and smashed it with all his strength through the large window. The glass collapsed in the frame and tinkled away into the night. At once the foetid smell of the jungle wafted into the room, but now Ruth found that she could draw breath without the constricting pain in her chest. She struggled to her feet, gasping.

'Dan, who's out there? Is there someone – something – in the hallway?'

When he didn't answer she followed his gaze to the door. Paint was flaking off. The door seemed to be bulging. The sound of straining timber sang a low steady note of protest. There was a metallic screeching as the hinges were forced out of their seatings.

'What is it? For God's sake, tell me!'

Dan was crouching, arms hanging limply, his face drained of expression. 'They're growing in the corridor,' he said faintly. 'I don't see how, because there's nothing to eat out there. The food's in here. But they're growing all the same . . .'

A crack appeared in the centre of the door and something white started seeping through.

Ruth grabbed him, her nails digging into his arms.

Jen appeared in the doorway, mouth working, eyes wide with shock; behind her Art shouted hoarsely, 'They're breaking in! How do we stop them? Dan!'

Dan shook his head helplessly. 'What can we do? They must be everywhere by now.'

He glanced up as the ceiling creaked. A woman scuttled into a corner, screaming through her hands. Dan stared upward as bits of plaster showered down and a jagged crack opened up with a noise like a rifle shot. He couldn't believe it. The pressure! Pulpy soft bodies surely wouldn't have the strength? But their combined weight might do it, packed tightly together, struggling and squirming for growth, for expansion, for life.

Epitaph: 2052

I

I watched the six-year-old, body smooth and brown, straight blond hair that shone like a silvery cap in the sunshine, perform a twisting triple somersault from thirty feet and dive cleanly into the sparkling green waters of the lake. Spray lifted and hung and settled slowly like glittering gossamer in the low gravity.

Watching from the shade of a jacaranda tree and sipping cold drinks, Dan and Jo, the boy's parents, applauded proudly. On the other side of the placid water, beyond the terraced tiers of residential gardens, I could see the cylindrical core: a polished shaft of fretted aluminium three hundred metres in diameter, rising several thousand metres in the air.

Insects zoomed and ticked in the undergrowth; a butterfly wafted erratically by; somewhere a bird sang, claiming territory or looking for a mate.

'Did you teach Nick?' I asked, watching the boy's bright head, named after my closest friend, break the surface. My grandson could leap and twirl like a lithe brown seal.

'All the kids are brilliant divers,' Dan said. 'They don't need teaching. There's a kid in Nick's tutor group who can stay in the air so long you'd swear he was actually flying. I tried it once and went arse-over-tip and landed flat on my back. You need natural low-g coordination, which youngsters have and we don't. I'll stick to hang-gliding; at least there your earthbound conceptions and reflexes aren't violated.'

'I don't know about that,' Jo said archly, prodding him with her bare foot under the table. 'Your earthbound reflexes adapted quite well.'

'Pure instinct,' Dan grinned. 'And of course the trampolinists' revised edition of the *Kama Sutra* was a great help.'

I hid a grin as Jo kicked him again, harder.

It was late afternoon and the mirrors were angled by computers to throw slanting rays that mimicked the setting sun. Three light planar mirrors, each ten kilometres by three, beamed the sunlight into the revolving island colony through huge transparent panels tinted blue to mimic the impression of a natural sky. As the day wore on the mirrors were tilted fractionally to give an approximation of the sun's path through a 180-degree arc and were then turned away for the eight-hour night. It turned out that human beings *needed* darkness.

Seen from a distance, the colony had the appearance of a large silver globe attached by tubular spokes to a doughnut. Here, inside the central globe, were the recreational areas, parklands and, because of its reduced gravitational stress, the homes of the older residents. Its proper name was Globe City, although of course it was known to everyone as Geriatric Gardens. Our three-room apartment – Ruth's and mine – was a few hundred yards from the lake. Being six years younger than me, Ruth objected in typically blunt manner to this insulting description.

Five spokes or thruways connected the globe to the outlying torus: the encircling tube that housed the main population as well as the multi-level crop-beds and animal farms.

At the topmost level in enclosed chambers, fishponds stocked with a wide variety of edible species filtered down and irrigated the lower levels, supplying waste effluent that fertilised the wheat, soybeans, vegetables and forage below. Given the near-perfect conditions of sunlight, temperature, humidity and nutrients – and a controlled supply of carbon dioxide – each of the seven-hundred-acre fields could produce seventeen hundred pounds of grain crops and forage a day, enough to feed a population of ninety thousand people. Half a million fish stocks provided everyone with a ten-ounce fillet once a week.

Canton Island had originally comprised just the central globe, with living space for ten thousand people: the first settlers, scientists, technicians, engineers and construction workers. The torus and connecting thruways had been added later; work was still going on to complete the external radiation shielding.

Even now, after all these years, the concept and execution of the enterprise still seemed to me like a miracle – or a dream. I can remember where I was and who first told me about it, and my incredulity. I was in the sickbay, and that person was Boris Stanovnik.

2

It was the blue crystalline light filtering through narrow smoked windows that I couldn't get used to. Inside was fluorescent-bright; outside there was only a glimmer of shiny spheres and tall steel spires, giving off sparkling highlights. I'd pondered them for hours and come to no conclusion. Exactly what the hell *was* this place? And where?

Having finished his rounds, Dr Pazan paused at the door and said, 'How do you feel? Strong enough?'

'Strong enough for what?' I asked.

'Some answers. I'll send your visitor up.'

'Visitor? Who?'

Dr Pazan disappeared with his enigmatic smile.

'How are you, my friend?'

I could only gape. 'Is it really you?'

Smiling broadly, Boris Stanovnik stood in the doorway. He ambled in and clasped my hand in both of his. He was still big, but more shrunken than I remembered him, his features thinner, more angular. The deep rumbling voice was the same. 'Your son is well – Ruth also. Dr Pazan has told you?'

'That, and not much else.'

'He was very worried, my friend. But now you're over the worst and the good doctor has allowed me to see you.'

'How long have I been here?'

'This is the seventeenth day. For two weeks you were in a toxic coma.' Boris smiled. 'It must feel like you arrived here only a couple of days ago.'

'Not even that. I've lost all sense of time and geography. Boris, tell me, please – what *is* this place? It's driving me mad not knowing.'

'It's called Emigrant Junction,' Boris said. 'It was once a small town – no, hardly that – in Death Valley on the Californian border.

Now it has become one of seven bases, three in the United States, two in Russia, one in Canada and one in Sweden. Emigrant Junction now covers the length and breadth of Death Valley; it is isolated from the outside world by a gamma-ray protection system. The only way in and out is by air. For that purpose we have a fleet of almost three hundred transporters and tactical airborne craft.'

'You mean gunships.'

Boris gave a ghost of a smile. 'You know how the military love their euphemisms.'

'So the rumours I heard about this being a concentration camp with a deathray fence are true. I thought it was a scare story.'

'True in part – and also a scare story,' Boris said. 'It was deliberately invented and spread to keep the prims and O-zoes away, and anyone else who might want to come in uninvited. Yes, there is a "deathray fence", but its purpose is defensive. Emigrant Junction is not a concentration camp, my friend, but a colonisation base.'

I sat up straighter in bed. 'Colonising what?'

'Space. Six "islands" as we call them are in the process of construction and three more about to be started. Then there are plans—'

I grabbed his sleeve. 'Islands? You mean space colonies?' I could feel my heart hammering. 'Do you mean they're actually building space colonies here? At Emigrant Junction?'

'No, no, no, not here.' Boris patted my hand. 'The programme is named the "Island Option" and it's been in progress for more than seven years. America, Russia and China are the principal partners, with co-operation from many other nations.' He raised his eyes to the ceiling. 'The colonies are being built *in space*.'

'My God.' I felt suddenly weak, falling back on the pillows. 'We saw lights in the sky and thought they were UFOs and all the time they were *rockets*?'

'Shuttles. Three lift off from here every fifty-six days with supplies and technical personnel; a similar programme goes on at the six other bases. Most of the "groundwork" – not a suitable phrase in the circumstances,' he chuckled, 'has been completed. It has taken nearly three years to transport and establish large-scale storage facilities for the life-support materials, namely oxygen and water. These are now in place and work is proceeding on the construction of the islands themselves.'

This achievement in itself was difficult to believe. Another factor I found even more incredible.

'Are you saying there really is genuine cooperation between the Americans and the Russians and the Chinese?' I couldn't keep the scathing disbelief out of my voice. 'Or is it the usual race to see who can get the first colony ready as a missile platform?'

'Not this time.' Boris was shaking his head soberly. 'It's mankind's last chance and everyone knows it. There is complete cooperation and interchange of information. Our head of projects here, Colonel Gary Zittel, who started the "Island Option", insists on it.' He could see I wasn't convinced. 'Believe me, this is true, Gavin. It is a fact. At Emigrant Junction there are Americans, Russians, Europeans, Asians, Africans, all working together for the common good. They know they have to work together . . . or perish together.'

'And how long have you been here, my Russian friend?' I asked.

'Less than a year. After Nina died I stayed on in the cabin in Oregon, but the flood of refugees from the south made life very difficult. I couldn't defend myself; I was forced to move further north. You know, they would have pushed me right up to the Arctic Circle if a patrol hadn't come along—'

He broke off. 'Ah! I understand! The reason for your question – how did they find *you*.'

'Exactly. I'm still pretty hazy about what happened back there. We were trapped in the Tomb and there was no way out.'

'You were exceedingly lucky. The search-and-rescue party nearly turned back without investigating because they thought Desert Range was abandoned. Then I requested – no, no, I *insisted* – they send a patrol to check it out and make sure.'

'Thank God they did,' I said, heartfelt. 'And thank God for you, Boris!'

He turned and gestured through the narrow windows towards the misty blue shapes, the domes and towers sparkling in the distance. 'The first colonists will be leaving soon. They will set up home on Canton Island and start planting crops.'

'Canton is the name of the island where Theo Detrick carried out his research.'

Boris was smiling. 'I suggested – no, once again, I *insisted* we name the first island in his honour, so that we should always remember Theo and the debt we owe him. Each colony will be named after an island.'

'How many people?'

'To go and live there, you mean? Sixty thousand.'

'In just the one colony?'

Boris could see my amazement, and deliberately, mischievously I thought, went on matter-of-factly, 'Canton Island is thirty-seven point six kilometres in total diameter. The first six islands to be completed will be the same size, the rest larger, up to seventy or eighty kilometres in diameter.'

'With what kind of population?'

'You mean in total numbers? One hundred thousand to one hundred and twenty thousand for each island, something of that order. And there are plans to build at least a hundred such islands, more if time allows.'

I distinctly recall my reaction; I had no other response than to close my eyes and sink back on the pillows. I took in a deep breath and slowly let it whisper through my nostrils.

Ten million people living in space. Incredible.

3

Young Nick ran up the shelving beach of white sand and jumped, wet and dripping, into my lap. 'Take me to the flying fish. Take me, Grandad, please!'

'Nick, now stop that!' Jo reprimanded him sharply. She reached for her son and flashed a look at Dan, who gave a slight shrug.

'I think we're too late today, Nick,' I told him with a rueful smile. 'They don't allow visitors after four o'clock. Some other time, okay?'

The experimental fish farms within the cylindrical core were a favourite and endlessly fascinating attraction for children and adults alike. There in zero-g, freed of gravity, which made their gills collapse, fish swam weightlessly through an atmosphere of one hundred per cent humidity, which kept them moist. To see fish 'flying' through the air was almost dreamlike.

When we returned to the apartment, Ruth and Jen were preparing a meal. Young Nick settled down to watch one of his favourite programmes, *Psychic Space Cats*, about a race of cunning telepathic cats that had adventures on exotic worlds in distant galaxies. I still had a problem figuring out whether the cats were puppets, animated models, or the real thing; they were so amazingly lifelike.

'When's your next lunar trip?' I asked Dan as we were eating.

'Six weeks from now, October tenth,' Dan said. 'We're flying out to Censorinus where the new mass-driver is being installed. They're planning to lift seven thousand tons of graded ore for aluminium smelting. Hey' – he suddenly remembered – 'the whole thing will be televised. You'll have a chance to see it in operation.'

'Where's the ore being processed?' Ruth asked.

'The construction shack off Long Island.' Long Island was a colony nearing completion. Dan picked at a chicken leg. 'You know, we get enough oxygen as a by-product of the smelting process to sustain all the islands and to use as rocket propellant. About forty per cent of lunar rocks are oxidised.'

The bulk of the building materials for the colonies had come from the moon: it was easier and cheaper to transport vast quantities of ore with the low-energy mass-driver from the lunar surface and process it in one of the four smelting shacks that were re-orbited in the vicinity of the island under construction.

Each smelting shack weighed more than 10,000 tons, with a power plant of 3,000 tons, and housed 2,300 workers in thirty-six modules.

Mercifully, Dan didn't have to endure the weeks of tedium suffered by the crews out there. As one of the transporter coordinators he was able to fly in, do his job and return by fast passenger craft. The round trip usually took about three weeks.

Jen helped herself to more salad. 'Did any of you see the newscast last week of the shuttle from Emigrant Junction?' She shook her head sadly. 'Those poor people . . .'

Jo said, 'It's amazing, really. I thought conditions on Earth were so bad that no one outside a sealed enclosure could remain alive; yet they keep coming. It has to end sometime.'

'It isn't the same everywhere,' Ruth said. Her smooth tan and the sweep of greying hair over her forehead successfully camouflaged the disfiguring scar. 'Some places have survived even with a thirty per cent drop in oxygen levels. I read a story about an isolated village in the Philippines where the way of life had hardly changed.'

'Ah yes, I remember that,' Dan put in sardonically. 'They were living off giant frogs. I wouldn't call that "normal", would you?'

'Oh – *you*,' Ruth snorted. 'It might have been normal for them. How do we know?'

'Sure it was,' Dan said, straight-faced. 'Frog quiche. Frog à la mode. Frog on toast. Frog Supreme. Frog—'

Ruth held up a stick of celery threateningly.

'—Maryland. Ouch!' Dan fell back laughing as the celery hit him on the chin.

'Is Daddy being silly again?' Nick enquired gravely. Like most six-year-olds he was severely disapproving of adult humour.

While we were drinking coffee on the small flagged terrace, the shadows lengthening all around, a golden thread of sunlight on the lake, I thought it a good time to tell them about the last shuttle. I'd been near to mentioning it earlier and hadn't because it wasn't yet official. But this was his family, and anyway, it would be released any day now. 'They're already evacuating the colonisation bases and bringing the service personnel up.'

'How do you know?' Jen asked me.

Dan was slightly put out. 'I haven't heard a whisper about that.'

'Jervis Cooper called me a few days ago. Jerv was our tech genius at Midnite-Net in Pittsburgh. He now works in Immigration Control. From what I can gather, there's been a wrangle going on behind the scenes. It was finally put to a vote and carried by thirty-one to fifteen, with one abstention. There's to be an announcement soon.'

'And that's it?' Jo rested her head on her hand. 'No more people from Earth?'

I drank some tea and put my cup down. 'The last one will lift off from Narken in Sweden and after that the bases will be closed down. Apparently the people applying now are genetically damaged in some way – and we all know the rules: no medical clearance, no transit visa. Simple as that.'

There was a silence, a long one, which no one was anxious to break. Sooner or later it had to come; we all knew that, had been prepared for it . . . and yet.

The final severance with Earth, the home planet.

'It's very nearly three years to the day since we came up,' Jo said reflectively. 'September 5, 2049.'

'Was that when we came to Canton?' Nick piped up. 'Our Leaving Day?'

His mother smiled. 'You'll have to remember that date always, Nick. You were too little to remember the shuttle ride, but never forget the date.'

'Bryn says he can remember his Leaving Day. I don't believe him. Bryn tells fibs. He said he went for a fly with the flying fish. Can I fly with them, Mummy?'

'You're right, that is a fib,' Dan said, 'flying with the fish. But he was a year older than you when he came to Canton, so maybe he's telling the truth about remembering it.'

'What's the final tally?' Ruth asked me.

'Jerv says it's not far short of five million. It should have been more but the programme didn't go ahead as quickly as planned. I remember Boris telling me that they were hoping to build a hundred islands with an average population of a hundred thousand per colony. So far they've completed forty-seven, with three more being built. There's no doubt we'll need more as the population increases.'

'Thank God for the moon,' Dan said fervently. 'Our handy neighbourhood mineral resource. We'd have been sunk without it.'

'I was thinking of Boris only today,' Ruth said. She reached out and squeezed my hand. 'Would they have allowed him to come, do you think?'

'You mean because of his age?' Jo said.

'I don't see why not,' I said. 'No one was rejected due to age, providing he or she received clearance and was fit enough to travel. Boris would have been eighty-seven the year we came up. Perhaps he didn't want to leave Earth after all.'

The mirrors were tilting, the sun was nearly gone. Way off in the distance, beyond the ranks of terraced gardens, the core gleamed with a dull rich light like a pillar of fire. And further still, beyond it, the terraces on the far inner side of the globe rose into a purple misty twilight.

'Will we ever go back?' Jen said wistfully. She was thinking of her husband; not a day went by when she didn't think about Nick. She had a daughter and a grandchild and friends to be grateful for, but there was a hollow ache in her heart that would never go away. It was just over a year after they arrived on Canton Island that Nick was diagnosed with anoxia. His lungs must have been affected back on Earth, and there was no cure that could save him. There had been times when Jen would have gladly throttled Nick, but now she felt desolate.

I could almost read her mind, and my thoughts followed the same track. More and more these days I dwelt in the past. I said to her, 'I think about him too.' I started to cough, my throat tight and dry. 'I used to think he was crazy.'

'He was,' Jen said, 'bonkers. He never took anything seriously.'

'Sometimes I wonder how come we liked each other, or even became friends. Strange, really. I think I always saw the world as tragic. Nick saw beyond the tragedy and thought it was a comedy. Isn't there a saying? "The person who thinks sees the world as a tragedy, while the person who feels sees it as a farce."'

'What's farce?' young Nick said.

I patted my knee and he clambered up. 'Don't pay any attention to us, Nick. We're old and past it and we've made a fine mess of things. But you'll do better – much, much better, I hope. You'll show us how it ought to be done, won't you?'

'Will you take me to the flying fish?'

'If you promise me faithfully to do better.'

'Better than what?' asked Nick sensibly.

'Better than us old farts.'

He frowned up at me. 'What's old farts?'

'This young man is a budding philosopher,' I said proudly. 'Questions, questions, questions.'

'He takes after his grandfather,' Ruth said briskly.

'More than likely,' I said, 'but which one?'

'I guess it depends on the answers.'

I kissed my grandson on the forehead. 'Nick'll find them,' I said. 'He's the perfect balance: tragedy and farce combined.'

4

The island colonies ringed the Earth like a swirling necklace of glittering white diamonds.

High above the grey-and-yellow miasma of the poisoned planet they spun like silver cartwheels in the empty blackness and subzero temperature of space: islands of warmth and light and humanity, with five million of the species *Homo sapiens* who had fled their dying planet in the hope of starting anew.

There was to be no return for many generations to come, I knew. It had taken the planet 300 million years to evolve a biosphere capable of supporting life. Every creature and plant had fitted in somewhere, each dependent on all the rest, all dependent on the cycles and rhythms of the complex interweave of forces that kept in equilibrium the land, the oceans, the air.

It might take ten thousand years for the planet to regenerate itself. Or it might take as long as it took to create it in the first place, or it might never happen. There was no God-given guarantee that it would ever again be a habitable place for the human species.

From the window of my study I could view the sliding stars through the transparent panels several hundred feet above. The Great Bear drifted by, pointing to the unseen Pole Star. As with the other colonies, Canton Island's angle of declination was such that the Earth couldn't be seen from inside the colony itself. It was possible to see the Earth (in rather uncomfortable circumstances) by taking a stroll along one of the six-kilometre-long thruways that connected Globe City to the outer torus. But the motion of the colony made it a stomach-churning experience.

Its constantly spinning orbit made the mother planet appear to whirl all over the sky, above and below the watcher, in a series of dizzying spirals.

Orbital sickness was unknown, except when someone was rashly tempted to take a peek at the old homestead; I had tried it once, never again.

The sad and tragic truth was, there was nothing to see: a muddy ball wreathed in haze. No brilliant blue oceans or dazzling white clouds; no landmasses or islands or polar caps. Just grey nothingness masking every feature, like a once-beautiful woman shamefully hiding her aged, crumbling face behind a soiled veil.

At any given moment, I realised, we could be passing over Desert Range, yet failing to see anything through the miasma. Somewhere far below was the Tomb, with its endless labyrinth of tunnels. Deep below on Level Three was my office and my desk and the drawer with my notebook locked away inside. Would it be discovered and read by future inhabitants a thousand years from now? If there were to be any future inhabitants, that is.

The thought of my notebook lying there, waiting to be found, brought back the recollection of Ruth asking me about it.

When she wondered what I was 'scribbling' and why I was so secretive about it, I made the stupid mistake of telling her it was a Future Diary, which had the opposite effect I intended of making her even more curious. I remember Ruth saying (as if it was just this morning) that this was a contradiction in terms because a diary was a record of *past* events, not ones in the future. And how could I record events that hadn't happened yet anyway?

Another contradiction. Apparently I was full of them.

The last thing I wanted, though I pretended otherwise, was for Ruth to read my Future Diary. (Daft title anyway, which is why I changed it to *Epitaph 2052*, as you will know, reading this now.) The reason was simple: Ruth had remarked on the UFOs in the northern latitudes that everyone had seen. Conditions at Desert Range were perfect for spotting them: a perfectly dark sky with no light pollution for a hundred miles. Several times I heard groups of people in the rec room speculating that the ascending spears of light were, or might be, missile trails or the exhausts of booster rockets. They rose straight up, on a fixed trajectory, before arcing into deep space; obviously they had to be the result of a command and control system, or in other words, man-made.

That led to febrile notions that they were in fact cargo-carrying shuttles heading for orbiting space platforms. When Ruth asked my opinion, I was always vague and evasive, because I was ninety-nine per cent certain that I knew what they were and weren't.

They weren't missile trails or booster rocket exhausts. They were actually gigaton burps of methane trapped deep within the Arctic permafrost; and as it melted in the warming oceans, the permafrost ejected vast plumes into the atmosphere, some of which ignited to form incandescent flares. It was the Earth burping flaming methane.

Perhaps I should have told Ruth and the others what I knew the UFOs really were. I just didn't have the heart to crush their illusions with the cruel truth . . .

There would always be victors and vanquished. The eternal law of survival of the fittest would still apply, as it always had. Though now the fittest would be those best able to thrive in an atmosphere with only the merest trace of oxygen. They might be methane-breathers, with a physiology alien to that of a human being. They might feed off dioxin, the deadliest poison known to man, and produce offspring that drank carbonic acid and breathed in sulphurous smog as if it were an invigorating sea breeze. There might be new forms of life so grotesque that it was beyond the wit of man to conjure them up, even in his most demented imaginings.

And while this was taking place, the species that had failed the semester course in planetary management would be gazing down at what had been theirs and was now lost, wilfully and cheaply thrown away. The Earth didn't care. Nature was indifferent to the fate of a single species. The brute thrust of growth went on in other directions, explored other avenues. As far as the planet was concerned, humankind was only one more species to add to the long list of failed experiments.

True, humankind might have made a greater impact than all the rest, created more havoc, interfered like a spoiled ignorant brat in things he didn't understand, and yet the earth abided.

5

It was the discussion with young Nick at the fish farm that stirred the accumulated sediment of memories. We were standing on the walkways where you could look down into huge shallow tanks and see thousands of fish – some, like the white amur, a Chinese delicacy – that could grow to over a foot in length in less than a year. Other varieties were being cultivated that would grow to edible size in three months.

In the warm, shallow water, fed with precisely the right amounts of phosphates and other nutrients, diatoms bloomed. These microscopic one-celled plants living on minerals, sunlight and carbon dioxide provided food for the fish, just as they had on Earth.

But on Earth, as I pointed out to my grandson, the diatoms had performed another, more important, function too.

'They gave us oxygen, Nick, which is in the air all around us. We breathe it in and it keeps us alive. Without it we die.'

Nick had a good look around. 'I can't see it.'

'No, but it's there. If it wasn't, we wouldn't be here.'

'Would we be dead?'

'Stone-cold dead in de market.'

Nick pressed his chin into the plastic mesh, eyes swivelled down as far as they would go, watching the streaking fish.

'Mummy said you and Grandad, my other grandad, the one who's dead, used to swim under the ice.' He frowned up at me, the grid imprinted on his chin. 'Ice is little. I have some in my orange drink. Did you swim in the freezer?'

'You've seen snow and ice on TV, haven't you? Well, on Earth some parts of the land and ocean were once covered in deep snow and thick ice. Your other grandad and I used to dive in the sea, underneath the ice. It was colder than in the freezer, so we had to wear rubber suits to keep us warm.'

'Was it dark?'

'Yes.' I smiled, remembering, 'and we had to take very big, very bright lights to see with.'

'What were you looking for?'

'Those tiny green plants down there.'

'Is that all?'

'That's all.'

'What for?'

That was a tough one. How to explain marine biology to a six-year-old in a few simple sentences? At the time it was research for its own sake, without any specific purpose. It was only later – months or years? – that the work we'd been doing at Halley Bay Station took on dramatic significance.

The sediment had been disturbed and memories began to float to the surface: about diving underneath the ice, for instance. Funny how I could recall every detail as vividly as if it were yesterday, when more recent events, even those that had happened yesterday, had been forgotten.

The cold in the Antarctic – Christ, I could feel it now! – cold enough to freeze gasoline and make steel as brittle as porcelain. How you had to stop breathing when adjusting instruments with your mittens off so that your fingers wouldn't become frozen to the metal by the condensation from your own breath. One guy had lost so many layers of skin that his fingerprints had peeled off.

I leaned over the notebook, mulling through the pages in the lamplight. The pages were crammed to bursting with quotations I'd copied from books and articles over the years. I was searching for something, but didn't know what exactly. On one page I came across this:

There is a goal, one that has the potential to unite every man, woman and child on this planet, which, if reached, will enable them to build at last that 'land fit for heroes'. A home which they can be proud they helped to build, one in which they can live in harmony with the wild things, retaining the beauty of the mountains, the lakes, the rivers, the fields, the vast oceans and the sky.

But this needs effort and requires a genuine desire on the part of every one of us to make this dream reality.

Something like that was needed to set the tone, as a prologue or the opening passage. Then I had second thoughts; the quote might be better at the end than at the beginning – as a summing up, a plea perhaps, an admonition. Or even a warning.

THE END

AFTERWORD

By definition a book set in the future must be speculative. I should like the reader to be aware, however, that this speculation is based on scientific evidence and prediction models, as well as on actual events. I will confine myself to just a few examples to illustrate the point.

As the ice cover in the Arctic thins out and disappears, the exposed dark surface of the ocean absorbs more heat from the sun, leading to the melting of more ice and so on in a runaway positive feedback effect. This will continue until the entire Arctic Ocean is without ice cover, resulting in rising sea levels all around the world.

Another deleterious effect of this process, as noted in a study in the science journal *Nature* in 2013, is that as the permafrost beneath the East Siberian sea thaws, a vast amount of locked-in methane (fifty gigatons) will be released into the atmosphere. Methane is a much more powerful global-warming gas than carbon dioxide and this amount is the equivalent of at least 1,000 gigatons of carbon dioxide. (Human activity has caused the release of around 1,475 gigatons of carbon dioxide since 1850.)

Things are not going any better at the other end of the planet. The melting of the West Antarctic Ice Sheet, according to Eric Rignot, a glaciologist at the University of California, 'has passed the point of no return.' If the ice sheet is absorbed into the Pacific Ocean (and there is no scientific reason why it shouldn't be) and eventually melts, it will add ten to thirteen feet to global sea levels.

Increasing acidity of the world's oceans is a serious concern for climate scientists. The oceans absorb roughly one third of the carbon dioxide produced by industrial society, which reacts with sea water to form carbonic acid. Sir Mark Walport, the UK's chief scientist, warns that acidity levels have increased by twenty-five per cent since the industrial revolution, caused mainly by manmade emissions. He told BBC News, 'If we carry on emitting carbon dioxide at the same rate, ocean acidification will create substantial risks to complex marine food webs and ecosystems.' The current rate of acidification is thought to be unprecedented within the last sixty-five million years.

Carbon dioxide continues to build up in the atmosphere. The amount has more than doubled since 1800 and the rise has accelerated dramatically in the last sixty years. It is now measured at slightly more than 395* ppm (parts per million) and currently rising at a rate of approximately 2 ppm/year and accelerating. The daily average measured at the Mauna Loa Observatory in Hawaii first exceeded 400 ppm on 10 May 2013.

The present concentration of carbon dioxide in the Earth's atmosphere is the highest it's been in the past 800,000 years; and likely the highest in the past twenty million years.

Global temperatures today are higher than they have been since instrumented records began. If the present trend continues, climate models predict an increase of between 1.5° C and 5.5° C at the Earth's surface before the end of this century.

Professor Freeman Dyson of the Institute for Advanced Study at Princeton has pointed out that in a world in which acres of forest are being felled every minute, nobody seems to be doing any research into oxygen depletion. In fact, no reduction in the oxygen content of the atmosphere has been detected anywhere in the world. Yet.

T. H.

Lancashire, Cornwall,

Tunisia, USA

1979–2015

---

* I've had to update this figure. When an earlier version of *The Last Gasp* was first published, thirty-two years ago, the level of carbon dioxide was 330 parts per million.

ACKNOWLEDGEMENTS

I should like to thank the following people and organisations for their invaluable advice and assistance in the research for this book:

Dr Leslie F. Musk and Dr David Tout, Geography Department, University of Manchester; Dr E. Bellinger, Pollution Research Unit, University of Manchester; Dr F.W. Ratcliffe, librarian and director of the John Rylands University Library of Manchester. Special thanks to Dr Phillip Williamson, then of the Wellcome Marine Laboratory, Robin Hood's Bay, Yorkshire, for hours of fruitful and enlightening discussion.

The following publications and research papers were extremely useful: *Climate Monitor*, issued by the Centre for Climatic Research, University of East Anglia; *World Meteorological Organisation Bulletin; Yearbook of the Scripps Institution of Oceanography*, San Diego, California; 'National Climate Programme' in *Oceanus*, vol. 21, no. 4; 'Continuous Plankton Records: Changes in the Composition and Abundance of the Phytoplankton of the North-Eastern Atlantic Ocean and North Sea, 1958-1974' by P.C. Reid of the Institute for Marine Environmental Research, Plymouth, in *Marine Biology*.

Of many other useful sources of information, I should like to acknowledge the following: National Oceanic and Atmospheric Administration, US; Woods Hole Oceanographic Institution, US; PP Shirshov Institute of Oceanology, Academy of Sciences of USSR, Moscow; Scottish Marine Biological Association, Argyll, Scotland; Institute of Terrestrial Ecology, Huntingdon, UK; Natural Environment Research Council, Swindon, UK; Marine Biological Association of UK; World Meteorological Organisation (an agency of the UN); World Climate

Research Programme (joint venture of the WMO and the International Council of Scientific Unions); World Climate Conference held in Geneva, 1979; Global Weather Experiment; POLYMODE: the Mid-Ocean Dynamics Experiment, US and USSR; NORPAX: the North Pacific Experiment; CLIMAP: Climate and Long-Range Investigation Mapping and Prediction; National Center for Atmospheric Research, Boulder, Colorado; World Oceanographic Data Center, Washington, DC: US Council on Environmental Quality; Interagency Coordinating Committee of Atmospheric Sciences, US; International Conference on the Environmental Future (Iceland, 1977).

As reference sources, I made use of the following: *Population, Resources, Environment*, Paul R. Ehrlich and Anne H. Ehrlich (Freeman, 1970); *Planet Earth* (Aldus Books, 1975); *Journal of Environmental Management; Environmental Pollution; Science; New Scientist; Only One Earth*, Barbara Ward and René Dubos (André Deutsch, 1972); *The Closing Circle*, Barry Commoner (Jonathan Cape, 1972); *Pollute and Be Damned*, Arthur Bourne (J.M. Dent, 1972); *The Doomsday Book*, Gordon Rattray Taylor (Thames & Hudson, 1970); *The Ultimate Experiment: Man-Made Evolution*, Nicholas Wade (Walker & Company, 1977); *Colonies in Space*, T. A. Heppenheimer (Stackpole Books, 1977).

In preparing and writing the new and revised version of this book, I am grateful to the following people for providing information and scientific expertise used as background research: Andy Boocock, Dr Jonathan Dugdill, Ray Dugdill, George Kelsall, Dr Keith Mullen, André Street; and a particular mention to Dr David Cromwell and David Edwards, co-editors of *Media Lens*, an invaluable resource for media and current affairs, political opinion and scientific stories. Find it at medialens.org.

Special thanks, and much merited, must go to my agent, Tanja Howarth, for her enduring optimism and dedication; also to my publisher, Jo Fletcher, who has been wonderfully encouraging and supportive and single-minded in making this book the best our talents could make it; also to my desk editor Nicla Budd, and copy-editor Julie Crisp for their close attention, insightful comments and valued creative contribution.

And finally – last but certainly not least – I should like to offer my thanks and appreciation to Nick Austin, who, thirty-seven years ago (yes, thirty-seven!) over a bottle of Chivas Regal, gently dropped the idea into my mind and waited for something to happen.

SOURCES

This section contains links to recent articles and news reports in science journals and the mainstream media which form the factual basis for the fictional narrative of this novel.

Storms of My Grandchildren / Bloomsbury, 2011
The Venus Syndrome
If we burn all the fossil fuels, the ice sheets almost surely will melt entirely, with the final sea level rise about seventy-five metres (250 feet) ... After the ice is gone, would Earth proceed to the Venus syndrome, a runaway greenhouse effect that would destroy all life on the planet?

[Written in 2009] James Hansen: [former NASA scientist, now adjunct professor in the Department of Earth and Environmental Sciences at Columbia University]

BBC News / February 2013
Siberian permafrost thaw warning sparked by cave data
Evidence from Siberian caves suggests that a global temperature rise of 1.5° C could see permafrost thaw over a large area of Siberia. A study shows that more than a trillion tonnes of the greenhouse gases CO_2 and methane could be released into the atmosphere as a result.

http://www.bbc.co.uk/news/science-environment-21549643

NASA Jet Propulsion Laboratory / June 2013

Warm ocean causing most Antarctic ice shelf mass loss

Ocean waters melting the undersides of Antarctic ice shelves are responsible for most of the continent's ice shelf mass loss, a new study by NASA has found. Antarctica holds about sixty per cent of the planet's fresh water locked into its massive ice sheet.

http://www.jpl.nasa.gov/news/news.php?release=2013-202&rn=news.xml&rst=3831

BBC News / July 2013

Antarctic's Pine Island glacier produces giant iceberg

A crack has opened across the full width of the Pine Island Glacier, spawning a new berg. The longest and fastest flowing glacier in the Antarctic has spawned a huge iceberg, about 720 square kilometres in area – roughly eight times the size of Manhattan Island in New York.

http://www.bbc.co.uk/news/science-environment-23249909

The Independent / July 2013

Massive ice sheets melting 'at rate of 300bn tonnes a year', climate satellite shows

A satellite that measures gravity fluctuations on Earth due to changes in the massive ice sheets of Greenland and Antarctica has detected a rapid acceleration in the melting of glacier ice over the past decade, which could have a dramatic impact on sea levels around the world.

http://www.independent.co.uk/news/science/massive-ice-sheets-melting-at-rate-of-300bn-tonnes-a-year-climate-satellite-shows-8708117.html

The Independent / July 2013
'Rivers of rain' to make severe floods twice as likely by end of century

Severe winter flooding in Britain could become twice as likely by the end of the century because rising global temperatures are increasing the chances of huge 'atmospheric rivers' that transport massive volumes of water vapour in the air.

http://www.independent.co.uk/news/uk/home-news/rivers-of-rain-to-make-severe-floods-twice-as-alikely-by-end-of-century-8728874.html

The Guardian / September 2013
Arctic sea ice delusions strike the *Mail on Sunday* and *Telegraph*

When it comes to climate science reporting, the *Mail on Sunday* and *Telegraph* are only reliable in the sense that you can rely on them to usually get the science wrong. This weekend's Arctic sea ice articles from David Rose of the *Mail on Sunday* and Hayley Dixon at the *Telegraph* unfortunately fit that pattern.

http://www.theguardian.com/environment/climate-consensus-97-per-cent/2013/sep/09/climate-change-arctic-sea-ice-delusions

New Scientist / October 2013
The oceans are heating, acidifying and choking

We know the oceans are warming. We know they are acidifying. And now, to cap it all, it turns out they are suffocating, too. A new health check on the state of the oceans warns that they will have lost as much as seven per cent of their oxygen by the end of the century.

http://www.newscientist.com/article/dn24351-the-oceans-are-heating-acidifying-and-choking.html#.VQ74XvzkdqJ

Reuters / October 2013

Shift to a new climate likely by mid-century – study

Billions of people could be living in regions where temperatures are hotter than their historical ranges by mid-century, creating a 'new normal'. Temperatures in an average year would be hotter by 2047, give or take fourteen years, than those in the warmest year from 1860-2005 . . .

http://www.reuters.com/article/2013/10/09/us-climate-shift-idUSBRE9980W820131009

The Independent / October 2013

Pacific Ocean 'warming fifteen times faster than ever before'

Deeper regions of the Pacific Ocean are warming fifteen times faster now compared to previous warming phases over the past 10,000 years . . . the recent 'pause' in global surface temperatures may be due to large amounts of heat in the atmosphere being absorbed by the deep ocean.

http://www.independent.co.uk/news/science/pacific-ocean-warming-15-times-faster-than-ever-before-8916297.html

New Scientist / October 2013

Earth, 2100 AD: four futures of environment and society

You may have heard last week that Earth in 2100 is likely to be between 0.3 and 4.8 °C warmer than it was in the late twentieth century. Why such a broad range? Because the rise in temperature depends largely on what we choose to do now – where our energy and food come from . . .

http://www.newscientist.com/article/mg22029372.700-earth-2100-ad-four-futures-of-environment-and-society.html#.UlGOBNK-ruA

BS News / October 2013
The ocean is broken
Exactly ten years before, when Newcastle yachtsman Ivan Macfadyen had sailed exactly the same course from Melbourne to Osaka, all he'd had to do to catch a fish from the ocean between Brisbane and Japan was throw out a baited line. But this time, on that whole long leg of sea journey, the total catch was two.

    http://bsnews.info/ocean-broken/

The Guardian / October 2013
Rate of ocean acidification due to carbon emissions
is at highest for 300 million years
The oceans are becoming more acidic at the fastest rate in 300m years, due to carbon dioxide emissions from burning fossil fuels, and a mass extinction of key species may already be almost inevitable as a result, leading marine scientists warned.

    http://www.theguardian.com/environment/2013/oct/03/ocean-acidification-carbon-dioxide-emissions-levels

The Independent / November 2013
Exposed: the myth of the global warming 'pause'
Scientists can now explain the 'pause' in global warming that sceptics have used to bolster their arguments . . . A new study has found that global temperatures have in fact continued to rise as fast as previous decades, during which we have seen an unprecedented acceleration in global warming.

    http://www.independent.co.uk/environment/climate-change/exposed-the-myth-of-the-global-warming-pause-8945607.html?google_editors_picks=true

The Slate / December 2013
We're still losing ice at the poles
One of the key indicators and consequences of global warming is ice loss at the Earth's poles. As the planet warms, on average and over time, every summer more ice melts. It refreezes in the winter, but again as temperatures rise, in general we'll see less ice as compared to the year before.

http://www.slate.com/blogs/bad_astronomy/2013/12/14/global_warming_ice_loss_continues.html

The Guardian / February 2014
**World begins 2014 with unusual number
of extreme weather events**
There have been heatwaves in Slovenia and Australia, snow in Vietnam and the return of the polar vortex to North America. But temperatures in parts of Russia and the Arctic have been 10° C above normal. Meanwhile, the southern hemisphere has had the warmest start to a year ever recorded . . .

http://www.theguardian.com/environment/2014/feb/25/world-2014-extreme-weather-events?CMP=twt_gu

Reuters / February 2014
**Wild weather puts climate back on global agenda
before 2015 deadline**
Bitter cold in the United States might appear to contradict the notion of global warming, but with Britain's wettest winter and Australia's hottest summer, extreme weather events have pushed climate change back on the political agenda.

http://www.reuters.com/article/2014/02/18/us-climate-world-idUSBREA1H1OG20140218

American Geophysical Union / March 2014
New study shows major increase in West Antarctic glacial loss
Six massive glaciers in West Antarctica are moving faster than they did forty years ago, causing more ice to discharge into the ocean and global sea level to rise. The amount of ice draining collectively from those half-dozen glaciers increased by seventy-seven per cent from 1973 to 2013.

http://news.agu.org/press-release/new-study-shows-major-increase-in-west-antarctic-glacial-loss/

Scientific American / March 2014
Earth will cross the climate danger threshold by 2036
The rate at which the earth's temperature has been rising eased slightly in the past decade, but calling the slowdown a 'pause' is false. New calculations indicate that if the world continues to burn fossil fuels at the current rate, global warming will rise to two degrees by 2036 . . .

http://www.scientificamerican.com/article/earth-will-cross-the-climate-danger-threshold-by-2036/

Perth Now / March 2014
Western Australia's 'mad' summer is proof of climate change: BoM expert
The weather bureau says Perth's record-smashing summer was 'madness' and it has used temperature and rainfall data to lash out at climate change sceptics. And the state's top meteorologists are warning West Australians they face hotter, drier and more extreme summers.

http://www.perthnow.com.au/news/western-australia/was-mad-summer-is-proof-of-climate-change-bom-expert/story-fnhocxo3-1226842388364

Medical News Today / March 2014

WHO: air pollution responsible for 1 in 8 global deaths

According to a World Health Organisation report released today, around one in eight of total global deaths – seven million deaths annually - are as a result of exposure to air pollution. The figure of seven million more than doubles the previous estimate of annual air pollution-caused deaths, making air pollution now the world's largest single environmental health risk.

http://www.medicalnewstoday.com/articles/274510.php

Climate Rocks / March 2014

Irreversible climate change a few years away

Most scientists concur that two degrees of warming above the temperature during preindustrial time would harm all sectors of civilisation – food, water, health, land, national security, energy and economic prosperity. ECS is a guide to when that will happen if we continue emitting CO_2 at our business-as-usual pace.

http://climatecrocks.com/2014/03/26/mike-mann-irreversible-climate-change-a-few-years-away/

Yahoo Finance / March 2014

Big climate report: warming is big risk for people

If you think of climate change as a hazard for some far-off polar bears years from now, you're mistaken. That's the message from top climate scientists gathering in Japan this week to assess the impact of global warming. In fact, the dangers of a warming Earth are immediate and very human.

http://finance.yahoo.com/news/big-climate-report-warming-big-risk-people-040615058.html?soc_src=mediacontentstory

Eco Watch / March 2014

How scientists are moving climate change conversation forward

It boils down to three main points — ninety-seven per cent of climate scientists agree that climate change is here and now, that this means we risk abrupt and irreversible changes to the climate, and the sooner we act, the lower the costs and risks we face.

http://ecowatch.com/2014/03/27/scientists-climate-change-conversation/

The Mirror / April 2014

Iceberg larger than the Isle of Man floats into ocean and is so big NASA is tracking it

NASA has been called in to monitor the huge block of ice, which broke off from an Antarctic glacier. Known as B31, the iceberg covers an area of 255 square miles and is a third of a mile thick.

NASA glaciologist Kelly Brunt said: 'It's one that's large enough that it warrants monitoring.'

http://www.mirror.co.uk/news/world-news/b31-iceberg-larger-isle-man-3451206

Open Democracy / April 2014

Book review: *A Quiet Word*

What do the following policies have in common: NHS privatisation; fracking; academies and 'free schools'; tax cuts for the rich; corporate tax loopholes, and the Private Finance Initiative? And what do they share with the decisions not to regulate sugar, tobacco, alcohol, pesticides and banks; not to address climate change and not to reform Britain's anti-democratic electoral system?

https://www.opendemocracy.net/ourkingdom/tim-holmes/book-review-quiet-word

The Independent / March 2014

Official prophecy of doom: global warming will cause wide-spread conflict, displace millions of people and devastate the global economy

Climate change will displace hundreds of millions of people by the end of this century, increasing the risk of violent conflict and wiping trillions of dollars off the global economy, a forthcoming UN report will warn.

http://www.independent.co.uk/environment/climate-change/official-prophecy-of-doom-global-warming-will-cause-widespread-conflict-displace-millions-of-people-and-devastate-the-global-economy-9198171.html?google_editors_picks=true

The Conversation / March 2014

PCC preview: deep trouble brewing in our oceans

If you'll pardon the pun, the ocean is in deep trouble, and that trouble will only get deeper if we don't deal decisively with the problem of climate change. The argument is pretty simple. Human activities are increasingly affecting the oceans, which are the cornerstone of life on our planet.

http://theconversation.com/ipcc-preview-deep-trouble-brewing-in-our-oceans-24721

Nature World News / March 2014

Deep sea currents may be slowed by climate change

In deep Antarctic waters, researchers have observed the mass of cold, salty, dense water that makes up the deep ocean current to be shrinking. This is concerning, the scientists say, because the currents are able to 'hide' heat and carbon from the atmosphere.

http://www.natureworldnews.com/articles/6410/20140321/deep-sea-currents-may-be-slowed-by-climate-change.htm

The Daily Climate / April 2014

Deforestation, drought push Amazon towards destruction by fire

Fire and drought, exacerbated by deforestation, could tip the region into large-scale destruction, flipping the Amazon into net carbon emitter. 'We could be missing huge amounts of carbon.'

http://www.dailyclimate.org/tdc-newsroom/2014/04/amazon-deforestation-fires

Climate Progress / April 2014

Last month was the fourth-hottest March on record

But looking at the entire globe – as scientists do when they track things like global warming – 2014's month of March was the *fourth-hottest* one on record. Only 2002, 2010 and 1990 were warmer.

http://thinkprogress.org/climate/2014/04/23/3429721/last-month-was-the-fourth-hottest-march-on-record/

USA Today / May 2014

Carbon dioxide in atmosphere at record level

For the first time in human history and likely for the first time in at least 800,000 years, the average level of carbon dioxide (CO_2) in Earth's atmosphere topped 400 parts per million for an entire month. Carbon dioxide is the greenhouse gas considered to be most responsible for global warming.

http://www.usatoday.com/story/weather/2014/05/01/carbon-dioxide-400-ppm-april-mauna-loa/8575651/

Climate News Network / May 2014

Rising sea temps affect phytoplankton and photosynthesis

Phytoplankton are the single-celled plants that are the basic building blocks of most marine life. In particular, they sustain zooplankton – tiny animals that are eaten in turn by fish.

http://www.climatenewsnetwork.net/2014/05/plankton-loss-threatens-marine-food-web/

New York Times / May 2014

Scientists warn of rising oceans from polar melt

'This is really happening,' Thomas P. Wagner, who runs NASA's pro-grammes on polar ice and helped oversee some of the research, said in an interview. 'There's nothing to stop it now. But you are still limited by the physics of how fast the ice can flow.'

http://www.nytimes.com/2014/05/13/science/earth/collapse-of-parts-of-west-antarctica-ice-sheet-has-begun-scientists-say.html?_r=1

Climate News Network / May 2014

East Antarctic ice basin 'may be at risk'

Part of the East Antarctic ice sheet may be less stable than anyone had realised, researchers based in Germany have found.

http://www.climatenewsnetwork.net/e-antarctic-ice-basin-may-be-at-risk/

The Guardian / May 2014

Doubling of Antarctic ice loss revealed by European satellite

Antarctica is shedding 160 billion tonnes a year of ice into the ocean, twice the amount of a few years ago, according to new satellite obser-vations. The ice loss is adding to the rising sea levels driven by climate change and even East Antarctica is now losing ice.

http://www.theguardian.com/environment/2014/may/19/doubling-of-antarctic-ice-loss-revealed-by-european-satellite

The Guardian / June 2014

Australia experiences its hottest two years on record

Australia has experienced its hottest two years on record and high temperatures are set to continue through winter in a clear sign of climate change. May 2012 to April 2014 was the hottest twenty-four-month period ever recorded in Australia.

http://www.theguardian.com/environment/2014/jun/02/australia-experiences-its-hottest-two-years-on-record

Climate Progress / July 2014

The amount of carbon dioxide in our air just reached a new record, and scientists are worried

The finding is troubling to climate scientists, a reminder that humans are still pumping too much carbon dioxide into the sky. If the trend continues, carbon levels will soon surpass 450 ppm – a level that would create a level of global warming too difficult for some humans to adapt to.

http://thinkprogress.org/climate/2014/07/01/3455026/400-ppm-carbon-dioxide-three-months/

Truthout / August 2014

Climate change: point of no return

Extreme weather conditions, including rising temperatures, droughts, crop failures, melting sea ice, rising sea levels, disappearing glaciers and the loss of plant and animal species all point in only one direction. The tipping point towards the sixth great extinction is taking place right now.

http://www.truth-out.org/opinion/item/25448-the-climate-change-point-of-no-return

Fox News / August 2014

Hundreds of methane plumes erupting along east coast

In an unexpected discovery, hundreds of gas plumes bubbling up from the sea floor were spotted during a sweeping survey of the US Atlantic Coast. Even though ocean explorers have yet to test the gas, the bubbles are almost certainly methane, researchers report in Nature Geoscience.

http://www.foxnews.com/science/2014/08/25/hundreds-methane-plumes-erupting-along-east-coast/

Climate Progress / August 2014

The really scary thing about those jaw-dropping Siberian craters

Russian scientists have determined that a massive crater discovered in a remote part of Siberia was probably caused by thawing permafrost. The crater is in the Yamal Peninsula, which means 'end of the world'.

http://thinkprogress.org/climate/2014/08/01/3466466/siberian-craters-permafrost-climate-change/

Washington Post / January 2015

The US has caused more global warming than any other country

The US has caused more global warming than any other country. Here's how the Earth will get its revenge.

http://www.washingtonpost.com/news/energy-environment/wp/2015/01/22/the-u-s-has-contributed-more-to-global-warming-than-any-other-country-heres-how-the-earth-will-get-its-revenge/

The Guardian / January 2015

**Rate of environmental degradation puts life
on Earth at risk, say scientists**

Humans are 'eating away at our own life support systems' at a rate unseen in the past 10,000 years, two new research papers say.

http://www.theguardian.com/environment/2015/jan/15/rate-of-environmental-degradation-puts-life-on-earth-at-risk-say-scientists

Scientific American / March 2015
Global warming could hit rates unseen in 1,000 years
This finding comes from new research also showing that the Arctic, North America and Europe will be the first regions to transition to a new climate.

http://www.scientificamerican.com/article/global-warming-could-hit-rates-unseen-in-1-000-years/

Scientific American / March 2015
Arctic Sea Ice Dwindles Toward Record Winter low
Sea ice extent is crucial to the Arctic's ecology and economy, affecting wildlife habitats, weather patterns, and shipping lanes. Sea ice is a key part of the habitats of animals like polar bears . . .

http://www.scientificamerican.com/article/arctic-sea-ice-dwindles-toward-record-winter-low/

The Guardian / March 2015
Russian scientists say climate change to blame
for mysterious Siberian craters
Russian scientists have now discovered seven giant craters in remote Siberia, a geologist told AFP on Thursday, adding that the mysterious phenomenon was believed to be linked to climate change.

http://www.theguardian.com/world/2015/mar/12/siberia-russia-craters-climate-change

USA Today / March 2015
Earth had warmest winter on record
The Earth just had its warmest winter on record, the National Oceanic and Atmospheric Administration announced Wednesday. Winter is defined as the months of December, January and February in the Northern Hemisphere . . .

http://www.usatoday.com/story/weather/2015/03/18/record-warm-winter-globe/24957737/

University of Texas / March 2015

East Antarctica melting could be explained by oceanic gateways

Researchers at the Jackson School of Geosciences have discovered two seafloor gateways that could allow warm ocean water to reach the base of Totten Glacier, East Antarctica's largest and most rapidly thinning glacier.

http://www.jsg.utexas.edu/news/2015/03/east-antarctica-melting-could-be-explained-by-oceanic-gateways

Washington Post / March 2015

Global warming is now slowing down the circulation of the oceans

Global warming is now slowing down the circulation of the oceans – with potentially dire consequences.

http://www.washingtonpost.com/news/energy-environment/wp/2015/03/23/global-warming-is-now-slowing-down-the-circulation-of-the-oceans-with-potentially-dire-consequences/

The Independent / March 2015

Methane meltdown: The Arctic timebomb that could cost us $60trn

The sudden release from the melting Arctic of vast quantities of methane – a greenhouse gas at least twenty times more potent than carbon dioxide – is an 'economic time-bomb' that could explode at a cost of $60 trillion (£40tr) to the global economy, a study has concluded.

http://www.independent.co.uk/news/science/methane-meltdown-the-arctic-timebomb-that-could-cost-us-60trn-8730408.html

The Guardian / March 2015

The film that reveals how American 'experts' discredit climate scientists

For Naomi Oreskes, professor of scientific history at Harvard, there's no more vivid illustration of the bitter war between science and politics than Florida's ban on state employees using terms such as 'climate change' and 'global warming'.

http://www.theguardian.com/environment/2015/mar/15/climate-change-denial-florida--global-warming-naomi-oreskes-interview

Washington Post / March 2015

The melting of Antarctica was already really bad. It just got worse

A hundred years from now, humans may remember 2014 as the year that we first learned that we may have irreversibly destabilised the great ice sheet of West Antarctica, and thus set in motion more than 10 feet of sea level rise.

http://www.washingtonpost.com/news/energy-environment/wp/2015/03/16/the-melting-of-antarctica-was-already-really-bad-it-just-got-worse/

Washington Post / April 2015

Climate-change deniers are in retreat

What began as a subtle shift away from the claim that man-made global warming is not a threat to the planet has lately turned into a stampede.

http://www.washingtonpost.com/opinions/climate-change-deniers-are-in-retreat/2015/04/06/942eb980-dc9f-11e4-be40-566e2653afe5_story.html?hpid=z2

Truthout / April 2015

Melting accelerates in Antarctica: so far, 2015 is hottest year yet

The dramatically rapid melting of the earth's poles is the biggest news in this month's climate dispatch . . . There is no pause in human-caused global warming. If anything, we've been lulled into a false complacency.

http://truth-out.org/news/item/30063-melting-accelerates-in-antarctica-so-far-2015-is-hottest-year-yet#

The Independent / April 2015

Scientists say temperatures could rise by 6° C by 2100

There is a one-in-ten chance of the world being 6° C warmer than it is today by 2100 which would lead to cataclysmic changes in the global climate with unimaginable consequences for human civilisation, leading climate researchers have warned.

http://www.independent.co.uk/environment/climate-change/global-warming-experts-say-temperatures-could-rise-by-6c-by-2100-with-cataclysmic-results-10193506.html?google_editors_picks=true

Motherboard / April 2015

The last time oceans got this acidic this fast,
96% of marine life went extinct

The biggest extinction event in planetary history was driven by the rapid acidification of our oceans. So much carbon was released into the atmosphere, and the oceans absorbed so much of it so quickly, that marine life simply died off, from the bottom of the food chain up.

http://motherboard.vice.com/read/the-last-time-our-oceans-got-this-acidic-it-drove-earths-greatest-extinction

The Independent / April 2015
'Letter: Cimate Change: Time is shorter than we think
Letter in *Independent* from scientists.

http://www.independent.co.uk/voices/letters/letters-climate-change-time-is-shorter-than-we-thought-10182804.html

Time magazine / May 2015
Glaciers are crumbling in Southern Antarctica
faster than previously thought
Multiple large glaciers that were previously not thought to be in danger of melting have been crumbling since 2009 . . . with some dwindling by as much as 13 feet per year. The glaciers had not shrunk significantly before 2009.

http://time.com/3894137/antarctica-glaciers-melting/

Morning Star / May 2015
The terrifying truth about the 2° C climate target
Western aims on climate change are beyond feeble, and can only lead to disaster for our children and grandchildren . . . 'clean energy progress is falling well short of the levels needed to limit the global increase in temperature to no more than 2° C.'

https://www.morningstaronline.co.uk/a-1663-The-terrifying-truth-about-the-2C-climate-target#.VWTN6WA-CRu

Think Progress / June 2015
'It is climate change': India's heat wave now the
5th deadliest in world history
A searing and continuing heat wave in India has so far killed more than 2,300 people, making it the fifth deadliest in recorded world history. If the death toll reaches more than 2,541, it will become the fourth deadliest heat wave in the world, and the deadliest in India's history.

http://thinkprogress.org/climate/2015/06/02/3665123/india-heat-wave-5th-deadliest/

Washington Post / June 2015

Study sees a 'new normal' for how climate change is affecting weather extremes

Every time the world witnesses a weather related disaster – most recently, extreme flooding in Texas and Oklahoma, a deadly heatwave in India – the attribution battle begins. Some scientists and commentators seek to explain how the event could have been worsened by climate change . . .

http://www.washingtonpost.com/news/energy-environment/wp/2015/06/22/study-sees-a-new-normal-for-how-climate-affects-weather-events/

BBC / June 2015

Earth 'entering new extinction phase' – US study

'We are now entering the sixth great mass extinction event,' a study by three US universities has concluded, and humans could be among the first casualties. The report by Stanford, Princeton and Berkeley Universities, said vertebrates were disappearing at a rate 114 times faster than normal.

http://www.bbc.co.uk/news/science-environment-33209548

BBC / July 2015

'Irreversible change' to sea life from CO2

A major report warns that life in the seas will be irreversibly changed unless CO_2 emissions from industrial society are drastically cut. Twenty-two experts in the journal Science say the oceans are heating, losing oxygen and becoming more acidic – all in response to our carbon dioxide.

http://www.bbc.co.uk/news/science-environment-33370591

The Guardian / July 2015

Nearly 9,500 people die each year in London because of air pollution – study

More than twice as many people as previously thought die prematurely from pollution (toxic gas NO2) in UK capital, according to new research.

http://www.theguardian.com/environment/2015/jul/15/nearly-9500-people-die-each-year-in-london-because-of-air-pollution-study

The Slate / July 2015

Glaciers will melt 10 times faster than previous estimates

The study – written by James Hansen, NASA's former lead climate scientist, and 16 co-authors, concludes glaciers in Greenland and Antarctica will melt ten times faster than previous consensus estimates, resulting in sea level rise of at least ten feet in as little as fifty years.

http://www.slate.com/blogs/the_slatest/2015/07/20/sea_level_study_james_hansen_issues_dire_climate_warning.html

Huffington Post / July 2015

First half of 2015 was hottest ever recorded

Off-the-charts heat is 'getting to be a monthly thing,' said Jessica Blunden, a climate scientist for the National Oceanic and Atmospheric Administration. June was the fourth month of 2015 that set a record, she said.

http://www.huffingtonpost.com/entry/first-half-of-2015-was-hottest-january-june-ever-recorded_55ad7b8ce4b0caf721b3a968

Daily Mail / July 2015
ASSASSINATED? The astonishing claim made
by a Cambridge professor

A Cambridge professor has claimed that three scientists investigating climate change in the Arctic may have been assassinated. The trio had been studying the polar ice caps – with a focus on sea ice – when they died within a few months of each other in 2013.

http://www.dailymail.co.uk/news/article-3174599/Have-three-climate-change-scientists-ASSASSINATED-astonishing-claim-Cambridge-professor.html#ixzz3h6IUR4LS

The Telegraph / August 2015
Scorching 'heat dome' over Middle East makes it feel
like 162° F in Iran

Iran is buckling under the pressure of a massive heatwave passing across the Middle East. The heat index was recorded by a group of astonished weather experts who predict the country could be enduring some of the hottest urban temperatures ever endured by mankind.

http://www.telegraph.co.uk/news/worldnews/middleeast/iran/11777843/Scorching-heat-dome-over-Middle-East-makes-it-feel-like-162F-in-Iran.html

Rolling Stone / August 2015
The point of no return: climate change nightmares
are already here

The worst predicted impacts of climate change are starting to happen – and much faster than climate scientists expected. Historians may look to 2015 as the year when shit really started hitting the fan. In just the past few months, record-setting heat waves in Pakistan and India each killed more than 1,000 people.

http://www.rollingstone.com/politics/news/the-point-of-no-return-climate-change-nightmares-are-already-here-20150805#ixzz3hz9RYv4p

The Real News / August 2015

Climate change: have we reached the point of no return?

For scientists, the debate has been long over. Droughts, killer heat waves, extended wildfires, drastically melting glaciers, typhoons, and extreme rainfalls leading to floods and landslides as well as sea level rises and mass die-off of animals all make it rather clear.

http://therealnews.com/t2/index.php?option=com_content&task=view&id=31&Itemid=74&jumival=14473

Think Progress / August 2015

Hottest July on record

NASA reports this was the hottest July on record. So we are now in 'bet the mortgage' territory that 2015 will be the hottest year in NASA's 125-year temperature record. In fact, 2015 is likely to crush the previous record – 2014 – probably by a wide margin . . .

http://thinkprogress.org/climate/2015/08/14/3691940/hottest-july-hottest-year-record/

Carbon Brief / August 2015

Climate change set to fuel more 'monster'
El Niños, scientists warn

The much-anticipated El Niño gaining strength in the Pacific is shaping up to be one of the biggest on record, scientists say. With a few months still to go before it reaches peak strength, many are speculating it could rival the record-breaking El Niño in 1997/8.

http://www.carbonbrief.org/blog/2015/08/climate-change-set-to-fuel-more-monster-el-niños,-scientists-warn/

Reuters / August 2015

**Sea levels worldwide rose an average of nearly
3 inches (8 cm) since 1992**

In 2013, a United Nations panel predicted sea levels would rise from 1 to
3 feet (0.3 to 0.9 meters) by the end of the century. Low-lying regions,
such as Florida, are especially vulnerable ... normal spring high tides
cause street flooding in sections of Miami.

http://www.reuters.com/article/2015/08/26/us-environment-sea-
level-nasa-idUSKCN0QV2B020150826?feedType=RSS&feedName=en-
vironmentNews

takepart / August 2015

NASA says three feet of sea level rise is unavoidable

Scientists say coastal cities around the world are all but certain to face
catastrophic flooding in the coming decades. The findings looked at
sea levels, the amount of heat that's already stored in the oceans, and
how much water is being added by melting ice sheets in the Arctic
and Antarctica.

http://www.takepart.com/article/2015/08/27/sea-levels-are-
rising-3-feet-unavoidable

The Independent / August 2015

**Climate change: 2015 will be the hottest year
on record 'by a mile', experts say**

Climate scientists are predicting that 2015 will be the hottest year on
record 'by a mile', with the increase in worldwide average temperatures
dramatically undermining the idea that global warming has stopped – as
some climate-change sceptics claim.

http://www.independent.co.uk/environment/climate-change/
climate-change-2015-will-be-the-hottest-year-on-record-by-a-mile-
experts-say-10477138.html